#CraveSeries praise on social media for Tracy Wolff's Crave series

"It was everything I ever wanted and more."
—@ballerinareads on *Charm*

"Tracy Wolff totally knocked it out of the park."
—Paige and Abby, @thelaundryroomscene on *Charm*

"It. Is. Stunning."
—Phoenix G., @wolfieinx on *Charm*

"Truly magical."
—Katie B., @kberry310 on *Charm*

"Just might be my favorite of the series, it was that good."
—@BookNookMandy on *Court*

"[Y]ou will be BLOWN AWAY by this masterpiece."
—Megan D., @snowwhiteandthe7morechapters on *Charm*

"I read the series and FELL IN LOVE with it."
—Robin E., @robin_hereforindiebooks on the Crave series

"Beautifully written and everything I could've wanted as a reader."
—@madsinlovewithbooks on *Court*

"This book was so amazing!"
—Christy M., @anerdybooklife on *Crave*

"Wow!!!! Emotional!!!! Swoon-Worthy!!! EPIC!!!!
Exceeded all my expectations!!!"
—Andra P., @andra_bookmom on *Charm*

"If you haven't read the series yet, you are missing out!"
—Barbara E., @calleycat61 on the Crave series

"I think this is going to be my new obsession."
—Sharon L., @bebalovetwilight on the Crave series

"Tracy's writing style is a work of art."
—Megan H., @meganmariehusted on *Court*

cherish

ALSO BY TRACY WOLFF

cherish

#1 *NEW YORK TIMES* BESTSELLING AUTHOR
TRACY WOLFF

Entangled Publishing, LLC
644 Shrewsbury Commons Ave., STE 181
Shrewsbury, PA 17361
rights@entangledpublishing.com

Entangled Teen is an imprint of Entangled Publishing, LLC.

Visit our website at www.entangledpublishing.com.

Edited by Liz Pelletier
Cover art and design by Bree Archer
Stock art by BlackJack3D/GettyImages,
ptasha/GettyImages, Renphoto/GettyImages
Interior endpaper design by Elizabeth Turner Stokes
Interior design by Toni Kerr

ISBN 978-1-64937-316-8 (Hardcover) ISBN 978-1-64937-556-8 (B&N)
ISBN 978-1-64937-557-5 (BAM) ISBN 978-1-64937-488-2 (TARGET)
ISBN 978-1-64937-555-1 (WALMART) ISBN 978-1-64937-317-5 (Ebook)

Manufactured in the United States of America

First Edition May 2023

10 9 8 7 6 5 4 3 2 1

To the people I Cherish:
Steph, Adam, Noor, and Omar.
Forever and always.

At Entangled, we want our readers to be well-informed. If you would like to know if this book contains any elements that might be of concern for you, please check the back of the book for details.

A Ribbon for
Your Thoughts

"**D**o you think we're ever going to see this place again?" The question slips out as Hudson and I walk past the campus to the diner where we're supposed to meet Eden and Heather.

Originally, we'd settled on the university center, but the coffee is better at the diner, and I think Heather's trying to impress a certain dragon.

"Of course we'll see it again," he tells me, sliding a comforting hand into mine. "What even makes you ask?"

I shoot him a look. "The last time we were in the Shadow Realm, it took us years to find our way back to this world. *And I forgot you.*"

The guilt of everything I'd forgotten has danced at the corners of my mind for months, but now that I have my actual memories of our time in Adarie back...it's like a punch to my heart.

All I want to do is turn around and go home, so I can just *think* about everything. So I can be with Hudson as I sort through the memories, cherish all the things that made me fall in love with him that first time—including those damn bird calls of his.

The fact that he had all this inside him for months since our return, and I didn't have a clue... The pain of it is indescribable. It makes my stomach churn and turns every part of me to an open, gaping wound.

Which only gets worse when Hudson laughs down at me and adds, "You say that like it's a crime."

"It feels like a crime," I answer, battling against the tears that burn the backs of my eyes.

He squeezes my hand, rubs his thumb back and forth over the double promise ring on my left ring finger—half from Giant City, half from the Shadow Realm. "I already told you, I'm the guy who's lucky enough to have his girl fall in love with him twice. I don't feel bad about that."

"For now."

He lifts a brow even as he looks at me with teasing blue eyes. "Does that mean you're planning on falling *out* of love with me?" he asks. "If so, I'm not okay with that part of the plan."

"Obviously I'm not *planning* on falling out of love with you," I tell him with a snort. "But I didn't plan on falling out of love with you the last time we left the Shadow Realm, either. Shit happens." Not to mention we still don't even know *why* I lost my memories. As soon as I'd gotten my memories back, Hudson had suggested it might have something to do with the giant-ass amount of time-dragon magic that slammed into me, but I have my doubts.

"Well, then, I'll be the guy who has the distinct honor of having his mate fall in love with him three times. There are worse things in the world."

"Yeah, because it worked out so well the last time." I shake my head. "I can't believe how much I—"

"Hey." He cuts me off, pulling me into his arms here on the busy sidewalk, right between a drugstore and my favorite fish taco place. "It did work out well the last time. We're here, aren't we?"

"Now," I answer. "*Now* we're here." But there were a lot of months wasted where we weren't here. A lot of pain, a lot of suffering, a lot of heartache. Is there any wonder I'm not anxious for either one of us to have to go through it again?

"*Now* is all that matters. You're my mate. You're always going to be my mate, and I am always going to love you. How could I not?" His eyes twinkle as he adds, "Hey, 'I came across time for you, Grace. I love you. I always have.' And I always will."

It's ridiculous, but even knowing he's quoting one of our favorite movies from our months trapped in his pseudo-lair doesn't stop my heart from melting. Then again, melting my heart—and the rest of me—has never been a problem for Hudson. Even from the beginning.

That doesn't stop me from busting his balls a little bit, though. "James Cameron called. He wants his line back."

He laughs. "Caught that, did you?"

"The fact that you just *Terminator*-ed me? Yeah, I caught that."

"It's not my fault that movie has so many great lines."

"No, but your absolute and abiding love for it is *completely* your fault." I take his hand, tugging him along and into the drugstore.

"What can I say? I'm a romantic at heart." He looks around. "What are we doing in here?"

"Checking out the gift-wrapping section. I want to see if they have any sparkly ribbons," I answer as I lead him toward the back of the store.

I didn't think it was possible, considering the way he's been looking at me since I told him I remembered everything that happened in the Shadow Realm, but Hudson's eyes go even softer. "You want to pack her more ribbons?"

His voice is as rough as my aching heart as we both remember the tiny umbra he loved like a daughter. The one who sacrificed her life to save his. No, she isn't dead. I have to believe she's out there, waiting for Hudson to find her again.

"Don't get all mushy on me now. It's pure selfishness on my part," I say, coughing a little to clear my suddenly tight throat. I pick up a thick roll of sparkly gold ribbon and study the package. "I need Smokey to like me."

"She *does* like you."

I turn from my contemplation of glittery red versus shiny pink ribbon to give him an are-you-kidding-me look. At which point, he hastily gathers up both spools of ribbons—and an extra glittery silver one as well—and heads for the nearest cash register.

"Maybe 'like' is a strong word." He pauses to grab a box of cherry Pop-Tarts off the snack display on the way to self-checkout.

"Maybe 'like' is just a full-on *lie*," I counter, taking out my credit card to pay.

But Hudson beats me to it, as usual, tapping his black American Express. I take the purchases to put in my backpack as we leave the store.

He doesn't say anything else as we walk, but he's holding my hand like it's a lifeline.

I can't help but wonder if he's more worried about this trip than he's letting on, but before I can ask him, he murmurs, "She's going to be there, right?"

"She is," I answer, squeezing his hand back extra hard. "We're going to find her, Hudson. We'll start at the farm, and if Smokey isn't there, we'll keep looking until we figure out where she is. She's there, just waiting for you to find her again. And we will. I promise."

He nods, but I can tell he's still worried. And I don't blame him. Smokey hated me, but I couldn't help but love her, if for no other reason than she loved this boy who'd never known love but deserved it all. And now that I remember the Shadow Realm and everything that happened there, her absence destroys me. I can't even imagine what it's felt like for Hudson all these months.

"Hey," I tell him, moving us into an alcove between buildings. "Listen to me. We're going to find that ridiculous little umbra."

I try to put as much confidence as I can in my gaze, hoping the fear that Smokey didn't make it is buried down so deep that Hudson can't see it. Because, as much as we know that time-dragon fire resets timelines and sends those who enter the Shadow Realm to the point they were at just before they entered Noromar...I have no idea what would happen to a creature who was actually *born* there.

I grit my jaw against any thoughts that Smokey is gone forever and hold Hudson's gaze, willing him to believe me about Smokey being okay.

When the corners of his eyes crinkle, a crooked smile lifting one side of his mouth, I let out a long breath of relief. He shakes his head. "She really is ridiculous, isn't she?"

"So ridiculous. And if she wants to come back here with us, then we're going to find a way to bring her back, too."

"And what are we going to do once we get her here? She doesn't exactly blend in."

"We'll hide her, of course. Like Lilo did Stitch—only a lot better."

He laughs, exactly as I want him to, but I can still see the worry lingering in his eyes. It kills me. Hudson has done so much for me, has always made sure that I feel safe, even in the middle of the worst situations imaginable, and almost never asked for anything for himself.

This is one thing that he needs—to know that Smokey is happy and healthy and okay. There's no way I'm not going to move heaven and earth to make sure it happens for him.

He stares at me for a second, his eyes searching mine for the answer to a question he doesn't even know he's asking. "I love you, Grace."

"Across time. I know," I tease.

"Across everything," he says, and he's never looked more serious.

"I love you, too." I lean in and kiss him, reveling in the little zing of sensation that works its way through me the moment our lips touch. "No matter what."

He moves to deepen the kiss, and I let him, because I never want to say no where this guy is concerned. And also because I get lost the second he scrapes one of his fangs across my bottom lip.

Shivers shoot down my spine and my fingers curl in the front of his shirt as I give myself to him—to this—for just a few more seconds.

Then I force myself to take a step back, even though I want nothing more than to drag Hudson home and have my wicked way with him. Or the other way around.

But we've got things to do and people counting on us, so I smile up at him and say, "We need to go. Heather and Eden are waiting."

He nods, then leans forward and nips at my lower lip one more time. I almost say to hell with it. They've waited this long—they can wait a little longer.

But then I remember Smokey and Mekhi and everything else we need to take care of. I reach for Hudson's hand.

"Let's go," I tell him.

He rolls his eyes but doesn't argue, and we head back onto the busy sidewalk. We've only gone a block or two before Hudson suddenly steps in front of me, his shoulders tensing.

"What's wrong?" I ask, trying to see around him as my heart kicks up in my chest.

But he's too busy scanning the surrounding area to answer.

"Hudson?" I query when several seconds go by and he doesn't relax his vigilance or his stance.

"Sorry," he finally tells me, stepping back. "I thought I saw something."

"What?" I look up and down the street as I take a few calming breaths. There are several college students in school sweatshirts outside an ice cream shop, men and women in business attire bustling to and from work, and a mom pushing her baby in a stroller, but that's about it. At least as far as I can see.

"I don't know. I just…" He shakes his head as he takes my hand again. "It was nothing."

"I guess so," I agree as we resume walking, but I can't help glancing behind us, just in case.

As we turn and cross the street, Hudson asks, "We're not really going to let Heather come with us, are we? She's human."

"Hey!" I make a face. "Don't say it like it's such a bad thing. I was human for a lot of years."

"You know what I mean. I'm worried about something happening to her."

"Me too," I answer. "Which is why we'll let her come along for now. But the second we figure out how to get to the Shadow Realm, I'm buying her a plane ticket back here."

"Oh, she'll love that."

"I'll make it first-class," I say, sticking my tongue out at him. "And she *will* love it—certainly more than dying at the hands of the Shadow Queen or who knows what."

"Good point," he admits as we turn the corner to the diner, the shiny front door no more than ten feet away now. "Besides, you've already got one needy person to take care of. You can't be dividing your attention too much."

"Oh yeah?" I ask, brows raised. "Are you feeling needy?"

"Please." He gives a proper British sniff as he holds the door open for me. "I was referring to Flint."

I crack up, because he's not wrong. But we've got this. As long as Hudson and I are together, everything is going to be okay.

I smile at him as I walk through the door and into the diner…and then straight into a very upset Jaxon and Flint.

Heart's in the
Wrong Place

The second I realize who I just ran into, I throw myself at both of them. They catch me—of course they do—and one of my arms goes around each of their necks as I hug them as tightly as I can.

It's been more than a month since we've been together in person. Now that Hudson and I live in San Diego and they live in Manhattan, we don't see each other nearly as often as I'd like. And FaceTime may be the next best thing, but it just isn't the same.

Flint laughs as he brushes a few of my wayward curls out of his face. Then he tugs me away from Jaxon and twirls me around a couple of times. "Looking good, New Girl."

I fake-grimace at the old nickname, even as it makes me smile. Flint and his teasing never change—something I'm grateful for in a world that so regularly tilts beneath my feet.

"Wish I could say the same about you, *Dragon Boy*," I shoot back. "That's one hell of a shiner you've got there."

But he just snickers. "You should see the other guy."

As Flint and I continue to joke around, Jaxon clears his throat in a pay-attention-to-me kind of way. It's Flint's turn to grimace at me, even as we both pivot toward my ex-mate.

"You look good, Jaxon," I tell him in a there-there voice.

"Too little, too late," he answers. But then he's wrapping me up in another hug, and the comforting scents of fresh water and oranges wash over me.

"The Dragon Court seems to agree with you," Hudson comments as he joins us.

"At least something does." Flint grins as he gives Hudson a hearty slap on the back. Because, apparently, that's what men who used to be enemies but are now friends do.

Jaxon snorts in a way that doesn't sound entirely teasing as he tells Flint, "I think he was talking to me."

Flint's grin fades as he murmurs, "I know."

But Jaxon is too busy studying Hudson to notice. "San Diego looks pretty good on you, too, brother. Better than the Vampire Court, certainly."

Hudson holds his gaze, and as I glance back and forth between them, it looks like they're saying a lot more than what we're hearing.

"Who knew vampires could tan?" Hudson finally replies as we head over to our table, where Eden and Heather are staring googly-eyed at each other across a plate of French fries. Or at least as googly-eyed as Eden gets…which, at the moment, is more than I ever expected.

"Guess that ring Remy gave you is coming in handy." Flint nods down at the ring on Hudson's finger that lets him drink human blood and still walk in the sun.

Lucky me.

"It is," Hudson answers, and the glance he shoots his brother, then Flint, tells me he's picked up on the same thing I have. That Jaxon is looking pretty tan himself even though he *doesn't* have a ring. "Now, let's get this party started."

As we settle down next to Heather and Eden, I can't help wondering if Jaxon's tan means he's not feeding from Flint. And if he isn't, why not?

I make a mental note to ask Flint if they're having problems when there aren't so many people around. I hate the idea of things being off between them, especially when they're both trying so hard to make their budding relationship work at the Dragon Court.

Heather immediately wraps her arms around me, and I squeeze her back. We were apart for so long, it is such a relief that we're close again. I'll never get tired of seeing my best friend. We exchange a few comments about recent stormy weather but stiffen when Eden shrieks.

"Holy shit!" she exclaims after finally looking away from Heather long enough to notice the rest of us. She's staring at Flint's black eye, and I know why she's so surprised. It's rare to see a dragon with a bruise like that—partly because they don't get hit hard enough to bruise very often and partly because they heal so quickly. "What happened to you?"

Jaxon answers for him. "What happened is, he refused to run when I told him to."

"Seriously?" Flint gives him an incredulous look. "What the hell was there to run from? There were barely a dozen of them."

"And yet, somehow, you still have a black eye," Jaxon replies.

Flint's brows shoot up. "Not from *them*. From you throwing that one guy at me without so much as a heads-up for me to, I guess, finish where you left off."

"I didn't realize you weren't paying attention." Jaxon leans back in his seat and crosses his arms in a move I know all too well. "And who shouts when they throw something anyway?"

"Umm, everyone," I tell him. "It's, like, the first thing you learn playing ball on the playground."

He makes a disbelieving sound in his throat. "Well, that's boring."

We all laugh, because how can we not? But then Hudson asks, "So who were these people who made the bad life choice of attacking the two of you?"

That stops the laughter in a hurry—at least for the two dragons and the dragon-vampire sitting at the table.

"Shit's going down at the Dragon Court," Eden finally answers.

"What kind of shit?" I ask, my eyes going wide. "Are Nuri and Aiden okay?"

"They're fine for now," Flint answers. "But, to be honest, we're not that far from full-on civil war among the dragon clans."

"Civil war? That seems impossible. We were there only a few months ago for Wyvernhoard, and everything seemed like it was perfect."

"Yeah, well, a lot can happen in a few months," Jaxon says.

"There's a lot, and then there's *a lot*," I counter. "What the hell is going on?"

"There's growing dissent from clans who think my mother isn't capable of ruling now that she doesn't have a dragon. They've asked her to step down, and she's refused, so they're working to bring a vote of no confidence against her within the Dragon Court."

A vote of no confidence? Against Nuri, the most badass dragon queen imaginable? It seems inconceivable. "They won't win, will they?"

"I don't know." Flint picks up Eden's water and drains it in a single sip. "There's more of them every day."

"But there must be something the Montgomerys can do about it," I suggest.

"I don't know what. The other clans appear to want us all gone." He says it flippantly, like it doesn't matter. But I can see the pain in his eyes, hear it in the studied blankness of his voice.

"What they want," Jaxon snaps, "is for you to stop flaunting a vampire around their precious Court. And for their ruler to have her dragon heart back."

"Yeah, well, neither of those things is going to magically happen," Flint bites out. "They're just going to have to get used to it."

"What about your father?" Hudson asks quietly. "Can he rule in her stead?"

Flint sighs. "He's royal by marriage only, and that's not enough for the throne without my mother."

"Right." Hudson nods like that makes sense, even though it sounds ridiculous. Then again, the whole right of royal primogeniture seems archaic to me. To Hudson, too, I know. It's one of the many reasons he announced he would be abdicating, though that won't be "official" until a ceremony in a few weeks.

"So what's going to happen if this whole no-confidence thing succeeds?" I ask.

"What's going to happen or what *should* happen?" There's a touch of bitterness in Jaxon's tone.

"Is there a difference?"

"Fuck yeah, there is," he tells me. "What *should* happen is Flint stepping up and taking the fucking throne."

"You know why I can't do that." Flint shrugs.

"I know why you *won't* do it," Jaxon mutters. "It's not the same thing."

Tension stretches between them, taut as a circus highwire, and I can't think of anything to say to defuse it. But then Eden comments, "You never did tell us who attacked you guys. Surely it wasn't someone on the Council?"

She seems as tense as they are as she waits for the answer, which I can totally understand. It's one thing to be bringing a no-confidence vote. It's another to brazenly attack the crown dragon prince with no fear of reprisal.

"Yeah, right." Flint scoffs. "They only do their work in dark rooms where no one can see their faces. They hired someone to attack us."

"One of the outlying dragon clans?" I ask, because I can't imagine who else would be short-sighted enough to do something like this.

"Worse," Jaxon says with a disbelieving laugh. "Humans."

"They hired humans to try to take you down? That doesn't make any sense."

But even as I say it, I think back to that moment on the street when Hudson stepped in front of me. He'd sensed some kind of threat, though neither of us picked anything up when we scanned the street. Could someone have been following us to get to Jaxon and Flint?

The thought horrifies me. The last thing I'd ever want is to bring something to my friends that might hurt them, even inadvertently.

But when I mention it to the group, Flint shakes his head. "Don't worry about it, Grace. I already know they're watching my every move. There's nothing you could do that would make their scrutiny of us any deeper. Besides, Jaxon and I can handle whatever comes our way."

"It's not about what you can handle," I counter. "It's about not putting you in the situation to begin with. Believe me, we all know you and Jaxon are badasses."

"Hey, what about me?" Eden squawks.

"Oh, you're definitely a badass," Heather answers, batting her eyes. "Though, I have to say, who knew dragons were so needy?"

"Everyone," I answer. "*Everyone* knows dragons are needy."

"Excuse you! I am the least needy one here," Flint exclaims.

He looks so insulted that we all crack up, which only insults him more.

On the plus side, the last of the tension dissipates just as the waitress comes to take our order.

Once she leaves, though, we all kind of stare at one another like we're not sure what to say next. Until Hudson finally breaks the silence by asking, "So shall we talk about Mekhi dying?"

3

Great Minds
Think a Lot

His words hit like a slap, and the last of our levity falls away.
I expect everyone to rush to talk over one another with ideas,
but instead we just sit in silence as the weight of what we have to do
presses down on us all. I definitely feel it resting on me, making my
shoulders slump and my stomach churn. How can I not, when Mekhi
is dying and we need to come up with a plan to save him?

And not just any plan. A great plan—one that has more components
than "storm the Shadow Queen's castle and demand she cure Mekhi
of the shadow poison." And, equally important, we need a plan that
everyone at this table is going to come back from.

I've already lost too many friends as it is. I'm not going to lose any more.

That includes Mekhi, who's already been gone for what feels like
a year, even if it's only been five months.

"How much longer can Mekhi stay in Descent?" I ask. The Bloodletter
had put him under as soon as we'd realized he'd been infected by shadow
poison in the Trials, but I know there have been problems.

"We don't know for sure, but not much longer. Weeks, not months,"
Eden answers, and the words settle like an anvil on my chest. Even
expecting the worst, I didn't think it would be *this* bad. "The Bloodletter
says she's already given him more elixir than any vampire in history,
and still he keeps coming around every few days. Any more and"—she
shrugs sadly—"the cure might be worse than the poison."

Jaxon flinches at her words, at the reminder of just how precarious
his friend's grasp on life truly is right now, which only has my heart
tightening more.

I know he blames himself for Mekhi's situation and for the deaths
of the other members of the Order. But now isn't the time for blame.

Right now, we need to focus on what's directly in front of us: getting to the Shadow Realm and curing Mekhi. Everything else can wait.

Speaking of which—I realize with a jolt—something, or someone, is most definitely not right in front of me. And she definitely should be.

I turn to Flint, eyes wide. "Where's Macy? I thought you guys were meeting up with her and coming together?"

Jaxon and Flint exchange a long look that has my stomach sinking. Because old habits die hard, and we've been through too much for me to ever take my cousin's absence lightly.

"What's wrong with Macy?" I ask even as I dig in my pocket for my phone with fingers that are suddenly shaking.

"Nothing's wrong with her," Jaxon assures me, placing a hand over mine before I can text her. "She just got kicked out of another school yesterday, and Foster and Rowena brought her back to live at the Witch Court with them. But she's currently on house arrest."

"House arrest?" Eden repeats with a smirk. "They don't really think that's going to work, do they?"

The others laugh, and if I wasn't so worried about my cousin, I would, too. Macy's had a really hard time these last few months since Katmere was destroyed and we found her mother at the Vampire Court. She's now been kicked out of all three schools Uncle Finn has tried to put her in, and her magic has turned dark enough to have us all worried about her. And a little afraid—*for* her and *of* her—if I'm being honest.

"Who knows?" Flint leans back in his chair and pops one of Eden's French fries into his mouth. "Apparently, Rowena has been bringing down the hammer since we got her out of that shithole."

"So no Macy on this trip." It sounds weird to say it out loud. "Which means we only have to pick up Remy and Izzy—"

"No Remy and Izzy, either, I'm afraid," Jaxon interjects. "They can't get away from Calder Academy."

"Can't get away, like they're bogged down with schoolwork?" I ask, brows raised. "Or can't get away, like they're prisoners?"

It's Hudson's turn to raise a brow. "Surely it's the former. Can you imagine any headmaster strong enough to hold my half sister against her will? Or Remy?"

It's a good point—one that finally settles my racing heart. Well, that and the thumb Hudson is rubbing soothingly over my knuckles from across the table.

"So it's just us, then?" I clarify, glancing from face to face. "Just the six of us?"

Jaxon leans forward, crossing his arms on the table. "I assure you I am more than capable of retrieving one little antidote from the Shadow Realm."

"You say that because you've never met the Shadow Queen."

"And you have?" he shoots back.

Of course Jaxon doesn't know Hudson and I have been there. Hudson has never said a word about what happened during our time trapped together, and I've only just remembered. I expect Hudson to update everyone now, but he doesn't. Instead, he looks over at me in question.

"Hudson and I fought her," I answer, diving right in. "I feel like that should count for something."

Hudson laces our fingers together now, his touch letting me know he's got my back as I catch everyone up on my missing memories. Well, as much as I feel comfortable sharing with Jaxon here.

"So you're saying…" Jaxon eventually starts. "You were trapped in this Shadow Realm with Hudson for much longer than four months?"

"I was," I tell him, uneasiness crawling through my belly like ants. Because there's a lot in that simple statement, and as Jaxon's dark eyes meet mine, I can tell that he knows it, too.

Even before Heather's cup of tea rattles on the table between us.

"Umm, what was that?" Heather gasps, looking around a little wildly, as if expecting the Big One to hit us at any second.

"Just a tremor," Hudson says but glances at his brother with somber eyes.

"This *is* San Diego," I add, trying to help him cover for Jaxon. But judging by the way Flint is suddenly staring at Jaxon like he wants to flip our table and pull him closer, nothing I say is going to help.

"When did you remember?" Eden asks, completely ignoring the sudden tension. Or maybe she's just so wrapped up in Heather that she doesn't feel everything else going on.

"Today," I reply. "And there's a lot for me to unpack in the memories. But I think I need to shelve that for now. Mekhi needs to be our focus. And yes, the Shadow Queen is scary as fuck, even worse than Cyrus. Shadow magic is the oldest magic in the universe, and she can do all kinds of twisted shit with it. She nearly killed us and did kill a lot of other people. Still, if Mekhi is dying from shadow poison, I agree she's our best chance of finding a cure."

"There's a difference between knowing how and being willing to do something," Eden comments.

I nod. "I know. And trust me, I'm not excited to *ever* face her again."

Flint shakes his head, looking more than a little freaked out. "Is she really worse than Cyrus?"

"Deadly plus bugs," Hudson answers, deadpan, and we all kind of shudder, remembering the Trials. Everyone except Heather, who wasn't trapped in that hellish room with us. "The shadow-bugs-covering-every-inch-of-your-skin experience will haunt you forever, Heather."

Flint runs his hands along his arms, as though checking for bugs without realizing it, and I get it. Those bugs are enough to bring even a dragon to their knees.

Jaxon leans over to whisper something in Flint's ear. Something that sounds suspiciously like, "I won't let any shadow bugs close enough to touch you."

A quick glance at Hudson shows my mate ready to jump in with a snarky comment, but a swift—if gentle—kick under the table keeps his mouth shut. Though it doesn't stop him from winking at me.

Hudson continues. "Plus, in the Shadow Realm she's upgraded from just bugs to a full menagerie of shadow creatures, some with sharp teeth and claws."

Heather squares her shoulders. "Well, I'm willing to fight whatever it takes to save your friend. What are we waiting for?"

Before anyone can answer, our waitress comes back with our order, mainly coffee—and a hot cocoa for Flint, of course.

As she walks away, Hudson scratches his jaw. "Actually, I'm not sure we have to *fight* anyone to save Mekhi." He must see the nonplussed expression on my face because he adds, "She wanted the mayor to reset the timeline to before she was cursed. So she fought us because we were trying to stop him, and ultimately, stop her. But she lost, obviously, and now that she has no means of escape, maybe we can bargain with her."

I blink. It's not a bad idea, except for one fact. "She's trapped for a reason, Hudson. We can't find a way to set her free. She's pure evil."

"Is she?" Hudson raises one eyebrow.

"Umm, bugs. Remember?" Flint says, shuddering again.

"Don't get me wrong—I'm not saying she's perfect," Hudson clarifies. "But I think there's a real chance she's not as evil as we believe."

"Were you not in the Trials, man?" Eden barks out. "She tried to *kill* us."

"We don't know for sure that she was the one attacking us during the Trials. Other people can wield shadow magic, too, for all we know."

Eden sniffs. "Well, she's the only one we actually know has that kind of power. So I'm assuming it's her until we know otherwise."

"Maybe that's fair, but we also know that in the Shadow Realm she only attacked Grace and me to save her people. She could have attacked at any time we were in Adarie, but she only fought us to the near death when we were trying to stop the mayor from resetting the timeline and freeing her people, even if he didn't know that's what he was doing in saving his daughter." He pauses, holding my gaze steady. "Have I not done worse for less? Am I evil, Grace?"

My heart squeezes as I remember just how much that question tortured him when we were in the Chamber in the Aethereum prison. "No, you could never be evil, Hudson."

"Then maybe she's not, either," Hudson says, his words hanging in the silence like a knife, each of us considering things we've done to save the ones we love.

Eventually, Heather asks, "So, what's the plan, then?"

"I suggest we trade the antidote for helping free the Shadow Realm." Hudson shrugs.

"Well, obviously that's your plan," Jaxon drawls. "Let's just go destroy a *realm*."

"I didn't say 'destroy,' I said 'help free,'" Hudson clarifies with an eye roll, as though that explains it all.

"I think everyone at this table is absolutely amazing," I start, and Flint puffs out his chest, clearly liking where this is going. "But I'm not sure how we can just"—I make air quotes—"'free a realm' cursed by a god a thousand years ago."

"You're looking at the problem from too far away, Grace. Think smaller." When I can do no more than blink in response, Hudson shakes his head and adds, "The Shadow Realm is a *prison*. And what do prisons have?"

"Walls. They have giant fucking walls," I answer, not even trying to hide my confusion now.

Flint snaps his fingers. "Oh, and guards. And usually loads of weapons, too."

"And really bad food." Eden gets in on the fun before Hudson interrupts.

"Jaxon, can you help out here?" Hudson pleads.

"Locks," Jaxon answers, and the two brothers' eyes meet. "Prisons have locks."

There's a total shared moment hanging between them, which I'm loath to interrupt, but— "Sincerely, I still have no clue where this is going," I admit.

"Locks can be *un*locked, Grace," Hudson says.

My eyes widen. "Or broken," I add, and Hudson grins.

"Or broken," he echoes.

"We don't need to free an entire realm," I say, awed at how simple Hudson has made the problem. God, I love how that boy's brain works. "We just have to break a lock and open a door."

We're both grinning at each other now, my eyes one hundred percent sending the message I'm going to adore the brains out of him later if the slight reddening in his cheeks is any indication.

"As much as I love breaking shit, any idea where a master key might be, brother?" Jaxon asks, and everyone holds their breath, hoping beyond hope that Hudson has one hidden on him now.

"Not a clue," Hudson replies, and five sets of shoulders sag as one. He leans forward again and picks up my hand across the table, rubbing his thumb over my promise ring. "But I know someone who does know."

4

"Well, by all means, let's add more drama and tell us slowly." Eden rolls her eyes, and we all chuckle at Hudson's unintentional theatrics. Heather is mid-sip when she snort-laughs—and nearly chokes on her coffee, until Eden reaches over and starts rubbing circles on her back to calm her lungs.

"I apologize." Hudson offers Eden a slight nod. "I keep forgetting that you guys don't know what Grace and I learned about the Shadow Realm. Let me speed this up. The Shadow Realm was built as a prison after the Shadow Queen upset a god. And, as Flint pointed out, this prison is like most and has very badass prison guards—called guardians, aptly enough. Therefore, it stands to reason that the god who created these guardians likely holds a key to the prison as well, so his guards can come and go."

"Jikan," I blurt out, then turn to the others and explain excitedly. "We were told the guardians, which are these scary-as-fuck time dragons, were created by the God of Time—we just didn't know who that was while we were there. But we know now. *Jikan* created them!"

Hudson adds, "Jikan might have even created the prison itself, Grace. Either way, I bet he has a key… And maybe, with a little luck, he'd be willing to give us the key to trade for the cure for Mekhi."

Jaxon shifts in his seat and grumbles, "I doubt Jikan would give us the key to the bathroom if we were about to piss our pants."

We all laugh because, well, he's probably right, but before my stomach twists itself into a pretzel, Hudson holds my gaze, the corners of his eyes crinkling in that way that always calms my nerves, makes me feel a little gooey inside. Then he says, "I'm not expecting him to give us the key because *we* asked. But I don't think there's anything Jikan wouldn't do for the Bloodletter or, I'm hoping, the Bloodletter's granddaughter."

And it's true. I get spanked if I freeze one measly person, but Jikan let my grandmother freeze her entire army for a thousand years.

"Do you really think he'll help?" I ask, excitement making my voice quiver.

"Only one way to find out," Hudson replies, then reaches up to rub his chest. "Besides, I think a thousand years is long enough for anyone to be kept prisoner, don't you?"

A stillness comes over the table, even Flint pausing mid-stir of his hot cocoa, as we all think of Hudson and Jaxon's half sister, Izzy. She was held captive by her father for that same length of time, and Hudson's right—no one deserves that punishment, even the Shadow Queen.

I squeeze Hudson's hand and agree softly, "I do."

Just then, the waitress stops by our table again. She refills our coffee mugs one last time, asking if we need anything else. Hudson hands her his credit card with a smile and a compliment about the sunny scarf she has tied around her neck. The woman, not a day under sixty, blushes like a schoolgirl before walking away. The best part is he means every word.

"So, let's do this," Heather says, gathering up her phone and putting it into her cross-body bag.

I start to push back from the table as well, but before I can, Artelya reaches out to me telepathically. *We've got a problem, Grace.*

What kind of problem? I ask, my stomach clenching. *My grandparents—?*

Are fine, she answers in her brusque way. *But I'd rather show you the problem than try to explain it like this. When can you come?*

I'm on my way, I answer, my heart racing in my chest.

Then it occurs to me it's Thursday night across the pond. And that if we head to the Gargoyle Court, I can kill two problems with one quick trip across the Atlantic...

5

Love, Love
Me Don't

"Ireland!" Heather gasps as she steps out of the portal between San Diego and County Cork. It closes behind us in a swirl of purple magic that sparkles and snaps like a live wire, as if the witch who made it intentionally wanted us to know she could just as easily incinerate us as deliver us to the other side. "We're in *Ireland*!" She spins around, her braids swinging behind her, before jogging toward the edge of the moonlit cliffs. "And we got here in a couple of minutes, like it's no big deal."

"It's a very big deal," Flint grouses as he comes up behind me. "I still want to know how you have a portal and we don't."

"Because you're dragons? You've got wings and you fly everywhere," I reply.

"Umm, okay, *gargoyle*. What are those things you usually have on your back?"

I roll my eyes. "Yes, I have wings. But Hudson doesn't, and he's usually traveling back and forth with me. Not to mention he needs to have access to the Vampire Court, too."

"I guess." Flint shrugs. "I still feel like the Witch Queen is playing favorites, only making a portal for the gargoyles."

"Imogen is definitely not playing favorites. In fact, I'm pretty sure she hates me." I start walking as a stiff breeze comes off the water, making me shiver.

Flint falls into step beside me. "You say that," he teases, "but the portal says something different."

"The portal is a result of hours of shrewd negotiating. You should try it."

Hudson makes a disbelieving sound deep in his throat. "Shrewd negotiating? Is that what you call it?"

"Hey. Just because what she wanted was absurd doesn't mean I didn't negotiate," I answer.

"Oh yeah?" Now Flint looks intrigued. "What did she want?"

"To be in charge of the upcoming investiture ceremony. I got the portal in exchange for letting her plan everything."

"Everything?" he asks, brows raised.

"Everything," I answer. "But what do I care what flowers she wants to use to commemorate my ascension to the Head of the Circle? Or what color dress she wants to put me in? I was more than happy to let her take the reins."

"That's seriously what you traded to get a portal?" Flint looks amazed. "Flowers and a dress?"

"Music, too, I think. And food. But since I've never been to one of these ceremonies, it definitely feels like I got the better end of the deal." I shrug.

"Umm, yeah. Definitely," he agrees before sprinting to catch up with Eden and Heather, who are walking several yards ahead of us.

As he runs away, I can't help noticing that he's barely got a limp at all now. I've hated watching him struggle to acclimate since he lost his leg on that damn island, but he's obviously healing well and getting used to his prosthetic.

"You sure you're up for this?" Jaxon asks, walking beside Hudson and me as we allow the stars to guide us over the rocky path that weaves along the cliffs overlooking the Celtic Sea.

I know he's referring to seeing Jikan, and I get it. It's never exactly fun to deal with the God of Time. But in this case, Jikan really does seem like our best chance to save Mekhi.

"Absolutely," I reply.

Jaxon doesn't look convinced. "And you're sure he's going to be here?"

"It's Thursday," I answer.

"Is that supposed to mean something to me?" Jaxon frowns.

"Jikan's always here on Thursdays. It's kind of his thing."

Jaxon raises a brow. "That's a weird thing to have, isn't it?"

"You'll see," I say, hoping to cut off his questions about the time god. Not because I don't have the answers to them but because this is the first time I've had Jaxon and Hudson alone since I regained my memories of the years I spent in the Shadow Realm.

I have better things to talk to them about than Jikan. Especially when the next couple of days are going to be rough and we have no idea how they're going to end up. This may be the last time I ever get a chance to say what I have to say to the two of them.

We can try to bluster our way through all of this, pretending it's not a big deal. But the truth is, going back to the Shadow Realm is dangerous as fuck, and none of us knows if the Shadow Queen will even be willing to listen to us. If I'm being honest, she's just as likely to try to kill us all, key or no key. Last time, Hudson and I barely escaped with our lives—and I didn't escape with my memories.

If that happens again, or if something worse does, there's something I need to say first.

I've loved both of these guys, and while Hudson is my mate—the person the universe created just for me—Jaxon will always be special to me. And no matter what's going on with him and Flint, I know that I'll always be special to him, too.

We may not care about each other the way we once did, but that only makes what I have to say more important—for all of us.

With that thought in my head, I reach for Hudson's hand and bring it to my lips. Then I reach for Jaxon's and squeeze it tight.

He squeezes back, a quizzical expression on his face as he glances down at me. "Everything okay, Grace?"

"I'm sorry," I blurt out. It's not the most eloquent apology out there, but it is the most heartfelt. "That goes for both of you."

"Sorry?" Jaxon seems bewildered. "For what?"

Hudson doesn't say anything. He just wraps a supportive arm around my waist and waits for whatever I'm going to say next.

"For everything that happened after I got back from the Shadow Realm." I look from my mate to my former mate and back again. "I hurt you both so much, and you didn't deserve that. You didn't deserve any of it."

"You're not responsible for what happened," Hudson tells me. "You lost your memories."

Yeah, but *why* did I lose my memories? Maybe it was because of the time magic that the dragon hit me with, like Hudson said. Or maybe it was because I didn't want to remember. Maybe I didn't want to have to hurt Jaxon.

Just the thought makes me shudder, has my stomach twisting and my heart beating way too fast. Because I never wanted to hurt either of these guys and, in the end, I hurt them both unbearably. Now that I remember the entirety of my time in Adarie, everything that's happened since feels so much worse, even though it was never anything but awful.

"I don't know that that matters," I say. Jaxon makes a protesting noise in his throat, and I turn to him. "But I think it's important that you know something about what happened with Hudson—not just for our relationship but also for your relationship with Flint."

Now it's Hudson's turn to protest, but I ignore him. He's spent so much of his life playing the villain, he doesn't understand that sometimes showing he's the good guy is actually the way to go.

"When we were trapped in my head, both Hudson and I could see the mating bond between you and me."

Jaxon jerks backward, his body arching like I just hit him. I can't see his face very well in the darkness that surrounds us, but I don't need to see him to know that I just hurt him all over again. So I rush ahead, determined to say what needs to be said. Determined to make him understand.

"What I mean is, we also knew when it disappeared. It didn't happen for a long time, and when it did, we were both sure you were dead. I couldn't feel you anymore—at all—and mating bonds are forever. Everyone knows this. So when ours disappeared, Hudson and I were devastated. We both felt like we lost you, though in very different ways. And it took a long time, even after the bond was gone, before either of us so much as looked at the other person."

"It doesn't matter—" Jaxon starts, but I grab his face and hold it between my hands, effectively shutting him up.

"It *does* matter," I tell him fiercely. "Because you need to know that both your brother and I love you so much. Neither of us would ever deliberately hurt you the way we did. We grieved for you, Jaxon. And we missed you so much. The love we have for each other—" I break off, shaking my head as tears form on my trembling lashes. "It didn't start to grow until after we'd finally come to terms with losing you."

I inhale deeply, then let it out slowly even as I step back to wrap my arm around Hudson and hold him as tightly as he has always held me. "I love Hudson with every breath I have inside me," I say to both of them. "And I know he feels the same way about me. But if either of us had had any idea that you were still alive, we would never have gotten together."

Because the words feel wrong even as I say them—Hudson is my mate, and I will always be grateful that we found each other—I add, "At least not until we'd all had time to figure out that the mating bond was fake, and we had a chance to come to grips with that knowledge. Maybe it seems ridiculous for me to apologize for this now, maybe it doesn't matter to you at all, but I need you to know that your brother didn't betray you. And neither did I."

They remain still for several long, painful seconds, and I can't help wondering if I somehow just made everything worse. But then Jaxon grabs me with one hand and Hudson with another, dragging us toward him into a group hug that feels like it's been far too long coming.

"I didn't blame you," he whispers, his voice breaking with each word. "I didn't blame either of you."

"I know," I answer. "But I also know it would hurt me to think of you cheating on me when we were still together. I don't want that hurt for you, now that I know for sure it never happened."

"I'm sorry," Hudson starts. "I didn't think to—"

"It's okay." Jaxon cuts him off, clearing his throat a couple of times before pulling away. "Everything that happened. It's all okay. *We're* okay."

It's my turn to nod even as I hold on to Hudson just a few seconds more. Even as he holds on to me the same way.

And when I finally step out of his warm embrace, I realize that we've made it. Not just emotionally, past the ugly, painful hurdles of our past, but physically as well, to the huge iron gates of the Gargoyle Court.

My Court.

6

"It's beautiful," Heather breathes as we come to a stop in front of the gates, taking in the millennia-old castle before us, all lit up against the darkness. "Where in Ireland are we, exactly?"

"Home," I answer, because for me, that's exactly what the Gargoyle Court has come to represent. My people and my home.

"*This* is the Gargoyle Court?" she asks, her face glowing with wonder as she looks from one end of the keep to the other. "Why would you ever want to move the Court to San Diego when you could be *here*?"

"Because San Diego is home, too," I say, making sure to catch her gaze with mine.

When I do, and when she realizes what I'm saying—that San Diego is my home at least partly because she's there—her huge brown eyes go wide. But then she grins and says, "Yeah, well, if it means living on these kick-ass cliffs in an even more kick-ass castle, then home—and I—can definitely adopt an Irish accent."

We all laugh at that as I admit, "Well, just the ruling portion of the Court is moving to San Diego, so I'll still be visiting here often, and you can join me, too. The main army is remaining in Ireland. This is *their* home."

I walk up to the gate's keypad and enter the combination, then push the heavy iron open. Even though it's only been a few weeks, excitement thrums through me at the thought of seeing my people again. Hudson and I try to get over here as often as we can, but with school ramping up and assignments coming fast and furious, we aren't traveling as often as we used to.

That's another reason I want to move the ruling Court to San Diego.

With all the degrees Hudson wants to rack up, I'm pretty sure we're going to be there for years to come. And while all those degrees may not be at UCSD, they are likely going to be at schools up and down the coast. Going back and forth between Ireland and California isn't practical, even with Imogen's portal.

"Hey, I didn't think about this when we were walking through a portal," Heather says nervously. "But it looks pretty official in there, and I didn't bring my passport."

At first, I have no idea what she's getting at, but when it hits me, I start to laugh—as do the others.

"You know, right, that Grace is in charge here?" Eden asks, running a hand through her bangs. "She can bring whoever she wants with her, whenever she wants."

"Not to mention, paranormals don't really worry so much about human laws," Flint adds with a lift of his chin.

Heather looks unimpressed with Flint's imperiousness. "So, you just do whatever you want?" she asks, shaking her head.

"Yes," Jaxon answers, sounding bored. Because of course he does. Jaxon is nothing if not succinct when it comes to who he is and what he can do.

If possible, Heather looks even less impressed by Jaxon's answer. She doesn't show him that, though. Instead, she moves so he can't see her and rolls her eyes at me.

I shoot her an I-feel-that expression, because yes, they're both sounding a little too big for their britches now. But when I turn to share the joke with Hudson, he doesn't even seem to have noticed.

He's too busy scrolling through his phone with serious eyes and a definite frown on his face.

"Everything okay?" I ask, laying a hand on his arm.

The familiar zing goes through me as our bodies make contact. It's enough to distract him, too, to have him glancing away from whatever has him upset to give me that little half grin of his that still makes my heart beat way too fast.

"Absolutely fang-tastic," he jokes, but I realize the smile I love doesn't quite reach his eyes this time.

I want to push a little, but with the others standing here around us, this isn't exactly the time. Hudson may be more open with me than he's ever been with anyone, but he prefers an aloofness in front of others—even when those others include his closest friends.

As if to prove my thoughts, Hudson shoves his phone back in his pocket and teases, "Shall we go show Jikan who's boss? And by boss, I mean you, of course."

I smile, like he knew I would.

"Actually, I need to see Artelya first. But if you want to head down to the training fields, he's probably already there," I suggest.

"Believe me, there's no hurry," Jaxon drawls. "We'll wait for you."

"So, the God of Time just hangs out at the Gargoyle Court?" Heather asks, sounding completely bewildered. I'm not sure if that's because she didn't know the God of Time existed before a few hours ago or because she really has no idea what he would be doing hanging out in Ireland.

To her credit, she'd taken the news that there are gods just walking around in our world with admirable calm back at the diner, asking only a couple of questions before focusing on the fact that witches can build portals to anywhere they've already been.

Then again, that's pretty much Heather to a T.

From the time we were little, she's always kind of taken a second to think things through and make a plan before heading into a situation with a ton of confidence and even more swagger. Considering my inclination to rush in without thinking at all, Heather's moments of planning saved us more than a few times growing up.

I can't help smiling as I think of the way my mom would sit us down and lecture us whenever Heather and I got into some ridiculous scrape or another. She never freaked out, but she definitely spent a lot of time trying to infuse us both with a little more reticence. It never worked, much to her chagrin. Still, my mom was always there to bail us out...until she wasn't.

A wave of sorrow swamps me as I think about her and the way she used to scold us one minute and give us a cookie the next. I can't believe it's been more than a year since my parents died—and more than a year since I started on the journey that brought me here, to

Hudson and to my Court.

I've learned not to fight it when the sadness hits, so I take a deep breath and let it wash over me. Then let as much leave my body as I can when I exhale. It never eases the pain entirely, but it helps.

"He does on Thursday nights," I answer Heather after taking another slow breath in and out. "But if you really don't want to head down without me, you guys can grab something to drink while I check in with my general."

"Good plan," Flint says. "I could totally use a snack."

"We just left a restaurant," Heather tells him, looking bewildered, since he was the only one who ordered a sandwich with his hot cocoa and still ate all of Eden's fries.

"So?" he answers, his trademark grin stretching across his face.

Eden leans toward Heather and mock whispers, "An ego that big requires constant feeding."

"Hey, it takes a lot to keep my dragon in kick-ass condition," he jokes, waving a hand down his body as we walk toward the lowered portcullis that guards the front door.

"I rest my case," Eden shoots back.

Flint responds by stretching his neck for a second, then blowing a small stream of fire right at her.

Heather gasps, but Eden just dodges and shoots a stream of ice square at his chest, immediately turning his T-shirt to a hard sheet of uncomfortable-looking frost. "Two can play that game, Montgomery."

"Ouch," Flint barks, rubbing at his chest and knocking the ice loose. He looks like he's about to respond with an ice blast of his own, suspiciously focusing on Eden's long black hair, but before he can do much more than open his mouth, the portcullis in front of the castle door is raised and six members of my army race outside, swords at the ready.

It's a very different welcome than my first time here—when Alistair and I visited the court when it was frozen in time and had no worries of being attacked by any other paranormals—but one I'm getting used to. Now that gargoyles are unfrozen and back in the timeline again, they're a little bit overzealous with their determination to stay here.

Not that I blame them. A thousand years frozen in time after being poisoned, tortured nightly by the souls of your fallen friends and family members desperate to be welcomed home, would make anyone skittish. I'm still traumatized by what I saw—and what Hudson did to protect us then. Why would my people be any different?

Still, all six guards stop abruptly when they see me, giant grins replacing their scowls as they lower their swords and drop into deep bows.

Behind me, Heather gasps.

"Strange watching Grace the queen, isn't it?" Flint whispers to her.

"Soooooo strange," she answers.

I turn around just long enough to make a face at both of them before stepping forward to greet the soldiers.

"I've told you a million times, you don't have to do that," I say to the guards, gesturing with both hands for them to stand back up. When they don't immediately take the hint, I just flat out ask, "Please, get up."

Funny how, when I first got here, all I wanted was some small sign of respect from these people. Now that I've got so much more than that, there's a part of me that wants nothing more than for things to go back to the way they were when I was just any other gargoyle to them.

It's not that I don't want to be their queen, and it's not that I don't take my responsibilities seriously—because I do. Very, very seriously. I just wish those responsibilities didn't also come with a whole lot of pomp and circumstance that only manage to make me very uncomfortable.

At least they heard my pleading as an order. They all straighten at once.

"How are you, Dylan?" I ask, extending my hand to the young warrior at the front with golden-brown skin and short dark hair.

"Ready to serve," he answers, taking my hand. But instead of shaking it, he bows his head and kisses my ring.

"Oh, umm, that's really not necessary," I tell him as I try desperately to extricate my hand.

I'm saved when Hudson steps forward, eyes crinkling with affection, and claps the young soldier on his shoulder. "I hope you've been practicing that jump move I taught you last week."

Dylan immediately drops my hand and takes Hudson's, bowing over his as well. "Yes, sir. I think I've mastered it now. I even took the general in a hand-to-hand trial earlier this week, sir."

The two men separate as Hudson leans back to gives the guard a measured look. "You bested Artelya? That's impressive, Dylan. I look forward to seeing that demonstration at next week's training." He raises one brow. "We'll see how you fare against a vampire, eh?"

Dylan's eyes widen with excitement, as if Hudson hadn't just offered to give him a beatdown. "I'll be ready, sir."

"I'm sure you will," Hudson answers, his voice thick with pride. He'd been working hard to find his own place within the Gargoyle Court, a use for a king, and he found it on the training grounds a couple of months ago. Now that I have my memories of our time in the Shadow Realm, I'm not surprised that even here, he gravitated toward a teaching position.

I've just started telling Dylan he should never be this excited to face a vampire on the battlefield when I see Artelya stride across the courtyard.

She's dressed in green shorts and a matching shirt, but the long braids she usually wears in a coronet are gone. In their place is a beautiful afro that frames her high cheekbones and makes her eyes look huge in the very best way. She takes one look at me and bursts into a jog, a smile on her face. "Grace!"

I have one moment to flash back on my brand-new memories of her—of her guiding me in the Shadow Realm and then of watching her turn to dust by dragon fire—before she envelops me in a tight hug.

Sorrow overpowers me, has my stomach clenching and my chest tightening, as I realize that she doesn't have the same memories. Her timeline reset the moment I failed to save her from the time-dragon fire that consumed her, and now she remembers nothing of the Shadow Realm or our friendship there.

For a long time, I didn't remember her, either. But now that I do, I can't help but think about everything she sacrificed for the people of Adarie. She spent a thousand years trapped with only a beast for company, just to be yanked back here to spend another thousand years frozen in time.

The isolation, the loneliness, the agony... Her death may have saved her from the memories of her imprisonment in the Shadow Realm, but I'm pretty sure the emotional trauma of those years lingers somewhere deep inside her still. The same way my feelings for Hudson lingered deep inside me long after I lost my memories of him.

Even worse, it's robbed her of the knowledge of the many people her sacrifice saved. So she doesn't even have that to hold on to when the loneliness imprinted within her rears its ugly head. Instead, all she has are shards of pain she has no memory or understanding of.

It's a terrible thought—one that has my heart aching for the soldier I knew in the Shadow Realm and the general I've gotten to know here in the Gargoyle Court and on the battlefield. She deserves so much better than that.

But as she lowers me back to the ground, I tell myself I can't let my newfound memories of the sacrifices she made haunt me. They were her choices to make, not mine, and they eventually led her here. Not just as a soldier before me, but as a dear friend and the general of my entire army.

She leans over and claps Hudson on the shoulder. "I wasn't expecting you guys to get here quite so fast. Give me a second to change, and then we can head in."

"Head in where?" I ask, watching her step away and transform once again into my serious-faced general. Her gaze darts to my friends before coming back to mine, her jaw a little tighter.

"Let me get changed," she repeats as she starts walking back toward the front of the castle. "Then we'll talk."

Now I'm even more concerned. I look to Hudson, but he's already on it. "I'll take care of the others. You go do what you need to do."

Thank you, I mouth, then follow Artelya.

"Where do you want me to meet you?" I ask as we walk into the castle entryway. I can see that my grandmother has been busy remodeling again. The heavy gray stones have been painted a dark navy that somehow manages to look both intimidating and royal at the same time. She's also hung some beautiful landscapes of Ireland on the wall, though I'm pretty sure that's my grandfather's influence.

Another time, I might spend a few minutes taking it all in, but right now I'm more concerned about whatever it is Artelya wants to discuss, so I barely give them a cursory glance.

"The interrogation room," she answers as she turns down the hallway, and my heart speeds up.

"I'm sorry. The what?" I choke out. Then clear my throat. "We have an interrogation room?"

"Of course we do. Where do you think Alistair and Chastain used to torture their enemies?"

I have absolutely no idea, and to be honest, I don't want to know. My grandfather and my respected former general torturing people isn't something that has ever crossed my mind. I don't say that, though. Instead, I go with, "And when did they last torture someone?"

She stops to look me in the eye. "The Second Great War was brutal, Grace. Things had to be done."

"Well, the Second Great War is long behind us," I answer, squaring my shoulders and staring right back at her. "And we don't torture anyone in my Court."

I've signed on for a lot of things since I joined this paranormal world. Mating a vampire. Being a demigod. Even accepting the gargoyle crown. But I absolutely, positively draw the line at torturing anyone.

Artelya sighs, looking disappointed—though I'm not sure whether it's with me or just because she doesn't get to torture anyone. Either way, I'm not particularly impressed.

"Yes, well, we still have to interrogate the spy," she finally says. "So let's meet downstairs, the room just past the cells at the end of the east hallway, in twenty minutes. I'm covered in dirt and need a quick shower."

And then she walks away, muttering, "Though I'm not sure how you expect us to get the enemy to talk."

As she disappears from view, I can't help swallowing the bile rising in my throat at her word choice. There's an enemy at the Gargoyle Court.

7

Don't Have a Field Day with This

Okay, twenty minutes to kill without going stir-crazy trying to think of what "enemy" is being held captive right now? Only one thing to do, really.

Which is why I don't waste a second before turning and jogging back down the hallway. I pick up speed as I head into the main hall, then hang a sharp right and out the double doors—straight for the training arena in the back.

As my feet pound against the packed earth, I can't stop thinking about how many prisoners Artelya has tortured for information over the years, if one more doesn't even warrant delaying a shower. I'm not naive. I know the Gargoyle Court has mainly existed during a much more brutal world than now, but still…I shudder. The whole idea of harming someone held captive and helpless is revolting to me.

Thankfully, I catch up with my friends just as they round the makeshift bleachers.

"Jikan's training with the gargoyles?" Flint sounds incredulous as I skid to a stop next to him.

"Not exactly," Hudson answers before locking eyes with me and raising his brows in question.

I give my head a quick shake, letting him know now isn't the time to discuss what Artelya wanted, and thankfully he crosses his arms and turns back to Flint.

"What does that mean? He's either—" Flint breaks off as he gets his first good look at the arena—and what happens to it every Thursday.

"Soccer?" Eden's eyes go wide. "We're here for a *soccer* game?"

"I think you mean football," Hudson comments mildly.

"Excuse me," she says in an outrageously fake British accent as she makes a face at him. "We're here for a *football* game?"

"Forget *us* being here," Flint tells her. "*Jikan*'s here for a football game?"

I start to explain, but before I can, everyone on the field—and in the stands—freezes. Everyone, that is, except Jikan, who tosses a giant green foam finger on the ground and proceeds to stomp on it.

8

What's Good for the Goose
Is Good for the Gargoyle

"Well, that's a sight you don't see every day." Flint smirks, his voice dripping with sarcasm.

"*That's* the God of Time?" Heather asks incredulously.

"Oh, that's him all right," Flint answers with a rueful shake of his head.

Jaxon mutters to Flint, "'God' seems like a bit of an overstatement."

For the most part, Jaxon's just bitter—he and Jikan have never gotten along. But to be fair, a grown man/god having a full-blown temper tantrum over a sports call is a sight to see. Especially when that man/god is currently dressed like the most rabid sports fan in the history of sports fans.

Green T-shirt. Green hoodie. Green sweatpants. Green socks. Green hat. He's even wearing green-and-gold-checked *loafers*. I didn't know such a thing existed before this moment, and to be honest, I could have gone my whole life without knowing it, let alone *seeing* it. Whoever said ignorance is bliss obviously knew what they were talking about.

Jikan stamps a foot on the giant foam finger a couple more times, then slides back into his seat and waves his hand, the arena coming instantly back to life and the game continuing as though the God of Time hadn't just frozen everyone on the field. To throw a tantrum.

"What's got his rubber ducky boxers in such a twist anyway?" Eden asks.

Before anyone can make a guess, a long, loud shout of "gooooooooooooooooal!" echoes through the air. Everyone wearing blue in the stands starts cheering.

"It appears green is his team." Hudson glances at the metal

scoreboard, two hooks with numbers dangling from each on big square cards. "And they're having a very bad day."

Considering the score is currently seven to zero in blue's favor, I can't disagree.

"Maybe now isn't the best time to approach him," Heather comments as Jikan leans forward and once again picks up his foam finger. This time, he tosses it onto the field before flopping back in his seat, arms crossed over his chest. "He looks like he might turn us all into pocket watches if we get too close."

"I'm pretty sure if he was going to smite anyone, he would have already done it to the green goalie." Flint's eyes are wide as he stares at a rather energetic goalie flying loop de loops over the goalposts.

When the goalie lands, then leaps back up, throwing his body into a midair somersault, all the while ignoring the ball heading straight downfield toward him, I wonder if Flint is right about the smiting. But if we don't catch Jikan now, we won't have another chance until next Thursday. And Mekhi doesn't have that kind of time to waste— especially since we're already here.

Besides, how pissed off can one god *really* be over a friendly soccer game, especially when the team rosters change each week as the captains—Jikan and Chastain—take turns picking players?

Apparently, the answer is *very* pissed off, as we climb the bleachers, and the ref—also known as my grandfather Alistair—throws a red card for one of the green players.

Jikan's back on his feet, grabbing the railing in front of him. "Are you kidding me? Did all those years living in a cave make you unable to see under the lights or something?"

"Wow," Jaxon murmurs as he settles into the seat next to Jikan's and props his legs up on the metal bar. "Someone needs a nap."

Because antagonizing an already pissed-off god who we need to ask for a favor seems like a good idea to my best friend and ex-mate.

"All that hair drains the sense out of him," Hudson comments softly in my ear. "There's no other answer for how bloody ridiculous he is."

"It's that or the dragon heart," I reply.

"Hey, I heard that," Eden complains. "Don't go blaming that boy's arrogance on dragons. That's pure vampire." She gives Hudson an arch look to enhance her point.

Jikan just glares at Jaxon—thankfully no smiting—as he very deliberately picks up his water bottle and puts it in the cupholder on the other side of his seat—away from Jaxon.

"No wonder we're losing," Jikan snipes as he pulls his green baseball cap down lower over his dark-brown eyes. "The goth harbinger of doom is in the house."

"Pretty sure that's a step up from Goth Boy," Hudson murmurs.

"Shut it, Book Boy," Jikan tosses back.

But Hudson bursts out laughing at the intended insult, and I can see why. Book Boy is definitely not an insult—at least in his mind, I'm sure.

Before he can mention that, though, Chastain—decked out entirely in blue—comes bustling up the bleacher stairs. The stocky former gargoyle general is carrying two hot dogs, a bucket of popcorn, a reusable cup in the same shade of blue that he's wearing, and two giant rainbow lollipops.

"You're in my seat," he tells Jaxon. But instead of waiting for him to move, he partially shifts and flies over all of us so that he can settle into the seat on the other side of Jikan.

He starts to hold a hot dog out to Jikan, but Jikan's too busy glaring at the field to notice.

"What'd I miss?" Chastain asks, finally shoving the hot dog into Jikan's hand.

"Nothing important," he grumbles back.

"Oh, is that why there are three more goals on the scoreboard than when I left?" Chastain asks drolly.

"Not my fault you took an hour to get concessions." The God of Time takes what can only be described as a sulky bite of his hot dog.

"May I remind you that there isn't actually a concession stand here?" Chastain says. "And, in case you forgot, you're the one who wanted the damn rainbow lolly."

"Rainbows are smiles upside down," Jikan answers.

"Upside-down smiles?" Heather whispers loudly, looking completely baffled as she glances among the rest of us. "Is he trying to say rainbows are *frowns*?"

"That or he's trying to say they're upside-down smiles," Flint tells her with an it-could-be-anything look on his face.

She stares at him. "I don't even know what that means."

"Join the club." Jaxon snorts as he stands up, walking over to Flint. "The man never makes any sense. In fact, he—"

Jaxon's entire body freezes mid-sentence.

"Seriously?" I groan at Jikan, then catch Flint's eye to warn him to let me handle this. Surprisingly, he appears to be enjoying this more than he should, leaning back as he takes in the full view with a grin. I turn back to Jikan, hands on my hips. "You yell at me for doing that all the time, but it's okay for you to do it?"

"I yell at you because *you* don't know how to freeze time without ripping a giant hole in the universe," he answers with an arched brow. "And also because what's good for the goose isn't always good for the gargoyle."

"I don't think that's how that saying is supposed to go," Eden murmurs as Heather waves her hands back and forth in front of Jaxon's face like she's trying to get him to respond.

"That won't work," I tell my bestie. "He's—"

"Are you kidding me?" Jikan yells, jumping up from his seat again to glare downfield. "Are. You. Kidding. Me? Are you drunk, Alistair? Is that it? Did Cassia make you a few too many mimosas at dinner this evening?"

Alistair is either too busy picking up the red card he just threw on the ground to answer Jikan or he's deliberately ignoring him. Whatever the reason, he doesn't even glance in our direction.

Which only pisses Jikan off more, judging by the amount of trash talk regarding Alistair and the blue team that starts coming out of his mouth. Alistair, looking hale and hearty and almost forty—which I'm still getting used to, considering he's my who-knows-how-many-greats-grandfather—still doesn't give Jikan the satisfaction of so much as a hint he's aware of his antics.

At least not until Jikan gestures at the stands of fans dressed in green and yells, "How do you think Cassia would feel about you screwing this many people at once? You know she's the jealous sort."

Alistair doesn't pause as he walks to the opposite end of the field. He does, however, flip Jikan off with both hands.

While it's a much milder reaction than I expected, Jikan seems satisfied with having provoked Alistair at all—at least if the way he settles back down in his seat and sucks on his *lolly/frown* is any indication.

I pull my phone out of my pocket and check the time. I've got ten more minutes until I need to get back and meet Artelya, so when the green team scores its first goal, I figure this is as good a time as any to try to talk to him. Especially since it's Chastain's turn to throw a fit and trash-talk my *very patient* grandfather.

"Hey, Jikan." I shift around Statue Jaxon, who is thankfully a couple of feet to the side of the seat, and settle down beside Jikan. "I'm sorry to bother you, but you're actually who we came here to see."

"And the spankings just keep on coming," he answers before reaching over and grabbing a handful of popcorn out of Chastain's bucket.

Heather turns to Flint. "Does he mean hits? The *hits* just keep on coming?"

Flint shakes his head at her in a don't-ask kind of way. Jikan is definitely an acquired taste—which he's yet to acquire.

"I was wondering if we could talk for a few minutes—" I start again.

"Is the game over?" he asks, not taking his gaze from following the ball down the field.

I blink. "No, but—"

"Then you've questioned your own answer, haven't you?" He barely takes a breath before leaping up and shouting again. "Damn it, green! Could you at least pretend to know how to play this thrice-fucked game?"

"'Thrice-fucked' seems a bit ambitious," Hudson comments as he settles down next to me.

"Keep it up and I'll freeze you, too, Book Boy," Jikan tells him. Then shouts onto the field, "I should probably freeze all of you! Maybe then you'll actually be able to stop a ball!" He plops back down and mutters under his breath, "Or at least nothing else will happen until Artelya gets back."

"Artelya's on your team?" I ask, my stomach sinking as I realize she *had* been dressed in green when I first saw her. How the hell am I supposed to break it to him that if she's showering now, she's definitely not coming back?

"Yes, finally!" He nods at Chastain. "He's won the coin toss every week for the last three months to pick first and has chosen her every time. I finally won the toss today, picked Artelya, and *foosh*!" He makes what looks like an exploding gesture with his hands. "She vanishes ten minutes into the game."

"Your bad luck." Chastain tries to sound sympathetic, but it's pretty hard to buy when his eyes are dancing with glee. "You know she's a general with huge responsibilities *as well as* a superior footballer, right?"

"Yeah, well, she's managed to do both every single week she played for *you*," Jikan fires back. "It's pretty suspicious the one week I've got her, she suddenly has somewhere more important to be."

He's got a good point. If I didn't know about the prisoner back at the castle, I might actually buy his conspiracy theory.

For a second, I want to do what he's threatening to do—freeze everyone on the field until it's just the two of us and he has to talk to me. But then I remember what happened the last time Jikan and I got into a god-power pissing contest.

Not only did I lose, but I also ticked him off so much, he almost left all my friends frozen forever. I'm a lot better at controlling my powers these days, so I don't think that could happen anymore, but I don't want to take any chances, either.

Especially since Jaxon is currently still frozen, and Flint's humor is turning more to annoyance by the minute.

So instead of telling Jikan we're in a hurry like I want to do, I decide I should just head back to Artelya—and whatever awaits there—and tackle Jikan when he's not so distracted by all of this losing. Before I leave, though, I say, "I won't bother you again until the game is over. But do you think you could unfreeze Jaxon while we wait?"

That gets his attention.

Jikan turns away from the field for pretty much the first time since we got here, glancing between Jaxon and me like he's actually contemplating my request.

But then he says, "I kind of like him like that. It's the quietest I've ever seen him," before returning his attention to the game.

I think about ignoring him and unfreezing Jaxon myself. But if I do that, there's no way Jikan is going to give us the key to unlock the Shadow Realm. And as much as Jaxon will hate this when he's unfrozen, I know he'd suffer through it again if it meant a chance at saving his best friend.

So instead of unfreezing Jaxon, I give my friends a be-patient head shake and stand up to leave Jikan and Chastain to watch the rest of the gargoyle equivalent of a casual Sunday game in the park...like it's the freaking World Cup.

I shoot Hudson a sharp look, wordlessly letting him know I want him to join me, and we both maneuver around Jaxon. "We have to take care of something, but you guys enjoy the game, and we'll see you after," I tell the others.

And do my absolute best not to notice when a *pigeon* lands on Jaxon's head.

9

Prey for Me

"**A**rtelya told you nothing else about the prisoner?" Hudson asks after I catch him up as we head back to the castle.

"Nope. Just that there's a prisoner who needs interrogating—and by interrogating, I get the strong sense she definitely means torture," I answer, glancing up at my mate. His jaw tenses as he remains focused on the double doors thirty feet ahead of us, his long strides eating up the distance so fast I have to bump my speed a bit to keep up.

"Excellent. I haven't enjoyed a good torture in a while." His accent is crisper than usual when he says it, and I legit can't tell if he's kidding or not.

I try to tell myself that he is, but the truth is I just don't know. Our San Diego college student lifestyle makes it easy to forget that Hudson was raised in a brutal society. And that he feels a million times more comfortable than I do in this deadly world that I'm still trying so desperately to fit into.

Because I don't know if he's joking—and I need to before we go in that room—I reach out and snag his elbow, pulling him to a stop. "Hey, you're not serious, right?" When he doesn't meet my gaze, focusing over my shoulder instead, my stomach fills with cement. "We don't torture people, *right, Hudson*?"

The muscle on the side of his jaw tics for a few more seconds before he turns his intense gaze on mine, and my knees full-on tremble at the storm raging in their blue depths. "That would depend on what their intentions are, *Grace*."

"Meaning?" On this one point, he's going to have to spell it out for me.

"Meaning, I would do anything to keep you and our people safe."

That doesn't mean torture. It can't mean torture. Except I know how Hudson feels about me, know just what he would risk—and what he would do—to keep me safe. And now that he's made a home here at the Gargoyle Court, now that he cares so much about *our* people, it's hard to imagine that same protectiveness won't extend to them.

We're in this together. Gargoyle queen and king, which means he has as much say in what goes on here as I do. And it's not like I thought we'd see eye to eye on everything when it comes to leading, but this... this is a big one not to agree on.

Still, now isn't the time to hash this out. Not when Artelya—and the prisoner—are waiting below. Maybe we'll get lucky and they'll sing like a canary the minute they take in the expression on Hudson's face. I know I would.

Deciding now isn't the best time to argue about something that may never happen, I plaster on a smile I'm not really feeling and say, "Well, then, let's hope it doesn't come to that," then open the castle door.

The tension between us is so thick that my skin feels tight and itchy by the time we reach the basement—which, now that I'm down here, I realize is really just a dungeon. And a surprisingly creepy one at that. Damn it. I truly thought that gargoyles, the keepers of balance and arbiters of justice, were above having a place to keep people prisoner, but judging from the chains embedded in the walls, I've been far too naive.

I just wish I knew what to do about it.

Thankfully, Artelya comes rushing toward me before I can get any more inside my own head. "I'm sorry it took me so long," she says as she pulls a long skeleton key out of her pocket.

"Who's in there?" I ask, nodding to the unmarked wooden door of the interrogation room. "I mean, who could you possibly need to interrogate right now?"

"We found one," she replies with grim satisfaction.

"Found one of whom?" I blink, baffled.

"A hunter," Hudson answers, and Artelya's eyes narrow on his.

"Yes," is all she says before she snaps the key into place and turns the lock.

We all know the Crone's been training hunters to kill paranormals, but honestly, we haven't actually seen much evidence of that in months. Not since she was freed from her island prison, at least.

Of course, the Circle had discussed looking into the matter further at our last council meeting, keeping an eye on their activities, but I had no idea that plan had evolved to the let's-kidnap-one variety.

Artelya inclines her head, correcting herself with, "Actually, *she* found *us*."

"She came here? To the Gargoyle Court?" I ask, cheeks flushing and fists clenching. "She seriously had the nerve to show her face on our cliffs?"

Outrage, ice-cold and livid, slices through me. Not enough to make me want to torture this woman, but more than enough to make me want to kick her ass in a fair fight. Who the hell does she think she is, marching right up to the home of my people, of my grandparents, with her misinformation and unfounded hatred?

"We think she's a spy, though I'm not sure, since I haven't had a chance to inter—*question*—her."

"I'm surprised the Crone would risk venturing this close when she's done everything to remain hidden up till now," I say.

"Because we are her biggest threat," Artelya answers, looking insulted. "The Gargoyle Army is the only thing standing in their way now when it comes to paranormal genocide and world domination."

I'm not sure it's the only thing, but I don't say that. Instead, I watch her reach for the door handle as she asks, "Do we know if they've been sneaking around the other Courts, too?"

"Not yet," I tell her at the same time Hudson responds, "Yes."

I turn and shoot him a we-will-talk-about-this-later look, which he has the brains to answer with a sheepish half nod.

Artelya raises her brows, then asks, "Ready?"

Not even close. I have absolutely no idea what I'm supposed to do in that room. But I've been faking it till I make it for a year now. What's one more hour?

"Absolutely," I decide. Then take a breath and follow Artelya into the dank, dismal room.

And immediately wish I were anywhere else.

10

Fashion à la
Murder

I'm not one to care much for interior design—that's definitely more my grandmother's department, now that she's over her whole frozen-murder-cave phase—but even I can tell this place needs work. Just being in here scares me. Or maybe that's the point.

I'm used to being surrounded by weapons—the gargoyles do love their broadswords and battle-axes—but what's in this room is a step above all that. A big step. From the chains embedded in the walls, to the various knives and tools I can't even imagine the use of displayed on giant hooks and shelves, to the stone floor stained a dull orange-red, this room clearly has only one purpose: to cause a lot of pain.

My stomach churns with horror, but I swallow down the bile burning its way up my throat. Nothing like that is going to happen here today, even if I have to wrestle Hudson to the ground. That's pretty much the only thing I can guarantee about whatever's coming next.

"What's your name?" Artelya asks as Hudson closes the door behind us with a sickening clang, then leans against it to size up the spy with a predatory gleam.

The hunter—who is currently sitting on a chair in the center of the room, her arms and legs shackled by chains as wide as my arm—doesn't answer. In fact, she doesn't so much as glance our way. Instead, she keeps her gaze focused on the wall directly in front of her.

The lighting is dim, but I can't help but notice that the table against the back wall is covered in a plethora of pouches and vials in various sizes and colors.

More instruments of torture, I wonder as I walk closer to the display, *or something else entirely?* I'm leaning toward the latter, given the closer I get to the jars and other paraphernalia, the more agitated the hunter becomes. She still doesn't say anything, but I can feel the turmoil rolling off her in waves.

Because her reaction intrigues me, I lean forward and pick up one of the glass vials. It's small and hourglass-shaped, with a cork stopper that keeps the viscous yellow liquid inside from pouring out. I have absolutely no idea what it is or what it does, but the second I lift it up to the light, the hunter strains against her bonds.

Artelya and I exchange a glance, and I put the vial down in favor of a royal-blue pouch with a drawstring. Curious, I open it up, but all that's inside is a strange white powder.

I close it quickly, with thoughts of anthrax-laced envelopes dancing in my head. Even with my back turned to her, I can feel the hunter's angst lessen the second I put the pouch down.

"What's your name?" Artelya asks again from behind me.

Again, silence.

"What are you doing at the Gargoyle Court?"

No sound at all. Not even breathing, really.

I glance over at Hudson, curious to see if he might step in, but he's still leaning against the door, between two very large maces on either wall. His arms are crossed as he studies the prisoner with a bored expression now—but his eyes are laser focused.

"I'm going to ask you one more question, and you'd better answer it," Artelya says, and I can hear the annoyance rising with each word she bites out. I turn around to see if I can defuse the situation, just in time to watch the hunter flip Artelya off.

Artelya's teeth snap together with a sharp click that has the hair on the back of my neck standing up. Before I can think better of it, I've put myself between them, which makes Hudson bristle, but he doesn't move.

Artelya makes a low sound, but she stands down as I take the lead. Or whatever it is I'm doing right now.

To begin with, I pull up a chair so I can sit facing the hunter. I make sure to stay several feet away, out of reach of her hands and feet and the chains that currently keep her shackled, and take my first good look at her.

She's not young by human years, but she's not particularly old, either. Maybe forty, forty-five, with blond hair cropped close to her scalp in uneven waves. She's tall—even chained and sitting down, I can see that—and the left half of her face was obviously badly burned at some point, because her skin is ridged and discolored there.

But the most interesting—and horrifying—thing about her isn't the burn or her unusual hairstyle. It's the clothes she's wearing.

At first, I thought she was outfitted with snakeskin leather pants, but now that I'm sitting across from her, I realize the reptilian pattern isn't snake. It's dragon.

Oh. My. God. She's wearing pants made of dragon skin—and since dragons don't molt, there's only one way she got them. Suddenly, the burn on her face makes a lot more sense.

As I take a deep breath to combat the bile once again churning inside me, I realize dragons haven't been her only prey. Her jacket is real fur, a beautiful, fluffy white-and-gray coat that I know is a wolf's pelt—partly because of the color and partly because of the claw she left attached like a brooch that's currently hooking around her shoulder. Circling her wrist is a bracelet of vampire fangs, and hanging around her neck is a chain with a ring attached. I notice the large moonstone before I spot the witch's bony finger inserted through the ring.

And on her hand, sticking straight up from the center of the ring she herself is wearing, is a chunk of a brilliant red gargoyle heartstone.

Suddenly, *interrogation* doesn't sound so bad.

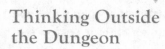

11

Thinking Outside
the Dungeon

Nausea swamps me, has my stomach pitching and rolling with horror. Only the rage burning deep inside keeps me from throwing up, because there is no way I will give this bitch the satisfaction of seeing my weakness *or* my horror.

So I swallow down the sickness and stay exactly where I am, arms crossed in front of me and legs curled under my chair as our gazes lock. I can see in her eyes that she's waiting for me to speak, waiting for me to be the one to break the silence that stretches between us like shattered glass.

But my father taught me a long time ago that in a game of wits, the person who moves first always loses. In children's games, that never bothered me. Here, today, locked in this staring contest with this heinous murderer, it bothers me a lot. Hell will freeze over before I blink first.

Next to me, Artelya shifts uncomfortably. But—like the general she is—she doesn't say a word. Instead, seconds turn into minutes as the spy winds a long piece of nylon string around her index fingers and then pulls it taut. Over and over again as I just wait and watch.

"You can torture me all you want," the hunter suddenly blurts out. "I'm not going to tell you anything."

"I don't remember asking you anything," I answer mildly. "That was the general. As for torture? You're not worth the mess you'd make. I actually like these shoes."

Artelya doesn't utter a sound at that, but I can see her standing straighter out of the corner of my eye, as if my words have reinvigorated her.

"Then what do you want from me?" She shifts in her chair, pulling against her bonds.

"What makes you think I want anything from you? You're the one who came to my Court, wearing the *heart* from one of my people." I nod toward her ring, doing my best to ignore the anger and the sorrow still coiling inside me. "I think I should be the one asking what you want."

"What all hunters want. To free the world from the pestilence of all paranormals. You are a blight on this land, a plague on—"

"Oh, please." I fake a yawn I'm far from feeling. "You don't really believe all that hunter propaganda, do you?"

Her eyes narrow. "It's not propaganda if it's true."

"Is that like 'you aren't paranoid if they really are out to get you'?" I shoot back.

"Just go ahead and kill me already. I've taken enough of your kind with me to die with pride."

"I have no idea how killing anyone can be a matter of pride," I answer, standing up and crossing to the table loaded with her belongings.

"Because you've never suffered the way I have," she snarls at me. "You've never lived in fear the way we humans have to every day—"

"From each other. Not from paranormals," I interject. "Humans are brutal creatures, and we both know it."

"*We're* brutal? You hunted us long before we formed our army to hunt you. How do you think the *Bloodletter* got her name?" She sneers. "She slaughtered humans a dozen at a time and never thought anything of it. Werewolves and wendigos eat us. Witches cast spells to force us to do their bidding. Dragons burned down our homes for centuries until we finally chased them into hiding. You don't think any of that is brutal behavior?"

She snorts and continues. "Hell, look at the last vampire king. He raised an army to try to subjugate and kill every human on earth. You think we're brutal? We're only brutal because that's the way you taught us to be. If we don't kill you, you'll kill us. You've proved that much over and over again."

She's breathing heavily by the time she finishes her little speech, and as much as I want to knock her down a few pegs, I can't. Not because I think she's right, because I don't. But because it's obvious she's a zealot, and like any true zealot, she picks and chooses her truth.

Did Cyrus try to kill humans? Absolutely.

Did a group of paranormals stop him from enacting his plan at great personal risk to themselves? Damn right we did.

Humans didn't stop him. We did, by regulating our own the way I wish humans would regulate theirs. But how can they, when contingents like this are so busy blaming someone else that it never occurs to them to try to solve their problems using anything but violence?

Not to mention the fact that she is literally sitting there dripping in the trophies of paranormals she's killed, while I have never hurt a human in my life. Hell, I spent most of my life thinking I was one.

"Nothing to say to me?" she taunts as I once again study all the strange vials and pouches spread out in front of me.

They're weapons of some kind—that much I'm sure of. I just don't know what they do or how much damage they'll cause. Are they designed to kill paranormals, or will they hurt anyone in their path? And if so, do they work on all paranormals or only some?

These are questions we need answers to for our own protection. But I don't believe that any amount of interrogation will get those answers from the woman in front of me. Which means holding her is pointless.

Which also means there's only one thing to do in this situation.

"General, come with me." It's as close to an order as I've ever given in peacetime, and I can see Artelya's eyes widen as she turns her back on the prisoner. She doesn't say a word, though, as she and Hudson follow me from the room. None of us do until the door is shut firmly behind us.

"You can see that there's no reasoning with her," Artelya starts.

"No, there isn't," I agree. "But interrogating her will also be a waste of your time. She'll give you nothing and—"

"You don't know that," Hudson interrupts.

"I *do* know it. And so do you, if you're honest with yourself."

Artelya looks like she wants to argue, but in the end, she doesn't. Because she knows I'm right, as does Hudson—I can see it in their eyes. "You can't actually expect me to just let her go, do you? Did you see what she was wearing?" Indignation slams through each syllable.

"I did," I answer, the flames of anger still turning my organs to ash. "And no, you're definitely not going to let her go."

"Well, thank heavens for—"

It's my turn to interrupt. "You're going to let her escape."

"You want me to do what?" Artelya's lips pull tight with fury.

"I want you to let her escape," I repeat. "Without all those little potions and powders she's got with her. And then I want you and a couple of your best soldiers to follow her and see where she goes. Torture won't work on a woman like that, but subterfuge just might."

"She already thinks she's smarter than us," Hudson adds, and Artelya nods as the plan comes together in her mind.

"Then we should give her the chance to prove that to herself," she says.

"Exactly," I tell her. "And if we're lucky, she'll lead us straight back to the Crone and this 'army' she mentioned, so we can put an end to the hunters once and for all."

"And if we're not lucky?" Hudson raises one brow.

"If we're not, we'll cross that bridge when we get to it. And in the meantime…"

"In the meantime, we have a god to reason with," Hudson reminds me.

"And I have an escape to plan," Artelya says, a grin finally spreading across her face.

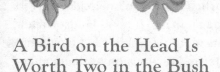

12

A Bird on the Head Is
Worth Two in the Bush

Hudson and I make it back to the game with less than a minute on the clock. A quick glance at the scoreboard shows that Jikan's team has made a miraculous comeback in our absence, which is a relief, given we really need to ask for his help if we hope to save Mekhi—and Jikan being in a winning mood will definitely make that easier.

The literal second the game is over, Flint demands, "Can you please unfreeze Jaxon now?"

Despite the use of the word "please," it doesn't sound like a question, and every one of us knows it, including Jikan. Which is probably why he gives Flint a look so mild it has fear icing its way up my spine even before he pops one last piece of popcorn in his mouth and stands up to stretch.

His casual insolence is the last straw for Flint, who steps forward, looking like he wants to throttle the god. Thank the world for Hudson, who positions himself between them so smoothly that it looks like an accident.

I know it's not, just like I know Hudson isn't nearly as amused as he seems that his brother has been frozen for so long.

Jikan must sense it, too, because he yawns—right before he waves a hand and unfreezes Jaxon, *who still has a pigeon on his head*. The bird freaks out the second it realizes he's alive, letting out a squawk that echoes through our entire section before flying away in a very affronted flap of wings.

"What the fuck?" Jaxon says, more than a little disturbed as he stares after it, trying to figure out what he's missed. "What happened to the game? When did you guys sit down? And why was there a *pigeon* on my *head*?"

He looks so befuddled and disturbed that I can't help it. I start to laugh. Seconds later, Heather and Eden join me. It takes Hudson a few more seconds, but eventually he joins in, too. Flint doesn't laugh, but he does duck his head to hide a smile, and the tension of the moment dissipates like so much smoke.

Jikan, on the other hand, leans a hip against the railing and crosses his arms over his chest. "So what is it you want from me now?" he asks, heaving a long-suffering sigh.

He looks so put-upon that I'm tempted to shift and toss him over the balcony and down to the field below, especially since he's making it sound like we come to him for favors every other day. Which we do not. This is the first time I've spoken to him since the battle with Cyrus, and it's not like I asked him to show up there. He's the one who's usually sticking his nose in where nobody needs or wants it.

But since I do need him this one time, I grit my teeth and try not to think about how satisfying it would be to smother him with a giant foam finger. Instead, I say, "We had a few questions to ask you about the Shadow Realm."

"Noromar?" he asks, sounding surprised. "I would have thought that's the last place you'd want to think about ever again."

I swallow the anger rising in my throat. Jikan *knew* I'd been there—knew what I'd forgotten—and didn't say a word. What an ass.

He squeezes past us, then sets off at a quick pace, leaving me to scramble after him. The others have no problem keeping up with him, but my short legs don't cover the same ground theirs do, and I end up feeling like a little kid trailing after her teacher.

Despite his long legs, Hudson keeps stride with me, but when we're halfway back to the keep, he turns to Jikan and says, "We know you created the Shadow Realm—and all the shite rules that trapped Grace there *and* stole her memories."

Hudson has obviously hit a nerve, because Jikan stops walking long enough to lock eyes with him. "You don't know shit, vampire."

Hudson just lifts a brow. "Want to try me?"

Several tense seconds pass as the two of them stare each other down.

But no matter how right Hudson apparently is, given Jikan's reaction, I need to break this up. Fast. Especially since Jikan looks like he's two seconds away from smiting Hudson. No matter how tough Hudson is, nobody wants to be smote by a full god. Certainly not a god capable of creating the Shadow Realm like it's nothing.

My mind is racing, trying to come up with a way to alleviate the tension, when Flint rushes in to say, "I've been meaning to ask. What kind of hair products do you use, Jikan? Because your ponytail always looks spot-on."

For a second, we all stare at Flint in shock. And then we're laughing again. Even Jaxon cracks a smile. Jikan, on the other hand, looks at Flint like he has no idea where he came from or what he's thinking.

But then he chuckles, too, before he turns back around and continues walking, this time at a more reasonable pace.

"Jikan," I begin, though I'm not sure what I'm going to say next—only that I need to say something. "I'm sorry if our coming here for help upsets you."

"It doesn't upset me, Grace," he answers softly, sounding resigned. "But nobody likes having their mistakes thrown back in their face."

"Is that what the Shadow Realm was?" Eden asks, her purple eyes watchful. "A mistake?"

"No, it was more than that," he answers. "It was vengeance."

13

Your Mosa Is
Actually Mi-mosa

When we reach the castle, Jikan pulls open the heavy wooden doors with a sigh.

"Mimosas, anyone?" the Bloodletter asks as she greets us at the door. "I've already set Alistair up with one in the parlor."

Mimosas at midnight? Heather mouths to me. I shrug back, even as I try desperately not to grin. I can definitely imagine what Heather was expecting someone called "the Bloodletter" to be like. In her mind, she should probably be handing out goblets filled with blood from people hanging over buckets in the corner, *not* handing out champagne cocktails.

I don't bother telling her that my grandmother has been there and done that, even before Jikan answers, "I'll take one, Cassia." Then seems to reconsider as he says, "Actually, make that two."

"Double fisting the champagne, are we?" Hudson comments dryly.

"After the dragon urine that just went down on that field, I'd be triple fisting if I could," Jikan answers with an edge to his voice.

"Dragon urine?" Flint makes a face.

"I think he means dragon shit," Eden tells him, looking no less disgusted.

"He means bullshit," the Bloodletter says wearily. "He speaks every language on Earth—and understands half of them."

Heather snort-laughs, and I think Jikan's going to swing his head around and freeze her, but instead he replies, "Hey, I resemble that."

We all laugh this time—not sure whether he intended the misstatement or not, which only makes it funnier.

"Now, can I pretty please have a drink?" Jikan asks and tosses the

Bloodletter a wink. A *wink*.

But she's having none of it. "Well, with the way you behaved, you're lucky I'm even letting you enter my house, much less touch my champagne."

"Yeah, well, if your mate wasn't drunk every time he got on the field, I wouldn't have to correct him, Cassia."

"Perhaps if you didn't berate him so much, he wouldn't have to *be* drunk every time he has to referee one of these *friendly* games," the Bloodletter counters with a toss of her head, but I notice she hands him both glasses before she turns to walk us toward the parlor—wherever that is. Since she and Alistair have moved back into the Court, it looks majorly different than it used to. Kind of like the Bloodletter herself.

Gone is the old woman I first met. In her place is a slender woman in her thirties, with unwrinkled brown skin and long locs pulled up in a head wrap the exact shade of her flowing red caftan. Only her eye color is the same, a swirling emerald green that changes intensity with her emotions.

Heather is looking everywhere but where she's going as we follow the Bloodletter down the grand hall. "This place is amazing!" she whispers as she stares at the huge stone hallways filled with weapons and tapestries.

I flash back to my first hours wandering the halls at Katmere Academy, part awed, part overwhelmed, as I tried to figure out how my life had taken such a strange and abrupt turn. I have a moment of wishing I could have shown Katmere to her before Hudson and Jaxon had to bring it down to save us all, but then I let it go.

Because, as Jikan would probably say, if beggars were horses, wishes would ride...

Besides, with the team the Circle has put together to rebuild Katmere, I know it's going to be better than ever. I just wish it could be better than ever now.

The Bloodletter finally stops in front of what used to be a pretty utilitarian meeting room, if I remember correctly. But as she throws open the mahogany French doors, I realize exactly why she's calling this the parlor now. Because there's absolutely nothing utilitarian left about it.

Instead of light-gray stone, the walls are now covered in a pale-green fabric decorated with birch trees and flowers and flying birds. The drapes are teal, and so is the very fancy rug that now covers the rough stone floors. Crystal chandeliers hang from the ceiling, and the furniture all looks comfortable and ladylike.

Especially the Queen Anne armchair that Alistair is currently sitting in as he sips a very large mimosa.

"Grandfather," I say, crossing to him.

"Grace!" He leaps to his feet and meets me halfway. And while he may look young, he still hugs like a grandpa, his arms as strong and comforting as the old-fashioned scent of Aramis that wraps itself around me. "I was hoping you'd stop by the house to see me!"

"I wouldn't leave without at least saying hello," I tell him as he pulls me over to sit next to him on one of the dainty rose-gold couches.

"Too bad Jikan can't say the same," he answers with a scowl directed at the God of Time.

Jikan is completely unfazed, of course. So unfazed, in fact, that he sets one of his now empty glasses down, reaches out, and snatches the mimosa out of Alistair's hand before sitting in one of the delicate armchairs and draining it in one long sip.

Alistair raises an imperious brow. "Excuse you?" he growls.

"You've already had too many," Jikan responds airily. "Though it's nice to see that common sense prevailed at the end."

"You wouldn't know common sense if it bit you in the—" Alistair breaks off when the Bloodletter shoots him a dark look.

"Aorta?" Jikan fills in the blank for him.

"Who wants to be bitten in the aorta?" Heather asks, wide-eyed.

Eden chuckles. "Who wants to be bitten in the ass?"

She makes a good point, and Heather must think so, too, because she ducks her head before finding a seat next to Eden on a couch opposite the chairs.

"Another mimosa, Cassia dear?" Jikan asks. "It's been a trying evening."

"Made so by you, Jikan *dear*," she answers with fake sweetness. But she pours him another of the orange-juice-and-champagne drinks before settling down next to Alistair with one of her own.

"There's no try in team." Jikan shoots me a sly glance. "Just ask Grace."

"There's no I, either," I comment as I lean forward.

"Exactly. Because that would spell time. Speaking of which…" He drains his own mimosa as quickly as he drained Alistair's. "I have a trapeze lesson in an hour, so let's make this quick."

I start to remind him that I'm not the one holding up the conversation—I've been waiting to talk to him for a while—but in the end, it's not worth the fight. Not if we want to get out of here with the answers we need—the favor we need.

So instead, I consider my words carefully. If I've learned anything about dealing with gods, it's that they rarely like to answer a question head-on. "I wanted to know what you could tell me about the Shadow Realm."

He lifts a brow. "You've been there. What more would you need to know?"

"Let's just say, the last time I visited, things didn't go as planned," I admit. "But that's why I want to know more. In case we have to return."

"You want to go *back*?" he asks. He sounds amused as he scratches his cheek, but his gaze darts to my grandmother's concerned expression.

Before he can continue, though, the Bloodletter lets out an alarmed cry.

And disappears between one breath and the next.

14

All of the Circus,
None of the Tense

I gasp at the sudden disappearance of my grandmother, but one glance at Jikan and Alistair—both still relaxed in their seats—has my heart rate slowing again. Whatever just happened, if they're not worried, I guess I shouldn't be, either. Although I *am* quite curious.

In fact, I'd have thought Jikan had just poofed her himself, he'd been looking at her so strangely, except my grandfather doesn't have him by the throat, demanding answers. What can I say? We're a take-action kind of family.

"Well, that's something you don't see every day." Heather's gaze darts around like she expects someone or something to come along and make her disappear next.

"All of the circus, none of the costumes," Hudson tells her in a soft aside. "It's definitely the motto around here."

"From what I understand, the same can be said about you," Jikan answers. But it lacks his usual sharpness—probably because he's staring vacantly off into space as he says it. A few seconds later, he snaps back to us, nodding to himself as he settles deeper into the settee.

"I do so aim to entertain," comes Hudson's dry response as he lowers onto a small green love seat. I watch him unfold like a lawn chair, stretching his long legs out in front of him and crossing them at the ankles as he leans back against the couch. Even before he folds his arms over his chest, I know exactly what the pose is saying—namely, that he's as relaxed as he is unwilling to put up with any bullshit today.

It's a good look on him. A very good look.

The sarcasm goes way over Jikan's head, though. "Yes, well, you're certainly not weighing your pull in that department. But what else should I expect from Goth Boy's brother?"

His gaze slides slyly to Jaxon, who bares his teeth the tiniest bit but keeps quiet. The fear of being turned into a statue once again is obviously stronger in him than he wants to admit.

While Jikan is clearly a little disappointed that he couldn't provoke Jaxon, in the end he just takes another sip of his mimosa. Then he focuses his direct mahogany gaze fully on mine.

"You were going to tell us more about the Shadow Realm?" I prompt, eyebrows raised.

"I don't get your sudden obsession with that place." He waves a dismissive hand. "But it was created as a punishment, not a vacation destination."

"So you *did* create it?" Eden asks, pointing at Jikan. "You can just do that?"

"I'm a god," he shoots back. "I can do almost anything."

"And Noromar is a punishment for whom, exactly?" I prompt again. At least he's answering questions, so maybe this means he'll help, with a little luck.

Well, that and a whole lot of begging. We are talking about Jikan, after all.

"The Shadow Queen, of course. Who else?" Jikan yawns like he's bored, but there's a watchful look in his eyes that says he's anything but.

"But why?" I sigh, frustrated because getting a straight answer out of him is like pulling arms, teeth, and everything in between at the best of times.

And this is definitely not shaping up to be one of those times.

Alistair holds Jikan's gaze for several long, inscrutable seconds. Some kind of silent communication is going on there, obviously, but I can't tell what it is.

Eventually, though, Alistair tells him, "Go ahead." He makes a strangely formal flourish with his hand. "Tell the kids what they want to know."

At first, it seems like Jikan is going to argue, but in the end, he just stands up and announces, "I'm hungry." Then he takes off toward the kitchen like we weren't just in the middle of a very important conversation.

"How can he be hungry?" Heather asks in a low voice. "It's been less than ten minutes since he ate the better half of a concession stand."

I don't have a clue, but I'm not about to make the mistake of asking him about his food intake. Instead, I get up and follow him down toward the kitchen, Hudson and my friends trailing a little behind.

My grandfather stays in the parlor with his pitcher of mimosas, probably to wait on my grandmother's return.

It turns out she's been busy decorating more than just the parlor since I was last here. She's also changed the tapestries that lined the ancient stone walls, exchanging the battle and nature scenes for beautiful black-and-white photographs of Alistair, Artelya, me, and many of the other gargoyles as well.

Scenes depicted range from battle practice to our weekly soccer game, from huge "family" dinners to Alistair's lone figure walking the cliffs just beyond the iron fence. The effect is somehow both welcoming and haunting.

I love it.

Within minutes, most everyone takes a seat in high-backed barstools around a massive granite island. Jikan slips on a chef's apron that reads, The Last Time I Cooked, Hardly Anyone Died. Comforting.

Then he opens the larder and starts yanking things out of it in a way that says, very clearly, that he has no actual plan for his midnight snack. Everything from Oreo cookies—Alistair's newest obsession— and pickles to dried pasta and canned pineapple ends up on the counter next to the mimosa he carried with him from the parlor.

"So, he's not actually going to mix all that together, is he?" Heather whispers, sounding horrified.

I have no idea, and since I'm still hoping to convince him to help us, I'm sure as hell not going to say anything to offend him about his culinary choices. I even manage not to wince when cinnamon and dried mustard join the growing pile on the counter.

"Fill a pot with water, will you?" Jikan tosses over his shoulder as he continues to rummage in the larder.

"Of course." I move to do it, but Eden is already there, pulling a giant copper pot down from the rack above the center island and carrying it toward the sink with a this-is-exciting expression on her face, and I chuckle.

Jikan finally emerges from the closet with a triumphant crow, a pack of chocolate chips in one hand and a jar of peanut butter in the other. He holds them up like spoils of war before dropping them on the counter next to the rest of his plunder.

"I need orange juice and eggs," he announces to the room in general, like saying it will make it so.

Then again, I'm the first one to hightail it to the fridge and pull out giant containers of both before Jikan can even make it around the corner of the center island. The faster we get him what he wants, the faster we might actually get him to tell us about the key to the Shadow Realm—get him to *give* us the key.

I'd be lying if I said my skin wasn't itching to just stop this god-dance we're doing and plead with Jikan to help. After the whole prisoner-in-my-basement scene with Artelya, I haven't wanted to admit I might have to choose between Mekhi's need for a cure right-this-fucking-second and an army of hunters possibly organizing to attack with the same alacrity. But it's fifty-fifty Jikan can even help—a solid zero if we upset him—and a hundred percent we're not going anywhere unless he does. Math was never my strong suit, but even I know those odds mean I need to plaster a smile on my face and keep on waltzing.

I set the containers on the counter near the other random ingredients with a "here you go" and hop back onto my barstool.

"What exactly are we making?" Flint asks, eyeing the food combination with the same glee rounding Eden's eyes in wonder.

Hudson didn't take one of the barstools, preferring to lean against the opposite counter, arms crossed, and we exchange a humorous look. *Dragons.*

Jikan reaches for the jar of pickles and pops it open. "Dessert pasta."

"With pickles?" I blurt out before I can stop myself.

But Jikan just rolls his eyes. "Obviously not, Grace. They're for eating while we cook."

As if to prove his point, he grabs a fork and fishes out two of the small pickles to pop in his mouth before walking to the sink to wash his hands.

When he's done, he turns around and claps his hands together. "Okay, where did we leave off?"

I'm not sure if he's referring to the dessert pasta, the pickles, or the story he's supposed to be telling us, but I decide to hope for the best. "You were about to tell us why you created Noromar to punish the Shadow Queen."

15

Aghast from
the Past

"**O**h, that's right," he agrees. But he doesn't say anything. Instead, he reaches for the jar of pickles and pops several more into his mouth.

Then, with a mouth full of pickles, says, "It's all the Shadow Queen's fault."

"We assumed as much, given the whole you-made-a-prison-for-her-like-a-god move," Hudson jokes, but his eyes are following Jikan carefully.

"Honestly," he says, then sighs long and hard as he reaches behind his head and tugs his ponytail tighter. "This whole story is proof of why it's just a good practice to avoid falling in love. Ever." He takes a swig of his mimosa and chases it with another pickle before adding, "Better to have never loved so you can't get lost, as the saying goes."

"You fell in love with the Shadow Queen?" I bite out the question—because that would be all kinds of fucked up if he then built a prison for her.

"Why in the world would you think that?" he asks, his eyebrows hitting his hairline as he pauses in the middle of opening a bag of pasta. Then adds, "She fell in love with a mortal," as if that explains everything.

Shrugging, he resumes cooking, if you can call it that, while the rest of us watch him warily. Jikan's not a bad guy, but he is unpredictable—which makes trying to anticipate his behavior more than a little stressful sometimes.

"She fell in love and got married." He reaches for a small saucepan and puts it on the stove next to the water pot. "And here we are."

"I'm pretty sure we're going to need more explanation than that,

Jikan," Hudson drawls as he pulls his phone from his pocket and starts scrolling without missing a beat. "People don't tend to go from falling in love to trying to overthrow a god without something in between. So what set her off?"

"The pregnancy, obviously." Jikan makes a disgusted face. "Isn't that what always sets women off?"

"That's sexist as fuck, isn't it?" Hudson interjects mildly, more proof that he's listening despite the fact that his thumbs are now flying across the screen.

The God of Time's eyes narrow in annoyance as he drops a heaping spoon of peanut butter in the small pan in front of him. But then he must think about what Hudson said—and what he'd said to provoke it—because he sighs.

"You're right. I apologize. In this instance," he stresses, "what set the Shadow Queen off is falling in love with—and getting pregnant by—a human time wizard."

I stiffen, and my gaze jumps to Hudson's. I mouth, *The mayor?* at the same time that he raises an eyebrow.

We'd never considered that the Shadow Queen and the mayor were allies, and I can see the cogs turning in Hudson's brain now. If the mayor was trying to reset the timeline to save his daughter... Maybe the Shadow Queen wasn't fighting us to be free of the prison as much as she also wanted the timeline reset to save *their* daughter.

Jikan continues, unaware that my mind is exploding. "Because she's from the shadows, a wraith, the Shadow Queen is immortal. But her mate was mortal, which made her deathly afraid that—"

"Her child could die," Alistair finishes from behind us.

Considering the last time I saw him, he was happily ensconced in the parlor with his mimosa, I wasn't expecting to hear his voice right now. But he must have decided to follow us after all, because he's currently leaning against the kitchen doorway, staring blankly into the distance. But there's a softness—and a sadness—in his face that makes me wonder if he's remembering his own daughter with the Bloodletter. The thought of her—and the pain my grandparents must have felt when they lost her—has my chest tightening.

"What did she do?" I ask, biting my lip with unwanted empathy for the Shadow Queen that makes the tightness in my chest even more pronounced.

Whatever she did next, however awful it must have been to lead to being sentenced to an immortal life in prison, a part of me can't help but wonder just what lengths *I* would go to in order to save the life of the child Hudson and I might one day have.

Suddenly, getting the key from Jikan and releasing her from her prison seems like the absolute right thing to do, whether she helps Mekhi or not.

Jikan adds a splash of orange juice to the rapidly melting peanut butter before cracking an egg on the side of the pan and adding that, too. Heather makes a small gagging sound, but thankfully Jikan ignores her as he continues the story. "While pregnant, the Shadow Queen became obsessed with finding a way to keep her child from eventually dying. She begged the child's father for help, which he refused several times, as this kind of magic is both forbidden and highly unstable."

Jikan stops to add a giant pinch of salt and the entire pack of linguine to the now boiling pot of water on the stove. Then he tosses a pinch of salt over his shoulder—"For luck"—before rapidly stirring the peanut butter, orange juice, and egg concoction he'd just assembled and reaching for the cinnamon and dried mustard.

"So, what happened?" Heather asks eagerly. "Did her husband ignore her pleas for help?"

"He should have," Jikan tells her with a disgusted shake of his head. "But no. Love made him soft, too. And when she eventually gave birth, he couldn't resist his mate's desperation, and he performed a spell using forbidden time magic that would let their daughter live forever."

"Let me guess." Hudson finally glances up from his phone with a lifted brow. "Something went wrong."

"You could say that." Jikan grabs his champagne flute and tries to take a sip of his mimosa, but the glass is empty. And because I know we're not getting any more story out of him until he has another drink, I start to head back to the fridge to grab the pitcher of mimosas I noticed there earlier. But before I can hop down from my barstool, Jikan just waves a hand and his glass is full again.

I want to ask him why he nudged my grandmother for more when he can just fill his own glass like that, but Hudson gives me a look I can't quite decipher, and I let the question drop.

Jikan takes a long sip of his drink, then steps into the larder again. When he comes out, he's got a bag of shredded, sweetened coconut that he drops next to the Oreos and chocolate chips already on the counter. "Get me a measuring cup, will you?" he once again asks the room in general before continuing his story.

"Anyway, the ill-planned spell didn't bring the baby eternal life like they'd hoped—because she was pregnant with not one child but two. Instead, as she gave birth to the second twin, it bound the children's souls"—he breaks off to dart a quick look at Alistair before continuing—"forever."

I turn to my grandfather, my heart racing. "Like the Bloodletter and the Crone?"

"Not quite," Alistair says but doesn't elaborate, as though this is a story he wants Jikan to tell in his own way.

Jikan takes the measuring cup Eden hands him with a nod of thanks. "At first, she and the wizard thought everything was fine—in the first few years of their lives, both twins thrived. Sure, one was a little smaller, a little more sickly than the other, but supposedly that can happen with twins. Still, both were fine. Until…" He pauses, shaking his head sadly even as he dumps a ton of chocolate chips into the measuring cup and tops it off with a second one of shredded coconut.

"Until they weren't," I press, deliberately ignoring whatever gastronomic misstep he's about to do next.

"Precisely. Even worse—" He pauses just long enough to dump the chocolate and coconut into the peanut-butter mixture on the stove. "The sickly little girl's well-being was tied to that of her sister. The stronger and healthier that one sister grew, the weaker the other became. But part of the time wizard's spell had worked—as long as their souls were linked, neither could ever die."

"Did the strong one feel bad?" Heather gasps, and she's literally wringing her hands right now, completely spellbound by the story

Jikan is weaving.

He appears equally fascinated as he turns to stare at her. "You're a human," he says suddenly.

She arches a dark brow. "Is that a bad thing?"

"I haven't decided yet." He seems to think about it, his head tilted to the side for long, painful seconds as the kitchen fills with a noxiously sweet odor.

In the end, Jikan shrugs and answers her original question. "Siblings are complicated." As though that says it all.

I glance between Hudson and Jaxon and have to wonder if maybe it does.

"What happened next?" I prod, both intrigued by the story and also wanting to get to the end so I can ask the real question I came here for.

"What do you think happened? It didn't take one twin long to figure out that every time her sister got hurt, she grew stronger."

Heather isn't the only one who gasps this time. The whole group of us exchange horrified looks, totally disgusted at the turn the story has just taken.

But it's Flint who finally says what we're all thinking.

"She started hurting her sister in order to become even more powerful."

Jikan looks Flint up and down like he's seeing him for the first time. "Looks like you've got far more going for you than your royal spleen after all, dragon."

Flint seems confused, like he's never considered his spleen before—royal or otherwise. But I can see the second he decides to just roll with the compliment, because the wide grin that's as much a part of him as his dragon spreads across his face. "Thank you."

Jikan harrumphs, then pops a lid on the pot of pasta that's only been cooking for about two minutes before carrying it to the sink to drain. I can only imagine the crunchy mess he's about to unveil.

"What did she do?" I press once the drained pot is safely back on the stove. "Did she end up killing her sister?"

"How could she kill her? I already told you the time wizard performed a dark-magic spell to make the girls immortal by irrevocably tying their souls together." He takes the lid off and reveals what looks to be perfectly cooked linguine—apparently the God of Time doesn't have to abide by basic cooking times—and pours the icky peanut-butter mixture over the pasta and begins to toss it slowly. So, so, so slowly that for the first time, I realize Jikan is stalling.

"Is Cassia back, Alistair?" he asks out of what seems like nowhere.

My grandfather shakes his head, but it's impossible not to see the sudden empathy in his eyes. "Not yet."

Something passes between them, a look that's so much more than a look, and I realize that Jikan is *waiting* for my grandmother. He doesn't want to tell the rest of this story—at least not without the Bloodletter here. But what does she have to do with shadow twins? It doesn't make sense.

"So, if she couldn't kill her sister, she just tortured her over and over again so that she could grow stronger and stronger herself?" Heather asks, her face wide with shock. "That's horrible."

My skin chills, and I glance over at Hudson. He's still leaning back against the edge of the counter, texting like he doesn't have a care in the world. But his jaw is so tense, I'm afraid he's going to break a fang. At first, I don't think he even notices I'm watching him, but then he shifts a little, and I realize he is very deliberately not looking at me, though I know he can feel my gaze on him.

I hate that he won't look up, that he won't let me share this moment with him. Because I know he's thinking about the same thing I am right now—the way Cyrus tortured him over and over and over again. Sending his son back into Descent every month for nearly two hundred years because he, too, wanted to be more powerful. It's not the same as what happened between these two sisters, but it's not all that different, either.

The bastard. Maybe eternity locked in the Bloodletter's cave isn't enough of a punishment for him. Or for that bitch of a shadow twin, come to think of it.

Then again, it wasn't her vicious behavior that upset a god. It was her mother's. I shudder a little, even as I ask, "What did the queen do?" And how could it possibly have been worse than what the dark shadow twin did?

Jikan lets out a long sigh as he reaches for the Oreo cookies. Several seconds pass as he crumbles them in his hand while staring down at the noxious pot of "dessert pasta" he's just assembled. Eventually, though, he drops the broken-up Oreos on top of the pasta and reaches for a kitchen towel to wipe his hands.

"Anybody want some?" he asks as he reaches for the plates, and both Flint and Eden shout "yes" in unison.

The rest of us decline—some of us more forcefully than others—but Jikan is so wrapped up in whatever he's thinking about the Shadow Queen that he doesn't notice the insult. In the end, he dishes up four plates, offering two to the dragons and one to Alistair...who takes it without so much as a grimace.

But now that the food is ready, Jikan must finally want to get through the story, because he stops glancing out the kitchen doorway, looking for my grandmother. And he stops stalling.

"Obviously, the parents weren't particularly impressed with their daughter's sadistic impulses, especially when the victim was their other daughter," he says. "After trying everything they could think of to protect both their daughters—and failing spectacularly—the Shadow Queen decided the only way to keep both of them safe was to sever the bond between them."

"Is that even possible?" I ask, wondering if my grandmother ever tried to sever her soul bond with her sister, too.

"Wingo!" Jikan gives me a fond nod, like I've finally done something to impress him. "The queen was told it was impossible by many people over and over again. Including me," he adds with a sniff. "But desperate measures call for desperate times. And she wouldn't stop, no matter how often she was told her quest was fruitless.

"Until one day she heard about someone who might know what she was going through, someone she believed went through something similar. So..." He pauses and sighs, then shoves a bite of peanut-butter pasta into his mouth and chews. When he swallows, he glances at Alistair, who is also eating his dessert, before continuing again. "The Shadow Queen went to find this woman who it was rumored also shared a soul bond with her twin sister and beg her for help."

My neck starts to prickle at the realization of why Jikan has been trying so hard to wait for the Bloodletter to return before he finishes the story.

"And the woman could actually help her?" Heather looks skeptical. "Sever the bond between two souls?"

Jikan shakes his head. "Of course she couldn't, but the Shadow Queen believed her when she said she could. She said she would tell the Shadow Queen what she knew about severing a soul, in exchange for a vial of shadow poison."

"Who would just ask for that, knowing what it does?" Eden asks, and now she looks even more disgusted.

"Who do you think?" Hudson counters, meeting my gaze finally.

Nausea churns in my stomach as I realize exactly who it was—and exactly what she needed that shadow poison for. My voice is scratchy as I choke out, "It was the Crone, wasn't it? She wanted the shadow poison. Because it was the only thing she could use to poison the Gargoyle Army."

Jikan raises his glass in mock salute, and my stomach does a series of flips that leaves me dizzy. Sweat beads my forehead, and I take a few short, quick breaths as I attempt to swallow the bile down as best I can.

I frantically look back at Hudson, his gaze still holding mine, his phone completely forgotten. He walks over and reaches for my hand, runs his thumb along my palm, and leans into me, whispering, "It's going to be okay. I promise."

I shake my head. How can anything be okay? The Shadow Queen gave the Crone the poison that nearly killed the entire Gargoyle Army. The same poison that caused the rest to be trapped in a frozen Court for a thousand years, that forced my grandparents to give up their only child, and that ultimately resulted in the reign of Cyrus and the death of so many of our friends and family.

And now, to save Mekhi, I'll have to beg for this bitch's freedom and show her a mercy I don't think she'll ever deserve.

16

It's Pasta Time
You Knew

"**H**oly shit," Jaxon breathes as he looks among Hudson, Jikan, and me. "That's what they used to poison the whole army?"

"It is," Jikan agrees.

"And the Shadow Queen just gave it to her? Knowing she would try to kill an entire people?" Finally, I'm understanding why Jikan decided she needed to be punished. Forever.

"Maybe she didn't know," Heather says quietly. "Maybe all she cared about was saving her daughter, and she tried to ignore what the Crone would do with the poison."

"Like that matters?" Eden asks, incredulous. "It was a *poison*, which by definition is used to hurt someone or something."

"She probably didn't let herself think about that," Heather answers. "She probably only thought about her daughter."

"Who was weaker but not dying." Eden looks at Heather like she can't believe she's even trying to make a case for this.

It's Heather's turn to look like she can't believe what she's hearing, but I can't help thinking that Eden is right. I mean, I love Hudson more than anything, but killing thousands of innocent people just to stop him from being hurt? I couldn't do that.

Would I hate every second that he was hurting? Yes.

Would I despise myself for casting some kind of spell that made him suffer like that? Of course.

Would I search forever for a way to make it right? Abso-freaking-lutely.

But would I risk anyone's death just to give him a chance at a better life? I don't think I could do that. More, I know he would never want me to do it. It's one of the million reasons I love him so completely.

"What happened then?" Flint looks as grim as I feel. "Did the Crone give her a way to save her daughter?"

"Of course she didn't," I murmur. Because I've met the God of Order.

I glance down at my arm, at the tattoo delineating the magical bargain I so naively made with her—and the favor I still owe her.

"You must not know her if you can ask that," Jikan says to Flint, shaking his head. "She took the poison and then upheld her end of the bargain. She told the Shadow Queen exactly what she knew about severing a soul bond between two twins. Namely, that it's impossible and can't be done."

After dropping that bomb, Jikan forks a huge bite of pasta into his mouth and makes rapturous noises as he slowly chews. Once he finally swallows, he turns to my grandfather and asks, "So, Alistair, are we going to talk about the fact that you're obviously too infirm to referee a football game, or are we going to pretend everything's normal?"

"I don't know," my grandfather answers as he twirls his own pasta around on his fork absently. "Are we going to talk about the fact that you act more like a spoiled toddler in need of a timeout than a god, or are we going to pretend everything's normal?"

I wait for Jikan to explode—my grandfather did just fire a cannonball across the bow, after all—but the God of Time just raises his glass to Alistair.

"Wait a minute." Flint jumps up from his barstool next to Jaxon. "That's it? You're not going to tell us the rest of the story?"

"What else is there to tell?" Jikan looks truly mystified. "Considering what you've been down to in the past several months, I have to assume you know the rest."

He means "up to," but I don't have the heart to correct him. Not when I realize that so much of what's happened in the last year can be attributed to this one moment, this one bargain. When the Shadow Queen went to the Crone over a thousand years ago, she set in motion all the events that we've lived through—and that the people we love have died for.

It's funny. I've always known someone has been playing chess with our lives. I just thought it was Cyrus and the Bloodletter. Now I realize that it's been the Crone all along.

Not that there's anything concerning—or terrifying—about the fact that we're at the mercy of a sadistic god who has been in the wind for months. Nope, nothing disquieting about that at all.

"That's why you punished the Shadow Queen," I say slowly as Hudson squeezes my hand again. The look on his face says he's already realized what I'm just now figuring out. "Because she gave the Crone a poison to kill the gargoyles, forced the Bloodletter to give up her own child, and your best friend, *my grandmother*, was suffering."

Jikan takes another bite of pasta, chases it with a sip of his latest mimosa. "Let's just say that I had no choice but to seal their fate in that realm with my time dragons. The Shadow Realm was created by a fury so wild and unchecked, its very existence is as unstable as the magic holding it together."

"Well fook," Hudson mutters, and I couldn't agree more. Unstable magic is not something any of us should be messing with. Ever.

"Yes," Jikan says, his gaze narrowing on Hudson and me. "So you see, there's no point in asking. I can never release the Shadow Queen *or* her people from their prison."

"How did you—?" I start, but I realize it doesn't matter how he knew what I was going to ask. At least now I won't have to beg for mercy for that bitch.

Hudson crosses his arms. "And if we wanted to *visit* the Shadow Realm without disturbing time, without awakening a time dragon?"

I hold my breath, waiting on Jikan's answer. Maybe there's still a bargain we can make with the Shadow Queen, a way to convince her to help save Mekhi.

Jikan shrugs. "There's a proper way to do things, of course. Visitors are allowed—even in a prison."

"So what is the proper way to visit the Shadow Realm?" Hudson asks, sliding the question in so smoothly that I can't help being impressed.

Especially when Jikan starts to answer. "You have to find the access points, of course. Where the shadows are—" He breaks off, eyes suddenly focused over our heads.

"Where the shadows are what?" I wave my hand, determined to get his attention again.

But it's too late. Because when I turn to follow his gaze, I realize the Bloodletter is back. And she doesn't look good.

17

Pretty Freeze with a
Cherry on Top

"Cassia?" Alistair springs forward to wrap her in his arms. "What's wrong?"

"I'm okay." She brushes a reassuring hand over his cheek, but when she turns to the rest of us, the look in her eyes is grave. "I've just come from the Vampire Court."

I glance at Hudson and realize he's gone from watchful to intense between one breath and the next. "Is there a problem?"

"Of course there is, but that's not what I'm concerned about." She looks between Jaxon and me. "I'm sorry, but there's nothing else I can do for your friend."

Alarm slams through me, has my heart pounding and my palms sweating. "Do you mean Mekhi?"

"I know I warned you that this was the last time he could be in Descent, but he's woken up much sooner than even I thought he would. As you know, the sleeping potion loses efficacy over time when it's used with the elixir. Unfortunately, due to the nature of a vampire's metabolism mixed with the poison, his body is simply metabolizing it at increasingly faster and faster rates. The amount required to put him under again would kill him instead."

Jaxon lets out a strangled cry at the news, and I flinch—we all do.

I start to reach for him, but Flint gets there first, his arm sliding around Jaxon's waist. "It's okay," he murmurs, their earlier discomfort with each other nowhere to be seen in the face of this latest development. "We'll find a way to save him."

Flint sounds confident, but the look he shoots me is anything but. Which I get, because I'm pretty much feeling the opposite of confident right now as well.

How the hell are we going to convince the Shadow Queen to give us an antidote to the poison that's killing Mekhi without a bargain to release her from her prison? Not to mention, we still don't even know how to get *into* the Shadow Realm without a horde of time dragons hunting us immediately. It all seems impossible right now.

Panic burns in my stomach. It makes my hands shake and threatens to buckle my knees. To stave it off, I take several quick and shallow breaths, then shove it down as hard and as deep as I can. I'm going to push through—I have to push through this, for Mekhi's sake.

As my mom always said, the best way to achieve any goal is to tackle it one problem at a time. And our first issue, the one I'm still certain Jikan can answer for us, is: "Jikan, we really need to find out how to travel to the Shadow Realm safely."

"I still don't understand why you'd ever want to go back there, Grace." A minute ago, it had seemed like he was going to answer the question, but now he's back to stalling.

Frustration eats at me. "Shadow poison? Mekhi? Dy-ing?" I bite out each syllable.

Jikan is too busy staring at the Bloodletter to pick up on the urgency in my voice. "I really don't think this is a place you should be going, dying friend or not."

Before I can tell him I don't have a choice, he continues. "You did hear me when I said it was created with a very unstable magic, right, Grace? Probably best to avoid that, too."

He's still locked in some kind of silent communication with my grandmother, and it takes everything in me not to throw a foam finger on the ground and jump up and down on it right now. One of my best friends is dying, and these two are tiptoeing around some ancient mistake they apparently want to forget ever happened.

I rack my brain, trying to come up with the right thing to say to get Jikan to give us the information we need. But before I can, Heather steps forward, shoving a braid behind her ear as she does.

"So, I've been listening to everything, and I'll admit I don't understand a lot of it, but I know this much…" Heather holds up a single finger. "The way I see it, we only have one choice. We need help from the Shadow Queen. It's the only way to save Mekhi. Her poison. Her cure." She extends another finger. "But to get that, we have to be able to travel to the Shadow Realm without attracting time dragons." She extends a third finger. "And we are definitely going to need a way back home." She extends a fourth finger. "And if we can make all *that* happen, we're still going to need a bargaining chip to force the queen to help cure Mekhi or—" Now she curls her fingers into a fist but extends her thumb, gesturing with it to Jaxon on her right. "High Testosterone Vampire here is going to try to beat it out of her. In which case, we will probably all be fucked."

Everyone chuckles at that. Well, everyone except Jaxon, who stands a little taller. "I could take her," he murmurs, and Heather rolls her eyes.

"Like I said, we're probably all fucked if this guy ever gets going. He is bad. Ass." She tosses Jaxon a wink, and I swear he stands another inch taller, if that's even possible. His shoulders certainly look broader.

But Heather's already moved on, both hands on her hips as she squares off against Jikan with narrowed eyes and a determined look on her face. "So, while the Hudson-Grace brain trust tries to figure out leverage against the queen—which something tells me the Bloodletter here is going to know how to get, since it was her evil sister who started this whole mess—we need *you* to stop dicking us around and give my bestie here a straight answer about how to travel between realms safely. So, do you think you can do that, or are we going to have a problem?"

Silence descends on the room as Heather finishes her speech, and I have to fight the urge to applaud. Because oh. My. God.

My best friend is…amazing. Beyond amazing. She's freaking incredible.

I mean, she's also definitely about to be smote, but still. That was *awesome*. I don't even bother to hide the giant grin spreading across my face. She may think Jaxon is the badass of the group, but I'm pretty sure she could give him a run for his money in that department anytime she wants.

Considering she's been aware of this world for less than three months, I have no idea how she's been following all the strange new things about it. Then again, I always knew she was the smarter of the two of us. And now everyone else knows it, too. Including Jikan, who is currently sizing her up with eyes as cold and flat as a king cobra's.

"I've met humans," he begins. "They're weak. Silly. Scared. *You* are not human."

Heather narrows her eyes more. "I kicked the last man who tried to tell me what I was and was not *in the nuts*."

As one, my friends and I take a step closer to her, and I've never loved my found family more. If Jikan wants to smite Heather, he'll have to go through all of us first.

The thought has barely occurred to me when Jikan waves a hand and freezes everyone except the Bloodletter, Alistair, Heather, Hudson, and myself. Which, okay, way to reinforce the fact that we wouldn't *actually* be able to put up that big of a fight against the God of Time. Still, surely he doesn't want to upset his best friend by killing her granddaughter *and* her granddaughter's best friend and mate, especially not right in front of her.

"Jikan?" The Bloodletter's voice is pleasant as she nods toward Heather, but there's a warning in it nonetheless.

"I'm aware, Cassia," Jikan answers with a loud sigh. He doesn't look impressed as he shoves his hands deep into the pockets of his green sweatpants and studies Heather for a minute.

Then he turns his gaze on mine and says, "But I also won't be helping you eliminate time dragons—not because I don't want to but because I literally can't. There's no shortcut to eliminating them, no cheat code that will shut them down. They are the worst thing I've ever created, and they are nearly undefeatable, as you and Hudson figured out the hard way. My advice, Grace? Enter the Shadow Realm in a way that doesn't cause a tear in space-time."

"And that way in would be?" I ask, holding my breath as I wait to see if he'll finally answer.

His gaze darts to the Bloodletter's for half a second before capturing mine again. "You already know. It's where the shadows converge."

"The shadows?" I repeat.

Jikan looks at me expectantly, but when I just stare back, baffled, he gives another heavy sigh. "The fountain in the Trials, where you first encountered the shadow bugs. It doesn't just exist there. It exists—"

"In Turin!" I exclaim as memories of the piazza outside the Witch Court come flooding back. "I knew I recognized that fountain from somewhere. I saw it the first time we went there for help."

I can't believe I forgot it.

"But wait," I continue as another thought occurs to me. "That means the gateway into the Shadow Realm is in the Witch Court."

Jikan harrumphs. "Just remember, it's not getting into the Shadow Realm that's hard. It's getting out. It *is* a prison, you know."

Well, at least Hudson was right, I guess. The Shadow Realm is a prison. That's not concerning at all. "Do you have any suggestions on how to escape?"

"I actually don't." He looks disgruntled, jabbing at the remains of his dessert pasta with a scowl. "That being said, I know there are ways and people who know how to negotiate them. You just have to find one."

My gaze searches out Hudson's, and we both say the same thing at the same time. "Blue jeans." I give him a huge smile, remembering how he'd borrowed a pair from Arnst on the farm and we'd realized there *were* things in Noromar that weren't purple. You just had to know the right people or—as we are obviously both guessing right now—the right smuggler to get them for you.

Heather raises a hand. "Okay, I'll ask. How do blue jeans get us out of the Shadow Realm?"

"What's one thing every prison has?" Hudson asks, an eyebrow raised at me.

"Walls. Huge fucking walls." I repeat back to him what I said in the diner what feels like an eon ago, then toss him a wink and turn to Heather. "And contraband networks."

Hudson smiles. "We'll just have to get ourselves smuggled back out."

He makes it sound so simple, but I can't help my stomach twisting at the possibility that we're wrong and we get stuck there forever. Or worse, we make it back but I forget him again. Because something tells me it's going to be harder than he makes it sound—I doubt there's a laundry cart filled with purple T-shirts we can hide in heading out. But at least there probably *is* a way back. That's got to count for something.

"Watch your back, Grace. The Shadow Realm is pure chaos. Everything is far more dangerous there than it seems, with a complete lack of rules or—" He breaks off as my grandmother rolls her eyes and interrupts.

"I'll take it from here, Jikan," she tells him. "Now, why don't you head home? If you don't have a few minutes to rest after your travel, you'll end up tossing your cookies all over your trapeze class."

"I think you mean tossing my pasta. And that hardly had *any* cookies." But they share another look before he eventually nods. "A pleasure, Cassia. As always."

Then, between one blink and the next, Jikan is gone. The only thing left to signify that he'd been here at all is his empty plate and mimosa glass, standing forlornly on the corner of the bar.

I have one second to wonder how all these gods manage to disappear whenever they want before everyone becomes unfrozen at once.

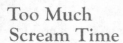

18

Too Much
Scream Time

Between being frozen and Jikan's sudden departure, everyone's more than a little worked up. Jaxon is one hundred percent tired of being frozen. Eden keeps loudly reassuring herself that the God of Time hasn't given Heather an extra limb, considering she did threaten to junk-punch him. Flint just looks bewildered.

And Hudson—Hudson has gone back to texting furiously.

Once I get everyone settled again, I turn to address my grandmother—and realize she and Alistair must have snuck away during the chaos. Which stinks, because I really need to talk to her.

Something tells me Heather was right when she wondered if the Bloodletter knows more about how I can bargain with the Shadow Queen than she's let on so far.

Which is why I clap my hands to get everyone's attention. "Listen, I'm sorry Jikan loves to freeze people, but the good news is that Heather and I know how to get into the Shadow Realm now. The entrance is at the Witch Court." I pull my phone out of my pocket and glance at the time, not surprised to see it's past one. "Let's all head to our rooms and get some rest, then meet back here at nine and discuss strategy."

"But we still don't have anything to trade the Shadow Queen for Mekhi's antidote," Eden worries.

"I know, but I'm working on that." I bump her shoulder in reassurance. "For now, let's get some rest. We'll all think more clearly in the morning."

Everyone grumbles but agrees, and we shuffle off in the direction of the guest suites. Eden offers to show Heather to her room as I tug on Hudson's elbow, urging him to hang back with me.

"Hey," I breathe, slipping my arms around his waist and squeezing hard.

He responds by pulling me tight against his chest and murmuring, "Hey, back," in my ear.

He smells good—like warm amber and spices—and I want nothing more than to rest my head against him and stay right here in his arms, forever. Eventually, though, responsibility rears its ugly head and I have to step back.

The space between us sends an instant chill along my skin that I struggle to ignore as I ask, "What's going on?" I nod in the direction of his phone, which he's still got gripped in one hand.

He shoves the device into his pocket and offers a half smile that doesn't quite reach his eyes. "Nothing for you to worry about."

The way he says it *does* worry me a little, and I start to tell him that there are never things for me and him to worry about separately—that we're in this together, always—but he rushes on. "Besides, don't you need to be figuring out how to charm a certain former vampire queen into helping us bribe the one woman she might actually hate more than her sister?"

I sigh because, in this instance, he's right, even though I wish he wasn't. "Yeah, that."

Still, I hate that he's keeping a secret from me. Because I feel the distance of it between us, I take his large hand in mine. He curls his fingers around mine and squeezes, and I let the rush of electricity chase away the chill.

"It's funny. I never think of the Bloodletter as the vampire queen," I say, making air quotes around the title, "and yet it's kind of right there in her name."

Hudson gently guides a few of my curls off my forehead and behind my ear. "She's the OG." This time, his smile reaches his eyes. "Like her granddaughter."

I roll my eyes at his silliness. "I'm definitely not the original gargoyle queen."

"Aren't you?" he asks, the question so simple. "The Bloodletter was the gargoyle queen for a time, but by marriage only. And we know how these royals feel about their bloodlines."

I bite my lip, unsure how I feel about being the very first gargoyle queen who is actually a gargoyle. Then I give him a pointed look. "You're just trying to distract me from asking about your phone. We will be coming back to this, Hudson." Proclamation delivered, I run a hand through my hair. "But you're right. I need to figure out a way to convince my very stubborn grandmother to help us—if she can."

"She can," Hudson says. "I've never seen *anyone* drag a story out as long as Jikan did—and I lived with Cyrus."

"You noticed he was stalling, too, eh?" I ask, but it's rhetorical. Hudson notices everything.

"I'm just unsure if it's because there's not more to the story or because he didn't want to be the one to tell it," he says, then releases my hand to squeeze both my shoulders. "I need to go find my brother, make sure he's not still upset about the pigeon. Do you want to go deal with *Grandma* now or in the morning?"

"Now," I say firmly, earning a quick kiss. I love that he gave me the option to leave a bill in the drawer, as I have a bad habit of doing. But Mekhi's life hangs in the balance.

I don't have a choice. I'm going to have to face the Bloodletter, whether she's ready for the confrontation or not.

19

Hate the Game, Not the God

Imake it to my grandparents' suite of rooms in a matter of minutes and knock softly on the huge double doors. Not because I hope she doesn't answer—but she *is* a vampire, as I was just reminded, so it's best not to sneak up on her.

The door swings open, and the Bloodletter is on the other side. She's still dressed in her red caftan, but she's exchanged the red head wrap holding her hair on the top of her head for a long gold one, her locs tumbling past her narrow shoulders now.

"It took you long enough," she says with an imperiously raised eyebrow. "Probably making out with that mate of yours instead of tending to business."

I raise an eyebrow right back at her. "Jealous much?"

She lifts her chin, but I can hear Alistair chuckling in the background. He walks up behind her and grips her waist, leaning forward to kiss her cheek. "Leave her be, dear. We used to be young and in love, too."

"We are *still* young," she snaps back, but there's no bite to her words.

"Yes, you are, dear," he agrees with a twinkle in his eyes, and I can tell this is an argument they have often. "I, on the other hand, am as old and weathered as a stone and need my beauty rest. So let me pass and give you two women some time to catch up so we can all head to bed soon."

She gives an elaborate sniff but moves to the side.

"I'll be back in a bit, Grace, to say good night."

"Okay," I say, but he's already halfway down the hall.

The Bloodletter ushers me into the sitting area of her suite with a flourish, murmuring under her breath, "He's still very young, too."

Something in her tone makes me pause, study her unlined face. All the talk tonight about humans and immortals has me asking, "Will you outlive Grandfather?"

I don't know how long gargoyles live, though I assumed very, very long. But now, I'm not so sure, and suddenly I need to know.

"Gargoyles live a very long time," she answers, then adds softly, "but not as long as vampires. Not as long as gods."

My stomach twists as her words sink in. She will outlive her mate, my grandfather, and the sadness turns her eyes into a swirling green as dark as a forest.

"I'm so sorry, Grandmother," I choke out. Then I force myself to ask, "I'm a demigod. Does that mean I am immortal as well?"

"Yes, Grace. You and Hudson will be mated for all eternity."

For a moment, the idea of eternity stretches out endlessly before me. I simply can't take it in.

And then I realize, Hudson didn't know I was a demigod when he fell in love with me, became my mate. Come to think of it, neither did Jaxon. My heart blossoms with pain, passion, and disbelief. Could it be these two beautiful boys chose to be mated to me even knowing an eternity of sorrow awaited them after I was gone?

The same sorrow that awaits my grandmother.

The Bloodletter is not the touchy-feely sort of family, but I can't help myself. I throw myself into her arms and squeeze her tight as I repeat, "I am so sorry, Grandmother."

She squeezes me back for a second, maybe even two, but then she sets me aside, blinking away any moisture in her eyes as she points across the room to an elaborate chess table framed by two blue chairs. "Come along, Grace. Let's play a game, shall we?"

"Of course," I reply, accepting the subject change as I cross to the chessboard.

She falters for a moment as she moves to sit but recovers quickly and slides into her chair. I sit across from her, then watch as she reaches out and picks up the king that was laying on its side, standing it upright as she arranges all her chess pieces in their proper starting positions.

As our eyes meet across the board, I can't help thinking this is going to be much more than a game. And while I'm nowhere near prepared to match wits with my grandmother—I mean, who is?—I've got no choice. I need answers, and if this is the way to get them, then so be it.

I take a deep breath and begin to organize my own pieces as well.

"You're white," she says as we both finish with our setup. "Which means you've got first move."

I stare at the board for several seconds, trying to figure out where to start. Chess isn't exactly my game, but I've watched Hudson play himself enough to have a few opening moves spinning in my brain. In the end, though, I pick up the marble pawn in front of my king and move it out two spaces. It's an opening I saw my father make countless times while playing with Heather's father, so I feel fairly certain I haven't embarrassed myself yet.

That is, until the Bloodletter says, "So your first instinct is to expose your queen, then?"

Okay, so not a game. Or at least, not *just* a game. Big surprise.

Ignoring her question, I ask my own instead. "I think Heather was right. You've got an idea of how I can convince the Shadow Queen to cure Mekhi, don't you?"

She moves the pawn in front of her king to directly in front of the pawn I just moved, exposing her queen as well, although I don't point this out the way she did to me. "Of course I do, Grace." She looks up at me with the swirling green eyes I've finally grown used to. "But so do you."

Do I? I wasn't aware I had any idea how to bargain with the Shadow Queen, but as I examine the board and everything I've heard today, I realize I *do* have an idea.

Still, I'm not sure it's the *right* idea. I think it over as I study the board for my next move. Knight or bishop?

In the end, I go with my knight, shifting it on the king's side diagonal to my moved pawn, then lean back and state, "The Shadow Queen would do anything, even risk poisoning an army, to save her daughters. I can use that."

The Bloodletter gives me an arch look. "Can you, now? Even though everyone has said over and over that two souls cannot be separated once tied together?" She shifts her opposing knight to mirror my moved one.

I return her look with interest, and I can't help wondering what she's getting at. I know that when souls mate, they're tied together, except... "My mating bond with Jaxon was severed." I ignore the twinge at the memory of that painful separation as the Bloodletter's eyes narrow. Intriguing.

I look away from the board, spend a minute taking in the restrained opulence of her sitting room as I give myself time to consider my next words. This is too important not to think through.

"Granted, our mating bond was an engineered bond, but still. The question is, would a spell performed by a time wizard not result in an engineered bond as well?"

When she doesn't immediately answer, I start to move my bishop. But before I touch the more powerful piece, another glance at the board has me going for the pawn in front of my queen instead. I move it two spaces forward, then meet her gaze.

"And you think it did?" She moves her pawn to capture mine.

"I do." I use my knight to take her pawn. "But that's not the right question, is it? What I need to be asking is: Do you know how to undo it again?"

"Of course I do," she answers, and I can tell she's as startled by her words as I am. As if to offset the unscripted moment, she moves her untouched knight into position, putting pressure on both of my revealed pieces. "However, their bond was created with dark magic. It'll take something very, very powerful to break it."

"How powerful?"

She inclines her head. "You're still asking the wrong question, Grace."

"Right." I take a deep breath and consider thoroughly before trying again. "It isn't about how much power is needed. It's about what it will take to capture that power," I tell her, grinning as I reach out and take one of her knights with mine. "Luckily, I am just as relentless as my grandmother."

She leans back in her chair and studies me, the board—and our game—forgotten.

Eventually, though, she nods and says, "I can see that you are, Grace. So I will warn you that two souls bonded by dark magic for this long may be impossible to break apart—"

I start to interrupt, but she waves a hand for silence.

"I said *may* be impossible, Grace." She sighs. "It will definitely be more dangerous than you believe. But I know if I don't tell you, you'll do something even riskier trying to find out."

"I would do anything to save Mekhi," I say, crossing my arms.

She nods. "As you should."

My eyebrows shoot up. Well, that was unexpected.

"What?" she asks. "I assure you, loyalty is a trait I value greatly, Grace."

"As you should," I repeat back to her, and I can tell I've impressed her. "So what will it take to break this bond?"

"Celestial Dew," she says as though the answer was as simple as sipping a soda. "One of the twins needs only drink it. Now, the getting of it is a whole other matter."

I can't help it. My heart races with unexpected hope. Celestial Dew is an item, and my friends and I are very good at fetching items from impossible places. How hard could it be? "Where can we find this Dew?"

"Near the Bittersweet Tree, of course," she answers. "But first, you'll need to go see the Curator and make an impossible trade for the location. The Bittersweet Tree vanishes and moves by the whim of the stars, and only the Curator knows the location at any given time."

An old idiom pops into my head, making me want to jump up and blurt out that I need to see a man about a dog, but I don't think my grandmother would get the joke. Either way, this doesn't seem as hard as she was making it sound earlier. Of course, if I've learned anything about this world, it's that *everything* is harder than it seems.

"So first we need to go see this Curator—" I begin.

But the Bloodletter cuts in. "No, first you need to go to the Shadow Queen and make a bargain. You will trade the elixir—which may or may not work but is her only chance to save her daughters—in exchange for her healing Mekhi."

I shake my head, getting up to pace the room. "Wouldn't we have better luck making the deal if we had the elixir first?"

"She has an army and home-field advantage, Grace. What do you think?" She turns in her chair to watch me walk back and forth between a small love seat and a bookcase on the other side of the room.

She's right. There's nothing stopping the Shadow Queen from simply taking the elixir and then not helping Mekhi at all. Hell, after what happened the last time Hudson and I were in the Shadow Realm, she's as likely to kill us all if given half a chance.

The Bloodletter's gaze softens ever so slightly as she considers her next words. "I have to warn you, Grace. Celestials are immensely powerful. This item will not be easy to collect. You may not survive— none of you. And there is a war coming to this world, as I'm sure Artelya has told you already. A war we have a better chance of winning with you in it."

That comment brings me up short, and I stop pacing to stare sightlessly at the bookshelves, my stomach twisting into knots. Is a war really coming? Is that what a spy in our Court means? And if so, can I choose Mekhi over everyone I'm charged with protecting?

I know the answer even before Artelya bursts into the room, my grandfather right behind her with a devastated expression on his face.

20

Not-So-Happy
Hunting

Artelya is dressed in her usual training uniform of leather leggings, a white T-shirt, and a cross harness for her weapons. Other than rushing into the room, she looks calm and collected, like she hasn't spent half the night chasing a hunter whose main goal in life is to kill her.

"What happened?" I ask, because even in the middle of my discussion with the Bloodletter, I've been on tenterhooks waiting for her to come back with news of the hunters. "Did she figure out you were tailing her?"

"She had no idea we were behind her. She was nervous at first, constantly checking, but the farther away she got, the more relaxed she became." Artelya shakes her head like she still can't believe what she's about to say. "She led us straight to a large group of soldiers."

"So the Crone *has* been amassing an army," I tell her as my stomach sinks. We just got out of one battle. Gargoyle Army or not, what my people need right now is peace, not more war.

"How many are there?" I ask.

"It looks like she's been amassing hunters for months. And from what I overheard, this isn't the only hunter stronghold she has. There are several other camps."

My stomach goes from sinking slowly to bottoming out. "How many others?"

"I don't know." She shakes her head.

"Any idea how many hunters we're talking about? If not in all the camps, then at least in the one you were just at?"

"Thousands," she answers grimly. "Their number indicates that the Crone is clearly aware of the Circle's vulnerability right now and is hoping to attack while we're at our weakest."

I start to ask why we're at our weakest, but all the pieces I've learned over the last several hours are finally starting to fit together.

Still, I have to ask. "Is this really about the Circle? Or is this about someone inexperienced leading the Gargoyle Army?" There, I said it, and I count to ten in an effort not to throw up on my grandmother's very beautiful new rug.

"It's about the *vampires*," the Bloodletter informs me. "They've always been the most formidable group, even before Cyrus took the throne. Without your mate to lead the Vampire Court, there's a total dearth of leadership there. The Vega line of succession ends with Hudson, as both Jaxon and Isadora are unwilling, and a millennium of Vega rule left the Court unprepared for an alternative. The remaining vampire aristocracy is feuding for control, trust and suspicions high as the Court is splintering into unlikely alliances."

I think of Hudson frantically answering all those texts. "But this isn't just about them, is it? The vampires alone aren't enough to destabilize the entire Circle. There's unrest in the Dragon Court as well."

"So you do know about that," she replies. "I wondered."

"I just found out." Still, I'm embarrassed that I didn't see it sooner. Jaxon and Flint told me the dragons were in trouble. I knew Hudson wasn't stepping up at the Vampire Court. How could I be so shortsighted as to not figure out what was going to happen?

But is it really as bad as they're implying? Cyrus has been gone barely five months, and the Crone is declaring World War III on all paranormals? That seems a bit bold, even for her.

Then again, court intrigue has been a thing forever. And Aristotle wrote that power abhors a vacuum. It's no shock that we're here. The only shock is that I never saw it coming. Even sitting in the diner, when we talked of a dragon civil war, it never occurred to me that the entire political structure of our corner of the paranormal world might actually fail.

"This isn't right," I whisper. "It isn't fair."

"There's nothing fair about politics, Grace." Artelya gives me a puzzled look. "I thought you would have figured that out by now."

I have. God knows, I have. But that doesn't mean I have to like it.

"So without the dragons and the vampires, that leaves the wolves and the witches in charge of the Circle?" It's a horrifying thought for so many reasons.

"And you," my grandmother reminds me, as if I can forget.

Well, shit.

Is it really any wonder the Crone sees an opportunity to take us down once and for all?

The Vampire Court has no king.

The Dragon Court has no heart.

And the Gargoyle Court has me—a teenager in way over her head, still trying to figure out the rules of this world.

Which leaves only one thing for me to do.

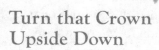

21

Turn that Crown
Upside Down

"**I** can't go to the Shadow Realm," I say as the truth of these new circumstances settles around me. "I can't leave with the Crone amassing an army. Not even for Mekhi."

It hurts to say it, hurts even more to think about not being part of the rescue mission for one of my closest friends. Not to mention sending my mate and my other friends off to the Shadow Realm to confront the Shadow Queen on their own.

It's a no-win situation. One that has panic racing through my bloodstream, making my chest ache and my heart pound triple time. Any decision I make is going to hurt someone, leave someone I care about vulnerable. But I am the Gargoyle Queen.

It's my job to lead my army, my job to protect all the paranormals in the world who can't protect themselves. I can't just abandon them now, when a terrible threat is on the horizon. The Crone and her hunters cannot be allowed to hurt those under my protection.

"They're not mobilizing yet," Artelya tells me. "They're still growing, training. It will be a while before they march on us."

"She's right, granddaughter," Alistair affirms. "They aren't coming for us tomorrow. Soon, yes, but you've got a week or two at least. There's time enough for you to take care of Mekhi."

"Can you guarantee that?" I ask him before turning to Artelya. "Can you? Because if you can't, I have to be here. What kind of leader would walk away when her troops need her most?"

"The kind who comprehends that gargoyles stand for everyone, including poisoned vampires," Artelya answers. "And the kind who knows the importance of building alliances."

"Alliances? With whom?" But I'm already figuring out where she's going. "The hunters are coming for all paranormal creatures. We *all* have a vested interest in stopping them. Even wraiths."

"Exactly," Artelya agrees. "The army supports this. While you take these next few days to save Mekhi, pay attention to where you are."

"And who I can recruit to our side," I finish for her. I scratch absently at my palm, weighing my options. I understand what everyone is saying— there is time to save Mekhi *and* be ready when the Crone attacks. I can do both. I don't have to choose.

But the Bloodletter's warning about Celestials still rings in my ears.

Yes, there is time to do both, *if* I survive the first impossible task of saving Mekhi. And if I don't, I risk losing the Crown to the Shadow Realm forever. That is something I simply cannot allow.

"Grandfather," I say, and my chest tightens when his faded gray gaze focuses on mine.

"Don't say it, Grace." He starts to turn away. "You will make it back."

I don't know whether to be hurt by the dismissal or flattered by his faith in me. "You don't know that."

He doesn't answer for a long time, just stands there staring at me like he can see into my soul. And, for all I know, he can. His centuries chained in that cave left Alistair with some freaky talents, not the least of which is making me feel really, really uncomfortable whenever he forces me to meet his eyes for any length of time.

"What is it you want to do, granddaughter?"

"It's not what I want to do. It's what I *have* to do, and you know it." I hold his gaze, begging for his understanding. And I thrust out my hand, hold it between our still bodies.

At first, I don't think he's going to return the gesture. But then, after what feels like an eternity, he slowly holds his hand out to mine.

I press my palm to his.

For one second, a fiery heat burns its way across my hand, and I gasp at the searing pain.

But the pain fades as quickly as it came, and when I pull my hand back, the Crown is gone. It's now emblazoned on Alistair's palm, where it lived for more than a thousand years.

"Are you certain this is what you want?" he asks.

For a second, I want to say no. I want to grab his hand and accept the Crown I know he's more than willing to cede back to me. But I can't do that. Not now, and—depending on how things go in the Shadow Realm—maybe not ever.

Because the Crown is bigger than any one gargoyle—as is the power it carries within it. And while I accept the power and the responsibility that comes with it, I also accept that the likelihood of me dying on this quest into the Shadow Realm got a whole lot higher with the Bloodletter's revelations.

But if my general is telling me there is time, I will listen to her and go. Mekhi is my friend—one of the first friends I made at Katmere after my cousin, in fact. There is nothing he wouldn't do for me or I him. But the Crown and its power must stay here. Mine to reclaim if I make it back from the Shadow Realm. Alistair's to hold, and to wield, if I don't come back.

"I'm certain," I tell him, even though I'm not. Even though I'm terrified I'm leading the people I love most into another slaughter like the Trials.

But what other option do I have? Sneak away alone? Leave Hudson and the others here and try to find my own way into the Shadow Realm?

Hudson would never stand for that—and I don't blame him. Because if he snuck away to protect me simply because he thought something was too dangerous for me, I would never forgive him. How can I even think about doing that to him—or any of my friends, for that matter?

"Thank you." I finally break the silence in the room. Artelya watches with a solemn expression as I bow slightly to my grandfather, the newly reinstated gargoyle king.

He nods but doesn't say anything. Nor does he make any move to turn away again.

For the first time in a long time, the silence between us feels uncomfortable. Oppressive. Then again, that could just be the thoughts weighing so heavy on my mind.

Either way, I take a step back. My friends are waiting for me—and so is Mekhi.

"Is it permanent?"

I freeze at the question, at the wary concern that Alistair doesn't even try to hide.

"No," I answer as honestly as I can. "It's for a week, maybe two. Just long enough for us to cure Mekhi and bring him home. But I can't take it with me to the Shadow Realm, either. If something were to happen to me there, I don't want the Crown to die with me."

"Are you sure the Shadow Realm is the real reason for your abdication? Or is it about your mate?"

"Hudson?" The accusation startles me so much that I blurt out his name. "Why would this have anything to do with Hudson?"

Surprise flashes across Alistair's face, but it's gone so fast that I can't be sure I didn't imagine it. "I must have been mistaken."

"I don't believe that," I shoot back. Since he broke free of the fog of the Unkillable Beast, Alistair has been super sharp. Way too sharp to make an accusation like that without something serious—and tangible— to back it up. "Tell me the truth, Grandfather. Why would you think me giving you the Crown has anything to do with Hudson?"

He glances to the Bloodletter before answering, but her face is impassive. Alistair sighs, then says, "Because the rules of primogeniture are preventing the Vampire Court from stabilizing. Since the abdication ceremony hasn't occurred, it is not too late for Hudson to rescind his abdication and take the throne, but your mate is refusing to do so because it would mean asking you to abdicate instead...or leaving you."

My grandfather's words go off like a bomb, sending shock waves slamming through me so hard that it takes every ounce of energy I have not to show how shaken I am.

"Hudson's not leaving me," I tell him when I can finally find my voice.

"Hence the reason your grandfather was concerned about you giving him back the Crown." The Bloodletter eyes me critically. "It *is* just temporary, isn't it?"

"Of course it's temporary!" I squawk, even as my heart beats like a metronome at its highest tempo. "As long as I make it back from the Shadow Realm alive, I plan on reclaiming the throne."

But even as I say it, doubts start to creep in. Not just about what might happen in the Shadow Realm—those doubts have been there all along—but about Hudson as well.

If what my grandparents are saying is true—and they have no reason to lie—then something bigger than he's letting on is going on at the Vampire Court. And he hasn't told me anything about it.

For a second, I flash back to the way he's been glued to his phone all day. Not just using it for cover while he thinks, like he usually does, but actually texting. A lot. Even though most of the people he would be texting were in the room with him. With us.

Still, it doesn't make sense for Hudson to omit something like this. Something this big, especially when it affects both of us so completely.

My stomach pitches as I consider Hudson's options and why he might not have told me himself about what's going on in the Vampire Court. He'd have no problem telling me everything if he was refusing the vampire crown—we discussed his abdication extensively before he brought the decision to the Vampire Court. But he would struggle with telling me about a harder choice.

I rush to say good night to my grandparents and Artelya as fast as decorum will allow, unable to hear a word they say over the heartbeat pounding in my ears.

Because there's an answer I desperately need, and only my mate can give it to me.

I need to know if Hudson is planning on leaving me.

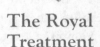

22

The Royal Treatment

When I finally make it up to my room, Hudson is laying on our bed, still texting on his damn phone.

Big surprise.

There's a part of me that can't wait to share the conversation the Bloodletter and I just had about how to save Mekhi. But I know I can't have that conversation yet. Not when all I want to do is confront him about keeping some pretty important secrets from me.

I swallow the bile rising in my throat and realize I may not be ready to have that conversation, either.

So instead of saying anything, I start toward the bathroom, determined to take a shower and wash away all the grime and difficult questions from the day so I actually have a chance of sleeping tonight.

But I barely make it past the bed before Hudson asks, "Everything okay?" without so much as looking up.

And for some reason, it gets all over me. Just crawls right up my ass and pisses me off in a way he hasn't managed since he was stuck in my head.

"Were you ever planning on telling me?" I demand, stopping to yank open the pajama drawer of the dresser where I keep a few changes of clothes for when I'm here. "Or were you just going to keep me in the dark forever?"

That gets his attention, though I'm not sure if it's the questions or my aggressive way of asking them. But Hudson finally puts his phone down on the bed and sits up warily. "Can I have some context for that question?" he asks, smarmy British accent in full residence. "Or am I just supposed to guess?"

"Seriously? You're hiding so many things from me that you don't even know which one I'm asking about? That's reassuring." I grab the first pair of pajamas I find and then slam the drawer so hard, the entire dresser rattles.

Now he's off the bed, too, fading next to me with his arms crossed over his chest and a what-the-hell look on his face. "I'm sorry, but you just came at me out of the fooking blue. You want to tell me what went on in that bloody meeting with your grandparents, or am I just supposed to guess?"

"Why didn't you tell me about the Vampire Court?"

His outrage turns to wariness in an instant. "What about the Vampire Court?"

"Seriously? That's the answer you want to go with?" I storm toward the bathroom, but he stops me with a gentle hand on my shoulder.

"What did they tell you, Grace?" His blue eyes are steady on mine as I turn around to face him, and try as I might, I can't find any hint of subterfuge or guilt there. Which only makes me madder, considering he's been lying to me for months.

"What you should have," I retort, shoulders slumping as weariness and worry replace my fury. "We're partners, Hudson. If you're being pressured to take the crown as the vampire king, don't you think that's the kind of thing we should talk about?"

He sighs, looking anywhere but at me. "To be honest, not really," he finally answers.

Hurt arrows through me. "Seriously? If you can't trust me to talk through this kind of major life decision with you, then what are we even doing?"

"It's not that I don't trust you. Obviously. It's that it doesn't matter what the Court wants. I never considered assuming the role of vampire king for a moment."

Now I'm the baffled one. "Why not? I mean, I know you decided to abdicate months ago, but if the Court needs you, it's the logical choice—"

"There is nothing bloody logical about it," he snaps. Then runs a frustrated hand through his hair as he takes a deep breath and lets it out slowly.

"You're the gargoyle queen, Grace. Which makes me the gargoyle king. And that means I can't also be vampire king—or you vampire queen. And we sure as hell can't petition for a role on the Circle as such. There's no way they'd ever permit us to hold two powerful positions each. It would disrupt the entire Circle."

"From what I just heard, the Circle is already disrupted," I shoot back.

"Yes, well, maybe that's not such a bad thing," he mutters as his phone buzzes with another string of texts.

We both turn to look at it, and Hudson curses under his breath. But he doesn't move to pick it up, which makes me happier than it probably should.

I want to ask him what he means by his last comment, but I have bigger things to focus on. Namely: "You really don't think we should talk about this? You have a right to be king."

"I *am* king," he answers.

I roll my eyes. "You know what I mean."

"Yes, but I don't think you know what *I* mean. The Vampire Court has given me nothing but bloody misery my entire fucking life. There is nothing about that place that I want to rule. And even if I did, you're the goddamn gargoyle queen, Grace, and no one deserves it more. There's no way I'd ever think about asking you to give that up."

"Well, maybe you should," I tell him, and my knees tremble.

His eyes narrow. "What exactly does that mean?"

"I'm not sure." I shake my head. "I just can't help thinking that I'm not very good at this, you know? You'd be a way better vampire king than I'll ever be a gargoyle queen."

He laughs, and the tension leeches out of his stance. "Now I know you're exhausted. And, apparently, delirious. You know you're a kick-ass queen."

"I'm really not," I tell him. "A lot of the time I don't have a clue what the hell I'm doing."

"But being able to concede that is more than half the battle. Most rulers are way too arrogant to admit when they don't know something. Maybe if they did, things wouldn't get so bollocksed all the time."

He wraps his arms around me, starts to pull me into his chest. And while I think about resisting, the truth is I want to be held by him as much as he wants to hold me.

But that doesn't mean he's completely off the hook. "I still think you should have at least mentioned it to me."

"Fair enough." He rests his cheek against the top of my head. "I'm sorry I didn't say anything. Since I have no intention of taking up the crown, I really didn't think it was important."

"We're partners. If something is affecting you, it's affecting me. Understand?" I give him a fierce look as I angle my head so our eyes can meet.

It's his turn to roll his eyes. "Understood. As long as you understand that it isn't affecting me. I am exactly where I want to be."

I tuck my head under his chin and whisper my greatest fear. "For a minute, I thought you didn't say anything because you didn't know how to tell me you were leaving me."

His entire body stills, not even his chest rising with his next breath. "The only way I will ever give you up, Grace, is if you ask me." His voice is as rough as sandpaper. "Are you asking me to leave?"

I don't hesitate to give him the only answer I can. The answer he deserves. "Never."

I didn't realize he was nervous about my response until he exhales with his entire body, like that one word just took the weight of a thousand thrones off his shoulders. I reach for him then, but he's already pulling me closer and closer still, holding me in the space between one breath and the next as the warmth of what we have chases away the specters of what we never want to be.

Then he puts a finger under my chin and tilts my face up so that he can slowly, sweetly brush his mouth against mine.

The moment our lips meet, I can feel the tension leave me in a rush. And for a moment, just a moment, things feel normal. Like we're back in San Diego, going to classes, building a life together, spending every night wrapped in each other's arms and every day texting ridiculous things to each other.

There's no Crone who wants to destroy the entire paranormal world, no friend whose life depends on us not messing up, no secrets between us that I don't understand.

There's just Hudson and me and the never-ending heat that wells between us.

He must feel it, too, because he pulls back just enough to look me in the eye as his strong, talented hands cup my face. "I love you, Grace Foster," he whispers.

"I love you, Hudson Vega," I whisper back, right before I tangle my fingers in his hair and pull his mouth down to mine.

And the moment our lips touch, it feels just like I need it to.

He feels just like I need him to.

Familiar and safe and hot and exciting all rolled into one. All rolled into Hudson.

It feels amazing. We feel amazing. And so do I, when he's in my arms.

Heat wells inside me, making me ache for him in a way that I hope never goes away, and I slowly walk us toward the bed. What I want to do with him right now will definitely benefit from us both being horizontal…

Hudson must have the same thought, because it only takes a second for him to fall backward onto the bed, pulling me with him as he goes.

I land directly on top of him, my body stretched out over his lean hardness in a way that has every nerve ending inside me standing up and scrambling to attention. All I can think about—all I can need—is Hudson.

When I first started this, I thought I wanted it to be gentle and soft—thought I wanted to let the heat between us build as slow and steady as the love I have inside myself for him.

But it's hard to be gentle when desire barrels through you like a bullet train.

Hard to be soft when every part of you aches for every part of him.

And it sure as hell is hard to be steady when you're being ravaged by the man you love like you're the very air he needs to breathe.

Which is exactly what Hudson's doing to me right now.

My Hudson.

My mate.

The man with as many secrets as the Sphinx and as many depths as the Pacific Ocean that's fascinated me my entire life.

His mouth is plundering mine like this is our first—or our last—time.

Because just the thought of the latter disturbs me, I shove the thought out of my head. Bury it deep inside my mind in a place I don't let myself go to very often. And concentrate instead on making Hudson as hot, as achy, as desperate as he's already made me.

As he always makes me.

I start by shoving his T-shirt up and out of the way. Then I rake my nails down his lean, muscular chest, relishing the way his entire body stiffens with the same need pulsing inside me.

"Grace." My name is a gasp on his lips as he drags me down until I'm stretched out over him, every part of my body touching some part of his.

"Hudson," I murmur back, and if there's a teasing note in my tone right now, it's because sometimes turning the tables on him is just plain fun.

And this is definitely one of those times, I decide as I slide my tongue along his lower lip before pressing open-mouthed kisses across his jaw, down his neck, over one broad, beautiful shoulder.

He bucks against me as I do, groans low and deep in his throat in a way that sets the tiny hairs on the back of my neck to standing straight up even before his hands tighten in my curls.

Once he does, heat pours over me like lava from a volcano—molten hot and devastating but so good I never want it to stop.

Never want this to stop.

So I do it again, only this time I add my tongue—licking and sucking and nibbling my way over his collarbone and down the chest I have spent entirely too many hours thinking about.

His hand finds its way from tangling in my hair to gripping my hip as something wild breaks free inside him.

I can see it in his too-bright eyes.

Hear it in his uneven breathing.

Feel it in his powerful fingers digging into my flesh.

Suddenly, his mouth is everywhere—my lips, my neck, the sensitive spot behind my ear—before moving down.

In the blink of an eye, I'm the one on the bottom and he's the one above me, his fangs scraping over my collarbone, down my breasts, across my stomach, to my navel and then lower, lower, lower.

It's my turn to cry out, my turn to clutch the sheets in my hands, my turn to arch and shudder against him as he takes me higher and higher and higher until I worry we'll fly too close to the sun.

And then we do, and I forget to care about sunburn or melted wings or anything else that might happen because it feels so good. He feels so good. Even before he moves back over me and we race toward the surface of the sun together.

Later, much later, when it's over and we're done free-falling through the atmosphere back to earth, I wrap myself around him and hold on as tightly as I can. Because this is Hudson and me, and I am never, ever letting go.

Even if in the morning the world is going to try its damnedest to make me do just that.

23

Seed You Later

"**O**f course we're not going to let you go find some Bittersweet Tree alone." Heather is the first to speak after I outline the situation while we're all eating breakfast outside the next morning. "I don't even know what makes an elixir celestial, but I'm totally in."

She looks at the others questioningly.

Hudson doesn't answer, because he doesn't have to. I know he's got my back, that he'll always have my back. That's never been a question. Besides, I already told him everything from the meeting with my grandmother last night, and he is in agreement with me. We save Mekhi, whatever the cost. And when we succeed—and we will—we come back and kick the Crone's ass to the curb as well.

"We're *all* in," Jaxon says, thankfully drawing the attention away from me. "You know that."

"Yeah," Flint agrees. "When have we not been in?"

As we clean up our breakfast dishes, I think back to the time he and Macy were so full of anger that they left us at the lighthouse without so much as an explanation—and dragged us straight into the mess at the Vampire Court. But that was then, and this is now. Besides, I've hauled them into messes plenty of times myself. Messes that, in the end, were a lot worse than what happened in London.

For a second, Liam's face flashes before my mind—the way he looked right before he died. We still haven't discussed why he betrayed us. We can't face it yet. And because the thought has bile churning in my stomach, sadness welling up inside me, I push it away.

I push everything away except for the task at hand—namely, finding the Shadow Queen and striking a deal with her that will help us save both her and Mekhi.

"Thank you," I tell them.

"You don't ever have to thank us, Grace." Eden wraps an arm around my shoulders as we make our way through the castle to the front door. "We're in this together."

"I do have a question, though." Heather looks back from where she's the first one out the double doors. "What happens if we get to the Witch Court and no one knows how to activate this magical portal fountain?"

"Someone will know." Hudson speaks up for the first time in a while.

We turn as one to look at him, but he just lifts a shoulder in a negligent shrug. "When people live as long as paranormals tend to, someone always knows something."

"Yeah, but witches don't live as long as dragons and vampires," I respond.

"Still, Hudson's got a good point." Jaxon grins. "Try keeping a secret when half the Court can brew a truth serum. Or cast a location spell. Or use a scrying mirror to—"

"We get it," Eden says with a roll of her eyes. "No one's got any privacy in the Witch Court."

I hope that's not true, considering I need to have a private moment with the one Witch Court insider I actually trust to give me straight answers.

"But first," I say, "we need to go to the Vampire Court and fetch Mekhi."

Pandemonium breaks out. Everyone starts shouting—we need to let him rest, he can't make this journey with us.

I hold a hand up. "I know. I know." My gaze lands on each of my friends' concerned faces, one by one. "But Hudson and I have a theory that the poison's effects will slow in the Shadow Realm." Without going into detail about Artelya, I quickly explain that we knew someone suffering from the poison, but it was acting much more slowly on their body than on Mekhi here. "Either because time works differently there or because it's where the poison originated—whatever the reason, we think it's our best chance to buy us the time we need to make this bargain with the Shadow Queen."

Jaxon starts to say, "I don't want him—"

But Hudson nails him with a piercing look. "He's dying, Jaxon. We can't stop that right now. At least we have a chance to slow it in the Shadow Realm."

Jaxon's jaw muscles tighten, but he gives a quick nod. I don't miss that he leans back against Flint's chest. I can only imagine how hard this is for him, and once again I'm grateful he and Flint have found each other, even if they appear to be having troubles. At the end of the day, they know they can count on each other, and that's all that matters.

"So who's flying with whom?" Eden breaks the silence. "I'm assuming there's no always-open portal between here and England, is there?"

"No, the Vampire Court is not interested in a direct line of communication at this time," I answer, glancing at Hudson.

"Oh, wait!" Flint reaches into his pocket and pulls out a small black velvet bag. "I almost forgot that Macy gave me these."

"Gave you what?" Hudson asks, brow raised as he looks doubtfully at the bag.

"Magic seeds!" he answers triumphantly.

"I don't think a giant beanstalk is what we need right now," I tell him.

"Pretty sure that was a bean, not a seed." Flint rolls his eyes. "Besides, these are from Macy. She felt guilty and said we should use them anytime we need a portal."

"A portal?" I look at the bag with fresh eyes. "Are you telling me Macy charmed a seed so that it will grow into a portal?"

"That's what she told me."

"Where would she even learn that?" Eden asks, reaching for the bag to look inside it.

"Maybe from that all-witch academy she was at before she got kicked out?" Flint shrugs. "I don't know. I just know she said they worked. But she said, like her regular portals, they can only go where she's visited before. Good thing the Vampire Court is on her been-there, done-that list!"

"Well, I guess there's no time like the present to find out." I look around, ensuring everyone's got their travel stuff ready to go, then look at Flint. "Do you want to do the honors?"

"Hell yeah! I've been dying to!" he answers, retrieving the bag from

Eden. Then he pulls out a single iridescent black seed.

We all take a couple of steps backward as he performs the spell Macy taught him before tossing the seed into the dirt a few feet in front of him.

And then we all watch in awe as Macy's seed blossoms into an actual portal. It's the most bizarre and most amazing thing I've ever seen, and I'm captivated by the entire process. How can I not be, when it literally burrows into the ground in front of us under its own power?

Several seconds pass as it continues to bury itself in the dirt, and then, in the blink of an eye, a tiny green seedling breaks through the topsoil. It's tiny at first, a little shoot of a plant just beginning to bud. But then it grows and grows and grows.

Branches sprout out of it in two directions, and within seconds, they're curving upward as they grow larger and larger. Seconds later, they're tangling and twisting together at the top, forming a circular shape that brings to mind Snow White's evil stepmother's magic mirror.

But this little seed hasn't grown into anything as mundane as a mirror. No, this is a portal sparking with power and electricity, strength and rage—exactly like the magic that created it.

There are no rainbows here. No kaleidoscope of colors that welcomes you in the way Macy's portals normally do.

No, this portal is filled with a dark, swirling magic that fascinates me even as it makes me worry for my cousin all the more.

"I'm not sure if I'm ever going to get used to this," Flint murmurs.

I don't know if he's talking about the seed or the ominous overtones in Macy's new magic, but I feel him on both fronts. Maybe that's why my heart is beating at a frantic tempo when I take my first hesitant step into the portal.

The second I step inside, a chill sweeps through me that sinks all the way to my bones. It makes me shiver uncontrollably and ache like my body is starting to give out. At the same time, thorns skate across my skin, pricking me one after another—not enough to draw blood but more than enough to make me hurt.

One digs deeper than the others, and I gasp as I finally stumble out the other side of the portal and land—as I nearly always do—on my ass.

24

Home Not-So-
Sweet Home

I have a few moments to glance down and make sure I'm not actually bleeding before Hudson walks out like he's taking an early-morning stroll along the Thames.

The jerk.

"Well, that was fun." Sarcasm drips from his words as he reaches a hand down to help me up.

"No kidding. What the hell *was* that?"

He looks like he wants to say something, but in the end he just shrugs and walks away from the portal. Which has me wondering exactly what kind of portal we just went through. Because something about it didn't feel right to me—and Hudson's reaction is only reinforcing that fact.

Once I'm on my feet, I take a moment to dust off my butt and look around, trying to figure out where the portal has dropped us. I know we're at the Vampire Court, but we're definitely not in a part of it that I recognize.

The Vampire Court I know is all creeping shadows, torture devices, and concrete crypts.

This room is decorated in three varying shades of…white. White on sort-of white on creamy white. The furniture is minimalist, dark wood when not covered in more white. White cushions. Off-white lumbar pillows. Even the massive rug covering the dark hardwood floor consists of swirls of varying shades of white.

And it's all fucking gorgeous.

But definitely *not* the Vampire Court.

"Umm, no offense, but I think Macy's internal GPS is a little off this time," Flint comments as he emerges from my cousin's portal seconds later. He, too, looks a little worse for wear.

"I don't think it works that way," Eden tells him, but as she looks around, she doesn't sound very convincing. Or convinced.

"Well, something's sure as fuck wrong, because this doesn't look like home sweet home." Jaxon strides to the nearest doorway and peers down the hall.

"Like there was ever anything sweet about your home," Flint mutters.

"Touché."

"So, if we're not in the Vampire Court, where exactly are we?" Heather asks.

"The Vampire Court," Hudson finally answers as he walks back to us, "updated edition."

Jaxon turns on him. "Dude. What did you do?"

"Gave it some class." Hudson smiles in that bared-teeth way he has that makes everyone but me nervous. Judging from the sudden looks on my friends' faces, today is no exception.

"I think it's amazing," I say, my gaze softening on Hudson. "It's like someone threw open the windows and let the light in. Finally."

Heather spins in a slow circle, eyes a little bit dreamy as they take in every detail of the room. "It's beautiful. Really, really beautiful."

I've always thought gothic architecture was gorgeous, with its flying buttresses and vaulted ceilings, but this white minimalism—I don't know what else to call it—goes way beyond elegant.

It feels like a home.

The ceilings are still as high as ever, but instead of the pointed arches and decorative columns that were here the last time I visited, now everything is smooth, rounded, soaring.

The room we're in obviously works as a meeting place—long, streamlined couches and comfy chairs are grouped in different-shaped sections around the room, all in shades of white and tan that beg people to congregate.

The floors are a warm chestnut, the walls paneled with what looks like dark, rich, petrified wood—a mixture of crushed espresso bean color with spots of copper and jade woven throughout. The back wall is lined—floor to ceiling—with cream-colored bookcases filled to bursting with books bound in shades of black, gray, and brown leather.

The lancet windows are covered with slate-gray screens to block out sunlight, if not the view of London down below, and the chandeliers are works of art in and of themselves. Each one is comprised of dozens of flutelike cylinders floating at different elevations that, when combined, somehow manage to look like a deconstructed, crystal version of stalactites.

The effect is awe-inspiring and yet inviting.

And that's not even counting the soaring gray-and-black Rothkos hanging in strategic positions around the room. I recognize them from images Hudson was obsessed with a couple of months ago. When he asked me to pick my favorite, I didn't realize it was so he could buy it and hang it here.

"It's…" Jaxon's voice trails off.

"A new start," Hudson says quietly. "After everything that happened with Cyrus, this place—and our people—deserve something different. Something better."

"But how did you get the Court to agree?" I ask. Considering neither Vega is currently willing to take the throne…

Hudson raises one imperious brow. "I don't need their permission. This is my family home. I can do whatever the hell I want to with it, including deciding whether I will allow the Court to remain here."

Oh. My eyes widen. I mean, I knew this was the home he grew up in, but I guess I assumed the building belonged to the Vampire Court, not his family.

"Damn, the Vegas are almost as rich as a dragon," Flint jokes, elbowing Jaxon, and we all laugh.

"But Cyrus still owns it, doesn't he?" I ask, not sure why I'm harping on what Hudson's done here. But it just doesn't sit quite right with me that everyone else is learning facts about my mate's childhood home at the same time I am.

Hudson shrugs. "My mother had him give it to me last month in exchange for her not feeding from him for the next year. I guess that first stretch was rough—and she really does have a soft spot for me, after all."

He says the last bit like it doesn't matter, but I know it does. In fact, I know how much all of this must mean to him.

And there's a part of me that's incredibly proud of him for doing this. I mean, getting rid of Cyrus's fingerprints here is a great idea—a chance for the Court to blossom again, a chance for Hudson to reclaim the space after a millennium of fear and pain here.

I just wish he'd asked my opinion about more than just a Rothko painting—or, for that matter, told me anything about this. I've involved him in every step of the planning for the administrative wing of the Gargoyle Court I'm building in San Diego, from picking an architect to working out the design of the Court to approving the plans, which is the step we're on now. And I intend to involve him in all the other steps that come along, too.

Or at least I did. Now, standing here, I'm less sure if I should. Not only did he not involve me in any of this, he didn't even mention that he was doing it. I can't help wondering why. And I can't help writing my own scenarios to answer the question.

The fact that none of the scenarios are good doesn't exactly put my mind at ease. Especially not with everything I've been worried about since I talked to my grandparents.

And to him.

He said he isn't interested in taking over the Vampire Court, but this doesn't look like someone who isn't interested. If getting involved in the Court is what he feels like he needs to do, then I support him— of course I support him. But he needs to talk to me, not shut me out. And not feed me lines about never giving up his place at the Gargoyle Court for the vampires.

"Don't you think you should have run some of this by me?" Jaxon asks, and for a moment I feel like he can read my mind. But then I realize that he feels as betrayed as I do about this. Maybe even more, as this is his legacy, too.

"You've been pretty busy playing house over at the Dragon Court," Hudson answers. "I figured if you wanted to know what was going on here, you'd stop by. Or at least ask about it."

For a second, it looks like Jaxon is going to take a swing at his brother, but then he just shrugs. "You know what? It doesn't matter. This place isn't worth fighting over."

"Precisely," Hudson agrees. Which seems like a strange sentiment for a guy who has obviously spent as much time, energy, and money redesigning this place as he has.

Still, ogling the new architecture—and feeling wounded at being left out of any decisions Hudson has made here—isn't why we came to the Vampire Court. We've got bigger things to worry about.

Besides, Hudson and I are fine. He loves me. I love him. He's my best friend and my mate for eternity. What more could a girl ask for?

Someone who confides in her the way she confides in him? a little voice deep inside me whispers just a little slyly.

But I push it away, shove all the tiny frissons of fear that come with the shrewd question down deep inside myself. Tell myself I'm not being fair, to Hudson or to our relationship.

And then focus on something far more pressing—and far more easily definable.

"Is Mekhi in the crypt?" I ask, as that's where Hudson, Jaxon, and Izzy were put for their Descents.

Hudson looks surprised by the change of subject, but then his face goes inscrutable. It's one more thing that makes me beyond frustrated— the inability to read him when he doesn't want me to—but again I force myself to focus on his answer and not the uncertainty that's suddenly beating at my insides like a wounded bird.

"I believe your grandmother had him moved to one of the guest suites before she headed back to Ireland." He fires off a quick text. "Let me find out which one."

Then he reaches out a hand for mine, and the moment our skin presses together, all the noise inside me quiets. Because despite my worries, despite the fact that something doesn't feel quite right, the uncertainties fade to the background under the feeling of rightness that comes from being near him. From loving him.

"I really do like what you've done with the place," I say as we head for the door. "It's incredible."

Another flash of *something* in his eyes that's gone too quickly for me to identify. "I'm glad."

His phone dings and, after a quick glance at it, he turns us left down the hallway. "He's on the third floor, in the east corner," he says as we head for the nearest staircase.

As we walk, Hudson doesn't say anything else. And neither do I. Behind us, everyone is talking about different things.

Eden is telling Heather about Mekhi.

Jaxon and Flint are cataloging all the changes—of which there are many—they see along the way.

At least until Hudson passes between the two members of the Vampire Guard the Bloodletter apparently assigned to protect Mekhi and knocks on the door. As we wait for him to answer, I can't help stealing glimpses at the two guards.

I don't recognize them from the time we spent captive here, but that doesn't keep my stomach from tightening anyway. Hudson hasn't gotten around to changing the uniforms yet—a fact that surprises me, considering all the other changes he's made—and seeing them again makes it impossible not to think about everything that happened to us here and on the battlefield near Katmere Academy.

Impossible not to think about all the pain and loss and torture and devastation we suffered.

When there's no answer, Hudson knocks again, firmer and louder this time. The sound jolts me out of my bad memories, and I tell myself to focus on what's really important here: Mekhi.

He doesn't answer the second knock, either, and when Hudson goes to knock a third time, his brother stops him with a hand on his wrist.

"Just open the door," Jaxon says, and there's a thread of fear in his voice that echoes the terror bottoming out my stomach right now.

Hudson does as he asks, pushing the door open and standing aside so Jaxon can be the first in the room. But he only makes it a couple of steps before letting out a pained cry—one that has Flint and me rushing into the room right behind him.

I want to comfort Jaxon, but my first glance at Mekhi wipes everything but total and abject terror out of my head.

25

In Need of a Revamp

Asleep on an enormous four-poster bed, Mekhi looks like a ghost—or worse, like a shadow of his former self.

His normally rich brown skin has turned an unhealthy gray color, as if the poison creeping through his veins is slowly turning him into one of the very shadows that sought to destroy him.

Even the locs around his face—usually so well taken care of—are growing out.

And he's swimming in his clothes, the outline of his shoulder and collar bones in sharp relief against the thin cotton of his T-shirt.

Even worse, his breathing is as fast and shallow as a pneumonia patient's.

Panic rips through me, along with a desperate need for denial. This isn't Mekhi. Not fun, full-of-life, friendly Mekhi.

Please don't let this be Mekhi.

But it is, clearly.

Just enough of his former self remains for me to recognize him. And it breaks my heart.

I'm not the only one. Eden shrieks when she sees him, a high-pitched, terrified sound that is like nothing I've heard come from her before. Flint starts swearing, low and long and vicious. And Jaxon—Jaxon is beside himself, pacing the room and muttering, wild-eyed.

"Why didn't she tell us?" Jaxon demands, his voice little more than a hiss now. "We thought he was safe in Descent."

"She did tell us," I say softly. "That's why we're here."

"Too late," he snarls, and I can't even argue with him. Because I thought Mekhi was okay these last few months, too. Not great, obviously, but not like this—this person hasn't had their metabolism slowed for months. This person, asleep or not, has continued to be ravaged by shadow poison.

"We never would have let him get to this point if we'd known," Jaxon continues bitterly. "It's like Descent didn't slow a damn thing down."

Flint moves to Mekhi's bedside, grabbing a blanket from the bottom of the bed and pulling it over the vampire, who is shivering and muttering incoherently in his sleep.

"Do you think we can even get him to the Shadow Realm?" I ask the question that's been eating at my insides from the moment we walked into this room. "Because he doesn't look like—"

"Oh, we'll get him there," Jaxon says. "I'll carry him the whole way if I have to. I just hope you're right and the Shadow Realm slows the poison."

"We still have to get him to the Witch Court first," Eden points out, and the tough-as-nails dragon looks frightened in a way I've never seen her before.

Heather notices and moves to her side, but before any of us can propose how to move him, there's a loud knock on the door.

It startles me, has my back tightening and my heart beating fast as I whirl toward the door. I know it's silly, know Cyrus is locked up thousands of miles away and can't hurt us anymore. But being here—even with the changes Hudson has made—gives me the creeps.

I'm afraid it always will.

Though I try to hide my reaction, Hudson sees it. He stiffens for a second, too, then fades to the door in a blink.

As he passes me, I feel the faint brush of his hand over my curls. It's not much, but it's the reassurance I need to relax just a little bit—and to remember that there is no longer anyone or anything to fear here.

Hudson opens the door, and I get a glimpse of the two men who were guarding the room earlier. Then he steps into the hall and pulls the door partially closed behind him.

It obscures my view of the two men but does nothing to stop me from hearing their conversation. One guard vaguely mentions a meeting for a couple of matters Hudson needs to take care of. He tries brushing the guards off, but they're insistent. Apparently, these matters have been needing his attention for a while now.

"It's okay," I say, crossing the room to stand next to him in the hall. "We still need to figure out how to move Mekhi. Take a few minutes and deal with this and then we'll go, okay?"

He looks like he wants to argue, but I give him a soft push on the shoulder to get him moving. "We can handle this," I tell him again. "This is your Court. Go do what has to be done."

"It's not my Court," he answers. But he allows me to usher him gently down the hall. "I'm going to find out where his nurse is and get him back here."

As I watch him leave, I can't help but become aware of the fact that the two guards in the hallway somehow tripled to six in the time we were inside Mekhi's room. And all of them are trailing expectantly behind my mate.

Which only makes the uneasy feeling inside me grow, even though I know Hudson is safe with them. Not to mention he could kick any of their asses if he wanted to.

Maybe it's the fact that I know he doesn't want to and never would that makes me uneasy. Hudson is the kind of vamp who cares for anyone and everyone he takes under his wing, so to speak. I just wish I could understand how he's taken these people—who fought against us such a short time ago—into that care.

"Well, we need to figure something out!" Jaxon snaps behind me, and I turn around. "Because there's no fucking way we're leaving here without him."

"I'm not suggesting we leave him," Flint growls. "I'm just saying—"

He breaks off as the door opens and a vampire in black scrubs bustles in like his long blond ponytail is on fire. "I'm sorry," he apologizes as he rushes to Mekhi's bedside. "I've only been gone fifteen minutes or so."

His hands are shaking as he moves to take his patient's vital signs— surefire proof that Hudson ran into him on the way to his meeting.

"We have to bring him with us," I say after the nurse removes the stethoscope from his ears. "How do you suggest we do that without hurting him further?"

"I have a sleeping draught to give him," he answers. "I'll have to wake him briefly, and then it will take about half an hour for him to metabolize enough for it to be effective, but once he goes under, you should be able to move him without causing any undue pain. I warn you, though—it won't last long."

"A sleeping draught?" Jaxon asks suspiciously.

I lean forward so that I can rest a hand on Mekhi's. "It won't make him worse, will it?"

"There's not much that can make him worse at this point, Your Majesty," the nurse answers, a look of pity on his face.

That's not what I want to hear—what any of us want to hear. But it's honest, and I guess that's all we can hope for right now.

"If you'll step out, I'll administer the draught and get him ready for the journey," the nurse adds. "I'll watch over him for as long as you need."

I don't want to leave—it's obvious that none of us do—but it's not like we're doing anything standing around his bedside freaking out, either. So we nod as one and file into the hallway.

Then keep walking as I do my best to ignore the sound of Mekhi's desperate moans...and the terrifying silence when they abruptly stop.

26

I Don't Trust You
as Far as I Can Throne You

I want to find Hudson and speed things along, but I'm not willing
to expose Heather to whatever an *urgent meeting* looks like at the
Vampire Court—she may be brave, but she's still a human—so I leave
her outside Mekhi's room with Flint and Eden as company. Last I hear,
Flint is complaining loudly about what I'm pretty sure is a genuine
Miró—whether to entertain Heather or distract them from Mekhi's
chilling silence, I'm not sure.

As Jaxon and I follow a long curve in the hallway, I can't help
marveling at all the changes Hudson's made to the Vampire Court. I
also can't help wondering why he's done it. Yes, he said earlier that
it's because the people here deserve a fresh start after everything that
happened under Cyrus, and I believe he means that.

But I also think there's more to the story than he's telling me. These
alterations are too radical, too polished, too *everything* to just be about
giving vampires a pretty new Court.

Neither Jaxon nor I say anything about the Court's new look, but
I know he's noticing it, too. It's impossible to miss.

I'm not sure where we're going, but Jaxon must, because when we
get to the end of the hallway, he guides me to the left. We stop in front
of a closed door the color of onyx with an elaborate door handle.

"Are you sure Hudson's in here?" I ask as Jaxon reaches for it.

"It's the war room. There's nowhere else he would be right now."

He says it with such certainty that I don't ask again. And it turns
out he's right. The second the door opens, I can hear Hudson talking.

I can't make out what he's saying, but he doesn't sound happy. And
neither do the people he's talking to.

Jaxon must be thinking the same thing I am, because instead of knocking, he suddenly slams the door against the wall hard enough to make the hanging artwork rattle.

Conversation stops as everyone in the room turns to stare at us. Hudson lifts a brow—a definite welcome to the party if I've ever seen one—while everyone else looks outraged at being disturbed.

But since my mate's the one in charge, and I don't have a lot of—meaning any—respect left for anyone else in this godforsaken Court, I don't actually give a shit.

"Everything okay?" Hudson asks, rounding the table in the center of the room to meet his brother and me.

"The nurse is with Mekhi," I answer. "Thank you for arranging for him to come back so quickly."

He nods before returning to the people gathered around the table—two men who look vaguely familiar from Cyrus's rule and a woman with a tight black updo whom I'm sure I've never met before.

"Aunt Celine," Jaxon says as he crosses the room to press a very perfunctory kiss on her powdered cheek. "What an unpleasant surprise."

Her lips pucker in a bizarre version of a smile as she reaches up and pats the scar on his face. "Is that any way to talk to your aunt when I've come all this way to help you with this Court mess?"

"Is that what you're calling it these days? Help?"

I glance at Hudson to see what he thinks of Jaxon's strange interaction with his aunt, but he's just leaning a shoulder against the wall, arms crossed over his chest and an amused half smile on his lips. When he catches my questioning look, he gives a slight shrug as if to say, *What can I do? Jaxon will be Jaxon.*

While that is absolutely true, I'm still confused by what's happening here. It doesn't surprise me that there's no love lost between Jaxon and Hudson and this woman who must be Cyrus's sister, if her chilling vibe is anything to go by, but I don't have a clue what she's doing here. Or why they're letting her be here when it's obvious they want nothing to do with her.

"Well, I have heard that there's some question of who will be taking over my dear brother's throne now that he is...indisposed. And of course, since you abdicated as well, Hudson." She waves a hand. "I know the formal ceremony isn't for another couple of weeks, but I thought I would come and volunteer the services of Rodney and Flavinia for when your abdication is final. My heirs stand ready to assume the mantle of leadership."

My stomach pitches. Hudson swore to me last night that he has no interest in being vampire king, and I believe him. We both considered the formal ceremony nothing more than pomp and circumstance. But standing here, looking at this woman with avarice in her eyes and cheeks stained pink with excitement, I can see why not assuming the role of king may not actually be the same as rejecting it.

Hudson may not want it for himself the way Celine, Rodney, and Flavinia obviously do, but he doesn't want them to have it, either, because his people deserve better than the new-and-unimproved Cyrus 2.0. Which leaves him in one hell of a conundrum.

More, it leaves *us* in one hell of a conundrum.

"How kind of you," Hudson tells her in a voice that says she is anything but. "We are managing to muddle along here in London, though. I'm sure you'd be much more comfortable back home in Stoke-on-Trent. You know how Rodney misses Mummy if you're gone too long."

I can't help it. I turn to give Hudson a what-the-hell-is-even-happening-right-now look. Stoke-on-Trent? Mummy? Who are these people, and what have they done with my mate?

But he just smiles placidly back at me, as long as I don't look too closely at the wicked gleam in his eyes.

"Yes, well, perhaps we should wait until later to discuss this in more depth. We don't want to air our not-so-clean laundry in front of the non-vampires in the room."

Considering I'm the only non-vampire in sight, I try not to be too offended by that. Then again, if it wasn't for Hudson and Jaxon, I wouldn't care at all about what went on among these hideous people in this hideous war room, as long as it didn't affect the world outside it.

But I do care about Hudson and Jaxon, so I keep a smile plastered on my face even as Hudson tells her, "The non-vampire is my mate.

And she's not leaving until I do."

"Of course not, dear Hudson," she answers slyly. "We know you would never dream of putting the Court before your mate. Though that's not a problem that my dear Rodney has…"

"Goodbye, Aunt Celine," Jaxon grinds out as he links his arm with hers and escorts her firmly toward the hall. And he doesn't bother to kiss her cheek before he shuts the door in her very affronted face.

"Any other business we need to take care of?" he asks as he turns around. "Or can we get on the road?"

Hudson grins, waving at the two other men to dismiss them. "I'm done here."

But I can't help wondering…is he really?

27

An Epic
Throne Down

"I think you've spent your time changing the wrong things around here, Hudson." Jaxon gives his brother a shrewd look as we start walking back toward Mekhi's room.

"Oh, I'll get to that, too," Hudson answers grimly. "Believe me."

"What if you don't have to?" Jaxon asks.

Hudson looks incredulous. "You want me to leave those three creeps on the advisory council? They'll have us back at war in a few months, if not earlier."

"No." Jaxon swallows. "I want you to abdicate—"

"I *am* abdicating. I assure you," he says as he reaches down to take my hand in his and squeeze. "Just not to Rodney." Even I know that's a bad idea, and I have no idea who Rodney is. But if he's anything like his mother...

Jaxon clears his throat again, then swallows a second time. "Luckily, Rodney isn't next in line for the throne. I am."

Hudson and I both stop in our tracks. "I'm sorry?" I ask, because I'm certain that I didn't hear him correctly. Jaxon has never wanted the throne. Even before, when he thought Hudson was dead, the idea of actually ruling the Vampire Court was anathema to him.

"You know that doesn't solve anything, right?" Hudson tells him. "You'll have the same problems with the Dragon Court that I'm having with the Gargoyle Court. The Circle—"

"The Circle can get fucked," Jaxon snarls.

It's not the most king-like answer, but I don't point that out. Partly because he's trying really hard to do something nice for Hudson and partly because I know exactly how he feels. When I'm dealing with Court business, I want to tell the Circle and the rule makers in this world to get fucked at least once a day.

"That still doesn't solve the problem," Hudson says after a few long seconds. "There is no way the Circle will allow you to have that much power—to sit on both thrones."

"Then I'll just sit on this one," he answers.

"Jaxon." I touch his arm. "That's a huge sacrifice—"

"What, only one Vega brother is allowed to sacrifice for the other?" he asks, his voice thick with emotion.

Hudson's gaze turns watchful. "That's not at all the same, Jaxon."

"You found love, man. Our whole lives, we never thought a Vega would be able to do that. But you managed it. And then I fucked it up. Just like I'm fucking everything up for Flint. He wants the dragon throne more than anything, and taking it will restore balance to his Court. But he can't do that with me by his side."

He clears his throat one more time, runs a frustrated hand over his hair. "Maybe this is how things were always meant to be."

My heart breaks at the anguish in his tone and at his determination to do his best by his brother, by me, and by Flint. But sacrificing his and Flint's future so that Hudson and I can have one? That's not something either of us is willing to let him do.

"I think you forget how long it took Grace and me to get *our* shit together," Hudson tells him mildly. "We didn't start out like this."

I laugh at just the thought of it. "No, we definitely didn't."

"If you take up the vampire crown, you'll lose any chance you have of finding that same happiness." Hudson puts a hand on his shoulder. "You deserve to be happy, too, Jaxon."

He looks away, shakes off Hudson's hand. "You don't know... Flint and I are a fucking mess, bro."

"Everyone's a mess," I tell him. "That's just how most relationships are."

"Yeah, well." Jaxon shrugs. "At some point, relationships are supposed to make things better for the people involved, aren't they? All being with me has done is made things worse for Flint."

"This isn't a sacrifice you need to make," I tell him. "We'll find another way."

He shakes his head. "I don't know."

"Exactly," Hudson says, wrapping an arm around his brother's shoulders in a one-sided hug. "And until you do—until we all do—no one is making any drastic decisions."

"Not even you?" Jaxon asks, brows raised.

I lean forward, as interested to hear his answer to that question as Jaxon is.

"My decision has already been made. The rest is minor details."

"Pretty *important* details," Jaxon corrects.

Hudson doesn't say anything, just looks at him steadily until Jaxon exhales in a series of curses. "We're not done talking about this."

It's Hudson's turn to shrug. "We'll see."

"Yeah," his brother tells him. "We will."

My stomach is in knots now, all these impossible problems with no solutions running through my brain at top speed, over and over and over again.

We can't put another Cyrus on the vampire throne. If we do, we'll eventually end up right back where we were just a few short months ago.

Jaxon can't take the throne, because if he does, he'll lose any chance he and Flint have of working through their problems and coming out on the other side of them.

Izzy can't take the throne, at least not yet. She hasn't been out of Descent for long enough, not to mention her...unpredictable tendencies.

And Hudson can't keep the throne, at least not as long as I hold on to mine.

It's a complete and total clusterfuck—one I have no idea how to fix, especially not when most of my brain is focused on trying to figure out how to save Mekhi from the shadow poison and everyone else from these damn hunters who are gaining power and followers by the day.

Before I can say anything else, Jaxon's cell phone dings. He glances down at it, then says, "Flint wants to talk to me about something, so I'm going to meet him where the portal dropped us. We'll catch up with you at Mekhi's room in fifteen minutes."

Even as I nod, part of me wants to beg him to stay. Because as long as he's here, Hudson and I won't be able to avoid the discussion that neither of us wants to have.

28

It's Sledge(Hammer) Time

After Jaxon leaves, we walk slowly and silently for a couple of minutes. I don't know what Hudson is thinking about, but I'm definitely trying to get my thoughts in order. Definitely trying to figure out what I need to say to him—about the throne, about the changes here at Court that he hasn't talked to me about at all, about us.

But before I can, we make another turn and end up in a corridor that looks hauntingly familiar. Which doesn't make sense, considering there are huge swaths of the Vampire Court I haven't explored yet and likely never will, since I absolutely despise the place, even with Hudson's improvements.

Still, the farther we walk down the hallway, the more convinced I am that I've been to this specific spot before. There's something about the odd configuration of the windows on the left side of the hallway that feels familiar. As do the giant wooden double doors I see at the end of a hallway directly to the right of us.

Despite the doors' familiarity, I almost keep walking right on by them. But there's something about the sudden deliberate blankness on Hudson's face and the shuttered look in his eyes that has me approaching them and reaching for the door handles.

He moves like he's going to stop me, which is strange in and of itself, but in the end he just shrugs and lets me go.

The second I open the doors, I know exactly where we are. I've only been in here once, but I recognize it right away. Or should I say recognize the remnants of what it once was. Cyrus's perfectly curated, perfectly decorated office.

No one can accuse it of being perfectly anything now—except, maybe, perfectly, extraordinarily destroyed. While the outer doors remain intact, inside the room, it looks like a bomb has gone off. And unlike the other rooms we passed that are currently under renovation, no one has made any attempt to clear up the mess of the old room to make way for the new. It's all just sitting there—overturned couches, broken paintings and sculptures, ripped-up books, torn curtains—lying under the detritus of destroyed walls and ceiling and light fixtures. The circular table that once dominated the middle has been demolished, pieces of the inlaid map—which Cyrus once used to plan attacks on paranormal factions—scattered across the floor.

I spot a sledgehammer leaning against the insides of what used to be a wall, and I realize that someone whacked away at things in here until it looked like this. Then they walked away and left it for who knows how long. Judging by the amount of plaster dust settled on everything, this wasn't done today. Or anytime recently, for that matter.

I'm one hundred percent sure of that. I'm also one hundred percent sure that Hudson is the one who did this. And the one who left it here, like this, to rot.

He's been to visit the Vampire Court to handle business several times since we imprisoned Cyrus, and I never thought anything of it. Now I can't help thinking that maybe I should have. The thought of Hudson, all on his own, just whaling away at this room with a sledgehammer, makes me want to cry.

Because there's more than rage in this shrine of rubble. More than disdain or hate or a need for vengeance. There's also devastation. And I have no idea what to do about that—not when Hudson hasn't spoken to me about any of this.

Not the changes to the Court.

Not the pressure to take on more responsibilities and perhaps even the throne.

And definitely not this wanton destruction. When a man who wields as much power as Hudson chooses to use a sledgehammer instead of a simple thought, you know it's personal. More, you know there's a lot still left to uncover.

And right now, with our friends in the middle of this quest to save

Mekhi, I just wish I had a clue where to start.

"We should get going," Hudson says from beside me. His voice is as stiff as his upper lip, his British accent so formal that if he wasn't looking straight at me—and we weren't the only two people in this hallway—I would guess he was talking to a stranger.

"Are you okay?" I ask, stepping forward so I can rest a hand on his biceps. Because no matter how hurt and confused I am by his silence on all of this, he's still Hudson. Still my mate. And the thought of him hurting destroys me.

"I'm fine," he answers. But there's something in his eyes, something in the way he's holding himself, like he might shatter right here in what's left of his father's office, that makes me think he's far from fine.

Even before he pulls me against him and wraps his arms around me so tightly that I can barely breathe.

"It's okay," I tell him, stroking my hands over his hair, his neck, his too-tense back. "Whatever this is, it's going to be okay."

His cheek is pressed to the top of my head, and I feel him nod.

I also feel the deep, shuddering breath he takes and the shaky way he lets it out.

And then he's pulling away, a half smile on his lips that doesn't feel like it belongs there. But the light is back in his eyes as he looks down at me, and that makes it easier for me to believe he's okay for now.

And much easier for me to go along with it when he says, "It's been close to twenty minutes. We should probably get to Mekhi."

There's so much I want to say right now, so much I want to ask him. But I know he's right—just like I know this isn't the time or the place for my questions. Hudson doesn't like being vulnerable on a good day. Trying to get him to let his guard down here, in the middle of the Vampire Court, where he spent most of his life being tortured?

To borrow a phrase from his book, not bloody likely.

So instead of pushing like I really want to do, I thread my fingers through his hair and pull him down for a kiss...or three.

The fourth kiss gets interesting, has my heart beating too fast and my blood roaring in my veins. But this isn't the time or the place for our intense chemistry, either. Hudson was right when he said we need to get back to the others.

I give myself—give us—just a few more seconds. Just one more kiss. Then I pull reluctantly away. "You're right. We should."

When he grins down at me this time, the darkness and distance is gone from his eyes—at least for now. In its place is the wild, desperate, infinite love that I'm so used to seeing there. The same wild, desperate, infinite love that I know is in my eyes when I look up at him.

It's not enough—we still need to talk, and I still need answers about what's going on with him—but for now, as we hurry down the hallway to Mekhi's room, it feels like a step in the right direction.

29

It's the Motion
of the Potion

Hudson and I make it back to our friends just as the nurse opens the door to let us in to see Mekhi again.

My heart is in my throat as I move toward the bedchamber, terrified of what we're going to find when we walk in there. But Mekhi looks fine—definitely better than he did when we left him with the nurse. The sleeping draught has obviously taken effect, as the lines of pain are smoothed out from his face.

The nurse hands Eden a small black parcel. "There's another sleeping draught in there, in case you need it to get him where you're going. But that's all you can give him. He's too weak to metabolize more right now."

"So he's going to be suffering?" Jaxon asks, voice hoarse.

The nurse gives him a sympathetic look. "There's nothing to be done to stop the suffering. The draught makes him comfortable for a little while, but anything else will only exacerbate the effects of the shadow poison."

"So how are we going to do this?" I move straight into logistics in an effort not to dwell on Mekhi's suffering. "We're using one of Macy's seeds to get to the Witch Court, correct? But how are we going to move Mekhi through the portal?"

"I'm carrying him," Jaxon answers in a tone that brooks no argument.

"That's okay, right?" Eden asks the nurse. "It won't hurt him to be carried?"

"He has to be moved," he replies. "And that's definitely the most practical way to get him through the portal."

It's impossible to miss the fact that he didn't answer her question.

Then again, that's an answer in and of itself. Moving Mekhi will hurt him, but there's not much we can do about that right now.

"Where's the closest exit?" Flint asks, pulling out Macy's bag of magic seeds again.

"There's a garden around the corner," Hudson answers, moving next to his brother. "We should be able to open a portal there."

"I'll head out now. Give me two minutes to get it open and then bring Mekhi," he tells Jaxon, who nods.

Eden follows him with the sleeping draught while Heather grabs a couple of blankets before leaving the room, too, with one backward concerned glance for Mekhi.

"Thank you for your help," I tell the nurse as Jaxon moves to Mekhi's bedside. "We appreciate it more than we can say."

"Of course. I hope he'll be okay," the nurse responds.

"Thank you." This time it's Jaxon who answers, voice thick with the emotions that are running through all of us right now.

"You ready?" Hudson asks quietly.

"No," Jaxon answers. But then he bends over and picks Mekhi up in a fireman's carry. "Let's get the hell out of here, shall we?"

He doesn't need to ask me twice. I rush to the door and hold it open for him while Hudson fades down the hall and does the same with the door into the garden.

Part of me expects Jaxon to fade, but instead, he walks down the hall as slowly and carefully as if he were carrying a newborn. When we finally get to the garden, Eden and Heather are already gone and Flint is holding the portal open for the rest of us.

"You okay?" he asks Jaxon as he steps up to the swirling black-and-purple magic.

Jaxon ignores the question, though. And then he's stepping through the portal, Mekhi securely hooked over his shoulder. As they disappear, I really hope the portal is easier the second time around. For all our sakes.

30

Like a Goth
to a Flame

Turns out, the portal is even worse the second time around. I swear, for a minute I'm certain I'm being flayed alive.

But thankfully, all my skin is intact, and so is the rest of me, when I finally tumble out of the portal and onto the ground in Turin, Italy. Everyone else is, too, including Mekhi, who is still sleeping peacefully— or at least as peacefully as anyone can when draped over Jaxon's shoulder.

Once I'm on my feet, I take a moment to brush the city grime off my butt, then look around to try to figure out where the portal has delivered us. I was kind of hoping we'd be inside the Witch Court, but the traffic whizzing by on the street behind us definitely negates that idea.

A quick spin tells me exactly where we are: in the heart of Il Piazza Castello, right in front of the Witch Court. I'd recognize this place anywhere—not just because of the distinctive architecture of the buildings all around us but because of that damn creepy statue directly in the center of the piazza.

For the most part, it's just a pile of rocks balanced on top of a fountain, but when you add in the sculptures of barely clothed men languishing on the side of it and the dark angel standing watch at the top, it gives off some very menacing vibes. It's given me the creeps from the very first time I saw its double in the Impossible Trials, and now that I know it's also the gateway to the Shadow Realm, it seems even worse.

But I have no time to obsess over statues right now. Not when I still have to figure out how to *open* the portal. I mean, it's a fountain—so it's not like we can just turn a knob and walk through a doorway. Clearly there's a spell or something that activates a portal inside the fountain.

I just need to find the right witch to ask...

The late-afternoon sun is blocked by gray clouds as we move toward the entrance of the Witch Court. A cold wind sweeps through the air around us, making me shiver.

"So who's going to knock?" Flint asks as he saunters up beside me. I haven't had a chance to ask him if he wants to talk about what's going on at the Dragon Court, but given the way he seems to be avoiding Jaxon's glances right now, I'd wager political intrigue is probably the last thing on his mind.

I shoot off a quick text to Macy, then wait to see if she'll answer immediately. If she does, she might be exactly who we need to get into the Court without a lot of fuss, or she might even know who can tell us how to open the statue-portal. Besides, I'd just like to see my cousin, check on her. Maybe ask about the whole spooky-painful-portal thing.

"This place gives me the creeps," Jaxon mutters as we wait for Macy's response. "It's so...extra."

"I can see how that's a problem for you, considering how cozy the Vampire Court is," drawls a familiar voice from behind us.

I turn just in time to see the shimmery edges of a portal disappear—right after my cousin steps out of it.

"Macy!" I squeal, running to her. "I thought you were grounded. I wasn't expecting the immediate meetup!"

She runs a hand through her shaggily cut hair. She's changed the color since I saw her last—now it's a dark, gorgeous sea green that somehow looks both beautiful and dangerous. Which is a pretty accurate reflection of everything about Macy these days.

Gone is the sparkly, bubbly cousin who always looks on the bright side, even when bad stuff happens. In her place is a witch who's embracing her power in new and mysterious ways—one who definitely appears to be choosing chaos over joy.

"There's grounded and then there's grounded," she tells me with a roll of her big blue eyes. "Besides, it's not like they can actually keep me prisoner if I don't want them to."

There's an edge to her voice—one that I choose to ignore as I wrap my arms around her in a huge hug. Obviously, Macy is still pissed about

Uncle Finn lying to her, letting her believe her mother had run off and left her *by choice*—and honestly, I don't blame her.

To have your child believe their mom ran away and abandoned them, rather than tell them she was in prison... I still grapple with understanding that decision. But to also welcome the person holding her captive at your home numerous times throughout those years? That's a slap in the face that I know is going to take Macy a while to get over.

I'm still hurt that my parents never filled me in on the whole gargoyle thing. If they'd kept a secret like *this* from me? I don't know what I'd do.

Macy lets me hug her for a breath. Then she's stepping back, putting some distance between us. Flint and Eden move to hug her as well, but she just gives them an awkward wave as she takes another step away.

It stops them dead in their tracks, has them looking back and forth between Macy and me. Only Hudson seems to know what to do, holding a casual fist up to her. For a second, an impish smile reminiscent of the old Macy flits across her black cherry–colored lips. But it's gone as quickly as it came.

Then she's reaching out and bumping her fist against his before saying, "So are we just going to stand around here waiting to get dragged into the daily tea ritual, or is there some kind of plan?"

"I'm pretty sure *you* are our plan," I answer.

"You know sneaking the head of one Court into another Court could be considered an act of war, right?" she asks.

"The witches should get so lucky," Hudson tells her with a roll of his eyes. "Grace declaring war on them would finally put them on the map."

Macy snorts—the closest thing to a laugh that I've heard from her in quite a while. "True. The Gargoyle Army could make quite a stand here."

"To be clear," I interject in my most queenlike tone, "the Gargoyle Army is *not* taking a stand here. And I am most definitely *not* declaring war on anyone."

Been there, done that, and if I can avoid it with the hunters, I don't ever plan to repeat it.

"Chill out, New Girl," Flint tells me with a grin. "No one thinks you're girding your loins for battle."

"Really?" Heather curls her lip. "*That*'s the description you want to go with?"

"I was just saying—"

"Not to interrupt a totally meaningless conversation," Jaxon talks over them. "But I don't know how much longer Mekhi is going to be able to sleep."

"We'll get to it," Macy assures him, sweeping her hair back from her face. "I've just got one question. Who are you here to see?"

"Not Linden and Imogen." I blurt out the king's and queen's names, because the more I thought about it, the more convinced I've become that there's no way they're going to be of any help. "How about Viola?"

Based on my previous experience here, Imogen's sister seems the most likely witch in the place to actually be helpful. But that's if we can find her without attracting too much attention—or raising too many alarms.

I say as much to Macy, who shoots me a grin that's way more wicked than I'm used to from her.

"I think that can be arranged." She waves a hand, and a giant, spinning portal appears right in front of her. "Last one in has to eat an entire jar of eye of newt."

The last thing I hear as I step through the portal is Heather asking, "Eye of newt? Is that actually a thing?"

I start to tell her that Macy is just joking, but before I can get out more than a "don't worry," the portal has me.

31

Unlike the portals that come from the seeds we've been using, this one doesn't hurt. It just feels like Macy's portals always do—like I'm being stretched and compressed at the same time.

A few seconds of discomfort, even fewer seconds of feeling like I'm going to implode, and we're done.

The moment I feel normal again, I open my eyes. The first thing I see is an ornately carved archway in shades of gold and cream, followed by wallpaper in the same colors.

So, yep. Macy definitely got us into the Witch Court. And she got us to Viola, I realize as I find myself staring directly into the witch's startled eyes.

The only problem? Viola just happens to be sitting in a drawing room filled with a whole lot of other witches.

So much for not making an entrance.

I contemplate turning around and diving back through the portal before any fresh hell can spring from this, but before I can so much as move, two very different things happen.

Heather comes tumbling through the portal and lands at my feet. And several of the witches jump up, spells flying.

I manage to grab Heather before she's hit by one, but I'm not so lucky with Flint, who gets stunned as soon as he steps out of the portal and ends up falling flat on his face.

Followed immediately by Eden getting hit by what I'm pretty sure must be a jellification spell, as she turns into a gummy blob right in front of me.

"Wait! Please!" I hold up both hands even as I race to put myself in front of the portal entrance, shifting into my gargoyle form in an instant. The last thing we need right now is for Mekhi to get hit by some random spell that sends his body completely over the edge.

"We're not here to hurt you! I just need to talk to Viola for a few minutes," I yell.

But they're obviously not impressed, as more spells fly my way.

I manage to dodge a couple of them, but then I end up getting hit by three at once. None of them work on me, thankfully, but they do still hurt like hell when they hit.

On the plus side, Jaxon and Mekhi pass through the portal just as the spells hit me, giving Jaxon a couple of seconds' reprieve before more come bouncing his way. I throw myself in front of one of them even as Eden rolls over in full gelatinous form to try to protect them as well.

As she does, she gets hit with another spell—one that turns her from a blob into a long, skinny snake. Of course, it doesn't get rid of the first spell, so now she looks an awful lot like a giant purple gummy snake lying there.

Flint has managed to roll himself over. But he's given up on trying to sit and is instead inching his way along the floor like an upside-down earthworm. In the meantime, Hudson steps through the portal right after Jaxon.

There's no way I can leave my spot protecting Mekhi to get to him, but before I can shout a warning, Flint yells, "Heads up!"

Hudson looks straight up, like he's expecting a ball to come shooting down at him from somewhere, and ends up getting hit with a balding spell. Seconds later, all of his perfectly coiffed hair falls out, leaving his head as bald and shiny as a mirror.

On the plus side, he looks surprisingly good bald, though the look on his face says he doesn't agree.

"What?" he asks archly.

"Never heard the phrase *heads up*?" I ask as I continue dodging spells.

Several more are speeding toward Jaxon, Mekhi, and me. I manage to take several—and can I just say, *ow*—but at least I block them from hitting Mekhi. I can't stop Jaxon from getting hit, though, and he ends up shrinking to the size of a mouse between one blink and the next.

I dive for Mekhi, throwing myself over him as he hits the ground. At the same time, Macy saunters through the portal like she's got all the time in the world.

Her eyes widen as she sees what's going on and shouts, "Stop!" while jumping out in front of all of us with her arms raised.

Apparently, it works much better when a witch does it than when a gargoyle does, because the spells stop flying immediately. Thank God.

I crawl off Mekhi, and with Hudson's help, I roll him over on his back to make sure he's okay. And find a tiny, tiny Jaxon buried underneath him.

"Looks like someone finally got cut down to size," Hudson drawls as he scoops his brother up.

Jaxon responds by punching one tiny fist straight at his nose. It doesn't make much of an impact, though.

"Don't you dare torture him," I scold Hudson, even as I turn around to face the witches.

"I'm sorry!" I say, moving to stand next to Macy. "We should have warned you we were coming."

"That would be the normal thing to do," Viola tells me tartly. "Then again, when have you ever done what's expected?"

I feel like I should be insulted, but the truth is, she's probably right. "We just wanted a few minutes of your time without..." I trail off, not sure how to say what I'm thinking without insulting her family.

"Without all the ceremony?" she asks, brows raised.

"Something like that," I answer.

"Fair enough." She waves a hand, mutters a few words, and all the spells are lifted.

Flint and Eden spring to their feet, Hudson's hair grows back in ten seconds flat, and Jaxon just grows and grows and grows—which looks pretty hilarious, considering Hudson is still holding him in his hand when he first starts to change back.

He drops him, of course, and then everyone is back to normal. Except Heather, who is currently standing in the corner of the room, laughing her ass off at the rest of us. Apparently, my best friend has quite the mean streak.

"Well, you're here now," Viola says after everyone is back to their regular selves. "What do you want to talk about?"

32

I Spy with My Little Lorelei

I take a deep breath. Do I really want to discuss this in front of a bunch of witches I don't know? But this seems like a now-or-never kind of moment, so I exhale slowly, then say, "We have a problem."

Viola's gaze falls on Jaxon, who is currently crouching over Mekhi to check on him. "I can see that."

"We have to take him to the Shadow Realm, which means we need help opening the portal in the piazza."

Her expression goes from vaguely interested to completely blank. "I have no idea what you're talking about."

I want to call her bluff—no one goes that blank that fast without a reason. But considering Viola is our biggest ally in the Witch Court, antagonizing her seems like a really bad idea.

"And why would you want to take him there?" Viola asks.

"He's suffering from shadow poison, and we believe its effects will be slower in that realm." I take a deep breath and decide to trust her with the entire plan, hoping beyond hope that I read her right and she's the kind of witch who would help us. "We're going to find a cure for the Shadow Queen's twin daughters, a way to separate their souls, and trade it for a cure for our friend."

Her eyes go wide as the other witches gasp. "There is no way to separate two bound souls, Grace," she says gravely. "And offering such to the queen and not following through would mean a certain and painful death."

I shake my head. "We have a way to do it. We just need to find the Curator to locate something for us. But that's only after we first go to the Shadow Realm, slow the poison killing Mekhi, and make a bargain with the queen she can't renege on. Will you help us?"

I bite my lip, afraid I've overshared and put the whole plan in jeopardy. But Viola holds my gaze and then gives me a short, curt nod. "You are a woman after my own heart, Grace. No secrets. No subterfuge. Just candor." She turns to the witches alongside her. "It's so refreshing to see at Court, is it not, ladies?"

A tall, elegant witch with long brown curls whispers to another older and rounder witch with bright red hair. Their murmuring draws the attention of Viola, who asks, "Should we reward such behavior, witches?"

My heart is pounding in my chest as I realize this is it. They'll either help, or they won't and Mekhi will die. Jaxon must figure this out as well, as I see him start to step forward, but I give him a sharp look, and for once, he gets it and remains still.

The three witches seem to come to a decision without consulting the rest of the witches in the room, so I guess this trio is in charge here. Viola turns back to me and says, "Honesty is always the best policy, my dear. Therefore, we will grant your request and offer a spell that will activate the portal to the Shadow Realm. However, this doorway only works in one direction. You will need to find your own way home."

My shoulders sag with relief. "We have an idea how to get home. Thank you, ladies. Thank you so much."

"Lubella here will teach Macy the spell while you and I share a private word, yes, dear?"

It's a statement, not a question, and I nod, wondering what she has to say to me that she doesn't want said in front of the others. I reach out and give Hudson's hand a squeeze, mouthing *I'll be back* before following the regal witch through a door in the corner.

Once we're both safely on the other side of the door, in a small room with two couches and an ornate coffee table dominating most of the space that must be used for intimate gatherings, Viola turns to me.

Her eyes narrow. "Is there another reason you've come to my Court, dear?"

Of all the things I was imagining she wanted to discuss, a secret motive was not one of them. "I mean, I hoped I'd see my cousin while I was visiting, too," I say.

One brow arches. "And no one else?"

"I definitely didn't come to see the king and queen, if that's what you're asking," I say on a half laugh.

"Hmmm," is her only response. Eventually, she adds, "Well, then perhaps this occasion is fortuitous for us all, for today you seek to save not only the life of your friend but also the life of someone I've helped protect for longer than I care to remember."

"But the only other people we might help are the twins—" I gasp as understanding dawns. "One of them is here, isn't she?"

"She is," she agrees. "But I still haven't decided if it's wise to let you meet her and possibly get her hopes up."

"We won't hurt her," I assure the witch, my mind racing at the possibility of talking to her. "But I would love a moment with her to discuss strategy—what she knows of her mother, her eagerness for a bargain, her sister."

"Is that all?" Viola asks, and I'm not sure what she's referring to, so I remain silent. Wherever this conversation is going, I need to let Viola take us there. There's a long period of silence before she says, "Lorelei doesn't know how to cure shadow poison."

"I never said I needed her to," I reply slowly, the wheels in my brain turning. Where have I heard that name before? Then I shrug and add, "Although that would have been nice."

After another interminable pause, she says, "Yes, I think you should see exactly what—and who—is at risk if you fail." And with that, Viola moves back toward the door, tossing over her shoulder, "Well? Are you coming, or am I just supposed to wait until you're ready?"

"I—" My voice breaks, so I clear my throat and try again. "You're going to take us to her?"

"I'm going to ask Lorelei if she wants to talk to you. If she does, fine. If she doesn't..."

"We'll leave her alone," I tell her. "I promise."

She nods, then opens the door and walks back into the room with my friends. She motions for Hudson to join us but tells Macy to remain there and watch over "our visitors." Then we leave through another door and follow her down the hallway to a long, circular flight of stairs.

She ushers us up it, then up three more flights as well.

Hudson shoots me a look, so I mouth, *The Shadow Queen's daughter.* His brows shoot up, but he nods, taking the development in stride.

"We're almost there," Viola tells us as she guides us up what I'm pretty sure is the final flight of stairs. She doesn't seem worried at all, but by the time we get to the top of the stairs, my senses are ultra-heightened, and I'm balanced on the balls of my feet. Not because I actually think there's a problem but because everything about this situation sets my nerves on edge.

"It's going to be okay," Hudson murmurs as he presses a gentle hand against the small of my back.

At the top of the stairs is a narrow iron door. Viola waves a hand in front of it, her fingers moving in a pattern that reminds me of the safeguards at the Bloodletter's cave, invisible magic put in place to keep unwanted visitors from wandering into her lair uninvited.

As I watch Viola weave the spell to undo the safeguards here, my heart beats faster and faster. There's an oppressive heaviness in the air around us now. I try to ignore it, but it weighs on me, makes me feel like maybe this isn't the best idea after all.

Makes me worry that I'm leading Hudson into some kind of trap.

I shift uneasily at the thought, wipe a surreptitious palm down the side of my jeans to dry it off. What if this is a mistake? What if—

"It's okay." Hudson rubs slow circles on my back as he murmurs softly in my ear, "It's just the safeguards."

The oppressive feeling gets worse, has my chest aching and my heart racing all over again. "I don't—I can't—"

"Almost there," Viola murmurs. Her hands are moving faster now, the near-silent spell spilling from her lips at an astonishing rate.

As the heaviness gets so bad I can barely breathe, I lean into Hudson, who has managed to stay calm through all of this. But the moment my back touches his chest, I realize that he's not as calm as he looks. He's shaking slightly, and now that I realize it, I can feel it in the hand he still has pressed against me and the fingers that continue stroking soothing circles over my back.

"It's the safeguards," he murmurs again, moving closer until his chest is pressed against me. "They're meant to make us feel like this." He slides his hands around my waist, and at this point, I can't tell whether it's to lend comfort or to keep me from bolting.

And to be honest, I don't really care. I sink into him, let the rich, spicy scent of him wrap around me like a blanket. And hold on to his words like the lifeline I know they're meant to be.

This is not a panic attack, I tell myself as the feeling of doom grows more oppressive with every second that passes. It's just part of the safeguards. They're meant to make whoever tries to breach them feel like this, meant to make us want to turn around and run away as fast as we can.

Just the safeguards, I tell myself. Everything's okay. Not a panic attack.

Even as I realize safeguard magic wouldn't work on a gargoyle like me.

I take a deep breath, try to let it out slowly.

Still, the pressure gets worse and worse.

It's a buzzing in my ears now.

A heavy weight pressing down on my head and shoulders so hard that it feels like it's crushing me.

A lack of oxygen in the air around me, making me gasp like a fish washed up on the beach.

Just when I don't think I can take it anymore, just when it feels like there's no more oxygen left in my body—the heaviness lifts.

"Done," Viola murmurs with satisfaction. "That was the last one."

She doesn't need to say it. I can feel it—and so can Hudson. The pressure is gone, just like that, and so is the strange buzzing that felt like it was coming from deep inside me.

I take my first real breath in several minutes, reaching down to squeeze Hudson's hand in a silent thank-you for helping me through whatever that was.

In response, he bends down and rests his chin on my shoulder. His warm breath brushes against the curls near my cheek, and for a second, everything feels right in my world. It feels like we're back home in San Diego, going to class, meeting with the architect for the Gargoyle Court, living the lives we're both so grateful to have.

There's no dangerous quest looming in front of us, no Vampire Court secrets hanging between us, no Circle edicts bent on making our lives as miserable as possible. There's just Hudson and me and the never-ending feelings that stretch between us.

Viola leads us through a small antechamber to one more door. "I'm going to go in and let her know you're here," she says, waving a hand over the door so that the lock disengages from the inside.

I give her the best smile I can muster. "Thank you."

"Of course. Though I can't guarantee she'll want to meet with you. She hasn't been feeling very well the last few days."

"We understand."

As she slips inside the room, I exchange a worried look with Hudson. He wraps a reassuring arm around my shoulders and pulls me in for a hug. "It'll be fine," he whispers against my temple.

"I know," I say, even though I don't.

I can't shake the fact that the Crone is gathering an army while I'm heading into the Shadow Realm, yet Mekhi is getting sicker every second we waste. And that's before I let myself think of the midterms I'm going to miss if we don't wrap everything up quickly and hightail it back to school.

But if Lorelei has any suggestions for how to deal with her mother, it would behoove us to take a moment and listen. Too many times, I've rushed into situations without gathering all the facts. For once, I know the right thing to do is to take a breath and gather information—before we head into what is still most likely going to be the death of us all.

Mirroring my thoughts, I take one, two, three deep breaths, trying to calm my racing heart.

"Hey, if you want—" Hudson breaks off as the door swings open.

Viola stands there, looking a little grim. I brace myself for the worst, but all she says is, "Lorelei is happy to see you both."

I nod and exchange another glance with Hudson, who just smiles encouragingly at me. Okay, then. Guess we're doing this.

"Thank you," I murmur quietly to Viola as she moves aside to let us in.

And am completely unprepared for what I see.

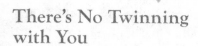

33

There's No Twinning
with You

As we enter, I can't help but notice that neither the suite of rooms nor Lorelei is anything like what I expected. Then again, maybe it's because Lorelei is nothing like I expected that the apartment looks the way it does.

To begin with, posters cover every available inch of wall space. BTS and Shawn Mendes and Quincy Fouse war for space with signs touting funny sayings and a slew of travel posters. The main room contains a huge, comfy-looking sectional that could easily seat ten people facing a fireplace big enough to walk in. Off to the right, I can just make out a stately four-poster bed with furry turquoise pillows. To the left is an oversize granite kitchen with clusters of tiny, globed lights hanging over the island. There's a closed door between the main seating area and the kitchen, and I find myself wondering if she has a hallway leading to more bedrooms. Overall, the entire apartment looks set up for entertaining—like a giant dorm room—although I can't imagine any guests relishing passing through those wards, should they want to visit.

Lorelei herself is sitting in the center of her sectional, cross-legged. She's dressed in a BTS T-shirt and a pair of zebra-print pajama bottoms, and her long black hair is twisted up into a bun on the top of her head. She looks around seventeen, comfortable and happy, and not at all like she's spent what must have felt like an eternity being tortured by her evil twin.

At least not until I get closer and see the dark circles under her eyes. The frailness of her arms. And the way she holds herself, like she's trying to sit very still, so as not to move and cause herself any pain.

It makes me feel awful for her—plus furious all over again at the

Shadow Queen. How could she let one of her daughters treat her other daughter like this? I know she probably physically separated them to keep Lorelei from getting hurt any more than she already had been, but she obviously did it too late. Even after all this time at the Witch Court, Lorelei looks like a stiff wind could blow her over.

And suddenly, I realize exactly where I've heard the name Lorelei before. I actually can't believe I didn't realize it the second I walked in the door. The family resemblance is striking.

Lorelei is the Shadow Queen's daughter. But she's also Mayor Souil's.

Unbidden, images of everything the mayor did—everything he risked and everyone he hurt—to save his daughter from pain come to mind. I know Hudson and I did the right thing when we were in Adarie. The right of one girl to live pain-free wasn't more important than the lives of every other person in that town.

But the good of the many versus the good of the individual is an easy distinction to make—when you're friends with the many. When you come face-to-face with the individual's suffering, though, it's a lot harder to be nonchalant. Even more, it's harder not to feel partly to blame.

So I approach her slowly, trying to think through my words, what I want to say, to ask. But what do you say to someone who has suffered so much? And whose bond with her twin you want to blow apart?

Turns out I don't have to say anything, because the moment we get close to the couch, she starts doing the talking. "I can't believe it's really you!" she says, reaching both hands toward Hudson and me.

When I just stare at her, dumbfounded, trying to figure out what she means by that, she smiles. "You two are the best!"

"Oh, well, I wouldn't say that exactly—"

"I would," Hudson interrupts as he moves to shake her extended hand, a charming grin on his face. "But please, feel free to tell us more."

I know he's playing up the vanity for Lorelei's benefit, but come on. I roll my eyes behind his back, which makes Lorelei chuckle.

"You're funnier than I thought you'd be."

"Thank you," Hudson answers.

I'm beginning to suspect she's confused and actually has no idea who we are. I mean, why would she even be thinking about us at all?

I start to introduce myself to her, just to avoid any awkwardness when she figures out we're different people than she was expecting, but before I can say anything, she makes a face at Hudson and says, "I was talking to Grace."

"Oh, well, I am very sorry, then." Hudson lays on the proper British accent extra thick for her. "I didn't mean to steal the spotlight from my mate."

It's Lorelei's turn to roll her eyes. "I always knew you'd be funny. It's Grace who surprises me."

"Oh, well...ouch?" I say.

She laughs again. "You know what I mean."

I don't, but I'm not about to say that to her, so I just smile a little cluelessly.

"Sit down, sit down." She gestures to the other end of the sectional, and we take a seat. "Tell me what you're doing here. When Viola said you wanted to see me, I couldn't believe it. I mean, what could *the* Grace and Hudson possibly want with me?"

The Grace and Hudson? She makes us sound like celebrities or something.

"Actually, we came because we're in the middle of a problem and realize we could use your help before we go any further," I tell her.

"My help?" Now she looks as confused as I feel. "With what?"

Hudson's leg brushes against mine in a supportive you've-got-this move, and I let the warmth of his touch flow through me. Then I just go for it.

"Our friend Mekhi was infected with the Shadow Queen's poison," I start, then lay the entire situation out for her. By the end, though, I realize we shouldn't be here asking for her help as much as her permission. We're about to separate her soul from her sister's. Surely she should get a say in that. So I plunge forward with, "I understand we're asking a lot. She's your sister, and you probably have a lot of complicated feelings around that. But the only thing of worth we have to trade your mom for a cure is finding a way to separate the two of you, as that's what she's wanted for a millennium. But obviously, if you don't want it, then there's no way we could ever—"

"Oh, I want it!" Lorelei eagerly leans so far forward, she's almost in our laps. "I want it more than anything."

"Really?" I exchange a relieved look with Hudson. "Are you sure? Because the last thing I want is to pressure you—"

"I didn't want to interrupt your story while you were telling it, but I don't think you have the real picture," she explains. "If you did, you wouldn't worry you were pressuring me at all."

"Oh, umm—" I look between her and Viola. "We'd love to hear the full story, if you wanted to share it."

"I'm more than okay telling you anything you want to know, Grace." Her smile is so big now, it crinkles the dark corners of her eyes. "First off, my mom is not evil. You need to know that. At least I don't think she is. I haven't seen her since I was five. But I believe she loves me."

I shoot Hudson a quick glance. Evil or not, it's clear we need to tread carefully here—we *are* talking about her mother, after all.

Hudson returns her winning smile. "It's wonderful to hear she loves you so much. I'm sorry that your sister has treated you so poorly, then, and your mother was unable to prevent it."

"Well, it's not my mom's fault she couldn't help me, is it?" she asks. "She's trapped in the Shadow Realm."

It's clear this is getting us nowhere, so I try again. "Why don't you tell us why you're hiding in the Witch Court, with protective wards on the doors, if you're not afraid of your mother and sister?"

She nods. "Well, you were right that my sister, Liana, and I share an unbreakable soul bond. However, you're wrong that she is still hurting me to gain power. At least not now. When we were younger, she was kind of a mean little brat to me, I'll give you that. But I wasn't so innocent, either." She sighs. "And our mother saw that we could very easily hurt each other, especially when we were mad, which is why she did something terrible to try to undo my father's magic. I don't know what it was, no one would tell me, but it was so bad that a god banished her to a prison realm with my sister. I was with our father then, and we were practicing time magic—I was awfully adept as a child, if I do say so myself—when the prison walls came down."

Tears well in her eyes, but she quickly blinks them away. "Liana and I were trapped on opposite sides of this wall. But she had recently won our power struggle—so a piece of my soul is trapped with her in that prison." She gestures toward the door. "My body was left weak, but worse, my soul yearns for the other piece of itself. And so, if Viola does not keep me locked inside, for my own good, I feel compelled to try to cross to the Shadow Realm to reconnect with the rest of my soul."

My eyes widen, and I reach for Hudson's warmth. "You've been imprisoned here? All this time?"

She raises a hand. "For my own good! I cannot cross realms—part of my soul is also trapped here. But still, I try…"

Her voice trails off, and my eyes search out Viola, who adds, "When she tries to activate the gateway to the Shadow Realm, she receives a massive shock. And in her weakened condition, if we don't keep her locked up, it could kill her."

I gasp. "Then why live so close to the fountain at all?"

Lorelei shrugs. "Any farther away and the agony to reach the Shadow Realm is too much to bear." She idly draws circles on the sofa cushion with her finger as we absorb everything she's saying. "At least in the Witch Court, it's more of a dull ache, manageable as long as I stay in here."

I swallow the bile rising in my throat. My God, the Shadow Queen's actions have caused *two* daughters to spend their lives imprisoned. I still hate that bitch—no matter what Lorelei says, I know she's evil as fuck—yet I can't help but feel sad for her, too.

I lean forward and squeeze Lorelei's hand. Her gaze rises to meet mine as I say, "Lorelei, we will find a way to separate your souls. Not just to save our friend but because you are suffering as well."

Lorelei's features soften into another wide smile. "Of course you will. Macy has told me so many stories of your adventures—I know you and Hudson can do anything you set your minds to."

Ahhh, so that's how she knew about us. I love the idea that Macy has befriended this girl, even if she did tell her some obviously tall tales about me.

"Well," I start, "we will do our—"

Hudson's and my phones both start dinging multiple times in a row, and we pull them out of our pockets at the same time. But as I read the texts from Macy, my stomach sinks.

"It's Mekhi," I whisper on a ragged breath. "The sleeping draught is no longer working."

34

You're So Kind-Blooded

"What does that mean?" Lorelei asks. "Is your friend going to be okay?"

I shake my head, typing as quickly as I can to ask for more details. "The sleeping draught was the only thing keeping the poison from causing immeasurable pain—before killing him."

"Let me see him," she says, and the request is so unexpected that I stop typing to stare at her. "Bring him to me, and I will try to help."

Fear for Mekhi has me blurting out, "How?" before I can think better of it. I don't mean for the question to be rude, and from her expression she didn't take it that way, but still...how could this girl, weak with half a soul, possibly help our friend?

"Because I am half my mother's daughter, of course," she says, like that explains everything. And maybe it does, because Hudson reaches over to pat her hand.

"Thank you so much, Lorelei, but we can't ask you to weaken yourself in any way to help our friend." His smile is soft and sweet. "You are incredibly brave, but we will find another way."

The poor girl blushes a fierce red, but she tilts her chin and says, "He should feed from me. My blood will most likely offer some immunity for him, since it's shadow poison affecting him. It won't last, but it will give you time to win my mother's help. I only wish I could go with you and convince her to help regardless. I haven't seen her in so very long, but I've heard that she has grown cold over the years, filled with rage at what she's done, so I am not surprised you feel you need to bargain with her to help your friend. But just know, she is not an evil woman. Promise me you will not hurt her in your quest, and I will keep your friend alive as long as I can."

I echo Hudson's words. "You are very brave, Lorelei, but I have to agree with Hudson. We cannot ask you to risk your health for his."

But she shakes her head. "Come on, Grace. We can donate a little blood without any risk of injury." Her gaze flashes to Hudson's, then back to mine. "Do you not share blood with your mate?"

O-kay. Now we're getting into some seriously personal territory, although I doubt she knows how...interesting...feeding can be between mates. Still, I cough awkwardly—while Hudson chuckles under his breath—and say, "If you're sure that it would be no more than a very small amount and would in no way jeopardize your own health, then yes, anything you could do to ease our friend's suffering...I would be forever grateful."

"And you promise not to hurt my mother?" She raises a brow, then rushes to add, "Or my sister?"

I sigh. I really was looking forward to curing Mekhi, saving the twins, and kicking the Shadow Queen's ass. In that order. "Fine. I promise."

Lorelei claps her hands together. "I get to meet two vampires in *one* day! This is so much fun!"

35

Baby's Got
Sad Blood

"Fun" isn't exactly how I'd describe seeing Mekhi in pain again. The sleeping draught has obviously worn off, and he is suffering because of it.

"We didn't want to give him the other draught," Jaxon tells me when I grab another blanket from the closet and pull it over a shivering Mekhi. It turns out that closed door in Lorelei's apartment did indeed lead to a hallway with several guest bedrooms. Fortunately, the others didn't have to fight through the safeguards as they carried Mekhi up the flights of stairs. "We thought we might need it to get him to the Shadow Realm."

To her credit, Lorelei wastes no time after she lays eyes on Mekhi. "Put me down," she tells Hudson, who very carefully deposits her on a chair beside Mekhi's bed.

Viola had to leave to attend to business, but she sent up another witch whom she said is trained in healing and assured us she would not leave Lorelei's side. As the tall, waiflike woman flutters around Lorelei, taking her pulse and then Mekhi's, the tension in my shoulders slowly starts to ease.

"My name is Grace," I introduce myself when the witch is finished taking their vitals.

"Caroleena," she replies and shakes my hand. She's got a thick Irish accent that immediately makes me feel a little homesick for my own Court. "I will look after them both. You need not worry." She nods to Mekhi, whose eyes flutter open but remain unfocused. "How long has he been like this?" she asks.

"Five months or so," Hudson answers.

"Five months? Really?" She looks astonished. "How has he survived?"

Hudson explains Descent to her, as well as the elixir the Bloodletter has been feeding Mekhi for months, and she seems fascinated by the very idea of it.

"Well, it obviously worked," Lorelei says as she scooches her chair closer to the side of the bed and lays a hand on Mekhi's sweaty forehead.

"I don't know if that's true," Jaxon tells her. "He's in really fucked-up shape."

"He is. But he's alive, and that has to be because of what you did. No one lasts five months with shadow poison in their veins. Not even a vampire."

Since she seems to know more about shadow poison than I thought, I can't resist asking, "How long do you think we have?" I'm trying to figure out how fast we can accomplish everything we need to do to save him. The problem is, I don't know exactly what we have to do yet. I don't know how to find the Curator, and I sure as hell don't have a clue what it's going to take to find the Bittersweet Tree, either, nor capture celestial magic."

"I'm not sure," she answers. "I might be able to find out."

Lorelei reaches down and places her hand on the center of Mekhi's chest. At first, nothing happens, but after several seconds, his labored breathing becomes a little easier. Not normal by any means, but at least he's not actively gasping for air right now.

"I won't hurt him," she says, and in that moment, her voice is as solemn as an oath.

Carefully, Caroleena picks up Lorelei's wrist and asks, "Are you ready, lass?"

Lorelei gives a sharp nod, and the witch slashes her sharp nail downward, slicing through the soft skin of her wrist with magical precision. Then she holds Lorelei's arm just above Mekhi's mouth until a few droplets of blood fall to his lips.

At first, Mekhi doesn't react, and my stomach starts to twist and turn with fear that this isn't going to work. But then he strikes, fast like a cobra, faster than I thought he could even move in his condition, one hand grabbing her wrist as his canines explode through his gums and sink into her arm.

Almost instantly, his gaze comes into focus as he feeds, his moans of pain shifting to moans of solace.

The witch only lets him feed for a minute or two before she taps his shoulder with her wand, and he falls back into a deep and restful slumber. Then she applies a salve to Lorelei's wounds and covers them with a bandage.

When she's taken care of Lorelei, she turns to the rest of us and says, "Your friend is not in pain now. He will sleep for some time, and I will let Lorelei feed him a small amount again. They'll both be fine, although this is not a permanent solution. Her blood will eventually not be enough to counteract the poison in his veins."

Her words are as much an omen as they are a respite, and everyone knows it.

"I don't like this," Jaxon grouses as he paces at the foot of Mekhi's bed.

"Me either," Flint agrees from his spot on the other side of the bed, and while he's not pacing, he's not exactly relaxing, either. More like just standing there curling and uncurling fingers that have suddenly become talons. "But you need to calm down, Jax."

Jaxon starts to say something back to him, but in the end, he must think better of it because his teeth snap shut with an audible click. But the look he gives the dragon has uneasiness crawling up my spine. Because it's not just stress and worry I see there. It's a deep-seated anger that has me wondering just how many factors provoked Jaxon into offering to take the throne in Hudson's stead.

I suddenly feel uncomfortable observing this moment between them and glance over to Heather...who looks back at me like someone's kicked her puppy. Or worse, her.

Since we got here, she's been unusually reserved, besides her amusement at everyone getting spelled. But I just chalked it up to the fact that there's so little she can do to help as a human, and Mekhi appears so sick.

But as I watch Eden walk over to Macy, who's currently facing the wall with her arms wrapped tightly around herself, I can see why Heather seems so lost. She and Eden have pretty much been inseparable from the moment they met. Which, okay, was yesterday, but still.

I start to tell her not to worry, that Eden and Macy are just friends. But there's something about the way Eden puts her arms around Macy—and about the way Macy lets her—that has me wondering what's up between the two of them. Even before Macy bows her head with a sigh and rests her forehead against Eden's shoulder.

"Heather—" I put a hand on her arm, but she shrugs me off with a smile so bright, I'm pretty sure I can see my reflection in it.

"It's fine," she tells me, though it patently isn't. "We've got way more important things to worry about anyway."

We both turn to look at Mekhi. There's a little more color in his cheeks, a little less gauntness, but as I glance at Lorelei and see the devastated look on her face, my stomach bottoms out and I feel slightly dizzy. I reach out with one hand to use the wall to steady myself, but Hudson fades to my side in a blink and pulls me close.

"I thought my blood would do more," Lorelei says softly, and it's like we all hear the ding of a nail being hammered into Mekhi's coffin, the sound echoing through the quiet room with deadly precision.

Jaxon explodes with a litany of curses while Hudson asks Lorelei, "Should we take him to the Shadow Realm instead?"

"No, my blood did stave off his death more than I believe the Shadow Realm would. You would be wise to leave him here," she assures us. "But I had hoped it would buy you a month, maybe even two."

"How much time *do* we have?" I ask, the words raw and painful in my throat.

"Two weeks at most," she says, then bites her lip. "Maybe less."

I knew he was gravely ill. We all did. Probably even knew deep down we had very little time left as well. But to hear it stated so bluntly—it's like someone lobbed a ticking bomb in our direction.

And I'm afraid none of us will survive if it explodes.

36

Fountain of Poof

Once the gates of the Witch Court are closed behind us, we all kind of stand around looking at one another. Macy said she'd meet us here in a few minutes. Presumably she's off to grab more magic portal beans or something. At least, I hope that's what she's doing.

The statue is in the center of the piazza, but none of us takes a step toward it. Not yet.

It was painful leaving Mekhi behind, but Lorelei assured us she and Caroleena would look over him until we could return with an antidote. Which means we need to get to the Shadow Realm *now*.

And still, we don't move.

It's almost like the weight of potential failure has us unable to lift our feet. I mean, even if the Shadow Queen makes a deal with us, we still don't even know where the Curator is or who does—

My phone vibrates, and I glance down to find messages from an old friend.

REMY: Hey *cher*

REMY: You can find what you're looking for in Alexandria, Egypt

REMY: Sorry I can't be with you now, but you won't need me for a while. As soon as I can figure out how to break out of this place, I'll meet up with you. Hopefully it'll be in time

GRACE: We need to go to Alexandria?????

REMY: To the satellite location of the Ancient Library. I'll drop a pin

GRACE: I don't know if it's good or bad that you can tell the future

REMY: Welcome to my life

GRACE: How's Izzy?

REMY: Ghosting my ass

GRACE: Sounds about right

GRACE: Thank you so much

REMY: You got this

I shove my phone back in my pocket and turn to the gang. "That was Remy," I explain. "He dropped a pin on the Curator for us."

"Damn, that guy is freaky." Flint whistles.

I shrug. "Let's do this, eh?"

"Come on, New Girl." Flint grins. "You can say that with more enthusiasm. We're just about to hop in a portal to who knows where in a prison realm to make a deal with an evil queen who loves to sic poison bugs on you. We eat no-win situations like this for breakfast."

We all chuckle, as I'm sure he intended, and feel our bodies shrugging off our earlier hopeless inertia. As one, we head across the piazza to the center.

A minute later, Macy comes jogging over, skidding to a stop at the edge of the statue.

"I'm ready," Macy confirms, staring at the sky above the horizon, where the soon-to-be-setting sun is casting a golden haze over everything, even the scary-looking statue at the center of the piazza. Then she reaches out and begins performing a series of intricate moves with both hands. "Let's just hope this works."

I swallow—there are no beans in sight. "It better."

She does another set of complicated moves, and the water surrounding the statue begins to shimmer and vibrate.

"Where in the Shadow Realm do we want to go?" Macy tosses over her shoulder.

Hudson begins, "Ada—"

But I cut him off. "Our friends' farm." He turns and holds my gaze. "We have time," I assure him, and we do. The farm is not that far from Adarie. "Oh, but don't get us too close at first—we don't want to scare them," I add, though really I'm thinking of Hudson. He'll need some time to prepare himself for whatever we find at the farm...or, worse, *don't* find.

Macy nods, then reaches out a hand to hold one of mine. "Focus on the farm," she says. "Picture it clearly in your head. I'll drop us a bit away."

I remember the farmhouse where Hudson and I awkwardly shared a bedroom. Tiola, Maroly, and Arnst. The rows of purple vegetables. The lake...

The ring of water surrounding the statue turns a violent shade of purple and swirling black, the colors seeming to sink deeper and deeper into the ground.

My eyes widen. I kept waiting on a portal to appear in front of us, upright, like how Macy's portals usually stand. But as I watch the water swirl faster and faster, it's pretty obvious I had it all wrong. Macy isn't making a portal appear—she's just *turning one on.*

"The fountain *is* a portal!" Eden shouts, pointing to the stone circle surrounding the water and statue. "It's been here the whole time."

"Okay," Macy says, letting go of my arm to gesture to the fountain/portal. "Jump in."

She sounds like it's the best idea in the world, but I'm not so sure jumping into a demonic-looking fountain in a piazza known to house the gateway to hell is really the best life choice any of us could be making right now. But when I glance at my friends, expecting them all to have as much trepidation as I do, I realize that they're all grinning. Even Hudson looks excited to jump into a portal to God knows where, which makes me ask myself if it's them or if it's me.

I decide it's definitely them, even before Flint rubs his hands together and walks forward, saying, "Oh, I'm definitely jumping in first!"

But Jaxon shouts, "You wish," then fades over the edge of the swirling pond area—and is immediately sucked down into the swirling vortex.

"Damn you, Jaxon," Flint grumbles with a laugh and then jumps over the edge, feet first, with Eden racing right behind him.

Hudson turns to Macy and me, his eyebrows raised as if he's asking if we want him to wait, but I nod for him to go ahead. And then I turn to Heather.

"You've got your plane ticket, right?" I ask. "I sent you the email with the information on it last night, and a car should be coming to take you to the airport in the next few minutes."

"I've got it, but I don't want to go, Grace."

"I know you don't. But we've gone over this. You can't come with us—it's too dangerous."

"I'm okay with it being dangerous, and shouldn't that be my decision anyway?"

"On normal things, yes. There's nothing normal about this, Heather. I don't know what's going to be waiting for us on the other side of this portal. I have no idea if the Shadow Queen is going to accept the deal or try to kill us. I have no idea if we'll even find a way back from the Shadow Realm. What if we get stuck there forever?"

"Then we'll figure it out. We've been figuring things out together since we were kids. I've come this far. Let me see it through."

I want to say yes. Of course I want to say yes. But doing so is completely irresponsible. So instead, I say the only thing I can think of that might get through to her. "What about your parents?"

She jolts a little, like they haven't even occurred to her. "What about them?"

"I lost my parents, and there isn't a day that goes by that I don't wish I could talk to them, hug them, be with them. And I know what happened to them. I know that they're dead. Imagine what it would be like for your parents if you just disappeared off the face of the earth? If they had no idea where you'd gone or what had happened to you or even if you were alive or dead? You can't tell me you'd wish that kind of torture on them."

"Grace." Heather reaches over and hugs me as tight as she can. I hug her right back, because what I say for her I also say for me. If we don't make it back, this may be the last time I ever see my best friend. "I've tried to take care of you for as long as I've known you. Who's going to do that if I'm not there?"

"I'm going to take care of myself," I tell her. "And you are going to take care of yourself—back at school. And, hopefully, take really good notes that keep me from flunking out when I finally make it back. Okay?"

Heather nods against my shoulder and then pulls away slowly. "You better not get dead over there, or I'm going to be really mad at you."

"Fair enough. Now, it's time for you to catch your ride."

She grins. "And time for you to catch your portal?"

"Something like that." I give her a little wave. "See you soon?"

"You better."

And then I turn and walk toward the fountain—and the portal—and can't help wondering if I'm wrong and I'll never see my best friend again.

37

It's Just Another
Paranormal Pileup

"**W**ell, this sure as shite isn't the dignified entrance into the Shadow Realm I was imagining," Jaxon says in a voice as dry as burned toast.

Eden snorts. "Hard to be dignified when you're at the bottom of a dragon pile."

"I think you mean dragon, witch, vampire, and gargoyle pile, don't you?" Flint's voice rumbles just below me as I try to get my bearings.

"Whatever the fuck it is, I'm done," Jaxon growls.

The next thing I know, everything under me is moving—and that's when I realize we really are in a dogpile of bodies. I just happen to be on the top of it, along with Macy, while Jaxon, apparently, is on the very bottom.

No wonder he sounds so annoyed.

I scramble off just in time, because people go sliding and flying in all directions. Seconds later, Jaxon stands up and brushes his hands off against his black jeans. "There. That's much better," he says, voice rife with satisfaction.

"For you, maybe," Eden grumbles as she, too, stands up. "My hip may never be the same. Do you weigh three thousand pounds or something?" She glares at Flint.

"I *am* a dragon, in case you forgot," he answers as he reaches down and pulls Macy to her feet.

Eden simply raises one finger in response.

"You okay?" Hudson asks, a few feet from the rest of us as he crosses to me.

"Of course he didn't end up in the paranormal pile," I mutter to myself.

"She's fine," Eden answers with a roll of her eyes. "She was on top."

"Was she now?" Hudson's gaze takes on a distinctly wicked gleam that has my cheeks heating and my breath catching in my recently reassembled lungs.

"Let's not go there," I hiss at him as I look around to see who else is watching.

And spot something, or some*one*, that makes my heart stop beating.

Holy shit. *Heather?* "What are you doing here?" I screech at her.

"I decided you couldn't do this without me," she answers in an angelic voice.

"This isn't what we talked about! You were supposed to go back to school. You were supposed to—"

She shakes her head. "I heard you, and you made some very good points. But at the end of the day, I have to follow my gut." Her gaze holds mine steadily. "I don't know why, Grace, but I have this feeling that if I didn't join you, you'd never come back."

I bite my lip. There's so much I want to say to her right now... She has no idea the danger she's put herself in. But how many times have I made a decision based on nothing more than my instincts, then later found out it saved my life? All. The. Time.

So do I have any right to be upset that she followed hers?

"I'm not sure I can protect you," I admit.

Only to have her fire back, "Well, I'm sure I can protect *you*, so that's fine."

"Glad to have you along," Hudson says and reaches for my hand, squeezing it. "Grace was human once, too, and she helped kick some trolls' asses."

"Well, if that's the bar"—Heather grins—"I think I've got you covered. I eat troll for breakfast."

"Actually, I hear certain parts of a troll can be quite—" Flint starts.

But Eden shoves a finger in each ear and starts singing loudly. "La-la-la-la-la-la."

Everyone laughs, and the tension eases out of me. Hudson is right.

Humans aren't helpless—they just help in different ways.

"This is it?" Heather asks as she spins in a circle. "It looks like a purple Mars."

I smile, because that's as good a description of this part of the Shadow Realm as any. Like everywhere else in this place, everything around us is purple—the sky, the land, the trees, even the rabbit hopping by a few feet away.

But here, in this part of Noromar, the land is jagged and rocky with what look like giant fault lines running in all directions. And in the distance are the massive, craggy mountains Hudson and I climbed on our way to Adarie.

It's strange to be back here, strange to be looking at this place through familiar eyes when everyone else is stunned by it.

Jaxon is standing at the edge of a crater, looking down into it like it's the most fascinating thing he's ever seen. "Are we sure Noromar is on Earth?" he says, echoing Heather's earlier question. "I thought craters like this only happened on the moon."

"They're everywhere here," Hudson tells him. "Not when you're in the towns but when you're out in the wilderness like this."

"This is the wilderness?" Eden asks doubtfully.

"Wilderness as in desert," he clarifies. "They do have some forests here, but they aren't as dense as what we're used to."

"Is everything really purple?" Macy stares at the peaks not too far in the distance. "Like, even those mountains?"

"Even those mountains," I confirm. "You can see they're a dark violet when we get close to them."

"You've been here before?" Jaxon asks. "I mean, to this exact place?"

"We have," Hudson answers. His eyes are already on the mountains, and I know if the rest of us weren't here, he'd already be there, looking for *her*.

"Let's go," I say, shifting into my gargoyle form so that I can fly. Because now that I have my breath and my wits back, I realize that giving Hudson time to adjust might have been a bad idea. It feels like making him wait is torture.

"Go where?" Eden asks as she picks up a fistful of purple dirt and watches, fascinated, as it runs through her fingers.

"Toward the mountains," I say, heading that way. "There's a farm there."

"A farm? Out here?" Flint asks incredulously. "What do they grow, nightmares?"

"All kinds of things, actually, like porocli and purrots and paiz."

"Purrots?" Jaxon repeats, then shakes his head. "Never mind. I don't want to know. Trust food in the Shadow Realm to be even stranger than in our world."

"I swear it tastes good," I tell him. "At least most of it does."

"Well, thank God for that," Flint says dramatically. "If I have to eat something called porocli, I really want it to taste good."

"Pouspous is Grace's favorite," Hudson interjects slyly from his spot several feet in front of us. Which has every single one of my friends turning around to stare at me with wide eyes.

I wait for the questions, but only Flint is actually brave enough to ask, "I'm sorry, did he just say pouspous?"

"It's a grain-slash-vegetable thing," I tell him.

"Yeah, well, it sounds like an obscene grain-slash-vegetable thing," Heather tells me.

"It sounds like it, but it's not."

Flint snorts. "I guess we'll see about that."

Then Flint and Eden shift—Eden lowering a leg, which Macy shows Heather how to use to climb up before she hops on Flint's back. Jaxon chooses to fade with Hudson, and we all take off.

Part of me wants to tell Hudson to go ahead and fade to the farm as fast as possible so he can see if she's there, but another part of me is terrified. What if she isn't? What if our ideas about the timeline are wrong and she's not actually okay?

No way do I want him to have to be alone when he learns that.

Hudson must feel the same way, because every time he gets more than a few yards ahead of us, he slows down and waits for us to catch up. It's rare that I can feel the anxiety in him—he's usually much better at hiding it than I am—but right now, it's so obvious that it breaks my heart.

Which is why when we're about half a mile away, I shift back to just plain Grace. I may be slower like this, but I can walk beside him and put my hand in his. Whether he realizes it or not, he is going to need a moment to prepare himself for what may—or may not—be waiting for us at the farm.

He looks startled when I slide my fingers between his, but he doesn't pull away. Instead, he grabs on like it's a lifeline and smiles down at me. It doesn't quite reach his eyes, but then, I don't expect it to. Not now, when we're both so nervous I feel like we might explode any second.

"It's going to be okay," I whisper to him.

He shrugs in response. But his grip on my hand gets a little tighter. And for now, that's all I can expect.

"Is that the farm?" Jaxon asks suddenly. His eyes are narrowed as he stares far into the distance, and my stomach twists. I would be lying to myself if I didn't recognize how hard this must be on him as well. All of this must seem like the place where he lost me.

His gaze swings to mine, slides down to Hudson's and my joined hands before sliding away, and I want to go to him and tell him how sorry I am. But then he turns to Flint, who is flying straight toward us, one wing dipping at the last second and nearly sweeping Jaxon's feet out from under him.

I gasp, expecting Jaxon to yell at him, but he surprises me and laughs instead, shaking his head as he mutters affectionately, "Asshole." Then he takes off in a run, jumping up and shifting into a giant amber dragon at the last second—and chases after Flint, who is now flapping his wings like his life depends on it.

Macy is laughing so hard on Flint's back as he swoops hard left, then right to avoid Jaxon, that I think she might fall off. Eden joins the impromptu race, swooshing easily between the two male dragons in a here's-how-it's-done flyby that has Heather screaming like she's on the best roller-coaster ride of her life.

"Good God," Hudson murmurs. "They're all overgrown children."

I squint up at the dragon silhouettes racing against the bright sun and say softly, "Flint is good for Jaxon." I pause, then add, "Do you think they're going to be okay?"

"No," Hudson says, and my head whips to his. "One of them is definitely going to crash into the ground right now."

I pivot back to the dragons and gasp. One very large, amber dragon is locked in a death spiral with an even larger green dragon. My hand flies up to my chest as my stomach sinks, neither dragon letting go as they spin round and round, speeding closer and closer to the ground.

At the last second, they both fly apart, swooping within inches of the rocky surface before rising back up again on opposite sides of a giant crater.

"For fuck's sake," I mutter, my stomach permanently in my throat.

Hudson just chuckles and tugs on my hand. "Come on. You can scold the kids later. We're almost to the farm."

I turn back to the road and realize we've actually walked quite a way now. We've only got about a quarter of a mile before entering the main property, and we both come to a halt.

Within seconds, the others swoop down next to us and land. Heather and Macy hop off while everyone shifts back into their human forms, and we stand side by side as we take in the view.

"Is that it?" Heather asks, moving a few feet closer to get a better look.

Hudson nods. "That's it."

"It's bigger than I thought it'd be," Eden comments.

"You'll love it when we get there," I tell her. "There's a flower garden and vegetable patch that the owners have for their own personal use, plus several commercial crops as well. And there's a gorgeous lake surrounded by the most amazing trees—"

"Sounds like you and Hudson had one hell of a vacation here," Jaxon comments in a tone so brusque that it has both Flint and me turning to look at him questioningly.

He doesn't say anything else, though. Which isn't awkward at all.

"We only spent a few days here," I start to tell him. "We had to go on the run because—"

I break off as Hudson shoots me a very clear what-the-fuck look. I'm not sure what it's about—I was just trying to explain things to Jaxon—but since it's the same look Flint is currently giving Jaxon, I decide to shut my mouth and keep it shut.

Because, apparently, there's no winning about this right now.

The farm and its outbuildings become more visible to the non-dragon and -vampire folk as we near, finally reaching the outskirts of the farm.

As soon as we open the gate and step foot on the property, there's a part of me that starts looking around for Tiola, with her overalls and braids and gorgeous little face. But she's nowhere to be found, and neither is a certain umbra I've spent our entire walk obsessing over.

"It's okay," I murmur to Hudson, who becomes a little stiffer with each step we take. "We'll find them."

He nods like he believes me—like everything is fine—but I know it's not. I know he's as worried as I am that no one has come out to greet us. But just like with everything else, he's determined not to show it.

"She's going to be here." I say it as much for me as I do for him.

Again, he nods.

"Who are you talking about?" Jaxon asks, looking around like he expects someone to jump out at us from any direction. "The farmer?"

I'm still trying to figure out how to answer him without upsetting Hudson when we make it to the edge of the field—and are bum-rushed by dozens upon dozens of umbras.

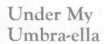

38

Under My Umbra-ella

They pour out of the field from all directions, shadows of all shapes and sizes. Some are in the guise of animals—lizards and snakes, birds and bugs, squirrels and chipmunks and tiny rabbits—while others look more like roly-poly little balls and other shapes. They tangle around our feet, rush for our hair and faces, slither up our legs to wrap around our waists.

As they change color, from shades of purple to lavender gray and back again, my friends freak out. Start trying to fling them off themselves.

"Grace, look out!" Macy screams, fire dancing around her fingertips as she takes aim at a group of umbras near my feet.

"It's okay!" I tell her, jumping in front of them. As I do, a giant snake slithers up my back and wraps itself around my neck. "They won't hurt you."

"The fuck they won't!" Flint growls, grabbing a shadow lizard off his leg and throwing it as far into the field as he can.

Jaxon reaches for a shadowy bird that's flying at him and snatches it out of midair. Seconds later, he sends it careening head over tailfeathers in the other direction.

Eden shoots a stream of ice out of her mouth at a couple giant shadow spiders that are at her feet, then snarls as they scatter before it can hit them.

"Seriously, stop!" I yell. "This isn't like the shadows at the Trials. These are umbras. They aren't trying to hurt you. They just want to say hello."

"They've got a very aggressive way of saying hello," Heather answers.

But she must decide to believe me, because she stops squirming and lets the curious little umbras move over and around her.

Eden hisses when one gets too close to Heather's throat and moves to intervene, but I step in between them. "She's fine, Eden. I swear."

And she is, despite the fact that dozens of umbras are currently slithering up her sides and tangling themselves in her shirt and pants and hair.

Heather laughs as one of them leans down and gives her what sounds like a smacking kiss right on the cheek. Then cries out a little as another one of them starts to tug at her braids.

"Come on, little one," I say, holding out a hand to the one pulling her hair.

It squeaks in protest, but eventually it gives up and scampers onto my hand and straight up my arm to bury itself in my curls.

"If these aren't shadow monsters, can I ask what the fuck they are?" Jaxon demands, brushing the last of the umbras off him.

The other creatures have obviously decided to give up on my hostile friends, because they are now swarming Hudson, Heather, and me.

"They're umbras," I say again. "Shadow pets, but real. If you hold one instead of fighting them, you'll see that they have mass. They just look like shadows."

"Shadow pets," Eden repeats, sounding unconvinced. But at least she's stopped trying to freeze them.

Jaxon and Flint also seem to be reserving judgment. They aren't actively attacking the umbras anymore, but both of them are still in fighting stances.

Macy, on the other hand, just goes all in, plopping down on the ground and letting the umbras swarm over her.

"Are you sure that's a good idea?" Eden asks, moving closer to her like she wants to protect her.

"It's fine," she says, and her laugh sounds like a tinkling bell ringing through the air. It's a laugh I haven't heard from my cousin in a while, and a soft smile lifts a corner of my mouth.

But now that I've got everyone else under control, I turn my attention to trying to coax an umbra salamander to let go of my curls long enough for me to put it on the ground. The others take the hint and slither back down to the purple dirt, but the salamander isn't budging. It keeps slipping and sliding along my neck, darting between my curls and into the collar of my shirt every time I get close to grabbing it.

I turn to share my amusement with Hudson, only to find him standing completely still. He's being swarmed by umbras, dozens of the little creatures wrapping and sliding and clawing their way across his chest, over his shoulders, down his legs.

But he doesn't even seem to notice. Instead, he's staring far into the distance, jaw clenched and throat working like every breath is a struggle. And that's when it hits me. None of the umbras currently winding their way around him is Smokey.

Devastation swamps me, and I close the distance between us in a single leap. I was so sure she would be here—so sure that the timeline would reset for her, too, since she was hit by time-dragon fire. Hudson was, as well. And now that she's not here, now that we were wrong…it feels like losing her all over again.

"I'm sorry," I tell him, wrapping my arms around his waist and holding him as tightly as I can. "I'm so sorry."

He doesn't move.

"Hudson, baby." I want to tell him that it's okay, want to tell him that she has to be somewhere in the Shadow Realm and we'll turn this place upside down until we find her.

But I just don't know if that's true anymore. I expected her to be here waiting for him—expected her to launch into his arms and coo at him like she did from the very first minute she met him. And now that she's not here, now that all of his hopes are dashed…I don't know what to say to him.

I sure as hell don't want to overpromise anything else. Not when giving him false hope just feels cruel.

Tears burn the backs of my eyes and clog my throat as I press my face against him and hold on as tightly as I can. Not finding her here is a giant hole inside me. I can't imagine what it feels like for him.

"What's wrong with him?" Jaxon asks from right next to us. He sounds as shaken as I feel.

"Nothing," Hudson answers in a voice I haven't heard him use since that night in my room when he asked me to stop. To just stop. I didn't know what he meant then, but I do now, and hearing that same voice come from him brings me right back to that moment. "I'm fine."

"You don't look fine." Jaxon isn't being an asshole. There's genuine concern in his tone and in the hand I feel him rest on Hudson's other shoulder. I get that he doesn't understand what's going on here—to him, his brother's freak-out comes out of nowhere—but I still wish he would just drop it.

"We need to get going." Hudson smooths a hand down my hair and then gently sets me away from him. "None of you have eaten in too many hours to count, and Macy and Heather need to rest."

"I'm pretty sure I'm doing better than you right now," Macy says, getting back up on her feet. "Is there anything we can do for you?"

Hudson shakes his head. "I'm fine," he repeats as he turns toward the house. And my heart breaks all over again. Because he's moving like he's broken, like every single part of him hurts, and I can't do anything to fix him. I can't say anything that will make losing her again any better.

I turn to look at our friends, all of whom have worried looks on their faces as they either watch Hudson or studiously don't watch him. Jaxon drops back a few steps to walk behind his brother, his shoulders braced like he's ready to catch him if he falls.

The others give him space, except Macy, who walks up on his other side and slides her hand into his. "I'm fine," he says a third time as he glances down at her.

"Yeah, me too," she answers. But she doesn't take her hand away. And he doesn't let it go.

"What the fuck is going on?" Jaxon whispers to me, but I just shrug. It's too complicated to explain Hudson's relationship with Smokey in one or two sentences, and I can't say any more right now. Not when he's like this.

"Later," I whisper back. Then I wrap my arm around Hudson's waist and hold on tight as we walk toward Arnst and Maroly's farmhouse.

The sun is still high in the sky, which means they may be out working the fields. But short of wandering their land looking for them—which we may still resort to—the house seems like our best bet.

Especially since the moment we make it around the fields, we see Tiola walking down the old farmhouse steps. She's got a backpack on her back and a bucket in her hands and several cat umbras trailing along behind her.

She's looking down, chattering away at them, all the while dropping treats for them to gobble up. It's not until she's done feeding them that she finally raises her gaze.

Her eyes lock on Hudson, and her mouth falls open for several seconds. Then she lets out a delighted squeal and runs straight for us.

39

Lost and Profound

"Hudson!" she yells. "Hudson, Hudson, Hudson!"

Her enthusiasm gets a smile out of him, which I didn't think was possible right now. He rushes to meet her and drops to his knees so she can hug him.

Which she does with extreme enthusiasm, wrapping her little arms around his neck and squealing like she's just received the best present of her life. "Mom and Dad said we'd never see you again, but I knew you'd come back! I just knew it!"

"Well, you were right," he tells her, and his accent is thicker than usual. A surefire sign that he's feeling extra emotional.

"I knew I would be! Come on, come on, we have to go tell Mom!" She grabs his hands and tries to pull him to his feet.

"Absolutely," he says. "But can I introduce you to my friends first?"

"Of course!" she squeals, clapping her hands. Then she looks straight at me and says, "I'm Tiola! It's so nice to meet you!"

I start to tell her that it's me, Grace. And then my stomach sinks like a boat, nearly pulling me under, too. Hudson and I had wondered if our timeline reset when we left. The arrow of time that impaled me seemed to go through him as well. But Tiola remembers Hudson and not me...which means only my timeline reset.

Why we never considered that before, given I lost my memories and Hudson didn't, seems foolish now. It makes complete sense. And yet, I kind of want to sit on the ground and bawl like a baby. I'd somehow thought when I got my memories back, it meant my timeline hadn't reset. But instead, it's much, much worse.

I finally remember everything that happened in Noromar—all the amazing, wonderful people I met here, too. And no one is going to remember me.

Not this little girl who I went on walks with and baked cookies with and read bedtime stories to.

Caoimhe and Lumi and Tinyati. It's so strange to think that I care about all of them, that I worry about them and think about them, and they have absolutely no clue who I am. Even Arnst and Maroly, who took us into their home and helped us so much when we were here, won't recognize me any more than Tiola does.

"I'm Grace," I tell her, shaking her little purple hand with all the dignity such an encounter deserves.

"It's very nice to meet you," she tells me in a singsong voice. "You have pretty hair."

"Thank you. I think your hair is very pretty, too."

"It is." She grins and shakes her head. "Mom tells me it's beautiful."

"Your mom is right," Heather says, bending down so she's eye to eye with Tiola. "I'm Heather."

"You're human!" Tiola's eyes go wide, and she claps her little hands. "I've always wanted to meet a human!"

The words are so similar to what she once said to me that it breaks my heart a little more. Heather seems charmed, though, and the two of them chatter for several seconds before Tiola moves on to Flint.

She takes her time working her way down the line of paranormals waiting to meet her. As she gets to the end—shaking hands with Jaxon— her backpack makes a loud cooing sound.

A loud, *familiar* cooing sound.

"Tiola." Hudson calls her name in the voice of a man who is terrified to hope. "Who's in your backpack?"

"You know who's in my backpack, silly!" she answers as she shrugs the bag off her shoulders. "I knew you'd come back, so I've been keeping her safe for you. I don't think she knows who you are—she didn't remember me—but I've told her all about you."

My heart is beating so fast now that I'm afraid it will explode before she actually gets the backpack open. Just in case we're wrong, I move closer to Hudson, clutch his hand in mine. And pray like I haven't prayed in a long, long time.

"Come on, girl," Tiola coaxes as she kneels on the ground and unbuckles the top of her backpack. "Hudson is finally here, and he wants to meet you."

There's another cooing sound now, and it's louder this time. Then Tiola reaches in and pulls out a tiny shadow puff no bigger than a softball.

My first sight of the umbra has my stomach dropping to my knees. She's not Smokey after all—she's way too small to be the umbra who followed Hudson around our entire time in Adarie.

But then Tiola turns around and crows, "Meet Baby Smokey!"

She's so excited that she practically screams the umbra's name as she thrusts her toward Hudson.

At first, neither of them move. They just stare at each other, wide-eyed. Then Smokey lets out a loud cry and dives for Hudson's chest. She spreads herself out as thin as she can, then crawls up him until her little face is right in front of his and she's looking him straight in the eye.

Then she chitters and chitters and chitters at him, a long discussion that I don't understand but somehow still sounds an awful lot like she's giving him what for.

As for Hudson, he doesn't say a word. He doesn't even make a sound. He just stares at her like he's seen a ghost. And then he, quite simply, crumbles.

I reach for him as his knees buckle, trying to catch him before his legs go out from under him completely. But it's too late. All I manage to do is get pulled to the ground next to him, and then we're there, all together. Hudson, Smokey, and me.

I reach out to stroke the tiny umbra, but Smokey hisses at me and pulls every particle of herself onto Hudson so that no part of her is touching any part of me. Apparently, lack of memories notwithstanding, some things never change.

"You're here," Hudson says in a voice that's filled with as much disbelief as it is joy. "You're really here."

Smokey, in her own way, seems to be saying the exact same thing to him. She slips back down his chest, and Hudson catches her, cradles her in his arms as he strokes her shadowy cheek.

Tiola says Smokey doesn't remember him, and maybe she doesn't. But if I've learned anything in the last few months, it's that the heart and soul remember things that the mind can't hold on to. If they didn't, I never would have known what to engrave that bracelet with that I got Hudson.

And as Smokey coos up at Hudson, staring deep into his blue eyes, it's obvious that there's a part of her that very much remembers him.

Thank God.

Eventually, though, the excitement of their reunion proves too much for Baby Smokey, and she curls into the crook of Hudson's arm and falls fast asleep.

I crouch down next to them as she snores contentedly and whisper, "I told you she'd be here."

He rolls those glorious blue eyes of his, but instead of the sarcastic comment I'm expecting, all he says is, "I should listen to you more often."

"I'm sorry, what did I just hear come out of your mouth?" I ask, looking back around at our friends, who all started doing their own things once the novelty of watching Hudson entranced by a baby umbra wore off.

"Don't believe him," Jaxon tells me. "He's obviously under the influence of something."

"Who knew Hudson would have to travel to the Shadow Realm before he found someone who could put up with him for that long?" Flint snickers.

"Excuse me, but what am I?" I demand.

"You don't count," he tells me. "You got bamboozled into being mated with him. I'm talking about everyone else in the world."

Hudson flips him off subtly so Tiola won't notice, taking great care not to disturb Smokey as he does. Then looks at Tiola and says, "Thank you for taking such good care of her for me."

Tiola grins, swinging her arms from side to side. "That's what friends do. They help each other out when they need it."

"You're right," I tell her, glaring at Flint over her head. "That's exactly what friends do."

He makes a talk-talk-talk gesture back at me, but I notice he's the first one to offer a hand to help Hudson up. The fact that Hudson actually takes it tells me more about how their friendship is evolving—and advancing—than anything the two of them say when they snipe at each other.

"Where do you put her when she's asleep?" Hudson asks Tiola as we climb the steps to the farmhouse.

"Usually my backpack. But she's got a cradle in my room. I tied a bunch of sparkly ribbons on it for her, since you wrote to me about how she likes them."

"That's—" Hudson pauses, clears his throat. "That's really great thinking, Tiola."

"I know," she says. "Mom says I'm super smart."

"Mom says a lot of things," an amused voice agrees as the door swings open. "Looks like you've brought us a whole party this time, Tiola."

"I did, Mama. And guess what! I brought you Hudson!"

"Hudson?" Amusement changes to shock as Maroly steps through the door. "Oh, Hudson!" She throws her arms around him and gives him a giant hug. "We've been so worried about you!"

Smokey screeches a bit at being disturbed, but she settles back down again once Maroly pulls away.

"I see you've found our favorite little umbra," she says with a fond glance at Smokey.

"I have indeed. Tiola told me she's been keeping her safe for me." His grin is bigger than I've ever seen it.

"She has," Maroly confirms. "She kept telling us you'd come back, but we didn't know whether to believe her or not."

"You need to trust me more, Mama," Tiola says, all sweetness with just a little steel underneath. "I'm a penumbra. I know about lost things."

"That's true," Maroly says as she holds the door open and ushers us inside. "But Hudson isn't lost anymore."

Tiola appears to think about that as she turns around to stare at Hudson with eyes that seem a million years older than her actual years.

Then, out of nowhere, she says, "I'm not so sure about that."

"Yes, well, that's not for you to decide," Maroly tells her as she scooches her toward the door. "Now, go wash up for dinner."

Maroly turns to the rest of us. "You'll stay, of course. You must be starving, and we have plenty. Plus, you have to catch us up on everything that's been going on in your life, Hudson."

Again, it hurts a little that she's speaking only to him. That she's forgotten me completely. I know I'm being ridiculous, though, so I force myself to shrug it off and introduce myself to Maroly as we follow her deeper into the house.

This round of introductions takes a little longer than it did with Tiola, largely because Maroly has more questions about each of us than her daughter did. Still, we're just about through with the intros by the time she leads us into the family room to sit down.

Flint's the last one to go, and he's in the middle of telling her that he's a dragon when he breaks off mid-word. I turn around, trying to find what's caught his attention. But before I can figure it out, he makes a choked sound and asks, "I'm sorry, but is that a *shrine* to Hudson Vega?"

40

"A shrine?" Jaxon repeats, his voice high-pitched in a way I've never heard from him before. "Where?"

Flint points across the room with a look of horrified fascination on his face. But I've already spotted what he's talking about. And while "shrine" may be a bit of an overstatement, there's definitely something strange going on here.

"Tiola insisted." Maroly smiles indulgently as I walk over to get a closer look. "Hudson is something of a hero around these parts, and she felt it was only right to commemorate his stay with us."

"Something of a hero?" Flint chokes out. "If this is what you do for Hudson, what do you do for a real hero?"

"Apparently, I *am* a real hero," Hudson comments placidly. "I don't see anyone building shrines to you."

But he's too busy cuddling Baby Smokey back to sleep to cross the room to investigate the maybe-not-quite-a-shrine-but-definitely-a-serious-display that's set up—I realize with dawning amusement—right where Hudson's favorite chair used to be.

I start to say something to Flint and Jaxon about it, but then I figure Maroly will wonder how I know where he used to sit.

But I am absolutely riveted. It's about time someone besides me realized just how fabulous Hudson really is. And, judging by the looks of the small purple table Maroly has set up to honor Hudson, someone definitely has.

In the center of the table stands a huge photograph of a smiling Hudson sitting on the front porch. Around that picture are other, smaller photos—him with Arnst and Maroly in the gardens, him having a tea party with Tiola, him playing with Smokey. There's even one of him alone, standing by the lake, and I have to squint at it for a bit because I'm pretty sure I used to be in that photo with him.

And can I just say, this whole being-erased-from-the-timeline thing is wild. What kind of universal magic is it that not only has people forgetting I exist but also works to erase me from photos and who knows what else?

I guess it's the butterfly effect—you change one thing and everything changes. The timeline is different now, and if I never existed, all these things happened without me, so nothing would have actually needed to be erased.

Except I did exist—I still exist—and standing here in this room, with these people I remember but who don't know me at all, feels beyond strange.

Not, however, as strange as the small marble statue of Hudson that's standing next to the picture of him at the lake. Or the teacup he used that's next to the photo of him and Tiola. Or the scrap of fabric that I'm pretty sure came from something of his, though I can't quite place it.

Jaxon, apparently, has no such trouble. Then again, he's a much bigger fan of Italian designers than I am. "Holy shit," he mutters as he bends down to get a closer look. "Is that Armani?"

I crack up then, because it is. Oh my God, it is. It's from the pants he was wearing the day we fled the lair. He left them here when we evacuated to the mountains because the Shadow Queen was after us, and it took weeks before he stopped whining about the inferior craftsmanship of the pants he was stuck with.

Never in either of our wildest dreams did it occur to us that a piece of them would end up on a table for the entire world to see.

All of a sudden, the front door opens and Maroly calls out, "Oh, Arnst! Guess who's come to visit!"

As she rushes toward the front of the house, Flint turns on Hudson and me. "Okay, I don't care how upside down this whole freaking world is—it's not normal to put someone's pants in the middle of some weird-ass shrine to them!"

"You've got to admit, that's some CSI shit," Macy agrees. "You know, like, serial killer–type shit."

"To be fair, it's just a piece of a leg. Not the whole pair of pants," I say.

"Like that makes it better?" Jaxon half whispers, half hisses. "Who the fuck are these people?"

"Our friends," Hudson answers in a tone that brooks no argument. "Our very kind, very helpful friends, who I'm spending the night with here, in comfort, before we end up having to traverse half the fooking Shadow Realm looking for Lorelei's dear old mom. You, however, are more than welcome to get the hell out."

"I'm not saying that, man. I'm just saying..." Jaxon looks around like he can't believe he, Flint, and Macy are the only ones freaking out. "Aren't you a little bit worried that they're going to try to make a pair of pants out of your skin or something?"

It's such a bizarre image that it breaks the underlying what-the-fuck tension in the room, and we all burst out laughing. Not just because the idea of the very sweet Tiola and Maroly skinning Hudson for any reason is an absolutely absurd one but because with his strength, it would take an army of wraiths to bring him down. He may not have his powers in the Shadow Realm, but he's still a vampire. And two farmers and their daughter don't stand a chance against him, let alone all of us together.

We're still laughing when Arnst walks into the room. "Hudson! You've returned to us!"

My mate has just enough time to thrust Smokey onto my lap before Arnst wraps his arms around him in a huge bear hug and lifts him several inches off the ground. "It's so good to see you!"

"It's good to see you, too," Hudson tells him. "I'm sorry to crash in on you like this."

"Don't worry about it." Arnst waves away his apology. "Two times makes it a tradition. So now we'll always look for you, never knowing when you'll drop by again."

He turns to smile at the rest of us. "And I see you've brought a lot of friends with you this go-around. By the time we finish dinner, it'll be late. I hope everyone's planning on staying the night."

"We would love to," I tell him. "If you'll have us."

"Of course we'll have you. Any friend of Hudson is a friend of ours."

Behind me, Flint makes a slight gagging sound—which stops, thankfully, the second I stomp on his foot.

"I'm sorry there's not enough room in the house for all of you," Arnst says. "But we've got a bunkhouse we use when we hire extra help for harvesting season. You're welcome to stay there."

"Anything is fine," Hudson tells him with a smile.

"Yes," I agree. "We're just grateful that you've got room for us at all."

"Don't be silly, Hudson. You won't be staying in the bunkhouse." Maroly pats his shoulder as she walks by him toward the kitchen. "You'll sleep in the guest room, like you did last time you were here."

"Of course he will," Flint mutters.

"The guest room sounds amazing. The bed is so comfortable in there." Hudson shoots Flint an evil smile as he says the last, and it's all I can do to keep from bursting into laughter again.

"Now, Maroly and I will have dinner on the table in just a few minutes." Arnst points in both directions. "In the meantime, there's a bathroom at the end of that hallway. You can take turns freshening up while we get everything ready for you."

I start to give Smokey back to Hudson—freshening up sounds like heaven right about now—but she wakes up before I can actually shift her into his arms. I freeze as her big purple eyes blink open once, then twice. I brace myself for her to lose it completely, but when she doesn't so much as cry out, I figure she must be okay with me holding her and decide to try to rock her back to sleep.

Which might go down in the books as the worst mistake I've ever made. And I've made some doozies.

When Smokey's eyes blink open a third time and she sees my face directly above hers, all hell breaks loose. She lets out a scream that shatters my eardrums along with, I'm pretty sure, the sound barrier. And then she really loses it—hissing and clawing as she throws herself out of my arms.

I make the mistake of trying to catch her—the last thing I want to do is drop any kind of baby, even a pissed-off umbra one—but that only makes her angrier. Because she whirls on me with a snarl and sinks her jagged little teeth into my hand.

"Smokey, no!" Hudson growls, sliding a finger between her mouth and my skin and popping her off. "We don't bite."

She turns on him with a snarl, then realizes who it is who's holding her, and the snarl turns immediately into a coo. She throws herself against him and crawls up his chest until she's wrapped gently around his neck.

"Are you all right?" Hudson asks, reaching for my hand.

"I'm fine," I tell him, because I am. Smokey's tiny baby teeth didn't even break the skin, though I'm pretty sure she tried. My pride is hurt, though. I know the old Smokey never liked me, but I thought I'd have a chance with this new Baby Smokey.

But apparently her hatred of me runs deep in her DNA. The little turkey.

"Are you sure?" he asks, lifting my hand up so he can get a better look at it.

"I'm positive." I pull away. "It's not even bruised."

"Still—" He breaks off as Smokey gently smacks her hands against his cheeks, chittering away at him as she does.

"We don't bite, Smokey," he reiterates as he bends over and puts her on the ground. "And we especially don't bite Grace."

Smokey lets out another high-pitched screech the second he lets go of her. Only this time, instead of biting, she flings herself on the floor and starts sobbing hysterically.

Hudson looks at me, horrified. "What do I do?" he demands.

"Why are you asking me?" I demand right back.

"Put her back in her backpack, obviously," Eden says, speaking up for the first time since she introduced herself to Maroly. "She needs to go to time-out for a while and think about what she did."

When we all turn to look at her, surprised, she shrugs. "Why do you look so shocked? I've got cousins."

We all crack up again—including Hudson—which only makes Smokey throw a bigger tantrum.

"All right, then, Tiola. May I borrow Smokey's backpack?" Hudson half yells to be heard over the umbra's caterwauls.

"I'll take care of it," Tiola says, picking up a squirming Smokey and sliding her expertly into the backpack and buckling her in. This obviously isn't Smokey's first temper tantrum. "I'm pretty used to her fits by now."

"Her fits?" Hudson asks, all raised brows and exceedingly proper British accent.

"Oh yeah. She has a lot of them." Tiola rolls her eyes. "But the good thing is they don't last long."

"Still," I say to Hudson. "You got her back, and that's what really matters."

In the blessed silence that follows, we all just stare at one another. At least until Flint claps Hudson on the back and says, "Be careful what you wish for, man."

"Truer words," Hudson answers as he stares at Tiola in obvious horror. "Truer words."

41

Dying Is
Snot an Option

Ten minutes later, we're sitting around Maroly and Arnst's large, round dinner table, eating a pouspous dish that's as delicious as I remember. Or at least some of us are—the vampires are making do with ice water. The beautiful chandelier lit by crystals above us shines just as bright as the last time we were here, casting a glow over the faces below it.

"So," Arnst says after everyone's been served. "How did you all meet Hudson?"

The question seems innocent enough, but I can't help thinking that what he's really asking is how someone of Hudson's stature came to know the rest of us.

After a quick drink of water, Hudson answers, "Well, Grace is my mate. The rest of the group came with her."

"Besides Jaxon," I comment. "He *is* your brother."

"Really?" Tiola squeals, bouncing up and down in her chair. "Grace, you're Hudson's mate?"

"I am," I assure her, reaching over to rest my hand on Hudson's knee under the table.

He shoots me a smile as he moves to gently cover my hand with his own.

"Is it difficult?" Maroly asks.

My brows hit my hairline. "Being mated to Hudson?"

"Yes, or being his brother. He's so brave—you must worry about him all the time." Maroly looks so concerned that I almost choke on my latest bite of pouspous.

Jaxon, however, seems to take it in stride. "Oh, it is definitely a trial," he tells her.

"I can imagine. But also a real honor, I'm sure," Arnst interjects.

Now it's Jaxon's turn to choke on his water. "It is, absolutely," I say for him, squeezing Hudson's knee in a silent apology for teasing him. "He's the best person I know."

"Me too!" Tiola squeals. The little girl only knows one volume. "Hudson is the best! He saved everyone!"

"I don't think that's quite what happened—" Hudson starts, but I cut him off with a grin.

"Now, now, don't be modest, darling. You truly did save Adarie single-handedly. It's the most impressive story I've ever heard."

Hudson flushes bright red—a first for him—while the rest of our friends struggle not to laugh. And even though the conversation is hilarious, mostly because of how uncomfortable it makes him, I remind myself to make sure he knows that, under all the teasing, I mean every word I'm saying.

"Grace is leaving her own accomplishments out of this discussion," Hudson tells our hosts smoothly. "As are the rest of my friends. They're really all amazing people."

"Of course they are," Maroly tells him. "They're friends with you, aren't they?"

This time, it's Flint who sounds like he's having trouble swallowing—I'm sure having his worth judged based on his friendship with Hudson is a doozy for him—but he doesn't say anything. In the end, neither does anyone else. They just kind of grin down at their plates while Hudson squirms in the proverbial hot seat.

Deciding to take mercy on him, because I'm just that generous, I clear my throat and prepare to shift the conversation to a different, equally important topic. "We do have a question for you, if you don't mind."

"Of course. Ask away," Arnst tells me as he serves himself another heaping spoon of pouspous.

"We're here because we need to meet up with the Shadow Queen. How do you—"

"The Shadow Queen?" Maroly interrupts, clearly horrified. "Why on earth would you want to have a meeting with her? The last time Hudson was here, she nearly killed him!"

"Like that would have been the worst thing in the world," Flint mutters under his breath. Then yells, "Ouch!" and glares at Macy, who looks completely innocent as she takes a bite of her dinner. Or at least as innocent as someone with heavy cat-eye liner *can* look.

She obviously took the words "freshening up for dinner" seriously.

"She's definitely not our first choice of people to hang out with," I tell Maroly. "But she's got information we need, and there's no one else we can think of to go to for it."

"What information are you looking for?" Arnst asks. "If it's something from Adarie, maybe we can help you."

I don't think that's true—if everyone in the Shadow Realm knew the cure for shadow poison, surely it would be common knowledge by now—but in the end, I figure it can't hurt to ask. "Our friend was bitten by one of her shadow bugs. We're trying to find a way to save him."

"He's been poisoned with the queen's shadow magic?" Maroly asks, horrified.

Tiola bursts into tears at the mere mention of the words. Which isn't terrifying at all.

"You mean he's going to die? That's howwible!" she tells us through her sobs.

"That's why we're here," Heather explains. "To stop that from happening."

"But he is!" she says as she climbs off her chair. "He is going to die." Then, to everyone's shock, she walks over to Hudson and throws her arms around him. "I don't want your friend to die."

For a second, the vampire looks stunned as he stares down at the sobbing little girl. Then he wraps his arms around her and pulls her up to sit on his lap. "It's okay," Hudson tells her as he rocks her. "I promise, he'll be okay."

She pulls back and looks him in the eye, tears still running down her face. "Do you pwomise?"

"I—" He breaks off, glancing around the table at the rest of us in obvious consternation.

"I promise," I tell her. "We're going to save him."

"Absolutely," my mate agrees. "We're here to find a cure for Mekhi, and we're not leaving until we have one. Of that much, I can assure you."

Tiola looks torn between believing her hero and believing what she knows about shadow poison, which is a lot, apparently. But in the end, Hudson's words must comfort her, because she stops crying. And then wipes her snotty face all over the front of his T-shirt.

"Tiola!" Maroly gasps, standing up and reaching for her. "I'm so sorry—"

"Don't worry about it. It's probably an improvement to the shirt," Hudson tells her with his easygoing grin.

"You think?" Tiola asks.

"Absolutely!" he assures her. "I love it."

"Me too." She snuggles closer into him, then lays her head on his non-snotified shoulder. "I love you, Hudson."

He gently pats her back. "I love you, too, Tiola."

Watching them together makes me melt on the inside.

"Well, a promise is a promise," Arnst says into the ensuing silence. "So we'd better figure out a way to help you keep it, hadn't we?"

42

I'm Not
A-Posed

We spend the next hour and a half trying to figure out the best way to get to the Shadow Queen. Apparently, there have been several assassination attempts on the Shadow Queen since Hudson's last battle with her in Adarie.

"There's a growing faction that believes killing the queen will protect Noromar from her attempts to free us," Arnst explains.

I gasp. "Why in the world would they think that?"

Arnst's eyebrows shoot up like the answer is obvious. "Because Hudson told us she was trying to reverse the curse that created the Shadow Realm."

Well, I guess technically that *is* true… "Do you and Maroly not want to leave this prison realm?" I ask.

"Oh no, dear," Maroly says, getting up to bring a pitcher of water to the table and refill the vampires' glasses. She turns to Arnst and smiles. "Why would we want to leave any place that brings us such happiness?"

"Because it's a *prison*?" Heather insists. She pushes her plate away, her food long forgotten.

"It's only a prison if you want to leave," Arnst says. "For some of us, it's home."

"And it's a wonderful home," Hudson insists. "But do you know how we might find the queen anyway?"

"She's gone into hiding at one of her fortresses throughout Noromar." Arnst rubs his stomach, pushing his own plate forward. "I'm sorry, but I have no idea how to find out which one."

All of our shoulders sag in unison, Mekhi on all of our minds. How are we going to save him if we can't find the queen?

"Nyaz might know," Maroly offers.

"Who is that?" Macy asks.

"An innkeeper in a town Hudson and—" I stop myself just in time and instead say, "Smokey stayed in."

"You know, Starfall *is* this week," Maroly says, changing the subject. "Are you going to perform again, Hudson?"

"Oh, I have to hear this," Jaxon drawls. "What kind of *performance* did Hudson put on last time, Maroly?"

Jaxon's sarcasm goes right over Maroly's head. "Unfortunately, I missed it, but I hear there are fan clubs ever since he—"

Arnst interrupts his wife, shouting, "They're back!" out of the blue before pushing away from the table and racing out of the dining room at top speed.

"Who's back?" I stare after him blankly.

"And does he need help with them?" Hudson stands up and heads toward the front door after Arnst.

"See?" Maroly says to no one in particular. "He's such a hero."

Even I have to roll my eyes at that. "Where's Arnst going, Maroly?" I ask as we follow Hudson toward the front.

We get there just in time to see Arnst grab a giant shovel off the porch and race down the shrub-lined path that leads from the front door to Maroly's garden, Hudson hot on his heels.

Seconds later, there are shouts, followed by several people running toward the edge of the farm.

"And don't come back here!" Arnst yells after them. "Or next time you'll meet the business end of my shovel!"

"These people are becoming bigger and bigger problems," Maroly says with a shake of her head.

"What people?" I ask, because the last time we stayed here, we never saw another soul. And I'd be lying if I said I wasn't suddenly terrified that a hunter had followed us to the Shadow Realm.

"Dirt thieves," Arnst spits out as he climbs back onto the porch and drops his shovel in the corner.

Hudson, who came back with him, and I exchange mystified looks.

"I'm sorry, Arnst. Did you say dirt thieves?" he asks.

"Yeah, they usually come in the middle of the night and steal dirt from the crops. But these people tonight were really brazen. The nerve of them, coming right up to Maroly's garden like that." Arnst shakes his head. "I don't know what the world is coming to."

"Is that common here?" Jaxon asks as we tromp back to the dining room. "Stealing dirt?"

"Not normally, no. But some people are of the belief that our dirt is special," Maroly tells him.

"*Is* your dirt special?" Heather asks.

Arnst and Maroly exchange a long look before Arnst finally answers, "Not in the slightest."

I want to question him—want to question both of them about this new and strange development—but before I can, Maroly says, "Let's not let this derail us. Before that unpleasant incident, we were talking about how to get the group of you in to see the Shadow Queen."

She whispers "Shadow Queen" like it's a dirty word.

"Yes, let's get back to that," Arnst agrees.

I still find something very strange about the fact that people have apparently decided that stealing dirt from a working vegetable farm is something they should be doing. But since Maroly and Arnst obviously don't want to talk about it anymore, I choose to help them change the subject. It's easier now that I know we aren't going to have to deal with hunters right this second.

"Does she come out for any sort of events or celebrations?" I ask.

"I don't think so. She's been quite scarce since her encounter with Hudson…" Maroly trails off as she turns to give Hudson a strange look. "Although I do believe just knowing you're back might bring her out all on its own."

"I agree. We need to figure out how to get her to notice us," Heather comments. "I'm pretty sure if she knows Hudson is out there waiting for her, she'll pay attention."

"If we breathe, I'm pretty sure she'll pay attention," I tell her. "The last time she saw us, Hudson threw her headfirst over a wall in front of a whole lot of her subjects."

"Seriously? Throwing her over a wall is the best you had?" Jaxon shakes his head as if he's ashamed of his brother.

"If you think you could do better, you're welcome to take your own shot when we find her," Hudson shoots back. "Maybe there'll be a window you can toss her out of. That's practically the same thing, right?"

"Can we please get back on track?" I ask to stop the brotherly sniping. "The whole point of this is getting ourselves in front of the Shadow Queen to make a deal. And while I think Hudson can attract her attention fairly easily, she doesn't strike me as the act-first-think-later kind of person. She came after us when we first got to Noromar, but when we evaded her, it took her years to try again—and only when she viewed us as a threat to her plans. We don't have that kind of time to waste."

"So, we need to make sure we *really* get her attention," Heather says.

"How about we leave it at this," I suggest as Maroly gets up to clear the dishes. "We'll spend the night here, and tomorrow, when we leave, we'll head to Adarie to see Nyaz. If he knows where she is, we'll make our way there and take drastic action, if necessary, to be brought to her attention."

"Sounds like the best plan we've had so far," Eden comments as she stretches her arm out so it lays against the back of Heather's chair.

Heather's eyes go wide and she kind of freezes, like she's not sure what's going on. But she doesn't pull away. In fact, she leans in her chair just enough that her back brushes against Eden's arm.

"Sounds a little boring to me," Macy grumbles. "But responsible, so sure. Count me in."

The others agree, too, and then everyone spends the next several minutes clearing the table and helping Maroly and Arnst clean up from dinner.

"Why don't you head to bed?" I say to the others. "Hudson and I will finish up in here."

"We can help—" Eden breaks off abruptly when I tilt my head as unobtrusively as possible toward Hudson, who keeps glancing at Tiola's backpack with sad eyes. "You know what, I am really tired."

"Me too!" adds Flint, who caught on instantly to what I was trying to say. He gives a huge, exaggerated yawn. "I could fall asleep right here."

Jaxon snorts. "Like that's anything new." But he starts following Flint to the door. "Thank you so much for dinner, Maroly and Arnst. We really appreciate it."

"You didn't eat anything," Maroly tells him with an amused shake of her head.

He nods as if to say *touché*. Then holds the door open for her so she can show them to the bunkhouse.

It isn't long before Maroly returns and Hudson and I are left alone with Tiola and her family. As we finish drying and putting away the dishes, I thank them both again. "You've been so kind to us, and we really are so grateful."

"No need to thank us," Arnst says with a smile. "I'd like to think someone would do the same for Tiola if she needed it. Besides, after everything Hudson sacrificed to save so many of us, this is absolutely the least we can do."

"He is a wonder," I say with an answering grin. Hudson shoots me a rueful look and mouths, *Sorry*, behind their backs, but I just shake my head. Because now that I've gotten over my initial sorrow at not having the same relationships with these people that I used to, I am totally on board the Hudson Appreciation Train.

He deserves a lot more of it than he's gotten in his life.

I can't help but notice when he glances at Tiola's bag again, and I elbow him gently. "Go get her," I murmur. "She's learned her lesson."

Hudson wastes no time fading to the backpack and flicking open the closure. He reaches in and scoops out the little umbra, cradling her in his arms and whispering nonsense in her ear. When she snuggles farther into the curve of his arm, I watch his shoulders relax and realize he was nervous she wouldn't forgive him for teaching her a valuable lesson.

Biting me is one thing. Of course I'll forgive her. But what happens when she bites someone really nasty? It's best she learn the no-biting rule now—however painful the lesson is for Hudson.

He comes back over to the rest of us, swinging his hips left and right as he rocks Smokey in his arms. I'm not even sure he knows he's doing it, which makes my heart melt even more.

"Tomorrow morning, Arnst will draw a map showing you the best way to get to Adarie," Maroly comments as she eventually leads us down the hallway to the same room we shared the last time we were here. "Then you can be on your way."

We thank her again, but she waves away our gratitude before closing the door behind her.

Once we're alone—or almost alone, considering Smokey is still snoozing in his arms—Hudson turns to me.

"I'm sorry," he says. "I didn't even think of how it would feel for you to meet up with people you care about, none of whom can remember who you are or even that they've met you before."

"There's nothing for you to be sorry for. It's fine. We didn't know."

He gives me a doubtful look.

"I'm serious. Was it a little weird when we first got here? Absolutely. But now I'm really enjoying it."

"Enjoying it?" He looks downright disbelieving.

But I grin at him. "Are you kidding me? How could I not be enjoying this? I particularly love the whole Hudson-shrine thing they've got going on out there."

He makes a give-me-a-break sound deep in his throat. "You don't need to say that. The whole thing is bloody ridiculous, and we all know it."

"I think it's *bloody* wonderful. You deserve all the accolades. And that statue is freaking fantastic."

"Where did they even get that thing?" he asks with a groan and a face palm.

"I have no idea. Maybe they had it made?"

"Had it made?" His accent is so thick with dismay that the words are barely recognizable now. "Don't you think the whole thing is a bit wonky? I kept thinking they were winding me up, but how would they know to have that whole table set up and ready?"

"It's not wonky at all!" I tell him. "It's incredible. They even got your perfect little coif right."

"They did not." His tone brooks absolutely no argument, but when have I let that stop me?

"Oh, they absolutely did," I tease. "It was brilliant! Now I just need you to pose for me."

One eyebrow shoots up. "Pose for you."

It's not a question so much as an expression of horror—which makes it even harder for me not to burst out laughing.

"Oh, come on!" I urge. "Do the pose."

In case he pretends to not know what pose I'm talking about, I mimic the statue myself. Head high, shoulders back, chest forward, hands on hips.

Now both brows are up. "Is that your poor attempt at an impression of Superman?"

"It's my attempt at an impression of your statue, and you know it!" I shoot back. "Now, come on. Do the pose for me. Just once."

"I don't think so."

"Pleeeeeeease, Hudsy-Wudsy."

Full-on dismay ripples across his face. "What did you just call me?"

"Hudsy-Wudsy?" I give him my most charming grin.

"*Never* call me that again."

"I swear I won't—*if* you pose for me."

He shakes his head, walking over to the dresser and pulling one of the drawers completely out. "There is nothing on this planet that will make me strike that pose for you."

Hudson carries the drawer to the side of the bed and sets it on the ground. He then grabs one of the pillows off the bed and tosses it into the drawer.

"Nothing?" I repeat, eyes open extra wide.

"Absolutely nothing," he tells me, getting down on his haunches to carefully lower the sleeping umbra onto the pillow. She makes a snuffling whiny noise but settles back into the pillow, sound asleep.

"That's okay," I say with a negligent shrug. "If I wait long enough, you'll just do it naturally."

He stands up again, his back ramrod straight. "I most certainly will not."

"Oh, sure you will. I mean, your chest never sticks out quite as much as that statue's does, but other than that? It's a carbon copy of your—"

I break off, breath whooshing out of me, as Hudson leaps across the room and tackles me onto the bed.

"Take it back," he says, his beautiful face inches from mine.

"Take what back?" I ask innocently.

He narrows his eyes. "Grace."

I narrow mine right back. "Hudson."

"This is seriously how you want to play it?" He grabs my wrists in one big hand.

I buck against him, twisting and rolling my hips in a playful effort to get him off me. But dislodging a normal guy built like Hudson would be a struggle for me on a good day. Dislodging a vampire who has absolutely no desire to go anywhere? Next to freaking impossible.

And that's before he pins my wrists over my head. "Take it back," he says again as he straddles me.

"Or what?" I ask, refusing to give an inch.

He doesn't answer, despite the diabolical gleam in his eyes. Instead, he just smiles his most charming smile.

And that's when I know I'm really in trouble.

43

The first thing Hudson does is slide his free hand underneath me. "No," I tell him, squirming with laughter. "No, no, no, no, no!"

He ignores me, his fingers sliding lower and lower along my side.

"Don't you dare!" I screech at him, my eyes going wide.

But it's too late. He's already reached the spot on my right hip that I don't share with anyone.

The spot that he found several months ago and has enjoyed tormenting me with ever since.

The spot that, no matter how hard I try to resist, turns me into a giggling, hysterical mess every single time he tickles it.

A bark of laughter escapes me the second his fingers skim over the sensitive spot, which only makes him dig in in earnest, tickling me until I'm laughing so hard I'm crying.

"Stop!" I gasp when I can't take any more. "Stop, please—"

He's not a total fiend, so he stops right away, lets me draw several breaths. And just when I think he's done, that the torture is over, he dives back in for another round.

On the plus side, I'm bucking so wildly now that he has to let go of my wrists, and I fling myself backward just far enough to snag a pillow with my fingertips. As soon as I grab it, I bring it down as hard as I can.

I'm rewarded with a satisfying *thunk* when it smacks him across the face. It's his turn to let out a shocked grunt. As he shrinks back in surprise, I press my advantage, hitting him with the soft, fluffy pillow in his shoulder, his chest, his face.

He retaliates by laughing and going back in for more tickles, but I'm ready for him this time. I smack him again with the pillow, in the side now, and I put all the force I've got behind it.

It doesn't hurt him—the pillow is way too soft for that—but it does dislodge the vise grip his knees have on my hips. It's all the in I need.

I shove him off me, all the while hitting him continuously. And when he rolls over on the bed, throwing both of his hands up in an effort to catch the pillow the next time I bring it down, I seize the opportunity and straddle him.

As he reaches down to grab my hips to pull me off, I raise the pillow above my head in an obvious threat. "You sure you want to do that?" I ask in my most menacing voice—which isn't very, at the moment, because I'm having entirely too much fun. But it's the thought that counts, or so I tell myself.

"Pretty sure," he answers haughtily, even as his fingers curl around my hips.

I narrow my eyes at him. "You know you're going to pay, right?"

"I'm counting on it," he answers right before he strikes, fast and clean and deadly.

He snatches the pillow from my hand, throws it across the room, and rolls us so that I'm lying facedown on the bed and he's straddling me from above.

"What have you got to say for yourself now, Gracy-Wacy?" he whispers in my ear.

"What do you want me to say?" I tease back, wriggling my hips against his.

His breath is hot against my ear as he murmurs, "I believe the word you're looking for is 'uncle.' Though I'll take 'I give up,' or even a white flag in a pinch."

"Wow, that's so considerate of you."

He shrugs. "I'm nothing if not magnanimous."

"Yeah, well, I'm nothing if not determined." And with that, I use every ounce of strength I have to roll us off the bed and straight onto the floor.

"Pretty sure we've been here before," he tells me as I land on top of him.

"Yeah, well, this time I'm the one on top."

I dig my knees into the sides of his hips, wrap my hands around his wrists, and stretch his arms above his head—or at least as far above his head as I can manage.

"Looks like you got me," he whispers, wicked blue eyes gleaming with interest.

"Looks like," I answer. "Now the only question is, whatever will I do with you?"

"I've got some ideas on that front—" He breaks off as a just-woken-up Smokey lets out a very loud, very annoyed caterwaul from her spot inside the drawer.

Seconds later, she wiggles her way out and chitters at us like we just took the last cookie from the cookie jar. Then she takes off toward the open window and slides into the night.

"Should we go after her?" I ask, starting to get up.

But Hudson grabs my hips and holds me in place. "Tiola told me she leaves the house every evening. Even though she's still a baby, she likes to hunt at night with the other umbras."

"Just like she always did." I smile down at him.

He smiles right back up at me. "Just like she always did."

And for this one moment, everything feels right in the world.

He must feel it, too, because he reaches up and tangles his hands in my curls before slowly, gently, *inexorably* dragging my face down to his. "You're so beautiful," he whispers.

"Not as beautiful as you," I whisper back.

His fingers weave their way through my hair until he's cupping the back of my head so he can bring me down closer and press kisses along my jawline. "I think we'll have to agree to disagree on that."

"I'm okay with that." I sigh, tilting my head back to give him better access.

He takes the hint, scraping his fangs along the sensitive skin beneath my ear before sliding slowly, slowly, slowly down my throat to my collarbone.

Heat explodes inside me like a sunrise, streaking along my nerve endings and melting me from the inside out. My hands clutch at his shoulders, my body arches against his, and I pull him closer.

It feels like forever since he's held me like this, touched me like this. And even though it was just last night at the Gargoyle Court, a lot of things have happened since then. And right now, I'm not thinking about any of them. Right now, all I'm thinking about—all I *can* think about—is Hudson.

His mouth. His hands. His *soul*. I want him. More, I need him.

I shift a little bit so he can sit up. Then, when he does, I tilt my head even farther to the side in a silent plea for more of him—for all of him.

Hudson's only response is a groan deep in his throat before licking his way back and forth across the pulse at the base of my neck.

Frissons of pleasure work their way down my spine, lighting me up from the inside. Spreading along my nerves, working their way into my very cells, until there isn't a single part of me that isn't aching for him. That isn't burning with want and need and love.

So much love that I can't hold it inside any longer. So much love that it comes pouring out of me and wraps itself around Hudson, pulling him closer, closer, closer.

Weaving us together even more tightly until all I can feel is him. Until all I can taste or smell or hear is him.

He scrapes his fangs against my pulse point again and again and again until I'm little more than a trembling, sobbing mess. I arch against him, shuddering, burning, aching.

"Please," I murmur brokenly, the words falling from my lips like cries—or prayers. "Please, Hudson. Please, please, please."

Again, he scrapes his fangs against my skin. Again, I shudder and arch against him in a desperate attempt to get closer. Right now, I'd crawl inside him if I could. That's how desperate I am to feel all of him, to have all of him.

The worries of earlier burn away in the wake of the supernova turning my skin to kindling and my insides to ash.

"Please," I say again, only this time it's as much order as it is plea.

Hudson must realize it, because he chuckles deep in his throat. Murmurs my name. And then strikes, his fangs slicing through my skin between one breath and the next.

Ecstasy explodes through me as he drinks, my body erupting a little more with each pull of his mouth against my skin.

He drinks and drinks and drinks, until I can't tell where I end and he begins. And then he drinks some more.

It's what I wanted—what I needed right now—and I hold him to me as tightly as I can for as long as I can. The future is uncertain—maybe even the next few moments are. But this? I've never been more certain in my life than I am about the heat, the connection, the power burning between my mate and myself.

When it's over, when he's broken the connection and licked away the trickle of blood that runs from my wound, he keeps me wrapped around him as he stands up and moves us back to the bed.

"I love you," he whispers as I spread out on top of him.

"I love you, too. So much."

And though there are a dozen things we need to talk about, a hundred questions I'm dying to ask him, I don't say another word. Because who knows what the next few days are going to bring, and all I want is to spend these moments in the arms of the guy I love. Everything else can wait for just a little while longer.

We spend the rest of the night that way, wrapped around each other as we drift halfway between waking and sleep. I know I need to rest, but I don't know how long it will be before we get to do this again, and I don't want to waste a second.

But time waits for no one. And as the world begins to stir beneath the vast purple sky, Hudson finally lets me go.

44

Never as Easy as
One, Two, Free

As I step into the shower a few minutes after finally rolling out of bed, a ton of questions assail me.

Are we going to be able to convince the Shadow Queen to give us the antidote for Mekhi?

Are we actually going to be able to do whatever impossible thing we have to do to help split Lorelei and her sister forever?

Are we actually going to be able to find the smuggler Hudson is sure exists and make our way back across the barrier?

I tell myself that we're going to be able to do everything we came here to do. That it's all going to work out. That, somehow, it always does.

But as anxiety wells inside me, making my stomach hurt and my lungs burn like they're running out of air, it's harder to believe that everything will be okay. And harder to ignore the fact that so much is still hanging over me. The Crone amassing an army of hunters. Hudson still not telling me about what's going on with him and the Vampire Court.

It's fine, I tell myself as I finish washing my hair and turn the shower off.

It's fine, I repeat as I dry myself off and pull on a magenta sweater and my favorite pair of jeans.

It's fine, I say one more time as I twist my hair into a clip at the back of my head to keep it out of my way.

But none of that seems to matter as a panic attack overcomes me and I tumble inelegantly to the floor.

I brace my hands on my crossed legs as I desperately try to drag air into a chest that suddenly feels like I've been underwater way too long.

It doesn't work.

I count backward from ten and try again to take a deep breath. Again, it doesn't work.

It feels like I'm suffocating now, and I claw at my throat, trying to open my airway. Trying to find a way to convince my body to just breathe.

"Grace?" Hudson calls. He sounds concerned.

"Just a minute!" I gasp out, trying to sound as normal as I can, considering a six-ton elephant has just taken up residence on my chest.

But I must not sound normal enough, because about two seconds pass before the bathroom door goes flying open and Hudson is standing there with a worried frown on his face.

He takes one look at me, bent over and struggling, and he's across the room in a single leap.

"You're okay, Grace," he tells me, gently pulling me back into a standing position. "You've got this."

I shake my head wildly. It doesn't feel like I've got this. In fact, right now it feels an awful lot like I'm drowning.

"Yes, you do," he says, calmly placing a hand on my chest. "Make my hand move up and down."

"I can't," I choke out.

"You can." His voice is steady, firm. "Take a small breath, Grace. Make my hand move just a little bit."

"I can't," I tell him again. But I try anyway, forcing my chest to rise. Forcing my lungs to accept just a little bit of air.

"That's perfect," Hudson says as his hand rises and falls very slightly. "Can you do it again?"

I nod, even though I'm not sure I can. Still, it's better than dying, so I take another, deeper breath before letting it out slowly.

"That's it. You're doing great. Let's take one more and hold it this time, okay?"

I do as he says, taking an even longer, slower breath, and this time I hold it to the count of five before letting it out slowly. Then I take another breath and hold it to the count of seven.

As I do, I can feel my racing heartbeat slowing down just a little bit. Can feel my stomach unclenching and my muscles relaxing. Not a lot, but enough that it makes the next breath—and the one after that and the one after that—progressively easier to take.

This time, when I count back from twenty, I can actually feel it working. I can feel my anxiety receding and the fears that have been circling in my head since I woke up this morning slowly shrinking back down until they feel manageable once more.

Still, I count one more time—this time up to twenty—before taking another long, careful breath and letting it out.

Then I move so I can rest my forehead against Hudson's chest. "Thank you," I whisper.

He shakes his head. "Nothing to thank me for. You did that all by yourself."

It's not true—I was really spiraling this time, and he helped ground me when I couldn't find a way to ground myself. He was there for me, like he's always there for me, and as he wraps his arms around my waist and presses soft kisses to the top of my head, I tell myself that it's enough.

At least until he says, "I know you're still worried about what you saw at the Vampire Court, but I promise you, Grace, there's nothing for you to worry about."

45

You're Just a Big Parmallow Inside

"It's not that I'm worried," I tell him after several seconds. "It's that I don't understand why you aren't talking to me about all of this."

Hudson doesn't answer right away. Instead, he stares over my head, straight into the mirror that doesn't show his reflection or his expression. The silence goes on so long that I can't help wondering if he's trying to find the best words to answer my question—or if he's trying to figure out the best lie.

In the end, he does neither. He just smiles down at me and says, "'Time does not change us. It just unfolds us.'"

For a moment, I'm certain that I've heard him wrong. And then I realize—"Quotations? You're pulling out time quotations on me?"

"Do you know where it's from?" he asks, and I can tell from the look in his eyes that he's suddenly very serious about this, whatever this is.

"I don't have a clue," I answer.

He steps away, shoves a hand through his hair. "The quote comes from the sketchbooks of a Swiss playwright. Max Frisch."

"Okay," I tell him as I play the words over in my head, trying to understand what he means. I'm usually an expert in obscure Hudson-isms, but this is a lot to unwind.

"I want to unfold for you, Grace. I want to tell you everything in my head. But I just can't yet, no matter how much I want to."

I don't say anything for several seconds as I try to unpack what he's getting at. I know it's something important, but I'm just not there yet. Finally, for lack of a better guess, I ask, "Is this about the Vampire Court?"

"Fuck the Vampire Court," he answers curtly. "What they want or expect doesn't mean a bloody goddamn thing to me. And it shouldn't matter to you, either."

"Your happiness matters to me—"

"I've never been happier in my life than I am right now," he tells me. "Being your mate. Being gargoyle king. Building a life with each other and with our people. Do you believe that?"

"I do," I say, after pausing to make sure it's the best, most honest answer I can give him. "I just don't want you to regret anything."

"What's there for me to regret?"

"Were we wrong for not thinking about giving up the gargoyle throne in place of the vampire throne?" I ask after several more seconds pass. "And if we were, should we be considering it now? Is that what you don't want to talk to me about?"

If so, I can believe it. How could I not, when I know Hudson would sacrifice anything, everything, for my happiness? Is this one more thing he thinks he has to give up for me to be happy? One more choice he doesn't want to ask me to make because he thinks he'll lose?

Just the idea is devastating.

"The Vampire Court is your legacy. If you want it—"

"That abomination is not my legacy," he snaps back.

It's the first real emotion he's shown since I discovered Cyrus's destroyed office, and it has me rearing back in surprise.

He notices—of course he does—and ends up taking a deep breath of his own and blowing it out slowly. When he starts again, his voice is perfectly pleasant, even if the look in his eyes is still a little hot.

"What you and I are building together is my legacy, Grace. The Gargoyle Court will be my legacy. Our life, our children, will be my legacy—our legacy. And if I want to tell the Vampire Court to go fuck itself, then that's exactly what I'll do. But the rest?" He shakes his head, lets out a quiet sigh. "Letting you see the shit going on in my head right now as I try to unravel everything that is and was? I'm not ready to unfold for you like that. Not yet. And maybe not ever. Can you be okay with that?"

I want to tell him that I can—that I will—but the truth is, I just don't know. I don't need him to tell me everything inside him, but the big stuff? The remodeling the Vampire Court/taking a sledgehammer to your father's office/coming up with a plan that you think will somehow offset our duties to the Circle? Yeah, that's the stuff I want to hear about.

But then I think about everything Hudson's gone through to get right here, to this moment. The pain and the trauma that will live inside him forever—and that he may never unfold for me to deal with alongside him. And the truth is, I have to be okay with what he's asking. He went through hell in that Court—at the hands of his father, yes, but also at the hands of everyone else who knew about it and never tried to stop it, either.

It's only natural that dealing with all of this—the Court, the abdication, the lack of leadership in the Court trying to pull him back—is stirring up the hellish trauma of his life there. He's spent a long time burying it, ignoring it, making himself and his life the way he wants it to be. But trauma never stays buried, and I can only imagine what all that pain is doing to him now that he can't ignore it. Now that he can't control it on his own terms.

And instead of helping him deal with it, instead of accepting the parts he's willing to share, I keep pushing for more. Keep pushing to understand what I don't think he himself can understand yet.

Which pretty much makes me the arsehole in this situation and not him.

Because it's never anyone's right to tell someone else how, when, or even if they should deal with their trauma. Even their mate.

"Hey." I walk over to him and wrap my arms around his waist. He's stiff against me, his whole body braced as if for another attack, and I hate that he feels like that. Hate even more that I'm now one more thing in his life he has to brace himself against.

"I'm in no hurry," I tell him as I rub soothing circles on his back.

He stiffens slightly. "I don't know what that means."

"It means I'm willing to wait as little or as long as it takes for you to unfold this part of your life for me. And if you never can, then that's okay, too. I just want you to know that whatever you do, whatever you say, whatever you decide about the Vampire Court, I'm here for you, Hudson. Nothing is going to change that."

He nods, but he doesn't relax, and for a second I'm afraid it's too little, too late. That I've already pushed too hard and doubted too much and his trauma won't let him find his way back from that. But then he shudders against me, his arms wrapping tight around me, and I know that when it comes to us, everything is going to be okay.

The rest of the world may burn, but we'll be at the center of it all. Fireproof. And for now, that's all that matters.

I start to tell him so, but before I can, Tiola stands at the open door and calls, "Can I come in?"

"Of course!" Hudson answers, so desperate to escape this conversation that he nearly stumbles in his effort to get away from me.

"Mama made breakfast, Grace," she says. "So you need to hurry up or it's going to get cold."

"Well, then, I'd better get a move on."

He glances back at me as we exit the bathroom, and I give him a sharp look, letting him know that I might be willing to wait for him to talk to me, but that doesn't mean we run in the middle of a conversation—no matter how uncomfortable.

Breakfast is the last thing I want right now, but it would be rude to say so when Maroly obviously went out of her way to make it for us. Plus, who knows the next time we'll actually get a chance to eat?

"Come on, Tiola," I say, holding out a hand to her. "Let's go see if your mom made any homemade parmallow rolls."

"She did, she did, she did!" Tiola answers, clapping her hands. "And they should be cool enough to eat now."

"Well, let's go get some. My mouth is watering already."

"That's because my mom makes the best parmallow rolls in the whole world."

I start to say that she really does—and I had plenty of the sweet breakfast rolls when I lived in Adarie, so I should know—but then realize I wouldn't know that if this was my first time here. I wouldn't even know what parmallow rolls are.

The thought has a weight settling in my stomach, but I ignore it as I follow Tiola toward the kitchen. And say instead, "Well, I can't wait to try them!"

When we get to the dining room, the others are already there, chatting with Arnst and Maroly while they eat. I scan my friends' faces as I sit down, trying to figure out how everyone is doing.

They all seem fine. Flint and Jaxon are sitting on opposite ends of the table from each other, which sadly seems to be par for the course lately, but they're acting totally normal otherwise, so I don't know what to think of it. Eden and Heather have their heads close together as they talk about something I can't quite hear. And Macy...well, Macy seems just like she did yesterday.

Her green hair is spiked out in all directions. Her eyes are heavily made up with black liner, just like yesterday, and today that same shade of black has made it onto her lips and fingernails.

Somehow it suits her just as well as the rainbow hair and glitter she was rocking when I first met her—she looks cool as hell like this—but it still makes me sad.

Ugh. No wonder she and Hudson are such good friends. Underneath all the surface stuff, they deal with their shit exactly the same way. By locking it deep inside themselves and putting up no-trespassing signs all over the place so they can suffer alone.

The fact that they are no longer alone doesn't seem to make it any easier for them to deal, no matter how much I wish it did.

It matters to me, though, and as soon as we fix Mekhi and Lorelei, I'm going to make sure they both know I am a gargoyle—I can be as patient as a stone. And while they both have a hell of a lot of resolve on their sides, I will wait as long as it takes, be the wall they lean on when they're ready to let someone in.

It's that thought that has me grabbing a plate and filling it from the spread in the kitchen before finding a seat next to my cousin.

"Hey," I tell her as I sit down. "I like the new lipstick."

She just nods before taking a huge bite of her parmallow roll, then making the can't-talk-mouth-full gesture. It's all I can do not to roll my eyes. But that's okay. Like I said, I can be patient.

Breakfast goes by quickly, with Arnst and Maroly giving us advice on the best way to get to Adarie, since last time we were here—or, in their minds, *Hudson* was here—we had to flee over the mountains.

Hudson and Smokey join us halfway through, and my heart still jumps just a little at the sight of him.

He's fresh out of the shower, his hair still damp and falling over his forehead in the natural look that is my favorite on him. And when he slides into the chair next to mine, he smells good. Really good, like amber and ginger and just a touch of sandalwood.

I don't say anything to him, but when he bumps my leg under the table, I can't help but glance his way. And the crooked little half grin he gives me—the one he uses when he knows he's in trouble and is ready to get out of it—has me melting despite my best intentions.

It pisses me off just enough that I narrow my eyes at him. Which only makes him grin wider, because he knows he's got me. The jerk.

I don't say anything, though. Instead, I just smile sweetly as I pour him a cup of tea. And do a little celebratory dance inside when I see the slightest bit of wariness creep into his gaze.

Apparently, he knows me as well as I know him.

I guess we'll find out soon enough if that's a good thing or a bad one.

46

A Very Gated Community

"I've got to say, not going through the mountains definitely makes this trip easier," I comment as we make it to the outskirts of Adarie several hours later. Being able to fly made the trip *substantially* quicker and easier than the last time Hudson and I passed through here.

"I don't know. I kind of liked the mountains," Hudson answers. His voice is casual, but when he glances at me, there's a heat in his eyes that has my heart stuttering in my chest.

I know he's remembering the cave—and everything that happened there—because I am, too. It feels nice to actually remember our first... everythings together.

"So now what?" Eden asks, staring up at the huge purple stone wall that surrounds the town. The new, fancy-looking gate—built after the Shadow Queen's breach—is locked up tight. Worse, there doesn't seem to be anyone around who can open it for us.

"We could fly over," Flint suggests.

"No, we ring the bell," I correct, pulling on the cord that connects to the watchtower.

The bell tolls, and a sleepy-looking guard peers down at us. Adarie's people don't go many places, but they also don't get many visitors, except during Starfall.

"State your business," he yells down at us.

"We've come for a visit," Hudson calls up.

His eyes widen when he hears the British accent. "Hudson?" he asks, and as he leans over, I get a better look at his face and realize he's Nyaz's oldest son.

Hudson must figure out the same thing, because a genuine grin splits his face. "Hi, Anill. I've brought some friends to see the town."

"Any friends of Hudson's are friends of ours!" Anill moves out of sight.

Within moments, a loud clanking sound splits the air, and the huge gate begins to swing open.

"Just like that?" Flint asks, looking between Hudson and the gate like he can't quite believe it was that easy.

"Just like that," Hudson answers.

By the time the gate finishes swinging open, Anill is at the bottom of the watchtower waiting for us. He's grown a bit taller since the last time I saw him, and his thick purple hair is cut short now, but it suits the lavender guard uniform he's wearing. "How are you?" he asks, holding out his hand so Hudson can shake it.

"We're good," Hudson answers, trying to include me in the conversation, but I subtly shake my head at him.

Anill has no idea who I am. We may have talked almost daily when I lived here and even shared several meals together, but that doesn't matter now. At least not to him.

Hudson's smile dims as he remembers, and he reaches for me, wrapping an arm around my shoulders in a very un-Hudson-like way. "This is my mate, Grace," he tells Anill, whose eyes widen again.

"You found your mate? That's amazing! Congratulations, man!" He turns to me. "And congratulations to you, too. It must feel unreal to be mated to such an incredible guy."

Jaxon makes a slight choking sound at that, but I ignore him.

Instead, I smile at Anill and resist the urge to ask how his mate—the very sweet Stalina—is doing. "You're right. It really does feel unreal sometimes."

Flint snorts at my response, and even Macy giggles a little. But Hudson just lifts a brow at me before turning his attention back to Anill. "Thanks for opening the gate, man. The security looks like it's gotten tighter around here since I've been gone."

"The new mayor insists on it. We keep trying to tell her that the chances the Shadow Queen will attack us again are really low, but she still wants us to be prepared." He sighs heavily. "Overprepared, really.

But better safe than sorry, I guess."

"I'm sure dealing with the aftermath of that last battle was hard," I tell him. "It was so brutal."

Anill gives me a strange look, and I remember that, in his mind, I wasn't in that battle. I had nothing to do with fighting off the Shadow Queen or breaking Souil's grip on Adarie. "Hudson told me about it," I rush to cover. "He said everyone who fought that day was really brave."

"He was the brave one. Everyone in the whole area knows what he did for Adarie."

"I'm so glad. He deserves it." And I mean it. The thought that people truly do know and remember Hudson as the hero he is fills me with joy.

Hudson obviously doesn't feel the same way, though. The smile is gone from his face as he looks back and forth between Anill and me. And I can see the frustration in his eyes, can see the desire to tell Anill that I was here, too.

But I don't need him to do that.

Does it suck that Anill doesn't remember me? Yes. Does it suck even more that when we go into town, none of the people I cared about will know who I am? Absolutely. But blowing their minds with alternate histories isn't going to make them remember me—and it isn't going to give me back the friendships I lost when I was yanked out of the timeline.

And if it doesn't do that, why does it matter if they know I was here fighting or not? I don't do the things I do because I want credit for them. I do them because they need to be done and because I care about the people who would be hurt if I didn't. As long as Adarie is safe, as long as all the people I cared about when I lived here are happy and healthy, nothing else matters.

"I'm okay," I whisper to him. "I promise, Hudson."

He looks like he wants to argue, his blue eyes narrowed in concentration as his giant brain tries to figure a way around several immutable laws of time. But they are laws for a reason, and there's no getting around them—a fact that he will eventually have to concede.

In the meantime, I smile brightly at Anill and say, "Thank you so much for letting us in. We really appreciate it."

He takes the gratitude for what it was—a hint that we need to get going—and steps aside. "Make sure you stop by the inn and get rooms for tonight. My dad will be devastated if you stay anywhere else."

"Devastated" seems like a fairly over-the-top description, especially since the Nyaz I remember didn't have that deep of an emotional well. But Hudson assures him that we will before we head through the gate en masse.

And then stop dead as we run smack-dab into a giant sign that says, WELCOME TO VEGAVILLE.

47

For several seconds, none of us move. We just stand there, staring at the giant wooden sign with what I'm pretty sure is Hudson's name on it. Vegaville? Have they seriously renamed Adarie *Vegaville*?

I love Hudson more than anyone on earth, and even my mind is boggling.

"What the actual fuck?" Jaxon asks the question that begs to be asked.

"I thought you said this place was named Adarie?" Macy gives me a questioning look.

"It...was," Hudson answers as he continues staring at the sign, unblinking. Ironically, I'm pretty sure he's the most shocked one of all of us. "I don't know what...changed that."

"You did, obviously." Macy gives him a good-job punch on the shoulder, which somehow only makes him look more bewildered.

I, however, am completely over the shock now and determined not to let this opportunity pass me by. "Go stand next to the sign. I want to take a pic," I tell him as I pull out my phone and turn it on.

The look Hudson levels at me is one I haven't seen since we were locked in his lair together. "I don't think so."

He starts walking—and not anywhere near the sign.

"What the actual fuck?" Jaxon repeats, still staring up at the sign like he expects it to spontaneously combust. Or maybe like he thinks it's going to suddenly flash the words "Just Kidding" in really huge letters. When it does neither, he finally shakes his head and follows Hudson—as does everyone else.

We walk the outermost block of Adarie—excuse me, Vegaville—in silence, but then Heather banishes the awkwardness when she says, "So, tell us more about Adarie, Grace. What's your favorite thing about this place?"

"I've got a lot of favorite things," I answer as we turn the corner. "But I think my absolute favorite thing is definitely—" I break off as we pass a souvenir shop—one with a giant poster of Hudson right in the middle of the front window.

"Is that…" Flint moves to get a closer look at the sculpted bust below the poster, then nods to himself. "Yeah, that's definitely your face, Hudson."

"It really is," Hudson says, sounding at least as concerned as he is befuddled at this point. The concern ratchets up to alarm as Macy and I all but race for the door. "Hey! Where are you going?" he asks.

"Where do you think we're going?" I call over my shoulder. And I know Mekhi and Lorelei need us to hurry, but we already decided this morning that we'd give ourselves a week to find the Shadow Queen. Time might work differently in the Shadow Realm—years here with Hudson was only months back at Katmere—but we don't want to assume we have any extra time because of that. Lorelei will text us with an update when we leave this realm, but she assured us she could help keep the poison at bay for at least the next week and a half. Guilt aside, this is too good to miss. Way too good.

Hudson catches up with us in a few steps. "You don't really think that's necessary, do you?"

"Are you kidding me?" Eden squawks as she holds open the door. "Nothing has *ever* been more necessary."

We're rushing in just as a guy in his early twenties walks out. He takes one look at Hudson and says, "Dude, great costume."

"What are you talking about?" Hudson answers in a very annoyed tone.

"Whoa. You've even got the accent down!" When Hudson continues to stare at him blankly, he finally says, "The H.V. costume, man. It looks totally realistic."

"That's because it *is* realistic," Hudson growls.

"Yeah, that's what I'm saying. Totally believable."

"H.V. costume?" Macy queries.

"Umm, yeah. Obviously your friend is rocking a premium Hudson Vega costume. One of the best I've ever seen, in fact."

"Hudson Vega costume," Jaxon repeats like he's finally heard it all.

"Yeah, it's, like, the most popular costume in Vegaville."

"Of course it is." Jaxon nods toward the store. "Do they sell them in here?"

"They sell everything in here. It's like full-blown H.V. worship."

"Hudson Vega worship?" Flint nearly chokes on the words. "I'm sorry, but did he just say Hudson Vega *worship*?"

"Pretty sure he did," Eden replies, and pure mischief twinkles in her eyes.

"I don't— I can't— What does that—" Eventually, Flint gives up trying to formulate a full thought and just throws his hands up in the air.

"Tell them, dude," the guy says to Hudson. "You obviously get it."

"I don't know about worship." Hudson puts his tongue firmly in his cheek. "But I am the president of the Hudson Vega fan club."

"What the actual fuck?" Jaxon mutters under his breath once more.

The guy grins. "And here I thought that title went to my girlfriend. It's why I'm here, in fact. Their collectibles are second to none."

"Collectibles?" I repeat.

"Oh yeah. There's, like, an entire aisle over that way." He points toward the left side of the store.

"What the *everlasting* fuck?" Jaxon says this time.

He starts to say something else, but I'm too busy heading in the direction the guy pointed to listen. I just hope I'll be able to find what he's talking—

I turn down an aisle and freeze. Because there is *absolutely no chance* of me missing the collectibles he's referring to. No chance at all.

They take up the entire aisle. *The entire aisle.*

There are T-shirts with "Hudson Vega Forever" scrawled across them. Cups with "Bloody hell" written on them in red letters. Notebooks with his smirking face staring out from the cover. Kitchen towels with vampire fangs and a variety of Hudson's favorite Britishisms embroidered on them. Statues—so many different kinds of statues that

I lose count somewhere around the twelfth pose I find.

And, maybe most surprisingly, vials of dirt labeled "Authentic dirt from TAM farm, touched by Hudson Vega."

Suddenly, that moment when Arnst ran out after dinner last night to chase away the dirt thieves makes so much more sense. As does his and Maroly's evasiveness afterward. Those people were there to steal dirt that just might have possibly been touched by Hudson Vega.

And here I've been low-key worried that it was the hunters. This is so much better.

Not to mention, the question of where they got the statue of Hudson has also been answered. They didn't have to have it specially cast after all—they just needed to walk into the closest souvenir shop.

My mind is boggled. Actually, it's whatever word is beyond boggled. Because nowhere in my wildest fantasies could I possibly have imagined something like this happening—to Hudson or to anyone else for that matter.

Except maybe Harry Styles.

I glance at Hudson to see how he's taking this latest development and find him staring at a statue of himself flexing his arm muscles up near his head with a truly horrified expression on his face.

When he sees me watching him, his face smooths out. But he gives another one of those British sniffs he's so fond of and says, "I'm fairly certain I've never made that gesture in my life."

"Don't worry, babe. It looks to me like they've taken a lot of artistic license here." To prove my point, I hold up a shot glass with directions for Hudson's favorite "Bloody Cocktail" on it.

"I can't drink anything in this beverage," he says as he squints to read the tiny writing on the sides of the glass.

"Exactly." I smile up at him. "I say forget about the inaccuracies of it all and just enjoy it. I mean, who else do you know who has a whole aisle devoted to souvenirs of himself?"

"Not to mention his very own fan club," Macy teases, and for the first time in a long time, there's an impish gleam in her eye. "I think we should join, Grace."

"I completely agree," I answer with a laugh. "I can spill all his secrets."

Hudson rolls his eyes. "You're hilarious."

"This is my favorite," Eden tells him, picking up a Hudson mask from the costume section and putting it over her face. "How do I look?"

"I'm in hell," Jaxon opines to no one in particular as he stares in horror at the shelves. "In actual hell."

"You'll be okay." Flint plops a snow hat that reads "I do it like Hudson" on top of his boyfriend's head, then pulls out his camera. "Here, let's take a selfie."

I've never seen Jaxon move so fast in my life, and that's saying something.

"Over my dead body," he quips with a half smile, finally seeming to see the humor in all of this, but he still wastes no time yanking the hat off his head and tossing it back to Flint before racing for the store exit.

"Is that your way of saying you like the baseball cap better?" Flint calls after him, which has all of us cracking up as we head toward the exit as well.

"What the bloody hell is happening here?" Hudson murmurs to me as we make our way through the aisles.

"I don't know, but I really do think you should enjoy it."

"Enjoy it?" He looks nearly as horrified as Jaxon at the mere suggestion.

"Yes, enjoy it. People have finally figured out how fabulous you are, and I, for one, am here for it."

"There's a difference between not being reviled and having people dress up as you for costume parties," he tells me.

"There is," I agree, sliding my arm around his waist to give him a hug. "But there are way worse people they could dress up as."

He just rolls his eyes again, but I can see the pleased flush creeping up his cheekbones. He may be totally embarrassed by the excess of what we just saw, but I know the lost little boy inside him well enough to recognize he's just a bit pleased as well.

Which is why I grab a Mrs. Vega hat the second he takes Smokey out to get some exercise. After all, if everyone else in this town is going to be wearing one, I figure his real mate had better be wearing one, too.

And it's totally worth it when he sees me outside, because he laughs and laughs and laughs and laughs.

"It's a good look on you," he tells me, tugging on the brim of the bedazzled black-and-red cap I couldn't resist.

"You're a better look on me," I murmur while everyone else is too busy checking out Adarie—Vegaville—to notice.

"I am at that." His eyes grow dark. "In fact, maybe when—"

He breaks off as an artsy wraith with tufts of purple hair sticking out around a very shiny purple bald spot walks up to us. "Hudson? I heard Anill telling some people you were actually in town. Man, what an opportunity! You're excited, right?" he asks, extending a purple card.

"Excited?" Hudson asks, nonplussed, arms crossed over his chest.

"Oh yes," the man says, rubbing his hands together. "We are about to make *history*, man!"

48

Talk About
Star(fall) Power

"I have trouble imagining that," Hudson answers, studiously avoiding taking the guy's card. I, however, accept it with a smile, taking a moment to appreciate the glittery edges.

"My name's Aspero, and I'm a concert promoter here in town. I've been waiting for you to come back to Vegaville *forever*, and how perfect is it that you came right before Starfall? I can do so much with that."

"Concert promoter?" Jaxon asks as he steps closer, sounding equal parts fascinated and amused.

Aspero doesn't take his eager gaze from my mate. "I would love the chance to sit down and talk numbers and dates with you, Hudson. Your performance at Starfall is still the most talked-about concert in the history of Noromar, and I'd love the chance to duplicate it—with tickets and an exclusive venue this time, so we can both make a lot of money."

"I'm not a singer," Hudson answers and starts walking toward the inn. He's not trying to be rude. I know Hudson well enough to know that. He only sang to save me from embarrassment, and now he's looking ten shades of uncomfortable at the reminder. I reach for his hand and squeeze, but he doesn't meet my eyes.

"Don't be so modest, brother." Jaxon claps him on the back.

"We all know that isn't true," Aspero tells Hudson, rushing to catch up, not the slightest bit put off by his lack of interest. "Your voice is great, your looks are pretty good, and you've got that star presence that's so hard to find. Plus, you've already built up a base of loyal fans."

"Yeah, Hudson, your looks are *pretty good*." Jaxon is outright chuckling now. "You should get up on stage and give all the kids a thrill. Make those handsome Vega genes work for you."

Jaxon snickers like a rabid hyena—but stops abruptly when Aspero's eyes narrow on him and he asks, "Do you sing, too?" He looks Jaxon up and down. "Now, you're some *real* eye candy. The fans would go wild for you."

And I can't help it. I snort-laugh so hard I almost choke on my own spit. Hudson and I meet eyes—and both roll them at the same time. He shakes his head and murmurs to me, "It's the hair."

Jaxon levels a glare on the promoter that has the man shuffling his feet to get to the other side of Hudson. "Do not speak to me again, should you wish to keep your head," he bites out, then turns a goofy grin back on Hudson like the concert promoter is already forgotten. "It's more than the hair, bro, and we both know it."

Aspero nods over and over, and I'm honestly not sure which of Jaxon's statements he's agreeing with. At least until he says, "But Hudson has his bravery and courage giving him additional sexy points."

Even Macy laughs at that, calling out to Eden. "Hey, you hear that? They give out sexy points for bravery in Vegaville."

"I always wanted to be rich," Eden jokes back, and Heather joins in the laughter.

None of it is said to make fun of the promoter, but I doubt he'd notice any rudeness anyway. He seems completely focused on Hudson and convincing him to put on a repeat performance.

"Come on, man," Aspero urges. "Just imagine the fans going wild." He moves a hand in front of us to emphasize each word: "One. Night. Only." He drops his hand and grins. "We'll make history!"

Hudson's teeth snap together with an audible click. "We don't have time for that."

Jaxon addresses the rest of the gang. "What do you think, everyone? Because I'm certain we could make time if it means giving Hudson a chance to connect with his *fan base*, right?" He turns back to Hudson. "You could sign their arms and everything."

"Oh, I definitely think he should do it. It would give me something to live for," Eden answers.

Flint guffaws. "Well, then, now you've got to do it, Hudson."

"I'm not interested." My mate deliberately speeds up his walk in an effort to shake the concert promoter.

But he's obviously underestimated Aspero's determination, because it isn't long before the man is running full-out behind Hudson in an effort to keep up, the rest of us trailing behind. "You haven't...even heard...my pitch."

He's breathing heavily, but he's managing to hold his own as Hudson turns the corner and gets even faster.

"I don't need to hear your pitch to know I have no desire to get up on a stage in front of who knows how many people—"

"Thousands!" Aspero pants. "That's what I'm trying to tell you. Give me...five minutes...I know I...can change...your mind."

"I don't want you to change my mind. And I don't want to give a concert," Hudson replies in a strained voice that I know means he's at the end of his patience. Aspero, however, definitely hasn't clued in to that fact yet.

"But your fans would go wild! A little publicity, a brilliant album— which you're already on your way to composing, I have no doubt. A little fan baiting. You'll be rich before you know it."

"I *am* rich," Hudson answers as he steers me around the next corner.

"No such thing as being *too* rich," the promoter encourages. "I can double your fame and your fortune with just a few days of prep work."

"Aww, come on, Hudson," Jaxon taunts. "Everyone knows you want fame and fortune!"

This time, Hudson doesn't even bother answering. He just fades away—which is an answer in and of itself, I suppose.

Aspero finally figures out he's not going to be able to keep up and yells after him, "Call me before you sign with anyone else," and then disappears as suddenly as he appeared.

Thank God.

Of course, his disappearance gives Jaxon and the rest of the gang a golden opportunity to catch up to Hudson and rib him mercilessly about his fan base and touring schedule. All of which Hudson does his best to ignore as we get closer and closer to Adarie's—I mean Vegaville's—downtown.

As we finally make the turn onto the main street, my own excitement gets the better of me and I rush ahead, anxious to see the town square without Artelya and Asuga in it. Anxious to prove to myself that me getting written out of the timeline isn't the only thing that's changed.

Intellectually, I know it's not.

I've met Artelya at the Gargoyle Court.

Fought beside her in the final battle against Cyrus.

Consulted her several times on matters regarding the Court since I've become queen.

And I watched her question a hunter in Ireland two days ago.

Intellectually, I know that. I do. But that doesn't mean my mind isn't playing tricks on me. And it doesn't mean that I don't need to see with my own eyes an empty spot where her frozen body used to rest.

Since finding out about the paranormal world and falling in love—first with Jaxon, and now with Hudson, forever—I've had to take so much on faith. Had to believe things that I had no proof of and that didn't make sense when held up to everything I'd learned until I was seventeen years old.

And now I have to believe—have to accept—that I was ripped out of the timeline here. That all of these memories of people and places and Hudson, so many memories of Hudson, are all true even though they don't actually exist anymore. At least not anywhere that isn't in his head and mine.

I can believe that. No matter how hard it is, I can even accept that it had to happen that way. But that doesn't mean I don't want just a little bit of proof. Just a little bit of confirmation that I'm not the only one this strange, bizarre, unbelievable thing has happened to. And that the reason Artelya doesn't remember me is because she was yanked out of the timeline, too.

So yes, I rush ahead to Noromar's town square, determined to prove to myself that the statue of the gargoyle and the dragon that was in it the whole time I lived here is actually gone.

And it is.

My first step into the square shows me that Artelya and Asuga really are gone.

Everything I remember really did happen. Relief sweeps through me, even before I realize another statue has replaced the one that stood in the center of town for a thousand years. And this one is so. Much. Bigger.

"Are you fucking with me?" Jaxon says as he, too, steps into the square. "You're just fucking with me at this point, right, bro? This can't actually be real."

But even Hudson is taken aback by this newest statue that seems to tower over every building that edges the square—even the multiple-story inn. Because this isn't just any giant statue.

No, this statue is *special.*

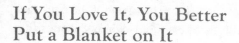

49

If You Love It, You Better Put a Blanket on It

Carved out of shining purple marble and standing at least thirty feet tall is a very lifelike rendition of a *very* naked, *very* well-endowed Hudson.

"I'm trying not to look at it," Macy chokes out, and by "it" I know she means a certain unmissable part of the statue. "But it's impossible."

"It really is," Eden agrees, looking half impressed and half terrified.

"It's just, like, right there," Heather says. "Just, like, right there, Grace. Really big and right there."

I nod, because she's absolutely right. It is *really big* and *right freaking there*.

"It's okay, baby." Flint pats Jaxon's back soothingly, even though he, too, seems to be mesmerized by the statue. "I still think I got the better brother."

"Are you *fucking kidding me*?" Jaxon says again, and this time I don't know if he's talking to Flint, to all of us, or to the universe itself.

Eden's shaking her head by this point. "You poor girl."

"Grace." It's the first sound Hudson's made since he's seen the statue, and it sounds really strained.

"You okay?" I ask, because while the statue is gorgeous and obviously a piece of art, I can see how it might feel like a violation, especially to someone like Hudson, who keeps so much of his true self hidden from the world. And while this is just his physical self, it's still a whole lot of exposure.

"I can't—" He breaks off and takes a deep breath, then blows it out slowly. "How am I supposed to walk past that thing to get to the inn? I feel so…"

"Naked?" Macy quips.

"That," he agrees quietly. "Exactly that."

Smokey, who slept through most of the trip and our entire walk through town, chooses this moment to peek her head out of the backpack slung over one of Hudson's shoulders. She squeals when she sees that Hudson is still carrying her and chitters away at him for several seconds before crawling out of the backpack and scooting up to his neck.

But she's barely settled herself there when she makes a loud squealing noise, followed by what can only be a gasp. And then she throws her little baby hands over her little baby eyes and lets out a loud, keening cry.

"It's okay, Smokey," I tell her, reaching up to rub her head.

She snaps at me in response, her teeth coming together so hard that they make a clicking noise. And then she complains to me and about me in a series of squeals and snarls. I have no idea what she's saying, but it sounds an awful lot like she holds me single-handedly responsible for the fact that there's a naked statue of Hudson in the town square.

"I didn't do it!" I tell her, careful to keep my hand—and all my other body parts—away from her mouth this time. And every other part of her as well.

"Smokey, it's okay," Hudson tells her, pulling her off his shoulder and cradling her in his hands.

She stands up as tall as she can and looks him in the eye, her little hands on either side of his face as she studies him for long seconds. I don't know what she sees there—maybe his embarrassment about the statue, maybe something else—but she lets out a long, high-pitched wail.

And then scampers out of his hands and down his body to the ground.

"Wait! Smokey! Where are you going?" Hudson starts to fade after her, but I grab his arm to hold him in place.

"Give her a second," I tell him. "She's not leaving the square, so you can keep an eye on her and catch up to her if you need to. But she's obviously got something going on."

"That's an understatement," Macy says as we all watch Smokey race across the square to the patch of purple grass that Hudson and I had more than one picnic on during our time here.

It turns out a couple is in our favorite spot near the wishing well right now, lavender quilt spread across the bright violet grass and picnic basket open.

Smokey heads straight toward them, zipping over the grass and stopping right in the middle of their blanket. Once there, she starts to tell them something, because her little arms are flapping and her head is bobbing and her squeaks are filling the air as she moves closer and closer to the people.

They start backing up, not sure what to do with what looks to them like a pissed-off, out-of-control umbra. But the more they retreat, the more Smokey advances on them. And while she is small and adorable, she also looks ferocious as hell right now, and I get why the people are scrambling away from her.

"Maybe you should—" I start, but Hudson has already reached the same conclusion I have and is fading across the square to get Smokey.

He's one second too late, though, because she sees him coming and bobs and weaves in an attempt to evade him. The couple uses the distraction to put some real distance between them and Smokey, which apparently was what the umbra was waiting for all along.

Because the second they leave the blanket, she lets out a triumphant screech. Then she snatches it up, basket and food launching into the air, and speeds back across the square.

"What is she doing?" Macy asks as we all watch, transfixed by the tiny umbra with the giant attitude.

"Terrorizing the locals?" Flint answers dryly.

"Obviously," Macy agrees. "But she's got some kind of plan—"

She breaks off as Smokey's plan becomes clear when she makes a beeline toward the statue of Hudson.

"Wait a minute," Heather says, mouth open in surprise. "Is she going to—"

"Yes," I tell her with a laugh. "That's exactly what she's going to do."

Hudson almost catches her at the base of the statue, but she darts between its legs with a squeal. Then, under everyone in the square's fascinated eyes, she scurries up the statue's right leg all the way to its hip.

She gives another loud and disapproving squeal as she comes face-to-face with the body part that's caused so much commotion. Then she races around it over and over again until she somehow manages to tie the quilt around Statue Hudson's hips, sarong-style.

"Is it me," Jaxon asks, "or is my brother now wearing the skimpiest towel in history?"

"Maybe not in history," Heather tells him. "But it's pretty skimpy."

"It covers everything important, though," Flint chimes in.

Jaxon breathes a sigh of relief that I have no doubt Hudson is echoing all the way across the square. "Thank God."

I watch as Smokey shimmies back down the leg of the statue to where Hudson is waiting. But instead of leaping into his open arms, she rushes around the base of the statue several times, wiggling and jumping and waving her hands in the air.

Macy sounds as amused as she does worried when she asks, "What's she doing now?"

"A victory dance?" Heather suggests.

I realize she's right. Little Baby Smokey is doing her very elaborate, very complicated version of a touchdown dance. In fact, if there were a football anywhere around right now, I'm pretty sure she'd be spiking it.

When she finally finishes, she zips back toward Hudson—who's been watching her with wide eyes and a giant grin on his face—and dives into his waiting hands. But since everyone in the square has been gawking at her, all that attention transfers immediately to Hudson.

It only takes a moment for them to recognize him. And then all hell breaks loose.

50

I'm with the
Vamparazzi

People race toward Hudson from all directions—including the couple whose picnic blanket is now providing Statue Hudson with a modicum of modesty.

"Do we need to get in there and save him?" Eden asks as the crowd descends on Hudson. "Or is this a good thing?"

"They built a giant statue in the middle of their square to honor him," Heather answers. "I think he'll be okay."

"Eventually," Eden agrees. "After he kisses a bunch of babies and shakes a bunch of hands."

"A *bunch* of hands," Flint echoes, watching the crowd grow and grow and grow.

"So what are we supposed to do in the meantime?" Jaxon comments with a yawn. "Tell me we aren't going to stand around waiting for him to extricate himself from that mess."

He sounds just caustic enough to get my back up. "'That mess,' as you call it, is a group of very nice people," I say as I recognize Tinyati and Nyaz and so many of the other people we knew when we were here. "They care about him and just want to say hello."

Jaxon rolls his eyes. "I'm not saying they can't say hello, Grace. I'm just saying I don't want to be here for *all* of it."

Fair. "I suppose we can check in to the inn now," I muse. Though it will take almost all the money Arnst gave us. Then again, we left so abruptly last time that everything we abandoned might be exactly the same. Not for me, obviously, but for Hudson. Things like his bank account, for instance.

I make a mental note to tell him to check it before starting across the street toward the inn. Nyaz is out in the square, gathered around Hudson with all the others, but he's got an assistant working behind the desk. The name tag attached to her sweater reads Amnonda, and her eyes widen when I approach her.

"You're the group with Hudson Vega, aren't you?" she asks.

"We are, yes," I answer warily. "How do you know that?"

"You mean besides the fact that you're one of the few paranormal visitors we've had through here outside of Starfall in quite a while?" Amnonda says with a shrug.

"Oh wow, I didn't realize tourist business had declined," I say, although I suppose it makes sense without the Shadow Queen needing to chase foreigners to Adarie in the hopes that one would bring a time dragon to the former mayor.

"It's okay. Vegaville is a huge draw among wraiths all over Noromar who want to see where the Hero of Adarie saved the Shadow Realm." She offers us a huge grin. "Besides, Anill told us to expect you. Nyaz has already set rooms aside for you, and he wanted me to tell Hudson that they're on the house for tonight."

"Hero of Adarie," I repeat and find myself smiling. I like it. "But Nyaz doesn't have to do that. We've got money." I reach into my pocket and pull out the bills Arnst gave us before we left the farm. "Besides, we really need to speak with Nyaz. Do you know when he'll be coming back?"

"If you stay another night, you can talk to Nyaz about that," she says, waving my money away. "But for tonight, his orders are clear. Hudson and his friends stay for free." I start to protest again, but she holds a hand up to stop me. "It's the least we can do."

I nod, letting the matter go.

"And to answer your other question, Nyaz said he's coming back later tonight to work the late shift," she says. "I'll leave him a note that you need to speak with him. For now, please enjoy your rooms."

"That's very nice of him," Flint tells her from behind me.

"Well, we can't have Hudson staying anywhere else, nor his friends." Her smile gets wider. "I still can't believe Hudson is here. He's really here!"

"He really is!" Jaxon says with fake enthusiasm, and I stamp my foot on his.

Amnonda doesn't seem to notice—or she's too excited to care. "I was away at school when Hudson was here before," she tells us as she pulls the keys for our rooms off the pegboard behind her. "But I've heard all the stories."

I want to ask her what stories she's talking about. What do Hudson's days here look like if I've been erased from the timeline? Was he still a teacher? How many time dragons did he actually have to kill? How did he eliminate Souil, as he doesn't have the same kind of powers that I have?

There are so many other questions bouncing around inside me that I want answers to. So many questions about what's real and what's not real about his time here—about *our* time here.

It's like the old adage about the tree in the forest. If a tree falls and no one is around to hear it, does it actually make a sound? If I was here but no one remembers me, did my time here even exist?

Intellectually, I know it did.

I fell in love with Hudson here.

I met Arnst and Maroly, Tiola and Smokey, Caoimhe and Lumi and Nyaz here.

I killed a time dragon and fought a time wizard and battled the Shadow Queen herself. That has to count for something, right?

So why do I still feel so lost? Why do I still feel like something important has broken and I don't know how to put it back together again?

"Thanks for checking us in." I give Amnonda the best smile I can muster as I distribute the keys among my friends. Hudson and I are in one room, Jaxon and Flint in another, and everyone else has their own room.

"Why don't you all go put your stuff in your rooms and relax for a little while?" I say as we walk toward the stairs. "I'm going to see if I can remove Hudson from the chaos outside so we can hit the town and try to figure out where this smuggler is."

And it is total and utter chaos right now. More people have joined the original crowd, and while I can see Hudson—with Smokey perched on his shoulder—trying to make his way toward the inn, he barely gets a couple of steps before someone else stops him to say hello and ask how he's doing.

If they were strangers, I think he'd find it easier to just wave and move on. But they're not. Most of the people in the square know Hudson—they served him food, sold him clothes and other things, or even had kids in his class during his time here.

I slide through the crowd and wait for there to be a small lull between people.

As soon as there's more than a five-second pause between one person and the next, I swoop in for the kill—or in this case, the rescue.

"I'm sorry," I say as I loop my arm through his. "But I've got to steal Hudson for a little while."

A disappointed murmur moves through the crowd, and I hold up a hand. "I promise I'll bring him back later, though. In fact, Hudson wants to reacquaint himself with all his old haunts, so he'll be around a lot in the next few days."

The disappointment changes to excitement at the thought of Hudson visiting their stores and restaurants, and the crowd parts a lot more easily than it did at first.

A few more hands shaken, a few more hellos called to old friends, and I've gotten him through the square and into the inn.

"Are you handling me?" he asks as I move him toward the stairs.

I shoot him a look. "No offense, but somebody had to, or you would have been there all night."

"Believe me, I'm not complaining. That was…"

"Amazing," I tell him with a smile. "Absolutely amazing."

"A little overwhelming," he corrects with a bemused look. "But, if you say so, who am I to argue?"

"They're so proud of what you did for them, and obviously so happy to see that you're okay after our very abrupt departure."

"Yeah." His grin fades. "I'm sorry they don't remember you."

"I'm not." I shake my head. "I mean, it feels strange, almost like that time didn't happen, but I'm not the least bit sorry not to be the center of attention. I'm more than happy to leave that to you."

We're at our room now, and as the door closes behind us, Hudson grabs me and pulls me against him. "That time did happen, Grace. Fucked-up timeline or not, we *were* here together. Even if they don't remember, even if you'd never remembered, it still happened. I will always remember you."

"I know, Hudson." I hug him back because he's trembling just a little now—whether from the emotional overload of what just happened in the square or because of the emotional overload that still occasionally hits one or the other of us when we think about those first months when I brought him to Katmere with me. "I loved you when I didn't remember, and I love you now that I do. Nothing is going to change that."

He pulls back just enough to look into my eyes. And I see all the love I have inside me for him shining down at me.

Part of me wants nothing more than to curl up in this room with Hudson and stay right here forever. Things were simpler when we were in Adarie. Easier. And right now, simple and easy sound really good.

But no matter how good it sounds, it's not to be. Not when we have a Shadow Queen to find and a barrier we still need to confirm *can even be crossed* to reach the Curator—all as quickly as we possibly can, so we can save Mekhi from certain death and keep Lorelei from suffering any more than she has to.

"What are you thinking about?" Hudson asks right before he lowers his head and drops a soft kiss on my lips.

As he does, I wrap my arms around his neck, hold him close, and steal a few more kisses. Not enough to have either one of us eyeing the bed in the corner—the same bed we shared for our entire time in the Shadow Realm—but definitely enough to muddle my thoughts and chase away the chill that slithers through me when I think of everything we have waiting for us on the other side of the barrier.

"I love you," I whisper against his lips, relishing the way his mouth instantly curves into a smile.

"I love you more," he answers before slowly, reluctantly pulling away. "You didn't answer my question."

"What question is that?" I'm not prevaricating. I really don't remember what he asked me. It's not the first time I've had that problem when Hudson is touching me, and I'm pretty sure it won't be my last.

"What were you thinking about a minute ago? You looked…"

"Serious?" I fill in the blank for him.

He shakes his head, those blue eyes watchful as all hell now. "Scared, actually. You looked scared. I just wish I knew why."

51

Sugar and Spice
and Everything Ice

"I'm not scared," I tell him, and it's true. Or at least I want it to be true, and that's pretty much the same thing, isn't it? "I'm just nervous about whether or not we're going to find a smuggler to help us get back to our realm. If we don't, then our entire plan is ruined before we even really get started."

"We'll find one," Hudson says confidently.

I bite my lip. "There's something else I've been worrying about," I say.

Hudson reaches up to smooth a curl behind my ear and asks, "And what's that?"

"If smugglers really *can* get contraband in and out of a prison, then why didn't the mayor use one to leave? He stayed here for a *thousand years*, Hudson. While Lorelei was out there suffering without him." I can't keep the plaintive tone from my voice.

But Hudson just gives me a soft smile. "You just answered the why, Grace. He lived here for a *thousand years*...and didn't age, which we found out was because he had absorbed that first dragon's time magic." He shifts his hand down to hold mine. "Jikan said this prison is unstable, held together by his time dragons. I think that means time magic is literally the steel cage keeping everyone trapped inside—wraiths, umbras, and time dragons."

I take in this explanation, chew on it for a second before working up the courage to ask, "Do you think that means I can't leave?"

His eyebrows shoot up. "Why would the mayor being trapped here by absorbing time mag—" He shakes his head, squeezing my hand. "Because the arrow of time entered you, right?"

"Well, yeah," I say and thump my chest for effect. "*Three* time dragons' worth of magic slammed into me, Hudson. And I can assure you, I would have no idea what was still bouncing around inside me—it's a mess in there."

He chuckles, as I knew he would, before saying, "Well, I know what's in there, and it's all beautiful. I also think that magic is what took your memories and reset your timeline." He gestures over my shoulder to the town square outside our window. "Just look at the effects. No one remembers you. That must have taken a lot of time magic to reset all of these people's memories, don't you think?"

"I guess we'll find out," I say, but I can't keep the skepticism from my voice. "And we still need to talk to Nyaz."

"He said I should stop by later, when he's working. He has some errands to run right now, but he'll be back tonight."

"I'll come with you," I tell him as I pull him down for one last kiss before heading to the bathroom to wash my face and try to tame my hair into some semblance of order.

Hudson, in the meantime, pulls a blanket and pillow out of the closet and arranges them into a comfortable-looking bed under the window. Then he coaxes the now exhausted Baby Smokey out of his backpack and onto the bed.

"She wore herself out." I cross to my backpack and pull out the glittery silver ribbon we bought at the drugstore. "Here, give her this."

"You should give it to her," he says, stepping back so I can get to her.

I roll my eyes. "One sparkly ribbon isn't going to make her like me."

"No, but it may make her *dislike* you less," he answers with a self-satisfied grin that makes me want to strangle him with the ribbon in question.

I settle for sticking out my tongue at him instead. Which makes the very tired Smokey yowl at me in reprimand even as she snatches the ribbon from my hands and wraps it around herself.

"Seriously?" I say, looking between her and Hudson. "You can't take the ribbon from me and be mean to me at the exact same time."

She chitters back at me, and while I don't understand what she's saying, I definitely understand the tone—which is completely snarky in all the worst ways.

"It appears that she can," Hudson tells me in a voice so innocent that I know it's taking everything he's got not to laugh.

I shoot him a glare that promises all kinds of terrible things if he gives in to the urge, and he responds with his suavest, most charming smile. The fact that it works on me, even when I know exactly what he's doing and why he's doing it, only makes me grumpier.

There was a chill in the air earlier, so I trade my magenta sweater for a warmer, plusher dark-green one and pull it on over my T-shirt before heading for the door.

Hudson pulls on a purple sweater, then asks, "Where do you want to go while we wait to talk to Nyaz?" as we begin to round up our friends.

"I was thinking..." I knock on Macy's door first and am unsurprised when she throws it open less than two seconds later. She may be lost and depressed at the moment, but Macy is still Macy. And that means she's always the first one in line for an adventure.

He glances down at me with a serious expression. "Maybe we could start at Gillie's."

My heart kicks into overdrive—and not because my mate just read my mind. "Do you think she's okay?" I whisper. "We saw her get hit by time-dragon fire, so her timeline should have reset. But she looked so... so..." *Dead.* I can't get the image of her throwing herself in front of the mayor out of my head—her limp body, right there in the town square—

Hudson saves me from spiraling. "Smokey is here. I think Gillie will be, too. Let's go find out for sure."

"Who's Gillie?" Macy asks before banging on Eden's door.

"The best baker in Adarie," Hudson answers, his hand rubbing soothing circles on my back. "Though even she couldn't teach Grace how to make a simple pastry."

I roll my eyes at him, but his ribbing works. My stomach has settled from extreme nausea to simple nerves, because he's right—Gillie *will* be at her bakery, ready with perfect baked goods and all of the town's gossip.

The bakery may not be at the actual center of town, but in all the ways that matter, it really is the town's center. Hudson may joke about the fact that I only lasted a day working there—my choux was truly terrible—but we both whiled away many an hour in the place during our first trip.

Not only does Gillie make the best pastries in Adarie, and maybe the entire Shadow Realm, but she also makes a mean cup of tea. One Hudson rarely went a day without during our time here.

Once we've got the others, we hit the town.

"So where do smugglers hang out?" Flint asks no one in particular in a low undertone.

"The docks, normally," Heather answers. "At least on TV."

I shake my head. "That may be so, but Adarie's landlocked. So I'm pretty sure there are no docks here."

"I think you mean Vegaville," Flint teases.

"How could I forget?" I wink at Hudson. "We're going to Gillie's bakery first regardless."

Of course, to get there we have to cross through the center of town square, right past the giant statue of Hudson. I deliberately try not to look at it, but it's so in your face that ignoring it is pretty much impossible.

On the plus side, Smokey's picnic blanket seems to be holding its own for now, so that's one less thing to worry about.

"The bakery where you got fired after the first day?" Heather asks. "You actually still want to go there?"

"I got fired because I was completely incompetent, not because Gillie was a bad boss," I tell her. "Besides, nothing happens in this town that someone at Gillie's doesn't know about."

Five minutes later, we're huddled around two of the small white-and-pink ice cream tables that line the bakery's window.

I can't spot Gillie, but the bakery itself looks the same as it did when Hudson and I were living here. That's got to be a good sign, right?

The place is crowded right now, and while a bunch of the customers and employees keep shooting looks at our table, no one approaches.

I'm not sure if that's because they all got their chance to say hi to Hudson earlier or if they're too shy to approach the group of us. Either way, it's kind of a bummer, because it's pretty hard to pump people for information if they don't want to talk to you.

In the end, I send Hudson and Jaxon up to the counter to get teas for everyone and snacks for those of us who don't survive by drinking blood. "What kind of pastries do you want?" Jaxon asks as he pushes back from the table.

"Anything that isn't made with choux," I answer. Because while the pastries made with Gillie's choux really are a marvel, it's going to take longer than it's been before I'm willing to eat the dough made from flour and butter.

A lot longer.

"I don't know what that means," he tells me.

Hudson grins. "That's okay. I do." He reaches down, squeezes my hand.

"Ask about her," I tell him quietly, fighting down the nerves churning in my stomach. He nods.

The two of them head to the front of the bakery and are intercepted before they make it halfway to the front counter. Not by someone who wants to talk to Hudson, specifically, this time—or at least not only because of that. No, from what I can overhear, they're just super fascinated by vampires.

Which is what I was counting on when I sent them up there. People in Adarie really do hold paranormals in high esteem.

"Can you do that dragon thing you do?" I ask Flint.

He lifts a brow. "You mean shift? Breathe fire? *Fly?*"

"I was talking about a bakery-appropriate activity, like the forget-me-nots you made bloom for me that time in the library. Can you do something like *that* again?"

"I suppose. Any particular reason why?" He brightens. "Are we going to make Hudson jealous?"

"That wasn't my goal, no," I answer.

He sighs dejectedly. "Can't blame a guy for trying." Then he holds out his hand and blows on it softly. Seconds later, I watch as an ice flower forms, petal by petal, in the palm of his hand.

"Oh wow!" I say loudly enough to attract attention. "That is the coolest thing I've ever seen! Can you do it again?"

"I'm not a trained seal," he tells me with a frown.

I pluck the perfect little flower out of his hand and hold it up. "I never imagined that you were," I tell him softly. Then in a much louder voice, I squeal, "This is amazing! It's perfect!"

A glance toward the counter tells me that the older woman behind the cash register—I don't know her, but she does look familiar, with short lilac hair and laugh lines around her eyes—is paying extra-close attention to us. Exactly as I'd hoped. If Gillie is in the back, she'll hear about the paranormals in no time.

"How can you do that?" I ask, again much louder than I normally would.

Flint gives me a what-the-hell-are-you-doing look. Then says, "Because I'm a dragon. It's kind of what I do."

"Well, I love it. Will you make me a whole ice bouquet? Please?" Then, in a softer voice: "Will you just play along with me?"

"I'll play along," Eden says right before she opens her mouth and blows out a whole stream of ice crystals. They form into the most perfect rosebud I've ever seen—complete with long, thorn-free stem.

"That's gorgeous!" I exclaim, and this time I'm not even playing it up. It puts Flint's pretty little daisy to shame. "I didn't even know dragons could do something like that."

Eden just gives me a smug half smile, then reaches over to the next table and hands the flower to Heather.

Heather's eyes widen, and she looks between Eden and the rose like she can't quite figure out what's going on. And I get it. Every time I've turned around lately, Eden and Macy have had their heads together in a way that does not look strictly platonic.

Heather's been moping and specifically not talking about it, but it's been obvious she's upset. At least until this evening, when she got dressed up, put some makeup on, and has spent the last half hour talking to everybody but Eden.

"Thank you. It's beautiful," she whispers, bringing it up to her nose like she might actually be able to smell it.

Eden gives her a little eyebrow lift/chin nod in response.

Flint snorts. "You act like that's hard or something." In just one breath, he creates a giant rose in full bloom.

"I didn't realize this was a contest," Eden shoots back. Then blows out a long stream of ice crystals that coalesce into a full bouquet of flowers—roses, daisies, lilies, and even a couple of orchids, if I remember my flowers correctly.

"Seriously?" Flint says.

Eden just shrugs and plucks one of the lilies from the bouquet and holds it out to him.

"I can make my own, thank you very much." And then he sucks in a breath so big and long that I have visions of him single-handedly starting a new ice age right here in this bakery.

But before he can start to blow anything out, the woman from behind the counter stops right in front of us with a couple of large jars in her hands. "I thought you might need these," she says, her eyes alight with wonder. "It seems a shame to let the flowers go to waste."

She holds one of the jars out to Eden, who takes it with a grin. Then she plops the huge bouquet of ice flowers into it before handing the jar back to the woman. "I hope you enjoy them."

She gasps in delight, and though she's not Gillie, I know we've found one thing we were looking for. An opening to ask some questions whose answers just might lead us to a smuggler.

52

Such a Sweets
Little Baby

"Is this your bakery?" I ask when she sets the heavy ice bouquet down on the table.

"It is." She smiles at me. "Are you new in town?"

My heart plummets. What does this mean? How could Gillie's bakery be here, exactly as it was, if she isn't here to own it?

"We came with Hudson," I force out, nodding to where he and Jaxon are— Oh my God. I almost rub my eyes to be sure, but yes, that really is my mate tickling a baby in a carrier propped up beside the cash register. I guess the "kissing babies" jokes from earlier are all too real. Jaxon catches me staring and shoots me an I-can't-believe-you're-making-me-do-this look, but I don't even feel bad about it.

It's good for him. Whatever's going on with him and Flint is making him more taciturn than usual, and that has to stop. Whether he's going to be the future vampire king or the future dragon king, eventually he's going to have to give up part of the tall, dark, and surly demeanor he's so fond of and actually talk to people. The sooner he gets used to playing nice, the better.

"Oh, Hudson is just wonderful," the woman gushes. "His students used to love him so much. They were always talking about him."

"He is pretty lovable," I tell her, pleased that he still became a teacher in their memories.

Flint makes a disbelieving sound in his throat, then shoots her his most charming grin. "She has to say that. He's her mate."

"Oh, you're the girl everyone is talking about!" She glances around the group. "I wasn't sure which one of you he was mated to, and it seemed rude to ask."

"It's not rude at all," I tell her with a smile. "Would you like to join us for a few minutes? Jaxon and Hudson are getting tea—"

"Oh, I'd love to, but I can't. Everyone wants to check on Hudson, see how he's doing, and get a look at his friends, so things are really busy in here tonight. But it was very nice to meet you all." She holds out her hand. "I'm Marian."

"I'm Grace." I shake her hand, then introduce the others in turn. "Before you run off, I have to ask, though. Where did you get these adorable little tables? I love them so much, and I can tell by the color that they aren't from around here."

"Aren't they precious? Polo got them for me, though I don't know from where. He's got a real talent for finding the most obscure things in Adarie."

"Polo?" I ask, searching my memories for someone who fits that name, but no one jumps to mind.

"He's got a booth at the midnight market. It's on the last row—you can't miss it, or him."

"Why is that?" I ask.

She grins. "Because he's the only chupacabra in town."

As soon as she says it, I flash back to that last battle with the Shadow Queen and the chupacabra who fought right alongside Hudson and me. Of course Polo was his name—how could I possibly have forgotten?

"If you go down to find him tonight, tell him Marian sent you," she says. "And that I said to give you a discount."

"We'll do that," Flint tells her as he picks up the ice bouquet and holds it out to her.

Her cheeks turn a dusky purple as she takes it. "Are you sure you don't mind?"

Flint grins at her. "We can make more. Besides, those are definitely for you."

"Thank you so much." She blushes a little more, then tells him, "I'm going to put them in the freezer so I can enjoy them for a long time to come."

Then she heads back to the counter, and I hear her announce that "whatever Hudson and Jaxon order is on the house."

Flint sinks back with a satisfied smile.

"You've still got it," I tell him dryly.

He gives me his most innocent look. "I have no idea what you're talking about."

"Sure you don't. It's not like you didn't try that charm on me when we first met." I roll my eyes.

"Try?" he snorts. "You fell for it hook, line, and sinker."

"Oh, absolutely," I deadpan. "Because nothing says Prince Charming like tossing a girl out of a tree."

"Seriously? You're going to bring that up after all this time?" He shakes his head. "We've covered a lot of ground since then, *New Girl*."

"Just reminding you where we started, *Dragon Boy*. And that your charm doesn't get you out of everything, no matter what you think."

He glances at Jaxon up at the counter, and the smile fades from his face, replaced by a look that can only be described as pensive. "Oh, believe me, that's a lesson I've learned really well recently."

I start to ask him what he means—and what all the tension I keep sensing between him and Jaxon is about—but this isn't exactly the place for it. Besides, Jaxon and Hudson choose that moment to fill the table up with two large trays.

One holds seven cups of tea, and the other holds nearly three times as many decadent desserts. Considering only five of us are going to be eating them, it seems like they went more than a little overboard. At least until I glance at Flint, who has already claimed two pieces of cake and a giant chocolate cookie.

Maybe they knew what they were doing after all.

"Any luck?" Eden asks them once they settle back into their chairs.

"You mean besides getting loaded down with every dessert in the case that doesn't contain shoes?" Jaxon asks. "Nope. Despite wearing blue jeans and a bright pink top, the waiter we talked to really didn't seem to know anything."

I have to bite the inside of my cheek to keep from laughing at the way he mixed up choux with shoes but decide not to correct him. He *is* a vampire, after all. How often is he really going to have to worry about ordering pastries?

Besides, there are way more important things to be talking about right now than my ill-fated day as a baker. Even more important than finding Gillie, though worry about her still scratches at the back of my mind. "We might have gotten a lead," I tell them.

Hudson puts an arm over the back of my chair and smiles down at me. "Why doesn't that surprise me?"

"Because I'm a genius?" I suggest.

"True story." He snags one of the cups of tea and takes a slow, cautious sip. "So what's the lead?"

"There's a guy named Polo who has a booth at the night market," Heather tells him as she snags a slice of carrot cake.

"The midnight market," I correct, because "night market" implies that it will open when it gets dark, but things don't exactly work like that here. "It opens from midnight until early morning six nights a week."

Hudson nods in agreement, then says, "Polo? The chupacabra?"

"So you remember him?"

"Of course I do. He saved my ass in that last battle with the Shadow Queen."

"He saved both our asses. But I still totally forgot his name." And I feel terrible about it.

"Don't feel too bad," Flint tells me. "Compared to forgetting your mate for several months, forgetting a total stranger—even one who helped you out—really isn't that bad."

"Gee, thanks. You really know how to make a girl feel better," I reply, voice dripping with sarcasm.

But he just smiles at me and says, "I do what I can."

The others enjoy their pastries, bickering and laughing, and while I'm happy to see them having fun, my stomach roils as I turn to ask Hudson, "Did you happen to spot Gillie in the back?" I try to sound casual, but my voice betrays my nervousness.

"Yes, I did see her. She's okay," he confirms immediately, and my heart soars. "She's just a little, umm...slobbery."

"Slobbery?"

Instead of answering, he points toward the counter—toward the lavender baby Marian is now cooing over. My eyes go wide. "That's..."

"Marian is Gillie's mother," Hudson confirms. "This is her bakery."

"Gillie's timeline reset to when she was a baby, just like Smokey," I say, and my heart aches at the realization that I won't get to talk to my good friend. But Hudson squeezes my shoulder comfortingly, and I smile up at him.

"At least she's alive. That's all that matters." He presses a kiss to my curls.

"Agreed." I sip my tea, letting the warmth seep through me. "Though personally, I wouldn't go through my tween years again for all the money in the world."

He grins, and I do, too.

"Midnight is still several hours away," Macy says to the whole group, glancing at the large cookie clock on the wall. "And Hudson said Nyaz doesn't come on for the night shift until even later. So what do you say we fill those hours with a tour of this place?"

"Yeah, but not one filled with tourist spots," Heather adds. "I want to see the places you hung out when you were here."

My stomach clenches just a little bit at the thought. Not because I don't want to show my friends those places but because this whole trip is hurting more than I thought it would.

There's a part of me that was excited to come back here, excited to see the town where Hudson and I lived, where we fell in love.

But I just got those memories back. I haven't even had a chance to go through them all and think about them, really think about them. And yet here we are, back in Adarie-turned-Vegaville, and it's like none of those things actually happened. I haven't even had a chance to sort them out in my head, and they're changing, morphing, being taken from me.

It's a very weird feeling.

Still, my own issues aren't anybody else's, and I can see why my friends want to explore this place. They were worried about me and looking for ways to save me the whole time Hudson and I were here—is it any wonder they want to see what our life was like when they were so convinced that something horrible was happening to me?

So I shove down all the weird thoughts ricocheting through me and ignore the discomfort I just can't shake, focusing instead on giving my friends the best tour of Adarie that I can give them.

And maybe at midnight we'll even get lucky and find a chupacabra who can answer once and for all if I've still got time magic in me—if I'm going to be stuck here forever, in this place that forgot me.

53

"So what do you want to see first?" Hudson asks after we've managed to put a dent in as many of the free pastries as we can.

Jaxon shoves back from the table. "I don't know. What did you two do for fun here?"

"The same things we did for fun at Katmere, I guess," I say as we head for the door.

"Oh, really?" Macy raises her brows. "There are a lot of snowball fights in the Shadow Realm, are there?"

"Not quite." I laugh before looking at Hudson. "I know where we can take them."

He grins. "The Mark, right?"

"Exactly!"

"What's the Mark?" Heather asks as we head away from the bakery to the outskirts of town.

"You'll see," I tell her as excitement thrums through me.

Hudson and I found this place after we'd been in Adarie several months. We were wandering around town on our day off, looking for something fun to do, when we ran into the old warehouse. And while I wouldn't exactly call us regulars here, we came enough that we got to know the place fairly well.

As we walk through town on our way to the Mark, it's hard not to fall into a weird mix of nostalgia about this place as well as a yearning to stay that I don't quite understand.

I mean, I love the life Hudson and I are building in San Diego. I love going to school there, and I love the idea of creating a new Gargoyle Court in my hometown. And most of all, I love being with Hudson.

But there's something about our walk through these streets, this town, that just feels right. Things weren't perfect when we were here—how could they be, with time dragons stalking us and trying to kill us? And with Souil up to his horrible schemes?

Still, despite all that, it was easier than the life we have now—especially once we'd resigned ourselves to staying here forever.

No responsibilities beyond taking care of ourselves and each other and our very regular jobs.

No life-and-death decisions that affected not just us but all of our people as well.

No fear of making a mistake that would destroy everything we had worked so hard to build.

I don't *dislike* being the gargoyle queen. How can I, when I get the honor and the responsibility of serving my people? But it's not something I would have chosen for myself, either. It's not like fifteen-year-old Grace ever sat on her bed and dreamed about what it would be like to rule someday. Queen definitely wasn't on my list of dream jobs.

So yeah, as we walk past Hudson's old school and point out his classroom to our friends, or stop to look in the windows of the boutique where I finally found a job I could do, it's hard not to think about our life here. Hard not to wish that the life we're building together now could be as uncomplicated.

Does it suck that no one here remembers me? Yeah, it kind of does. But the more we walk, the more I realize that it's also kind of freeing. Here, I can be anyone. I can do anything. Back home, I'm too busy trying to balance school, the Circle, and the gargoyle throne to worry about who I am or who I want to be.

"Grace used to work there, too," Hudson says as we pass the blacksmith shop that I apprenticed at for exactly two days.

"You were a blacksmith?" Heather asks, wide-eyed. "Really?"

"Um, more like someone who was auditioning to be an apprentice to a blacksmith," I tell her. "It wasn't really my thing."

"Really? What was it about standing over a two-thousand-degree fire and molding metal for hours on end that wasn't your thing?" Flint asks, crossing his arms with a smirk.

I roll my eyes at him before answering, "I'll have you know that I didn't mind the fire *or* the molding metal. I just happened to suck at it. Like, I really, really blew."

"She did," Hudson agrees, then laughs when I elbow him gently in the stomach. "What? You did."

"Yeah, well, you didn't have to sound so gleeful when you pointed it out."

"Sorry. I'll show more restraint next time I'm documenting one of your failed job attempts," he promises with a roll of his eyes.

I start to tease him some more, but then we turn the corner at the end of the shopping district and excitement zooms through me. "There it is!" I announce to my friends as I stop to get a better look. "The Mark."

"Umm, isn't that just an old warehouse?" Macy asks, staring at the sprawling building in front of us.

"Bite your tongue!" I tell her as I start rushing everyone toward it. "It's so much more than what it used to be."

"Which was an old warehouse," Macy repeats.

"You're going to regret your snap judgments once we get inside," I tell her before taking the steps that lead to the front door at a run. "This place is amazing!"

And then I'm pushing open the door and letting my friends into one of the coolest places I've ever been.

"It's a museum?" Jaxon asks, looking at the huge pieces of art hanging on the wall opposite the front door.

"More like a working artist co-op," I tell him as I lead the way inside. "A ton of artists live and work in here, sharing space and tools as they create some of the most awesome works of art I've ever seen."

"Did you paint here?" Heather asks, another reminder that she knew me in a different life—different from my life here, in Noromar, and my life at Katmere.

"Yes. All the time." My gaze darts around until I find what I'm looking for. An old purple couch pushed under a window in the corner. The springs were half poking out in places, the cushions ratty as fuck, but Hudson would lay there for hours, reading and watching me paint by the light streaming through the huge windows.

As I take in the collection of art on the adjacent wall, I realize it's more like a shrine than a display, consisting of about fifty different-size paintings—all featuring the same subject matter. Hudson.

And that's when I see it. Hanging among the collage of other paintings.

My heart races as I walk over and stand about thirty feet in front of one of the pieces, my eyesight suddenly blurry with unshed tears.

"Dude." Flint lets out a long whistle, staring at the wall, too.

"Seriously," Jaxon says as he steps a little closer to the display than me, his head bouncing as he takes in painting after painting. "I get people being grateful you saved them, but this is some next-level shit."

It's not said with an ounce of bite or jealousy, and I get it. When we first got to "Vegaville," I thought it was amusing. Awesome. Amazing that so many people could see how incredible my mate is. But I recognize now it's more than just hero worship.

There's a painting of Hudson playing pisbee with a bunch of people in the park, Hudson grinning in the foreground and the others at the farthest end of the field. There's one of him lifting a giant timber single-handedly above his head in front of a half-constructed house. Hudson throwing giant boulders from a cave entrance covered by a landslide. Hudson waving from a rooftop, a small child in his arms. There's even one of Hudson with his arms crossed, one eyebrow raised as he struggles not to laugh at a group of kids coated in paint, the building beside them also covered in random splashes of color.

And my personal favorite: Hudson standing with one foot on the neck of a dead time dragon, knee bent, hands on hips, townspeople crowding around him and cheering. The only thing missing is a cape…

"Oh my God," I whisper. "Vegaville is *Smallville*!"

Heather gets the connection immediately, as she should, given our mutual love of comics. "Hudson didn't just save the town when the queen attacked, Jaxon." She turns to him, then waves at all of the paintings before gesturing to Hudson behind us. "Clark Kent there never put on his glasses. He *lived* with them. Kept them safe. Made them feel loved."

Eden grins. "Can you imagine growing up with Superman living next door? For reals?"

"Well, there's loved and then there's *loved*," Macy says, staring at the two-foot-by-four-foot painting in front of me. "I'd be worried this artist is thinking of making a dress out of your skin."

"Hey," I say and playfully jab her in the arm. "I resent that."

Five heads swivel as one from the painting to me, and my cheeks suddenly feel very, very warm. I've never been the kind of artist overly comfortable with people looking at my artwork, so this is ten levels of self-inflicted hell right now.

"*You* painted this," Eden says, pride lacing her voice, and I give a quick nod.

And then we all just stand there, staring at the painting of Hudson.

I remember exactly when I painted it, too. It was the day after he told me he loved me the first time. When I told him I loved him, too. And it's evident in every pull of the brush against the canvas, every streak of paint left behind.

I swallow back an ocean of tears clogging my throat.

I don't want anyone to see what I'm feeling right now, but Hudson sees. He always sees. And when I feel him slide his arms around my waist and tug me against his chest, I wrap my arms around his and hold on as tightly as I can even as a sea of emotions rises up and threatens to swamp me.

It's not just the embarrassment of my friends studying the painting I did of Hudson that is suddenly making it hard for me to breathe.

It's not even the love I have for this boy exposed in every brushstroke I made of the creases next to his eyes and the flecks of navy in his bright blue irises that is twisting my stomach into knots.

And it's not the realization that in front of me—right in front of me—there is finally proof that I was here, that I *did* matter in this place that has chosen to forget me that is currently making my knees tremble.

It's that this painting represents a lot more than just its parts. And one of the other things it represents, one of the reasons why it matters so much, is that the act of painting is now just one more thing I used to do. One more thing I used to love.

Because other than what I painted for art class back at Katmere, I haven't picked up a brush since living in Adarie. Sure, I still have my old paints and brushes, but I haven't looked at them once in the last several months. In fact, I'm not even sure what closet they're buried in back in San Diego.

My love of painting is just one more thing this world has taken from me, just one more part of who I am that's gotten lost beneath the crush of being the gargoyle queen.

Heather gives me a strange look, but she doesn't say anything else about my art, which I'm grateful for.

Hudson rubs soothing circles between my shoulder blades as he guides us to the left out of the entryway. I flash him a grateful smile, but he doesn't smile back. Instead, he just studies me with watchful eyes that see way too much.

Which leaves me no recourse except to turn to my friends and start babbling on and on about this place. "So what floor do we want to start on? It's kind of divided by art forms so that the different equipment is easily accessible to anyone who needs it."

"What kind of equipment are you talking about?" Eden queries.

"All kinds," I answer. "The bottom floor is where most of the painters and photographers are, but when you go to the second floor, there's a sculpture studio with every kind of chisel you can imagine. Also pottery wheels and ovens and a ton of clay."

"And the third floor has looms and sewing machines and a bunch of yarn and textiles," Hudson adds.

"That's the neatest thing I've ever heard," Macy tells him, cherry black–colored lips tilted in a slight smile as she stands in the center of the warehouse and looks at all of the murals on the walls around us. "Do the artists pay for it themselves?"

"Actually, the town of Noromar pays for it," I say. "It's why it's open to the public. It's one of the town council's pet projects."

My friends are as fascinated by the co-op as Hudson and I are, and we spend a couple of hours wandering the different floors, looking at art and meeting artists. It's a little disconcerting because more than one of them is actually working on a piece of Hudson at the moment, which freaks him out a little, especially when they ask him to pose for a few photographs that they can use in their work.

He's pretty much taking it in stride by the time we make it through all three floors, though, and wander outside to one of my favorite parts of the co-op—the giant graffiti garden that stretches the length of the warehouse.

Between two massive walls that run parallel to each other, the garden stretches with flowers and stone pathways and benches with a different scene on each one. There's a huge fountain in the center of the garden, also with benches around it so people can sit and admire the graffiti walls.

Both of them are covered in small murals, tagging, and random phrases that make me smile. Everything from hearts with people's initials inside them to statements on life, both positive and negative, to quotes from favorite poems and songs.

"What's this?" Flint asks as he wanders over to the huge metal cabinets set up at one end of the garden. I feel bad as I realize he's limping a little—going up and down all the metal staircases inside must have aggravated his leg.

"The best part," I tell him with a smile.

But then Flint stumbles over an out-of-place rock and Jaxon fades to him in a blink, grabbing his arm to help steady him. Which is apparently the wrong move, judging from the look Flint shoots him and the way he yanks his arm away.

Jaxon growls deep in his throat, but he doesn't say anything. Just blows out an exasperated breath and stays where he is as Flint struggles the rest of the way to the cabinet on his own. Jaxon's ebony gaze is focused on Flint as he stumbles a second time on the rocky path, but I can tell he's respecting Flint's unspoken boundary coming through loud and clear—if Flint wants Jaxon's help, he'll ask for it.

I can't imagine how hard it's got to be for both of them. Jaxon with his overprotectiveness on hyperalert because he wants to keep Flint from getting hurt again. And Flint determined to be independent and do things on his own.

Not knowing what to do to help them except try to ease the awkwardness, I hurry toward the cabinets and throw the doors wide open so everyone can see what's waiting for them.

54

Spray a Little
Prayer for Me

"Spray paint?" Flint laughs as soon as he sees the contents of the industrial cupboards. "Are they for anyone?"

"Absolutely," I answer, reaching in and pulling out a couple of different cans, which I hold out to him. "What color do you want?"

He looks at the different-colored lids in surprise. "So they aren't all shades of purple?"

I realize he's right. The spray paint comes in dozens of different colors, which is why the graffiti wall is so beautiful. It's a mixture of every color imaginable, and I never realized it before. Or if I did, it didn't register that the spray paint—and a lot of the art supplies, like the paints I used for my portrait of Hudson—had to come from somewhere else. That it couldn't possibly be from Adarie or even somewhere else in Noromar.

Like the bakery tables and Souil's sofas and the colored clothes so many people in town enjoy wearing, they must have been smuggled in. More proof that there really is at least one smuggler—Polo or someone he knows—working in Noromar. And if that's the case, maybe Hudson's plan on how to get back across the barrier really will work.

But it's still several hours before midnight, so I decide to think about the smuggler later. Right now, I just want to have fun with my friends.

I grab a couple of cans for myself, blue and silver, then wait for my friends to do the same before heading over to the wall. We fan out and start spray-painting in whatever open space we can find.

Hudson draws a giant red heart and puts our initials in it, because he's just that sappy. I roll my eyes at him, but he grins and adds several extra hearts floating around the main one.

"You're a little gross. You know that, right?" Macy says as she paints a giant black spider right beside Hudson's hearts.

Hudson sniffs. "I prefer to think of myself as romantic."

"Yeah, well, I prefer to think of myself as awesome," she tells him. "Doesn't make it true."

"It's absolutely true," I say, pausing in my own drawing of a wave to look at her. "You're the most awesome person I know."

"Gee, thanks," Hudson deadpans.

I roll my eyes. "You're my mate. You already know I think you're awesome."

"Yes, well, it never hurts to hear it." But he's grinning as he adds *4-Ever* to the spot right below our initials.

Macy fake gags. "I think I'm going into sugar shock here."

She sounds so different than the Macy I used to know that I have to remind myself my cousin is still in there. Under the goth makeup and the new piercings *and the suffering*, Macy is there. I just need to figure out how to help her through the pain.

Eden comes running by then, a can of purple spray paint in her hand. She tags right next to Macy's spider with a quick pair of dragon wings before sprinting away to mess with Flint and Jaxon.

"Dragons," Hudson says with another very proper sniff, but amusement is gleaming in his eyes, even before he fades after Eden and draws a pair of vampire fangs right next to her dragon.

Macy and I sit out the next half hour as the others have a blast tagging on one another and spray-painting everything they can get their hands on. I'm hoping it will give me a chance for us to talk—*really* talk—but every time I try to bring something up that isn't totally superficial, she shuts me down.

Until, finally, I stop trying.

Eventually, the others wind down and come to sit next to us. Hudson plops down on the other side of me while Eden, Heather, and Jaxon sit on the ground around us. Flint chooses the fountain directly across from us and, with a sigh of relief, stretches his prosthetic leg out along its bench.

There's a breeze going, and it wafts the heavy scent of flowers by every so often. Even though it's after ten, the sun is still up, and as it beats down on us, it keeps the wind from feeling too cold. Add in the gurgle of the fountain and the gentle chirp of the birds in the purple magnolia trees, and it feels good to be out here.

More, it feels relaxing.

That's not a word I associate with hanging with my friends very often—at least not when we're almost all together like this. Since we graduated from Katmere Academy, we've only met en masse like this when there's a problem to solve or a battle to fight.

While I know there's a problem waiting for us as soon as we leave this garden—several problems, really—for now it feels so good to sit with my friends and talk about stupid stuff. Classes we're worried about and the last movies we saw and if concert tickets for our favorite bands are overpriced.

I've almost allowed myself to relax when Macy glances at her watch and announces, "It's half an hour before midnight. Time to see if a chupacabra knows someone who can help smuggle us home—or if purple is my new favorite color. Forever."

And just like that, our perfect moment fades like dusty drapes over time, replaced with silence and responsibilities and an unrelenting fear that follows us all the way across town.

55

Doppel-Tweeners

"Where to next?" Flint asks as we walk back toward the center of town.

"We've still got a little time before the midnight market opens," Hudson answers. "Is anyone hun—"

He breaks off with a choked sound that has all of us turning to look at him in concern.

"Are you all right?" I ask, resting a hand on his lower back.

But he's too busy staring across the street to pay any attention to what I'm saying.

I turn to follow the trajectory of his gaze and gasp. Because walking down the sidewalk toward us is a group of about ten young wraiths who are probably around thirteen or fourteen. And they are all dressed up like...us.

And when I say dressed up, I mean like full-Halloween-costume dressed up.

"Oh my God!" Heather squeals before they reach us. "Look at the tween Eden! She's adorable."

"She does have good taste in tats," Eden admits after she spends a second studying the little purple girl currently wearing low-waisted pants and a crop top. She's got temporary dragon and fire tattoos running up and down her arms and has twisted her long purple hair into two space buns with messy tails.

"Tween Flint looks great, too," Flint says as we walk a little closer. The kid has naturally curly hair like Flint, but unlike Flint's normal 'do, he's tugged it as high as it will go.

The fact that he's also wearing giant boots and worn jeans with a green T-shirt whose sleeves are rolled up to show off his nonexistent biceps is pretty freaking cute, too. Not to mention the dragon tattoo it looks like he's drawn on one of those tiny purple arms.

Tween Heather has her hair done in a million little box braids and is wearing a bright purple zip hoodie and sweatpants with the waistband rolled down. She's also got a ton of tiny sparkling rings on her lilac fingers, just like my bestie likes to wear.

As for the *two* tween Macys… Both are dressed in tiny black half shirts and shorts, with chunky boots and ripped, striped stockings. One is wearing a spiked collar around her neck while the other one has grommet bracelets around her wrists. Plus, they've painted/dyed their hair green, or as close to green as purple hair can get, and painted a ton of heavy black goth makeup around their eyes and lips.

One of them is carrying what I think is supposed to be a magic wand.

"They're darling," I agree as the kids get closer. "I think Jaxon's my favorite, though."

"What are you talking about?" Jaxon looks confused. "There's no Jaxon."

We all look at him like he needs glasses. "Are you kidding? He's right there." I point Jaxon's mini-me out.

"In the jeans and white T-shirt? The hair's wrong, but I like the leather jacket." He nods to himself. "Yeah, okay, I can get behind that kid."

"That's supposed to be me, you tosser," Hudson tells him with a roll of his eyes.

"You're the one in all black, Jaxon," Macy supplies helpfully.

"The one in all— No way!" He looks completely flummoxed. "That is *not* me."

"Really?" Heather looks him up and down, making a point of lingering on his tight black T-shirt and black jeans. "Who else could it be?"

"I don't know. Macy? I mean, look at the hair."

"Exactly," Flint teases. "Look at the hair."

"My hair does not look like that," Macy tells him.

Jaxon seems furious. "Well, neither does mine! Obviously." He runs a hand through his longish wavy hair as if to prove the point.

But that only makes it messier—and makes it more closely resemble the hair in question on the tween. Which is a woman's wig with floppy black hair that was obviously much longer before someone—an amateur, by the looks of things—took a scissors to it and tried to create Jaxon's signature shaggy cut.

"Dude, your hair looks just like that," Eden tells him. "They've even got the whole covering-your-eyes vibe going."

"I just hope they don't trip," Macy worries.

Flint shrugs. "Jaxon manages not to trip."

"Because my hair doesn't look like that!" Jaxon snaps, outraged. "Do you know how much I spend on this haircut?"

"Ah, the truth comes out," Hudson teases.

"I don't know." Eden looks between the kid and Jaxon. "They're either a hair-styling savant or you're being ripped off. Because, dude. The hair is exactly the same."

"And so are the pants," Macy comments helpfully.

Jaxon narrows his eyes at her. "The pants? Seriously? Theirs have sequins on them. I have never worn a sequin in my life."

"Yeah, but do you know anyone else in the group who wears pants that tight?" Heather asks him.

"They have sequins on them! And they're flares!" he roars, pointing at the hemline.

"I see absolutely no difference." Hudson pokes the already pissed-off vampire just because he can. "What do you think, Grace?"

"I mean, they do look tight enough to cut off circulation, which is a signature part of Jaxon's look. Besides, does anyone here know what flares are?" I ask the group.

Everyone shakes their heads.

"Not a clue," Hudson adds.

Eden looks confused. "Do you mean the gun thing that shoots off the little light when you're in trouble?"

"We rest our case," I tell Jaxon with a small shrug.

"You know what? Fuck all of you," he growls. "I don't look like that."

Tween Jaxon chooses that moment to race up to the tween Flint and pretend to bite his neck. At which point all of us—sans Jaxon—crack up.

"Well," Hudson says when he finally stops laughing. "It doesn't get much more obvious than that."

"Whatever," Jaxon says as they finally get within hearing distance of us. "They're just kids."

"Kids who—" Hudson freezes mid-joke, his eyes going wide.

"What's wrong?" I ask, whirling around. And then I nearly die. Because coming toward us from the left are no fewer than six high school–aged mini Graces, complete with long curly hair, tank tops, and very, *very* padded bras.

Oh. My. God.

Now would be an excellent time for the ground to open up and swallow me whole.

It's Jaxon's turn to laugh—and everyone else's. And that's before the leader of the Graces, for want of a better moniker, stops in front of Hudson and tosses her hair.

"Hey there, big boy," she says in the breathiest voice I have ever heard.

Hudson's eyes go wide, and then he takes two giant steps back to hide directly behind me. "Umm, hello," I answer, because I don't know what else to do. "You look very…"

"Whatever." She rolls her eyes as she very neatly sidesteps me so that she can sidle up to my mate. "You look handsome today, Hudson." As she speaks, she tilts her head back in an effort to elongate her neck as far as she can.

"Umm, I, we…" Hudson chokes. He just full-on chokes and abandons ship, pushing past the rest of us and walking very, very fast up the sidewalk.

"Hudson, wait!" one of the others calls out. And then all six of them are chasing him down the sidewalk like little ducks. If little ducks were tossing their wigs, giggling, and doing their best to get big, bad Hudson Vega to suck their blood. "You're going too fast! We can't catch up!"

He doesn't so much as pause in his headlong flight down the street.

Out of nowhere, one more fake Grace appears. Only this one isn't chasing him down the street. She's leaping from a four-foot-tall planter, tiny little plastic wings outstretched, just as Hudson passes by.

I gasp, but Hudson reaches his arms out on reflex toward the little girl, catching her—bride-style—in his arms.

All the little Graces freak out. They scream like they're at a Hudson Vega concert and rush him like he's onstage.

Hudson, to his credit, very carefully, very gently sets the girl on her feet. He even pats her on her head. And then he fades away faster than he has ever faded before.

56

I'm Trying What
You're Selling

The midnight market was another one of Hudson's and my favorite things when we lived here. Considering the sun only sets in Noromar during Starfall, it's easy to see why the market is so busy, even at midnight. But we didn't get to it all that often, simply because we were usually tired from work and life. The few times we went, though, we always had fun.

However, tonight isn't about fun. It's about finding Polo and convincing him to tell us who his source is for the goods he sells. There's a part of me that thinks he might be the source—and the smuggler—but I have nothing to base that on but a gut feeling.

Still, it's a good gut feeling, the strongest I've had in a while, so I'm not ready to discount it yet. Not until I talk to Polo and see what he has to say—and what he looks like when he's saying it.

"Do you know which booth we need to go to?" Jaxon asks as we make our way through the old iron gates that block off the open-air market when it's closed.

"Only that it's near the back of the market," I answer. "But things are pretty organized in there. It shouldn't be hard to find him—or ask someone to point us in the right direction."

"You think someone will help?" Eden asks, and she looks surprised.

Which surprises me, at least until I see how they're all holding themselves—not like they're looking for a fight, but definitely like they don't plan on running from one. Even Heather looks tense, like she's one sideways glance away from activating her fight-or-flight mechanism.

Only Hudson looks completely relaxed, like he's going for an evening stroll through Adarie. Which, in essence, is exactly what we're doing. Just with an agenda that we can't afford to mess up.

For about the hundredth time today, I wonder how Mekhi is doing back at the Witch Court. I wish our cell phones worked in the Shadow Realm. Lorelei promised to text if there was any change in Mekhi, but we won't get those texts until we leave. We have no choice but to trust her claim that we have more than a week to find an antidote.

We've got no other options, so I'm just going to keep my fingers crossed and hope for the best. And if that plan of action makes my stomach start flipping again in all the bad ways, well, then nobody needs to know about it but me. Besides, there's no use borrowing trouble. Not when I have no doubt that it will find us on its own soon enough.

"So, do they have a directory?" Heather asks as we turn down the last aisle of the market. "Maybe we can find him that way."

"No need," Hudson tells her, giving a little nod toward a booth filled with merch in every color imaginable. Bright lanterns in reds and greens and purples hang from strings that crisscross the top of the booth. One table is filled with colored stone jewelry, and another is filled with blue jeans and T-shirts in every shade of the rainbow. The center of the booth has multicolor blankets folded into piles that stand six or seven feet tall, plus furniture and paintings and colored glass that reminds me of the collection my mother used to have in her office.

She filled hers with herbs and flowers that she used for her teas, and as we approach the booth, I can't look away from the pretty amber apothecary bottles, crimson atomizers, and jade pitchers. I swear I can almost smell the sweet-and-spicy scent that used to wash over me every time she was blending.

It's an odd feeling—one that makes me sad even as it brings me an amazing amount of comfort. It's strange how just a glimpse of these containers can bring me back to all those hours after school when, under her supervision, I stuffed her bottles with the roots and flowers and berries that she had grown and harvested and dried on our dining room table.

"So what's the plan?" Flint asks as we approach. "Do I need to be the muscle?"

Hudson laughs. "The day I need a dragon to be the muscle for me is the day I walk into the sun without my ring and let myself burn."

"The fact that the sun can do you in should be proof enough that dragons are stronger," Flint answers.

Hudson just rolls his eyes. "The fact that dragons are mortal should prove just the opposite."

"What is it about vampires, man? Always throwing the immortal card in our face like it's such a flex." Flint sounds completely disgruntled, which only seems to amuse Hudson more.

Especially when Jaxon chimes in: "We don't need to flex. We're *immortal*."

"So, what he's saying is we don't have a plan," Heather says to all of us, and there's general chuckling.

"What I'm saying is that the plan is simple," Hudson tells everyone with a sigh. Then he turns and strides into the booth like he owns the place.

Polo is helping a customer who seems very interested in a pair of jeans, but he breaks off mid-negotiation when he catches sight of my mate. He's wiry and not especially tall, but I know from our fight against the pack of wolves that he's hiding a lot of strength beneath his plain white T-shirt. His black hair curls around his ears now, and he's got a new tattoo on his arm of an eagle with its wings spread, but otherwise he looks exactly as I remember him—right down to the wolfish grin he shoots Hudson's way.

"Hudson Vega!" he all but yells as he crosses the booth to shake Hudson's hand. "I heard you were back in town. I didn't believe it after everything that happened, but here you are."

"Here I am," Hudson agrees with a grin.

Polo smacks him on the back in a friendly fashion. "How the hell are you?"

"I'm good. Really good. How are you?"

"Can't complain," he answers with a laugh that sounds a lot like a howl. "Business is booming, my mate and I just had a baby, and that Shadow Bitch hasn't shown her face around here since you tossed her out like the trash she is. Life is good."

"That's fantastic news, man." It's Hudson's turn to clap him on the back. "A new little chupacabra running around! Boy or girl?"

"Girl. She looks just like her mama, gracias a Dios. She's gorgeous."

"I bet she is."

"What's her name?" I ask, because I feel awkward just standing here. And also because I don't want Hudson to have to carry the conversation all by himself. Especially considering the direction he needs to move it in.

"Her name is Aurora," he answers. "Because she's our light."

"That's beautiful. I'm so happy for you and your mate." After everything he went through in that last battle, Polo deserves all the happiness he can find.

"This is my mate, by the way." Hudson wraps an arm around my waist and pulls me close. "Grace."

"What? The great Hudson Vega found his mate?" Now he does let out a loud howl—one that sounds celebratory in nature. "Congratulations, dude. That is stellar." Then he jolts like he just remembered I'm standing here as well. "Congratulations to you, too," he tells me. "You've got a good one here."

"I absolutely do," I agree.

"So what brings you two to Vegaville?" Polo asks after a few seconds. "And please tell me you didn't bring any of those fucking time dragons with you."

"We didn't," Hudson assures him. "But that's actually what we want to talk to you about."

"Time dragons?" Polo looks wary.

"No, definitely not time dragons," I say. "We were actually hoping you could point us in the right direction. We're looking for someone who knows how to cross the barrier between the Shadow Realm and our world."

"Well, you did it three times now, right?" He looks at Hudson. "Coming, going, coming. So why should this time be any different?"

"The first time I came, I brought a time dragon with me—and an unfortunate encounter with a time dragon is how I made it home," Hudson explains. "But considering what happened the last time I brought a time dragon to Noromar, I wanted to go a little more low-key this go-around. So I found an easier way in, but it was a one-way trip. Which means my friends and I are stuck here forever. Unless…"

"Why'd you come to me?" Polo asks after several seconds pass in total silence. "What makes you think I know anything about how the barrier works?"

"Well, you're not a wraith, so you weren't born here—which means you crossed the barrier, the same as I did."

"Yeah." He inclines his head in acknowledgment of Hudson's logic. "But that doesn't mean I know how to cross back—or that I know anyone who does."

"Maybe *you* don't," Hudson agrees. "But I feel like you definitely know someone who does. Am I wrong?"

Now Polo just looks annoyed. "Even if I know something, and I'm not saying I do, you don't want to leave that way, dude. Trust me."

"Why not?" Eden asks, and Polo turns to her.

"Because most people who leave that way never come back," he says like that explains everything. When it's clear none of us understand why that's such a terrible thing, he adds, "Like, *never.*"

"Ohhh," Eden murmurs, and a shiver races along my spine.

My gaze narrows on Polo's, and I follow my instincts and ask, "But *you* go through it all the time, don't you?"

Polo raises one bushy brow. "What if I do?" he answers, which is no answer at all.

"Then you know how to get out safely," I reply.

But Polo just shakes his head, a wide grin stretching his lips. "Polo here is special." He spreads his arms wide to encompass his tables of merchandise. "It's why I have such a thriving business. Sadly, though, what I know won't be of any use to you, other than where the tunnel out starts. That's the best I can do."

"Works for me," Hudson says with a nod. "If you can just show us the way in a few days, we'll take it from there, Polo."

The chupacabra studies both of us for a second, like he's trying to figure out just how serious we are about going. I don't tell him that right now, the answer is as far as it takes. We've already done all this—there isn't much we wouldn't do to save Mekhi.

"First, I'm going to need you to sign all the Hudson merch I have in the back before you leave," he says, nodding to a storage area off to the side. "As payment for guiding you. I have a smuggling reputation to uphold."

"Done," Hudson answers. "I'd have signed the merch either way, though, for having my back in that last fight."

"Nah, I always do all right with Vega memorabilia," he says, a twinkle in his eyes. "But now? It's gonna be worth quadruple."

"Why's that?" Macy asks, speaking up for the first time, but Polo is already moving to help a new customer at the other end of his booth.

Without breaking stride, he tosses over his shoulder, "Shit, man, everyone knows autographed stuff like this sells for a *fortune* posthumously."

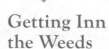

57

Getting Inn
the Weeds

"That doesn't sound good," I say, trying to calm my racing heart. But Polo's already gone, helping a customer who's interested in one of the brightly colored coats he has on display.

I turn to Hudson as our friends crowd around. "That doesn't sound good," I repeat.

"It'll be fine," he assures me. But there's an extra-cautious look in his eyes that wasn't there before.

"It has to be," Flint says as we start to make our way out of the market. "So it will be—one way or the other."

"That's a good way of looking at it," Heather tells him. "It has to be okay, so it will be. I'm going to steal that for when I'm freaked out about something."

"You mean you aren't freaked out about someone literally banking on our death?" I ask her as we cross through the gates.

She shrugs. "Not really. I figure you and Hudson have everything under control."

"That's a bit of a stretch, but I admire the vote of confidence."

Hudson doesn't say anything, but he does take my hand and lace our fingers together—Hudson/Grace shorthand for *we've got this*.

"Let's head back to the hotel," Eden says. "Maybe Nyaz has started his shift by now."

"Not to mention my bed is calling my name," Heather adds. "No wonder you never had time to text me back while you were at Katmere, Grace. Your life is exhausting."

"You have no idea," I tell her with a grin. "But I still should have texted you back."

"When? In between wrangling with gods and bargaining with smugglers?" She shakes her head. "Nope. I officially declare you get a pass for everything that happened before."

I start to make a joke, but I'm too choked up to say anything. Because it's just like Heather to let me off easy, even though she probably shouldn't.

"Yeah, well, from now on, I'll make sure to text no matter how dangerous the situation," I finally manage to get out. "In fact, expect nothing short of fawning attention."

"Well, I always love a good fawning," she answers with a smile.

Eden raises a brow. "Is that your philosophy on all things or just friendship?"

And on that note, I start walking faster. Some things I don't need to know—even about my bestie.

But speaking of besties… I pull my hand from Hudson's, and he gives me a surprised look. At least until I jerk my chin surreptitiously toward Macy, who is walking a little in front of us, head bowed and hands in her pockets. She wasn't paying attention to Eden or Heather, so whatever this is, it's not about them.

Hudson nods and drops back to let Jaxon and Flint hassle him some more about being a superhero. On the plus side, at least the two of them aren't fighting about anything when they have the common goal of messing with Hudson.

Hudson can more than hold his own, though, so I hurry to catch up with my cousin.

"Hey," I say as I gently bump her shoulder with mine. "How's it going?"

She shrugs. "Apparently well, since we aren't going to be trapped here forever after all."

"It's definitely one of many things to be thankful for," I tell her.

"Of course, I'm betting that whatever that Polo guy was referring to kills us on the way out regardless." She slides me a weak smile to let me know she's kidding. Sort of.

"Hey, we got this." I shoulder-bump her again. "Besides, that's not what I meant. You still have things—and people—to be thankful for,

Macy. You know that, right?"

"I know." But she doesn't say anything more.

I let a couple of minutes of silence pass before I try again. "If you want to talk about—"

She cuts me off. "I don't."

"Okay, then. Maybe 'want' was too strong a word. What I meant—"

"I know what you meant, Grace." She shoots me another small smile that *almost* makes it to her eyes.

I sigh. "I just love you, Mace."

"I know." She swallows. "Love you, too."

"Whatever you need, I'm here," I whisper. "Hey, you had my back when I first arrived at Katmere, remember, roomie?"

A tiny spark starts to flicker in her eyes, so I push ahead. "Maybe I should buy *you* a hot-pink comforter." This time, a half smile lifts one side of her mouth, and I sling an arm around her neck. "With sparkles and sequins and maybe even a feather fringe."

For a second or two, she stays tense as hell, but then slowly—so slowly I barely feel it—she lets her guard down a tiny bit.

I wish I had just the right thing to say to get her to open up. I know she's in a rough spot, know she's hurting. And I know from experience, you can't just go *around* pain... Eventually, you have to wade through it. But it's not my right to tell her when that should happen. It's hers. Still, she deserves to know she doesn't have to walk through it on her own.

"You'll find your way through this, Macy. On *your* terms," I whisper. "But I need you to know you are not alone. I'm here for you. Pink comforter and all."

Eventually, she nods, bending her head to the side so that she can rest her cheek on the top of my head. Then whispers back, "I know." Right before she pulls away.

It's not a lot, but I hope it's enough for now. Hope she knows that I've got her, no matter what.

We make it to the town square a couple of minutes later, and though it's past midnight, there are people everywhere. Eating in sidewalk cafés, shopping in stores that have stayed open late, listening to music in the center of the square. It's obvious Starfall is coming—the streetlamps are decorated with colorful purple flower baskets, and food tents are starting to set up downtown.

For a second, I consider suggesting hanging out in the square and listening to music for a while—but I think that's just the memories getting to me. I can't believe I forgot Hudson sitting in front of the crowd and singing "Little Things" to me. It's got to be one of my top ten favorite moments from our time here.

"Nyaz is at the front desk," Hudson says, nodding toward the picture window of the inn. "Want to try and catch him now?"

"Absolutely," I agree. "We need to make sure we can find the Shadow Queen. Because if we can't, the whole plan falls apart."

Hudson turns to the others. "You can head upstairs if you want, get some sleep while we figure out if this is going to work."

"And miss out on all this?" Flint asks, nodding toward the way people keep getting closer and closer to us, as if being in the same general area as Hudson will make him fall in love with them. Or at least get him to offer up a picture or twenty. "I'm just waiting for one of them to work up the nerve to approach you. Once that happens, I'm betting you'll end up at the bottom of a dogpile before the night is over."

"Your concern for me is overwhelming," Hudson responds dryly.

Flint shrugs. "I just call 'em like I see 'em. And I'm definitely not missing it."

We head to the inn, where we're met at the door by a grinning Nyaz. "Out showing your friends the pre-Starfall activities, I see, Hudson."

"I took them to the midnight market and the Mark."

Nyaz's smile grows even wider as he turns to the rest of us. "The Mark is my oldest son's favorite place. Did you enjoy it?"

"Loved it. The whole town is idyllic," Heather tells him with an answering smile.

"We work hard to keep it that way." He ushers us to the array of empty tables at the small restaurant in the corner of the lobby. "So I hear you need some help with something. How can I be of service?"

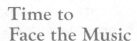

58

Time to
Face the Music

Before any of us can answer, Nyaz spends a minute waving down the lone employee in the place and ordering us drinks and some pachos and spicy punnion pings.

Once that is done and he's settled into the empty chair near Jaxon, I just dive right in with, "Arnst told us you might know where the Shadow Queen's secret fortress is located?"

His eyebrows shoot up as his shoulders stiffen. "Why in the world would you want another encounter with the Shadow Queen?"

"We have business to conduct with her," Hudson answers. "No fighting this time."

"Well, that's unfortunate," Nyaz says, settling back into his chair again. "She has several fortresses spread around the realm, and we never know which one she's residing in." He cups one side of his mouth as if to share a secret with us, and I find myself leaning forward to hear it. "I don't know if you're aware, but there's a bit of civil unrest in Noromar, with a rogue faction sending assassins to kill the queen."

"That's why she's in hiding, right?" I ask, nodding. "Because of the attempts on her life? We heard a rumor."

"And the disquiet through much of Noromar. She hasn't made life as pleasant in the rest of the Shadow Realm as it is in Vegaville, so most wraiths elsewhere want the curse ended so they can leave." He shrugs like he can't fathom it. "I don't know why they don't just come here. Or turn their own towns into a place like this."

I'm not sure a cushy place to live is enough to placate people who want freedom, but what do I know? Nyaz knows the wraiths here way better than I ever will.

"What do you suggest a person do to get her attention, then? To lure her from her fortress?" Hudson asks after Nyaz's rhetorical question hangs in the air for a few seconds.

The innkeeper blinks at us for several seconds, then slaps the table with a resounding thud. "No way. You are not asking my advice on how to bring the Shadow Queen down on this town again, are you? We've barely recovered from the last time that monster was here, and now you want to bring her back?" He shakes his head. "I can't let you do that, Hudson."

"Hey, believe me, no one wants to tangle with that bitch less than we do!" Heather tells him, hands up in a don't-shoot-the-messenger stance.

Everyone else makes a sound of agreement.

"We don't have a choice," Hudson tells him quietly. "And no, we have no interest in provoking her enough to make her attack Adarie. That's definitely not the end goal here. We just need to talk to her. And if we can get her attention, I believe we can make her an offer she'll actually be interested in accepting—and all without fighting."

"How do you plan to do that?" Nyaz crosses his arms over his chest and gives us a very unimpressed look.

"The goal is to get her attention—on us, not on Adarie," I assure him.

"I still don't see why you would want to do that. She wants to kill your man."

I don't have the energy to tell him that she will probably want to kill me equally as much if she ever remembers me. So I look to Hudson to explain, since he *is* the only one here who Nyaz trusts.

As Hudson explains more of our problem to the innkeeper, I rack my brain for a non-aggressive reason to bring her out of hiding.

After Hudson's explanation, Nyaz shakes his head again. "I'll admit, you might be the only thing the queen desires more than freeing the Shadow Realm, Hudson. I believe she *would* come out of hiding if she knew where to find you." I start to get excited, but then he adds, "Of course, that won't happen here. We have false Hudson sightings weekly because the townspeople are so eager for your return, so one more rumored return likely won't get her attention in the slightest."

"Good Lord," Jaxon murmurs. "He's like Elvis."

"He's just a hunka, hunka burnin' love," Flint sings in a fair imitation of Elvis, and we all laugh—even Jaxon.

The waitress arrives with a heavy tray loaded with our drinks, and Hudson jumps up to help her, which makes her blush and stutter, and she nearly drops the entire tray on Macy's head. Eventually, we get the drinks sorted out and sip our waters in silence.

I set my glass down and roll my eyes. "Come on, people. We need ideas! Chop-chop!"

Immediately, everyone starts tossing out suggestions—the wildest being the gang doing a flyby and tagging her statue in the palace gardens with spray paint. I'll admit, that one would be hilarious, but I'm not sure it would put her in the right mood for a calm discussion.

It's not until Macy leans over to me and points out the window that a real plan begins to formulate.

Reaching into my pocket, I pull out the card I'd taken in jest earlier. "I've got an idea," I tell the table at large.

"Oh yeah?" Nyaz doesn't sound impressed. Then again, he is currently afraid we're about to bring the full wrath of the Shadow Queen down on his little town, so I get it.

I turn to Hudson. "How's your voice feeling?"

"My voice?" he asks warily. But then his eyes fall on the card on the table and the wariness turns to full-blown alarm. "Oh, fook no, Grace."

Jaxon has obviously already caught on to the idea because he starts laughing like crazy. "Dude, that's fucking perfect."

"I'm not doing it." As if to underscore his flat-out refusal, Hudson, too, crosses his arms over his chest—and goes so far as to look in the other direction from me.

"Pretending I'm not here isn't going to make the idea go away, you know. Especially not when it's this good."

"It's not good. It's bloody terrible," he growls.

"Actually, it's bloody perfect," Eden crows as she also figures out what I'm suggesting.

"Can someone fill me in on what's so good-slash-terrible?" Nyaz asks as the waitress brings out our food. It smells delicious, and as she puts everything on the table, I realize that I haven't eaten a real meal since breakfast.

Everyone else must be feeling it, too, because Flint, Eden, Heather, and Macy dig into the pachos and punnion pings with gusto.

I try to show a little more restraint, mostly because Nyaz is still waiting for an answer. But I still can't resist grabbing at least one pacho and eating it before answering, "A concert promoter wants to put on a *widely publicized* concert during Starfall with Hudson."

Macy grins—the first real smile I've seen from her in months—adding, "And there is *no one* more equipped to make a Boomer stand up and pay attention than thousands of teenage girls."

59

Sing Work Makes the Dream Work

J axon snickers. "Hudson Vega: Hate on Tour. It's got a nice ring to it."
"Excuse me?" I ask, completely offended on his behalf. "Hudson isn't a hater."

But Jaxon is on a roll. "Hudson Vega: No Wonder Tour. Hudson Vega: Who Needs Eras When You've Got Centuries? Hudson Vega: I Have No Faith in the Future Tour."

Even Hudson is looking affronted now, but I've finally caught on to what Jaxon is doing. "You can make fun of him all you want, but *you* are the big, bad, dark-and-broody vampire who knows the names of all the huge pop tours going around at the moment."

"So that's what that was?" Eden snickers.

"Shawn Mendes, Taylor Swift, Louis Tomlinson, *Harry Styles*." I tick them off on my fingers, glaring at him extra hard when I say the last two names. Making fun of my mate and Harry all in the same sentence? He's lucky I'm on my best behavior right now. "I mean, it's no Of Course You Don't Remember Darren Hayes for Savage Garden tour, but whatever."

"Wait. He's touring?" Jaxon asks, whipping out his phone before he realizes it doesn't work here. "Slick, Grace. Very slick."

Everyone has a good laugh, even Nyaz.

"Anyway..." I turn back to Hudson. "It's a good idea."

"It's a great idea," Macy seconds. "You'll sell out the place, and she can't help but notice."

"Especially if we make the publicity a condition of the concert," Flint adds, looking thoughtful. "You know, like those contract riders stars attach to their appearances. Hudson will only perform if they can publicize the concert all over Noromar."

"And only if it's outside of Adarie—excuse me, Vegaville—so that Nyaz and the people of Adarie feel safe," I add.

"I can get behind that," Nyaz says, nodding. "My underground network can get the word out, too. Make it even harder for her to miss."

"That's brilliant," I tell him. "When we talk to the concert promoter, we can see if that will work for him, too."

"It will have to work for him," Flint says, sounding every inch the dragon prince. "Especially if he wants this as badly as he says he does."

"So, we've got a plan, then?" Heather says, ticking tasks off on her fingers like I did with pop stars, as if it's all just that easy. "Grace will contact the concert promoter with Hudson's demands. Nyaz will use his network to help get the word out. The rest of us will organize the concert venue. And, Hudson—"

"Yes, please, enlighten me," comes my mate's dry-as-burned-toast voice. "What is it exactly that Hudson will be doing while all this is going on?"

To her credit, Heather doesn't wilt. In fact, she doesn't so much as blink. She just looks him straight in the eye and says with a smile, "Putting together a kick-ass set list, obviously. The talent has to pull his weight, you know."

When Hudson smiles back at her, there's a little more fang showing than I would normally be comfortable with. Then again, we are asking an awful lot of him.

I say as much in an effort to placate him, and he turns that too-fangy smile on me. "Oh, is that what you're doing? Asking something of me? Here I was under the impression that I was being told what to do."

And apparently the vampire prince/gargoyle king/alpha male that is my mate is not particularly fond of being told what to do. Who would have guessed?

"It's the best idea we've got to get her to come to us. Mekhi can't wait much longer. You know that, right?"

He frowns, then begrudgingly admits, "I know."

"And you're going to be great. You know that, too, right?"

He shrugs. "Maybe."

"So what's the problem?" Jaxon intervenes. "Just take one for the team, bro."

Hudson's eyes narrow to slits. "You keep calling this a team, but I'm the one who has to keep taking the hits for it. You want to explain that to me?"

"Dude, there was a pigeon on my head. You didn't hear me whining this much."

"There was a pigeon on your head because you're an arsehole who can't keep his fooking mouth shut," Hudson shoots back, his accent getting thicker and thicker with each word. "It's not precisely the same thing."

"Oh, boo-hoo!" Heather interjects without bite but with a whole truckload of sarcasm. "The entire fucking Shadow Realm wants to see you in concert, Hudson. They love you *so much* they've built *statues* to you and renamed an *entire town* after you. How *will* you go on?"

"What if they don't?" Hudson mumbles so quietly that I'm pretty sure I'm the only one who heard him. And the last of the pieces clicks into place.

"Is that what you're worried about?" I ask. "That no one will come to see you sing?"

"I'm not a singer, Grace. Why on earth would anyone actually pay money to hear me sing?"

"Oh, babe." I clasp his hand between both of mine. "They're going to come."

"You don't know that."

"Oh, I'm pretty sure I do." I put a finger on the side of his chin and turn his head so that he can see what Macy pointed out to me earlier. Namely, that the entire sidewalk in front of Nyaz's inn is crowded with little teenage girls pressing up against the glass, all dressed in different variations of I <3 Hudson Vega shirts and jackets and scrunchies and earrings.

"They're going to come," I tell him again. "I think the only problem will be mitigating disappointment when the tickets sell out."

Jaxon snorts. "Little do they know they're signing on to listen to ninety minutes of vintage British Invasion."

Annoyance at all his little digs reaches a flashpoint inside me, and I round on him with a look that shuts everyone at the table up—even him. "You know what? I think I've finally figured out what you can do. You've got so much to say about Hudson and this concert, then fine. It just went from a solo act to a duo. Brother bands are huge."

"What?" Jaxon's voice is so high at this point that I'm pretty sure only paranormals and dogs can hear him. "No way. I'm not doing that."

"Oh, you are doing it," I tell him, pointing a finger at his face. "The Vega Brothers has a nice ring to it, doesn't it?"

"This is bullshit! I can't even sing—"

"Yes, you can," Flint corrects. "You have an amazing voice."

Jaxon shoots him a look that would have decimated a lesser man.

"Come on, Jaxon," I egg him on. "Isn't it your turn to take one for the team, *bro*?"

"I'm pretty sure I've already done that, considering I'm the last member of the Order still standing," he snaps in such a snide tone that Flint reels back in his chair like someone hit him.

"Yes, you have lost a lot," I say, standing so I can walk over to his side of the table while I say my piece. "But look around, will you? So has everyone else sitting at this table, except maybe Heather. But she's new here, so give her a little time.

"Flint lost his leg. Hudson lost the girl he loved for years to his brother, not to mention nearly losing his sanity in the frozen Gargoyle Court. Eden lost her family. Macy lost her boyfriend and found out she's been lied to practically her entire life. We've all lost something or someone, but we're still here. Still fighting to make sure you are *not* the last member of the Order still standing. So get off the pity train, stop riding your brother's ass so hard, and get on board. Otherwise, don't let the door hit you on the way out."

Total silence greets my words as every person at the table stares at me like they can't believe what I just said. To be honest, I can't believe it myself.

I'm not usually the one to go off on someone like that—especially not Jaxon, whom I adore beyond measure—but this time, he had it coming. We've all suffered. We've all been hurt. Just because he and

Flint are going through whatever the hell they're going through right now doesn't give him the right to take it out on the rest of us.

Still, we can't all sit here staring at each other forever, so I clear my throat and try to figure out what to say to get things moving again.

But before I can come up with anything, Jaxon clears his throat and says, "Fine, but I get to be the cool Vega brother. He can be the nerdy one."

"Well, obviously you're the 'eye candy.'" I quote the concert promoter, reaching down to squeeze Jaxon's hand in thanks for turning things around.

When Hudson mutters under his breath, "His hair better not upstage me," everyone cracks up. And that quickly, it feels like we're back on track. I mean, sure, it may be riddled with potholes and bumpy as hell, but we're on it.

For now, that will have to be good enough.

We need this moment of levity and confidence, for all of us. This feeling that we can do anything as long as we do it together.

Because the one thing nobody seems willing to even consider yet is the fact that we're about to lure a hungry tiger out of its cage with a juicy piece of meat...and we really think it'll want to chat with us before it pounces and rips out our jugulars?

60

Sweet Dreams Are
Made of Us

O ur meeting with Nyaz winds down a few minutes later, and we all make our way to our rooms. As soon as Hudson and I open the door to ours, Smokey races straight for us. She slams into Hudson at a dead run, then scurries up his leg and torso until she's sitting on his chest.

I expect her to admonish him about being gone so long, but instead she just chatters away about who knows what. Hudson, of course, nods and smiles like he understands every word of her story, and she ends up finishing with a flourish that makes both of them grin.

Then she reaches up and pats both his cheeks with her little hands before hightailing it out the door and down the hall.

"Should we go after her?" I ask. "She's kind of young to be on her own in a new town."

"She's okay," Hudson tells me. "She's just going to feed and run around a little. She'll be back in a couple of hours."

I stare at him. "You couldn't possibly have gotten that from what she told you. You don't actually speak umbra...or whatever it is she speaks."

"I don't," he agrees. "But I've gotten very adept at understanding certain noises that she makes at certain times. Including the one for food."

I start to ask him what that noise is, then decide he probably has no desire to try to imitate the little umbra at the moment. Also, I have no desire to hear him imitate her. Not when my entire being is craving sleep like my life depends on it.

"I'm going to take a shower," I say after a few moments. "Will you order me something from room service before they close? I got so worked up downstairs that I didn't eat much."

"I noticed." He runs a hand over my curls. "Anything particular you want?"

"Food," I answer, because I just need fuel and to make my stomach stop growling.

One quick shower and a few bites of Adarie's version of a grilled cheese later, I'm drawing the blackout curtains and crawling into bed. Hudson joins me a few minutes after, still slightly damp from his own shower.

I don't care. When he reaches for me, I go, rolling over until I'm straddling him, my knees around his hips.

He murmurs my name as he threads his hands through my hair and gently pulls me down for a kiss. And then we're rolling again, until I'm on the bottom and he's on top, propped up on his elbows and staring down at me with eyes so intense, it almost hurts to look at them.

"Go ahead," I whisper, lifting my chin and tilting my head back so that he can take what I so desperately want to give.

He doesn't answer, doesn't say anything at all. But his hand moves to rest on my collarbone, and his fingers softly stroke the pulse point at the base of my neck.

His eyes are darker now, the deep blue of his irises nearly obscured by his blown-out pupils. I can sense the hunger in him, can feel it clawing at him from the inside. But still he watches me, still he doesn't move except for the fingers slowly—oh so slowly—sliding back and forth against my vein.

"Go ahead," I say again. And when that still doesn't work, I run my hands up his lean, muscular back and tangle my fingers in the short, cool silk of his hair. I try to tug him closer, but he doesn't budge so much as an inch.

Instead, he stays exactly where he is, eyes and skin and hair gleaming in the dim light of the bedside lamp. And as he stares down at me, mouth open just enough that I can see the tip of his fangs where they rest against his lush lower lip, I can feel the same hunger in his eyes beating inside me as well.

"Hudson." I murmur his name as the ache grows and grows, taking me over.

Making me want.

Making me *need*.

Making me desperate to have him in any way—in all the ways.

"Please," I whisper, tangling my legs with his as I arch against him.

"Please what?" he whispers back, and there's a wickedness in his tone that somehow has the desperation burning even hotter inside me.

"Do it. I need—" My voice breaks, and his control breaks along with it.

Hudson's eyes seem to catch fire, and then he's striking quick as a heartbeat, his fangs sinking deep into my skin.

Pleasure slams through me as he drinks and drinks and drinks, and I never want it to end.

My hands clutch at him, pulling him closer.

My body wraps around him, cradling him in place.

And my veins light up like a Mardi Gras parade, noise and chaos and joy tearing through me with every sip he takes.

"More," I whisper, holding him to my vein. "More, more, more."

I feel his lips curve against the sensitive skin of my neck right before he starts to drink more deeply, more ravenously.

I give myself up to him, to this, offering everything inside me for his pleasure and mine. *More* is a chant deep inside me. *More, more, more.*

But this is Hudson, my Hudson, and his concern for me will always trump his own pleasure, and he's pulling back way too soon.

"No," I whimper, clutching at him, but he's not having it. He holds me tighter, though. Lets his tongue linger on his bite mark as he slowly, carefully seals it up.

Then he's sliding down my body, leaving a burning trail of kisses wherever his mouth touches. A flash of fang, a tug of fingers, and my panties disappear. Then he's sliding up my body again. Moving slow and purposeful.

I cry out then, and he pauses, catching my gaze with those heavy-lidded eyes and blown-out pupils that somehow only make him hotter. "Okay?" he asks, leaning down to kiss me in a way that has everything inside me trembling toward ecstasy.

"More," I manage to gasp out. "Please. More, more, more."

He grins then, a wicked little twist of his lips that has me clutching at his shoulders even as I arch against him.

And then he's giving me everything I've begged for and more as he takes me higher, higher, higher.

Until there is no yesterday and no tomorrow.

Until there is just him and me and the inferno that rages between us, growing hotter and wilder and more all-consuming with every moment that passes.

Until finally, finally, finally, he takes me up and over.

My eyes flutter open, and I bask in the sexy warmth of his gaze as he stares down at me. I smile back, reaching up to run a finger along his sexy lower lip for one second, two.

"I love you," I whisper as everything inside me yearns toward him. "I love you so much."

"Grace," he murmurs. "*My* Grace."

It's a plea as much as it's a demand, and there's only one answer I can give. "Yes."

Eventually, he gets up and turns off the lamp, cracks a window for Smokey so she has a way back in, locks the door, and grabs a bottle of water from the mini-fridge as I watch him with sleepy eyes.

"Here," he says, handing me the water as he climbs back into bed. "You need to drink."

"I think you just like bossing me around," I tease as I crack the water and take a long sip.

"Yeah, well, I've got to take advantage of it while I can," he says with a little smirk that makes me want to kiss him all over again. "Considering this is the only time you let me."

"Please," I scoff. "You'd be bored if I made it too easy for you."

He laughs as he pulls the covers over us. "You're probably right."

Hudson kisses me one more time, then rolls us over so that he can wrap himself around me. Because he always knows exactly what I need.

Most nights, he's the little spoon and I'm the big spoon—being on the outside helps keep my anxiety from rearing its ugly head when I'm asleep—but tonight I'm worried, really worried, and the feel of Hudson wrapped around me makes it seem like everything is okay. Even if my brain is telling me otherwise.

But sometimes the illusion of security is all you've got, and as I finally drift off to sleep, I tell myself that no matter what happens next, everything is going to be okay.

Now if only I could get myself to believe it.

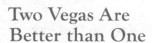

61

Two Vegas Are
Better than One

We spend the next couple of days in Vegaville eating a ton of Marian's pastries and getting ready for the concert. It turns out the concert promoter was really easy to track down—and even easier to convince to do things our way. As Flint thought, Aspero is willing to do anything to have a Hudson Vega concert—including turning it into a Vega Brothers concert.

I believe his exact words were, "How can I go wrong? The only thing better than one Vega is two!"

Heather and Eden went flying every morning, looking for venues, and we end up making the event an open-air concert a few miles outside of the gates of Vegaville. Normally, I'd still be freaked out at the idea of putting the town that close to danger—especially since so many town residents plan to be at the concert—but the others assure me it's going to be okay.

We have no intention of fighting the Shadow Queen, after all. In fact, the whole point is to surrender to her and get captured so we can make a deal.

On the plus side, the act of actually getting her attention seems to be right on track. Posters have gone up throughout the realm, I'm told, and Noromar is abuzz with talk of the concert of the century.

Hudson and Jaxon, however, are not nearly as excited as everyone else. In fact, every report from the concert promoter makes them turn a little more green.

"You said this was supposed to be a *concert*," Hudson hisses at me as the group of us walk/fly outside of town to help set up the stage the morning of the event. The promoting team doesn't need our help—and is, in fact, a little horrified that the talent and their entourage want to be so involved—but if I have to sit in a hotel room with a growly Hudson for five more minutes, we're going to end up in a giant fight, and neither of us wants that.

Which is why it seems better all in all to put him—and his equally-freaked-out little brother—to work for as many hours as we can. It figures Hudson would go from worried that no one would show up—the concert sold out within minutes of the tickets going on sale—to the stage now being too big.

"It *is* a concert," I tell him. "On a very large stage."

"It looks more like a three-ring circus to me," he answers. "Why all the colors? And weird decorations? Not to mention, I'm pretty sure half of Adarie would fit on the stage alone. I thought Jaxon and I would just be singing a few songs. Kind of impromptu."

I kind of love that—for all his usual vanity—Hudson is the only one who hasn't gotten used to calling the village by its new name. It's like just the idea of having a town named after him is so over-the-top he can't even wrap his mind around it.

And while I want to argue with him about the stage, the truth is, he's not wrong. Of course, I can't tell him that or he'll just spend the rest of the day thinking about tonight's performance.

I'd be lying if I didn't admit I was slightly nervous about the Vega boys hitting the stage together despite never making it through a single rehearsal without one of them calling the other a talentless hack—or something even more colorful. But I know these two well, and when they're really in a jam, they always come through for each other. Either that, or tonight's event will be equally entertaining for the crowd as the ultimate cage match: Superman versus Batman.

Regardless, what my mate needs right now is a solid distraction. "What?" I challenge. "You think you don't have the charisma to fill that stage?"

He recognizes my words for what they are, but knowing that I'm deliberately messing with him doesn't keep him from responding exactly how I expected him to. He lifts a brow and gives one of his singular British sniffs. "As if."

"Exactly. So what are you worrying about anyway?"

He gives me a little side-eye, but the corners of his mouth are definitely tilting up in the beginnings of a grin. "Jaxon messing up, obviously, and everyone blaming me."

"Obviously," I agree in the most British voice *I* can manage.

"Yeah, I'm the one you should be worried about here," Jaxon calls from several feet in front of us. "At least my ego will actually fit on that stage."

"But will that hair?" Hudson deadpans at him. "Maybe you should try it and make sure."

"It's not a real test unless your ego's up there with me," he shoots back. "Good thing I can fly—otherwise I might get pushed off the stage."

"Don't you mean float off like a blimp?" Hudson asks.

Jaxon doesn't answer—at least not with words. Instead, he shifts into his dragon form and takes to the sky.

"Looks like flying to me," Heather snarks.

At which point Smokey pops her head out of the top of Hudson's backpack and shakes her little fist at Heather—and Jaxon—all the while chittering away at the top of her lungs.

And Hudson takes his first breath in hours, because he's finally out of his own head. Mission freaking accomplished. Especially as he starts carrying Smokey in his arms, letting her talk to him and pull on his hair and hug him as much as she wants.

She's spending tonight during the concert back at the hotel. If the guard comes for us, that's where she'll stay until we can get back to her—Nyaz has promised to look after her for as long as it takes. But it makes every second we can spend with her right now more precious, especially for Hudson, who is already devastated at the idea of leaving her behind for even a little while.

Not as devastated as he would be if something happened to her at the Shadow Court, though, so it's a trade-off he can't help but make. No matter how much it sucks.

"What do you want to do first?" I ask as we approach the stage, where groups of people are carrying speakers and cables and other equipment across the platform on dollies.

"I think I'll help out up there," Hudson answers, leaping onto one of the lighting ledges in a single bound. Once there, he starts flinging equipment around like it's nothing, lifting with one hand what it was taking three wraiths to manage.

"I've got to say, being mated to a vampire has to be the most badass thing ever," Heather comments, watching him. "Does he, umm, throw you around like that, too?"

I grin. "Maybe you should find yourself a vampire of your own and figure it out."

"Believe me, I'm thinking about it." But then she nods to where Eden and Flint are flying above the stands, stringing fairy lights along the huge scaffolding set up all around the makeshift arena. "Though dragons are pretty cool, too."

"As are gargoyles," I tell her, shifting just so the others don't get to have all the fun.

"Well, obviously gargoyles," she agrees with a roll of her eyes. "I thought that went without saying."

"It does," Macy says as she comes up behind me. "So they're all showing off how big and bad they are at the moment. What do you think we should do?"

I look around the enormous, empty arena and decide this might be a perfect time to see if I can tempt the old Macy out to play a little bit. "How about we create some ambiance?"

Because I'm watching closely, I see a tiny flicker of interest in the depths of her eyes. "What kind of ambiance?" she asks.

"I don't know, but I'm open to suggestions. Something that will make tonight feel magical for everyone who shows up?"

She doesn't answer right away, just thinks for a minute. But then she lifts her hands, swooshing her wand back and forth several times, and says, "Something like this?" Seconds later, thousands of multicolored twinkles come to life, swirling and spinning in the air around us.

"Well, that sure as shit puts their little fairy lights to shame, doesn't it?" Heather comments.

Macy makes a *tsk*ing sound in the back of her mouth. "I'm just getting started."

Next, she does a small, complicated hand spell in the air before throwing her arms out wide. The entire open-air arena comes to life in a burst of sparks in every color of the rainbow.

"Show-off," Heather teases with a giant grin, but I can tell she's very impressed.

Macy just blows on her nails and then wipes them on her torn black shirt in the universal damn-right-I'm-a-bad-bitch sign.

Not to be outdone in what has obviously become a competition—at least judging by the way the dragons are now doubling up on stringing lights at the highest heights of the scaffolding—I take a deep breath and reach inside myself for my earth magic.

It doesn't come. And that's when I remember I can't use it here in the Shadow Realm. None of us can use our extra powers—no telekinesis for Jaxon, no poofing things for Hudson, no demigod magic for me. Only Macy has use of her magic because it's who she is—like flying and shifting are for the dragons and me, or superstrength and speed are for Hudson.

"Well, there goes my plan to decorate with flowers," I say with a sigh. "I was going to cover this whole place with them."

"That's a great idea!" Heather enthuses.

"Yeah, but—" I hold up my hands. "I've got no earth magic to make that happen."

She looks at me like I'm completely out of touch. "Yeah, but there are a ton of flowers in the nursery we walked by on our way out of town. We could just do the *human* thing and buy them."

I crack up, because she's right. I've become so accustomed to using my powers for everything that I've forgotten what it's like to just do things the human way. Which could be fun now that I think about it—especially since I'm doing it with my best friend.

"Let's go," I tell her, because it will give us time to talk. Besides, I spent seventeen years of my life doing things the human way. How hard could it possibly be?

62

R eally freaking hard, it turns out. We buy out all the flowers the
nursery has, and we even convince them to help us cart them
to the arena so we don't have to take multiple trips. But carrying the
bushels of flowers up and down the stage, creating a ring of intertwined
flowers all the way around the front of the set… Well, it's exhausting.

"Why did I let you talk me into this?" I tell Heather when we finally
finish.

Sweat is pouring down both of us, and we collapse on the nearest
bleacher bench we can find as Jaxon and Hudson do sound checks.
"Because no way were we going to let a bunch of dragons and vampires
outclass us," she says, holding up a fist for me to pound.

"Yeah, you're right." I rest my head on her shoulder as the sound
technician makes Jaxon repeat the same line several times because
he sounds pitchy. Which he does, but I'm not sure if that's the sound
system or nerves. Now that I'm sitting in the audience, among rows
and rows and rows of seats, I'm beginning to realize just how big this
concert is going to be.

"I'm glad you came," I tell Heather quietly. "I know I gave you a
hard time about it—and I'm terrified something is going to happen to
you—but I'm still glad you're here. It's been nice doing stuff together
again."

She laughs. "What, are you getting sentimental on me in your old
age, Grace Foster?"

"Maybe I am," I answer. "You got a problem with that?"

"Not even a little bit." Then she lays her head on my nestled one.
"I'm glad I came, too. Even though you really need a shower." She waves

a hand under her nose to indicate that I stink.

"Right back atcha," I tell her as I stagger to my feet. "I think the technician area behind the stage has a shower trailer for volunteers who won't have time to go home before the concert. I'll race you for first dibs."

Heather doesn't even bother to agree. She just takes off running. Which, if I was still only human, would be a problem, because she always could kick my ass in a race. But the great thing about being a gargoyle is it comes with wings. And if she's going to cheat by taking off early, all bets are off.

I fly right over her—and the others, who are watching the sound check—and am actually fully in the shower before Heather even makes it to the trailer.

"Cheater," she calls out from the sitting area in the front of the trailer.

"Takes one to know one," I shout back.

Fifteen minutes later, I'm dressed in my official Vega Brothers Concert Staff gear and heading to the front of the venue with Heather to work the ticket booth.

As soon as we get there, we realize *exactly* how big this concert is, as crowds of concertgoers are lined outside the arena as far as the eye can see.

"Holy fuck," Heather whispers, her eyes as wide as saucers. "It'll take us a year just to collect all the tickets."

She's not far off, I suspect, and I motion to the promoter to add a few more people to the ticket collection team.

As seven more volunteers rush to the counter, Aspero waves his arms out wide and shouts, "Who's ready to make history tonight?"

Everyone cheers, Heather and me included, with giant grins on our faces as we get into the spirit. When he swings open the doors of the arena to let the first excited fans shuffle inside, I take a deep breath and start collecting and stamping tickets.

Two very exhausting hours later, I leave Heather with the rest of the ticket workers to rush backstage to give Hudson some last-minute moral support. He's going to need it, if the number of people we let in tonight is any indication.

I hustle into Hudson's tent as he's arguing with Mila, the hairstylist, about the perfect amount of coif for his hair. I'd say it was just nerves, but this is Hudson, and everyone knows his hair is sacred.

Either way, they get it worked out and he looks gorgeous in the end—just like he always does. He's dressed in his Armani jeans and a deep-purple button-down with the sleeves rolled up to just below his elbows, and he looks good. Really, really good.

"Why are you looking at me like that?" he asks as he settles onto the couch next to me.

"Because you look amazing," I answer, sliding closer to him so I can wrap my arms around his waist. "If you weren't about to go up onstage, I might be tempted to mess up that fancy hairstyle of yours."

His eyes spark with interest. "I'm sure I could talk Mila into coming back and doing it again," he says, right before he lowers his mouth to mine.

It's a good kiss—just like every kiss we share—but I pull away before it can get too interesting. Partly because I'm afraid I'll get carried away and actually mess his hair up and partly because I want to talk to him before he goes onstage.

Hudson doesn't seem to have the same worries I do, though, and he grumbles a little when I pull away.

"Hey," I tell him, putting my hands on either side of his face so that he's got to look me in the eyes. "You okay with all this?"

"As long as I don't let myself think too much about the Shadow Queen's henchmen grabbing you while I'm still onstage, then yeah. I'm fine with it."

"You sure?" I ask. "You haven't even shared the set list with me."

"I happen to think some things should be a surprise," he answers before pulling me onto his lap for another kiss. "But I'm good, I swear. Totally steady."

"Well, that's an impressive turnaround. And while I appreciate it, I have to ask—what's changed since this morning?"

He shrugs. "I got used to the size of the place. And I got to meet the musicians who will be playing with us during rehearsals, and I couldn't wait all week to surprise you." His eyes twinkle as he says, "Turns out they tapped Lumi and Caoimhe to back us up, along with a few of their friends."

"Lumi and Caoimhe are here?" I ask as excitement roars through me at the thought of seeing them again—at least until I remember that they won't be nearly as excited to see me.

Hudson nods. "They are. And they'll be onstage with Jaxon and me. They know Vemy, and when they realized he was stage-managing this show, they asked to be able to sit in. So they'll be up there with me."

"That's fantastic!" I give him a huge hug. "I already knew you guys were going to kick ass tonight. Now I know it'll be even better than that."

"I'll settle for Jaxon and me not embarrassing ourselves, but sure. Let's go with kickarse." His grin fades. "If something happens—if the Shadow Queen's army takes us off the stage—"

"I'll be there," I tell him. "I won't let them separate us."

"I appreciate the protection," he says a little dryly. "But that wasn't what I was going to say." He takes my hand, holds it to his chest. "Whatever happens to me, I want you to remember what we're doing here. What we need to do to save Mekhi."

"Nothing's going to happen to you," I tell him immediately. "We're going to talk to her and—"

"I'm sure you're right." He wraps his arms around me and pulls me closer, but I'm too stiff now to let him. "But let's say that Nyaz is right, that she's out for revenge and she thinks the best way to get that is to come after me—"

"I won't let that happen. We won't let it happen—"

"That's what I'm trying to say. I don't want you to get yourself killed trying to protect me, Grace. I want—"

I stop him the only way I know how—by slamming my mouth down on his. And kissing him and kissing him and kissing him until he stops trying to talk and ends up kissing me back.

He doesn't pull away, and neither do I, until someone clears their throat from the front of the tent. "We're ready for you, Hudson," Vemy says with a smile.

He nods, then leans forward and rests his forehead against mine.

"Grace—"

"Go," I tell him. "I'll be right there watching you the whole time. And I'll be right here waiting for you when you're done."

For long seconds, he doesn't move. He just stares at me with eyes the rich, dark blue of forever. But eventually, he nods and steps away from me. "Wish me luck."

"I think you mean break a leg."

He gives me a lopsided grin. "As long as it's not my heart, I'm good with it."

"Seriously?" I make a gagging noise. "Corny much?"

"Only about you," he answers.

"Glad to hear it. Now, get your arse out on that stage and don't break any body parts. We've got shit to do."

63

Viva Las
Vegas

I make it to the side of the stage before Hudson and Jaxon do. Macy and the others are already there, so I join them. We thought about going down in the front of the crowd to watch, but there are a lot of really enthusiastic girls down there, and the idea of being crushed by them in their mad desire to get to the Vega Brothers isn't appealing to any of us. Then again, neither is the idea of the Shadow Queen's guards coming for us and trampling a bunch of innocent teenagers.

Basically, watching from the wings seems like the safest bet.

As the lights go down in the audience, Macy's colorful sparkles stand out even more, and the crowd *ooh*s and *aah*s—at least until the stage lights go up and someone welcomes everyone to the show.

The music starts, and Hudson strolls onto the stage, taking a second to greet Caoimhe and Lumi, who are already playing their instruments. It's a song I don't recognize—maybe one of their own—but the crowd is bopping along to it as Hudson jogs along the edge of the stage, waving to the fans.

Then he circles back to the microphone in the center of the stage and says, "Helloooooooo, Adarie! How are you tonight?"

Boos fill the audience, and I can't figure out what's wrong until the crowd starts chanting. "Vegaville! Vegaville! Vegaville!"

Hudson looks astonished for a second. He covers it well, but I can tell he is completely overwhelmed by their response. And things haven't even gotten started yet.

"Okay, okay." He holds up a hand to quell the screaming. "Let's try that again. Helloooooooooooo, Vegaviiiiiiiiiiiille! How are you tonight?"

The crowd goes wild—so wild that I think the sound waves buffet

Hudson back a foot or two, because by the time they're done shouting he looks a little shell-shocked.

"I want to thank you all for coming out tonight. Your reception has been, ummmm, a little astonishing." He pauses, kind of thinks to himself. Then says, "Yeah, astonishing is a good word."

The crowd laughs, and next to me, Macy groans. "Seriously? This is his stage patter? Has the guy never been to a concert before?"

"What do you think he should do?" I ask a little acerbically, because I don't see her ass out on that stage, taking one for the team. "Ask them to throw their underwear at him?"

As if the concert gods heard me, a bright-purple bra comes spinning up onstage and hits Hudson right in the face. Lumi and Caoimhe don't miss a note as they continue to play.

And if I thought Hudson was astonished before, it's nothing compared to his expression when he peels the lacy lingerie from his face. He holds it away from him, one of the straps pinched gingerly between two fingers, and it looks like he's torn between throwing it back or trying to hold on to it because he doesn't want to hurt anyone's feelings.

In the end, though, he holds it up and says, "I think one of you lost this? Wave your hand and I'll throw it back to you?"

The next thing I know, ten thousand hands are in the air and every single woman in the place is screaming for Hudson to throw her bra back to her.

"Okay, then," he says, looking back and forth between all the adoring, screaming fans. "Looks like I'll be keeping this."

Lumi and Caoimhe play a particularly complicated riff behind him as he wraps the bra around his microphone stand like one of Steven Tyler's scarves.

"Smooth," Heather says as the crowd starts screaming all over again. "I didn't think he had it in him."

Hudson leans toward the mic stand again and says, "So, um, I think it's probably time to, uhh, introduce you to, umm—"

He breaks off as the stage is literally flooded with bras and stuffed animals and Hudson Vega statues. A small one bounces off his left leg, and he jumps back. "Bloody hell!" he chokes out, which only makes the crowd get more frenzied.

"Is he all right?" Flint comes down from his flying patrol long enough to ask.

"I don't know. He looks like he's limping a little," Macy answers.

Heather pinches up her face. "I'm beginning to think he should have asked for hazard pay for this gig."

"Poor Jaxon." Flint looks super sad as he shakes his head. "If they're acting this way over Hudson, can you imagine what they're going to do when my man finally makes it onstage?"

I start to make a snarky comment back to him, but Hudson chooses that moment to look over at me wide-eyed, and I think he wants me to give him some advice on what to do. But I've got nothing, except to suggest that maybe he hurry things along. Maybe they'll stop throwing things at him if he's actively singing.

I roll my hands in a speed-it-up gesture, and he gives me an aggrieved look, as if to say, *What the hell did you think I was trying to do?*

But when he turns back to the audience this time, he grabs the microphone and yells, "I want to introduce you to someone! Do you want to meet him?"

The crowd screams and whistles and stomps their feet in reply.

Hudson grins, a little more confident now that he has something certain to say. "Let me tell you a little bit about this guy before I bring him on out to meet you."

The lights grow a little dimmer, and for the first time since he got onstage, Lumi and Caoimhe bring the background music down to something a little more soulful.

Hudson walks to the edge of the stage and crouches down to touch all of the little purple fingers thrusting up from the standing section right at the front. "He's my baby brother, and he's a pretty cool guy. I mean, he's got a soul-searing obsession with the color black, but other than that, he's a pretty stand-up guy. If you don't count the way he used to steal my colored pencils when we were little."

The crowd whistles and *awwwwwwwwwww*s at that, and Hudson raises a brow. "Wait a minute. Are you cheering because he stole my crayons?" he asks. And when he shifts the microphone from one hand to the other, I know he's finally starting to feel a little more comfortable.

The crowd responds by cheering even louder.

Hudson laughs. "Well, if you're that excited by a little crayon stealing, I'm guessing you're going to be really excited when you see how he can handle a pair of drumsticks."

The crowd roars their approval.

"I'm going to bring him on out. But you've got to do me a favor. From this point on, you need to refer to my little, tiny, baby brother only as…" Lumi plays a really loud riff on his guitar, strumming chords in quick succession to ramp up the introduction. "Jaxon 'the Hair' Vega! Come on, everyone, give a real Vegaville cheer for 'the Hair'!"

64

The Best
Shade Plans

Jaxon runs onstage as Hudson's voice echoes through the arena. And the already frenzied crowd somehow manages to take it up another notch or ten as he slides behind the drum kit and plays a complicated set of beats.

Apparently he's been building up a lot of energy waiting to be called onstage, because the more the crowd cheers, the longer his drumming intro goes, until he ends with a crash of cymbals and a spin of his sticks really freaking high in the air.

I expect him to pull another pair out of his pocket, but apparently I've underestimated the younger Vega's showmanship. Instead, he fades to the front of the stage and catches them before tipping a fake hat at the audience.

"Bloody hell!" Hudson says with a roll of his eyes. "I neglected to tell you that the reason he has all that hair is to cover his giant head."

The crowd roars with laughter, and Jaxon bends forward, doing a head-banging kind of move à la eighties hair bands everywhere, then fades back to his drum kit. Hudson walks to the edge of the stage, picks up his electric guitar, and hangs it over his shoulder before crossing back to the mic stand with its lone purple bra still waving in the wind.

The other musicians stop playing as Hudson runs his fingers up the neck of his guitar in a quick chord progression that culminates in the most plaintive note I've ever heard.

It echoes across the stage and out into the audience, a sound so pure and sad that it sends chills down my spine, and for a second I imagine that this is the sound of Hudson's soul. The sorrow and the beauty and the agony of living all rolled into one perfect minor key.

Hudson holds the note and holds it and holds it until finally it starts to wobble just a little bit at the end. As if sensing the same thing I do about the music, Jaxon picks it up with the drums, and it's such an obvious *I've got you, brother* that my heart catches in my chest.

And then he's laying down a slow, soft beat that shares with the audience the first, glancing rhythms of the song.

Hudson starts to play again, and this time a melody takes shape. One note and then two, and as the brothers continue tossing the notes back and forth to each other, my eyes widen as I finally realize what song they're playing. It's got a slightly different composition here, played between the two of them, than it does on the album, and it's a little slower, a little edgier, but it's definitely the same song: "My Blood" by Twenty One Pilots.

My heart shatters at the realization. Because this song is about family.

Like it was written just for these two brothers, who have each other's backs against all the odds and against all the shit in the world.

Brothers who would rip apart anyone who came for the other.

Brothers who, despite their differences, are ride or die till the end.

And as Hudson leans forward and starts to sing the lyrics, I feel the truth of them—the love and the pain and the determination of them—all the way to *my* soul as these two guys I love so much finally find their way to each other.

The lyrics meander across the stage, slow dive into the audience, and I can see the exact second all the screaming people realize the moment they have found themselves privy to. The gift that they're being given.

Because Hudson Vega is singing to each and every one of *them* that they're his family, too. And he will keep them safe. He'll protect them. Like they're his blood.

When Hudson gets to the falsetto that the lead singer, Tyler Joseph, usually does…Jaxon leans forward into his mic and lets loose with it, and the crowd goes fucking wild. And my chest tightens until I think my ribs might crack as I take in the beaming smile of pride on Hudson's face as he watches his little brother shine.

This—this moment right here—is what this song is about. More, it's what Jaxon and Hudson are about. These two kids who'd been to hell and back before they'd even learned to read. Tortured by their parents, forsaken by their people, separated from each other until all they heard was the lonely echo inside of them. Yet here they are, playing together, creating harmony and light and joy for all these people. Filling up the loneliness inside of them with their love and trust for each other.

It's one of the most profound moments of my life, and as I glance at Flint, who is still beside me, I can tell he understands it, too. That he knows just how much these two have suffered and what it means that— despite everything—they've somehow found a way back to each other.

In the middle of the song, the music lowers to a hush, the other musicians softly playing in the background. Even Hudson stops playing his guitar, letting it go until his straps hold it. He grabs the mic with both hands—and sings to every single wraith before him.

Low, deep, like every word is a part of his soul and he wants it to be a part of theirs, too.

Hudson Vega has them in his hands, and he'd die to keep them safe.

The audience is straining forward now, hands stretched to the sky like they can catch the notes if they could just reach high enough.

And then Jaxon's falsetto joins. And then Lumi and Caoimhe and the entire band, doubling and tripling as the music grows and grows and grows, filling every crack and crevice in the arena until there's nothing but wave after wave of sound and hope and promise echoing through the space.

As the last note of the song slowly fades, the entire arena goes silent.

Hudson shifts awkwardly in front of the mic stand, but he doesn't need to be worried. Because the audience wastes no time bursting into wild applause. Cheers and whistles and shouts fill the air around us, and Hudson turns to give me a slow, perfect grin.

I smile back as more bras flood the stage, and just as Hudson reaches for the microphone again, he freezes—and his face shifts from joy into an expression so lethal and laser-focused that I shiver. He gives me a quick nod—our signal that it's started—and I watch his gaze swing to the front of the stage, to the hundreds of young wraiths down below crowding as close as they can get to him.

Then everything goes black.

Even Macy's twinkly lights are gone.

Seconds later, a group of guards swarms backstage. Macy shrieks as one of them grabs her and slams her face-first into the closest wall.

"Hey!" Flint shouts as he tries to intercede and ends up getting an elbow to the nose for his trouble.

Eden growls, starts to respond by kicking the guy's feet out from under him, but I finally manage to get her attention.

"Stop!" I whisper urgently, and though she looks like she wants to argue with me, she doesn't. Because the goal here isn't to fight a bunch of guards, even if we can take them. The goal is to get captured and taken to the Shadow Queen with as little fuss as possible. The last thing we want is for anyone in the audience to get hurt.

I manage to keep my resolve as they slam me face-first into the wall, too, but when they rush the stage and grab Hudson, it takes every ounce of concentration I have not to fight back. Especially when he just lets them throw him to the ground and kick him a few times.

The audience starts screaming as they realize what's happening, and some even try to rush the stage, which is now filled with guards. It's my worst nightmare, the thing I was terrified would happen, but before anyone gets close to the stage—or the Shadow Guards—members of Nyaz's underground converge on the front of the stage and start herding everyone out of the makeshift arena.

I nearly sob with relief, even as one of the guards yanks my arms behind my back and marches me past the stage and down the stairs to the rocky ground below.

They push Heather down right behind me, and she cries a little, just enough for me to hear.

"Are you okay?" I ask, trying to see her over the guards between us.

"Close your mouth!" snarls one of them. "And get your hands up. We'll tolerate no disobedience from any of you."

"Can you define disobedience?" Flint asks as they shove him down the steps as well. "Just so that I don't make a mistake and accidentally—"

He breaks off as the tip of a dagger is positioned precariously close to his neck.

"I'm guessing that counts as disobedience," Hudson mutters on his way down the steps.

"Can you two just take this seriously?" Jaxon snarls. "You're going to get yourselves killed because you don't know when to quit."

He glares especially hard at Flint, who rolls his eyes back at him. But the dragon doesn't say anything else to the guards.

"You're all coming with us," the guard who appears to be in charge growls as he—and his sword—guide us into a line in front of Hudson's tent. Aspero is running back and forth in front of us, wringing his hands and demanding to know the meaning of all this.

"I'll find help for you, Hudson," he promises as he tries to put himself between my mate and the two guards who are standing over him. "I'll call someone, and we'll figure out what to do. They can't just come in here—"

"It's all right, Aspero," Hudson tells him. Then he lowers his voice to say something else, but I can't hear him over all the shouting of the guards, no matter how hard I try.

Aspero is dragged away before he can say anything else, and while this is exactly what we want—exactly what we've been angling for since we got to town—it still feels strange to just stand here and let them take us. It feels stranger still to let them treat people who have been kind to us this way.

Especially when I'm pretty sure we can take them, even without any of our extra powers. These guards don't seem like they're particularly skilled at what they're doing.

But escaping isn't the point of the plan, so I leave my hands behind my back and try to look as unthreatening as possible as they line me up between Hudson and Macy.

"Nice hat," my cousin tells me as she eyes the I <3 the Vega Brothers beanie I've got on.

I grin back. "It's a statement."

"That's really what you want to be wearing for your mug shot?" Hudson asks with a shake of his head. But I can see the smile lurking in the depths of his blue eyes.

"Don't worry about my mug shot," I tell him. "You should be

thinking about your own, considering it will probably be plastered on fifty different types of merch in less than a week."

"Thanks for that visual," he says with a groan.

"Anytime," I answer.

"Silence!" the head guard bellows. "You are being arrested for crimes against the queen. Please put your hands out in front of you now and clasp them together."

Considering Hudson is the only one of us they know has been here before, it seems a bit abusive to arrest all of us for mythical crimes against the Shadow Queen. But again, we're getting what we wanted, so none of us says anything.

Instead, we do exactly what they ask.

I hold my arms out, lacing my fingers together and pressing my palms against each other. As soon as I do, one of the guards steps up and rests a hand on top of my wrists. Seconds later, a shadow cord appears out of nowhere, winding itself around and around my wrists and binding them together.

Another wave of his hand, and a blindfold covers my eyes. "Hey, what—"

I break off as something that feels an awful lot like tape slams down on my mouth.

And just like that, panic explodes in me.

I was okay with being arrested because it would get us where we need to go—namely, to the Shadow Queen. But being blindfolded? Gagged? I didn't sign up for that.

Beside me, Macy lets out a high-pitched squeak—the most she can do, I assume, with her mouth taped shut. And then the others are making noises as well, muffled shouts and cries echoing through the air.

I can identify Flint's and Jaxon's growls, Heather's cry, Eden's muffled snarl. But Hudson doesn't make a sound—not one sound.

Terror explodes deep inside me, has my stomach turning in sick somersaults and my heart beating way too fast. Where is Hudson? What have they done to him? Did they hurt him? Take him away?

I'm breathing much too fast now, nearly hyperventilating—which is horrible in any circumstance and triply horrible with my mouth sealed.

I'm trying desperately to take a deep breath to calm myself down, but there's only so much air I can pull in through my nose.

And the more I try, the worse it gets.

"Hudson!" I try to say, but it comes out all muffled and unintelligible. I try again. "Hudson! Hudson!"

I can't even understand myself, let alone expect anyone else to understand me.

But then he's there, the side of his arm brushing against my shoulder as he, too, makes a noise beneath his gag that sounds an awful lot like my name.

Because of course Hudson, the hero of Vegaville and the Shadow Realm, can find a way to talk with a gag over his mouth. If I wasn't so relieved to know that he's okay, I'd laugh.

I am relieved, though, and when he brushes his arm against mine again, I can feel the tension deep inside me unlocking just a little bit. My stomach unclenches, and while my heart continues to beat way too fast, it becomes a lot easier for me to breathe.

I remember one of the tricks Hudson taught me to control my panics and start doing math in my head. One plus one is two. Two plus two is four. Four plus four is eight.

It's okay, I tell myself as they start shuffling us down the street. Eight plus eight is sixteen. This is what we wanted. Sixteen plus sixteen is thirty-two. This is what we needed to have happen. I take a deep breath through my nose, hold it, then let it out slowly.

Of course they blindfolded us if they're taking us to the queen. Otherwise, we'd figure out the location she's tried so hard to keep secret.

It's actually a good thing, I tell myself as I concentrate on taking more slow, even breaths. Because the sooner we get to see her, the sooner we can make a bargain to save Mekhi and help Lorelei.

It's a good thing, I repeat again, like a mantra. A very good thing.

Even if, right now, it feels like anything but.

We walk for a while—one thousand and twenty-seven steps, to be exact—before one of the guards orders, "Stop!"

I do, so abruptly that Macy crashes into me from behind.

She makes a noise that I can't quite distinguish, maybe "sorry," maybe "ow," but we both manage to stay upright, so I'm calling it a win. At least until I hear the clang of metal doors—followed by the high-pitched whinny of an animal I can't identify.

There's another clang of metal against metal, and then I'm being shoved forward. "Step up," one of the guards tells me in a harsh voice. So I do, nearly tripping on the high step.

I move slowly, feeling in front of me with my feet until I realize there's another step. I creep up it and two more steps before I'm finally... somewhere. Though I can't tell where—or even what—it is.

"Hurry up!" the guard growls at me, giving me a hard shove between my shoulder blades that sends me careening forward.

I stumble several steps, determined not to fall on my face. When I don't crash into anything, I continue hesitantly moving forward until my fingers brush against what feels like a cold metal wall.

I take one more step forward and push against it as hard as I can, trying to determine how sturdy it is. Behind me, I can hear my friends shuffling and stumbling in as well. I try to call out to them, to tell them to keep walking, but all that comes out is a bunch of muffled grunts.

In the end, I just turn around and press my back against the wall, trying to stay out of the way as best I can—which isn't exactly easy, considering none of us can see where anyone else is.

Finally, though, we must all be in the cage or whatever this is, because the same guard who yelled at me snarls, "Don't cause any trouble, or the queen will hear about it."

Seconds later, the warning is followed by the sound of metal doors clanging. Then the rattle of what may or may not be a chain and a lock.

The second we're alone, every single one of us tries to talk. It doesn't work, of course. All that comes out is a series of squeaks and cries and grunts and moans, but at least the sounds are identifiable and easily assigned to my different friends.

Even Hudson makes a noise that's a cross between a sneer and a question.

I try to answer him—even though I have no idea what he was trying to say—but my answer is no more intelligible. It seems to calm him down, though, judging by the fact that the next sound he makes is more of a grunt.

I've just started walking toward where the Hudson-sounding noise came from when I hear a series of high-pitched whinnies outside our cage.

And then we start to move—fast.

65

All Caught Up

We all go flying, bodies slamming into metal walls or one another. I bounce off someone soft—Heather, maybe, judging by the smell of her shampoo—and end up falling onto my knees and face-planting in someone else's lap.

Someone who smells a lot like oranges and fresh water.

Fuck.

I start to push myself up as fast as I can, but that means pushing my clenched, bound hands down on Jaxon's thigh as hard as I can. He grunts, tries to shift to help me, and ends up knocking my arms out from under me again.

Which, of course, makes me face-plant. *Again*.

Another low grumble, followed by him pushing against me a lot more gently than I was just doing to him. As he does, he makes a noise that I have no hope of interpreting. But I say yes, anyway, just to make a sound back.

After I'm back on my feet, courtesy of Jaxon, I reach out and find the wall again. Then slide down it until I'm sitting on my butt. If we're going to be moving for a while, it seems a lot safer down here than risking getting sent flying twice.

All around me, I can hear clothes rustling and people grumbling as they, too, settle onto the floor. And then there's nothing for a while besides the loud rattle of the cage's wheels on what feels like a *very* bumpy path and the occasional sound of an animal making noise.

I just hope wherever they're taking us includes the Shadow Queen, as we'd planned. If it's not—if they're just going to leave us languishing in prison somewhere—then we're all screwed, Mekhi most of all.

I give a muffled, humorless chuckle as I realize we never even considered the prison option. I don't know if that's because I'm surrounded by people who have spent their whole lives thinking themselves total badasses and uncontainable—or because we're just shit at considering every potential outcome. To be fair—to myself, at least—I've always been terrible at facing possible consequences. I'm just a wee bit surprised I'm not alone in that department, when one of us should have definitely considered a lifetime prison jumpsuit option and pointed it out to the rest of us.

Every few minutes, Macy makes a string of sounds, like she's attempting to perform some kind of spell. Every time she tries, I can feel a ripple of hope move through me and the others. And every time she fails, the hope drowns in a wave of disappointment.

Part of me wants her to keep trying, wants to think there's some spell out there that will at least get these gags off if she can just find it. I don't mind being arrested. I don't even mind having my hands bound. But this shadow gag? I hate it so much that a part of me wants it gone and damn the consequences.

But even as I wish for it, I know it's a pretty far-fetched hope. If regular magic could trump shadow magic—the oldest magical force on earth—then we wouldn't be here. We would have found a way to break the magic of the shadow poison a long time ago, and Mekhi would be safe.

Eventually, though, she gives up making noises. And so do the rest of us. Instead, we ride in silence, with only the occasional stray grunt for company.

I'm sitting with my back to the wall of whatever they've got us in, and even though I try my hardest to remain alert, at some point I end up resting my head back against the cool metal. And some time after that, I find my eyelids drooping and my whole body feeling heavy.

I try to fight off the lethargy, but in the end, I just give in to it. After all, if I'm asleep, maybe I can stop counting every second that passes like it's going to be my last.

I don't know how long I doze, but I jerk awake when the vehicle we're in comes to a shaking, shuddering stop. My heart is beating superfast now, and I strain to hear any sound that means they're coming for us.

At first, I don't hear anything. And then there's the sound of shoes crunching on gravel right outside our vehicle. I hold my breath, feel everyone around me doing the same thing.

For long minutes, though, nothing happens. We just sit in silence, waiting and wondering what's going to happen when the door finally opens.

The longer we wait, the tenser I can feel myself getting. The tenser I can feel the others getting, too, until I expect one of us to explode at any second.

Maybe that's the point, though. Maybe they're just waiting to see which one of us freaks out first. If so, they're doing a good job of it. With every minute that passes, I can feel myself getting closer and closer to being the winner here.

I think it's the total loss of control that's doing it. It's not about being locked up, per se. But having my sight taken from me? Having my ability to communicate with my mate and my friends ripped away?

Yeah, that is putting me very much on edge.

It makes me wonder how Hudson handled being locked in Descent for all those years without losing his sanity completely. I don't think I could take this for even a few days. If I was trapped like this year after year, decade after decade?

I shake my head.

As I inhale another steadying breath, I have even more respect for him than I did just a little while ago, and I didn't think that was possible.

In fact, I—

There's a sudden scraping at the door that has me leaning forward, heart once more exploding out of my chest as I strain to hear what's going on, what's going to happen next.

More scraping, followed by the sound of metal clanging against metal.

Voices murmuring.

A key turning in a lock.

And then the door swings open and ice-cold air floods the space.

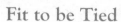

66

Fit to be Tied

"Get up!" someone growls harshly at us.

I try to follow directions, but it's not exactly easy, since my legs fell asleep hours ago from being in the same position for too long.

The others must be having the same problem, because someone keeps cursing at us. Then there's the pounding of feet against metal in rapid succession. Someone is climbing into the cage to get us. Several someones, if the number of feet I count coming up the steps can be trusted.

There's the sound of clothes rustling close to me, and then Heather cries out. Seconds later, Eden makes a low growling noise. I try to ask them what's wrong, but before I can get out much more than a low *mmmm* sound, someone grabs my hands and yanks me to my feet.

It's my turn to gasp as feeling comes flooding back into my legs, pins and needles jabbing at me until my eyes fill with tears. Whoever yanked me up starts propelling me toward the door, and each step is agony.

I refuse to give them the satisfaction of showing how much it hurts, though, so I keep my mouth closed even as they drag me down the steps.

When I get to the bottom, I keep walking until I bump into someone. Flint, I think, since the back I crashed into felt wider and more solid than Jaxon's or Hudson's.

Heather makes a small sobbing sound from right behind me, and I turn toward her instinctively. "It's okay," I try to say, but of course it doesn't come out sounding anything like that.

The guard holding my hands yanks me back around roughly. "Look forward," he barks at me.

I want to tell him I'm blindfolded and can't look anywhere, but I can't. So I just clench my teeth and promise myself that when we get out of this, I'm going to have a whole hell of a lot to say. And no matter how this ends up going—or what we might have to do in the future—I am never, ever letting anyone tie me up like this again. Not without putting up one hell of a fight.

There are several guards with us now. I can tell by the sound their... shoes? boots? make as they walk us over the gravel. Plus, there are a lot of different voices all blending together.

I try to differentiate them, try to guess just how many guards they've put in charge of us. But the voices are fading in and out, going close and far so fast that every time I think I've counted everyone, I realize I've missed someone. Or counted someone else twice.

I guess it doesn't really matter—it's not like we're about to mount an escape now that, hopefully, we're so close to the Shadow Queen. But I'd still like to know. Maybe it's a control thing. Maybe it's a fear thing. Or maybe, in the back of my head, I'm trying to figure out how to get us the hell out of here if things go any further south.

The fact that I've got nothing doesn't sit well with me. Especially not when so many people I love are stuck in this situation with me.

We walk forty-one steps before we turn a corner to the right. Walk another hundred and twelve steps before turning to the left. And then we go up seventeen steps, turn to the right, and walk one hundred and forty-five steps more before the guard holding my hands yanks me to a stop so roughly that I'm half afraid he dislocated my shoulder.

"Hey!" I try to exclaim, more because I'm pissed than because I expect him to understand me—or to care. It comes out like a cry of pain instead of an enraged complaint, which just makes me angrier.

And when he jerks me forward again just as roughly, I make myself feel better by fantasizing about punching him right in the middle of what I'm sure is his very obnoxious-looking face with a concrete fist.

It's a good fantasy, but it's not as good as hearing him suddenly grunt in pain. Twice.

I don't have a clue what happened to him—I know I didn't do anything—but whatever it is must have really pissed him off, because he suddenly hisses, "You're going to pay for that."

I don't know who he's talking to, but considering he's been in charge of me since we got here, I assume it's me. So I brace myself for the worst, expecting him to lash out at me a third time.

Instead, though, there's a solid thump to the right of me, followed by a muffled growl that sounds an awful lot like, "Sod off." And then a scuffle that leaves my guard groaning and, from the location of the noise, lying on the floor.

And just like that, I know exactly what's happening. Hudson took exception to my pained gasp and—even blindfolded and with his hands tied in front of him—made sure it didn't happen again.

There's an even louder scuffle behind me, the sound of more booted feet rushing toward us. Then a sickening thud that sounds an awful lot like someone getting hit with a bat or another blunt object. Several times.

"Stop!" I try to yell. "Stop, stop, stop!" When that doesn't work—when the hitting sound continues—I move toward it as fast as I can, determined to get between Hudson and whatever he's being hit with.

"Stop!" I say again, pushing myself forward. I get a hard, glancing blow on my shoulder from what feels like a cane. I clench my teeth against the pain of it, force myself not to make another sound that will get Hudson even more worked up.

But it's too late. He obviously heard the blow land, because even with his mouth taped up, he lets out a roar of fury that stops me in my tracks. And apparently, I'm not the only one, because the cane doesn't land on either of us again.

Instead, there's another scuffle that ends with the cane clattering to the ground at my feet—followed seconds later by what I can only assume is the person wielding it.

Someone lets out a sharp gasp of pain, which is followed quickly by two loud, low-pitched groans. And then the sound of a body hitting the wall several feet away.

"Hudson!" I cry out, terrified that what I heard was my mate being knocked unconscious.

But Hudson responds with something that sounds an awful lot like my name, and relief sweeps through me. At least until I hear something else collide with him.

Again, I try to get between him and the guards. But people are moving so fast and locations are changing so quickly that I can't keep up without some kind of visual. Terror grips me, has my hands sweating and my stomach dropping to my knees, as I imagine what a pissed-off group of guards could do to Hudson.

I can't let that happen. I just can't. Especially not when he started this fight to try to help me. But I don't know where to go, don't know how to help him. All I know is that something has to give, or he's going to get seriously hurt. We all are. Because these guards don't seem like the type to take an insurrection lightly.

I bend down, about to say fuck it and shift into my gargoyle form before racing toward the spot most of the noise is coming from, but before I can get there, everyone freezes at the sound of a door opening.

Even before a very prim, very proper voice announces, "The queen will see you now."

The Gag's Up and Down

It worked. Getting arrested really worked.

That's the first thought that comes to my mind upon hearing that the queen will actually see us.

The second is that—please God—we're finally going to get these restraints removed. The relief is so sharp I think I might cry.

I tell myself that when they let us go, I'm not going to do what I promised myself just a few short minutes ago. I'm not going to take a swing at my guard. At least not if Hudson looks okay. If, however, that bastard caused as much damage to my mate as it sounded like with all those thumps of a cane or whatever the hell it was, then all bets are off.

"What is going on out here?" asks a firm, authoritative voice as the door opens again. "Get the prisoners lined up and as presentable-looking as their type can be."

The distaste in his voice when he uses the words *their type* gets my back up all over again. But there's nothing I can do about it at this point, so I don't even bother reacting. I just stay where I am and wait to be freed.

One of the guards, obviously intimidated by the other's attitude, snaps, "You heard him. Line up, prisoners!"

I don't move—and, judging by the lack of noise coming from my friends, none of them do, either. To be fair, we can't see anything. We have no idea where we're supposed to move or even where our spots in line will fall.

"You heard me!" The guard is all but yelling now. "Get in line!"

Again, none of us move.

"What's wrong with you? Do you think we won't beat you before your audience with Her Majesty?"

"And here I thought their problem was that they can't see," comes a droll female voice from several feet away. "Are you planning on rectifying that before you bring them into my hall? Or am I supposed to have an audience with them when they look like rogues?"

I freeze as it registers that it isn't some assistant or lady-in-waiting who is speaking right now. It's the Shadow Queen herself. My fingers itch to rip my blindfold and gag off—there's so much I need to say to this woman—but the shadow bonds around my wrists make that impossible.

"Of course, Your Majesty," replies one guard.

"Right away, Your Majesty," says another one at the exact same time.

The others are all too busy tearing off our blindfolds and gags to answer her. The shadow blindfolds disintegrate as soon as they're removed.

The second mine come off—along with the shadow cords wrapped around my wrists—I bend in half and take giant gulps of air through my mouth, eyes shut. I was getting enough air to survive through the gag, but I definitely didn't feel like it was enough to function well.

As I draw several long, deep breaths in through my mouth, I finally begin to feel normal again. I take one more deep breath and force my eyelids open. Stabbing pain hits me immediately, but I blink past it. The longer I go without being able to see, the more vulnerable I am. And after the way I spent the last several hours, I am damn sick of being vulnerable.

As soon as I can see more than basic shapes, I whirl around and look for Hudson. He's already moving toward me, concern etched into his newly bruised face.

I narrow in on the forming bruises on his cheekbone and the slight scrape on the left side of his chin. "Are you all right?" I demand before he can ask me the same thing.

He laughs. "It'll take more than a guard or three to bring me down."

"Don't sound so proud of that fact," I answer.

I start to say more, but before I can, the guards usher us through the grand double doors and into the Shadow Queen's hall.

And what a hall it is.

The walls are made of midnight-purple glass broken into fascinating pieces and then reassembled into stunning geometric designs of all shapes and sizes.

The floors are the darkest purple jade, and from the ceiling hang giant iron sculptures in varying tones of violet that are both beautiful and intimidating as fuck at the same time.

Even the light fixtures are one of a kind, huge purple crystal chandeliers in abstract shapes that look like a shadow hellscape à la Salvador Dalí.

And scary as hell.

Scattered around the room are several groupings of chairs and couches, all upholstered in purple floral fabrics of what looks like suede and velvet. But perhaps the most disconcerting part of the entire room is the purple shadows climbing the walls and dancing across the ceiling.

Long shadows, short shadows, big shadows, small shadows, they cover almost every available space. They aren't umbras like Smokey and the other small shadows at the farm. No, these are something different. Something malevolent that reminds me of Hudson's and my last night in Adarie.

My skin crawls at the memory, but I have no time to dwell on it. Not when the Shadow Queen herself—dressed in purple robes and a purple diamond crown—is sitting on a violet velvet throne in the middle of the room, presiding over everything.

As we get closer to her, I can't help but wonder if the throne is supersized or if she's smaller than I remember. She's not ridiculously short, but judging by the way her feet barely touch the ground in front of the throne, she can't stand much taller than me.

It's a refreshing change, considering every other monarch I've met in the last year has stood head and shoulders over me. The thought of being able to easily look her in the eye when she stands up feels like a win to me. Not that I think we'll be having much to do with each other outside of what we need today. But still.

The guards direct us to a part of the room several feet away from the throne. "Line up," they hiss for what feels like the millionth time since the door to this room first opened.

"We're lining up," I mutter back as we do just that. I try to figure out what I'm going to say to her to break the ice, considering we've come here to ask a very specific favor of her.

"Why are you back in my kingdom?" she asks in a low voice that somehow radiates through the entire hall. "I was certain I had seen the last of you after that unfortunate night in Adarie."

I turn to Hudson, wondering how exactly he plans on answering such a leading question, considering what happened the last time he and the Shadow Queen ran into each other. But he just lifts a brow at me, and though it makes me nervous as all hell, I know he's right. I'm the one who has to negotiate with her. This is my fight to win, one queen against another. And I don't plan to lose.

68

What's Your Deal?

I step forward. "We want to strike a bargain," I say as regally as I can manage, and her gaze snaps onto mine.

"Letting people fight your battles for you now?" the Shadow Queen sneers to Hudson, though her eyes don't leave mine. "Have we met?"

I wish I could say, *Yeah, and we kicked your entire purple ass.* But instead I reply, "Not in this lifetime. I'm Grace Foster, and I'm here to strike a bargain with you. And it's one you'll want to hear."

"A bargain?" she repeats with a snide little laugh. "I don't bargain with friends of people who try to kill me."

"Maybe you should," Macy pipes up from behind me. "You'd probably be a lot safer."

The Shadow Queen narrows her eyes at Macy. "Maybe you should keep your mouth shut. You'd probably live a lot longer."

Macy shrugs. "You're assuming that's my number one priority."

"Careful what you wish for, little witch. Here in the Shadow Realm, it has a funny way of coming true." She shifts her gaze back to mine. "You should go. There will be no bargain here for you."

As if to underscore her point, some of the shadows around the room begin to wake up, elongating and squirming until the entire ceiling is undulating with their movements.

It's super creepy to watch, especially with memories of the Trials and Adarie fresh in my brain. My heart leaps up to my throat, and my hands start to shake so badly that I stick them in my pockets to hide them from her view.

"You haven't even heard what I want," I tell her. "Or what we're willing to give you in return."

"It doesn't matter. If it isn't that vampire's head on stakes in the middle of the Adarie town square, I'm not interested." She perks up at the mention of Hudson's death, her eyes gleaming with some kind of unholy light that comes from deep within her. "Then again, maybe I should make that happen anyway—no bargain necessary."

She waves a hand, and the shadows on the wall begin moving, too. Unlike the ones on the ceiling, they start to divide up—some small, some medium, some huge, and some extra small.

I don't know why she's breaking them up like that, but I'm smart enough to know it isn't for any reason that I might like.

But I also need to not back down from this woman.

Not now, not ever.

So instead of trying to placate her by throwing ourselves at her mercy, I look her dead in the eyes and say, "Threats don't work on us."

"Then you obviously haven't met the right threat," she answers. A flick of her fingers, and snakes start dropping from the ceiling. Not slithering down the walls but dropping from straight above us like they do from trees in the tropical rain forest.

It's one of the most disgusting things I've ever seen, especially when they start writhing and sliding on the ground at our feet.

Hudson doesn't flinch. In fact, he doesn't so much as look down. Instead, he just stays where he is, arms folded over his chest, and watches the Shadow Queen with eyes so bored I'm half afraid he will yawn right in her face.

I'm nowhere near as calm as he is. My heart is beating like mad, and there's a part of me that wants to scream my head off and run in the other direction. But I can't. If we're going to have any chance of saving Mekhi, we have to convince her that we can help her daughters. And she'll never believe we're strong enough to do that if I run screaming from this room like I so desperately want to.

So I stand my ground, refusing to flinch or move so much as an inch, even when one of the evil things slithers right over the top of my shoe.

She lifts a brow but doesn't say anything else. Then she flicks her fingers again, and this time, shadow bugs pour from the ceiling onto the ground all around us.

One plops onto my head, and I have to bite the insides of my cheeks to keep from screaming. Hudson reaches out, quick as lightning, and knocks it onto the ground, and I can take a breath again.

I want to just shout out Lorelei's name to get the queen's attention, but my gut is telling me now is the worst time to do that, when I need her mercy. She'll simply think it's a trick—or worse, go into a bug-filled fit of rage.

Thankfully, Macy extends both hands in front of her and murmurs a spell that sends fire washing over every single one of the shadow creatures, incinerating them on contact.

When I turn to look at her, wide-eyed, she shrugs. "I've been practicing. Just in case."

"Hell yeah you have," Eden tells her admiringly.

"You really think you just did something?" the Shadow Queen asks icily. "There are millions more where those came from."

Macy looks her straight in the eyes and sneers, "Ditto."

For a second, I think the Shadow Queen is going to pop a blood vessel. Her face turns a vivid, unbecoming shade of violet, and her eyes look like they're about to bulge out of her head.

But then she takes a deep breath and pushes to her feet as everything around us returns to normal.

"This is growing tiresome," she says. "What is the real reason for this picture of false bravado?"

Now that we're here, now that the queen seems actually willing to hear me out, my mind races with uncertainties. Should I mention Lorelei first, or Mekhi, or even the Celestial Dew? I know I'm only going to have one chance to convince her, so I need to choose wisely.

When I don't immediately answer her, she *tsk-tsk*s at me. "Come on now. Don't be shy, little girl. Let's hear that deal you've come so very far to offer." Then a devious smile lifts one corner of her mouth as she adds, "And it better be an *exceptional* bargain if you hope to keep me from moving on to the torturing part of today's events that I've been so looking forward to."

69

Breaking Up Is
Hard to Dew

The way she's talking to me—so saccharine and condescending— makes me not want to tell her anything. But the sooner we have this conversation, the sooner we can get the hell out of here.

In the end, I decide to start with why *we* need *her* and not Lorelei. I figure if she knows how badly we need her help to save Mekhi, maybe she'll be less likely to think it's a trick to play on her sympathies by mentioning her daughter. "I have a friend who's dying from shadow poison. He was bitten by a shadow bug in the Impossible Trials."

"And you're here to beg for his life?" She tuts at me in disappointment. "What a waste of time, trying to save another being. Caring about someone is a weakness your enemies can exploit."

"Is that how you rule?" I ask her, truly wanting to know her answer. "By not caring about what happens to your subjects?"

"Don't speak to me of subjects. You have no idea what it's like to rule," she replies haughtily.

The condescension is just too much. "I do, actually. I am the—"

"I know *exactly* who you are," the Shadow Queen interrupts, and my stomach clenches with fear that she recognizes me before she adds: "someone about to spend the rest of her life eating rats in my dungeon."

"Rat meat is actually—" Flint begins, signature cockiness on full display, but Eden stomps on his non-prosthetic foot before he can say anything truly disgusting.

"Enough," the queen snarls. "Get to the point. You're the one here asking for my help, after all. I haven't come asking you for help with one of *my* subjects."

"It doesn't matter if Mekhi is your subject. He's our friend. And we've never done any damage to your people—not the way you've done to mine."

She lifts her brows. "You're referring to the shadow poison currently working its way through his bloodstream?"

"You know that's exactly what I'm referring to."

"How am I to know?" She shrugs. "You pesky paranormals are so fragile. So very many things can go wrong with you. It's amazing you survive."

Her cavalier attitude toward Mekhi's suffering makes me blurt out, "You mean like Lorelei? It's astonishing she's lived as long as she has. But also terrifying to think that she's spent her entire life in agony."

The Shadow Queen loses her calm in an instant. "Keep my daughter's name out of your mouth!" she screams, her hand shooting out like a whip.

Seconds later, a shadowy rope wraps itself around my throat and starts to squeeze, closing my airway off a little more with each second that passes. I slowly shift to a portion of my gargoyle form, just enough that the stone helps keep the rope from constricting my airway too much.

I should probably start panicking right about now, except I don't feel very panicked. One, I still feel like we've got the upper hand despite the fact that I'm slowly being strangled. And two, I know Hudson and the rest of my friends will step in the second they think I need them to.

I'm actually surprised Jaxon hasn't already tackled the Shadow Queen and tried to pry her shadow whip off my neck. Hudson is balanced on his toes, ready to step in the second I make any indication that he should, but he's holding back right now because I haven't asked for his help. Jaxon, on the other hand, tends to leap before he looks.

A quick glance his way tells me I'm right, that it's taking every ounce of willpower he has not to intervene. I hold a hand out to him in a slow-your-roll gesture, then lock eyes with the Shadow Queen and wait her out.

Because she's smart and I can tell she's already thinking, can tell she's desperately trying to figure out how—

"How do you know about Lorelei?" she demands.

I gesture to the shadow she still has wrapped around my neck—the universal sign for *I can't exactly talk at the moment.*

She narrows her eyes, and for a second, the pressure gets worse, cutting off my air completely. But then, with an angry hiss, she pulls her hand back. Instantly, the shadow drops away from my neck, and I pull in several deep breaths.

"How dare you speak of my daughter when you don't know anything about her," she hisses, and now there's nothing slow in the way she walks toward me.

She doesn't stop until we're nose to nose, but that's fine with me. Bruised trachea or not, I'm more than ready to take a concrete swing at the Shadow Bitch myself. For what she's done to Mekhi, for what she had done to my friends and me when we were arrested, and definitely for what she allowed her other daughter to do to Lorelei.

"I know plenty about her," I snarl back. "It's why I'm here, after all. It's the bargain I want to strike."

"Don't you dare involve my daughters in your scheme," she tells me. But her voice is shaky, and her beautiful purple skin has turned a sickly lavender gray.

"I didn't involve your daughters," I snap at her, my own fury welling up inside me. "You did, a thousand years ago. And your tunnel vision nearly killed an entire species. So don't you dare stand there and try to take the moral high ground with me."

I didn't think it was possible, but somehow she gets even paler. Even so, there's no guilt in her eyes for the thousands of gargoyles whose millennium-long imprisonment she is directly responsible for, for the thousands of others who died from her poison. No remorse for the suffering of Mekhi and Lorelei or the suffering and deaths of my friends in Adarie at the hands of her maniacal time wizard of a husband. The same husband she convinced to cast the spell that led all of us here, to this very moment.

The knowledge that she doesn't feel bad about any of the pain she's caused, any of the death and destruction at her feet, enrages me. It makes me want to say to hell with these negotiations and leave her alone in a nightmare of her own making.

But the only people who will get hurt if we walk away now are the people who can least afford it. Mekhi, who grows closer to death with each hour that passes. And Lorelei, who's had to suffer with a fraction of a soul's life force for nearly a thousand years.

So I tamp down the fury scraping away at my insides and say, "I know how to separate your daughters' souls, which is something you—for all your power—can't do. So I'll give you one more chance to make a bargain with me that will sever them in exchange for my friend's life. All you have to do is decide if you want to take it or leave it."

70

Screwed and
Newly Tattooed

At first, she doesn't answer, and I'm terrified that I blew it. That I let anger get the better of me and that innocent people will suffer for it.

But then Hudson rests a hand on my lower back, and I can feel him lending me his strength and his resolve. Macy moves closer to me on my other side, until her upper arm presses against mine, and despite all the pain inside her, I can feel her steadiness and her determination to be there for me.

Together—along with the belief I can feel coming from all my friends—they give me the strength to keep my eyes locked with the queen's.

The strength to not apologize and not back down.

The strength to call her freaking bluff.

And call it I do, as long seconds turn into longer minutes and the tension in the air gets so taut that it feels like any wrong move will shatter it. Will have pain and regrets pouring down on me like shards of the sharpest broken glass.

But then, just when I decide this is the hill the Shadow Queen is going to die on, she yields.

"Come sit with me," she says in a voice as empty as the eyes I've been staring into for far too long.

She shuffles back to her throne, her walk a million times more labored than it was when she came forward to meet us.

There's nowhere for me to sit—her throne is isolated and alone in the direct center of the room—but I won't bend enough to mention it. Which ends up working out fine, because two members of the Shadow

Guard take care of it before we get there.

In a matter of seconds, they have a second chair positioned across from the first, with a table in between the two.

The Shadow Queen painstakingly takes her throne—again, moving more slowly than I've ever seen her—and I slide into the chair opposite her.

Several members of her Shadow Guard form a half circle behind her, and my friends move forward to do the same for me.

"Where is my daughter?" she asks once everyone is in position.

"Safe at the Witch Court," I answer.

Her eyes narrow to slits. "If you hurt her—"

"I would never hurt Lorelei," I tell her. "None of us would. We're here because we want to help Mekhi, Liana, *and* Lorelei. We just have to work together to make it happen."

"By separating my daughters' souls," she says.

"Yes," I reply. "We know how to do it—"

"Why should I believe you when you say you can do this thing? You think I didn't try? I did everything, asked *everyone*. And no one knew how to separate them. Everyone told me it was impossible."

"That's because you asked the wrong people."

"And I'm supposed to believe that you—a mere girl—knew the right person to ask, just like that? I turned the world upside down looking for an answer."

A spurt of sympathy hits deep inside me, but I shove it down. This woman can be deadly, and I can't afford to get sidetracked by feeling sorry for her. Even if what happened to her and her daughters sucks.

"I may be young, but I have resources. And I asked the *right* person. My grandmother, who is very, very old and even wiser than that. She told us exactly what we need to do. But it's dangerous—extremely dangerous. My friends and I have already agreed that we're willing to take the risk, as long as you agree that if we succeed—if we get what's needed to free your daughters—then you will help my friend."

For a second, she looks tempted. Very tempted. But then she shakes her head as if to clear it and demands, "Why should I help a vampire? He means nothing to me."

"It's not about helping him. It's about helping your daughter," I answer. "You can't leave the Shadow Realm. Which means you can't fix the mistake you and Souil made all those years ago."

"You think I don't know that?" she snarls, and for a second she looks so angry—so tormented—that I think she's going to strangle me again, for real this time. "My husband was a shadow's breath away from reversing our mistake before Hudson stopped him."

Her voice is plaintive and bitter, but there's no venom, and again I let my instincts guide me. "I'd wager that was his plan, not yours."

She raises one regal brow. "Would you really, now?"

She's bluffing. I don't know how I know, but she is. So I push more. "If he had succeeded in reversing the timeline, many of your subjects would never have been born." I lift my chin. "I don't believe you would cause another mother the same pain as yours, take her children from her, whether she'd remember them or not."

The queen watches me steadily, but she doesn't disagree.

"I'm not asking you to trust me," I tell her. "I'm not naive enough to think this deal includes you giving me the antidote first."

"Good," she snaps. "Because it absolutely doesn't."

I nod.

"Nor will I make a bargain that gives me false hope indefinitely."

I nod again. "No, that would be cruel. We will either bring you the answer you seek before the end of the week, or Mekhi will have died and the bargain will be unnecessary."

"That is an acceptable timeframe," she says with an imperial tone.

"Does that mean we've got a deal?" I can't help the excitement in my voice.

She studies me for several seconds, like she's trying to figure out if I'm telling the truth. Eventually, though, she says, "It means that if you follow through with your end of the bargain—which is to do everything you need to do in exactly the order you need to do it in *and* it results in the freedom of my daughters—then yes, we have a deal."

She holds her hand out to seal the deal, and while I am determined to follow through on our agreement, it still takes every ounce of willpower I have not to shrink away.

I promised myself I'd never do this again, make a bargain with someone so untrustworthy. But if I don't, then Mekhi dies. It's no longer about whether I want to do this. It's about the fact that I have to.

So I take a deep breath, use it to force the nausea and the revulsion down, and then I reach forward and clasp her hand in mine.

The second our palms meet, a flash of heat flares from her hand. A dark-purple shadow vine springs forward from the spark, wrapping itself around our hands and wrists and tying them together. As it does, the heat continues to grow and grow until—suddenly—there's a second flash.

The vine disappears, and when I look down, there's yet another tattoo on my arm. And as I stare at the glowing purple tree on the inside of my wrist, I know any chance I have of backing out is gone now.

The bargain has been sealed.

71

Go Smudge
Yourself

"Now what?" the queen asks as I pull my hand away as quickly as possible.

"Now we leave," Hudson tells her. "As soon as we have what we need to split your daughters' souls apart, we'll be back, and you can hold up your side of the bargain."

"I can't just let you walk out of here," the Shadow Queen counters. "No one knows where I am."

"Is that how you want to spend your life?" Macy speaks up for the first time since the negotiating started. "In hiding from your own people?"

The Shadow Queen glides across the room to a crystal bar set up against the back wall. For the first time, I notice that the whole wall is made of a conglomeration of murals depicting battle scenes. And while I wouldn't swear on it, I'm pretty sure the part she's stopped in front of right now depicts the fight she had with Hudson and me our first time in Adarie. Of course, in her version, she and her creatures are kicking his ass—which, to be honest, isn't far from how most of the battle went. I do wish she had included a representation of Hudson tossing her back over the wall, though.

If we were staying longer, I'd be tempted to sneak in here and paint it over the glass shards myself—just to see her face. Then again, reminding her of that moment probably isn't the best way to get out of here safely.

"I'm in hiding because I tried to free most of my people from this prison and reunite my daughters," she hisses at us as she pours herself a glass of wine, and I ignore how that's not entirely true. "And failed, courtesy of your friend here, so don't sound so sanctimonious."

"If you'd prefer to have your guards escort us out, we can live with that," Hudson tells her. "But it will be without restraints."

She takes a sip of her drink, staring at him over the rim of the delicate crystal glass. "Or else?"

He leans a shoulder against the nearest wall, looking bored. "Or else we're going to have a problem." It's a simple statement more than it is a challenge, but the Shadow Queen's eyes still narrow to slits.

But before she can say anything else, the side doors to the room fly open.

My friends and I turn as one to see a young woman sauntering toward us in no particular hurry, carrying a large bucket of purple popcorn.

My first thought is that she is the opposite of Lorelei in every way.

My second thought is that she's gorgeous but also somehow completely unattractive.

And my third thought is as much a warning as it is a thought. I should never, ever turn my back on her.

If eyes are the windows to the soul, then something really disturbing is going on inside this woman's. Looking into her eyes is like looking into an abyss—black, empty, totally devastating.

She's tall where Lorelei is short.

Hard where Lorelei is soft.

And dark in a way that Lorelei is just pure light.

Her skin is lavender here in the Shadow Realm, her eyes a deep, rich aubergine. Her long, dark hair is a beautiful shade of violet instead of the black of Lorelei's, and it looks like there's something tied to the end of every strand, though I can't quite figure out what it is.

At least not until she walks closer and I hear the rattling sound with every step she takes.

Jewels. She has tiny purple jewels tied to the ends of her hair, and they slide together as she moves, making her sound just like the diamondback rattlesnakes I grew up watching for in San Diego.

I'm not sure if I'm intrigued or revolted. I mean, who goes out of their way to deliberately sound like a rattlesnake? And is it a warning to her mother or the rest of the world?

Does it matter? Either way, something doesn't seem quite right, even before I get my first glimpse into her eyes—and the dark sadness there that she doesn't even try to hide.

She really is quite beautiful, but somehow that only makes the murkiness of her dark energy more prominent.

She doesn't stop until she's to the right of the Shadow Queen's throne. I expect her to speak, but instead she just stands there, meeting each one of our gazes individually.

Judging from the looks on my friends' faces, they aren't any more impressed with meeting her than I am. Eden looks annoyed. Macy looks revolted. And Hudson—Hudson looks very, very cautious.

My mate enjoys few things more than matching wits with someone new, so his concern makes me even more nervous that something could go wrong here. Especially since it's clear that the Shadow Queen loves this girl very, very much.

I can see it in the way she looks at her and in the way she moves quickly—very quickly—to put herself between her daughter and the rest of us, almost as if she considers *us* a threat to *her*. The idea is absurd, given some of the things we've heard about Liana, and yet...and yet it almost makes sense, too, as I get my first good look at her.

"What are you doing in here?" the Shadow Queen demands.

Liana holds up the bucket of purple popcorn like it's the most obvious thing in the world. "I stopped by to say hello on the way to movie night."

Her voice is ice-cold and contemptuous—and gets even more so when she looks us over. "So these are the paranormals you've been searching for? I have to be honest, Mummy. They don't look so scary to me."

The Shadow Queen blocks her path, refusing to let her get any closer to us. As Liana's eyes shine black, I can't help wondering if it's for her protection—or for ours. "Go back to your room, darling. I'll be there as soon as I can."

She ignores her mother, stepping around the queen to get a better look at us. "What do you want with them, anyway?"

When the Shadow Queen doesn't answer, she repeats herself, this time posing the question to us.

Except none of us answers, either. Making a deal with the Shadow Queen is one thing—getting in the middle of what looks like a very delicate relationship between her and her daughter is something else entirely.

"Guards!" the Shadow Queen calls.

There's an urgency in her voice now that is just as surprising to witness as the earlier softness directed at Liana.

"You can go," she tells us in a desperate voice as the guards forming a semicircle around the throne shift into a barrier between us and Liana.

"Just like that?" Flint asks, sounding as surprised as I feel. It seemed like she was settling in to do a whole spider/fly routine with us before letting us go.

Liana looks between her mother and us, and I can see the moment she figures out this has something to do with her sister. Her mouth tightens, her skin flushes, and her eyes turn into black pools of hatred and rage.

"You're going after Lorelei *again*?" she demands, her voice harsh. "After what happened the last time, you promised you would stop."

"I'm not the one going after her—"

"Even worse, you're hiring them to do it," she sneers. "More time, money, hope wasted because, as usual, nothing matters as much to you as your precious Lorelei."

The Shadow Queen waves for the guards to stand down, then turns to her daughter. "That's enough, Liana. Go to the movie room, and I'll join you as soon as I can."

"Don't bother." Liana gives her mother a look of complete and utter disdain, right before she turns the bucket of popcorn upside down and sends the kernels scattering all over the floor. "I'd rather spend another night in the dungeon than be with you."

And then she storms out, leaving us alone with a bunch of Shadow Guards and a very shaken-looking Shadow Queen. If she was anyone else, I might pity her. As it is, I just feel sorry in general, for the whole awful situation. And for the rest of us, who are going to have to risk our lives for at least two people who don't appear to deserve the sacrifice.

The Shadow Queen doesn't have much else to say after we meet Liana, although I'd be lying if I said the whole interaction didn't bother me at least a little bit. The last thing I want is to feel sorry for the Shadow Queen, but watching her with Liana and seeing how desperate she is to reunite with Lorelei… It makes it hard not to feel some sympathy for her.

Still, I'm more than ready to leave when the Shadow Queen turns to us and says, "My guards are waiting to take you wherever you want to go." As she does, the fact that she looks a lot older than she did just a few minutes ago isn't lost on me.

The thought of going back in that paddy wagon that brought us here has panic rising inside me. There's no way I'm letting them tie us up again. And there's no way in *hell* I'm letting them blindfold and gag us a second time.

My thoughts must show on my face, because the Shadow Queen gives us a thin blade of a smile. "You have my assurance that it will be a much more comfortable ride this time around."

"Could you be a little more specific?" Eden asks.

At first, it looks like the Shadow Queen is going to smite her—or whatever it is wraiths with too much power can do. But in the end, she forces her scary, scary smile back into place and concedes, "I'll have them pull the truck into the dungeon. That will circumvent the need for blindfolds. And since we've already struck a deal, there's no reason to restrain you, either."

"Is that what you want to call what they did to us?" Jaxon growls. "Restrained us?"

At the same time, Heather whispers to me, "There's really a dungeon?"

"There's always a dungeon," I answer with a sigh.

She shakes her head. "The paranormal world is *so* weird."

"You have no idea."

"Well, that's that," Hudson says as he reaches for my hand.

The guards look like they're more than ready to make us suffer for upsetting the Shadow Queen, but in typical Hudson Vega fashion, he's not about to give them an inch—even as he takes a mile. "Good, I'm glad you're here, mate," he tells the one with the most stripes on his uniform. "Can you show us to the truck that will take us to Adarie?"

"That little town?" The Shadow Queen sounds surprised. "Why on earth would you want to go back *there*?"

"I suppose I'm just sentimental," he answers with a smile that doesn't quite reach his eyes. Then he slaps the shoulder of the decorated guard. "Lead on, mate. The dungeon waits for nobody."

72

W e're all exhausted by the time we get back to Adarie—or Vegaville, as I've grown used to calling it.

The Shadow Guards pull their vehicle up to the gates of the town and shuffle us out of it before heading south across the rocky terrain. Thankfully, someone is still at the guard tower, and—after a very relieved greeting from them—we end up back at the inn within twenty minutes of being dropped off.

It's been one hell of a day, and I don't breathe easily until we say good night to the others and Hudson closes the door to our room behind us. And even then, I'm pretty sure I'm going to end up sleeping with one eye open. We may have struck a bargain with the Shadow Queen, but that doesn't mean I trust her anywhere near as far as Hudson can throw her. Not now, when we still have so much of the journey left to go.

"You did great at the Shadow Fortress," Hudson says, sweeping me into a hug that lifts my feet clear off the floor.

"*We* did great," I answer. "I can't believe we actually convinced her to help Mekhi."

"*You* convinced her," he tells me as he slides me down his body until my feet finally touch the floor again.

The familiar heat wells up inside me at the feel of my mate pressed against me, but I don't pursue it. Not the way I usually would. I'm sweaty and dirty and more exhausted than I've been in a long time, and all I want is a shower and bed.

Tomorrow morning, all bets are off, but for now, I settle for a long, slow kiss that gets both of our heart rates quickening. I pull away first and grin at him as he makes a sound of protest deep in his chest.

"Where are you going?" he asks as I start to rummage through my backpack.

"To take a shower. Then to sleep for as long as I possibly can, provided I don't have nightmares about that woman poisoning me—or all the millions of things that can go wrong between now and when I fulfill that damn bargain."

As soon as I mention it, the tattoo on my wrist burns—as if I need any reminders of my very necessary folly.

"She's not going to poison you," he says. "And nothing will go wrong."

I pause in my search for my PJs and toothbrush to look at him skeptically. "You sound way too sure about that to be believed."

He shrugs. "Let me rephrase. None of that is going to happen *tonight*."

"Again, you don't know that."

"Sure I do. The Shadow Queen's got to keep up her end of the bargain, which means waiting to see if we fail before she takes us out."

"We're not going to fail," I tell him.

"I happen to agree." He smiles. "And if we don't, then you won't have to worry about her poisoning any of us. She'll be so happy to have her daughters reunited and whole that she won't have time to poison anyone."

I study him for a second. "I'm going to choose to believe you."

"Because you know I'm right."

"Because I'm dirty and exhausted, and all I really want right now is a shower and a bed. Tomorrow is going to have to take care of itself."

Hudson gives me a rueful grin. "Nice to know you trust me."

"I do trust you," I tell him as I head into the bathroom. "It's her I don't trust."

Thirty minutes later, I'm sitting on the bed eating one of my emergency packets of cherry Pop-Tarts while Hudson finishes up his shower. As I eat, I can't help going over everything that just happened with the Shadow Queen.

I know I told Hudson earlier that I was afraid of the Shadow Queen poisoning us, but the truth is, I know he's right. She's skeptical of our deal—skeptical of what we can do—but she's also desperate to believe that we might be able to do everything we say we can. Which means she isn't going to try to hurt us unless we end up failing.

I can't believe it, but I think we've got more than a good chance of saving Mekhi and making it out of this bargain with all of us alive.

Is it going to be easy? No. But do I think it's impossible? Absolutely not. And right now, that's all that matters.

"What are you grinning about?" Hudson asks as he walks out of the bathroom, a towel wrapped low around his hips and another one draped over his shoulders. "When I went into the bathroom, you were afraid of being murdered in your sleep. Now you look like you're ready to take on the world."

"It's the power of the Pop-Tart," I answer, popping the last bite into my mouth.

"So that's your superpower?" He lifts a brow. "Pop-Tarts?"

"You're my superpower. They're just really, really good."

Hudson freezes in the middle of drying his hair, and when he looks at me, I realize the amusement is gone from his eyes. In its place is... his heart. And it's the most beautiful thing I've ever seen.

So beautiful that it makes me forget my misgivings about the Vampire Court and everything he's not telling me, at least for a little longer.

"Hey," I say, climbing out of bed to go to him. "You good?"

"I'm really good," he answers, pulling me close and lowering his forehead to mine. "You know we're going to be okay, right?"

I don't know if he's talking about the quest we're about to set out on or if he's talking about something more—something that has to do with him and me and the weight of the Courts, and the worlds, we carry on our shoulders. In the end, I decide he's talking about both.

"We're going to be more than okay," I tell him with a grin. "We're going to find that Bittersweet Tree and save the day. That's all there is to it."

"Exactly." He grins. "I mean, how hard could it be? It's a *tree*."

"Oh my God!" I shriek as his words sink in. "Hudson! You just jinxed us!"

He looks insulted. "I most certainly did not."

"You totally did!" I reply. "You have to take it back."

"Take what back?" Now he just looks mystified. "I didn't *do* anything."

"You asked, 'How hard could it be?' That's basically begging the universe to make sure that everything goes wrong."

He makes a "whatever" noise deep in his throat. "No, it's not."

"It totally is!" I give one of the dismissive sniffs he's so good at. "You're tempting fate."

"That's ridiculous, Grace." His accent gets more pronounced with each syllable, a surefire sign that he's getting more agitated.

"It's not ridiculous. You've got to take it back."

He looks like he wants to argue with me more, but when I give him my patented I'm-very-serious-about-this look, he just throws up his hands. "Fine. What do I need to do to take it back? Say that things are going to be really hard?"

"Yeah, right." Now I give him my are-you-kidding-me look. "Like that will be enough to fix things with the universe."

He returns my look with interest, but when I don't back down, he just sighs. "All right, then. Fine. What do I have to do to make you happy?"

"It's not me you have to make happy, Hudson. It's the universe."

He rolls his eyes. "Of course it is. So what do I have to do to make *the universe* happy?"

"You can start by spinning around five times and throwing some salt over your shoulder. It's not a perfect fix, but it's a start."

"I can't do that, Grace. I don't have any salt."

He's used my name twice in as many minutes—a definite tell that he's completely annoyed with me. I don't let it stop me one bit. "Well, you're going to have to find some. You can't do the thing without it."

"Do the thing?" He raises one sardonic brow. "That sounds so scientific. And where exactly do you expect me to find salt? This isn't a kitchen."

"I don't know." I pretend to think as I get increasingly absurd with my demands. "Are there bath salts next to the tub?"

"Bath salts?" he repeats, looking beyond annoyed. "Seriously,

Grace? Are you just fucking with me now?"

"I am, absolutely."

"You want me to turn around and throw bath salts over my shoulder? I'm a vampire, not a fucking witch. What do you think that's—" He freezes, eyes narrowing to slits. "What did you just say?"

"You asked if I was fucking with you," I tell him with a prim look. "And I said that I definitely am. Absolutely."

"Seriously?" He looks completely shocked, which is kind of the point of this whole thing. I mean, a girl's got to keep her mate on his toes, doesn't she? Plus, messing with him keeps my own anxiety under control.

"Seriously." I nod.

He shakes his head, starts to turn away. And then leaps across the room and tackles me to the bed.

I crack up and start kicking my feet in an attempt to dislodge him as he climbs on top of me. But I'm laughing too hard to put up much of a fight, and eventually he gives up and moves off me.

"You're going to pay for that one day," he says, staring at the ceiling with a bemused frown.

"Am I?" I ask as I roll over on top of him. "Am I really?"

"You told me to spin in a circle five times and throw salt over my shoulder," he says with an annoyed sniff that gets me way hotter than it has any right to.

"Better than telling you to streak naked through Vegaville." I pause as I imagine what that would look like. "Although, I feel like maybe that was a miscalculation on my part."

"Oh it was, was it?" He reaches up and tangles his fingers in my hair.

"Definitely," I answer as I kiss him until the annoyed smirk fades away and he starts kissing me back.

Eventually, he pulls away and asks, "So, you're okay with everything? You feel good?"

"I feel great," I answer with a grin. Then, tongue totally in cheek, add, "After all, we just have to find a tree. How hard could *that* be?"

Hudson groans in annoyance, then drags me back down for another kiss. And for now—in this room, at this time—it's more than enough.

73

Brit Bands to
the Rescue

A knock on the door has Hudson springing out of bed. "Are you all right?" he asks, reaching for me like I'm the one who woke us.

"Yeah." I sit up in bed, curls falling over my face and eyes heavy with sleep. "What's going on?"

"I don't know."

The knock comes again, harder this time. "What time is it?" I ask as Hudson walks toward our locked door.

Not that I expected a lock to keep a returning Shadow Guard out when I flipped it last night, but at least it gives us *some* warning.

"Six a.m.," he answers before calling, "who is it?"

I barely bite back a groan. We didn't get to sleep until after three, and three hours of sleep is so not going to cut it with the next several days we've got in front of us. Especially when those days tend to come fast and furious, with no breaks in between.

But then the person knocking answers, "Macy."

All thoughts of sleep abandon me in a rush, and I throw the covers back as Hudson opens the door.

"Are you okay?" I ask as I stumble toward the door in my PJs. I'm still half asleep, but I'm determined to wake up. This is the first time Macy has actually sought me out since she joined this trip.

"Yes. Sorry," she says as she walks into the room, then registers that we were both still in bed. "I didn't realize how early it is. I can come back later."

"Don't bother," Hudson tells her with a gentle smile. "We're up now."

"I couldn't sleep." She runs a hand over her face, and I can't help noticing that we're seeing the real Macy for the first time in months.

No heavy goth makeup.

No spiked jewelry wrapped around her neck and sticking out from the many new holes pierced in her ears.

No *keep out!* signs screaming at me from every direction.

She looks much younger this way. Much more like I remember her—and much more vulnerable. Which I suppose is the point of all the rest of the stuff. She's tired of being vulnerable.

I can't say that I blame her—not with what she's been through.

If I didn't have Hudson to keep me grounded and help me feel safe when the nightmares come at three a.m., I might be doing the exact same thing she is right now.

"Want to talk about it?" I ask, settling back down on the bed and scooting toward the middle so she can crawl in on one side of me while Hudson sits down on the other. "Or do you want to just watch TV or something?"

"I don't know," she answers, and she doesn't move from the spot she's claimed in the center of the room. "I really didn't mean to bother you two."

"You're my favorite cousin," I tell her. "You're never a bother."

That makes her smile a little bit, even as she shakes her head and looks at the ground.

"I think I'm going to go take a shower," Hudson announces to the room in general.

I shoot him a grateful look as he gathers clean clothes from his backpack. It's six in the morning, and he's willing to lock himself in the bathroom for God knows how long just so Macy and I can have the heart-to-heart she seems so desperately to need.

"You don't have to do that," Macy says, looking alarmed. "I'm sorry. I'll go."

"Bollocks," Hudson responds with a wink. "I wasn't sleeping anyway."

It's an obvious lie, easily contradicted by his sleepy blue eyes and the hair standing straight up on one side of his head. But neither Macy nor I call him on it—not when he is being so gallant.

After the bathroom door closes behind him, neither of us moves for several seconds. But when it becomes obvious that Macy isn't going to come to me—and she isn't going to say anything else from over there—I climb back off the bed and go to her.

"Hey," I whisper, pulling her in for a hug just as Hudson starts singing "Start Me Up" by the Rolling Stones at the top of his lungs. "What can I do?"

She doesn't answer, just shakes her head. But she holds on to me like I'm the only lifeline she's got. It breaks my heart, has me holding her just as tightly.

She doesn't let go, and neither do I. I just hug her as long as she'll let me, rubbing soothing circles up and down her back.

Eventually, she pulls away and there are tears in her eyes. She blinks quickly in an attempt to make them go away before I see them, but it's too late. I can't pretend they aren't there, any more than I can pretend that she's not suffering.

"Oh, Mace," I whisper, pulling her in for another hug.

And then she starts to cry. And cry. And cry.

I hold her through it all.

It takes a long time for her crying to stop, and the shower runs through it all, Hudson's vampire hearing keeping him exactly where he is, belting out everything from Radiohead's "Creep" to Elton John's "Rocket Man." Ecological guilt has me feeling terrible about all the water we're wasting, but thankfully, Adarie doesn't have the same water shortages our world does.

Eventually, though, Macy's eyes dry up, and her sobs become sniffles. "I'm sorry," she says for the third time since she came to my room this morning.

"Nothing for you to be sorry for," I tell her. "But I'm sorry. I really am."

"For what?"

"For everything that's made you feel like this," I answer. "You've been through so much the last few months, and I've been in San Diego for most of it."

She shrugs. "Nothing you could have done to fix it anyway."

"Except this." I push her hair back from in front of her eyes. "I've missed you, Macy."

"Me too." She takes a long, shuddering breath. "I'm so lonely, Grace. I'm just so lonely I don't know what to do."

Her words rip through me like a gunshot, leave a gaping wound where my heart used to be, and I press a trembling hand across my stomach. I nearly choke on the bile rising in my throat, my mind racing for the right words Macy needs to hear right now.

In the end, though, I can only find the truth. "This is all my fault."

74

Too Cruel
for School

Macy gasps. "This is *not* your fault, Grace."

"Oh, honey." I wrap my arms around her again and hug her as tightly as I can. "I haven't been there for you the way I should have been." The way she was for me when I was lost and alone and in a new place that I knew nothing about.

Guilt seeps through me at the thought. I've tried to keep up with her since Hudson and I moved to San Diego for school. I text her nearly every day, and we try to FaceTime at least once a week.

But it's not the same as me being there. I know it's not, just like I've known she was holding things back when we talked. I just didn't know how much she was holding back—and that's on me.

I should have known, should have read between the lines.

"What can I do?" I ask her. "What do you need?"

"My father not to have lied to me. My mother not to have run off to the Vampire Court knowing how it was probably going to end. Xavier to still be alive. Katmere to still be standing—and my friends to still be there with me." She gives a watery laugh. "Easy stuff, you know?"

"Super easy," I answer with a small smile.

"And these schools they're sending me to. It's ridiculous how awful they are."

"All of them?" I ask, one eyebrow raised.

"Yeah, *all* of them." She shakes her head. "The other students either want to suck up to me because they know who I'm friends with or they try to sabotage me as soon as I get there—also because of who I'm friends with. Or because they and their parents are loyal to Cyrus and are pissed about what happened last summer."

"Oh, Macy." Hudson and I are dealing with the consequences as well—the whole paranormal world is—but in some ways, we're more removed. Yes, we're both trying to find our way as good rulers of the Gargoyle Court, and Hudson is doing...whatever he's doing with the Vampire Court, so in some ways we're right in the trenches. But in other ways, we aren't.

I never thought about what it would be like for Macy, who doesn't have that position of power. And who is getting thrown into schools where she has no relationship to anyone. Of course some of the people were loyal to Cyrus. Of course some of the people wanted to see us fail in our attempt to liberate the Vampire Court from his abusive hold. And of course some of those people are all too happy to take it out on a barely seventeen-year-old girl.

Like leader, like follower, apparently.

I search for something to say, to try to make this nightmare sound better, but I've got nothing.

Which might actually be for the better, because Macy takes my silence as encouragement and continues. "And the teachers let it happen, because they've got their own issues with the Courts or the Circle or my parents or your parents or me. I don't know." She runs her hands through her hair in a universal gesture of frustration. "I don't know what I'm supposed to do. My mom tells me to just keep my head down and not make a fuss, but how am I supposed to do that when they're constantly stealing my shit and casting spells to fuck with me or coming at me in a group under the bleachers? I shouldn't have to take that."

"No, you should not." Outrage moves through me at the thought of Macy getting messed with that way. Of her being outnumbered under the bleachers or in some corner of the school somewhere, with a bunch of assholes fucking with her. "I didn't know it was like that."

"I didn't want you to know. It's humiliating."

My heart breaks for her, and I have to fight the urge to go to the schools she's been kicked out of so far this year and teach everyone what a real power imbalance looks like.

But since the low road isn't exactly an option here, I start by saying, "There's nothing humiliating about being singled out and bullied, Macy."

"There is when five months ago you were helping to save the entire paranormal world. And now you can't even go to Advanced Portals without getting ganged up on and sealed inside one."

"What the hell? They did that to you?" Screw teaching them a lesson. I want to obliterate the entire school off the face of the earth. "What did the headmaster say when you finally got out of it?"

"That using a spell to set their shit on fire wasn't a proportional response."

"You're damn right it wasn't," I snarl. "Setting *them* on fire would have been closer to proportional, in my opinion. Those portals fucking hurt."

"They really do," she agrees with a laugh. It's still a sad sound, but at least she isn't crying anymore.

I, on the other hand, am about to start crying. I can't believe this has been happening to Macy and I didn't know. Yeah, she didn't tell me what was going on, but still. I knew something was wrong, and I didn't push to figure out what it was.

I didn't want to upset her, didn't want her to feel like I expected her to deal with everything that had happened to her on some kind of a truncated timeline. I know what it feels like to try to grieve when the people around you think you should be able to just move on. I didn't want her to think that's what I expected her to do.

So I didn't push. I tried to be delicate, tried to respect her feelings. And instead, I went too far in the other direction and let her feel abandoned. I let her be tormented and tortured by other paranormals and didn't have a clue it was going on.

I feel like such an asshole.

"This is why you've been kicked out of so many schools since the year started?" I ask. "What about just staying home until Katmere is ready?"

She shrugs, and we both pause to listen as Hudson finishes Coldplay's "Yellow" and launches into "Bad Habits" by Ed Sheeran.

"At least he gets to finish his concert," Macy comments with a snort.

"It's always like this when he's in the shower," I joke. "He really is a one-vamp karaoke show. Of course, the days when he does his Beatles tribute are when it gets really interesting."

But we're not here to talk about Hudson—or his musical proclivities. "You never answered my question," I remind Macy after a few seconds of silence. "About Katmere?"

"Oh, Katmere won't be ready to actually open its doors until next semester at the earliest." Macy gives me a sad smile. "It's pretty much rebuilt, but there's a whole lot of politics going on around it right now with all the different paranormal groups. And instead of laying down the law, my dad is trying to please them all."

"Which isn't a recipe for disaster at all," I tell her dryly. If being gargoyle queen has taught me nothing else, it's taught me that.

"Exactly."

"So what are they going to do, then? They're really just going to ship you off to *another* school?" I ask.

She shrugs. "Apparently."

"But how is that going to solve the problem?"

"It's not. But my parents don't seem to care." She ducks her head so her moss-green bangs fall into her face, blocking her eyes from me.

"Oh, Macy. That can't be true. I know some school staff can be assholes, but surely Uncle Finn can talk to them—"

"He doesn't want to talk to them, Grace. He's so busy bending over backward to make my mother happy that he doesn't give a shit if I'm happy or not. And she doesn't want to listen to my side—all she wants to do is punish me for getting kicked out."

She stands up, starts to pace just as Hudson switches to a rousing rendition of the Clash's "Should I Stay or Should I Go." For a second, we both stare at each other, and then we crack up. Because Hudson's timing is impeccable, as usual.

Once we finish laughing, Macy flops onto the bed and covers her eyes with the back of her hand. "They don't get it, you know? It's the strangest thing. My mom comes back, and all of a sudden they want to tell me how to dress and where to go and who I'm supposed to be friends with and how I have to behave when I'm at school."

She shakes her head like she can't believe it. "I thought my mother *left me* years ago, and between his duties as headmaster and the time he spent supposedly looking for her, my dad's been nearly as absent.

Now they just want to pretend like it never happened, just pick up where they left off all those years ago. It doesn't work that way. I'm not a kid anymore."

"No, you're not." I reach out and cover her other hand with mine. "You're the best person and the most kick-ass witch I've ever met. They have to know that."

"They don't know anything," she tells me. "That's the problem. They say they love me, but who they really love is the good little girl I used to be. The one who never caused any trouble and did whatever they wanted me to. That girl died at the Vampire Court, and this Macy—the one who's a mess and can't get her shit together—is the one who took her place."

Just the thought that she might be right makes me furious. Because Macy is still one of the best people I know, and she doesn't deserve all the pain that's being heaped on her. She sure as hell doesn't deserve two parents who are so busy worrying about her messing up her life that they don't realize life has already messed with *her*. A lot. It's maddening.

"First of all, *you're* not a mess," I say in a voice that tells her I'm deadly serious. "You've had a string of really shitty things happen to you, and you've learned not to just roll over and take it. We both have—and I actually call that a win for us, not a loss.

"Second of all, your shit seems like it's together just fine to me. Have you been through a lot of really tough stuff? Yes. Did you come out the other side? Hell yeah, you did. Could you use some help dealing with it? Probably. There's nothing wrong with that. Maybe someone needs to tell your parents that."

"Maybe I do," she says, and there's such a look of relief on her face that it breaks my heart. Relief that I believe her. More, relief that I believe *in* her. And I damn sure am going to have her back from now on, whether I'm in San Diego or not.

I start to tell her as much, but Hudson switches to Queen's "We Will Rock You" and he's sounding more than a little hoarse at this point.

"Oh my God," Macy groans with a roll of her eyes. "Will you please go put that boy out of his misery before he works his way through the entire lexicon of British music? For all we know, he'll start on the Spice

Girls next."

"Hey, I bet he could rock 'Wannabe' if he wanted to." Still, I get to my feet.

"Hey, do vampires prune up when they stay in water too long?" Macy asks. When I turn to stare at her with a what-the-fuck look, she shrugs. "I'm just saying. Inquiring minds want to know."

"Can you see Hudson Vega looking like a prune?" I raise my brows.

"Well, no. But that's why I'm asking you. You know him better than anyone."

Again, I think of the changes at the Vampire Court. And wonder if that's actually true. Or maybe it is, and I know Hudson as well as anybody can. Just not enough to figure out what he's up to now.

As I knock on the door, I tell myself I'm being ridiculous. "Talk's over," I call out. "You can come out now."

The shower turns off immediately.

Ten minutes later, he comes out of the bathroom fully dressed and maybe—just maybe—a tiny bit prune-y, though I'm certainly not going to be the one to point it out. "We need to find Polo," he tells us as he slides on his boots. "And I want to let Nyaz know we're back and to see Smokey. Let her know we're okay."

"Why don't you do that while Macy and I grab something to eat?" I tell him as I head into the bathroom to get dressed as well. "I'm *so* hungry."

"Oh God, me too," Macy agrees. "Woman cannot live by renegade Snickers bars alone. Partly because nutrition is a thing, but mostly because I ate my last one when I got back to my room last night."

"We'll wake the others while you get dressed," Hudson tells me.

"I might go put on some makeup, actually," Macy says quietly, as if she's embarrassed. "I don't know if..." And I know exactly what she's saying—she might be starting to let her guard down around me, just a little, but that doesn't mean she's anywhere close to ready to go out in the world without her eyeliner armor.

And my perfect mate saves her from having to explain, saying, "I'll walk you to your room before waking the others, then. Grace, I'll see you in the lobby."

"Sounds amazing," I reply, going up on tiptoe to kiss his cheek, because he may have already brushed his teeth this morning, but I definitely haven't.

"You don't have to walk me to my room," Macy argues even as they head for the door.

Hudson just pulls it open and gestures for her to precede him through it. "Consider it full-service. You get company and a show."

"I really like your rendition of 'Start Me Up,'" she tells him with a laugh. "Though Grace and I think you'd do a bang-up job with 'Wannabe.'"

"Tell me what you really want," Hudson answers dryly.

Macy pouts. "Hey, that's not how the lyrics go—"

"I'm aware of how they go," he answers. "That's my way of telling you that it's never going to happen."

"Aww, come on. You'd make a great Posh Spice."

I can all but hear Hudson roll his eyes as he answers, "And here I was going for Scary."

The door closes behind them, so I don't hear anything else. Still, I can't help smiling as I strip down and step into the shower. Maybe I should have let Hudson handle the Macy crisis with me. The two of them just have a way of making each other feel better that defies logic but somehow works anyway.

On the surface, fashion is the only thing they really have in common. Yet, from the beginning, they've just kind of gotten each other, Macy's abysmal chess-playing skills notwithstanding. It makes me happy that two of the most important people in my life like and respect each other as much as Hudson and Macy do.

Figuring my mate used enough water for all of us, I take what might be the quickest shower of my life. When I'm out, I pull on my last clean pair of jeans—guess it's a good thing we're heading out today—and twist my hair up into a clip at the back of my head.

Then I stroll down to the small restaurant in the lobby. A parmallow muffin and some fruit sounds really good about now.

Hudson already has Smokey sitting on a chair next to him when I get downstairs. He has a cup of tea in front of him, and Smokey is

watching every move he makes like she's afraid he'll disappear again—
or worse, like she already knows he will, which means I guess they've
had "the talk."

Instead of taking the seat next to her, I grab a chair on the other side
of the table, as far from the pissed-off little umbra as I can get. She's
never actually hurt me, though I'm pretty sure she'd like the chance
to try right now. So distance definitely seems like the better part of
valor at the moment.

The waitress comes up to take my order as soon as I sit down, and
our friends straggle in over the next few minutes. But before my food
can arrive, I look out the window just in time to see a familiar face
walking toward us, one of Marian's choux pastry bags in his hand.

"Well, isn't that perfect timing for once," I murmur as the door to
the inn swings open. Maybe our luck is finally changing.

Hudson turns to find out who I'm looking at, a huge grin splitting
his face. "Just the person we need to see."

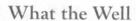

75

What the Well

Fifty-six minutes later, we check out of the inn and head across the square to the wishing well in the center of the park. It's strangely empty this morning—maybe that's why Polo was so insistent that we meet him now. The iridescent purple coins I remember filling the well are gone, replaced by an *extremely* ominous black hole that looks like it goes on forever. Because that's not scary at all.

"Remember to stay close to me," I tell Heather, who looks surprisingly unworried despite the warning I delivered to all of them as we finished our breakfast.

"I've got her," Eden says quietly. For once, the cocky grin I consider her signature look is missing. She seems serious and more than ready for whatever is about to come our way.

Or maybe that's just wishful thinking on my part.

We're almost to the well when Polo appears out of seemingly nowhere. We were completely surprised when he came to find us at the inn, but he'd insisted if we wanted even a chance of surviving our escape from Noromar, we had to leave immediately.

"You're late," he says when we stop in front of him seconds later.

"Actually, we're a minute early," I shoot back.

But he's not listening. His dark-brown eyes are locked on Heather, and I can practically see him tallying up "the human's" weaknesses.

"She's not going to make it," he says after a moment. "You should leave her here."

"And just have her spend the rest of her life in Noromar alone?" I ask, insulted.

He shrugs. "Guess so. She's just a liability. She's going to get you killed."

"She comes," Hudson says in a steely voice I rarely hear him use. "We'll get her through."

"Thank you," Heather murmurs, eyes wide.

Polo looks like he wants to argue, but in the end, he just throws up his hands. "Whatever, man. But I'm telling you now, if things go south, I'm leaving your bloodsucking ass and getting the hell out of Dodge. My daughter is not growing up without her father."

"Damn straight. I expect nothing less," Hudson tells him. "And thank you. We appreciate this more than we can ever say."

"Yes," I agree. "We'll never be able to thank you enough."

"Thank me when you get to the other side and you're not dead," is his cryptic answer.

"Now that we're here, can you at least tell us what to expect?" I ask, because really, the mystery is going to kill me faster than whatever awaits us.

"I hear it's a little different every time," he answers with a shake of his bangs.

"Wait, you don't know?" Eden asks, her eyebrows disappearing under her fringe.

"I'm a chupacabra," he replies, and his chest puffs out a tiny bit. When we all just blink at him, he shakes his head and elaborates. "Let's just say whatever is down there wants none of this"—he gestures down the length of his body, then taps his forehead—"and definitely none of this."

"That has to be the weirdest flex I've ever seen," Flint murmurs to Jaxon, who shoots him a half smile but says nothing.

"Basically, whatever *is* down there leaves ol' Polo alone. But that means they're smart and wily." He looks at each of us one by one. "But I've seen…*something* with others I've tried to smuggle out, and if you relax for even a second, they'll be on you. Whatever you do, do not let them swallow you."

Don't let them swallow you? That's the best advice he's got? Like, isn't that self-explanatory?

I exchange what-the-fuck looks with my friends as the tension in my stomach increases threefold. Don't let them swallow us? How the hell big are these things, anyway?

"No offense, Polo, but I feel like that's pretty generic advice," Flint comments. "Does anyone ever actually want to be swallowed by anything?"

"I'm not saying you *won't want* to be swallowed by them," Polo says with a half-hearted shrug. "By the end, you may be praying for it. I've seen it happen to others."

I've got nothing to say to that, and judging from the expressions on my friends' faces, neither do they. I do know, however, that the longer we stand here, the more freaked out I'm getting. I don't know if that's what Polo is aiming for—a last-ditch attempt to get us to change our minds—but I do know these kinds of nerves aren't going to do us any good.

It's time to either suck it up or get the fuck off the playing field. And since the latter isn't an option, I reach down deep. Then say, "Are we going to do this or what?"

"By all means," Polo says. Then he gestures to the wishing well. "Ladies first."

"Wait. That's it?" Jaxon asks. "We just need to jump into a well?"

"That's not *it*. But it's a start." Polo lifts a brow at me, as if asking if I'm brave enough to be the first one down.

Truth be told, I don't think bravery has anything to do with it. But a good leader never asks anyone to do what they wouldn't. And while I have no idea if I'm actually a good leader or not, I know that I want to be.

Besides, I've got to go down the dark, scary hole no matter what. I might as well be first and get it over with. And if something is waiting down there to swallow me, then maybe this will give my friends a better shot at not getting eaten.

"What do I do?" I ask, stepping closer to the well. "Just jump?"

But Hudson is already there. "I'll go first," he tells me.

Like I want him to be the first one to get swallowed if something is actually waiting at the bottom? No fucking thank you.

"Puh-lease," I say sarcastically and shift into my gargoyle form. "I believe the girl made of *stone* has the distinct advantage over the chewy vampire in the monsters-might-eat-us race."

Hudson raises one haughty eyebrow and gestures toward the well as though he were showing me the way to my throne. Cheeky bastard.

I turn to Polo and ask again: "Just jump, right?"

He nods. "Yep. You just jump."

As if to prove it to me, he shifts into his chupacabra form—which looks sort of like a coyote, if by coyote you really meant a giant fucking hellhound with menacing, foot-tall spikes along his spine and massive, razor-sharp fangs built solely for ripping flesh from bone like tissue paper at Christmas.

"I totally get the flex now," Flint murmurs to Jaxon, who rolls his eyes this time.

"Why didn't he do that when we were fighting together?" I murmur to Hudson, who just shrugs as if to say we shouldn't question our badass chupacabra guide.

The beast lets out an eerie growl that makes my friends take a healthy step back, and then he jumps straight down the well.

We stand there staring after him, and I can't help wondering if they're all thinking what I'm thinking—we're screwed if *that* is the level of monster that keeps the other monsters away.

Eventually, though, I turn to Hudson and say, "All right, then. See you at the bottom."

He nods and steps toward the well. But it's too late. Before he can so much as grab the brick edges of it, I'm tucking my wings as tightly as I can around my body and hurling myself over the edge.

And then I'm falling, falling, falling.

76

Gargoyles Are
Friends, Not Food

Wind rushes by me as I plummet through the darkness...down, down, *down*.

I have one moment to think about Heather—to worry whether she'll survive this fall and how I can possibly catch her when it's complete pitch-blackness all around me—then, just like that, I jackknife straight into water.

Because it's a well. Of course there's water at the bottom.

Which is great for Heather and everybody else. Not so great for me, since I made the genius move of turning into a brick.

When I first hit the water, I sink like the stone I am, plunging deeper and deeper, like an arrow seeking home. And though it only takes me a flash to turn back to my much more buoyant human form, it takes a lot longer to reach the surface and breathe again. Unfortunately, my lungs were totally unprepared for the huge mouthful of water they got when I first went under.

I spend the next several moments kicking my way back up to the surface—short arms and legs are a complete pain in the ass in situations like this—and finally make it just as someone drops into the water beside me.

He hits with a splash that sends water careening into my face and has my already spasming lungs spiraling into another coughing fit.

"Hey, you okay, Grace?"

So it's Flint who just nearly drowned me for the second time in as many minutes. Big surprise.

"Yeah, I'm fine." I direct my answer toward his voice. I can't actually see him yet in the darkness, but before I can start moving toward him, two more people drop in right next to us, followed by three more.

After we all check in on one another and make sure everyone's okay—especially Heather, thank God—we start to try to get our bearings.

"Now what?" Eden asks.

It's a good question, considering we're all currently treading water in the dark, with absolutely no idea of which way to go next.

"Does anyone see the chupacabra?" Hudson asks, and I've never been more grateful for the fact that vampires and dragons can see clearly in the dark. Or more annoyed by the fact that gargoyles can't.

"I think there's something up ahead to the right," Jaxon tells him, and then there's a whole lot of splashing as the rest of us take off to our right.

But some of us can't see the others—namely, the human, the witch, and the gargoyle—so our right turns end up being the *wrong* rights. Macy and I slam straight into each other, our rights apparently in direct contrast to each other.

"Could you be a little more specific?" Heather asks as she, too, gets tangled up with us. "For the mere mortals among the gods?"

"So what you're saying, Heather, is that I'm a god?" Flint teases.

"If you tow me out of this mess, I'll call you anything you want," she answers.

"God works," he answers cheerfully. And then must make good on his word because Heather brushes against me fast and hard, like someone is suddenly pulling her.

"I've got you," Hudson says as Macy and I untangle from each other. He doesn't tow us nearly as aggressively as Flint towed Heather, but he stays with us as we paddle our way through the darkness.

A couple of minutes into the swim, we turn some kind of corner and the world in front of us gets at least a little lighter. It's still near complete darkness to the tiny gargoyle, but there's at least enough light to make out a beach in the distance—and the chupacabra wading ashore and shaking himself like a dog on the sand.

"That's it?" Flint asks. "Seriously? A little water and a swim, and he thinks it's soooooo dangerous?" He strikes out toward shore without another word, his powerful biceps eating up the distance like it's nothing.

Heather takes off after him. As a lifelong member of the swim team, she's pretty much in her element in anything water, and Eden follows directly after her.

"Show-offs," Macy mutters, and I have to agree with her.

I love swimming—which is a good thing, given how I grew up a few steps from the Pacific—but loving it and being great at it are two very different things. Especially when everyone around me stands close to a foot taller than me, even Macy.

It isn't long before she leaves me in the dust, which isn't a big deal. I mean, sure, I never leave them when they're in a sticky situation, but what's a half-mile swim between friends...or mates, for that matter?

Jaxon and Hudson decided to race, and if their shit-talking is to be believed—I still can't see much of anything—they swim faster than they fade and are getting the rest of the gang to take sides and declare a winner. Which of course means everyone is now on shore except the short girl who is still very much in the creepy water, in the even creepier *fucking dark.*

No big deal. I'm not out here alone with scenes from *Open Water* playing in my head all of a sudden. Nope, not a big deal at all.

Though I have to say, after all Polo's warnings about how terrible and precarious this journey is, I'd be lying if I said this didn't feel kinda anticlimactic. A little cold water, an uncomfortably long swim...none of that actually spells terror the way Polo led us to believe.

The worst thing about it is the darkness, but the closer I get to shore, the more lights there are. Not just the sun leaking in from some hole above the beach, but a bunch of fireflies free-floating over the water that are beautiful. Like, really beautiful.

Maybe I'll try to paint them when I get back home to San Diego, see if I can get their color just right. They're a beautiful, glowing shade of purple I've never quite seen before. In fact—

"Grace!" All of a sudden, Flint yells my name and starts jumping up and down as he waves from shore.

I wave back and keep swimming, though I'd be lying if I said I wasn't taking my time at this point. I mean, why not? The others are drying off, and it's really beautiful out here. Besides, it serves them right to have to wait in wet clothes for *the friend they left behind*.

"Grace!" I guess it's Macy's turn to shout at me to hurry.

I start to wave back, but she's not waving like Flint. Instead, she's pointing behind me, a look of abject terror on her face.

Which, now that I think about it, isn't that different from the expressions of everyone else on shore. What the hell?

I stop moving forward and dog paddle in a circle, trying to figure out what it is that has them so freaked out, but there's nothing to see except unrelenting fucking darkness in one direction and those little purple lights in the other as I whip back around toward shore again.

Normally, I might not worry much, but I am an ocean girl—even though I don't see anything, this sure as shit feels like a *Jaws*, get-the-hell-out-of-the-water moment, so I start swimming as fast as I can, visions of sharks and giant squids and the Loch Ness fucking Monster suddenly dancing in my head. And that's before Hudson takes a running leap back into the water—aiming straight for me.

My heart is beating against my chest like a drum now, and I suck in as much air as I can between strokes and swim and swim and swim. But still, the shore seems miles away, even though logically I know it can't be more than a hundred yards.

"Grace!" Macy is screaming at the top of her lungs now. "Hurry, Grace!"

What the ever-loving fuck is going on?

I tell myself not to turn around again, tell myself to just keep going, but I have to know what's back there. I just have to.

So I turn around one more time—as my friends start screaming so loud that I think one of them is going to have an aneurysm. And that's when I see it.

Terror seizes the breath from my lungs as I realize that those beautiful purple fireflies weren't fireflies at all.

They were lures.

Dangling over me from the tail of the Shadow Realm's version of the ugliest, most disgusting-looking, bigger-than-a-fucking-*house* anglerfish.

And I am the ridiculous little blue Dory fish it has in its sights.

Shit. Shit, shit, *shit*.

It leaps at me, and I scream. Thank God a year of everything trying to kill me has given me pretty solid fight-or-flight instincts, because without even thinking, I dive deep to try to get away from it. The only problem is that a fish that's twenty feet tall has a pretty giant mouth, and I am right in the freaking center of all those massive, razor-sharp teeth.

The first time it goes for me, I manage to twist and dodge away at the last second, but I know that's not going to last. The second time, it gets so close that I feel the edge of a tooth scrape against my hip. And the third time…the third time, I'm pretty sure I'm screwed.

There's only so many ways to evade a colossal, gargoyle-hunting fish monster, and I'm pretty sure I've already used them all. So I do the only thing I can think of. I stop trying to swim away from the fish, and instead I whip around and pump my legs as fast as I can—and head straight for its giant mouth.

I barely even register my friends' near-desperate screams from shore now. I'm too focused on this beast. Timing is going to be everything as I get its face really, really, really close to mine.

Once I can see the milky whites of its eyes, I roll left at the last minute, just outside the range of its gaping maw that snaps closed with a sickening crunch. As its thrust carries it past me, I kick both my legs straight at its cheek and use every ounce of strength I've got—and its own momentum—to push myself away from it. It doesn't daunt the giant fish at all, but it *does* manage to propel my torso about three feet straight out of the water.

Which is all I need.

I reach inside and grab my platinum string, shifting as I continue to fly through the air. The second I've got my wings, I shoot straight up—just in time to avoid the angler's next attempt to catch me in its mouth.

But it's close, really close, and I pull my legs up as tight to my chest as I can manage, out of the reach of those wicked teeth. One still manages to get me, scraping all the way down the outside of my leg from thigh to ankle, but I don't bother to check. Instead, I race for shore with the fish leaping along behind me, over and over and over again.

Until it stops.

I'm about to take my first steadying breath since I first realized I was fish food when it occurs to me that my friends are all still screaming like someone's life depends on it. But if not mine, then—

My stomach leaps into my throat as I bank hard right and catch a glimpse of my mate powering through the water—directly in the range of the giant, pissed-off fish. And while Hudson's fast, I'm not sure he's paranormal-fish fast.

I don't even hesitate. I tuck my wings against my body and dive straight for him. I'm over him in mere seconds, and I reach down, grab onto the back of his shirt at the same time I yank my wings wide enough to catch some lift again—and I use all of my speeding momentum and every ounce of desperate, panicked, adrenaline-fueled stress I have to pick him up just enough to get him out of the water. And then I fly straight for shore with Hudson below me like a backward, freestyle-swimming Superman.

But even as a gargoyle with a bunch of adrenaline coursing through her system, I'm not strong enough to carry him very far for very long, and he slips out of my grip just as we get to shore and goes careening feet-first into a shocked and cursing Flint.

The two of them go flying ass-over-teakettle across the sand while I crash-land on the first available open space.

As I roll onto my back, blood gushing from the cut on my leg, Polo leans over me and says, "I told you not to get swallowed up."

77

Parthenon Crashers

"I'll just stay here a bit," I say to no one in particular, my lungs burning almost as much as the scrape down my leg. I wiggle my stone butt a little deeper into the beach, the cool sand taking the sting out of the wound.

Hudson fades to me in a blink, sliding on his knees to my side. He takes one glance at the blood pooling in the sand around my leg and looks like he might pass out.

"I will never let you live it down if you faint from the sight of a little blood," I croak out between breaths.

"A vampire who faints at the sight of blood." Jaxon snickers—but then something causes him to whips his head to Flint, all semblance of humor gone.

"Hey," Flint mutters to himself, lifting the edge of his T-shirt. "I think your belt cut me."

I roll my head to the side just enough to catch sight of a huge slash across Flint's abs—and Jaxon fading to *his* side, looking a little faint himself.

"Vampires have such weak constitutions." Eden rolls her eyes at Heather and Macy, and they all have a good laugh at the Vega brothers' expense.

Hudson tugs my hand in his trembling one, and my gaze softens on his as I whisper, "I'm going to be fine, babe. Promise."

He nods, blinking back the gathering moisture in his eyes, but he must not trust himself to speak quite yet. He just gives another quick nod and squeezes my hand.

Normally, I'd lay here for a minute, letting the earth magic slowly heal my stone body—my powers returned the second I hit the sand, so I guess we're officially out of the Shadow Realm—but I can tell Hudson is holding on to his shit by a thread. I would never want my mate to suffer a moment of anxiety over my health, nor I his, so I roll over onto my injured side to cup his face with my hand, rub my fingers along his strong jaw.

"I got this," I say. And to prove it, I draw energy from the earth into my wound, now packed with sand. It only takes a moment, and then I toss him a cheeky grin. "But you can give me a hand up."

He leaps to his feet and tugs me up with him in a single bound, and I shift back into my human form.

"See?" I ask, then gesture to the giant tear in my jeans and the wound-free skin below. "All better."

It takes a second, but then his eyes are widening and he's pulling me into his arms for a hug that feels as calming as watching a summer storm. "Thank fook," he breathes, dropping kisses all over my curls before sliding a hand under my chin and brushing his warm lips against mine over and over.

And I get it—I do. If I'd just witnessed Hudson get almost eaten by a monster fish and then watched his blood pool around him, I'd want to assure myself he was really okay, that everything was going to be okay. Which is why I lean into his warmth, give him whatever he needs to calm his racing heart.

Someone coughs off to the side, and we slowly, so very slowly, turn our heads to glare at Jaxon, who is apparently over his Flint scare and ready to get this show on the road.

I, on the other hand, refuse to move. At least not yet. Because: "I'm not going anywhere until *someone* gives me a pair of pants to wear."

"I got you, New Girl," Flint says and yanks a damp but serviceable pair of basketball shorts out of his backpack.

Hudson growls low and steady at him, and Flint shoves them right back into his bag.

"Hud-son," I whine, but thankfully my bestie comes to the rescue and offers a pair of her jeans.

Everyone turns around, and I quickly change into them, rolling the hem up several times to make up for the vast height difference. Still, though they're also pretty wet from the swim, they're not bloody, so I'll take it.

"We ready to get a move on?" Polo eventually asks, and we all nod. He turns and heads down a long tunnel that leads away from the beach, carved into a sheer wall of black rock that rises as far as I can see.

A couple of minutes pass before we stop again. "What's going on?" I ask, peering around Hudson's broad shoulders to try to figure out why we're not moving. Please don't let it be another lake crossing. Please, please, please don't let it be that.

But it turns out we're at a giant fork in the middle of the tunnel— one that breaks off in two different directions.

"What's this?" Flint asks Polo. "How do we know which one to take?"

"I've only ever taken the one on the right," Polo answers. "Every time I try to go down the left one, things get really weird."

"Weirder than huge lakes full of monster fish trying to kill us?" Heather asks doubtfully.

"Yes." We wait for him to add an explanation, but he just looks at us out of eyes that have seen far too much.

"Oooookay, then," Eden says. "To the right it is."

"Remind me to thank Jikan for creating a tunnel filled with something that freaks the chupacabra out so much he won't even go down it," Hudson says with a little bite.

Flint snort-laughs in response. "I'd pay to see that."

"Oh, I'll make sure you get a seat for free."

I put a hand on Hudson's back, hoping to comfort him. No one else may notice what's going on, but it's very obvious to me that underneath the dry, British humor, Hudson is *seething*.

I know it's because he watched me almost get Moby Dicked—and he could do absolutely nothing about it.

Hudson believes in fighting our own battles and doing whatever we have to do to get a job done. But he won't soon forgive Jikan for not giving us any advice about this world he created before setting us loose in it.

And I have to agree, it does seem like bullshit. I know the God of

Time told us not to come here, but he also knows us well enough at this point to be aware that we weren't going to heed his advice. I'm not asking for a ton of help—but a heads-up that actually would have given us a fifty-fifty shot of not dying in the barrier crossing would have been nice.

I'm sure when Hudson sees Jikan again, he won't level his objection anywhere near that diplomatically, though. Only the fact that Polo has been sneaking across the barrier all these years in a non-fish-enticing form—probably all those spikes down his back, now that I think of it—is keeping Hudson from being pissed at him as well.

Without another word, Polo leads us through the dark tunnel and up a steep incline to the surface. As we break through into the light, I say, "Thank you. I know you didn't have to do this for us, and I will forever be grateful that you did."

"Hey, turns out I'm the lucky one. You taught me something about the barrier that's going to make my life a whole lot easier in the months and years to come." He gives me a lopsided grin. "Swim faster."

"Too soon, Polo," I say with a shudder, and he cackles.

"Where are we?" Macy asks as we all squint against the bright light. "This doesn't look like Italy."

"Italy?" The chupacabra laughs. "You're about as far from Turin as you can get. You're in Kansas, baby."

"Kansas?" Heather sounds incredulous. "As in, there's no place like home?"

"Kansas isn't my home. And neither are these stick crop things." Flint bats at one of the crops to prove his point.

"That's wheat," I tell him as I lean forward and rescue the stalk from his hands.

He shudders. "Whatever it is, I'm not impressed. Isn't there a city around here somewhere?"

"Relax, City Boy. The food won't hurt you." Hudson rolls his eyes before addressing Polo. "I'll make some calls. By the time you get to the Piazza Castello to cross back over, I'll have a stack of jeans waiting for you at the Witch Court."

"Thanks, man. I appreciate it." He nods before turning to me and extending his hand.

I take it, murmuring, "Thank you, Polo, for everything."

He pulls me in for a quick hug, then whispers, "Take care of yourself, Grace. Hudson's a stand-up guy, and I don't think he'd do very well if something happened to you."

Before I can react, he steps back. Then, with a wave and an "adios, amigos," he shifts and hauls ass through the very large wheat field we are currently somewhere in the middle of.

"So, now what do we do?" Heather asks, looking baffled.

But Macy is already on it, spinning a portal open right here in the crops. "Have you ever been to Alexandria?" I ask my cousin as dark, colorful sparks fly. I'd told them all about Remy's pin drop on the Curator's location what feels like a lifetime ago.

"No, but I've been to Athens. I just looked it up. It's about a thousand miles from Alexandria, which is pretty much as close as I can get us."

"Athens? Seriously?" Eden looks impressed.

Macy shrugs. "There was some kind of paranormal education summit there when I was six or seven, so my parents made a family trip of it. I don't remember much, except the Parthenon."

"The Parthenon?" It's my turn to be impressed. "Really?"

She just nods toward her portal. "Next stop, the Acropolis."

78

Hex Marks
the Spot

It turns out the Parthenon looks exactly like it does in books and Disney movies. Sitting atop the Acropolis on the outskirts of Athens, the remains of the ancient temple are incredibly impressive—especially when I think about the fact that it was built in the fifth century BCE. Made of tall marble columns and built in the shape of a large rectangle, it doesn't feel like it should be as awe-inspiring as it is. But something about the feeling of standing atop a mountain filled with some of the most ancient ruins in the world is incredibly special.

Even before Hudson comes up behind me and wraps his arms around my waist. "It's a hell of a view, isn't it?"

I nod as I continue to stare at the lights of Athens spread out beneath the dark mountaintop. "I wish we had more time to take it all in."

"That's the story of our lives, isn't it?"

"Yeah." I turn in his arms and hug him as tightly as I can. "We need to come back here someday and actually explore—when Mekhi's life doesn't hang in the balance."

"It's a date," he promises me with a soft smile. "And no, that's not jinxing anything." Then he steps back so I can shift.

"Last one to Alexandria has to figure out where the Curator is," I call, right before I reach for my platinum string and turn into my gargoyle form.

"Already shared Grace's pin from Remy in a group text," Heather says, holding up her phone triumphantly. "We just need to fly a straight line between here and there and aim for the harbor. I'll fill you in when we get there."

Jaxon lifts his brows, obviously impressed by her thoroughness.

Even Flint grins at her and says, "Let's hear it for the human."

Heather flushes with pride, and I can't help smiling along with her. It makes me happier than I can say to have my oldest best friend getting along with all my new best friends. So far, she's also made it through the dangerous part of this world better than I ever could have imagined. I just pray that it keeps up, because the last thing I ever want is for her to get hurt, especially doing something that I made her a part of.

I give everyone a moment to have their laugh, and then I shut it all down with one well-placed phrase.

"We've got to go."

They nod, and then the dragons step back to shift in a flurry of rainbow sparks that lights up the whole night.

After a few minutes of prep, the others climb on the dragons' backs. Hudson on Jaxon, Heather on Eden, and Macy on Flint.

As the first stars begin appearing in the night sky, we take off toward Egypt, and I hope Remy's pin is in the right location.

Although we have a couple of missteps along the way, we make it to Alexandria, Egypt, around three in the morning. It's the downside of traveling by portal and dragon, but since we're about to ask the Curator for a really big favor, arriving at their place at three in the morning seems like a particularly bad idea.

Instead, we stop at an all-night café by the beach, and those of us who eat food fuel up on Egyptian bread, cheese, and stuffed vegetables— mashi, they call it. It's delicious, and it hits the spot. But I can't help thinking that we need to say to hell with social niceties. We need to go see the Curator *now*. Who cares if it's the middle of the night when someone is *dying*?

On that note, I resist the urge to text Lorelei again. She texted earlier that Mekhi was still holding his own, but something in the brevity of her texts hasn't been sitting well with me.

I glance at my cell phone yet again and convince myself that Mekhi will be okay for a few more hours. *Please*, I beg the universe as I read over his response to the text I sent when we first got to Kansas. *Please let him hang on just a little while longer.*

With nothing else to do after our middle-of-the-night breakfast, we wander down to the breakwater that runs along the length of the harbor in Alexandria.

It's a beautiful view, and the area is surprisingly busy considering the hour. Apparently, Alexandria is like New York in that it's a city that never sleeps.

Still, it's nice to walk along the harbor and gaze out at the Mediterranean. It's fun to think about what it looked like a couple of thousand years ago, when the Lighthouse at Alexandria was still standing on the Island of Pharos. Now there's a giant citadel there—also cool, but not as cool as the lighthouse.

Then again, maybe I just have a soft spot for them.

At one point, we all come to a natural stop, finding places to rest and wait along the breakwater. Hudson sinks down onto an open space on the wall and gestures for me to join him. When I do, he wraps an arm around my waist and murmurs, "Rest," as he pulls me closer to him. For the first time since we've been back from the Shadow Realm, his phone is in his pocket. I lean into him—he feels so good, it's impossible to resist.

After the long flight here and everything that came before it, part of me is amazed I'm not dragging more than I am. Still, the second I drop my head onto his shoulder, I pass out.

I wake up what must be about an hour later to the sound of the call to prayer ringing through the air around me. It's beautiful, rhythmic and melodious, as it goes out from what feels like one end of the city to the other.

"Hey there," Hudson murmurs, stroking a hand down my cheek.

I turn my face into his hand, press my lips to his palm. He smiles down at me in the early-morning light, and for a second, it's just the two of us. No quest, no fear, no Circle just waiting to close in on us when we're least expecting it. It's just him and me and this one perfect moment.

I press another kiss into his hand, then turn my face to watch as dawn paints the sky over the harbor a brilliant combination of fiery oranges and reds and yellows. The colors reflect off the water, turning the whole area into a blazing inferno.

"I love you," I whisper, because no matter what is going on—no matter how frustrated or annoyed or worried I am about what is going on inside him—that will always be true.

"I love *you*," he answers, his bright blue eyes blazing as fiercely as the sky around us.

I want to stay like this forever, want to say to hell with all our responsibilities—and, more importantly, all the political machinations that come with who we are. When we're just us, just Hudson and Grace, everything is as close to perfect as it can be when two headstrong people are mated. It's when all the other stuff gets added in that things get really difficult.

But that's who we are. Who we'll always be, whether I want it to be different or not. The good, the bad, and sometimes the royally fucked.

Some of my thoughts must show on my face, because Hudson's eyes turn cloudy. "You okay?" he asks, sliding his thumb across my lower lip in a gesture that always makes me melt.

Since today is no exception, I just nod and close my eyes, hoping that he'll go on touching me forever. Or at least for a little while longer.

But Eden chooses that moment to say, "We should probably get going."

"Yeah," Jaxon agrees, standing and stretching. "We should head out before the city really gets up and moving again."

I know he's right, but disappointment still slides through me as I move away from Hudson. A quick glance at him, though, tells me he's already pulled out his phone and is moving on.

As I reach for my own phone, I tell myself not to blame him for that. Every single one of us is looking up something right now. Including me, though after confirming I have no new texts from Artelya or Lorelei, I'm just pulling up the directions to the Serapeum of Alexandria that Heather looked up for me while we were at the café.

On the plus side, it isn't far from where we are, which is why we decided to spend the predawn hours here instead of trying to fly through the very crowded city as it begins to stir for the day.

Five minutes on Google in the café taught me that the Serapeum was a temple built to honor Serapis, who at one point was the guardian of the city. But more important to our purposes, I think, is the fact that at the time it was built, the Serapeum was referred to as the daughter of the Library of Alexandria.

It was a satellite building, housing much of the Library's overflow, and unlike with the Library, the Serapeum never burned.

It's destroyed now, I realize as we land several feet from the one remaining column on the site, and my stomach sinks.

Aside from some wall ruins and the catacombs that lay beneath the ground we're standing on, nothing remains. The Egyptians have used part of the site, away from the ruins, to put in a cemetery. But otherwise, there's nothing here.

I fire off a quick text to Remy, but I have no idea when he'll answer. I groan. It really never occurred to me that Remy might be wrong.

"*This* is where the Curator is?" Jaxon asks, looking around the ruins skeptically. "Did we get the wrong Serapeum?"

"This is the only one in Alexandria," Heather replies, her phone in her hand as she scrolls through information about the city. "There's another one in the south of Egypt, but, like...he dropped a pin. It's gotta be this one."

"No, this is definitely it," Macy says, walking straight toward the crumpled ruins. "Can't you feel it?"

"Feel what?" Flint asks, looking intrigued.

"The magic." Macy holds out her hands in front of her, like the ruins are a bonfire she's warming herself in front of. "It's everywhere in this place, but"—she pauses as she walks around the relics—"especially here."

The place she's standing doesn't look like anything special. The ruins are no more impressive here than anywhere else—just large white bricks dented by time and weather and more than two millennia of people touching and marveling over them.

They're cool to look at, absolutely, but there's nothing magical in them that I can see. Nothing that remains of the early power and potential of this place.

That doesn't mean Macy's wrong, however. Her magic is very

different than my own earth magic, and who knows what she's picking up here? I hope it's something, hope we can somehow follow it to where we need to be. Because otherwise, it feels like this is a bust.

I've seen how the Bloodletter and the Crone live, in houses that reflect who they really are. Even the ice cave my grandmother trapped herself in for a thousand years was loaded with her personality. I have no idea where Jikan lives, but I'm sure it's the same for him. So why on earth would the Curator choose to live here?

Plus, on a purely logistical level, where? There isn't a building in sight that might actually act as a home for anyone.

"Any ideas on where we should knock?" Eden asks, looking as unimpressed by the place as I am. "Because I'm not seeing a front door, let alone a welcome mat."

"Well, we need to do something," Heather says, her usual practicality ringing in her voice as she scrolls through her phone. "Because according to the site I'm on, this is it. The ruins here, the Victory Pillar there, and the catacombs down below. The temple is long gone, as are the statues to the twelve Olympian gods that once stood here. We're not going to find anything else, because nothing else is here. Some of the most noted historians in the world have signed off on that fact."

"They don't know what they're talking about," Macy says. "They can't feel the magic the way I can."

"Is it possible the magic you're feeling is coming from the ruins?" Eden asks. "Places like this, where so much has happened throughout history, have their own energy to them. But it's the energy of everything that's happened there rather than—"

"That's not it." Macy shakes her head, then walks in a small circle right in front of the pillar. And does the same thing again. And again. And again.

"This is it," she repeats after several long, silent seconds have passed.

"This is what?" I ask, glancing at Hudson to see what he thinks of this whole thing.

But his narrowed gaze is focused on Macy as she holds her hands straight in front of her and murmurs something I can't quite make out.

"What's she doing?" Heather stage-whispers to me.

But I just shake my head because I don't have a clue. This is the first time I've ever seen Macy do something like this.

Seconds turn into minutes as Macy continues to say what I can only assume is a spell under her breath. But nothing happens for what feels like the longest time, and I'm about to give up. To start trying to figure out where the other temple to Serapis was built in the south of Egypt and head there instead. Maybe we really did get the place wrong.

Except, just as I'm about to turn away in defeat, the air in front of us begins to shimmer with what looks an awful lot like a cloud of gold dust.

79

A-Muse Bouche Me

"What the hell is that?" Jaxon asks as we all scramble back as one. Everyone but Macy and Eden, that is, both of whom walk closer to the shimmer.

"I'd say it was a mirage," Eden comments quietly. "But we're not in the middle of the desert."

"This isn't the mirage," Macy tells her as the dust solidifies into a gorgeous building. "The ruins you saw when we first walked up are the actual mirage. *This* is what's really here."

What "this" is is a huge, circular building made almost entirely of gold and silver. At first glance, it sort of looks like an arena or a coliseum, with its high walls and round shape.

But that's where the similarity ends. A closer inspection makes it obvious that nothing else about the building is made for fighting—or for trade.

No, everything here screams pure artistic and erudite hubris.

The outer walls are lined with mural after mural done in gold overlay and finished off with glittering jewels. The murals themselves are works of art, even before you consider the historical scenes they depict—everything from the burning of the Library at Alexandria to what I'm almost certain is the moon landing.

Outside the walls is an elaborate garden filled with every type and color of flower imaginable. It's set up in the style of an English garden, with an abundance of flowering shrubs planted along neat gemstone-lined pathways and potted flowers grouped together every few feet. There are stairs leading to quaint little bridges that cover even quainter ponds filled with black, white, and golden koi, while floral archways and trellises situated every several feet are filled with roses, jasmine, and wisteria, just to name the ones I recognize.

Also in the garden, placed in significant spots around the building, are statues of nine women in various types of historical dress. *The muses through the ages?* I wonder as I step closer to get a better look. Then decide, yes, that's exactly what I'm looking at.

Urania in a space suit with a helmet under her arm.

Terpsichore in pointe shoes and an elaborate tutu, her hair scraped up into a perfect bun as she executes some ballet move I couldn't name if I tried.

Euterpe sitting at a drum kit, hair wild and face set in deep concentration at the moment her drumsticks meet skins.

I can see the other statues from where I'm standing, but I'm too far away to get a good look at them. I make a mental note to tour the gardens later if I've got time—Calliope has always been my favorite muse, and I can't wait to see how the Curator has had her depicted.

"This place is wild," Flint comments as he starts up the long, winding pathway to the front doors—which, from here, look like they're made of gold. The lion's-head door knockers are also made of gold, with emeralds as big as my fist in between their fierce teeth.

We follow him in silence, basking in the sheer opulence of the gardens.

"Wicked," Flint breathes as he pulls the emerald forward, then pushes it against the door to knock three times in quick succession.

"I didn't realize we were ready to do that yet," I tell him, pushing his hand away from the door knocker before he can do anything else. "I thought we needed a plan."

"The plan is to get the Curator's attention, then ask for their help with the spell, right?" Flint asks. "What else is there to talk about?"

So many things. But it's too late now, because the door is swinging open. And the person standing there is nothing like I expected the Curator to be. At the same time, though, she looks exactly like the kind of person who would design a place like this.

To begin with, she's tiny—shorter, even, than I am. Her chin-length black hair hangs in curled ringlets around her very pretty face, and her brown skin gleams in the sunlight.

Her septum and right eyebrow are pierced, and rings decorate every one of her fingers as well as most of her toes. Plus, she's got a dozen thin gold bangles and woven friendship bracelets piled on both her wrists. Elaborate henna tattoos decorate her palms and the backs of her hands, and multicolored feather earrings hang from her ears. And she's dressed in frayed jeans with holes over the knees and a vintage Joan Jett and the Blackhearts tour T-shirt that complements her gold-rimmed glasses.

Part boho, part punk rock, she's definitely on the list of coolest-looking people I've ever met. Not to mention the fact her eyes shout that she's something more than human—midnight-black irises with tiny silver flecks in them that look a lot like stars from where I'm standing.

"Come on in," she says, swinging the door open to let us pass. "I've been waiting for you since last night. Looks like you had a rougher time getting here than I anticipated."

"You knew we were coming?" I blurt out before I even know I'm going to say it.

She laughs. "Of course, Grace. All part of my godhood. You're going to have to have a lot more tricks up your sleeves if you don't want me to see you coming."

My gaze seeks out Hudson's, and I mouth, *Another god?* He shrugs, but I know he's thinking exactly what I'm thinking—how the hell did we not see *that* coming?

She leads us through a huge foyer whose walls are filled with original Rothko, Pollock, and Haring paintings that have both Hudson and me staring wide-eyed and lingering behind the others.

"They were a lot of fun to watch getting painted," the Curator tosses over her shoulder. "You can come back and check them out later. But I just finished making breakfast. You must be starving."

As if on cue, Flint's stomach rumbles loudly, and the rest of us laugh.

He gives the Curator a charming smile and a self-deprecating shrug that has her grinning back at him even before he says, "Breakfast is my favorite meal."

"I know. I made some blackberry-orange muffins just for you."

His eyes go wide. "How did you know those are my—" He breaks off as he remembers what she said earlier.

She winks in response, then leads us into a dining room.

"You can use the fountain to clean up," she says, nodding toward a four-tiered gold fountain in the corner, decorated with more gemstones and bubbling with soapy water. Next to it is a pile of snow-white Egyptian cotton towels.

We all line up to do just that—after everything we've been through since leaving Adarie, I figure everyone feels as grimy as I do. But while I like the Curator's style—a lot—I have to admit I'm a little skeptical about the fountain. At least until I thrust my hands under the pouring water. In the space of just a few seconds, everything from my hands to my teeth to my body and hair feels sparkling clean.

It's one of the most bizarre experiences I've ever had, but I absolutely love it, and I can't help wondering if she has a small one of these I can borrow to-go.

Once we're washed up, we sit down at the table, which is set with a mishmash of china with different patterns, an eclectic mix of crystal glasses, and several vases of multicolored flowers that I'm pretty sure came from her garden.

A wave of the Curator's hand has a selection of breakfast foods appearing on the table—everything from Flint's muffins to Florentine quiches to a tray of homemade breakfast sandwiches and a giant bowl of fruit so beautiful it looks fake. And, next to where I'm sitting, there's a box of cherry Pop-Tarts.

When the Curator catches me looking from them to her, she just waggles her brows at me before taking a long sip of what I'm pretty sure is the biggest mimosa I've ever seen. Because, apparently, all the gods have a taste for them.

Once we've filled our plates and started to eat, she props an elbow on the table and looks at each of us in turn with her fabulous outer-space eyes. Then asks, "So you really think you want to make the journey to the Bittersweet Tree? Because, I've got to tell you, Celestials are not to be trifled with."

"Oh yeah?" Flint asks around a mouthful of muffin. "Why's that?"

She shoots him a look like he's just asked the silliest question she's ever heard. "As a general rule, the greater the power, the greater the destruction and death that surround it."

"You just had to ask, didn't you?" Jaxon mutters.

80

Don't Brunch
Me Off

"I think 'want' is a strong word." Hudson responds to her original question, ignoring the dire warning of death like a champ. "But it's where we need to go if we have any hope of keeping our end of the bargain with the Shadow Queen."

The Curator jolts. "Cliassandra wants to try again?" She shakes her head. "I suppose hope springs eternal."

"Cliassandra?" I repeat. "The Shadow Queen's name is *Cliassandra*?"

"What were you expecting?" Eden asks, but she sounds surprised, too.

"I don't know. Medusa, maybe?" Flint chimes in.

"Medusa was a lovely woman. Her reputation was completely unearned," the Curator says. "Unlike Clio's."

"Damned by faint praise," Heather says dryly.

"Right?" Jaxon agrees with an annoyed shake of his head. "I'd definitely say the Shadow Queen's reputation is well-deserved."

Eden reaches for one of Flint's muffins and gets a dirty look from him in response—which makes her take two. "That woman has some world-class issues."

"We all have issues. Some of us just choose not to take them out on others," I say quietly.

I glance at Hudson to see what he thinks of this conversation, but he's back to frowning down at his phone and whatever text he's just received. It's good to be back in our world, but I can't say I miss the lack of cell service we had in the Shadow Realm. At least there I could pretend—for a little while, anyway—that Hudson doesn't have a whole slew of issues with the Vampire Court he's keeping to himself for now.

"So you've made a deal with Cliassandra, hmmm? A little Celestial Dew in exchange for the antidote to shadow poison. It's an intriguing trade, but aren't you worried you're about to play with fire here?" She takes another sip of her mimosa. "Which, coincidentally, is the name of quite a good song by the Rolling Stones, now that I think about it. Came out in 1965, I believe."

"We can't see another way to help Mekhi," Hudson answers, looking up from his phone. "Do you have a better suggestion?"

It's a sincere question, but his gaze is as watchful as hers as he waits to see what she has to say.

The Curator shifts her attention to him, and the two of them lock eyes. I'm not sure if it's some weird kind of pissing contest or if she's trying to figure out what's going on in his head. But when he doesn't look away, she seems impressed.

Then again, Hudson is a very impressive guy. And I'm not just saying that because we're mated.

"You're nothing like the last vampire king," she says finally.

"Small favors," he answers with a smirk.

She smirks back. "Favors rarely are."

"I'm not the vampire king." He inclines his head toward me. "I'm actually the gargoyle king."

"Are you now?" She isn't looking at him when she answers, though. She's looking at me.

The fact that a god asks that question rhetorically has the bite of apple I just took turning to cardboard in my mouth. Especially since the same question's been chasing itself around and around in my head ever since I talked to my grandparents.

Am I wrong in taking the Crown? In becoming the head of the Circle, running the Gargoyle Court? Would our world—and our people—be served better by us taking up the vampire throne?

My stomach twists into knots as I wait to see what Hudson is going to tell her, but he remains still. In fact, he doesn't say anything at all, and that only makes the knots in my stomach worse.

"The Bittersweet Tree is never in the same place twice," the Curator says after several uncomfortable beats of silence. "As soon as someone comes looking for it, it moves again."

"When's the last time someone came looking for it?" I ask.

She responds without missing a beat "1966. That's when Frank Sinatra's cover of 'Yes Sir, That's My Baby' came out. Have you ever heard it?"

She's looking straight at me when she says it, which I'm pretty sure means she already knows the answer. "My father used to sing me the chorus when I was little."

Hudson looks back up from his phone, surprised. Which must mean that somehow he never ran across that memory when he was in my head. I don't know how he didn't—my dad used to sing that song to me a lot.

But the Curator must be satisfied because she finishes her mimosa with a flourish. Then says, "The Bittersweet Tree is currently in South America."

"South America?" Flint repeats. "As in, like, below North America?"

"That is generally where South America is," Heather comments.

"I'm just saying. Jules Verne's got nothing on this trip." When Jaxon turns to look at him, obviously surprised, Flint makes a face. "What? Grace isn't the only one who knows how to read, you know."

The Curator pushes her chair back from the table and stands. "And on that note, if everyone's finished breakfast, I'll show you to your rooms."

"Our rooms?" I say, confused. "We weren't planning on staying. We would never dream of imposing—"

"Not an imposition," she answers with a smile. "I love having company."

"Oh, well…" I glance at the others for help, but they're all looking anywhere but at me.

Except Hudson, who says, "We're not sure we have the time to spare. Mekhi's not doing very well—"

"Yes, well, South America is quite large. If you want a more precise location, you'll come along. I don't have a lot of time to waste. I have waited *eons* for today." And with that, she turns on her very cool white sneakers and walks right out of the room.

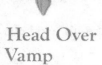
Head Over
Vamp

"What the hell was that all about?" Flint mutters to the room in general.

Macy shrugs as she gets up to follow the Curator. "She may be the coolest god we've met so far, but she's definitely a god."

"Truer words," Hudson says as he scratches his chest.

Heather looks at them, confused. "What does that mean?"

"It means gods like to have their own way," I answer as we follow Macy out of the room and down a hall lined with playbills. Everything from *Hamilton* and *Kinky Boots* to writing-only playbills for *The Elves* and *The Black Crook*, which date back to the 1800s.

Hudson stops in front of one for *Hadestown*. "And they've all got their own agendas."

I think of the chess game my grandmother spent nearly a thousand years putting together—much to the detriment of a lot of people I care about, including myself. "True freaking story."

"Well, what's the worst that could happen?" Eden comments, and we all gasp.

"You did *not* just jinx us with a god," Macy says and makes several sweeping motions in the air as though to cleanse the space.

Everyone else just keeps their heads down and their mouths shut as we follow the Curator through the curved halls that line the outside of her circular home, and then up two flights of stairs.

"Have you been to all these plays?" I ask as the parade of playbills continues.

She looks at me over the tops of her glasses. "I record history, Grace. I don't live it."

The Curator sounds so matter-of-fact as she speaks, but that doesn't stop it from being one of the saddest things I've ever heard in my life.

"So you've never seen any of them?" I ask.

"I've seen all of them," she answers. "But you asked if I had been to all of them. And that's a very different question."

Now I'm just confused. "But how did you see them if you didn't go to them?"

"How do you think I record history all over the world?" she asks, brows raised. "I can't be everywhere at once."

"You record history?" Macy sounds as fascinated as I feel. "How?"

As does Hudson. "And who's been recording history in the last hour that you've spent with us? What if something important happened while you were making breakfast?"

"One of the muses comes inside for a few hours every couple of days so I can sleep or shower or, occasionally, even entertain."

"A few hours every couple of days?" Heather repeats. "That's all the break you get?"

"History stops for no woman," is the Curator's obscure reply. "And on that note, I really do need to get back."

We turn one final corner and head down a very wide hallway, doors lining both sides.

"In the meantime, there are twelve bedrooms on this floor. Choose whichever ones you'd like," she tells us with a magnanimous wave of her arm. "And, of course, feel free to explore the grounds and the rest of the bottom floor. There's a pool, some gaming courts, several art galleries. I just ask that you stay off the second floor, as it's my personal quarters. Oh, and for those of you who need it, there's a laundry room at the end of this corridor."

With a friendly smile tipped in steel, she starts back toward the stairs, but she pauses after only a couple of steps. "I almost forgot. Lunch will be served at two on the first-floor veranda."

"At two?" I repeat. "But we need—"

I break off as she disappears. And it's definitely not a *walking back down the stairs* kind of disappears. No, it's definitely more of a *one second she's there and the next she isn't* kind of disappears.

Heather squeaks when it happens, her eyes going wide and a little wild. But the rest of us take it in stride. The Curator is a god, after all, and the laws of physics tend to work differently for them.

We spend the next few minutes exploring the entire floor. Hudson walks out to the balcony to take a phone call from someone at the Vampire Court, so I choose our room by myself. I pick the one next to the laundry room, because it's *Terminator* themed and it's only been a few days since Hudson was quoting the cheesiest—and the most romantic—line from that movie at me.

He's not the only romantic in our relationship.

Although I'd be lying if I said I wasn't half tempted to take the *Apocalypse Now* room, but with the way the last twenty-four hours have gone, I have to figure, why borrow trouble? Especially when we're *this close* to finally getting what we need to save Mekhi.

Hudson is still on the phone, pacing back and forth on the balcony as he talks. I think about going out and checking on him, but he looks more than a little frustrated at the moment. And since it's no use wishing he'd talk to me about what has him so frustrated—I did promise I'd let him process and unfold on his own terms, after all—I text him about what room is ours, then take our dirty clothes to the laundry room and start a load.

My phone dings, and I glance down to see a new message from Remy.

REMY: I'll be there

I tap out a text back.

ME: Where? When? What?

He answers right away with a thumbs-up emoji, followed by, When you need me most, *cher.*

It's just one of the many reasons I've got a soft spot for the time wizard. He always, *always* comes through for us.

And unlike with Hudson, I totally understand why he prefers to be vague and mysterious. He explained to me once back at the Witch Court that the future can always change. The more he's able to not influence it, the better he can see it—and help when I need it most.

I send my own thumbs-up in reply, then head back down to the gardens we saw earlier. If we have to waste a few hours here, I might as well satisfy my curiosity about the rest of the muses—and everything else the Curator's got going on in this garden.

It turns out it was worth the trip, because Calliope is dressed like a slam poet on a stage. Baggy pants, crop top, backward baseball cap on her head, and journal in her hands as she leans into a microphone. Melpemone is dressed like the Phantom from *Phantom of the Opera*, and Erato's sitting at a laptop, hair piled in a messy bun as she cranks out what I'm pretty sure is a romance novel, based on the words on the computer screen.

This god may be as persnickety as all the other gods I've met, but she's way fucking cooler.

I spend a few minutes looking for Kleo—my other favorite muse and one I thought would have a special place of honor here—but she's nowhere to be found.

After checking my phone to see if Hudson has texted—big surprise, he hasn't—I turn back to explore the rest of the garden. As I walk, I'm struck again by how amazing this place really is.

The fact that the Curator has managed to hide all this in plain sight at the ruins of the Serapeum is really badass. But more than that, the fact that she thought to do all this to begin with is incredible.

Besides the flowers and the trees—varieties from all over the world that somehow still flourish here, in one of the hottest climates on earth—the gardens are filled with numerous other whimsical surprises.

Painted birdcages filled with flowers.

Paths lined with multicolored gemstones.

Fairy-tale birdbaths that attract gorgeous birds of more species than I can name.

Elaborate windchimes in the shape of fantastical creatures.

And art—so much art throughout the whole garden. From a wall of hieroglyphics to ancient Roman statuary to gorgeous stained-glass sculptures resting on the surface of a koi pond. Everywhere I look, there's something else amazing to see.

As I walk through a series of circular arbors, I can't help thinking that Hudson would love this place. Not just the art but the sense of the absurd. He's totally the type to appreciate the trio of colorful painted frogs peeking out from under a flowering bush or the way the wind whistling through a series of oddly shaped hoops sounds like a song.

Maybe if we have time later, I can bring him down and see what his favorite things are.

In the meantime, I should head back up and move our clothes to the dryer. I have no doubt some of the others need to do laundry as badly as I did.

But as I turn and pass through a series of circular arbors for what I know is the second time, I can't help but notice a statue of the muse of history sitting at an ornate desk in front of a rainbow glass globe, scribbling away in a giant book. I stand and stare at her for several seconds, because I just passed through here. And while I noticed the giant globe—even walked up to it to see my reflection in it—I didn't notice Kleo at all.

She must have been there—statues don't exactly move around under their own power—but somehow, I missed her. I guess I was just too busy thinking about Hudson and the Vampire Court and the Circle to notice.

As I pass by the koi pond a few minutes later—also for the second time—I can't help but see something else I missed. Flint, sitting on the stone ledge that borders the pond, staring deep into the water as if looking hard enough will somehow reveal to him the secrets of the universe.

Or maybe just himself.

Either way, he looks like he could use a friend.

"Hey, what are you up to?" I ask as I walk up to him. "Besides doing your best Narcissus impression?"

"Definitely not in love with my reflection," he answers with a snort. "Though it might be easier if I was."

"Easier?" I lift my brows in curiosity.

"Aw, come on, Grace." Flint's usual grin is tinged with a sadness that it's impossible to ignore. "You know what it's like to love a Vega."

"You say that like it's a bad thing."

He shrugs. "I don't know."

"You don't know?" Everything inside me goes watchful as I ask,

"What does that mean?"

"It means you're down here alone in this damn garden, too." He scooches over, then pats the stone ledge next to him. "Sit down and tell Uncle Flint all about it."

"It's that obvious, huh?" I laugh, but it ends in a sigh.

"I've been in love with a Vega since I was fourteen." He shakes his head. "If it's any consolation, it doesn't get any easier."

"At all?" I ask, more than a little horrified by his words.

"Not even a little," he admits. Without looking up, he asks, "Did you know Jaxon plans to accept the vampire throne?"

"Yeah," I answer on a breath. "Although I'm not so sure he will—and I definitely don't think he should."

His gaze meets mine then. "You don't? But I thought—"

"What?" I interrupt. "That Hudson or I want Jaxon to sacrifice his happiness for a Court that has never cared about him?"

Flint goes back to staring at the pond, and we sit listening to the plaintive chirping of nearby birds for what feels like forever.

Eventually, Flint softly says, "Do you know what the real problem is with loving a Vega?"

"They always think they're right?" I suggest, one brow arched.

Flint chuckles but shakes his head. "That one's bad—I'll give you that. But that's not the *worst* thing about loving a Vega."

"Oh my God, it's their obsession with their hair." I chuck an elbow at him playfully. "Am I right?"

This time, he gives a full-throated laugh before adding, "They really need to just move a bed into the bathroom, the amount of time they spend before a mirror—"

He turns to me to finish the punchline of the joke, which I gladly do: "And vampires don't even have reflections!"

We're both holding our sides laughing now, and it feels good to have my old friend back. The one who loved to tease almost as much as he loved to be teased. Flint's sense of humor is one of the things I love about him most. One of the things Cyrus and this world seems to be slowly taking from him, his shoulders sagging again under a weight he's carrying that I can only imagine.

He kicks a pebble into the pond, and it hits the water with a *plonk* before sinking to the bottom.

His voice is as rough as the gravel path before us as he says, "The absolute worst, I-don't-know-if-we-can-move-past-this thing about loving a Vega, Grace, is they think they're the only ones who ever have the right to sacrifice anything."

He lifts his gaze to mine, his warm amber eyes shimmering with unshed tears. "I just hope it doesn't break you like it's breaking me."

82

Fit to be
Tongue-Tied

When Flint walks away, I let him go. I hate how upset he is, hate even more that I don't know what to say to him to help.

Then again, Jaxon is the one who needs to step up.

Actually, so does Hudson. Whatever is going on at the Vampire Court, whatever the constant texting is about, either we're partners or we're not. It's just that simple. I'm not asking him to process his trauma or reveal his inner life—just share facts that affect not only our relationship but his Court, my Court, and the entire paranormal world.

With that thought in mind, I head back up to our room only to realize Hudson is now nowhere to be found.

I start to text him—he can't seriously be on another call with the Vampire Court, can he?—but before I hit Send, Hudson walks in the door, arms piled high with our folded laundry.

"You're back," he tells me with a grin.

"You did the laundry." It's kind of a ridiculous thing to say after everything I've been thinking, but it's what comes out. Probably because I assumed he was so wrapped up in whatever's happening with the vampires that he wouldn't even notice I had put our clothes in the wash.

But I should have known better. When it comes to me, Hudson notices everything.

"I think it was more of a joint effort," he says, dropping the clothes in a neat pile on the bed so he can wrap his arms around me. "You did the first half. I'm just catching up with the second. How was your walk?"

"Illuminating."

He lifts a brow. "That's an interesting answer. Care to elaborate?"

"Actually, I do." But before I can say anything else, the alarm I set on my phone goes off. I sigh. "Later. We've got five minutes to get to the veranda. Something tells me the Curator doesn't tolerate lateness."

I grab Hudson's hand, start to tug him toward the door.

He doesn't budge.

"What's wrong?" I ask.

"I think that's supposed to be my line." His eyes search mine. "What do you want to talk about?"

I start to tell him that it's nothing, but that's not true. And Hudson and I don't lie to each other, even about the small stuff. I spent too much time lying to myself—and therefore to him—at the beginning of our relationship, and it did nothing but hurt both of us. I don't ever want to hurt him like that again.

So instead, I say, "Nothing that can't wait until later."

Now both brows go up. "You sure?"

And just that little check somehow makes me feel better. "I'm sure," I answer. "Now, let's go before she turns one of us into a frog."

"I don't think that's possible," Hudson says as we head into the hallway.

"You don't know that. She's a god. What if she turns one of us into a shape-shifting frog?"

"I don't think there are shape-shifting frogs," he answers with an amused grin.

I roll my eyes and repeat, "You don't know that."

"Pretty sure I do. I've been alive for two hundred years and have never run into one."

"You say that like it's a good thing," I tell him. And yes, I'm aware I'm being ridiculous. But if we don't have time to talk about what I really want to talk about right now, then I'd rather bring up something ridiculous. It beats having a normal conversation where Hudson tries a new conversational tack every ten seconds in an effort to figure out what I'm really upset about. I know my mate well.

"That neither one of us is a frog?" he asks, both brows still raised. "Yeah, I have to admit I think that's a good thing."

"You don't know. You might like a girl who can catch flies with her tongue." I stick my tongue out superfast to demonstrate.

Hudson's brow furrows. "Did you hit your head while you were in the garden?"

"Everyone's a critic," I complain as I start down the stairs with him right behind me.

"Not a critic. Just wanting to go on record as saying I like you—and your tongue—exactly the way they are."

"Now, that's a conversation you don't walk into every day," Heather quips as she follows us down. "Are you feeling insecure about your tongue, Grace? Or just something that you do with it?"

"I guess we know what you two have been up to," Eden says as she joins our line on the stairs *and* our conversation. "That's definitely one way to while away a few hours."

"Laundry," I tell her as my cheeks go pink. "We've been doing laundry."

"So that's what the kids are calling it these days." Macy grins as she joins in the fun.

I make a face at Hudson. "Do you see what you've done?"

"What I've done? You're the one who thinks one of us could be a frog shifter." He mock shudders at the thought. Although, to be honest, I'm not sure how mock the shudder actually is.

Eden cracks up. "I don't even want to know how that conversation started."

"I think I'm too young to know how it started," Heather adds, making a show of clapping her hands over her ears.

"Does anyone know where the veranda is?" I ask loudly, determined to derail this conversation before it gets even worse. I may have started it, but enough is enough.

"Looking for some flies to catch?" Macy deadpans.

Even I have to laugh at that one. Everyone does, except Hudson, who is watching me with those oceanic eyes that have always seen too much. *Soon*, I promise myself as we find the door to the veranda and make our way outside. Soon, I'll have the conversation with him that I need to have.

For now, we need to concentrate on pinning the Curator down on actual details about the location of the Bittersweet Tree and its Dew. Because there are a hell of a lot of trees in South America, and we really, really don't have time to check every single one of them.

83

Hide and
Speak

When we get to the veranda, which has a gorgeous view of the gardens I just spent hours exploring, the Curator is nowhere to be found.

"Did we get the time wrong?" Heather asks as we all mill around the beautifully decorated table.

"No, she said two o'clock," Jaxon tells her, checking the time on his phone. "And it's two now."

As if his words set something in motion, the French doors that lead to the veranda—doors we just closed behind ourselves—fly open.

Two people in black-and-white housekeeping uniforms step out, carrying huge trays filled with food—finger sandwiches, scones, pastries, fruit, and beautiful glass pitchers, some of which are filled with iced tea and others of which are filled with what I'm pretty sure is blood.

We watch awkwardly as they set the food on the table with its antique silver candleholders and elaborate bouquets of flowers. They leave as quickly as they came, without saying a word to any of us as we settle at the table. But once they're gone, we're left staring at one another and wondering if the Curator is going to show up or not.

"How long are we supposed to wait here?" Flint asks, and it's hard to miss the fact that he's sitting several chairs down from Jaxon. It's even more impossible to miss the way he refuses to look at him, even though Jaxon keeps trying to catch his eye.

"Until she shows up?" Macy suggests, but she sounds a little doubtful at this point.

"Maybe she got an important phone call," Heather suggests.

Jaxon runs a hand through his hair, obviously annoyed. "Or

maybe she just isn't coming. She wouldn't be the first god to give us the runaround."

"Speaking of her being a god..." Macy begins. "Has anyone wondered what a god called 'the Curator' actually collects?"

"Same," I say, and we smack raised hands. "Movie posters?" I suggest, thinking of the posters lining the walls downstairs.

"Vampires?" Flint offers, and Jaxon stares at him, which isn't awkward at all.

I rush to change the subject. "So, umm—"

Everyone's phone dings, and our collective eyes widen—it must be a text from Lorelei. Pandemonium breaks out as we all fumble to get our phones out. Well, everyone except Hudson, who was already on his and thus reads the text first.

"Fook." His accent is so thick, my stomach twists into knots.

My hand trembles as I unlock my phone and read the text myself.

LORELEI: Please hurry.

Two little words, and my heart shatters. Just breaks into a billion pieces.

Lorelei has been giving us frequent updates that Mekhi was doing fine, holding his own. But deep down, I knew he was doing worse and she didn't want to add to our pressure unless she absolutely had to. Which means...he must be on death's doorstep for her to send *that* text.

I stand up. "We need answers now."

"Yeah," Macy agrees. "But we can't exactly hunt her down in her own house and make her talk to us."

Hudson looks at Macy. "Are you sure about that?"

"I can," Jaxon says with deadly calm, shoving his chair back with a grating screech as he gets to his feet.

"That's exactly what I was thinking," I answer. "She said the second floor is off-limits, right?"

"Yeah, she said it was her personal space." Macy pushes back her chair as well as she glances toward the house—and the sweeping circular staircase that's only a few yards from the veranda we're currently sitting on. "Should we?"

It's not a question, but I answer anyway. "We should."

"Absolutely," Flint comments before shoving his own chair back and lumbering to his feet along with Eden and Heather. "What's the worst that can happen?"

"I'm a little afraid to find out," Heather answers, but she's the first to start walking toward the stairs—and by walking I mean marching like a general.

"We all are," Macy says, catching up to her in two strides. "But what's the alternative? Stay here waiting for her to remember we exist until Mekhi dies? We're not going to do that."

"No, we're not. But we're not going en masse to confront her, either." I glance at Macy and Heather, who've paused with one foot on the stairs. "Why don't the three of us go talk to her? Call in reinforcements only if we need them."

"You sure you don't want me to come?" Hudson asks.

"Do I want you to come? Yeah, of course. But I think that if we're going to her personal space unannounced, we probably shouldn't bring a huge group with us, you know?"

When my meaning sinks in, he looks absolutely horrified at the thought of catching the Curator in her skivvies—as do the others.

Jaxon looks like he could give two fucks if she were naked as long as she gave him the answers we need, but I quickly shake my head. He holds my gaze and says, "Five minutes."

And I'm impressed by his newfound restraint.

Heather, Macy, and I take the stairs two at a time to the Curator's floor. When we get there, it's to find that the floor breaks off into two wings, both of which lay behind elaborately carved wood doors.

"Which way do we go?" Macy asks as we look back and forth between them.

"Whichever way we can," I answer. "Check and see if those are unlocked, and I'll do the same for these."

I turn to the left and try both doors, but they don't budge. I glance back at Heather just in time to watch her push one of the doors on her side open just a crack.

"To the right it is," I say, moving to join her.

"Should we knock first? At least give her a chance to tell us not to come in?" Macy asks.

"I don't really want to give her that option," I answer. "But yeah. We probably should."

We knock, but when there's no answer, I decide I'm not in the mood to wait any longer. Every second we waste is a second that Mekhi gets closer to death.

I push the door open all the way and call, "Excuse me? I need to speak with the Curator?"

When there's still no answer, I give Macy a shrug and step inside.

I'm not sure what I'm expecting, but it's not the regular sitting room that we walk into. Pale-pink walls, cream couch, light wood coffee and end tables. Ancient books on the bookcases that line one wall. A few knickknacks scattered across the different surfaces.

"This is where the Curator spends all her time?" I ask skeptically.

"No," the Curator says as one of the bookshelves swings forward and all of a sudden she is standing in the doorway that was just created. "I spend all of my time in *here*. Though I do have to ask what you're doing in my suite when I remember giving very clear instructions for you to stay out."

The look on her face warns that our answer had better be good.

84

No Time Like
the Present

"We tried knocking," Macy tells her.

The Curator raises a brow. "And your standard response to someone not answering your knock is to walk into their home anyway?"

"I'm sorry," I interject before the sharpness in her gaze—and her tone—skewers my cousin straight through. "But we really need to speak with you about the Bittersweet Tree."

Her infinite outer-space gaze switches to me. "I understand that you are worried about your friend. I can see his situation is dire, but he still has time. I, on the other hand, do not. Please, show yourselves out."

And with that, she sweeps back into her inner sanctum, the bookcase/door swinging shut behind her.

"Looks like we blew that," Macy tells me with a giant sigh. "So what do we do? Just wait for her to emerge?"

"I guess so," I answer. But even as I say it, I'm walking toward the bookcase. "This is kind of like the door to your secret passage, right? There has to be a way to trigger it from both sides."

"You're not actually thinking about going in there, are you?" Macy asks, eyes wide. "After she just looked like she was one step from smiting us?"

"Gods don't smite demigods," I tell her with an airy wave of my hand. I have no idea if that's true, but I'm choosing to believe it is.

"Yes, well, do they smite witches? Or humans?" Heather counters, making an are-you-serious face at me. "Considering we aren't all demigods here."

"You make a good point." Still, I can't help myself from pulling books off the bookshelf one at a time, just to see if the door will swing open again. It doesn't.

"Hello?" Heather waves a hand in front of my face. "Didn't you just say I made a convincing point about the smiting?"

"I did." I reach for a hot-pink coffee-table book about rock bands and lean it forward. Nothing happens.

"So why are you still trying to open that damn door?" she asks, exasperated.

I pull out another book, this one about Beatles lyrics.

"Because we're out of time," Macy answers, and that really says it all. They share a look, and then they both start pulling books out with me.

After finishing the first three shelves, I squat and start pulling books off the second two shelves. There's got to be a way into that damn room, and I'm determined to find it.

"We could ask Hudson to poof the bookshelves," Macy suggests. "Although that would end in a definite smiting of someone."

"What if she really *is* busy, with some god-level stuff?" Heather asks, but she continues tugging on more books. "I mean, we don't even know what god things she does. She could be saving a village from a volcano right now."

At that moment, the door swings open again, and internally I crow in triumph. I must have found the right book—until I realize that the Curator is standing over me, glaring. "Yes, Grace. Maybe she really is busy," she says in a very annoyed voice.

"I know you're busy. I'm sure whatever you do takes a lot of time—"

"Takes a lot of time?" she repeats, brows raised. "Is that what you want to call it? How many people are there in the world, Grace?"

"Almost eight billion, I think."

"Actually, more than eight billion now. There are more than eight billion people on this planet, and I have to watch *every single one of them* and decide what matters and what doesn't. So yes, Grace, I'm a little busy."

"You watch all of us? All the time?" Macy sounds equal parts fascinated and horrified.

"'All the Time' is a song by Barry Manilow—1976," she says, and she doesn't sound angry anymore—just exhausted. "But yes, I do this job as close to all the time as I can manage."

It sounds impossible. Not to mention absolutely miserable.

And a little invasive, if I'm being honest. My eyes widen. Was she watching me decide between my purple heart underwear and the ones with little bunnies on them this morning?

"What kind of god are you?" Heather asks, one eyebrow raised. "'Cause I'll be honest, I'm not comfortable with the idea of you having watched me shower this morning."

The god in question narrows her eyes on Heather, and I move a step closer.

"I did *not* watch you shower this morning, or any other morning." She lifts her chin, straightening her spine to appear taller, although she's still just my height. "I will have you know that *I* am the God of History, and it is my responsibility to record every historic event—of which your shower was not."

My mind immediately snaps to some of *my* recent showers—a few of which Hudson may or may not have been a part of—and my eyes widen even more.

She swings her gaze to mine and deadpans, "Nor yours." Then she shakes her head. "I have enough work just keeping up with the big events of the day. I am exhausted—and that's sometimes giving up on smaller moments I desperately want to record as well."

"How do you do it?" I ask after a second. "I mean, how do you sleep? Or even find time to go to the bathroom?"

"And who was watching the world when you were at breakfast with us this morning?" Macy adds. I hope the Curator doesn't notice the fact that she sounds more than a little accusatory.

Apparently, she doesn't—or she doesn't care—because she just sighs. "I told you this morning. Kleo spells me a few hours every day. She was in here while I was with all of you earlier. But she can't spell me again so soon, so you are on your own for lunch and dinner tonight."

"Kleo?" Macy asks, and I can tell she's trying to figure out where she's heard the name before. "Is she a god, too?"

"She's a muse," I answer, thinking about how I couldn't find the statue of the muse this morning, until suddenly she seemed to appear out of nowhere. It still seems way too far-fetched to be believed. Then again, there are a lot of things in this world I can say that about. "But are you talking about someone real or just the statue from your garden?"

The Curator lifts a brow at me. "*You're* really going to talk to me about statues coming to life?"

"*I* turn *into* a statue, not the other way around. It's not actually the same thing."

She inclines her head. "Fair enough—which was the title of a song in 1997 by Beth Nielsen Chapman."

I don't know whether I should comment on that or not. She keeps saying song titles and dates like she's on a musical category of *Jeopardy!* or something, but I don't know if that's just because she loves trivia or if it's because she's a frustrated musician herself.

Eternity seems like a long enough time for her to learn an instrument—at least, if she didn't have to work all the time. I wonder if she's actually been to any of those concerts she has posters for, or if she just sees them in her crystal ball or whatever it is she uses to record history.

The thought makes me sad—this whole situation makes me sad—and for the second time in as many minutes, I start thinking about how both of us can get what we want out of this situation.

"So how does Kleo come to life?" Macy asks, still stuck on the Curator's marble helper. "If she's not a gargoyle—"

"She's not. A friend of mine charmed her for me years ago, so I could have an occasional break. But the charm only works for a few hours at a time. Once she's back in statue form, she can't take human form again until the sun sets and rises."

"So, just to be clear," I state. "For several hours a day, a statue who isn't really a person is deciding what history gets recorded and what doesn't?"

Heather snaps her fingers. "Ohhh... You *curate* history."

The Curator rolls her eyes but continues. "You make it sound worse than it is."

"It sounds pretty bad," Macy tells her. "Worse, even, than the fact that one person has been charged with recording all of the world's history. Forever."

"One *god*. And it's not like anyone else is volunteering for the job," she answers, and there's more than a touch of bitterness in her tone. "Jikan got to take a vacation a couple of months ago. Cassia spent the last thousand years on vacation. And Adria—" She snorts. "Does she actually do *anything*?"

"You mean besides make people miserable?" I ask as I glance down at the Crone's tattoo of impossibleness on my wrist.

The Curator laughs. "That *is* her singular talent."

"Don't we know it," Macy mutters.

"But speaking of recording history—and being miserable—I need to get back to it," the Curator says. "We can talk more tomorrow morning, at breakfast."

She turns around and starts to close the door/bookcase that leads into her secret history domain, but I reach out and grab it before she can.

"Do you mind if we come in there with you?" I ask.

She looks surprised—and more than a little suspicious. "I don't let people in this room."

"Yeah, the whole locked-door-and-secret-passageway thing kind of clued us in to that fact," Heather snarks.

Which has the Curator narrowing her eyes to slits. "It's been a while since I've smote anyone. Don't make me regret that fact."

Because the threat is real, I step between them. Then give my bestie a what-the-hell-are-you-doing look.

Heather just shrugs and looks bored, which has the Curator grumbling under her breath.

Not exactly the mood I was hoping for her to be in when I'm desperately trying to put the pieces together to make a deal here.

"I know this is your private space," I say in the most placating—and hopefully non-obvious—tone I can muster right now. "But I was hoping you could make an exception just this one time?"

The Curator's brows go up. "Because the gargoyle queen is so special?"

"Because I have an idea that might help us both," I answer.

She looks skeptical—and more than a little intrigued, which is exactly what I was going for. But before she can say anything else, a loud scream tears through the room behind her.

"Shit!" she mutters, just before she turns and disappears into her history-recording room.

But she leaves the door open.

I don't know if that's because she was in such a hurry to see what's going on or if it's actually an invitation to us. But there's an old saying that it's better to ask for forgiveness than permission, and this definitely seems like one of those times.

I glance at Macy to see if she agrees with me, and she's already leaning to the side, trying to see what's in the room. "So we're doing this, right?" she asks, and we're obviously on the same wavelength here.

"Hell yes we're doing it," I tell her.

And then I pull the bookcase open and step inside, Macy and Heather hot on my heels. Because some things really do have to be seen to be believed.

85

All the World's a ~~Stage~~ TV

"Holy shit," Macy breathes as the bookcase slams closed behind us. "Holy shit," Heather and I both echo.

I haven't spent a lot of time imagining what this room looks like—I did just learn of its existence, after all—but even if I had, I never would have dreamed that it looked like this. I think I was imagining some kind of hazy orb that lets the Curator drop into whatever moment in current human existence she wants to.

And I guess, to a certain extent, that's exactly what this is.

But there's no ancient magical accoutrements here, no mystical crystal ball for her to stare into that lets her see the present all over the world. Instead, there is wall after wall of *TVs*.

Only they are televisions like I have never seen before.

No, these aren't the large, rectangular screens that I'm used to—the ones that hang on the wall above the mantel and give you the clearest, most perfect HD images imaginable.

No, these are tiny, square TVs that look like they came straight out of the 1950s.

Painted gold or silver, with power and volume knobs right under the curved black-and-white screens, they are definitely relics of a not-so-distant past. And they are everywhere.

Everywhere.

Because in this room, there are no windows looking over the garden.

No modern art paintings by the masters.

No posters from the most famous concerts in history.

No, nothing in this room looks like the Curator's normal decorating aesthetic. How could it, when she has TVs stacked next to each other and on top of each other from corner to corner and from floor to ceiling? Thousands upon thousands of televisions, all on. All in black and white. All showing someone somewhere in the world doing something.

And the Curator sitting on a swivel chair in the middle of a circular desk in the center of the room. She has a thick journal open in front of her and a large cup of pens next to her right hand. As she leans over and starts to write in the journal, one of all of the thousands of TVs in the room turns from black and white to color.

"Holy shit," Macy breathes again. And I don't blame her, given I'm thinking the exact same thing.

I move closer to the colorized TV, try to figure out what it's showing—and where the footage is from. But before I can, the picture changes to somewhere else and goes back to black and white.

That's when I notice that all the pictures change pretty much all the time. They flicker onto something happening somewhere, play that footage for a couple of seconds, then move onto something else happening somewhere else. This happens on every single TV in the room over and over and over again.

Another TV turns to color for about three seconds, and I whirl toward it—just in time to watch it fade back to black and white. At the same time, the Curator spins in her chair—wait, no! her entire *desk* swivels with her on some sort of circular platform—and starts watching a different wall. About two seconds later, she starts to scribble in her journal, and one of the TVs on this wall changes to color as she does.

It's the strangest thing I've ever seen.

Obviously, the color flares are related to whatever she deems important enough to record in her book. If the Curator decides it matters, the moment bursts into color before fading back to black and white the moment she's done.

But how does it work? And is three seconds really enough time to figure out what's going on in any of these selected situations?

It must be, because another TV is changing to color right in front of me. Then another. And another. And another as the Curator continues to record in her book.

It's impressive how much she sees and manages to write down. But at the same time, I can't help wondering what else is getting missed. Because surely something important is happening at more than one spot in the world at the same time.

How does she watch both? Or does she have to choose what she thinks is most important? And what if it takes longer than three seconds to figure out what's happening in any given situation? Does something else get missed?

The whole situation seems totally bizarre to me. Then again, a crystal ball or scrying mirror would be equally bizarre, and that didn't freak me out. Why does this?

"So what's your idea?" the Curator asks after a couple of minutes.

"My idea?" I repeat, caught up in watching a little boy fall off his bike some place next to the Pacific Ocean.

He cries, and then the feed changes, replaced by what looks like two men on a fancy date. One of them pulls a ring box out of his pocket, but before I can see if the other man says yes, the feed changes again. This time to a classroom full of kids learning what I think is Pre-Algebra.

"You're blocking my view, Grace," the Curator says all of a sudden, and I realize that with each moment I've watched, I've crept closer to the display of televisions, until I'm standing right in front of several of them.

"Sorry!" I tell her, walking closer to where she's standing. "I just got…"

"Interested," she fills in for me as she starts writing something else down in her giant book. "Believe me, I understand. Fascinating things happen all over the world, every day."

"But how do you deal with not knowing how something ends?" I guess. "Especially if you think it's an important historical moment?"

"By assuming it ends badly," Macy interjects in a sly tone. "Obviously."

"Most things do," the Curator agrees. "But I can stay on situations longer if I want to. But right now, little moments are all that's happening—"

She breaks off as a TV to the left of me flares into color—and stays that way for nearly a minute as the Curator watches it and records what's happening at the same time. It's a political rally of some sort in a country that speaks Spanish, judging by the content of the signs people are holding up.

"Can you do me a favor?" the Curator asks as she continues to scribble in her book.

"Of course. What do you need?"

"In there"—she nods toward the only wall space in the room that isn't covered with TVs because it's actually a narrow door—"is a shelf full of blank journals. It's on the bookshelf just to the right of the door. Can you grab me one, please?"

"Sure."

I cross to the doorway and pull it open. A light comes on inside the room as soon as I do, and I can't help gasping at what I see. Because this is another huge room—maybe even bigger than the one with the TVs—and every available space is covered with these books.

Every. Available. Space.

Not just the bookshelves lining the walls—of which there are dozens—but every inch of floor space as well. There are piles and piles and piles of filled recording journals from floor to ceiling throughout the room, taking up so much space that the only spot to stand in the entire room is in front of the bookshelf to the right of the door, where the Curator directed me to find the empty journals.

I grab one, blinking when another magically appears to replace it, and hustle back out of the crowded, claustrophobia-inducing room as fast as I possibly can. "Is this what you're looking for?" I ask, laying it on the desk next to where the Curator is still sitting and writing.

She's now only a few pages before the end of her current journal.

"Excuse me," Heather says from her spot all the way across the room. "But this looks important."

"I've been doing this a very long time," the Curator says, voice rife with condescension. "I think I know what's impor—"

She breaks off at the same time the TV Heather was pointing at flares into color. Just in time to watch a car T-bone a semi at an intersection. I gasp. No one would have survived that wreck.

The Curator murmurs something under her breath in a language I don't understand. But she starts writing furiously.

Seconds later, the TV turns back to black and white, and she moves onto something else.

This goes on for another few minutes, and even though I'm fascinated by what I'm seeing on the screens, I'm still worried about the time we're wasting. All the seconds and minutes and hours trickling by while Mekhi is getting sicker and sicker.

And while I know my latest idea will only add more hours onto getting him help, I think it might shorten things in the long run. Because the Curator doesn't seem in any hurry to give up the information we need, and if we only get to talk to her an hour at a time, it may be days before she tells us everything we need to know.

And we don't have days.

We actually don't know how much time we have left—although I suspect my idea will solve that problem as well.

Which is why, when the Curator finally closes the journal in front of her—after filling it all the way to the bottom of the last page—and sets it aside, I take advantage of her break in concentration.

"So I've got a proposal for you," I tell her as she reaches for the blank journal.

"A proposal?" she asks, looking away from the TV screens for a split second to meet my gaze before darting back to the screens again. "What makes you think I'd be interested in anything you might want to propose?"

"Because you haven't had a vacation for a very long time," I answer. "And I can change that."

"You can?" she asks, sounding wary.

"You can?" Macy queries at the exact same time.

I ignore their question, remaining focused on the Curator. "It's more of a mini vacation than an actual vacation, but I figure you've got to start somewhere, right?"

The Curator laughs. And laughs. And laughs. "Let me get this straight. You actually think *you* can do my job?"

"No way," I tell her. "But I think the *seven* of us can."

The Curator's eyes narrow. "How mini is mini?"

"First let me ask—" I motion to the TVs. "If our friend Mekhi's situation were to worsen even more, would one of these TVs light up?

Or could you make it?"

That gets her attention, and her pen pauses for the briefest of seconds before she continues scribbling. "I could," is all she says.

"Then we can give you twenty-four hours," I say. Macy starts to protest, but I hold one finger up in the universal symbol for on-one-condition, and she settles back down. "But you would have to agree to tell us the *second* you returned *exactly* how to find the Bittersweet Tree...and we would have to turn one of these TVs"—I swing my arm to point to a wall of screens—"permanently on Mekhi, so we could be assured he was going to be okay until you came back."

She raises one brow. "One sick man cannot be the focus of a generation, my dear."

"This one is," Macy replies, and her tone says there is no debating this point.

I rush in to add, "We wouldn't be able to focus on recording history for you if we were preoccupied with worry for our friend."

Her desk spins several more times, the Curator furiously writing, but I can tell by the set of her chin she's considering my offer.

Eventually, she tells me dryly, "That is definitely a mini vacation."

She breaks off and scribbles in the new journal as a TV directly in front of her turns to color. She records the history she sees there, then more from another television. And another. And another. And another.

I'm beginning to think she's just going to ignore my proposal when she suddenly looks away from the wall of TVs and says, "Do you really think you and your friends can do this for twenty-four hours?"

"Absolutely," I tell the Curator, even as Macy shakes her head and mouths *no way* directly behind her.

"Twenty-four hours?" she repeats.

I pull my phone out of my pocket and shoot a quick text off to Lorelei.

ME: Do we have more than 24 hours?

Three dots appear, and I hold my breath. Please, please, please let Mekhi have more than a day left.

LORELEI: Best guess? Yes. Barely.

I sigh and shoot off a quick "on it" reply before I shove my phone back in my pocket and meet the Curator's gaze again. I smile as confidently as I can. "Twenty-four hours."

"You watch the televisions every minute of those twenty-four hours," she tells me. Then stops to record something else before turning back to me. "Every minute. And you record it in these books using only those pens."

She points to a *Moulin Rouge!* coffee mug jammed with pens sitting on her desk. "Only *those* pens," she reiterates.

"Absolutely," I tell her, even as I reach for one to check it out.

To my surprise, it doesn't look nearly as special as I expected from the only type of pen that can record history. In fact, it looks a lot like a regular Paper Mate Flair. Still, I have to ask. "Are they imbued with magic or...?"

"Yes." But she doesn't elaborate. "Plus, I just like them. I like what they feel like when they write, and I like what they look like on the page. So only those pens. Okay?"

"Okay," I agree.

"When in doubt—" She pauses to record something else. "Write it down. I can sort through what you've done when I come back. I've charmed the TVs to light up as a guide, although there is obvious discretion in the recorder, as some of the most momentous events in human history seemed inconsequential at the time. If you've recorded something you shouldn't have, I'll deal with it. But if you leave something out..."

"There's nothing you can do to record it later," Macy finishes for her.

"Exactly." She flicks a hand at one of the small TVs, and an even smaller vision of Mekhi appears, Lorelei perched on the edge of his bed and holding one of his hands. My heart squeezes tight to see our friend looking so ill and helpless, but at least he appears to be resting.

"Now..." She stands and hands the pen over to me with a flourish. "No time like the present to get started. In the meantime, you two grab your friend more journals. She'll need them. You all will."

"Lucky us," Macy mutters as she glares at me in a very definite what-the-fuck kind of way. At least that's what I think her look said. I'm too focused on grabbing a pen and sitting in one of the new chairs that magically appeared, each facing a section of TVs. Heather grabs the third chair in our trio and begins to feverishly write.

"Each chair is connected to its own desk, so they move together. This button stops the desk from spinning, which I assume you won't need if there are seven of you," she says, but I don't have time to see what she is pointing at now.

I'm too busy recording a fire in a small French museum to pay much attention.

A couple of minutes later, the Curator breezes out the door with a wave and a "see you in twenty-four hours."

I don't answer. I can't. I've got a battle being waged in Ukraine, a bank robbery happening in Prague, and top music awards being handed out in Italy. There's no time for me to do anything but write.

Still, the second the door closes behind her, Macy—who has also been recording—whirls on me with a gripe. "What the hell is wrong with you?"

"Twenty-four hours and we'll know exactly where the tree is," I rush out. "Trust me. Dealing with gods sucks, and she seems lonely. She could have dragged it out for weeks—and Mekhi has hours."

"Does he even have twenty-four—" She breaks off and starts scribbling furiously in the journal.

I'm scribbling, too. A scientist in Dakar just published their findings in a microbiology journal, and a lesser-known Norwegian royal just died.

It's several minutes—a lot is freaking happening right now—before I remember to say, "We can watch him. He's fine." I point to *his* TV. "We've got this. Besides, how hard can it be to write stuff down?"

Macy doesn't answer. And when I glance over at her, it's because she's writing too frantically to do anything but snort.

86

Write-or-Flight
Mode

Five minutes in, I want to call for help, but I'm too busy writing as fast as I possibly can—turns out the pens *are* special and write at inhuman speeds—to take time to reach for my phone.

Ten minutes in, I actually manage to pull my phone out of my pocket, but then I drop it in a rush when a building explodes on the south side of Chicago.

Fifteen minutes in, I've forgotten that help actually exists and I'm in full-out write-or-flight mode. I record a death in Ethiopia, an author on climate change signing books in São Paolo, the birth of a child in the Philippines. TV after TV flickers to Technicolor life, and I try to write faster than a god-spelled pen can write.

I assume it's the same for Macy, but I'm too terrified of what's going to happen next to risk looking away from the monitors long enough to check on her. But some truly strange noises are coming from her side of the room—squeaks, gasps, and even a couple high-pitched cries that send chills straight down my spine.

"Are you okay?" I manage to say when she lets out another sad-sounding squeak. And then I promptly write those same exact words into the record I'm currently taking of the UN's latest resolution.

"Damn it," I mutter as I cross them out, wondering if I'm allowed to cross things out when recording what's happening, even if it's obviously a mistake. The last thing I want is to tamper with history, especially when all I'm trying to do is record everything that matters. Although, is it really tampering if I'm crossing out words that should never have been there to begin with?

Then again, maybe Macy and me sitting here and doing this is tampering with history in and of itself. We don't mean to do it, obviously. In fact, we're both working as hard as we can to write down as many important things that happen as possible.

But who are we to decide what's important and what's not?

Maybe those Indian movie awards I just spent ten seconds recording— the magic pens also allow the recorder to understand *and* write in every language—didn't deserve more attention than the six seconds I spent recording that kidnapping in England I completely glossed over. Or maybe the explosion in Chicago isn't nearly as important as the car crash that just happened in Belize.

How are we supposed to know?

Heather, Macy, and I are seventeen and eighteen, and that is not enough living to have the perspective necessary to do this job—to make these decisions. And even our varying points of view and backgrounds aren't really enough to give a fair accounting of *the world*, are they?

But is our lens any worse than the Curator's? She's a god who has been locked up here pretty much from the beginning of time. Yeah, she's seen everything from this room, but has she actually experienced anything?

The thought makes me sad even as it frustrates—and worries—me. There's an old saying about history being recorded (unfairly) by the winners. But this somehow feels even worse than that. This feels like history is being recorded by people who've never even been on the field.

How is that real history? I wonder as I continue to scribble down information—this time about a rescue mission in a Chilean mine.

But my thoughts are interrupted when Heather makes a high-pitched sound—and then promptly bursts into tears.

"Heather! What is it?" I drop my pen, start to rush over to her. But before I can take more than a step or two, something else explodes on my screens. And because I took my eyes off them for a few seconds, I have absolutely no idea what it was.

I want to say to hell with this, Heather needs me, but the explosion looks important. As does the hurricane currently forming in the Atlantic.

Damn it!

"Are you okay?" I call over to her even as I lean forward to try to see what's going on with the aftermath of the explosion that is rolling across the suddenly colorized TV screen in front of me. "What happened?"

Heather doesn't answer, and when I glance over at her, I see she's still writing even as tears pour down her face.

I take another second I can't afford to glance at her screens—and as I zero in on the one currently in color, it's easy to see what has her so upset. There's been a truly horrible school bus accident in Morocco—one that has badly injured or killed dozens of young children.

"Oh, Heather," I say. "I'm sorry. I'm so sorry."

"This job sucks," she growls. "This whole fucking world sucks! Why the hell are we always working so damn hard to save it?"

She waves a hand at the screens to underscore her point. And I get what she's saying. God, do I get what she's saying. Sitting here, watching all these moments, reminds me of a time when I was a kid, maybe twelve or thirteen.

My parents took me to Washington, DC, to see the Smithsonian and a bunch of other really cool museums. One of the museums we went to was called the Newseum, which was dedicated to everything regarding the news. There were a ton of cool exhibits, but the one I remember the most was the one with every Pulitzer Prize–winning photograph ever taken. The very best and very worst of humanity up there on one wall for everyone to see.

These TVs—all these moments on display from all different people from all over the world—are like that. The absolute best and worst of what's going on in the world, and the people who are making it happen, on the wall in front of us, just waiting to be recorded...or not.

It's devastating. Not just the bad but the good, too. The best that we as people are capable of, juxtaposed with the very worst. How could it not be completely overwhelming?

No wonder Heather is crying. I'm pretty sure I will be, too, before long.

Except there's no time for that. A plane just crashed into the waters near Puerto Rico. And an article just came out about a North American leader that will either rock the country with scandal or be completely ignored. Which makes me unsure about what to do with it.

The article is followed by the exuberant birthday party of a seven-year-old boy in Berlin.

Which is followed by a patient in a hospital in Equatorial Guinea getting infected with Marburg virus disease.

Massive flooding in a young family's basement in Istanbul leaves them homeless.

And a large chunk of the Antarctic ice shelf is breaking off.

And literally a million other things, just on my wall of TV screens. Macy's more than got her hands full with her two walls, as well.

And there is nothing we can do about any of it except to keep writing, writing, writing.

My hand is already aching, and I feel like I'm getting further and further behind.

Macy gasps at something on her TVs, and I take a second to glance around in a desperate attempt to figure out where my phone has fallen. Because if we don't get some help soon, we're going to end up drowning...and I'm pretty sure the Curator won't be in any mood to bargain if we end up imploding her entire system.

Unfortunately, the time I take looking for the phone only puts me further behind. Screens flash by, and I didn't have a chance to look at any of them. I only have a second to hope I haven't missed anything too important before I have to start writing again, and *I still haven't found my damn phone*!

Regardless, someone needs to record the data on the newest viral outbreak, so I guess my phone will have to wait. As will the help we're all so desperate for.

But just as I start to write down the latest numbers, the secret bookshelf door swings open. And Flint is standing there, holding a tray of coffee, with the rest of my friends behind him.

"Anyone need a coffee break?"

87

Su-Shi's
All That

"Coffee break?" Macy shrieks, looking away from her screens for what I'm pretty sure is the very first time. "No one has time for coffee here!"

"Whoa," Flint says, putting the coffee tray next to me on the desk. "Someone's a little grumpy."

"Not grumpy—desperate," I tell him, not taking my eyes from the aftermath of the mass shooting in Florida that has my stomach clenching and tears burning in the back of my eyes. "What are you doing here?"

Jaxon lifts a brow. "Umm, we can leave if you'd prefer."

"Please God, no. Don't do that!" Macy all but whimpers.

"The Curator stopped by the veranda a couple of minutes ago on her way out and told us you'd traded a little work for helping Mekhi and said you might need some help." Hudson looks from me to Macy. "Apparently she's a master of understatement."

"You have no idea," I answer as I record the name of the player who makes the last goal in a hugely popular Vietnamese soccer game. "Can you go in that room over there and grab more journals? Then pick a section of TVs and start to record?"

"This place is completely badass," Jaxon says from where he's watching a section of black-and-white screens. "Do these TVs really show everything going on around the world right now?"

"Everything," I reiterate. "They go from grayscale to color on important events."

"Badass," he breathes again.

"You don't need to sound so impressed," Heather snaps as she continues to write. "Just go get the fucking journals and start helping out. Or, I swear, I'll leave you to it all on your own."

"Hey." Eden walks behind her and starts rubbing her shoulders. "It's going to be okay."

"Really?" She thrusts her free hand at the TV. "A sailboat is sinking in a storm in the middle of the Pacific, and no one is picking up their calls for help. That whole family is going to be in the *water* in the middle of a *storm* in less than ten minutes, and no one is going to know they're there. So, tell me, how exactly is that okay?"

She breaks down then, ugly sobs ripping through her as she—once again—continues to write even through her tears.

"Hey, hey." Eden wraps her arms around her from behind and hugs her close. "Take a second. Take a few breaths."

"I can't. I have to keep—"

Hudson walks over and eases the book from her hand. "I've got this. Why don't you go take a break for a few minutes?"

"I can't—"

"You can," he answers firmly, prying the pen from her grasp. "Eden, take her outside for some fresh air."

"But—"

"No buts." Hudson bends down so that he's looking her straight in the eye. "We've got this, Heather."

I have to go back to recording—there's some kind of late-night scandal about the Parliament of Australia that I've got to figure out—so I miss whatever else Hudson tells her. But whatever it is, it must work, because a couple of minutes later, Eden escorts a subdued Heather out of the room.

"So," Jaxon says after the door closes behind them, "what can we do to help?"

"Grab a bloody notebook," Hudson growls from where he's recording something from the wall of TVs directly in front of him. "And figure out what the fook is going on in Asia. Japan is blowing up right now, and I don't have time to look."

"The notebooks are in the room over there." I nod toward the closed door. "Once you get them, pick a wall and get busy, because I'm drowning here."

Jaxon and Flint do as I ask, each settling down in front of a wall different than the ones Hudson and I are watching so carefully. Eden, in the meantime, comes back and switches spots with Flint, who goes on to act like a pinch hitter, running back and forth between the different walls, calling out anything he thinks we might be missing.

Which works really well—right up until it doesn't.

One minute I'm recording the key points in a tense UN debate, and the next Flint is screaming, "Turkey farm!" from my right.

I'm so focused on the German chancellor's points regarding climate change that I jump about ten feet in the air. "What the fuck, Flint?" I give him a baffled—and aggrieved—look, which only makes him squawk louder.

He points at a monitor on the bottom row. "Turkey farm, Grace! Turkey farm!"

"Okay, sure." I nod to shut him up, then go back to the climate change resolution that's about to be voted on. The French prime minister has just taken the German chancellor's point up when Flint puts his face between me and my journal book and yells, "Turkey farm!" loud enough to shake the rafters.

"What about a fucking turkey farm?" I end up roaring right back at him, loud enough to have everyone turning around to stare at me like I've become an actual turkey.

He rears back from me then, looking completely hurt. "What the hell, Grace? I was just trying to help."

"I know you were." I take a deep breath, blow it out slowly. And can I just ask, how the hell has this become my fault when he's the one *screaming about turkeys at the top of his lungs*?

But assigning blame isn't going to solve the problem, so I take another deep breath and ask in the sweetest voice I can muster, "What do I need to know about the turkey farm, Flint?"

"It's on fire. And it's *November*."

At first, I have no idea why the month should matter—but then it hits me. I still don't think it's worth all this fuss when the UN is literally in the middle of trying to pass its most aggressive climate change resolution in history, but at this point I'm not about to argue.

Instead, I pick up my pen again and write, "Turkey farm on fire in—" I look up to ask him, but he's been reading over my shoulder.

"Minnesota," he supplies helpfully.

"Thank you," I answer as I write the state name. "Anything else I need to know?"

"No, that's it." He beams at me. "Looks like you've got this, Grace, so I'm going to go check on Asia now."

"Fantastic!" I breathe a sigh of relief.

"Fantastic," Hudson mutters under his breath.

Seconds later, Flint is freaking out again, this time about a major chain of sushi restaurants closing in Japan.

"But they're my favorite," he moans, poking a finger at the screen that shows one of the locations being boarded up. "You're getting this, right, Hudson?"

"Absolutely," my mate answers without glancing away from one of the screens that is currently in color.

"It doesn't *look* like you're getting it," Flint accuses.

Hudson rolls his eyes. "I'm getting it."

"Because this is super important. This is sushi history right here."

"That's what you told me." Hudson moves on to a screen showing a birth in China.

"Are you sure you're getting it?" Flint sounds a lot more doubtful now. "Because I don't think they have any restaurants in China."

"Oh, I think they do," Hudson replies mildly as he continues to write.

"I'm not so sure." Flint narrows his eyes suspiciously as he looks from Hudson to the TV screen and back again. "Hey! What's the name of the restaurant chain I'm talking about?"

Hudson ignores him.

"Don't worry about pronouncing it right. I know you don't speak Japanese."

Hudson still doesn't say anything.

"Unless you just don't know the name…because you're not recording it!" Flint points an accusing finger at my mate, which has Jaxon and me taking precious seconds to turn in our chairs and exchange slightly nervous glances.

Hudson doesn't usually like to be pointed at.

But my mate just sighs. "I said I'd record it, Flint."

"No, you said you *were* recording it. That's not the same thing."

Hudson's teeth come together with an audible click that would normally have me putting myself between him and whomever caused it. But there's some kind of poisonous gas leak in a plant in Waco, and I *have* to write the information down.

Flint, however, doesn't seem to notice the warning click—or maybe he just doesn't care about it. Either way, he asks again, "Then what's the name of the restaurant, Hudson?"

When Hudson still doesn't answer, he asks again. "What's the name of the—"

"Get fooked!" Hudson suddenly growls. "The name of the restaurant is *get fooked.*"

"Whoa, whoa. Dude!" Flint looks shocked as he holds up his hands in a simmer-down motion. "Who pissed in your cornflakes?"

"I don't eat fooking cornflakes, you bloody dragon's arse. But if you don't walk the fook away from me right the fook now, I'm going to drain every drop of blood from your bloody body and then I'm going to stake your sorry-arse carcass out in the garden for the ants and the rats and anything else that wants a shot at you to devour."

Each word is said in a low, calm voice that grows more terrifying with every second that passes—even before he ends with a smile so cold that Alexandria suddenly feels like Denali. And that's before I notice the tips of his fangs gleaming against his lower lip. "And if you don't believe me," he continues, "why don't you ask me one more fooking time what the arsed sushi restaurant's name is?"

Normally, that's the kind of threat that would make Flint engage, but even he must realize that he's pushed my normally unflappable mate past the point of no return.

Because under Jaxon's watchful eye, Flint takes a couple of giant steps back, then offers a narrowed gaze and says, "Fine. I'll go see if Eden needs some next-level help."

88

Eden freezes, pen midair, as she turns to look at me with wide eyes. *No, no, no*, she mouths, shaking her head wildly.

I just shrug and give her my most winning smile, because sometimes it's good to share the wealth—and this is definitely one of those times. Mostly because if Flint is bothering Eden, then he won't be bothering me...or Hudson. And judging from the fact that Hudson just snapped one of the Curator's pens in half by merely picking it up, I think he could probably use the break.

I know I could.

"You know, Flint," Eden starts out preemptively, "I'm actually good right now. There's some really cool stuff happening in South Africa with poaching resolutions and the dedication of a huge museum. I've got this. Maybe you should go check on Heather, see if she's doing okay."

"Are you kidding me?" Flint sits down at the desk next to her and kicks up his feet. "There are hundreds of TVs on your wall alone. How are you going to watch them all?"

"I've been doing fine so far," she mutters. I can't look at her expression to gauge her mood, because there's been a heroic rescue from a train derailment in Portugal, but she sounds unimpressed.

"Fine isn't good enough," Flint retorts. "Together, we'll do the best recording the Curator has ever seen."

"Ooooooor you can check out Jaxon over there," Macy suggests, still scribbling away. "He seems unusually quiet. He must be struggling."

"Nah. Jaxon likes to always go it alone," Flint says with a huge grin.

None of us are touching that—except Jaxon, whose pen only pauses for half a second before continuing to move across his page.

"You don't have to sound so disappointed," Jaxon says mildly.

"Why would I be disappointed?" Flint asks, his grin slipping. "Just because you don't need me doesn't mean someone else won't."

And just that easily, Flint makes me feel like a total jerk. From the minute he got into this room, he's been trying to make things easier for us. Is he succeeding? Maybe, maybe not. But he's still trying, despite his own pain, and that counts for a lot.

"You can help me, Flint. I have too many TVs to keep up," I tell him, noticing that Jaxon starts scribbling even more furiously. I point to a bank of TVs on my left. "Grab a notebook, and you can do that row right there."

"On it!" he says, racing to the closet to get one of the Curator's special journals.

Once Flint has a dedicated set of TVs, things go much more smoothly. It's still exhausting work, though. I can't imagine how the Curator does it almost completely by herself—god or no god. Not to mention the fact that she's been doing it pretty much forever, if the closet filled with journals is any testament, without so much as a day off.

It's unimaginable.

Sometime after six, Heather comes back to relieve a couple of us. And then we spend the rest of the night trading off.

When it's Hudson's and my turn for a break around five a.m., we stumble upstairs and fall into bed for a couple of hours of rest. But once I'm away from all those incessant TV screens, I can't sleep—even after I wrap an arm around his waist and cuddle up against him.

But when I close my eyes, all I can see is everything happening in the world—good and bad. I know that's life, know that shit happens in the world every day, even more so after spending the last twelve hours being bombarded with so much of everything.

Everything bad. Everything good. Everything...everything.

I thought I was keeping it together, keeping the job in perspective. But now that I'm closing my eyes, all I can see are the images coming at me like that over and over and over again.

It's a lot. Maybe too much.

Everyone else seems to be handling it—even Heather, after she returned from her break—but everyone else isn't a gargoyle.

My whole life, my parents told me I was too empathetic, that I had to learn to let some things go. But I've never been any good at that—even before discovering I was a gargoyle. I know some people can move on when bad things are happening, and I don't judge them for it. After all, most of the time it's just how they survive.

But I can't do it. The gargoyle in me wants to right every wrong. It wants to protect people who can't protect themselves and balance the scales of justice for every single person in the world who needs it.

Just the idea is impossible—and if I could, doing so would end up throwing off the balance of the world in other ways. I get that. I do. But it's impossible to pretend it isn't happening, either, especially after spending all those hours sitting in that room, recording so much bad stuff—and not recording even more.

It's definitely been one of the hardest things I've ever had to do.

Despite the warmth flowing in from the balcony doors, I'm chilled to the bone as I cuddle even closer to Hudson. He's half asleep, but he must feel me shivering, because he rolls over and pulls me closer, until my head is pillowed on his biceps and I'm half curled up on his chest.

His heart is beating slow and steady beneath my ear, his chest rising and falling in a slow, hypnotic rhythm that finally cuts through all the pain and horror and allows me finally—finally—to sleep.

For a little while, at least. Because I haven't been dozing long when all of a sudden, I become aware that something is wrong. I don't know what it is—I'm too asleep to figure it out—but something definitely is.

I sit up slowly, rubbing my eyes as I try to banish the sleepiness weighing me down like an anchor. I look around, trying to figure out what's wrong. But nothing stands out.

The room is still dimly lit, the sky outside the balcony still dark. My phone doesn't have any new texts or calls on it, and Hudson is sleeping peacefully beside me. Finally, I lay down, determined to go back to sleep. And that's when—out of nowhere—Hudson cries out and jerks against me, hard.

And then he does it again. And again. And again.

Is he sick? I wonder as I sit back up. But vampires don't get sick, at least not like that. So I reach over and click on the bedside light—only to realize that Hudson is having a nightmare.

And not just any nightmare, judging by the way he's jerking and trembling against me. He's having the nightmare of all nightmares.

"Hudson?" I whisper, pressing a soft hand to his chest. "It's okay, babe. You're okay."

He doesn't answer, doesn't indicate by so much as a flicker of his eyelids that he's heard me. Instead, he just lays there, stiff and completely unbending as I rub my hand up and down his arm.

When he still doesn't respond, I think he must have fallen asleep again. I wait for a few minutes, but when nothing else happens, I close my eyes as I sink down beside him—and then nearly go through the ceiling when he screams at the top of his lungs.

"Hudson!" I'm so startled that I'm yelling now, too. "Hudson, are you all right?"

But he's still asleep. He's breathing heavily, his chest heaving and body shaking as he stares unseeing into the distance.

"What's wrong, babe? What's going on?" I ask, but as he quakes and shudders it takes a second for me to realize that he's *still* not awake. That he's still locked in whatever nightmare has a grip on him.

I try to stay calm, to just rub a gentle hand up and down his back while I murmur to him. But somewhere in the middle of all this, a giant sob tears from his chest—racking his body—and it's so unlike him that it terrifies me even as it breaks my freaking heart.

"Hudson!" I call out more forcefully now, getting on my knees beside him so that I can try to get his attention better. "Hudson, wake up!"

Hoarse, terrifying noises continue to pour from his chest and throat. And I decide to hell with delicate and go straight for harsh, smacking him in the arm to wake him, to pull him from this nightmare.

When that doesn't work and the tortured noises continue coming, I shake him as hard as I can. "Hudson! Wake up! Wake up!"

And when that still doesn't work, I shake him even harder. "Hudson, damn it. Wake the hell up!"

He comes awake with a roar and a start, fangs bared and hands curled into fists even as he throws them up in front of his face in what is obviously a defensive move. And my heart breaks all the way open.

"Hudson, baby." Part of me wants to wrap myself around him, but I'm terrified of scaring him even more. The last thing I want is for him to think he's under attack.

"You're okay," I whisper to him, smoothing a hand over his hair. "I promise you're okay."

For long seconds, he doesn't move. Just stays exactly where he is, frozen in whatever horror was running through his dreams.

And I don't know if he's wrapped up in all the terrible things we saw in the Curator's room or if this is about something more. Something deeper. Something that has a lot to do with the sledgehammer he took to Cyrus's office and the two hundred years he spent drowning in the dark.

"Grace?" he finally says, running a hand over his face.

"Hey," I whisper, taking his other hand and bringing it to my lips. "You're back."

Hudson shakes his head, gives a half-hearted little smile. "I didn't know I'd gone anywh—"

His voice breaks before he can finish whatever joke he was going for, and my heart freefalls into a spiral of rage and pain and love.

"It's okay," I tell him as I reach for him. "You're okay."

"I don't know about that." He kicks the covers off, evading my embrace as he climbs out of bed.

Another time, I might be hurt at his rejection of my touch, but this isn't about me. And it's not about us. It's about all the terrible, terrible things that happened to Hudson before there was an us. And the deep-seated trauma that comes with all of them.

I suddenly realize the hardest thing my mate has ever asked me to do is let him work through this at his own speed. But that's what loving someone is all about, right? Offering them everything they need for their own happiness—even if that's space from you.

So instead of trying to cage him in my arms or offering comfort in any way, I let him walk away alone.

89

A Concert-ed Effort

Later, after Hudson has showered and remembered how to breathe, we head back down to the Curator's office.

It's close to ten in the morning, and we've only got a few hours before she should be back from her mini vacation. I'd be lying if I said I wasn't ready to hand all this back over to her. Well, maybe her and an assistant, because she definitely needs one, but still.

This is hard, brutal work, and I'm smart enough to know that I don't have the emotional capacity to do it for any real length of time. I'm glad that there are people out there who can look in the face of human suffering and depravity and find a way through it to the goodness on the other side. I just don't know if I'm that person.

We're on the stairs when my phone vibrates with a text, and I look down to find only one word from Heather. *Help.*

"What does that mean?" Hudson asks when I hold it up for him to see. But he's already fading down the stairs, and I'm flying after him, having shifted on the run.

We burst into the TV room about thirty seconds later, only to find Flint, Jaxon, Heather, Eden, and Macy all looking like they've been run over by a giant truck.

"Are you okay?" I ask, racing toward the center of the room, where they are draped over chairs and desks and the floor, pens dangling from their hands.

"I don't think I'll ever be okay again," Jaxon mumbles as he rolls over onto his back. "I don't think anything will ever be okay again."

"What happened?" I ask, turning to scan the screens for a nuclear explosion or some other cataclysmic event of existential proportions.

But the TVs all look pretty much how we left them. Awful and wonderful and brutal and beautiful and absolutely everything in between but still…normal. Still exactly how the world usually is.

"South America," Flint finally whispers.

"Africa," Jaxon says at the same time.

Macy shakes her head. "It was North and South America."

"More like Europe." Eden scoffs.

"I don't know what they're talking about," Heather says as she covers her face with her hands. "But *Asia* is what happened. Definitely all four point seven *billion* people in Asia."

The others seem like they're about to argue, but one look at Heather's haunted eyes and the way her braids are practically sticking straight out from her head like she's just spent the last three hours yanking on them has them all retreating again.

"Okay," Eden finally says with a groan. "Maybe it was Asia."

"No maybe about it," Heather grumbles as she climbs to her feet, sighing like every bone in her body hurts.

I'm looking from one of my friends to the next, totally confused. But first things first… "How are you able to know anything happened *by continent*?" I wave at the walls of screens. "The TVs aren't organized by geography."

"They are now," Heather says like she regrets all of her life choices. "There's a button next to the one that makes the desks spin that re-sorts the screens by all sorts of things."

Eden groans. "We thought it would be easier to all just take different continents."

"Big mistake," Jaxon deadpans.

"O-kay. Well, what can we do to help?" I ask, conscious of the fact that the TV screens are still going and nobody is currently recording what's happening.

"Were you not listening?" my bestie says in a voice that can only be described as a shriek and points to her right. "Asia. You can start with Asia!"

"Asia it is," I tell her, swiping the notebook out of her hand and heading over to the wall of TVs that covers that continent. "What's the last thing you wrote down?"

"I don't know," she answers as her eyes glaze over. "There was a trade summit that seemed really important and a K-pop festival that is supposed to have had the highest attendance in the world."

"K-pop?" Flint grumbles. "I could have been recording amazing stuff about K-pop instead of an earthquake that killed nearly fifteen thousand people? That doesn't seem fair."

Heather narrows her eyes at him. "Don't even start with me, Dragon Breath. If you'd wanted K-pop, you totally could have asked for—"

"Hey! Is that who I think it is?" I interrupt as I happen to catch a glimpse of the group taking the stage at a music festival in South Korea.

"That's Blackpink," Flint says, showing the first bit of actual enthusiasm since we walked in the room. "They're great."

"I know that, but I meant—" I point to two people in the front row. "The Curator's at the concert. With *Jikan*."

"Seriously?" Eden demands as they all lumber to their feet and crowd around me and the Blackpink TV.

"That's where she decided to go for her vacation? A concert?" Jaxon asks.

"Does that honestly surprise you? Have you seen this house?"

He inclines his head. "Good point."

"Why don't you take your break?" I tell him and Flint. "Go rest for a little while. We'll take it from here."

"We will?" Eden asks, sounding doubtful. "I think I'm broken."

"We *will*," I tell her. "It's just a few more hours. We can do it. Right?"

"Sure," Macy agrees, even though she looks like she'd rather have her fingernails and eyelashes ripped out one by one. "We've got this."

Jaxon and Flint exchange a look. It's the first time I've seen them *really* look at each other all day, and for once, they don't seem annoyed.

"We'll stay," Flint says with a magnanimous wave of his hand. "Seven of us have to be better at this than five."

"You don't have to—" I start, but Eden cuts me off.

"Sure they do," she says as she picks up a couple of notebooks and hands one to each of them. "Come on, guys. Chop-chop."

She claps her hands as the rest of us burst out laughing.

On the plus side, the crisis seems to have passed, and we spend the next couple of hours actually working pretty well together, until the Curator finally walks in the door wearing a Blackpink T-shirt and a flower crown and carrying a giant Manchester United pennant.

90

The Give-It-
Back Tree

"Thanks for holding down the fort," she says an hour later. We all sit down to lunch while Kleo mans the TV room.

"Don't thank us yet," I tell her. "We tried our best, but there's a lot going on in the world at any given minute."

The Curator smiles indulgently. "Isn't that the truth? But I'm sure you guys did great. Here, have some pasta." She grabs the bowl from the center of the table and slides it straight toward me like she's slinging beers in a bar. "Besides, if you messed up, who's to know?"

"Well, that's a terrifying thought," Hudson mutters under his breath.

"Thank you," I murmur to her before putting some on my plate.

"And these spinach fatayer. They're delicious," she says. Another bowl comes careening across the table at me.

I take one of the small triangular pastries and dig in.

By the end of the meal, I'm stuffed and also frustrated, because no matter how many times we try to bring the conversation back to the Bittersweet Tree, she's not having it.

The only thing making me—or Jaxon—not completely lose our shit on her right now is the fact that Mekhi actually looked a little better the last time we saw him on his TV screen. He'd just fed from Lorelei—which none of us had watched, because even when it's not between mates, it's still intimate—and had been sitting up in bed a little.

As she evades the question again, though, I wonder if she doesn't actually know where the Bittersweet Tree is. She wouldn't be the first god who'd tricked someone.

Eventually, I can't hold my tongue any longer and flat-out ask, "Can you tell us where the Bittersweet Tree is now? I'm glad you had an amazing day, and I'd be more than happy to talk about coming back here and giving you another day soon—"

As one, my friends choke on whatever food/water/saliva they are currently swallowing and look at me like I've suddenly grown another head. I shoot them a pleading look. At this point, I'm willing to do just about anything to get the location of this tree so we can help Mekhi— even go another round in the TV Room of Torment. After we find the Bittersweet Tree, that is.

The Curator pauses, her glass of wine halfway to her lips. "You're right. I'm sorry. I've been too wrapped up in my day. I need to just send you on your way. A bargain is a bargain, after all."

She looks so crestfallen that guilt assails me. "It's not that we don't want to stay and talk to you," I tell her. "It's just—"

"Your friend. I know. But you are all welcome back here anytime— though I promise not to put you to work on your next visit." Then she smiles sadly. "The tree you're looking for is outside a town called Baños. It's in Ecuador, near Las Lágrimas de Ángel."

"Las Lágrimas de Ángel?" I repeat, already googling the location on my phone.

"Yes. It's a waterfall." She pushes back from the table before continuing. "Thank you, Grace, for indulging me. Sometimes it gets lonely knowing *almost* everything."

She crosses to the end of the dining room and pulls one of the cabinets open. "You'll need this to hold the Dew," she tells us. And when she turns around, she's holding several of the most beautiful stained glass vials I've ever seen. "Here's a few in case— Well, you never know what might happen."

"Thank you," I say and take the vials from her. "We really appreciate it."

"Of course." She rests a soft hand on my cheek, and I think she's going to say something more. But then she stops and nods toward the front door. "You should go get your things. I believe your ride will be here any minute."

"Our ride?" Jaxon asks for the first time. "I thought that was our job. We—"

He breaks off as a portal opens in the center of the dining room, and all six foot four inches of Remy Villanova steps out, dressed in a white T-shirt, worn jeans, and a kick-ass pair of Dr. Martens.

He grins when he sees me, then glances down at Jaxon and drawls in his thick Cajun accent, "Now, come on, Jaxon. Who's going to send a dragon to do a wizard's job?"

And with a snap of his fingers, the portal closes behind him.

91

Grin and
Bear It

"So, where exactly am I plopping this portal down?" Remy asks the general room, and the Curator leans over and whispers something to him. He gives a quick nod and then gets to work creating a doorway to South America out of thin air.

Normally, I *love* being a gargoyle. And being a demigod of chaos comes in handy from time to time as well. But I'd be lying if I didn't admit how jealous I am right now that Remy can just fold space-time like a magician whenever he wants. I'd definitely spoil myself with frequent trips to art museums around the world if I could do the same.

"How are you here, anyway?" Flint asks as Remy makes another flourish in the air. "I thought you were stuck at that school, with no time off for good behavior."

"Yeah, well. There's different levels of stuck." He shrugs. "As long as I'm back for a test in three hours, all should be good."

"Three hours?" Macy sets a timer on her phone. "Then we need to get going."

Gold flecks begin sparking and moving around the circle he's making, and within seconds the portal is a huge circle spinning right in front of us.

"Ready to go, *cher*?" he asks me with a wink. "I'll do my best not to put you down in the middle of the waterfall."

"Somehow that doesn't inspire a lot of confidence in me," Jaxon mutters. I might take him more seriously if he didn't look like an actual thundercloud—gray and gloomy and ready to rain all over everyone and everything.

"That's because I'm making no promises about you," Remy says.

Jaxon flips him off, but there's no heat behind it—probably because he's so miserable. Remy must think the same thing, though, because he just laughs.

"It's gross how good you are at making portals," Macy tells Remy.

He side-eyes her with amusement. "And here I thought a thank-you might be in order."

"Of course, thank you," she says. "But also, you suck."

"I think you've got me confused with a vampire," he tells her, then steps back and with a very gallant hand gesture says, "Ladies first."

I'm beginning to think "ladies first" is just another way for guys to hang back and see what kind of trouble they're getting themselves into. But what the hell. The clock is ticking, and we're too close to waste any more time.

So with no further ado, I squeeze Hudson's hand and then step into the portal...and straight out of it on top of a mountain.

I can hear the roar of a waterfall close by, but since I'm not standing on the edge of it—or floating underneath it—I definitely call this a win for Remy.

As I wait for the others, I spin in a circle, trying to get the lay of the land—and gasp as I come face-to-face with a bear, who looks just as bewildered at seeing me pop out of nowhere as I am about seeing it at all.

92

On Your Bark,
Get Set, Go

Then again, it could be the gold rings around its eyes that make it look so surprised. I'm not so sure about me.

"Umm, hey there," I say, taking several big steps backward—right into Macy, who has just come through the portal, too.

"Oh, hey!" she starts, then freezes as she, too, sees the bear. "Huh. Guess we didn't think this through."

"What should we do?"

"Why are you asking me?" she demands. "Do I look like a bear whisperer to you?"

"You live in Alaska. There are bears there," I tell her.

"By that logic, you live in California. You've got one on your flag, for God's sake."

It's a valid point. "Should I turn into a gargoyle? Or do you think that will make it freak out?"

Before she can answer, the bear leans toward us, sniffing. Which makes both of us lean way, way back. So far back that we end up colliding with Heather, who does scream the second she steps out of the portal.

The bear rears back and lets out a roar of its own. And then turns and runs in the opposite direction.

"Huh," Macy says. "So that's all we had to do?"

"I guess so."

"What was that?" Heather demands.

"What do you think it was?" Macy asks as she walks toward the sound of the waterfall. "Hey, so is the tree supposed to be on the banks of the waterfall?"

"I don't know," I tell her before shifting into my gargoyle. "But I'm going to fly around a little, see what I can find."

Jaxon comes through the portal just as I launch myself into the air, and I wave at him before I fly over a huge copse of trees and off the edge of the world.

It is an absolutely breathtaking view. The sky is a gorgeous blue, without so much as the thought of a cloud in the sky. The mountains in the backdrop are gorgeous, including what I'm pretty sure is an active volcano that I'm just going to hope chooses not to be an asshole right now.

And the waterfall itself looks like it's more than two hundred feet tall as it cascades down the side of the mountain. There's greenery growing on either side of the fall, but the drop itself is pure sharp rocks that end in an area almost completely enclosed by neighboring mountains, making what looks like an enormous natural pool.

It's yet another amazing sight I wish I had time to go down and appreciate fully. As it is, though, I'm less interested in the waterfall than I am the trees growing all around it.

And I do mean all around it. How on earth are we supposed to find the Bittersweet Tree in a *mountain* of trees? I can't believe only now am I realizing I should have asked *someone* to describe this damn tree before now.

I do another lap above the waterfall and nearby trees, hoping to see something that I missed the first time. But nothing particularly jumps out at me, so I circle back to where the portal is—and find that I've been gone long enough for everyone else to make it through.

"See anything?" Hudson asks, holding a hand out to me as I land.

Behind him, Heather is telling anyone who will listen about the bear we ran into. Unfortunately, she's talking mostly to dragons and vampires, so none of them are particularly impressed—especially when she says it was her scream that scared it away.

"Trees," I answer Hudson despondently. "Lots and lots and lots of trees."

"We'll figure it out," he tells me as he strokes my hair. "One tree at a time, if we have to."

God, even the thought of it is exhausting.

I squeeze Hudson really tightly and wait for him to do the same to me, then pull away to see what everyone else is up to.

Jaxon is standing on the edge of the waterfall, looking down at its churning depths.

Flint has transformed into his dragon and is preparing to launch himself up and over the forest to do another layer of the reconnaissance I just finished doing, while Eden is already walking through the closest group of trees.

I get ready to take to the air again. But Macy, who has been talking intently with Remy for the last few minutes, calls Hudson and me over to talk to the two of them.

"What's up?" I ask as we get closer.

"We want to do a location spell. See if we can narrow this needle in a haystack down a little," Remy says as Macy hands him a pendant from her bag, which he hangs from a small branch.

"That's bloody brilliant," Hudson tells them.

Macy shakes her head. "Don't start praising us yet. One tree in the middle of all this is not exactly easy to pin down—even with a spell."

"Still, the fact that you thought of it impresses me," I tell them. "What can we do to help?"

"Visualize the tree," Remy tells me as he sends a steady pulse of power straight to the pendant, and it begins to sway back and forth just a tiny bit.

Heat blooms across my cheeks, and I tuck my chin as I admit, "I have no idea what kind of tree to visualize. I didn't ask anyone for a description."

"Hey, it's okay, *cher*," Remy says. "The Curator gave me a spell to get us close. We just need to find the right direction to walk in."

I groan. "But I didn't have the foresight to ask a *single* person what it looks like."

A crooked grin splits his face. "Then it's a good thing ol' Remy here doesn't need pesky things like details to work his magic." He tosses me a wink. "Just think of *what* it is. What it represents to you."

I nod and close my eyes as I think of Mekhi. Of Lorelei and Liana and the pain of souls trapped together for an eternity. And then I hope—no, I pray—that getting this far isn't just an exercise in hubris and the baseness of futility.

He adds more power, more pulses of energy coming from his fingers. But nothing happens. The pendant doesn't deviate from its forward-and-back rhythm at all.

After a minute or so, the pendant changes directions, now swinging from right to left—east to west. Remy gives it an extra boost, energy once again pulsing from his fingertips. And still nothing happens.

Until it does.

All of a sudden, sparks of light fly off the pendant each time it swings in one direction, each point of light floating in the air like a constellation of stars, reaching out and out in a straight line. I've never seen anything like it.

"So it's over there?" I ask, following the direction of the line of light pointing toward a huge grove of trees.

Jaxon looks to the trees and back again. "There's still a lot of trees to choose from over there."

"You are so observant," Hudson tells him dryly.

"Still, it's better than this whole area—"

"Relax." Remy cuts me off with a laugh. "We're not done yet."

Now that we have the general area, Macy starts making a series of quick hand movements, swirling her fingers in tighter and tighter circles until she suddenly pulls them apart like she's ripping open a present—and the swarm of floating lights takes off in one direction.

"Let's go!" Macy shouts, and we run, chasing the lights.

93

Let Sleeping
Bears Lie

We only have to run about fifty yards through the thick jungle before we skid to a stop at the edge of a giant meadow. In the center is a massive tree, hundreds of long, thick branches stretching out from the base of a trunk wide enough to rival one in Giant City.

We've found it.

We've found the Bittersweet Tree.

"Holy shit!" Flint crows as the others come running up. "We did it. We actually found the tree!"

"Who would have thought we'd come all the way to Ecuador to find the Bittersweet Tree, and it would turn out to be a simple elm tree?" Heather says, shaking her head in wonder.

"Is that what it is?" I ask. "An elm tree?"

"I'm pretty sure," she answers. "It's taller than a lot of elms I've seen, but the shape of it is straight elm. Look at how low and wide the branches are. Not to mention the leaves are super distinctive. See how they're shaped like a lopsided oval, with one side bigger than the other? It's definitely an elm."

Hudson walks up to me, sliding an arm around my waist as we take it in.

There's a small waterfall crashing into a crystal-clear blue lake a few feet away from the tree, and several of its long branches dip and sway into the water with the breeze. Behind the tree appears to be a small, rocky cave, and to the left of that is more thick jungle. But dotting the meadow in every direction are mound after mound of earth, with the most beautiful wildflowers in every color imaginable reaching up toward whatever spot of sunlight they can find under the thick tree's branches.

The entire spot is idyllic, and a sense of calm brushes along my skin with the gentle wind. I take a deep, centering breath as I realize everything is going to be okay. We just have to collect the—what did my grandmother call it?—Celestial Dew, or nectar from the tree...

"Do elm trees have sap?" I ask Heather.

She doesn't answer. She's too busy staring up at the tree. And up and up and up.

In fact, everyone seems mesmerized by the tree, their eyes wide, mouths parted in wonder. And I get it. This place is magical.

A soft smile lifts a corner of my mouth as I turn back to the tree myself, leaning against Hudson as I take in all of the long branches curving down to the meadow, weighted down by— I straighten up.

"Do all elm trees have so many honeycombs on them?" I ask, moving forward to get a better look. "There have to be hundreds of them here."

"More like thousands," Macy tells me.

She's right, I realize as I walk out into the meadow. There are hundreds upon hundreds upon *hundreds* of honeycombs hanging from every available spot on the tree's branches. And while the tree and its branches are absolutely huge, the honeycombs are all sizes.

Some are as tiny as a berry. Others are bigger than a beach ball, hanging off the longest, thickest branches. And every size in between.

I've never seen anything like it in my life.

"I hate to be the naysayer," Jaxon drawls as he, too, stares at the huge tree. "But are we sure this is the Bittersweet Tree? Elms aren't exactly native to this country."

"Exactly," Hudson tells him. "The Curator said it's never in the same place twice—which means it's likely not from this forest, yes?"

"And now it wants to be here," Heather breathes. "Surrounded by wildflowers of all colors on the bank of this amazing waterfall. That's kind of beautiful, when you think about it, isn't it?"

"Yeah," Eden answers. "But I'm thinking we need to hurry before the tree decides to relocate again."

"Do you think the nectar we need is really honey?" Flint asks, crossing his arms across his broad chest as he takes in the sheer number of honeycombs to choose from.

"I thought it was sap," I admit. "But I think you're right and it's actually honey."

"Why did the Curator tell us that we need a vial to collect it?" Jaxon wonders. "Can't we just break off a piece of the honeycomb?"

"Maybe it's fragile," Eden answers. "Besides, how much will leak out if you're just carrying it in your pocket all the way from here back to the Shadow Realm?"

"It can't actually be this easy, can it?" Flint asks, pointing to an especially large honeycomb hanging barely a foot off the ground. "The honeycomb is right there, waiting for anyone walking by to grab it."

"Does everything have to be hard?" Heather counters.

"In my experience?" Flint shakes his head. "Life has taught me that the only answer to that question is hell yeah, it does."

He's got a point. And I'm obviously not the only one who thinks so, as Eden is squinting up at the tree at least as hard as I am.

"It can't be," she says, agreeing with Flint—and me.

"It could," Heather insists, stepping closer.

"Doubtful," Hudson says, but he, too, moves toward to the tree.

The caution in his tone has me looking at the tree with even more scrutiny.

"What do you see that I don't?" I ask.

"It's not what I see," he answers. "It's what I hear."

"Fuuuuuck," Flint breathes, his eyes widening in alarm, and I realize that whatever Hudson is hearing, he's hearing it, too.

And so are Jaxon and Eden, judging by the twin looks of concern on their faces as well.

Panic skates down my spine—it takes a lot to intimidate a paranormal, especially ones as powerful as my friends. So if they look this worried, whatever they're listening to must be really bad.

"What is it?" Macy asks, because she doesn't have any special hearing, either.

"Bees," Jaxon answers. "Thousands upon thousands of bees."

"Seriously? That's what has you guys so upset? I can't even hear them," Heather tells him.

"You can't hear them because they're really high-pitched right now,"

Hudson explains. "Kind of like ten thousand dog whistles buzzing at the exact same time."

"Ten thousand?" Heather asks, suddenly looking more than a little freaked out herself.

"At least," Eden answers, shaking her head as if she's trying to clear it. "I think there's more."

"Well, I don't think ten thousand bees are a match for a bunch of paranormals," I tell them. "I mean, what's the worst that happens? We get stung a few times?"

"Only one way to find out," Jaxon says and walks about ten feet in front of us. Then he uses his telekinesis to break off a corner of the closest honeycomb and float it across the meadow toward us.

94

Nothing happens.

No bees swarm down from the honeycombs and attack us for taking their honey. No lightning flashes from the sky to strike us. No celestial force tries to protect the tree from our grasping hands.

But as Jaxon holds up his palm to catch the section of floating honeycomb triumphantly, it's hard not to notice that *something* is definitely wrong with him. Namely, Jaxon is suddenly moving in slow— no, make that *super* slow—motion.

I stare at him, eyes wide, as he starts to lower his hand.

And keeps lowering it.

And keeps lowering it.

And keeps lowering it.

And keeps lowering it.

Right about the time his arm finally makes it to *shoulder height*, a loud, high-pitched buzzing fills the air around us that even I can hear now. And about two seconds after that—before Jaxon can so much as lower the honeycomb a centimeter more—bees appear all over on the surface of the honeycombs themselves. A few begin buzzing around the honeycombs as well.

Still, it's nothing that has me panicked. I mean, we weren't expecting Slo-mo Jaxon—and I'm not relishing the trip home with him—but other than a little extra bee activity around the tree, the insects seem to be leaving us alone.

I let out a long sigh. Finally, the universe is going to give us a win, and I, for one, am here for it.

Flint and Eden take turns making wisecracks about Jaxon—who has now managed to lower the bit of honeycomb another centimeter—and I notice a huge droplet of honey forming at the bottom of it.

I look around for Hudson, to tell him I think I have a way to capture the nectar, but he, Macy, and Eden have started walking around the perimeter of the tree, I guess to get a better look at it. I shrug.

"No time like the present," I say to no one in particular as I slide my backpack off my shoulder. Unzipping the top, I rustle around until I find the pouch containing the vials the Curator gave me. I grab two, just in case, and sling the pack on my back again.

I pull the cork off of one of the vials, walk up to Jaxon, and position it just under the droplet of honey, careful to keep the forming blob over the center of the opening. I definitely do not want any of this slow-motion bullshit Jaxon is going through.

"Hey, can you guys stop giving Jaxon shit and look around for a stick or something to knock the honeycomb out of his hand?" I say with a pointed look at the two dragons, who shrug and head to the edge of the jungle to look for sticks.

Hudson, Macy, and Heather are still staring at the tree, I realize, and I follow their line of sight to find a cluster of bees buzzing around one of the largest honeycombs. The bees don't look like any I've ever seen before, though, and I have to swallow back the urge to shout, "RUN!"

First of all, the smallest of the bees—of which there are not many—are the size of a walnut. The bigger bees are more like the size of my fist—even bigger if you measure around the tall antennae shooting up from their head, massive wings keeping their fat bodies bobbing in the air, and a ridiculously long stinger sticking out of its venom sac.

As I stare at the giant creatures with their huge black eyes and fuzzy faces, all I can think is that I thought the shadow bugs were bad. Because, while I have nothing against regular bees, these are next-level bad.

And oh God...

I swallow hard.

They've spotted us.

That was my first thought.

My second?
Giant wings mean there is absolutely nothing slow about them.
And the swarm is heading straight for Jaxon.

95

To Bee or
Not to Bee

Flint must hear one of us scream, because he doesn't hesitate. He races to Jaxon and wraps his huge body around his—and accidentally nudges the honeycomb.

Flint, whose self-preservation instinct isn't always the best, must figure out exactly how screwed he is, because he starts to change into his dragon form, I'm guessing because a dragon's skin is so much tougher than our human skin.

But now he's also moving in slow motion.

Watching a dragon—or even a werewolf—shift is usually a beautiful thing, filled with rainbow shimmers and mystical light and a change that happens in little more than the blink of an eye.

Watching Flint shift right now is none of those things. Not beautiful. Not mystical. And definitely not quick. Instead, it's awkward as hell, not to mention terrifying, because, unlike when he normally shifts, we get to see every single thing that happens in close-up, slow-motion detail.

His skin starts to shift first, changing from warm and soft and brown to cold and scaly and green, one excruciatingly slow layer—and second—at a time. And while dragon scales are absolutely beautiful, especially Flint's, partially formed dragon scales slowly layering themselves over human skin is awful-looking.

Add in the fact that his head starts to shift at the same time as his skin, and the result is something truly monstrous. His bone structure starts to elongate, his jaw broadens, his teeth sharpen, and the skin above his temples, eyes, mouth, jaw, and cheekbones begins to form sharp, hard crests.

In other words, his human head becomes a dragon head—only it does it so slowly that he looks more like a demon than a human or a dragon.

The same thing starts to happen with his claws and his tail as well, until every part of him looks like some kind of human/monster meant to terrify small children—or anybody else.

Except, apparently, for the bees, who take one look at him—and the honey I now see on his hand—and head straight for him like their stingers are on fire.

Trapped as he is between his human and dragon form and slowed down to the speed of cold honey, he's a sitting duck for the bees and whatever horrors they want to rain down on him.

I glance down at the vial in my hand that now has a blob of honey sliding down the inside of the glass, and I slam the cork on top and shift into my gargoyle form. In my stone form, I'm completely impervious to beestings, so I throw myself in front of Flint and the attacking bees.

The noise is horrible, their buzzing so incessant that it makes it impossible to concentrate or even think. That doesn't stop me from trying to bat them away with my open palm, but it does prevent me from coming up with any kind of plan on how to deal with the attack. Add in the fact that Flint is also batting them away—without the benefit of being stone—and all three of us are in a world of hurt, something that Hudson must notice right away.

Because the next thing I know, all of the bees currently attacking us disintegrate instantly. I barely register that we're free before Hudson screams—a horrible, spine-chilling sound that has my heart stuttering in my chest—before falling to the ground a few feet from the water's edge, clutching his head in his hands.

96

You Can Run but
You Can't Hive

"**H**udson!" I scream, tearing around the tree toward him. "Hudson, are you all right?"

But he doesn't answer. He's too busy clutching his head and writhing on the ground.

At first, I don't understand what's happening to him—he's destroyed stadiums, poofed thousands of shadow bugs in the Trials, fought off gargoyle skeletons night after night and never had this reaction. It always hurts him to use his power, to experience all of those lives—one of the many reasons I hate for him to have to do it—but not like this. Never like this.

So what's different about a bunch of bees? What makes getting inside them so impossible for him?

"Hudson." I want to fall to the ground beside him, cradle his head in my hands, but I'm still clutching both vials and he's writhing too much for me to get close.

He just keeps moaning, over and over, "Souls. Souls. Souls. Souls. Souls."

And that's when it hits me. These bees do more than just protect the honeycomb. They make the honey. The honey is what we're here to get, Celestial Dew, the thing that somehow will break apart two bound souls. And if the honey is Celestial, then it's not a stretch to think the bees that make it are, too.

"Oh my God," I breathe, and my stomach twists like a braided rope. In disintegrating the bees, Hudson has put himself inside the mind of an ancient, Celestial being.

Fear swamps me as I wonder if there's any coming back from this.

Is there any way for his mind to let go of what it saw? What it felt? Or will he suffer with this kind of pain forever?

Just the thought has my stomach twisting again, but I do my best not to show it as I glance around the meadow. Hudson isn't the only one suffering right now.

Jaxon hasn't managed to drop the honeycomb yet, and a whole new set of gigantic bees is swarming him from all directions. Flint is trying to help him, but he's being swarmed, too. Both men have giant welts forming from beestings all over their exposed skin, eyes puffing up and nearly closing, hands swelling up like catcher's mitts. And still, the bees keep stinging them over and over and over until Flint stumbles to his knees.

I rush over to help bat the insects away, careful not to touch the honeycomb in Jaxon's hand, but there are too many.

Macy and Remy race to us and begin weaving spells in the air. Spells that form protective barriers around Flint and Jaxon that shatter almost immediately. Spells that fling bees back a few feet, but they never scoop many, and the few they do catch seem to only get madder when they fly back. In fact, absolutely nothing they do seems to have any real effect on the bees.

Eden is using her ice breath to try to freeze as many bees as she can. And while the cold does seem to repel them for a few seconds, the moment they manage to get out of the ice stream, they swarm again.

Heather has picked up a stray branch and is putting her years in middle-school softball to use as she swings for the fences. But more bees are coming than she has any hope of swatting away.

Then again, there doesn't seem to be much any of us can do against these bees.

Even worse, before my horrified eyes, the bees go from swarming only Jaxon and Flint to stinging all of my friends, and their tortured shouts fill the air.

Hudson is still on the ground, face pale, jaw clenched in pain. He's not yelling now, but I don't know if that's because the agony has lessened or because he doesn't have the energy to cry out anymore.

A glance back at Flint has a scream welling in my throat, and I rush to swat at more bees. He's stopped shifting, and his entire face is swollen with huge welts until it's nearly unrecognizable.

His jacket and shirt are ripped from long minutes of giant bee parts batting against them—legs, wings, antenna, stingers. All of them are so huge and sharp that they cause damage wherever they touch—which is everywhere, judging from the fact that every place his skin is exposed is swollen with enormous, pus-filled stings.

His neck, his hands, his chest, his abdomen, and even his nonprosthetic leg are three or four times their normal size with pus. I let out a scream when even his knees can no longer support him and he falls to his side, unmoving.

I'm sobbing now as I swat at the bees still on Jaxon, but he looks to be in even worse shape than Flint, though I wouldn't have believed it was possible if I wasn't seeing it with my own eyes.

When Jaxon took the honeycomb, his vampiric metabolism obviously slowed as well, because none of the beestings are healing on him and he's as unrecognizable as Flint. If anything, he looks worse than Flint.

Which is only reinforced when he tips over and—like Hudson—goes down face-first. Hard.

But unlike Hudson, he doesn't scream in agony. In fact, he doesn't make a sound at all, and somehow that is so much worse.

I turn to Eden and shout, "Get Macy and Heather out of here. Now!"

Remy is already on the ground. Unmoving.

As Eden takes off for the sky, part of me wants to just stand here and scream in horror while another part knows now isn't the time to lose my shit.

I need to stay calm. Everyone is counting on me. I am the only one of us that is immune to the bees, and I don't care that the guys aren't moving. They are not dead. I refuse to believe that. Not yet.

I glance over at Jaxon, who has succumbed to the pain and the venom. The bees have lifted off of him, too—all but the two humongous ones who have landed next to him and are gobbling the honeycomb from his relaxed fingers he's finally managed to let go.

They aren't stinging him anymore. In fact, they aren't doing anything to him or Flint, to Remy or Hudson, as if they know there's no longer a point. They'll soon be gone, their labored breaths coming slower and slower.

The panic I've been trying to hold back is like a freight train tearing through me now, and I open my mouth and scream and scream and scream. I scream until my throat is raw.

I scream until every single bee floats back to their fucking honeycombs, leaving my friends, my *mate*, alone to finally die in peace.

97

I Need an
Escape Claws

No. I can save them. I *will* save them.

I shove the vials in my pocket and rush to Hudson's side. I reach down with one hand into the grassy meadow and lay the other across my mate's shoulder—and breathe the earth's magic into my body, and then into Hudson's.

I reach inside him, looking for the worst effects of the bee venom, and send healing energy to his trachea, which has nearly closed completely. I feel the white-hot magic slowly, ever so slowly, begin to push the venom out of his bloodstream, feel his airways opening millimeter by millimeter.

When he takes a deep, shaky breath, I let the tears flow freely down my cheeks. He's going to be okay. *He will*, I convince myself.

And I know he needs more healing, but I can't focus on curing him completely yet.

A shadow crosses over me, and I realize Eden is flying circles overhead above the tree. Good. With her, Heather, and Macy safe, I can focus on what I need to do here.

I swing my focus over to Remy next, wrapping my hand around his ankle and sending as much earth magic as I can channel into his body. Flint and Jaxon are a few feet away, and I try to push earth magic along the ground to them as well. Everyone is critical, and my hands are shaking as I draw in more and more energy and send it into my friends' bodies.

When all three groan, take in deep breaths, I glance up at the sky and shout, "They're okay! They're going to be okay!"

Macy and Heather, though, just wave their hands and shout back,

"Look out!"

I don't have time to turn to see what has them so scared before something heavy slams into me and I go flying.

Holy shit. Whatever hit me plops down in the middle of my chest—and it weighs a metric fuck-ton. I think it cracked my chest—and my back—when it hit me, and though I want nothing more than to roll out from under it, I can't. It weighs thousands of pounds, and I am stuck under it like a roach under a shoe.

I gasp for breath—my chest really does feel like I've cracked my sternum or punctured a lung—and get my first real glimpse of what attacked me.

And the answer is—a bear.

A fucking bear.

And he looks pissed as hell.

With a roar, he starts swiping razor-sharp claws at my stone chest, over and over and over again. I've managed to get my arms over my face, but that's as much as I can do to protect myself. Panic squeezes my heart as I curl up as much as I can with a giant fucking bear camped out on my chest.

Hudson must sense my distress, because I hear him grunt painfully, one leg dragged along the ground, then another, as he manages to push himself to his knees. Unfortunately, his eyes are still swollen shut, so he has no idea where I am—nor can he see the bear on my chest.

I start to scream at him for help, but I stop myself, scared he might try to disintegrate this bear who, given he apparently hangs out near a Celestial tree, might just also be Celestial himself. If using his ability on Celestial bees brought Hudson to his knees, I can't imagine the damage to his psyche if he gets in this bear's mind.

Luckily—depending on how I'm measuring luck now—the bear must decide I'm not worth much more effort. He stops clawing at me and rolls off my chest in an impressive sideways somersault, then lumbers away.

"I'm okay, Hudson," I choke out after a minute and really hope he can't tell I'm absolutely lying. I am definitely, one hundred percent *not* okay. But I'm not dead, either, so at least there's that.

"The bees..." Hudson starts with a ragged breath. "The honey..."

He shakes his head, then tries again. "The bear…is a…soul eater."

Yes. I can agree with that. He's nearly devoured mine twice now.

I struggle to sit up, biting my lip not to make a sound so I don't interest the bear again. *God, please, not the bear*, I mentally groan, my gaze darting from the bear to Hudson, who has sunk back down to the earth, exhausted. I eventually get my weight onto my elbow as I keep one eye on the bear, who is under the tree now.

My eyes widen when I realize it's even bigger than I thought. And its fur is golden and shimmery, each hair burning as brightly as a full moon over the ocean on a clear night. If it hadn't just cracked my rib cage in half, I might even consider it majestic.

Suddenly, the bear turns to look at Hudson, and my heart flips into triple time.

I scramble to my feet as fast as I can, which is not as fast as I would like, and scream, "I'm the one you want!" I start limping toward the tree—and the honeycombs—as fast as my battered body can carry me. No way am I leaving this bear alone with Hudson. No freaking way. I'll die before I let him have my mate.

The bear meets me halfway, jumping forward with a roar that shakes the honeycombs in the branches. But I don't care, because as long as he's focused on me, he's not going after Hudson or Jaxon or Flint or Remy.

Behind his back, I lock eyes with Heather, who's sitting in front of Macy on Eden's dragon back. Eden is diving toward the bear, just as I am, and Heather's branch is raised like a bat.

"No!" I scream at her, throwing up a hand to ward her off. "Don't do it!"

But it's too late. She swings for the fences, hitting the bear in the back of his shoulder. He whirls around with a roar and hits Eden hard enough to send them all careening several yards away. Heather slams into the ground headfirst. And then goes still.

"Heather!" I shout. Hudson must somehow make out Eden's downed dragon body just as I see Macy trapped beneath her, because he fades to them and shoves at the heavy dragon until he can drag Macy out.

Terror and anger race through me, and I lash out with a stone fist, hitting the bear in his nose as hard as I can.

He bellows in fury as his head snaps back, and when his eyes meet mine, there's unholy rage in them. He rears up on his hind legs, and this time, when he swipes out at me, he hits me with everything he's got.

I fly backward, slamming hard into the side of the mountain beside the waterfall. And then everything goes black.

98

All of the Bitter, None of the Sweet

I come to slowly. My ears are ringing, and my entire body feels like it's just been run over by a tank—several times.

I blink, try to clear my foggy brain and figure out where I am. And that's when I see Remy laying on the ground near me, nearly unrecognizable from the damage inflicted by the bees but at least breathing. I think. Please please please don't let him be dead.

"Remy!" I whisper urgently. He doesn't stir, so I do it again. "Remy—"

I break off when he groans, a low, broken sound that strikes terror through me like a switchblade. I reach a hand out to him—just to feel the warmth of his body and reassure myself that he's still alive—and as I do, I realize I'm looking at my own skin.

My bruised and bloodied human skin. Somewhere between when the bear hit me the last time and me hitting the ground, I lost my gargoyle.

I reach for it deep inside me, try to wrap my hand around the familiar platinum string, but I don't feel it there. I don't feel anything but the pain of what's happened here today.

Fear claws through me, has my heart in my throat and ice trickling down my spine, as I turn my head and look for Hudson.

I don't find him right away. Instead, I see Jaxon and Flint on the ground, in the exact positions they've been in since this fight began. I can't see either of their chests moving.

The pain grows, pressing down on me with more force than that bear ever could. Stealing the air from my lungs, making it harder and harder to breathe. Even before I turn my head a little more and find Macy and Eden closer to the tree.

Macy is curled into a ball, her entire body tensed even in unconsciousness, braced for one more blow, while Eden, in her human form again, is laying on her side next to her. She, too, is unconscious—or worse. She, too, is bruised and battered and broken. But she's still reaching out for Macy, her hand just brushing against my cousin's sea-green hair.

Heather is several yards away from them, her crumpled body exactly where it landed when the bear knocked her away. And next to her, facedown and completely still, is Hudson.

My Hudson.

A sob wells up in my throat as I see his bloated, shattered body laying at an unnatural angle. Oh my God, the bear must have gone after him, or he it, after I was knocked out.

I start to call to him, but his name lodges in my chest, suffocating me. Terror, horror, agony washes over me, and I use every ounce of strength I have to push up to my knees, to try to crawl across the space between us to get to him. But my body is too broken—I'm too broken—and I fall back to earth with the first tiny forward movement that I make.

"Hudson!" I gasp his name out now. "Hudson, please."

He doesn't stir, and everything inside me turns to night. Because Hudson would never leave me suffering if he could prevent it. Hudson would answer me if he could. Hudson, my Hudson, would find a way to reach for me.

And he's not this time. He's just laying there, an empty shell of the man I will love for eternity. Which means he's gone. He's really gone.

Pain like nothing I've ever experienced wells up inside me. It rips through me like the ocean, rolls me over like the steady, relentless pounding of the waves. It drags me down like an undertow, burrowing deeper and deeper inside me until I'm drowning, and I don't even care.

I did this. *I did all of this.* The truth of the words ricochets inside me.

I was the one who didn't ask more questions about the tree. About the Celestial Dew. And *everyone* tried to warn me Celestials were not meant to be trifled with. But I ignored them, chose not to listen, not to ask, not to question a single thing that might result in us not trying to save Mekhi.

I buried my head in the sand, like I always do when I don't want to face something difficult, and I just kept barreling ahead.

And my friends have all paid the price.

My kick-ass, take-no-prisoners bestie has paid the price.

My sweet, sad, shattered cousin has paid the price.

My stubborn ex-mate and his loyal-to-a-fault boyfriend, my friend, have paid the price.

Even my friend who can see the future, who put his fate in my hands when he came anyway, just because he knew I'd need him, has paid the price.

And my mate, my beautiful, broken, tear-down-the-world-for-me mate, who has already suffered more than anyone should ever have to, has paid the price.

Because I bought into my own propaganda instead of taking care of them.

Because I didn't take one moment to think, to plan, before leaping headfirst into danger.

Because I let every single one of them down.

I've never felt more ashamed in my life—or like more of a failure. I'm supposed to be a leader, and instead I've become the executioner for everyone I've ever loved.

My parents died trying to protect me.

Xavier died because I wasn't strong enough.

Luca died because I couldn't save him.

Rafael, Byron, Calder, and even poor Liam died because I couldn't stop a war.

And now this.

I've injured or killed everyone I've ever loved because I haven't been strong enough or smart enough or good enough to save them.

Agony rips through me, and this time I don't whisper Hudson's name. I scream it. Over and over again.

He doesn't answer, but still I keep calling. Still I can't stop.

If I stop, it will mean he's really gone. And that can't be.

Not now. Not yet. Not my Hudson. Not my heart.

Not my mate.

I scream until I'm hoarse.

I scream until every last flicker of hope burning inside me dies.

I scream until there's nothing left. Of him. Of me. Of us.

And then I scream some more.

Eventually, my voice breaks under the stress, and I close my eyes, let myself drift away in a tsunami of pain so great that I don't think I'll ever be able to find my way back to the surface again.

I've fought this feeling, fought this wave so many times before, but I can't fight it anymore. Not now, when darkness is closing around me, pulling me into its arms—into oblivion—where I belong.

99

Just Dew It

I don't know how long I drift like that.

Long enough for the buzzing to stop and the bees to once more disappear.

Long enough for the soft lavender of dusk to paint itself across the sky.

More than long enough for the bear to pull down a honeycomb and drag it under the tree with him.

As I drift, caught somewhere between anguish and apathy, the world around us starts to change. The wind blows stronger. The grass grows longer. And the thousands upon thousands of wildflowers covering the area around the tree grow taller and taller and taller.

They grow up from beneath us and then they grow over us, wrapping themselves around our arms and our legs. Twining themselves around our bodies. Covering our hands and feet and heads until we're no longer visible. Until the wildflowers and the grass and the tree and the water are all that there are.

At first, I don't realize what's happening—don't realize what this means. But then the tugging starts, the flowers pulling me down, down, down into the dirt I'm laying on, and it hits me. These aren't just flowers. These are our funeral wreaths—in a meadow covered in graves.

The first trickles of panic meander through me as I realize what's happening. To Remy. To Jaxon. To any of my other friends whose lives might still be hanging on the brink. To me.

The earth is absorbing us, here in this garden of souls. Taking us back from whence we came.

The panic turns to anger, because this isn't right. This isn't our time. Once again, I turn my head and look at my friends. But none of them have moved. Even Remy is laying exactly where he fell. But at least I can see the shallow—so, so shallow—rise and fall of his back as he breathes.

And then I remember what I should have remembered all along. My strings, as vibrant and colorful as any patch of wildflowers.

I take a deep breath and blow it out slowly as I prepare myself for whatever I may find. And then I do what I should have done long hours ago. I dive deep inside myself and look for the strings that have become as much a part of me as my gargoyle.

They're there. Oh my God. They're all there. Macy's hot-pink string is thread slender, but it's there. Remy's rich, deep forest green string—so different than the blazing green of my demigod string—is thicker, stronger, but it's definitely tattered in places. Jaxon's black string, Flint's amber string, Eden's purple string. Heather's red string. They're all still there. Scuffed up and worn nearly clean through in places, but they're still there. Mekhi's yellow string is so translucent that it's barely noticeable, but it's still there as well.

And so is Hudson's. Oh my God, so is Hudson's. The mating bond is still there. Its shine has dulled, its blue has gone murky, and there's a spot—one terrifying spot that has my heart in my throat—that's so shredded that it looks like any movement at all will break it forever. But it's there, propped up—I see now—by my missing platinum string.

My gargoyle wasn't gone after all. It was just there, beneath the mating bond, holding Hudson and me together until I could do it for myself.

Which means we have a chance. We all still have a chance. And I need to make that chance a reality. I need to find a way to tap into all the strength, all the heart, all the soul that these people have shared with me this last year and find a way to get them out of here and bring them home.

My brain is still sluggish, my body is still battered all to hell. But I take a deep breath and force myself to think through the pain and the cloudiness. There must be a way. I just have to find it.

Turning my head to look at Remy, again, I can't help but notice the bear sitting comfortably beside the lake, shaded by the elm. He's got the honeycomb on the ground in front of him, and I watch as he devours a claw full of honey.

I'm still close enough to him to see it dribble down his chin and run between his razorlike claws. He licks at them for a moment before dipping his paw into the honeycomb and coming up with another claw full of honey.

Again, it dribbles down his chin, and this time he growls impatiently before wiping his mouth.

When he's done, he flicks his claw to clean it, and tiny little strings fly off in all directions. And then he does it again and again and again. Every time he does, little droplets of honey fly off his claws and float away on the breeze.

The bear is a soul eater. That's what Hudson said.

I watch as another string of honey stretches from the bear's lips to his claws, pulled thinner and thinner as he moves his paw farther from his mouth until it eventually breaks free, the gossamer thread glowing as bright as the bear's fur as it catches the breeze and floats away.

And I have the ridiculous thought that this is where our souls really come from—all of us, just little drops of honey flicked off this Celestial bear's claw and ignited with Celestial spittle.

I want to laugh at my absurdity, but it hurts too much to breathe. Instead, I just lay here and watch this ridiculous bear eat honey, little wisps floating from his mouth over and over. Every once in a while, his claws get too messy with strings of honey that refuse to float away, and he reaches out and dunks his paw in the lake beside him. The same pool of water just inches away from me.

And that's when a *truly* bizarre thought occurs to me. What if we were never after the honey at all? Watching as the bear rinses his claw in the water again, I can't help wondering if I was mistaken. My grandmother said we needed Celestial *Dew*. And dew is *water*, not honey.

If this bear is a soul eater, like Hudson said, and the lake water rinses away the honey... Can it really be that we need this lake's water to separate Liana and Lorelei's souls, like rinsing honey from a bear's claw?

Remy groans, and my heart starts pounding in my chest. He's awake.

I call out his name, and this time, when he moans my name back, I give a deep sigh of relief that he's really alive.

If Remy is alive, there's a chance. We have a chance.

Trying not to attract the bear's attention again, I whisper-shout to Remy, "Can you get us out of here?"

He shakes his head. "I can't walk," he answers in a voice broken with pain. "Or stand."

"I know that," I hiss back. "But I need you to suck it up and get us out of here." I imbue my voice with the urgency I'm feeling. There's so little time left for Hudson and for Mekhi that this has to work.

Remy's eyes drift closed, and for a second I think he's fallen back to sleep. But then he whispers, "I have an idea."

"Good," I answer.

I'm working up the energy to reach a hand in my pocket when I feel the ground beneath me begin to tremble. My gaze darts to the bear, my stomach in my throat, but the shaking ground must not be because of him, since he's still eating.

"I'm not sure I can get us all," Remy whispers, but I refuse to listen.

"We all go, Remy. All of us." And then I have an idea. "You reach for me, and I'll reach for them." And then I look deep inside myself and scoop up their strings in my hand. Because I *will* hold them, no matter what it takes. Nothing will make me let them go. Not now. Not ever. "I'll tell you when I'm ready."

He grunts what I think is a yes, and I reach into my pocket and pull out the empty vial the Curator gave me. I slowly, so very slowly, inch my hand closer and closer to the water, keeping my eyes glued to the bear. He's focused on his honeycomb dinner, though, and I dip the vial in the water and fill it to the brim. Then I cork it as quickly as I can.

Still, I'm not quiet enough. Because the bear looks up suddenly, a low growl rumbling from his throat as he comes charging toward me.

I reach one hand out to Remy's and squeeze the other one around my friends' strings. "Now, Remy, now!" I tell him.

The ground beneath us dissolves into a swirling pit of stars and colors. And then we fall.

100

My Get-Into-
Jail-Free Card

When we land, we hit the ground so hard that the entire floor rattles beneath us. My body aches anew from the impact—although, to be honest, it's hard to tell which pains are from this hit and which are from all the ones that came before.

It takes me a second to draw a breath—it feels like I was just donkey-kicked in my already bruised sternum. But once I can, I immediately dive inside myself to check the strings. They're all still there, even Heather and Hudson.

I force my eyes open, then, determined to find my mate.

The first thing I notice is how bright it is in here, the overhead strip lights nearly blinding in their intensity. The second thing is that the floor I'm lying on looks familiar, though I can't quite place it yet. And the third is a childish drawing carved into the metal wall right in front of me.

It's a stick-figure drawing, obviously done by someone very young, but it's some kind of animal on four legs. The animal has a strange hooked tail and a lion's head that it looks like the artist was trying to capture mid-shake.

It's a manticore, I realize as I blink to clear my eyes. In a little T-shirt with a giant C on it. So not just any manticore, then. Calder.

My heart starts to race again as I realize exactly where we are and that a young Remy must have made that drawing, knowing that he would eventually meet her here.

Panic rips through me, but before it can get a firm hold, Remy reaches a hand out and covers mine. "It's home," he tells me simply.

And I get it. Bruised, battered, broken nearly beyond repair, Remy took us to the only place he could manage—the prison that was his home for most of his seventeen years of life. The Aethereum.

"You can always find your way home," I answer. "Even in the dark."

"Exactly." He smiles faintly.

I turn my head then, in search of *my* home, and find Hudson laying on his back several feet away. He doesn't look good, but I can still see our string deep inside me. I hold on to that as I stagger to my feet and stumble across the slick cell floor to my mate.

"Hudson, baby." I drop to my knees beside him and lean down, my head on his chest as I listen for the solace of his heartbeat. It's still there, weak and a little thready, but there—and right now, that's all that matters.

I sit up and smooth his hair back from his face. He groans, grabbing my hand with one of his swollen ones as he rolls onto his side. He pulls my hand to his chest, curling around me. "I thought I lost you," he whispers.

"That's funny," I answer as I stroke his hair back from his face with my free hand. "I thought the same about you."

"You did bloody yell a lot, didn't you?" He laughs a little at that, which quickly dissolves into a coughing fit.

"Yeah, well, I would have stopped if you'd answered me." I pretend to be offended. "Thanks for that, by the way."

"So sorry to inconvenience you. I was trying not to die."

I make a disapproving noise deep in my throat even as happiness bubbles inside me. "And not doing a very good job of it, apparently."

"Apparently not," he agrees, leaning his head into my touch. "Fuck, it hurts, Grace."

"Just more proof that you're alive," I answer matter-of-factly.

"I think I could stand with a little less proof," he tells me dryly.

I shake my head. "Nope. After those damn bees, I want all the proof, all the time."

His chuckle is weak, but it's there nonetheless. "You make a compelling case."

"I thought you were dead." I mean it to come out a little flippant, a casual answer to his teasing comment. But it doesn't sound like that at all. Instead, it comes out shaky and terrified and devastated. So, so devastated.

"Oh, Grace."

He forces himself to sit up, and though it has none of his usual elegance and he's swollen up with beestings and bear swipes, he's still beautiful to me. Of course, he's looking at me the exact same way, and I know I'm an even bigger disaster than he is. Still, if I wasn't certain that it would hurt him, I'd throw my arms around him and hug him to me as tightly as I can.

I drop my forehead gently onto his chest—not to hear his heart beat this time, but just so I can feel close to him. Just so I can feel the rocky rise and fall of his chest as he breathes.

Around us, the others are starting to stir. They're not doing anything so wild as getting up or even moving around, but they are waking up.

Flint curses as he shifts back to his human form from the dragon/human hybrid form he's been stuck in all this time.

Jaxon rolls over from his stomach to his back, groaning.

Heather gasps as she comes to, arms swinging as if she's still trying to hit one of those damn bees, while Eden and Macy don't move at all. The only way I know they're awake is because their eyes are open—and they are all whimpering in pain.

Remy is sitting up like Hudson and me, but he's not looking good. His eye is somehow even worse—though I didn't know that was possible—with pus and blood streaming from it like a river.

He needs medical attention. We all need medical attention, but that's not really an option right now. Not when we have to figure out how to get out of this prison all over again.

On the plus side, the cell door is wide open, so we're not entirely *prisoners*. But we're not on the bottom level where we can just walk right out, either. At least not if the rules of this hellhole still apply, and I'm pretty sure that they do. Charon doesn't strike me as the type to like change, and neither does the Crone, who built this nightmare.

This whole damn paranormal world seems to have trouble with change. Not to mention a million different rules for a million different things that no one actually wants to tell you about. At the moment, I'm pretty pissed at the Bloodletter for her very abbreviated instructions about the whole Bittersweet Tree thing. I'm not saying she *had* to tell us the dew didn't come from the billion giant beehives, but a mention of the bees would have been nice. Or at least the bear. Something, anything to prepare us for what we just went through.

But nope.

Not even the Curator volunteered useful information—just *Celestials are not to be trifled with.* Understatement of the fucking millennium.

She blithely sent us on our way with an artsy vial and hoped we survived. Or maybe she didn't. Who knows with gods?

All I know is that if someone who doesn't have a clue what she's doing comes to little old demigod me and asks for help with a problem, I'm going to make it my mission to be as clear as possible. No obscure hints, no long-winded half stories that leave out the most important parts, no wave and "good luck" before I send her on her naive fucking way. Just straightforward answers that help them do what needs to be done. And, at the very *least*, I'm going to mention a billion Celestial bees and a goddamn Celestial *bear.*

I take a deep breath. My grandmother and I *will* be having words later.

But for now, I'm just glad we're okay. We survived *and* we got the Celestial Dew. Everything is going to be okay now. Mekhi is going to be okay.

Flint coughs, then groans immediately because the pain is too bad. And I just sit here, next to Hudson, trying to figure out what to do. How to get my friends and myself medical attention.

I know paranormals heal fast, especially vampires and shifters, but I'm not sure they'll heal fast enough. Not with the kind of injuries they have. And even if they are able to heal themselves, it doesn't help the rest of us.

So what the hell do I do?

Just wait here until some of us are feeling well enough to fight our way past Charon's little gauntlet? But if we do that, we risk getting slotted into the Chamber, and no one here can handle that right now.

Not to mention the fact that Mekhi's time has dwindled from days into what I hope is hours and not minutes.

"We need to get out of here," Hudson tells me, like he's reading my mind.

"I know," I answer. "I just don't have a clue how to make that happen. We can't even walk."

He nods, then lowers his head back to the floor, like holding it up is taking too much effort. And I get more freaked out than ever. If Flint and Hudson are too weak to so much as sit up, how the hell am I going to get the rest of our friends up and out of here before something terrible happens?

But before I can so much as get *myself* up, much less my friends, a tinny, rhythmic clinking comes from the passageway that runs in front of the cells on this floor, as if someone is clinking a key against the metal bars.

It's an ominous sound—one that has the hair on the back of my neck standing up. Even before I realize that it's not a key that's clinking but a ring. A ring that is currently on the finger of none other than the Crone.

101

I Have a Crone
to Pick with You

Fear slices through me as she walks into the cell like she owns the place—which, technically, I guess she does. Normally, I'm more than willing to go head-to-head with the Crone, but right now I'm not in any shape to match wits with her. None of us are.

Still, I struggle to my feet. If I'm going to have to deal with this woman, I'm going to do it standing up. Anything else seems like admitting defeat before even entering the battlefield.

It doesn't help my nerves that the tattoo on my forearm has suddenly blazed to life. I've been dreading this moment, but I have to say, it never occurred to me that it would happen in the middle of a damn prison after everyone I love has been beaten all to hell beside me. Then again, she always has been one to press her advantage.

"Well, Grace, I never thought I'd see you back here," she says as she looks around Remy's cell at all of my friends spread out on the ground. "Though I do feel like a hospital might be more in order than a prison cell."

Jaxon tries to sit up to face her and ends up collapsing with a pained groan, the back of his arm draped over his eyes.

"Actually, so do I," I answer. "We're planning on heading straight over there as soon as we can."

"A little late for that, isn't it? You're—"

Macy whimpers as she tries to move, an anguished cry that echoes off the cell's metal walls.

The Crone curls her lip as she turns to her. "Do you really need to do that here?"

Macy doesn't answer, and after several seconds, the Crone starts again. "This prison isn't exactly known for its easy escape. If you're in here, even by accident, it's going to expect you to be redeemed if you have any chance of getting out of here alive. Surely you remember."

"That bullshit only works once, Adria. I know exactly how to get out of this prison, and redemption has nothing to do with it."

Her eyes widen, though I'm not sure if it's because I called her by her first name or because I called her on her shit. And to be honest, I don't care. All I know is I'm not going to roll over for her anymore and pretend what she's saying or doing is okay when it patently is not.

"You don't know much, little—"

All of a sudden, Remy makes a gagging sound, and she jumps back about five feet, like she's terrified of being in the splash zone.

"What on earth is wrong with you creatures? I'm trying to have a conversation here, and you can't stop whining." She reaches into her pocket and whips out a small golden bottle. At first, I think we've driven her to drink, but then she flips open the lid, squirts some on her hand, and rubs it in.

Huh. Sanitizer. Didn't see that coming. I mean, I'm not sure how she thinks getting your ass kicked is contagious, but it takes all kinds.

"If you're going to do that, can you please go in the bathroom?" she demands, turning to Remy with an annoyed look on her face that quickly turns to horror.

She screams and stumbles backward. "Good heavens, what is wrong with you?" She points at his eye. "I've been alive for a very long time, and I've never seen anything like that before. There's not enough hand sanitizer in the world for me to be sharing this space with the lot of you."

And then, looking very put-upon, she makes a shooing motion with her hand as if to brush away a bee, which isn't ironic at all. Seconds later, a strange heat invades my body. It takes away the aches that are absolutely everywhere, but it's not until I glance over at Remy that I realize what's happened.

She's cured us all, not out of the goodness of her heart but because our ailments were disturbing her. That's a special kind of self-absorption. But it's not like I want her to take it back, so I decide not to kick the gift Crone in the mouth. At least I have a chance of getting my friends out of here if they can walk again.

The only problem with her sudden largesse is that now that she's not preoccupied with everyone's pathetic little weaknesses, she can focus all of her attention on me. Suddenly, my tattoo doesn't just glow. It burns—a lot. And I know exactly what that means.

It's time to pay up, whether I want to or not.

102

You're so Vial

"What do you want me to do?" I ask after a second. After all, it's not like we've exactly got time for small talk right now.

My friends may be healed, may be climbing to their feet and walking over to stand beside me, but Mekhi is still dying at the Witch Court. I'm deathly afraid that he'll run out of time if we don't get this elixir to Lorelei to drink very, very soon.

"It's not what I need you to do. It's what I need you to give me." She wrinkles her nose as Flint moves closer to me. "Ugh, why must dragons always smell so bad? Reptiles are horrible."

Eden makes a sound low in her throat, like she would love to show the Crone just how horrible dragons can be.

I hold a hand up—letting the Crone's barbs get under our skins isn't going to help us in the long run—and Eden stands down. But her purple dragon eyes continue to track the Crone's every move.

"I don't have anything with me that you might want," I tell her. Even my backpack got left behind in Ecuador—one more casualty of the bear fight.

"I wouldn't be too sure about that if I were you." She holds her hand out, then continues in a strangely formal voice, "I invoke my favor."

The tattoo on my arm goes from burning hot to freezing cold as she continues, "You must give me the Celestial Dew that you collected from the lake at the base of the Bittersweet Tree."

My friends erupt immediately. "No way!" Jaxon growls, striding forward like he wants to rip the Crone limb from limb.

Another flick of her hand has him landing on his ass several feet away.

Macy moves in front of me, clenched fists at the ready. "You're not getting near her!"

"Please. As if I want to have anything to do with a filthy little statue," she snarls, and another flick of her hand has Macy backed up against the wall, unable to move.

"Just give me the elixir, Grace, and I'll be on my way."

"It's the only thing that will save Mekhi," I beseech her. But even as I say it, I know it won't matter. She's never been interested in anyone but herself, and the fate of some vampire she doesn't know and will never care about definitely isn't going to change that. Still, our bargain had rules. "Your favor cannot cause the death of anyone, directly or indirectly."

"And it won't. Shadow poison is killing your friend—directly. And Clio's refusal to help—indirectly," she answers coldly. And this time, when she holds her hand out, it's palm up. "Now give me the elixir."

I start to argue, but I can tell by her expression that she knows she's won. In that moment, I curse every god I've ever met and their goddamn penchant for loopholes.

I don't want to do it. I don't want to give this evil bitch the only thing that can save my friend's life. But the moment I think about resisting, my hand moves of its own volition. And the harder I try to stop it from sliding into my pocket, the more quickly it goes. Seconds later, the vial of Celestial Lake water is in her hand, and she's looking down at it with the cruelest smile imaginable on her face.

"I have to hand it to you, Grace," she comments as she uncorks the vial. "I knew what you were up to, and I didn't think you had a chance of succeeding. Of finally securing the one thing that was powerful enough to separate my soul from my sister's."

"Why didn't you go yourself?" I ask. "If you've known about the Bittersweet Tree this whole time, why did you wait on me to do it for you?"

The Crone's eyebrows shoot up. "I keep forgetting how little you know about anything." She shakes her head. "Gods are forbidden from occupying the same space as a Celestial being, of course."

My grandmother and I are going to have a *serious* discussion about my education in this world when I get out of prison. Again.

For now, I narrow my eyes on the Crone. "And you just couldn't wait to hunt me down after I finished your dirty work?"

She laughs. A full-throated, evil-as-fuck laugh. "Oh, dear, I had *planned* on hunting you down, of searching for you far and wide to get my hands on this vial"—she holds the uncorked vial up—"but you hand-delivered it to me in my *own* prison. That's quite a blunder for a supposed queen to make, don't you think?"

And then she drinks every drop in the vial. She closes her eyes as a light shimmers to life in her chest for a second, two, three more, then fades as quickly as it appeared.

She opens her eyes, and the blue irises swirl with power.

Her words hit my chest like an arrow, exacerbating every worry I've had about leading the Circle for days now. Weeks. Months. But then I remember that I didn't choose this place. Remy did, for a reason that the Crone will never understand. Because it's his home. And strange as it may sound, it's the only place he feels truly safe.

Having that kind of love—no, the Crone will never understand that. It's what makes her such a bad leader and such a bad person.

But I can. I do.

That's what brought me here to this moment. Not this prison but these people. I don't have all the answers and don't pretend that I do. But I'll keep looking until I find them, keep asking questions until I figure it out. And I'll never, never quit on any of the people I care about or any of the people under my protection.

I have to believe that's what will not only make me a good leader but help get me and my friends out of this mess, too. I just need to keep asking questions, keep assembling the knowledge and the talents of the people around me until I've got the answers I need.

Hudson walks over, stands shoulder to shoulder with me as the Crone continues to berate me. "You think you're so smart, but you're just a child running around, doing exactly what I wanted you to do. And you, vampire," she sneers at Hudson. "You think you're so powerful? You think you're any match for me?"

She turns then, including all of us in her next statement. "You think any of you are any match for me? Dragons, witches, vampires, gargoyles?" She says the last with the same disgust Flint saves for cockroaches. "I've spent thousands of years figuring out how to destroy each of you, and there's nothing you can do to stop me now that I'm free of my sister. Did you really think you could?"

She leans over, gets right in my face. And I'd be lying if I said I didn't think about taking a swing at her perfectly made-up, red-lipsticked mouth. "I will never let that happen."

"You don't have a choice," Hudson answers in a tone so cold I get goosebumps up and down my arms. "There's no way we're going to let you destroy *our* people because of *your* hate. Not now. Not ever."

The Crone laughs, and it's one of the evilest sounds I've ever heard—which is saying something, considering I've spent the greater part of the last year matching wits with Cyrus Vega.

"It's almost cute the way you think you have a choice," she answers before spinning around and walking straight out of the open cell door.

I turn to Hudson, start to tell him that we need to get to the Shadow Realm before the Shadow Queen realizes we've lost the elixir, but before I can say anything more than his name, the Crone waves a careless hand from outside the cell.

And every door in the place slams shut, the heavy sound of metal clinking against metal echoing through the entire prison.

"You're never getting out of here," she tells us. "And just to make sure you stay busy..." This time, she doesn't bother to wave her whole hand. She just gives a flick of her shell pink–tipped fingers, and then my friends fall to the ground screaming.

Macy whimpers, folding her hands over her head like she's trying to ward off blows, while Eden drops to her knees with a shriek and sobs like her entire world is ending.

Jaxon starts to yell.

Flint, on the other hand, goes deathly, scarily quiet.

And Hudson... My poor Hudson curls into a fetal ball, clutching his head in his hands.

At first, I don't know what's happening, but as I look at his posture and take in the sudden horror on his face, terror moves through me.

Because I know what this is.

In all the time I've known Hudson, I've only ever seen him look like this one other time in our lives together. And that was months ago, right here in this room, after we lost the nightly Russian roulette game and were forced to enter the Chamber.

Bad to the
Crone

I glance back at Heather and Remy—the only other people in the cell
who aren't locked in some hell of their own mind's making—and
realize that my worst fear is correct.

The three of us are the only ones in this cell who aren't exclusively
paranormal.

"No! No, no, no, no, no!" I repeat, fear replacing every other thought
in my head as I race toward the cell bars that now separate the Crone
from the rest of us. "You can't do this to them!" I yell, pounding on the
bars in an effort to get to her. "You can't send them to the Chamber
tonight! They didn't do anything! They aren't—"

"Tonight?" she interrupts with a cruel laugh. "There you go again,
Grace. Always thinking small. I'm not putting them in the Chamber
just tonight. I'm extending the Unbreakable Curse to cover the entire
prison. They'll be in the Chamber *forever*."

"No!" I shout again as Jaxon starts to plead with some monster in
his mind. "You can't do this to them. You can't leave them like this.
I'll do anything—"

"There's nothing I want from *you*," she hisses, her strange blue eyes
glowing with an unholy light as she takes a step away from the cell—and
from me. "I'd wish you good luck, Grace, but I think we both know
that your luck has finally run out."

And then she turns to go.

Panic slams through me as Macy starts to scream. No, no, no, no,
no! The word is a mantra in my head, a pounding in my blood. This
can't be happening to them. It just can't.

Fear swamps me, pulling me under until I can't breathe, can't think, can't even *be* without wanting to jump out of my skin. I scratch at my face, claw at my neck, pound on my chest in an effort to make the panic stop. But my heart is beating too hard, my breath is coming too fast, and my entire body feels like it's being dipped in acid.

I can't let this happen.

I can't let this happen.

I can't let this happen.

No, no, no, no, no!

But it is happening. It is, and there's nothing I can do to stop it. Nothing I can do to keep them from suffering over and over and over again. Eternally.

No. Please, please, please, no. Anything but this.

The panic grows. It clouds my brain, bottoms out my stomach, makes my heart feel like it's going to explode once and for all.

"Grace!" Heather's voice, loud and sharp, arrows through the haziness surrounding me. "Grace! Stop. We'll figure this out. It's going to be okay."

Her words don't help. Neither does the firm way she grabs my shoulders like she wants to shake the anxiety out of me. But she does break through the panic and the horror just enough that I can think for a second.

And it turns out that second is all I need. I force myself to breathe, force myself to count backward from twenty. Force myself to press my hand against the metal bars just so I can feel the cold against my skin.

I concentrate on its coolness and on the metallic taste of blood in my mouth from where I bit my lip and on the soothing sound of Remy's voice as he calls me *"cher."* And I breathe.

Inhale. One, two, three, four, five. Exhale.

Inhale. One, two, three, four, five, six, seven. Exhale.

It doesn't bring me back completely—fear is still a wild thing within me—but it calms me down enough that I can think. And, more, I can finally remember.

"Remy," I tell him in a voice as sharp and rusty as a bucket of old nails. "What is it you told me once, when you wanted me to get my tattoo?" I hold my arm up to display Vikram's tattoo, which Remy had insisted I get in prison the first time.

"I told you a lot of things," he answers, sounding wary.

"You did," I agree, trying to block out the sound of Eden gasping for air as I turn back to him. "But you also told me you didn't know who your father was, but your mom would tell you a bedtime story that he gave you enough power to *level* this prison. Do you remember that?"

"I do," he answers, both his tone and his gaze suddenly resolute.

I take one more deep breath and let it out slowly. "Well, then, I think today's a good day to make that bedtime story come to life, don't you?"

"Hell, yeah, I do, *cher*!" he answers, his New Orleans accent especially thick and syrupy.

"Okay, then." I turn back toward the cell doors, determined to do whatever I can to help him.

"Are you sure he can do this?" Heather whispers. "He doesn't look strong enough to—"

"He's plenty strong enough," I tell her firmly.

Remy walks over and lays a hand on the prison wall, right above his scratched drawing of Calder. He takes a deep breath, closing his eyes as he exhales, and…nothing happens.

Not a single thing.

Jaxon lets out a pained scream that makes us all shiver, and Remy grits his jaw, pressing his weight into the wall.

And still nothing happens.

Eden's sudden shriek skates along my spine, and I can tell Remy is having trouble focusing. And I get it. I do. He's probably too in his own head, too crushed by the weight of every single person screaming in agony on him to save them, if only he could get his shit together. I would be.

So I do the only thing I can think of. I call out to Remy, "You know what Calder would say right now, yeah? She'd tell you to forget about the people crying out—just ignore them. Everyone's got troubles, and they ain't yours to carry." When he glances over at me under his lashes, I add, "She'd tell you to just focus on getting her to the nail salon. They have a new design she's"—I toss my hair over my shoulder in a fair imitation of the manticore—"just dying to get. Now hurry up, will ya?"

He chuckles under his breath, then leans back and shakes his hand a couple of times, rolls his shoulders. He tosses me a wink and says, "Do you think they'll paint little T. rexes on mine?"

"Wearing pink tutus," I deadpan.

"Well, all right then," he drawls. "Consider me properly motivated."

And then he slams his palm against the thick metal wall and mutters to himself, "Fuck this place."

One second, two…and the walls of the prison start to tremble around us. The floor shakes as cell doors begin to rattle against their hinges. But that's all that happens. No walls come down. The ceiling doesn't cave in. The floor doesn't crumble beneath us.

She must not have gone far, because the Crone comes strolling back to our door and laughs, a dark, sarcastic sound. "Do you really think the God of Order's construction would be easy—"

"Well, let's add a little chaos then, shall we?" I interrupt, one eyebrow raised as I lay a hand on Remy's shoulder.

I dig deep, grabbing my platinum string, shifting immediately, and then I grab my green demigod string with every ounce of energy I have— and pour my chaos magic directly into Remy, the dark forest green of his magic meeting and melding with the bright emerald green of mine.

He jolts when it hits him, his whole body lighting up in all the various shades of green as he starts to meld my magic with his own formidable power. And then, when he's stored enough up, he lets it all go, exploding out of him in all directions.

This time, the floor shakes hard enough to make the Crone stumble. Watching that sarcastic half smile get knocked right off her bitch face might be one of the most satisfying moments of my life.

But I can tell Remy is having a problem controlling this much power, can see the way he's nearly shaking apart under the strain of utilizing every ounce of both our magics. His feels like the most brilliant star in the night sky, but mine…mine is pure chaos. Wild and hungry and impossible to contain, no matter how hard Remy struggles to bridle it.

Remy strains against the power raging in him, and my eyes go wide. "You can control it, Remy," I say. "There has to be a way to control it."

Still, I'm not ready to give up. There has to be a way. There has to be—

"I've got you," Heather tells me as, all of a sudden, she reaches out and puts a hand over mine, right where Remy's and my magic meet.

"I don't understand." But even as I say it, I see the magic pulsing out of her. Not green like ours or gold like the Crone's, but a bright, stalwart, shining red that's impossible to miss.

There's not a lot of it—but what there is is pure and powerful and so, so strong.

"Gods and paranormals aren't the only ones in this world with magic, you know," Heather says. "Humans make order out of chaos every day. We build skyscrapers. We create symphonies. We write poetry, carve art out of boulders, travel to the moon. We love each other so much and so well that we can save the world over and over and over again. Do you really think there isn't power in that?"

"There is," I answer, because I can see it. More, I can feel it spinning and winding around deep inside me. It's exactly what I need right now. More, it's exactly what Remy needs.

I feel Heather's power flowing into me, flowing into Remy, giving him just the tiniest edge he needs to contain mine, to build a channel to funnel all of that chaos into the heart of this fucking prison.

The Crone shrieks, her rage echoing through the empty corridor, bouncing off the metal walls and ceilings, wrapping itself around us as she realizes what's about to happen. She throws her arms out, her own bright-gold power blasting in all directions as she tries to stop what we're so desperate to bring to fruition.

But it's too little, too late.

A scream builds in Remy's throat as he pulls one final blast of Heather's power inside himself—and releases every single particle of magic in him with a primal scream that makes the hairs on my arm stand up. And then the world around us goes completely silent...

Except for the clink, clink, clink, of cell doors opening one after another.

104

Here Today,
Crone Tomorrow

As soon as the doors open, the entire prison starts to roll and shake, the strain of metal shrieking in the distance skating along my spine as I realize Remy is doing it—he's leveling this entire place—with us still inside.

"You won't rid yourself of me this easily," the Crone snarls. "My hunters and I will come for you." And then—like every god I freaking know—she disappears.

I whirl around to check on my friends and realize that they are, slowly, coming out of the nightmare they've been locked in since the Crone activated the Chamber.

"What's going on?" Hudson asks as he climbs to his feet. He looks pale but okay, and that's what matters. "Are you all right?"

"We're bringing down the prison," I answer.

His eyes go wide. "The entire prison?"

"You have a problem with that?" I raise my brows.

"Fuck no, I don't. Let's do it." He reaches down and pulls a still-shaky Jaxon to his feet.

"What the fuck was that?" Jaxon demands, wiping a trembling hand down his face.

"The nightmare your brother and I had to live through for days the last time we were here," Flint answers as he helps Eden stand.

Jaxon swears again, reaching out a hand to brace himself on the nearest wall, but Hudson herds us toward the door. "We need to get out of here, now."

"Can you portal us out?" I ask Remy as a part of our cell's ceiling caves in.

He shakes his head, finally pulling a shaky palm from the prison.

"I'm too weak."

"I've got us," Macy says, though she's looking pretty scared herself.

"What about everybody else?" I ask, as more and more people go running down the corridor past our cell. "They won't all get out before the prison caves in."

"Jaxon and I will take care of it," Hudson answers. "But we need to go now."

"Already ahead of you," Macy calls over her shoulder as she spins open a portal.

"You okay, Remy?" Hudson asks the wizard, who's looking a little lost as he gazes around the cell that was his home for so long.

"Yeah," Remy answers. "Let's get out of here so we can make sure everyone else gets out, too. They've been prisoners of a broken system for far too long."

Hudson nods, then walks over to the edge of the wall where Remy had carved his little baby manticore into the metal so many years ago. And then, using his vampire strength, he rips the tiny picture from the wall and hands it to Remy.

"Let's go!" Jaxon shouts as another part of the ceiling crashes down.

We dive for the portal, and we end up tumbling onto the ground in the cemetery we'd escaped into our first time leaving this hellhole.

I scramble to my feet, checking to see if anyone besides us has made it out. But there's no one around. "Hudson—"

"On it," he says grimly as he springs to his feet.

Jaxon joins him, and seconds later the already shaking ground cracks wide open. At the same time, a whole section of earth explodes outward and disappears. Moments later, hundreds of paranormals start pouring out of the ground, flooding the cemetery as the prison begins to fold in on itself.

Remy stumbles, starts to sag, and I race to catch him. "Are you all right?" I ask. "Can you manage to portal back to school?"

He shakes his head. "I can't. My magic's gone."

"Gone?" Dismay pours through me. "What do you mean *gone*?"

I hold my breath, terrified that I already know the answer.

"I burned it out." He shrugs, but there's a sadness in his eyes that's impossible to miss.

My heart clenches. I did this. I asked him to do the impossible, and somehow he did. But I didn't know that meant he'd pay such a horrible price.

"It's okay, *cher*," he says, wrapping me up in a hug. "It was worth it. We freed all these people who had their lives stolen from them. What more could I ask for?"

"Your magic back?" I ask, hugging him as tightly as I can.

"It'll come back, eventually." He shoves the metal etching of the manticore in his backpack, then slings the pack over his shoulder. "It always does."

"You've burned it out like this before?" It took bringing down a prison built by an actual god to burn it out this time. What on earth has he done in the past?

"No," he concedes. "But I'm trying to be optimistic."

"Yeah, but what if it doesn't come back?" I choke out.

"Well, then, at least I lost my magic doing something important," he answers. But he's swaying on his feet now, and I can tell exhaustion is setting in.

Macy stands next to him, propping his arm over her shoulders for support. And then we all take a minute to recover from all the shit that just went down. A part of me can't believe we brought down the prison, but another part of me has never been happier about anything in my life. The Crone went out of her way to make this place a living hell for the political prisoners she kept here, and the fact that she'll no longer be able to have anyone sentenced makes me happier than I can say.

But Remy losing his powers? The Crone still on the loose? The elixir we meant to use to make a deal for Mekhi's life gone forever? My head is spinning with all the awful things that still have to be sorted out.

But the longer we stand here, the more exhaustion sets in. Any energy I did have, I expended helping Remy bring this place down.

I compromise by bending over and bracing my hands on my knees. But as I do, something presses into my thigh, reminding me I have something valuable in my pocket. I don't know how valuable, but maybe it's enough to trade for Mekhi's life.

The vial of Celestial honey.

105

Powered Down
but Never Out

Gripping the vial in my hand, I turn to Macy. "Can you get us to the Witch Court? And then take Remy back to school before Remy's three hours are up?"

Remy chuckles but there's little humor in it. "They're already up, *cher*." He turns to Macy and says, "But I *would* appreciate the ride."

She nods. "I'll get you home."

"That place isn't home." He looks out over the collapsed remnants of the Aethereum. "This is home. Or, I guess I should say it *was* home."

"You'll find another," I whisper as I squeeze his hand. "Thank you, Remy, for everything you've done for me. Everything you've sacrificed for all of us."

"Careful, Grace. You'll have me blushing soon."

I roll my eyes, because once a charmer, always a charmer. Power or no power, Remy's never going to change.

"Everybody ready?" Macy asks as she starts spinning a portal open.

"As we'll ever be," Heather answers with an exhausted sigh.

Eden rests a hand on her back. "We're almost done. Just a couple more stops."

"I know. We've got this." She even manages to punch a fist in the air for emphasis. It's a sad fist, lacking her earlier enthusiasm, but it's a call to arms nonetheless.

"I think you mean we *had* this," Flint says and has everyone laughing.

"Everyone's got to start somewhere," Jaxon answers, his gaze holding Flint's until Flint reaches over and slides his hand in Jaxon's, pulls him close. Whatever nightmare Jaxon experienced in the Chamber seems to have really shaken him up, if the way he pulls Flint to him, lays his forehead on the dragon's chest, is any indication. It's very rare to see Jaxon allowing himself to seem vulnerable, and I duck my eyes to give them some privacy.

"And here I thought we were ending," Hudson murmurs in my ear, and I don't know if he's referring to the prison or his brother's relationship. He rubs a hand down the center of my back, and in that touch I feel everything that's going on inside him.

Relief that, against the odds, we've made it this far.

Fear of what's going to happen to me when we get to the Shadow Realm and the Shadow Queen realizes I wasn't able to keep my side of our magical bargain.

And most of all, love. So much love for me that a part of me wants nothing more than to sink into him and just breathe for a while. Just be.

But the clock is ticking, and we're in the final countdown. Mekhi is dying, and I've lost the only chance we had at a cure. The Crone and her hunters are preparing to attack. And the Shadow Queen is just as likely to kill us all when we tell her we failed to save her children.

There truly is no more time.

And so I step into Macy's portal and let her whisk me straight back to the Witch Court.

106

Take a Jump on
the Wild Side

Macy's built her portal to come out right in the middle of Mekhi's room in Lorelei's tower, which I discover when I stumble out of it and nearly crash into the bed of a sleeping Mekhi.

Lorelei is sitting next to his bed, and she springs up when she sees me. "You came back!" she cries, right before Hudson comes strolling out of the portal, followed by everyone else.

"Of course we did," I say but don't meet her eyes.

"Did you get the elixir?" There's so much faith and hope in her voice that my stomach churns.

I shake my head, and my stomach twists even more. "It's a long story."

"Oh no." Her voice trembles as she looks at Mekhi. "How are we going to save him?"

"Throw ourselves on your mother's mercy and hope for the best," I tell her at the same time I propose my plan to the rest of the gang.

I watch as her shoulders sag. She lets out a sigh. "I don't know my mother very well, obviously, but from what I hear, she doesn't have a lot of mercy in her anymore."

"Yeah, that's kind of what we figured." I blow out a long breath. "But it's not like we have any better options. That's pretty much all we've got."

"I wish I could come with you," she whispers as Macy closes the portal behind her and Remy. "If I could, I could at least try to talk to her."

I don't tell her that I don't think there will be a lot of talking going on—that I'm pretty sure the time for all that is long past, especially in the Shadow Queen's mind. She's as likely to snap my neck with a shadow rope as she is to even hear out my proposal to trade the honey for Mekhi's life.

To be honest, the trade feels incredibly one-sided—even I can admit that—but if I've learned anything in this strange new world, it's that everything that can be bargained with can bring value. Surely there's something the queen wants that the honey can fetch her, even if it's not the one thing she wants most. I'm just not sure that value will be enough to save Mekhi—or the messengers.

I glance at my friends, the same friends whom I watched dying in a meadow less than an hour ago, and realize this isn't a trip we all need to make. "My friends here will help you find a way to make a better life for yourself, Lorelei." I take a deep breath, bracing for the storm about to unleash on me. "Hudson and I can take Mekhi to your mother."

"Bite me," snarls Jaxon.

Followed by Flint's equally succinct "fuck that."

Eden, Heather, Macy, and Remy have a lot more to say—all of it at the same time—and I can't help it. Tears well in my eyes, threatening to spill over, as I stare at all of my friends. My found family.

Despite everything, I really couldn't be luckier.

Eden fist-bumps Heather. "All for one..."

"Damn straight," Heather says, turning to fist-bump Macy, too.

"Now that that's settled—do you think he will be okay to make the trip?" Hudson asks as Mekhi starts to wake up—which is a good sign. He's not dead *yet*. There is still hope, however thin it is.

"I think he's got to be," I say at the same time Lorelei nods.

"He's very, very weak, but there's still a little time. I hope." As if on cue, Mekhi groans before settling back down into sleep. "Though, if my mother refuses to heal him, I'm not sure he'll be making a return trip."

Her voice breaks a little on the last word, and for the first time I start to wonder if there's something more going on between her and Mekhi than just plain friendship. I'd noticed back in the Curator's office that she'd never left Mekhi's side on the little TV screen.

"Remy and I need to get going," Macy says. "So if you want me to open the portal at the fountain for you, it needs to be now."

"Of course. We'll be ready in just a second." I turn to Lorelei. "We need to take Mekhi with us."

She sighs for what seems like forever but eventually nods, then leans down to lay her hand on his chest. "Mekhi," she croons softly. "Can you wake up, Mekhi?"

When he hears her voice, his eyes flutter open. A half smile lifts one corner of his lips, his voice weak and hoarse but full of affection. "Hey, Lori."

Hudson and I exchange a look but say nothing.

"Hey, you," I tell him after giving them a few seconds of privacy—or as much privacy as I can manage in a room crowded with people. "You ready to go fix this poison problem once and for all?"

He starts to laugh, but it turns to a cough pretty quickly—one that has him loudly sucking air into his lungs.

Lorelei bites her lip in an attempt to stifle a cry.

"I'm okay," he tells her, but even he sounds like he knows it's a lie.

"You will be very soon," Jaxon says with a smile that doesn't reach his eyes. "Can I help you up?"

Mekhi nods. "Thanks, man." He looks at the rest of us, his dark eyes clear for the first time in what feels like ages. "Thank you all. For everything—"

"Let's wait and make sure the plan works," Eden tells him in a deliberately light voice. "Don't waste your gratitude if we end up screwing everything up."

He laughs again, though it's a short-lived sound as the pain takes over, making him wheeze and cough.

"Come on. Let's get going." Hudson steps forward to help Jaxon get Mekhi up and steadied. Not that Jaxon couldn't do it on his own, but I think my mate needs to do something to keep from feeling so helpless right now.

I recognize it because I'm feeling exactly the same way.

Mekhi says goodbye to Lorelei—who, after everything we've done so far, still can't cross the barrier—while the rest of us pretend to be anywhere but in the room with them, and then we head out.

It takes a little bit of effort—mostly on Jaxon's and Hudson's part—but we get Mekhi through the Witch Court and out to the Piazza Castello in pretty quick order.

"You feel up to this?" Macy asks as we cross the street to the statue in the middle of the piazza.

"Not even close," Mekhi answers honestly. "But let's do it anyway."

She smiles. "You're my kind of guy."

While everyone else stops on the grass surrounding the fountain, Macy steps forward. I walk with her and say, "I'm worried about getting Mekhi through the Shadow Realm. Even if he makes it through the portal all right, he can't afford to wander around with us trying to find the damn Shadow Fortress."

Even as I say it, I'm pissed off at myself. Why didn't I think of this when we were at the Shadow Court? How did I expect to be able to find the queen and her fortress again?

Then again, maybe she'll be keeping an eye out for us this time. She does have everything on the line.

"Not to worry," Macy answers quietly. "I spelled a portal seed directly to the shadow bitch's fortress while she was distracted by making the bargain with you."

"You *did*?" Relief has tears springing to my eyes, and I hug her really hard.

Macy tolerates the hug better than the last time we were at the Witch Court, and it takes every ounce of willpower I have not to hug her even harder for it. But I push back and glance down at the tattoo of a purple tree that has gone from feeling like an uncomfortable prick on my skin to actual burning in the last several hours.

"So one quick hop through this portal"—Macy tosses her portal seed into the swirling fountain, then turns to the group—"and automatically through the next, and you'll drop directly outside the queen's fortress."

"Thank you," I say, giving her one last hug. "I love you. I'll see you soon."

"Geez, so much hugging," she moans, but she's smiling when she says, "I love you, too. Good luck."

"I wouldn't miss this party for all the money in the world," Flint says as he walks up to the fountain portal. "But there better not be any fucking shadow bees."

"Too soon, dude," Jaxon says. "Way too fucking soon."

True. Damn. Story. A collective shudder works through us, but we shake it off as best we can. And then we all jump in.

Getting Sticky
with It

Once we're through the portal, I look around and realize Macy has done it. While I've never seen the outside of the Shadow Fortress—the Shadow Queen was too cautious for that when we were here last time—it's hard to imagine that the craggy, intimidating, giant purple building in front of us isn't exactly what we're looking for.

"Well, that's not a nightmare you see every day," Flint comments as he scrambles to help Jaxon put Mekhi back on his feet after fireman-carrying him through the portal.

"Because anything on this part of the trip is?" Heather retorts, and I know she's thinking about all the difficult things we've done to get to this point.

I certainly am.

Just one more, I tell myself as I grab my platinum string and shift into my gargoyle form before starting toward the fortress. If things are going to go badly in there, I at least want the protection my gargoyle offers me and my friends.

As we get closer to the fortress, it's hard to miss the fact that every square foot in the front has its own designated Shadow Guard to protect it. I don't know if it's just a show of strength or if the threats have gotten so bad that she needs this many people to keep her safe in her own home, but either way, I feel sorry for her.

No one should have to feel that afraid in their own home—for themselves or their child.

I brace myself for the worst—a trip to the dungeon if we're not able to talk our way around the guards. But they must have standing orders to look for us, because the second we approach the fortress, the purple iron gates swing wide open.

And the Shadow Queen herself walks out to meet us.

She scans our faces, looking for...I'm not sure what. Her daughter, maybe, even though she knows better than us that it's impossible for Lorelei to cross between realms. But I suppose a mother's hope springs eternal.

"You came back." Her voice is hoarser than it was before, the eyes that meet mine darker and more shadowed. I guess the last few days have been as rough on her as they've been on us.

I don't want to feel sorry for her. She's the one who—long, long ago—started all the mess that got us here. If she hadn't tried to alter the laws of the natural world, of life and death, none of this would have happened. But she did, and now we're all paying the price.

And still, even knowing that, I can't help but feel for her pain a little bit. Especially since, as she walks toward us, I can suddenly see every one of the thousand-plus years she's been alive weighing on her with every step.

"Lorelei?" she asks when she finally stops in front of us. Her eyes are on Mekhi, and I'm wondering if she's observing his condition or if she's asking him how her daughter is, as he's the one who has spent the most time with her lately.

He stiffens when she gets close to him, but he doesn't back up. Instead, he meets her eyes and says, "She's okay."

Her gaze lingers on him for a second before sliding over to me. "I have refreshments waiting. Follow me."

She turns without another word and starts walking up the jagged, diagonal path that leads inside her fortress. It's slow going for her today—every step torturous, unlike her normal, smooth glide—and I can't help feeling as if she already knows that I failed. Knows that she'll never see her other daughter again.

"Please, help yourself," she says several minutes later when she leads us into her throne room. There's a table set up against the wall loaded with so many of the delicate fruits and pastries the Shadow Realm specializes in. Everything looks delicious, and still none of us even thinks of making a move toward it.

She smiles thinly as she notes our reticence. "Am I to take your reluctance as a sign that this isn't to be a celebration?"

"I'm sorry," I answer, biting my lip.

"You're sorry?" she repeats. "That's all you have to say for yourself? That you're sorry?"

She flicks a hand, and the beautiful china and glassware and food go flying in every direction, slamming against the wall and falling into pieces at our feet.

"You came here. You proposed a deal to me. You told me you could free my daughters. And now you have the nerve to come back here and tell me that you're sorry? Your apology means nothing to me," she snarls. "Less than nothing."

The shadows at the corners of the room start to respond to the agitation in her voice, writhing and spinning as they spread out along the ground.

"I understand—" I start, but she cuts me off with a slice of her hand.

"You understand nothing."

The shadows seethe and roil around us. And though they stay shadows and don't take the form of any of her normal creatures, that doesn't make them any less intimidating. It might even make them more so. I've had a lot of experience fighting shadow beasts, but I don't have a clue what to do with these disembodied things slowly slithering their way along the edges of the walls.

So I do the only thing I can do at the moment. I ignore them and focus on the Shadow Queen. If nothing else, I know my friends have my back.

"I'm sorry," I tell her, holding out a beseeching hand. "We did everything we could, but it wasn't enough."

She slaps my hand away, and the moment our palms come in contact, the tattoo on my wrist starts to burn like hell itself. "Do you think good intentions matter?" she screeches, and her voice bounces off the purple marble floor and glass-covered walls, echoing in the room and skating down my spine like the edge of a particularly sharp ice pick. "Do you think you can just get out of the deal we made? Because life doesn't work like that, little girl."

She lifts her hand, presses three fingers against her own magical bargain tattoo. And I don't know how it's possible, but the second she does, my tattoo starts to burn even worse.

I glance down at it—because I can't *not* look at it right now—and I half expect to see that it has branded straight through to my bone. But no. It's still just sitting here on my skin, sizzling like I've just poured acid all over it but not actually sinking any deeper.

"We had what you needed," I explain. "But it was taken from us. However, I brought something else of value. Maybe you can trade it with someone else for what you need to save your daughters?"

I start to reach in my pocket for the vial of Celestial honey, but her gaze narrows on mine. She flings her arms wide. "What bargain would you have me make from this prison?"

"We could help," I suggest, hope filling my chest just the tiniest bit. "If you can cure Mekhi, I have something just as valuable, which you could use to trade for the Celestial Dew."

"You. Have. Nothing. I. Want." The queen bites out each word. "And your bargains are worthless."

My eyes widen. "But—"

"No. You didn't complete your side of our bargain. But you brought him to me anyway. Did you really expect me to hold up my end of the deal even though you did not honor yours?" She sneers. "You think this boy matters to me? He may be wearing my daughter's talisman, but I will *never* care if he lives or dies."

"Talisman?" Confused, I turn to look more closely at Mekhi, who is currently leaning against Jaxon and Hudson like they're the only things keeping him from slumping to the ground. The fact that they probably are makes my heart ache for Mekhi and makes me even more determined to somehow find a way to reach this woman who knows more secrets of the universe than anyone should.

"What talisman?" I ask.

Another flick of her fingers, and Mekhi cries out, his knees going out from under him.

108

The Shadows
We Keep

The second Mekhi gasps, Hudson and Jaxon tighten their grip on him and catch him before he hits the ground.

The queen whirls away from us with a condescending laugh, and another flick of her fingers has the chain around Mekhi's neck snapping off and hitting the ground at Hudson's feet.

He reaches for it, but a shadow snatches it away before he can touch it and spirits it across the room to the Shadow Queen.

The shadow drops it at her feet, and for several moments she stares at the small gold necklace as if it's a shadow creature she's terrified will poison *her*. Eventually, though, she bends down to retrieve it, and the second her fingers close around the small pendant, her entire face—her entire being—crumbles.

She simply caves in on herself, shoulders slumping, body curving forward, head dropping to her hands as shudders rack her body.

My stomach roils at the sight of her agony, so raw and undiluted. If she was anyone else, I would go to her and try to do…something. Anything to take away the pain that has overtaken her entire aura.

But she isn't someone else. She's the Shadow Queen, and she holds Mekhi's fate in her hands. Because if she chooses not to help him…if she chooses not to help him, I'm completely out of moves.

"I gave this to Lorelei when she was five years old," she whispers into the cavernous silence of the room. "I told her to wear it always, to never take it off, so that she could be protected forever. She was wearing it the day this cursed place came into being, and I've—" Her voice breaks. "I've imagined her wearing it ever since. My magic, my love, keeping watch over her for a thousand years when I could not."

Her eyes narrow, turning a violent, vicious violet as she creeps closer to Mekhi. "How dare you take this from her?"

"I didn't," Mekhi chokes out, face livid with pain. "Lorelei gave it to me before I came here—"

"She would never," she snarls, then breaks off with an outraged cry, rounding on me. "Not unless you've convinced her that her mother doesn't love her anymore!"

"No!" I shout, holding a hand in front of me. "I would *never*."

But the queen is too enraged to believe me, and with a sweep of her hand, she sends the chandelier above us crashing to the ground. Glittering shards of purple glass shatter across the floor and the throne, but fortunately no one is hurt.

"Fate wouldn't be so cruel, to take my daughter from me twice."

"Maybe fate isn't trying to be cruel," I suggest, seeing my opportunity and seizing it because I don't think there will be a better time.

"Don't say it," she hisses at me.

Old Grace would have heeded that warning. She would have turned tail and run. But I haven't come this far, I haven't risked my friends' and my mate's lives, to lose Mekhi in the end anyway.

"Maybe your daughter was showing someone mercy for something her mother did," I say, disregarding her warning. "Maybe if you show—"

"I have no mercy in me," she interrupts. "Not anymore. Not since that woman sentenced me here. She built this prison, took my child from me, imprisoned my people for a thousand years. And for what? Because of one mistake?

"I am a mother, too. Am I not allowed to love my children beyond all reason, too? But did anyone care about me? Did anyone try to end my suffering? My children's suffering? Instead of offering mercy or help, I was sentenced to this prison made of vengeance and tears and pain. And my people, my innocent and blameless people, were sentenced right along with me. The walls going down and separating me from one of my children *forever*." Her voice cracks, tears streaming down her cheeks. "So why should I show any mercy? Why should I forgive a thousand years of suffering when she *never* has?"

Her pain is palpable, the rage and vindictiveness of earlier falling away in the face of her overwhelming sorrow. As she stands here in this room filled with shards of broken glass and memories unrealized, I no longer see the villain. The woman whose machinations brought about my own people's poisoning and imprisonment and everything that came after—everything that brought me here.

Instead, I see a woman who, in some ways, is as much a victim as the rest of us.

Did she make a bad choice? Yes. She made several bad choices.

Did she intend for things to go as wrong as they have? For the first time, I can't help but wonder if the answer to that question is *no*.

Maybe there is more to this story than I know. More than Jikan's interminable tale could tell us. And if that's the case, maybe there is still a way to reach her, a chance to save Mekhi. And, maybe, to help her, though I don't know how I could.

"I'm sorry," I tell her, and I mean it.

Her eyes flash to mine. "What did you say?"

"I said I'm sorry. I'm sorry that the Crone lied to you. I'm sorry that she tricked you. I'm sorry that Jikan—"

"The Crone?" She looks incredulous. "You think I'm here because of the *Crone*? You're right. She lied to me, but she didn't destroy my life. No, you foolish, foolish child. I am here because the Bloodletter put me here."

109

The Power
of Grace

"The Bloodletter?" I repeat even as denial races through me instinctively. "My grandmother would never—"

"Your *grandmother*?" Her eyes lock onto mine. "Your grandmother is the Bloodletter?"

"My grandmother didn't build this place. Jikan, the Historian, did. He wanted to—"

"Jikan? Is that what she told you?" She laughs, a cold and callous sound that bounces off the marble and sends shivers of fear racing down my spine.

"*She* didn't tell me anything. Jikan did." Did he lie to me? Although, thinking back to Jikan's exact words... He said the prison was a mistake, but I can't remember him actually saying he built it. "Why would he let me think he built it?"

"Because he's in love with her," Hudson says, and I swing my gaze to his.

There's a part of me that wants to disagree, to argue it's impossible. I mean, surely I would have sensed something.

Except...except maybe I did. I can't help but think back to the conversation before we played chess, about how she would outlive my grandfather one day—but not Jikan.

And fuck it. Just fuck it. Every time I start to think I know what's going on in this world, someone else—someone who's been here for a thousand years or more—comes along and drops a bombshell that yanks my feet right out from under me. And this is one hell of a bombshell.

Jikan? And my great-great-great-and-so-on grandma? Seriously?

The thought is mind-boggling...

As is the thought of the Bloodletter creating the Shadow Realm.

"Why?" The question bursts out of me as I move pieces around in my brain, trying to figure out what's happening here. Or, I should say, what happened a long time ago. "Why would she do such a thing?"

"Because her sister is a jealous hag. She tricked me into giving her the shadow poison to save my children."

"Tricked you?" Hudson lifts a brow.

She waves a hand and drops another chandelier next to him—which pisses me off but doesn't make him so much as blink.

"I didn't know what she was going to do with it," the Shadow Queen insists. "I didn't know she was going to use it to poison an entire race of people. All I wanted was to be with my children forever."

"Even if it meant taking someone else's child away?" I murmur. Because I'm slowly starting to understand what happened.

She made a deal with the Crone—one that resulted in her turning over shadow poison so that the Crone could make a deal with Cyrus to poison the Gargoyle Army in exchange for giving him her and the Bloodletters' children to turn himself into a god. But the Bloodletter didn't react the way the Crone could have ever foreseen—because the Bloodletter loved her child, and the Crone wouldn't know love if it bit her in her ass.

"The Bloodletter was forced to hide her child's power from Cyrus—her child who would have been immortal but was now a mortal human—and send her away so Cyrus could never find her—but nor could she," I whisper to no one in particular. The words twist in my stomach like knives, and my tear-filled gaze meets the queen's. "Her child died never knowing how much her mother loved her, how much she sacrificed for her."

I shake my head at the hopelessness of it all. "And then my grandmother—a mother enraged at the loss of her child, a wife enraged at the loss of her mate, a queen enraged at the loss of her people—went looking for revenge."

It was the Shadow Queen's—and the world's—bad luck that she was also a god with all the power and none of the caution needed to temper her quest for vengeance with mercy.

"I never meant for Ryann to die," the Shadow Queen says, and I gasp at the first mention of my great-something-grandmother's name.

"Ryann." I test the name on my tongue, a tear tumbling down my cheek. "Such a beautiful name."

The Shadow Queen's chin lifts. "I'm not a monster. I was devastated at the very idea of losing my own children. The last thing I would ever want is to take someone else's child from them."

"But you did," I say, holding her gaze until she looks away. She took my grandmother's child, and in doing so she cemented this vicious circle of death and retribution, sorrow and cruelty.

I swipe at the moisture on my cheeks and close my eyes, take a deep breath in an effort to process everything I've learned in the last few minutes. And when I exhale and open my eyes, I don't see a woman hell-bent on destruction and death.

Instead, I see a mother destroyed by the desperate quest to save her child's life, a woman subsequently destroyed by the loss of that child due to her own actions. And while I'm not a mother myself, and while there is nothing the Shadow Queen can do to make up for the pain she caused my family—and my people—I have to wonder if she's suffered enough. I have to wonder when all of the fights and the wars and the deaths and the prisons and the vengeance and the destruction and the pain, so much pain every step of the way, are enough.

No one can argue that what the Shadow Queen did wasn't wrong. Was it justified in her own mind? Yes. Does that make it right? Absolutely not.

But what my grandmother did was wrong, too. Did she also justify it because of her own unending grief? Yes. Does *that* make it right? Not even a little.

Wrong is wrong, and two wrongs never make a right. I learned that before I left kindergarten.

But as I stand here in this room, in this realm built of sorrow and rage, the issue of who is at fault is not the question that comes to my mind. Not today, and I hope not ever again. Because the real question, the important question, isn't who's to blame for this mess.

The question is, how can we ever make it right again?

People died. Hearts were broken. Wars were won and lost. And none of that can be diminished. None of that can be forgotten. The past is what it is.

It can't be changed, but it can be understood.

It can't be forgotten, but it can be accepted.

And maybe, just maybe, if we're very, very careful, it can be mended.

I look at my strong—and broken—mate.

At Eden, who lost her family, and Jaxon, who literally lost his heart.

At Flint, who lost his brother, his leg, and now, maybe his throne.

And at Mekhi, who may still very well lose his life.

Any of us could have chosen to give in to anger. Hell, Hudson could have started disintegrating the world. But he didn't. My beautiful mate always, always chose a path of mercy whenever he could.

If someone literally locked in the dark against his will for nearly two hundred years can still choose the light, then there is always hope. Always mercy. Always room for forgiveness.

And that's exactly what we need right now.

Because if we don't start learning from our parents' mistakes, our grandparents' mistakes, then we are destined to repeat every single one of them.

But I have to believe we won't. It's why we're still here. Why we came against all common sense to beg for Mekhi's life.

And it's why, even if we can't convince the Shadow Queen to do the right thing, it won't stop *us* from doing the right thing.

Because at some point, someone has to just roll up their damn sleeves and decide to fix this shit. Starting now.

No Woman
Is a Fortress

"**G**race?" Hudson steps forward and lays a hand on my lower back. "What can I do?"

I love that he knows me well enough to tell that I'm planning something. I love even more that he's the first one to step up and offer to help.

I turn to look up at him, and for a second I get lost in those oceanic eyes of his. So blue, so brilliant, so *kind* when the world has been anything but to him. And I know that whatever is going on between us, whatever secret he is keeping from me, it doesn't really matter. Because this is my Hudson, my forever, and I'm never going to give him up. Thank God I have an eternity to love him.

Though I'm not sure exactly what I'm going to do yet—or if what I'm *thinking* about doing is even going to work—I just smile and say, "Hang on to your fangs."

And then I look around at this room—this fortress—built of rage and fear and grief, and I decide enough is fucking enough. The Bloodletter built this prison with chaos magic, and maybe, just maybe, that means I can tear it down. I just have to figure out how.

Taking a deep breath, I close my eyes and dive deep inside myself. As I do, I see all of the strings inside me. Green and black and pink and red and platinum and blue. Always blue, right there, just waiting for me. I take one second to brush my hand against it, then smile as I feel Hudson brush right back.

And then I move on to my bright-green string—the one that burns as hot and strong as our mating bond. My demigod string, connecting me to all the power inside me. I haven't tried it in the Shadow Realm before—but now I feel it pulsing, rising to my chaotic intention. I wrap my hand around it and hold on as tightly as I can as I feel the magic begin to stir.

But unlike in the prison, I don't just let it roam free, unchecked, unbound. This time, I control it.

I feel it in my fingertips, feel the power and the beauty of everything that's inside me start to sprout.

Tiny branches running through my fingers and down my arms, my legs.

Vines curling and winding around them.

Leaves and flowers scraping against my skin as they blossom and bloom a little more with each second that passes.

Beneath my feet, I can feel the earth moving, spinning, pulsing with life, and I connect with it. Tap into it. Pull its strength—its magic— inside me and let it sink into my every pore. My every cell. Filling me up, taking me over. Bursting along my heart, my mind, my soul.

As it happens, I take a deep breath. Extend my hands out to my sides. And let just a little of the magic and the chaos inside me go.

The second I do, the ground shimmies beneath my feet. The marble walls and floor start to crack, and the glass decorating the walls of the throne room shatters all at once. Plants begin creeping in through the fissures in the floor and the walls, lush, luxurious, *green*.

And gold lightning booms across the purple sky.

"Umm, anyone else aware that the big one is hitting right now?" Heather asks, voice thin and high-pitched. "Shouldn't we be running for a doorway?"

"This isn't the big one," Eden answers. "It's Grace."

"I don't even know what that means." My bestie sounds shook.

"Just wait," Flint says, and I can hear the smile in his voice. "You'll figure it out."

He's right—she will. Because the power is growing inside me, bigger, stronger, more overwhelming than it's ever been, and I know it's only a matter of time before I'll stop being able to contain it.

I don't know if that's a good thing or a bad one, and right now—as I'm filled to the brim with the warmth of the sun and the soil and the streams that make up the world around me—I don't actually care. How can I, when the magic of the earth is spinning inside me?

I loosen my hold on the string a little more, and the ground around us goes from shimmying to rolling, from cracking to breaking wide open. I guess Jaxon isn't the only one who knows how to make the earth move. At least not anymore.

But even as the ground beneath the fortress buckles and brays, even as the vines wrap themselves around the throne and the columns and even the very studs of the walls, I know it isn't going to be enough. Because I'm going to bring down a lot more than this fortress before I'm through.

"Holy. Shit." Heather's voice echoes above the ruins. But I don't have time to explain right now. Not when I have so much more to do.

I yank my arms back, send the vines crashing through marble and walls, bringing the entire fortress down around our heads. When the ceiling starts to cave in, I yell to the others to go outside.

"Not without you," Hudson growls, and I can tell from the tone that it's nonnegotiable. But that's okay. There's no more for me to do in here, anyway.

I step over one of the crumbled walls and out into a garden. And the moment I do, the magic inside me leaps like it's just been given an infusion.

My friends, Jaxon carrying Mekhi, and the Shadow Queen flood out into the garden behind me. Once I know they're safe, I turn around and throw every ounce of power I have into bringing the entire fortress down.

Vines and branches erupt from the ground around us, slamming into the building, knocking it down one wall, one story at a time. And still I dig deeper, still I try to find more magic inside me. Bringing down a fortress is one thing. Bringing down an entire realm is another.

I know I can do it. I have to do it. I just have to figure out how Jikan is stabilizing my grandmother's magic enough to hold Noromar together. Because once I know that, I'll know how to take the whole damn thing apart.

I close my eyes again, send every ounce of my earth magic into the world around me to try to figure out how he's doing it. Branches explode from my fingertips, burrowing into the dirt in all directions. Vines and flowers flow from my hair, spreading down to the ground and then out, over the purple dirt, covering the world in all directions with chaos magic. With earth magic.

With *my* magic.

And that's when I remember. The Bloodletter uses chaos magic, but Jikan uses time magic. He has to be using his time magic to stabilize this entire realm.

So to take it down, I just have to figure out how to blow time itself apart.

111

I've Got the (Time)
Magic in Me

The time dragons make a lot more sense now. No wonder Jikan couldn't afford any tears in time—one too many might break this place apart and kill everyone inside it.

And while I do want to shatter the Shadow Realm to pieces, the last thing I want to do is hurt anyone. So whatever I do to destabilize it, however I choose to take on Jikan's magic, I know that I'm going to have to be very, very careful.

How does chaos beat time? How does earth magic trump the flow of the universe?

It doesn't, I realize, even as I smash the walls surrounding the Shadow Queen's fortress to rubble and let my magic—my vines and flowers and branches—pour out into the world. Or at least, it doesn't all by itself. It needs help. But what kind of help is the question...

All of a sudden, my chest starts to burn. It's a strange pain—a fiery, searing sensation that has me gasping for breath.

"Are you okay?" Hudson asks, voice thick with concern.

I nod even though I'm not so sure. The heat is getting worse until it feels like my heart and lungs are actually on fire.

I lift a hand to my chest, start to rub the spot that hurts the most. And that's when it hits me. The part that's hurting, the burning in my chest...it's the answer to my question.

Hudson told me he thought the reason I forgot everything about my time in the Shadow Realm was because I was hit with the arrow of time. It yanked me out of the timeline and sent me back to Katmere and, more importantly, to our world—where I've been ever since.

I haven't given the arrow much thought since Hudson shared his theory—I guess I figured it just dissolved or something when I made it back to my realm. But now, with this sudden kindling in my chest, I'm beginning to think that it's been lying dormant inside me all this time.

More, I think it just woke up.

It's as if it knew I would need it—and *when*.

It sounds foolish to even think such a thing, but the more I sort things through, the hotter the arrow burns.

As the world shakes and shatters around me, I keep my focus on the problem. When I was first learning to use magic, Jaxon took me to see the Bloodletter. She taught me—unsuccessfully, thank God—how to wall up Hudson in a corner of my mind. But when she was teaching me, her focus wasn't on the wall. It was on using magic with intention.

As long as I use it with intention—with an understanding of exactly what it is I want to do—magic can do anything. Especially magic as powerful as the freaking arrow inside me.

So what is it I want to do right here, right now? I want to bring down the Shadow Realm and reunite the Shadow Queen with her daughter. I may no longer be able to separate the twins, but I can bring them back together, at least healing Lorelei by reuniting her with the drained part of her soul. Not because of some promise I made or a bargain I struck to save Mekhi but because it's the right thing to do. And given how Mekhi was wearing Lorelei's talisman, I think it's what he would *want* me to do, too.

My grandmother suffered for a thousand years, as did Alistair and my people. The Shadow Queen, too, has suffered for a millennium. What's the point of being the gargoyle queen, of having power in the first place, if one can't use it to finally—*finally*—set things right?

So, once again, I close my eyes. I reach inside myself, and this time, I don't build a wall. This time, I grab Hudson's hand, not because I need his power but because I want *him*. My mate. My partner. My everything.

He holds on just as tightly, and I feel him all around me, in every part of my soul. Cherishing me and the world we're going to put to rights. The new world we're going to build together.

My friends move closer, gathering around us, as my power flourishes inside me. They surround us with their friendship and their laughter and their love. And as they crowd around me, I realize it's up to us to let go of the bad things that have happened to us, to let go of the old lessons we've learned at the hands of people and gods who ruled by fear and jealousy and rage. And to find our own lessons, our own truth, in the world we want to build. The world we want to rule.

Damaged in our own right, powerful in our own time, we have spent far too long at the whims of other people. People who have used us for *their* power, who have abused us to *take* our power. People who have hurt us time and time and time again in the name of their own ambition.

That ends here.

That ends now.

We are from here to eternity, and our aim is true.

One more breath. One more clasp of the green string inside me. One more moment to think and dream and be. And then I exhale and let the arrow go.

112

The world around us quite simply implodes.

The darkness falls.

The light flows in.

And the shadows stream behind us where they belong.

The sounds of joy fill the air—bells ringing, birds chirping, water flowing—as all around us, the purple cracks and crumbles and every color of the rainbow begins to take its place.

Purple dissolves into the bluest skies. Green grass. White clouds. And a big, bright, yellow sun shining down on every single thing it touches.

The Shadow Queen is free, and so are her people.

A thousand years in captivity ended in the moment between one choice and the next.

But there is still Adarie, still the farm and all the people who love their lives here. The last thing I want is to force them into yet another prison in our world, and so I do the only thing I can to ensure that they, too, always have a home.

I grab my green string, and I grow a thousand trees, huge and sturdy and everlasting, with the most steadfast trunks and the strongest branches. And I make a forest around Adarie and the farm, filled with chaos magic and near-constant daylight and purple dirt—and with these trees to keep the magic stable, not prison bars.

Behind me, the Shadow Queen gasps, and as I turn around I already know what I'm going to see. Lorelei walking through the shadow of the trees straight toward us, her steps steady and sure.

The Shadow Queen runs to her, and when they embrace, I feel one more part of our new world become whole. Even before Lorelei pulls away from her mother and walks to Mekhi.

He's on the ground now, his back against Jaxon's, as the pain of the poison grows too much for him to bear.

Lorelei drops to her knees beside him and cradles his head in her hands as she pleads with her mother. "Please. Please, save him."

"I can't," the Shadow Queen says, and there's a sadness in her eyes I never expected to see. "I never could. There was never a cure for shadow poison."

"You mean we did all this for nothing?" Eden asks as she, too, drops to her knees beside Mekhi. "We could never save him?" Outrage fills her voice.

"Not for nothing," Mekhi tells her as he looks around at all the colors that exist where only purple used to before. "Look at what we did."

"It's not enough," Jaxon grinds out as he holds his friend steady. "If you die, it will never be enough."

"It has to be," Mekhi answers. "Sometimes this is all you get. It's just my time."

"It will never be your time," I tell him, tears burning my eyes as I finish freeing this world and crouch at his feet.

"Hey now, Grace. None of that." He gives me one of his patented Mekhi smiles—the kind that made me feel like I had a friend in the halls of Katmere. He was Jaxon's friend first, but he was mine, too. From the very beginning. And I can't imagine what it will feel like to live in this brave new world of ours without him.

"It's all good," he whispers as Lorelei holds one of his hands and Jaxon grabs onto the other. "I've had the best friends and life and love. I can't ask for anything more than that."

"Mekhi. Mekhi, no," I gasp out as his eyes slowly close.

Not yet. Please, not yet. I'm not ready to lose him yet.

Beside me, Jaxon sobs—one single, desperate sound that tears right through me. And then Mekhi shudders out his final breath.

Lorelei's scream splits the air, and she falls forward onto his chest, her tears pouring like wishes down her cheeks as she cries over and over for Mekhi to wake up, just open his eyes one more time.

Then I see someone running across the garden, crashing through the vines and the flowers to get to us. Liana—but it's a Liana like we've never seen before. Her hair is black now, her skin a deep olive, and her eyes are a warm, dark brown.

But the purple isn't the only thing that went when the Shadow Realm collapsed. Because now that she's free, her previously flat and terrifying eyes contain the many multitudes of her soul.

"I'm sorry!" she says as she all but throws herself at her sister. "I'm so sorry."

"It's not your fault," Lorelei whispers to her. And when they finally pull away, gold sparkles hang in the air between them.

The sparkles flow back and forth between the two girls for several seconds before a large group of them arrows into Lorelei. She gasps when they hit her, but within moments her cheeks grow rosy and her hair takes on a new luster.

She barely notices, though, as she falls to her knees again and takes Mekhi's hand in hers—and jolts, her eyes widening on a desperate cry. Then she falls across his chest and sobs over and over: "My mate, my mate, my mate."

My stomach twists at the cruelty of finding your mate as he lies dying, knowing how brief your time will be together. "Why now?" I whisper.

"She didn't have all of her soul before," Hudson says, wrapping his arms around me as we both imagine the pain Lorelei must be feeling.

"Lorelei," the Shadow Queen says, and there's an urgency in her voice that won't be denied. "There is no antidote, but now that you have reunited with your sister and have your full soul, you *can* save him."

"How?" She blinks up at her mother, her eyes pleading for help.

"Use the bond," her mother urges. "You are a wraith, which means the shadow poison will not hurt you. Use the mating bond to pull it inside you and free Mekhi from its insidious grip once and for all."

"How?" she asks again, and I kneel beside her, pulling Hudson with me.

I don't know how, but I know I'm meant to help her. That I'm the only person who *can* help her—because I've done this before.

113

Way to Break
and Run

"**Y**ou can do this, Lorelei," I say, holding her shimmering gaze. "Now close your eyes and look inside your heart, and you'll see he's *already there*. He's in the pieces of your soul that make your chest tighten every time you think of him. His smile, his laugh, his teasing sense of humor." I turn to look at Hudson, trying to find the right words to describe a feeling. "Even the way he argues with every single thing you say…he's there. Right there. Waiting for you to reach out and grab ahold and never let each other go."

Hudson's oceanic eyes never leave mine as he says, "Your mate already found you, *chose* you, Lorelei. You just have to let them love you…and then follow their love back to you, take it in, let it consume you, until there is no you anymore—there's just an unending, unbreakable *us*."

"I see him," Lorelei breathes. "I found Mekhi. He's so incredibly beautiful—" She gasps, reaching to cup the side of his face. "I love you, too. Now will you come back to me? Please don't leave me, not when I've just found you. Do you hear me?" When Mekhi still doesn't move, she leans forward and presses her lips to his, then whispers, "Will you come home to me, Mekhi?"

His lashes tremble just before they sweep upward, revealing his gorgeous brown eyes. "Hey." His voice is rough and gravelly but strong.

Lorelei swipes an arm at the tears running down her face before saying, "Hey back."

"What? How?" Jaxon looks back and forth between Mekhi and the rest of us like he can't believe his eyes.

I know the feeling. I've seen a lot of things since becoming a gargoyle, but never in my wildest dreams did I think Mekhi and Lorelei were going to pull a real-life Sleeping Beauty right here in the remnants of the Shadow Realm.

"What happened?" Lorelei asks, but then she throws herself into Mekhi's open arms without waiting for an answer.

The Shadow Queen looks on indulgently, and even Liana has a smile on her face.

And while this is the most wonderful thing that could have happened and I'm so, so grateful, I'm also very confused. Because Mekhi was dead. I know he was. I saw him with my own eyes.

"This is real, right?" Hudson asks as he looks between his brother and Mekhi. And I can tell he's thinking the same thing I am. That this better not be some stress-induced mass hallucination, because losing Mekhi once nearly broke Jaxon. Having it happen twice would utterly destroy him.

"It is," the Shadow Queen answers as she wraps an arm around Liana's shoulders. "Mekhi is going to be okay."

"But how?" Jaxon asks again.

"The mating bond saved him—the way it saves most of us, in one way or another. I had trouble believing it, but I knew they were mates the moment Mekhi told me Lorelei had given him that necklace. But *he* didn't seem to know it, which could mean only one thing. So much of Lorelei's soul was trapped here, with Liana, that the mating bond couldn't function in your world. Once Grace brought the Shadow Realm down and my daughter was able to retrieve her soul—"

She pauses for a second, swallowing hard as if overcome by a thousand years of emotions flooding her system at this very moment, then clears her throat and continues. "Once Lorelei and Liana were able to touch, their souls realigned and Lorelei was able to reclaim all of herself. Which meant the mating bond could finally function the way it's supposed to. And since Lorelei's a wraith, immune to shadow poison, the bond automatically filtered the poison from Mekhi to her. And it will continue to do so for all time."

Jaxon slumps over with relief, and for the first time in months, the brackets of pain around his mouth and eyes are gone. He looks like the weight of a thousand pounds—or at least one two-hundred-and-twenty-pound vampire—has finally been lifted off of him.

Flint notices it, too, and he presses a supportive hand to Jaxon's shoulder. Jaxon lifts his own hand to cover Flint's, and when he turns his head to look up at Flint, there's a moment of understanding—of connection—between them that I haven't seen in months, if ever. I don't know what it means for them, but I hope it's good. They deserve to be happy together.

Hudson catches my eye, and we both kind of smile at each other. It's good to see Jaxon happy—or at least open to the possibility of happiness. God knows he's gone through enough to get there, and he deserves every ounce of joy that comes his way.

Mekhi and Lorelei finally break apart, and the vampire springs to his feet with more energy than he's had since he was bitten. His easygoing grin is back in place, and his warm brown eyes are finally, finally clear.

"Thank you," he says, looking all of us one by one.

Eden grins. "Pretty sure your mate's the one you need to be thanking here."

"It's all of you," Lorelei says. "You've all fought for him over and over again, and that's not something we will ever forget."

Taking compliments—or thank-yous—has never been my strong suit, so I duck my head and shuffle my feet back and forth as I wait for the awkward feeling inside me to pass.

But in true Mekhi fashion, he's not about to let me off the hook that easily. Instead, he grabs me and pulls me into a bear hug so huge that he lifts me several feet off the ground. And whispers in my ear, "'The rest is silence.'"

It's a reference to that long-ago Brit Lit class where we got to be friends, and it shatters the last of the awkwardness I'm feeling. "Uh, no," I tell him when he puts me back on my feet. "You've already done the death scene once today. You don't get a redo."

We all laugh, then, relief and joy coursing through the air around us.

"'There are more things in heaven and earth, Horatio, than can be dreamt of in your philosophy,'" Jaxon comments slyly.

I lift a brow. "Don't you mean heaven and hell?"

"Not today I don't." Jaxon and Flint smile ridiculously at each other while Hudson makes a slight gagging sound.

"Seriously? You couldn't let Mekhi have this one?" Hudson asks.

Flint snickers. "Always the attention hog." But I notice he still has a hand on Jaxon's shoulder.

Besides, Jaxon just grins and asks, "'Et tu, Brute?'"

At which point Heather demands, "What the fuck is happening here?"

When we all just look at her, she throws her hands up in exasperation and continues. "When did we go from saving the Shadow Realm to a Shakespearean throwdown? Because if you want to go there, I've got some great Shakespearean insults I can add to the mix."

"I bet you do," Eden says, wrapping an arm around her waist. "Maybe you can share a few of them with me later."

"Umm, sure." Heather looks happy, if a little confused. "Though I have to be honest. That's not the kind of dirty talk I'm used to."

"And on that note," Mekhi says with a giant grin. "I don't know about the rest of you, but I'm ready to blow this purple popsicle stand. I've been a little in and out recently, but if I'm not mistaken, we've got an important day to prepare for."

For a second, I'm so caught up in memories, I don't remember what he's talking about. And then it hits me. "Oh my God! What day is it?"

Hudson runs a fond hand over my curls. "We still have four days."

I sigh. Hard. "Thank God. But we have to go! There's so much to do!" I turn to the Shadow Queen. "I'm sorry to break and run, but I've got an investiture to attend."

"Attend?" Heather snorts. "I'm pretty sure you and Hudson are the headliners."

"As long as I don't have to put on a concert ever again," Hudson comments dryly.

"You're about to be king," Eden says. "Pretty sure that means you can do—or not do—whatever you want."

"That's not what being a ruler's all about, is it, Grace?" the Shadow Queen asks, holding my gaze. "We can do better."

It's an olive branch, and I don't hesitate to take it. "Yes *we* can."

She gives a tiny nod, and I know we're ready to try to heal, to find a path forward. And so I suggest, "All rulers have been invited to my investiture ceremony. If you've misplaced yours, I can have the invitation resent."

"I need to see to rebuilding for my people," she says, waving her hand to encompass the new Shadow Realm. "But I could maybe slip away for something so important. If you're sure?"

"The more the merrier," I tell her as I reach for my platinum string. "Besides, I'm all about building alliances."

"Then an alliance—and my gratitude—you shall always have," she says, and I feel the bargain tattoo on my arm slowly change shape, a beautiful purple crown appearing from the remnants of the tree that used to mark my wrist.

"Umm, anyone know how to get home?" Flint asks, rubbing his chest absently as he looks around the brightly colored Shadow Realm. "I really don't want to go well-jumping again."

"I think we can do better than that," the Shadow Queen says as she waves a hand once more, drawing a shadow from a nearby tree to us. "This shadow will take you where you wish to go."

And I know exactly where that is, because we've got one more journey to make, and this one has been a long time coming.

"Follow me," I say, and everyone does.

114

This time, when we land at the Witch Court, it's with all the pomp and circumstance that Imogen and Linden's tradition-loving hearts can handle—on dragon back and covered in brambles.

"I still can't believe the first thing you wanted to do after tearing down a realm was go back into said realm," Flint complains after shifting back.

"Hey, we had to go see Smokey," I tell him. "We couldn't just leave her there and not visit."

"That makes sense for you and Hudson," he agrees begrudgingly. "But what about Jaxon?"

Hudson laughs even as he delivers a shoulder bump to his brother. "I think he just wanted another chance to see his adoring fans."

Jaxon rolls his eyes, but he doesn't deny it.

Hudson's smile fades as quickly as it came, and I know he's thinking about Smokey. And how we've tried everything, used all of our combined powers, and come up with absolutely nothing that will let her cross from that realm to live with us in ours. Umbras can't leave the Shadow Realm, and neither of us, with all our powers, can find a way to change that.

On the plus side, the Shadow Queen built him a permanent portal between the two realms, so he can visit whenever he wants. Which has pretty much been twice a day since we brought the Shadow Realm down.

But the invocation is this evening, and she won't be able to come. He hasn't said anything about it, but I know it weighs on him. I just wish there was something I could do about it. At least we were able to spend several hours with her today—which is obvious from the dirt smudges Hudson is trying to wipe from my face right now.

Thankfully, we've still got several hours before we need to be at the ceremony site. With all the glamours they have at their disposal to use on my friends, surely the witches running the event can make even us presentable in that amount of time.

The witch queen, however, doesn't look nearly as certain as she gingerly approaches me. "This isn't quite the look I was going for, Grace," she comments, gazing down her long, aquiline nose at me.

"Sorry," I say, running a hand down my ripped T-shirt and jeans. "Hudson's umbra wanted to play a very enthusiastic game of Hide and Seek in the Shadow Realm today." What I don't mention is that the game was really I hide and Smokey seeks Hudson, leaving me in the brambles for at least thirty minutes until I finally crawled out. I just really don't think that image is what I want to put out there as they crown me head of the Circle today. So instead, I simply say, "She's enthusiastic with her love."

"So we've heard." Her normally disapproving face smooths into a real smile for maybe the first time ever. Or at least the first time that I've ever seen. "Nice job on the Shadow Realm. That's been a long time coming."

The praise startles me so much that I just stare at her for a second. Which has her sighing heavily. "Open mouths are so unbecoming, Grace."

And then she whirls around, the long skirt of her high-necked Dolce & Gabbana gown slapping me in the legs.

"Are we supposed to follow her?" I ask Hudson, completely baffled.

He shoots me an amused look. "Unless you plan on getting ready out here."

"It might be better." I sigh as we follow her through the front doors and down the long, elaborate hallway of the Witch Court. "God knows what she's got in store for us in there."

Turns out what she has in store is Macy, who's sitting in the middle of the bed in the room she leads us to.

"There's a second room through that door," Imogen tells Hudson. "Your valet and clothes are over there waiting for you."

He nods a quick thank-you and then—like the coward he is—fades at top speed to the other room. The last I hear from him is the door slamming and locking behind him.

"What about our friends?" I ask. "They need—"

"My ladies-in-waiting are getting them situated as we speak," Imogen tells me. "I know glamours don't work on you, so you might want to take a few minutes—or more—to avail yourself of the very nice shower in the other room."

"Is that your way of telling me I stink, Imogen?"

She sighs. "That seems a bit gauche, but there is a certain malodorous truth to it."

"Don't worry," Macy tells her with a wink. "I've got her from here."

"I certainly hope so, because otherwise you'll be in charge of running herd on the kitchen witches' Wingo games for many months to come. And Bettina is truly a wicked, wicked witch."

I burst out laughing, partly because of the joke and partly because I had no idea Imogen had it in her.

"Way to throw shade there, Imogen."

"Please." The witch pats her hair. "You aren't the only ones who know how to have a good time."

"Apparently not," I tell her with a grin.

She giggles. She actually giggles. And then, very gingerly and with a scrunched-up nose, pats my shoulder. "Your dress is in the closet," she stage-whispers like it's the biggest secret ever. "It's Vampire's Wife."

And then she slips out of the room in a swirl of crimson and gold ruffles.

"Oh. My. God."

Macy throws herself back on the bed and starts laughing hysterically.

"Oh my God! Who was that?" I stare at the closed door. "Are formal events what she uses to reach total and complete self-actualization?"

"That and about four shots."

I whirl on Macy, horrified. "What did you do?"

"Me? Nothing. Viola, however, suggested she might like a drink to calm her nerves. How were we supposed to know she'd have such a taste for whipped-cream vodka?"

"Oh my God," I repeat. I start to flop down on the bed next to her, then remember just what a sorry state I'm currently in and head toward the bathroom instead. "I'm going to take that shower, and then you can fill me in on all the deets."

Fifteen minutes later, Macy is doing just that as Esperanza, Imogen's personal glamour practitioner, "makes the most of what I've got." Which, surprisingly, is quite a lot under her expert touch, even if there's no real magic involved. Sure, the crushed-berry lip color is a little much for me, but I'm not about to fight her. Not when she holds the fate of my very curly hair in her hands.

On the plus side, it matches the dress in the closet perfectly.

After Esperanza finishes twisting my hair into the most perfect chignon it has ever been in—it only takes about an hour—she gives me a hug and wishes me luck before slipping out of the room.

"Holy shit," Macy says as she walks in a circle around me.

"It's not that big of a deal," I tell her.

"Holy shit," she says again.

"It's just the dress and the jewelry and—"

I break off as Macy takes hold of my shoulders and spins me around until I'm looking in the full-length mirror next to the dressing table. And can I just say: "Holy shit."

"That's what I've been telling you," she agrees.

I stare at the mirror, and for a second I really can't believe it's me.

Not because of the makeup and false lashes and fancy hairstyle.

Not because of the floor-length formal dress, though it is gorgeous, with its spaghetti straps, ivory tulle, and elaborate overlay of flowers and vines in shades of raspberry, periwinkle, gold, and the softest pinks and greens.

Not even because of the diamonds dripping from my ears and set throughout the platinum crown sitting on my head.

No, it's because for the first time since this whole journey began, I look like a queen. And maybe, just maybe, I'm beginning to feel like one, too.

115

Everything's
Coming Up Graces

M acy hugs me as gingerly as she can in an effort not to wrinkle the dress.

"It's okay," I tell her with a roll of my eyes. "You can wrinkle me. I'm still Grace."

"You're Grace, yes. But that dress is…" She trails off.

"Everything," I tell her. "I know."

"Everything," she agrees.

I look in the mirror one more time, marveling again that Imogen thought to pick out this dress for me. It's not something I ever would have thought about or even imagined existed. But the fact that Imogen thought enough about my earth magic and what it means to me to choose this dress… All I'm saying is that it makes me regret all those times I've been annoyed with her about this ceremony over the last few months.

"You've come a long way from that hot-pink parka," Macy says with a grin.

"I really have, haven't I?" For a second, I think about confessing to her just how much I despise hot pink, but in the end, I decide that's not even true anymore. It may never be my favorite color, but Macy is pretty much my favorite everything, and for that reason alone, I will always have a soft spot for hot pink.

"Today's a big day," she says, "and I thought you might appreciate a little reminder of those first days at Katmere to ground you for what's to come."

"You didn't have to do that," I tell her even as I turn into a giant gooey ball of emotion.

"Sure, I did," she answers. "By the way, have you seen the shoes Imogen expects you to wear?"

I have, in all their five-inch-heeled glory. I've also spent the better part of the last hour trying to pretend they don't exist. I'm not particularly nervous about being onstage in front of everyone today—especially since Hudson is going to be there, too. But I feel like wearing those is just asking to be humiliated in front of ten thousand paranormals.

"You got me shoes?" I squeal hopefully. And though I've never been a shoe girl, the thought of not being tortured for the next several hours by a pair of crystal-encrusted Louboutins has definite appeal.

She hands me a gift bag. "Guess you're going to have to open it and find out."

I do, and then I laugh like a hyena when I pull out the hot-pink satin ballet flats my cousin has picked out for me. "They're perfect," I tell her as I slide them on my feet.

"I know." She grins.

Before she can say anything else, there's a knock on the connecting door between Hudson's and my rooms.

"I think that's the sign for me to make myself scarce," my cousin says with a waggle of her brows. "But don't you dare let that man wrinkle you."

"Oh, I won't," I assure her.

To which she just laughs and says, "Oh, who are we kidding?" on her way out the door.

Hudson knocks again, and for the first time since we got here, butterflies take off in my stomach. It's stupid to be nervous about seeing him—he's my mate. Then again, maybe it's a good thing that just the thought of him still makes me all fluttery inside.

"Come in," I call when I can finally find my voice.

And then wish I'd braced myself, because I should have known. If I look this good, of course Hudson is on a whole next level.

He's dressed more simply than I would have expected of him—then again, Imogen would probably never forgive us if we clashed on the dais. But just because his tuxedo is a simple, black Tom Ford with a crushed berry–colored bow tie doesn't mean he isn't still the most devastatingly gorgeous sight I've ever seen. Add in his signature Brit-boy hairstyle and the small raspberry-colored flower in his handkerchief pocket, and I can feel myself starting to swoon.

Normally I'd quell the impulse—his ego doesn't need any help—but I figure he deserves the extra thrill on his invocation day. So I wave a hand in front of my face and give my lip a little nibble, just to see the way his eyes darken to my favorite midnight blue.

"Looking good, hot stuff," I tell him.

I expect him to grin and fire off some egotistical quip, but instead he just stares at me. And stares at me. And stares at me, until I start wondering if I've somehow ripped my dress.

"Is something wrong?" I ask, looking down at my skirt.

He fades to me in an instant. "I... I..." He clears his throat. "You..."

And oh my God. I suddenly realize what's happening. With the help of Esperanza and Imogen and Macy, I've made the ever-glib Hudson Vega speechless.

The tiny ball of nerves inside me that I didn't even know was there slowly relaxes.

"I'll take that as a compliment," I tease.

He shakes his head, eyes wide with wonder. And still doesn't manage to say anything.

"You want some water?" I turn toward the mini fridge hidden behind a panel in the dresser. But before I can take more than a step, Hudson fades to me, hands on my hips, and holds me in place.

"Grace." That's all he says, but there's such love and reverence and heat in that one word that I don't need him to say anything else.

"Yeah, I feel the same way every time you walk in a room," I tell him.

That finally breaks the spell, and he laughs, pulling me against him for a one-armed hug. "Hey!" I say even as I make absolutely no move to step away. "I'm under strict orders from Macy not to let you wrinkle me."

"Tulle always looks better with a few wrinkles," he lies outrageously, but he does back off, just a little.

I start to reach for him again, to hell with wrinkles, but before I can, he pulls out a giant bouquet of flowers from behind his back. They match the colors and types in my dress exactly.

I gasp when I see them, then reach for the bouquet—and him—with greedy hands.

"I thought you were under orders not to wrinkle," he teases as I press myself against him—while simultaneously burying my face in the flowers.

"Bite me," I growl.

"I would, but I'm certain that we would both end up with some severe wrinkles," he answers with the most choirboy look that has ever graced his face. "And I know we're not supposed to do that."

I roll my eyes. "You're not going to let it go, are you?"

"I'm never going to let *you* go. Does that count?"

"That might be the cheesiest thing you've ever said to me." The fact that it still manages to make my heart go pitter-patter is something I'm going to keep to myself.

"How about this," he says, setting the flowers aside and taking both my hands in his. "I dreamed you."

"Oh, Hudson—"

"Let me finish," he says in a voice so thick with emotions it barely sounds like his. "When I was trapped in that shithole for months and years, I dreamed you up. A woman so powerful and kind and strong that she'd be able to save the world, because if she could do that, then maybe she could save me, too."

His voice breaks right along with my heart, and I reach for him, the need to feel his heart beating against me a compulsion I have no desire to escape.

But he holds me off with a look and a shake of his head. "You've saved me, Grace Foster, a million different times in a million different ways. You've saved me, even from myself."

"You've saved me right back," I whisper, and forget wrinkling. I'm going to be sobbing in a second, and there are no false lashes built for that.

Hudson must know just how close I am, because instead of saying something else guaranteed to make me blubber like a baby, he just lifts a brow and says, "Damn right I did. And don't you forget it."

And just like that, we're laughing instead of crying. Which is exactly as it should be.

116

We're in Love with
the Shape of Us

"Hey, where's your crown?" I exclaim a few minutes later, after we've done our level best to wrinkle the hell out of both of our outfits.

"On the dresser in my room," he answers with an "obviously" look. "Some of us don't feel the need to flaunt our position every second of every day."

"Hey! Esperanza put this crown on, not me. She said it needed to go a certain way because of my ridiculous curls."

"Don't be saying mean shit about those curls. They're one of my favorite things about you."

"I thought my brain was your favorite thing about me."

He grins. "I have a lot of favorite things."

"Ditto."

"I do want to talk to you, though," he says, and his face grows serious.

Which has every electron in my body firing overtime as I scramble into a serious sitting position. Is he finally ready to share the secret I know he's been keeping?

"I've been thinking about the Circle."

"The Circle?" I ignore the disappointment in my belly. "What about it?"

He glances at his watch. "If things go according to plan, in about two hours, you and I are going to be the head of it."

I study his face, trying to figure out where he's going with this. It's not like this is news, after all. Unless he is trying to break something to me. "I mean..." I take a deep breath as I blurt out what I've been mulling over these past weeks, in between TVs, Celestial bears, and

Shadow Queens who are way too much trouble. "We don't have to be."

Hudson rears back like I actually balled up my stone fist and hit him. "What does that mean?"

"It means—" My voice breaks, and for a second the offer I want to make gets stuck in my throat. But then I remind myself that this is a partnership and a relationship that is going to last forever. For that to happen, both sides have to get what they need. If Hudson needs this, then I want to be the one to provide it.

And if he doesn't? Then at least I'll know that we discussed it, and we can start this next era of our lives free from coulda, woulda, shouldas.

The thought gives me the strength to clear my throat and finally say, "If you want to go up on that dais today and assume the role of vampire king and queen instead of gargoyle queen and king, then I'm with you."

He blinks at me. Then asks, "You want to be vampire queen?"

"I want to be whatever you and I decide together is best for us," I answer.

He lifts both brows, a sign of just how big a loop I've thrown him for. "I thought we already had. We're building a life in the Gargoyle Court."

"We are," I agree. "And I'm not proposing we give that life up altogether. They're still my people. They will always be my people. I just... You're my mate. And I don't need you to sacrifice something you've wanted or expected to have your entire life for me."

Hudson leans back to stare at the ceiling for several long moments. "I told you only a few minutes ago that what I've wanted my entire life is you. And now that I have you, what I want is to build a life together, doing something that we believe in somewhere that we can live and love and grow and thrive together. I thought that was the Gargoyle Court for you. I know it is for me."

"It is," I tell him. "I love the Gargoyle Court more than anything else on this earth...except for you. Which is why I had to be sure that it was right for *us*."

"It's right for us," he tells me with the utmost certainty. "I have a plan for the Vampire Court, but it does not include Jaxon or me. I haven't shared it because I haven't figured out if it's even feasible yet, but I think it is. And I think it will work. You just have to trust me, Grace."

There's a whole lot in that last sentence, and there's even more in the face of the man who said it to me. "I do trust you," I tell him. "I also know that you have a tendency to choose what's best for me over what's best for you. And that's why I had to ask. Because I want what's best for us, not just what's best for me."

I see the moment it sinks in, the moment he realizes—truly realizes—that I'm doing the one thing he swore he'd never ask me to do. Choosing him above everyone. Above everything. Forever.

And this time when he looks at me, his eyes shine as brightly as any star. "I love you, Grace Foster."

"I love you, Hudson Vega."

He grins. "I know. Which is why we're going to go to that invocation, accept the titles of gargoyle king and queen, and spend the rest of our infinitely long lives showing Alistair and the Bloodletter how it's fucking done."

I laugh, because if that's not the most Hudson Vega thing ever said, I don't know what is. "Damn straight we are."

"Okay, then. Stop trying to give your Crown away and help me figure out the answer to one last problem I've got."

"What is it?" I ask.

He pulls a notebook out of his pocket and spreads it open on the bed for me to see.

My eyes go wide when I realize what I'm looking at—and how closely it parallels something I've been thinking about since I brought down the Shadow Realm. Still, to see it spread out here in black and white? To know Hudson has been thinking of the same thing all along?

"They're going to lose their shit," I tell him.

He smiles grimly. "I really fooking hope so."

117

On the Portal
to Everywhere

An hour later, there's a knock on the door. I open it to find two of Imogen's ladies-in-waiting.

"They're ready for you, Your Highness," one of them says, bowing deeply.

I want to tell her it's okay, that she doesn't have to do that. But these women work for Imogen, and I have no doubt that she definitely requires them to bow. So instead of making us all uncomfortable, I just nod and say, "Thank you."

"The portal is set up in the back courtyard," the second one adds. "We will escort you whenever you are ready."

"We're ready now," Hudson says from behind me.

They do the whole bowing thing to him, and he bows back. It flusters them and has them giggling among themselves, and I make a note to do the same from now on. Though, to be honest, I'm pretty sure it's his smile that has them all aflutter instead of the return bow.

And that, I absolutely can't mimic.

After grabbing our phones and backpacks—the plan is to come back here after the coronation, but I kind of just want to go home—we follow the ladies-in-waiting down several halls to a pair of open French doors.

When we walk through them, it's into a courtyard crowded with witches and a huge, open portal. The witches have already started going through, and I have to admit to a tiny freak-out when I realize just how many of them are coming to the invocation.

But Hudson takes my hand and whispers, "It's going to be fine."

I choose to believe him, because it's better than the alternative. And worrying about the crowd isn't going to do anything but make me more nervous, and I really don't want that to happen. The last thing I need is to have a panic attack as we walk onstage to accept our induction into the Circle.

I don't even know why I'm nervous now. I've been fine all afternoon, even when Hudson and I were planning what comes next. But the second I walked into this courtyard, it's like all the nerves in the universe just ambushed me all at once.

Our friends come up behind us, all dressed in beautiful suits and dresses, too. I make a mental note to thank Imogen—I know she's behind this as well—and then we're making our way to the line for the portal.

Except the line disperses in an instant, and it's just our group standing at the opening of the portal. I turn around to the other witches, start to tell them that we're okay waiting in line. But Heather grabs my hand and hisses, "Don't you dare."

I give her a confused look, and she says, "You're a queen, Grace. A real freaking queen. And you're about to be head of this whole damn thing. I get that you don't want special privileges, but sometimes you're just going to have to take them. And if clearing out a line is your new superpower, I say run with it."

The rest of my friends laugh, and Macy even goes so far as to hold up a hand for a fist bump, which Heather returns with a grin. Then Hudson and I are stepping up to the portal, hand in hand…because apparently, when you're the king and queen, you get a double portal made just for you.

Just like that, my knees turn to jelly.

I've known my coronation day was coming—pretty hard to call myself a queen without one. But knowing it's coming in some nebulous future is very different than knowing it's coming *right now.*

"You ready?" Hudson asks before we step into the portal before us.

"No," I tell him, because I don't lie to my mate. And also because he already knows the answer.

He grins in response, and for a moment everything fades and it's just the two of us. Just Hudson and me and the world we want to build—the life we want to lead—together.

"Me neither," he agrees in his most proper British accent. "Why don't I create a distraction while you make a break for it?" He smiles, leaning down to whisper, "You're going to do great, Grace. I can't imagine a better queen."

And just like that, the nerves die away.

I know it's stupid, know I don't need validation from any man to make me feel important. But Hudson isn't just any man. He's my mate, and there's something about hearing him tell me he believes in me—something about him saying he knows I'll be a good queen—that makes me believe that I just might be.

I hold tight for just a moment, listening to his heartbeat. Breathing him in. Reveling in the warm, sexy scent of him—amber and sandalwood and confidence.

So much confidence—in himself, in me, in *us*.

It gives me the boost I need to lift my head and meet his oceanic eyes. They're filled with love, with pride, with *forever*, and as I gaze into them, I'm finally ready.

"Let's do this," I whisper.

"I thought you'd never ask."

And then he puts an arm on my lower back and sweeps me along with him, straight into the portal.

118

Crown,
Interrupted

We walk out of the portal onto the grounds of a Katmere Academy neither of us has ever seen before. When Macy told me a few days ago that the school was almost ready, I hadn't given it much thought. Hadn't given this moment much thought.

But as Hudson and I walk over the magically packed snows of Denali, I can't take my eyes off the new castle. In some ways, it looks just the same—gothic architecture, soaring towers, ornate parapets stretching across the top of it.

In other ways, though, it's very different. The entrance is much wider and more welcoming. There are a ton more windows on every floor—I assume because defenses have changed a lot through the centuries. And, maybe most importantly, the gargoyles are all gone.

Of course, I knew that already. They've been at the Gargoyle Court with me for months.

Still, it's nice to be here. And even nicer to know that Hudson and I will join the Circle here on Katmere's grounds, where it all began for me—and for us. The fact that, as far as I know, no one is planning a human/gargoyle sacrifice ritual is also a plus...

The dais where we will be crowned is directly in front of us, and as we walk toward it, I realize that the other members of the Circle are already here. *So many people* are already here and lined up in place around the stage. Including my friends, who are shuffling into the spaces reserved for them.

My grandparents approach with solemn faces. Alistair reaches for me, and I think he's about to give me a hug. But instead he goes for a handshake, pressing his palm to mine. As our skin meets, I feel the heat of the Crown burning against my palm. A quick shock follows, and then I look down to find the Crown emblazoned on my hand again.

"I thought you might have missed that, Granddaughter," he tells me with a smile.

"You have no idea how much," I answer as I curl my fingers over my palm.

He nods. "That's exactly what I expect to hear from the gargoyle queen."

And it's true. When I handed the Crown over to him, I felt relieved to be out from under the pressure of everything it stands for.

But the longer I was without it, the stranger and less like myself I felt, though I never really put the two together. Now that the Crown is back safely with me, however, I have no intention of ever letting it go again.

I thought the Crown was taking things from my life—my painting, my relationships, my normal, everyday joy—but I see now that being a ruler isn't overpowering those things. It's strengthening them, making them more precious. Sure, it's a lot of responsibility to carry the Crown, but it's one I accept with pride.

As he and my grandmother step back, I turn to look at my friends, hoping for one moment of normalcy—of levity—from them, but their expressions are as somber as Alistair's and the Bloodletter's. Even Heather, who I half expected to be pumped up with excitement, is as serious as I've ever seen her as she reaches out a hand to squeeze mine as I pass by.

"You've got this," she whispers to me, and I nod, even though I don't feel like I have this at all. Giving orders on a battlefield is one thing, or settling disputes at the Gargoyle Court. But heading up the Circle is something else entirely.

Still, I won't be doing it on my own. Hudson will be with me every step of the way. And if all of our challenges have proved nothing else, it's that we make a really good team. Plus, we've seen a lot of bad ruling decisions, and hopefully we've learned from them. Hopefully, when it's our turn to make the hard calls, we'll be ready.

I turn to Hudson and realize he looks as resolute as I feel. Looks like we're really doing this.

His smile says all the things I already know, just as I'm sure mine does. We take a moment for just the two of us in the midst of all this madness, and then, as one, we turn to the Bloodletter and Alistair, who—as the former gargoyle queen and king—are waiting to escort us to the stage.

And then I say, "We're ready." My voice echoes over the snowy fields to the mountains beyond.

We climb the stairs to the dais as the plums and grays of civil twilight begin to settle across the earth around us. In the center of the stage are two jewel-encrusted thrones that are a little much for me but right up Imogen's—and I think, secretly, Hudson's—alley. Behind them in a semicircle are six other thrones—just as large and gaudy as the ones set front and center for Hudson and me.

They're for the other factions, I'm sure. The dragons, the wolves, the witches. Only the vampires are missing, and while that's mostly our fault, I no longer let myself feel guilty for it. Hudson and I have made our decision, and we will stand by it as long as we are called to lead.

We sit in the chairs and look out at the miles of rolling snowy hills filled with paranormals, and one very special human, who have come from all over the world to celebrate this moment with us. I'm not naive enough to think they are all happy about Hudson's and my ascension to the head of the Circle, but when the entire field kneels before us, I can't help but hope that maybe, just maybe, we can mend the fissures that have been created through the centuries and eternities before us.

Our friends are the first people I see, kneeling right behind Alistair and the Bloodletter with proud smiles on their faces. I expect at least one of them to do something silly, make a face or try to crack us up. Flint, probably, or maybe Heather or Gwen.

They don't, though. Instead, every single one of their faces remains solemn. And as I meet each one of their gazes individually, they bow their heads. Even Jaxon and Flint, two princes in their own right.

It's a shock, but it's also one more reminder of the importance of what's happening here. Instead of letting it weird me out, I let their support steady me, let it flow through me and fill me with confidence as I finally let my gaze move beyond them to the snow-covered fields that surround us.

Fields that are filled with thousands upon thousands of gargoyles, all kneeling before me. I can see Artelya at the front, with Dylan and Chastain flanking her on either side. Behind them are the witches who opened the portals for us in the courtyard earlier.

Unlike everyone else on the field, they aren't kneeling. Instead, they're holding open a dozen more portals all across the field, and I watch in shock as people continue to pour through them.

Nuri and Aiden come through the first one, along with several members of their Dragon Guard. As dragon queen and king, they don't bow before Hudson and me as they make their way to their spot on the dais, but their guard does.

As our gazes meet, however, Nuri inclines her head, and in her eyes I see power and determination and respect. It's more than I expected, more than I ever would have thought to ask for after all that's passed between us, and I nod my head in thanks.

Out of another portal walk the wolf queens, Willow and Angela, along with their guards and several pack alphas, including the newest alpha of the Syrian pack, Dawud. They bend their head and their knee to me—after waving frantically.

A contingent of Katmere instructors who have yet to return to the school pour out of the third portal—Amka and Ms. Maclean, Mrs. Haversham and Dr. Wainwright, Mr. Damasen and Dr. MacCleary. They all smile at me proudly as they, too, kneel before me.

The fourth portal must go to Giant City, because Erym comes bouncing out, followed by Xeno, Vander, and Falia, who looks so much healthier and happier than when I saw her last. Erym waves her arms in the air to get my attention—as if standing several feet taller than anyone else on the field isn't enough—and it takes every ounce of willpower I have not to wave wildly back. Instead, I smile broadly as I nod at her and the others, all of whom also drop to their knees.

The next portal opens up seconds later, and out of it pours several members of the Vampire Court and guard. Mikhael and several people I don't recognize, along with Aunt Celine and two other vampires whom I can only imagine are Flavinia and Rodney.

And finally, the last portal opens and out walks the Shadow Queen, along with Liana, Lorelei, Mekhi, Maroly, Arnst, Tiola, Nyaz, Lumi, Caoimhe, and Polo. And while all of the other members of the Shadow contingent find their designated section and kneel, I can't help but feel Hudson's sadness that Smokey isn't able to be here, too.

The only people who couldn't come were Remy and Izzy. Remy insisted I shouldn't be worried, but there was just something in his voice, something screaming at me that not all was right with Calder Academy. But I trust that my friends will let me know if they need me, just like I will do should I need them.

Standing here before the rest of these people—people who have helped us in one way or another since I first got to Katmere—I feel very blessed. Teachers, friends, family—all here to watch Hudson and me take our place on the Circle. All here to honor the past and help start a new, better chapter for us all.

As I gaze out, I've never felt more humbled or more confident. Because seeing them here, remembering what each of them has taught me, makes me believe—really believe—that I belong here in this world. More, it makes me believe that I belong here, with Hudson, on this throne.

So much so that when Alistair steps forward and asks us to stand, I don't hesitate for an instant. And neither does my mate.

But before Alistair can say another word, the earth around us begins to shake. And the Crone's hunters pour in from all directions.

119

Sky Me
a River

They come in with guns and pouches blazing, the weapons the Crone has spent centuries developing against paranormals going off in all directions.

Attention! I mentally call out to my army, and they immediately take action.

They race to intercept the hunters, with Artelya at the head, followed by the guards from all the other factions.

At the same time, my friends spring into action, too, fading and flying toward the hunters at top speed. Hudson and I—along with the other leaders—race toward the edge of the stage. But before we can join the fray, the Crone appears in a flash of brilliant light right in front of us.

"I should have known it was you!" the Bloodletter snarls as she puts herself between her sister and me.

"Yes, you should have," the Crone agrees with a knife-thin smile that sends ice racing through my veins. "Now that we are no longer joined, there is nowhere on this earth that is safe for you and yours. I will hunt down and destroy every single one of you so that my people can thrive."

"You don't give a shit about your people," I snarl at her as the troops on the field engage the hunters in battle. Under my watchful eyes, several of my gargoyles race toward the portals instead of fighting, and at first I don't know what they're doing. But then I see that they're ushering all the non-guard and -army members back through the portals for their own safety—a move that makes me very proud in the middle of all this chaos.

"You use these hunters to get whatever you want," I continue, "which in this case is all the power that your sister and her mate wield."

"That's a very simplistic viewpoint," she tells me with a sneer.

"Sometimes simple is the best and truest answer."

"And sometimes it's just grounds for annihilation," she shoots back, right before she reaches in her pocket and pulls out one of the red pouches the hunters are using.

My grandmother takes one look at it and rushes her, knocking the pouch from her hand and sending her spinning across the stage.

The Crone screeches in outrage and comes back with a roundhouse punch to the Bloodletter's cheek—which earns her a kick in the stomach even as the Bloodletter reaches a hand to the sky and sends lightning careening across the stage.

"Ten thousand years, and you haven't learned a damn thing," the Crone tells her, voice clearly audible above the din of combat around us. "If you go for lightning right out of the gate, you've got no weapons to use later."

As if to prove her point, she holds a hand out and absorbs the lightning, then sends a stream of it flying straight toward a group of gargoyles racing across the snow.

"Plus, you make it even easier for me."

"I think I can keep up," the Bloodletter answers with a smirk. And this time there is no warning before lightning strikes the Crone right between her shoulder blades.

She screams then, a combination of rage and regret, as she gives up on the lightning and races straight toward my grandmother. As she does, the smell of sizzling flesh permeates the air around us, but she doesn't let that slow her down. Instead, she plows headfirst into the Bloodletter and sends her flying off the stage and straight through the air into the twilight around us.

Seconds later, the two of them are rolling across the sky, locked in the closest thing to mortal combat two gods who can't die can get, while Alistair races to join the fighting on the ground.

"Should we go after them?" Hudson asks as we both stare at the sky.

Part of me wants to say yes, if for no other reason than to see the Bloodletter finally kick a little ass. But it looks like my grandmother has the situation well in hand, and we have bigger problems to deal with than one spiteful god.

"I think we need to help the others," I tell him as three hunters race toward one of the wolf shifters, yellow pouches raised.

Two gargoyles rush to intercept them, but they are a couple of seconds too late. And as the yellow pouch hits the wolf, a scream of agony splits the air. Moments later, the young wolf disintegrates in a flurry of what looks like a strange, powdered version of silver.

The gargoyles finally reach the hunter, swords raised, but before they can stop him, he reaches inside his jacket and pulls out a purple pouch, which he throws straight into the face of my soldier Rodrigo.

I have one second to think he's going to be okay—one second when nothing happens at all. But before Rodrigo can so much as try to restrain the hunter, he—quite simply—blows apart, his stone shattering into a thousand different pieces.

120

Everything inside me recoils at the sight, and even though one of my other gargoyles, Cooper, strikes the hunter down, it's too late to do anything to help Rodrigo or that wolf.

Hudson sees it, too, and before I can so much as shift, he's already faded halfway across the field and snapped the neck of a hunter preparing to launch a green pouch at one of Imogen's ladies-in-waiting.

I jump off the stage, grabbing my platinum string as I do, so that I can shift into my gargoyle form. The only problem, however, is this damn dress. It was beautiful when I put it on back at the Witch Court, but right now it's nothing but a hindrance. So I reach down, say a silent prayer that Imogen forgives me, and rend the hemline in half, splitting the dress so I can fight and move and generally kick a lot of ass.

Three hunters run toward me, and I give the first a spinning concrete fist to his weak chin. He goes down instantly. A second hunter reaches into her pocket and pulls out a purple pouch that she aims straight at me, and though I manage to knock her hand away, in a flash she's got a purple pouch at the ready again.

I kick up the way Artelya taught me in practice several months ago, but as the hunter's hand comes forward, I brace myself for whatever pain comes next—and then suddenly, all three of them are gone, poofing out of existence between one blink and the next.

I whirl around to find Hudson staring straight at me, unadulterated rage on his face as he rips a hunter in half with his bare hands.

"Grace!" Macy screams from behind me, and I turn to see her running toward me at top speed.

As soon as she gets within range, she waves a hand in the air, and my dress transforms into my trusted battle gear. Leather leggings, T-shirt, leather vest.

Immediately, it feels like a weight is lifted, and I take off running straight toward Artelya, who is in the middle of decimating a contingent of hunters with several other members of the army.

Halfway there, I see Mekhi, who is fighting back-to-back with the Shadow Queen. A group of hunters has them surrounded, and I start to help, but before I can do much more than kick the legs out from under one of them, a wild array of shadow creatures springs out of the earth and swarms the ground around them.

Rats, snakes, spiders—Mekhi waves a hand, and they cover the hunters, who start screaming at the tops of their lungs as they fall to the ground.

I shoot him a hell-yeah look, then continue toward Artelya just as the Crone and the Bloodletter go rolling across the sky above me. Both look a little worse for wear, but they're going strong—kicks and punches and elbows and knees being thrown and absorbed by both of them.

Two gods in deadly but eternal combat, against a background of the cold Alaska stars.

And just like that, I decide enough is enough. I love humans, have spent nearly my entire life living with them and thinking myself one of them. But there is no way that my army, which has trained for a thousand years for just this eventuality, is going to fall to them. Not today. Not ever.

So as far as I'm concerned, it's time to stop playing with them and put a stop to this once and for all.

I call Artelya and several of her colonels over to me. By the time they get here, Hudson has also made it—along with Mekhi and the Shadow Queen.

"The only reason they're having any luck against us at all is because of those damn pouches," I tell them. "But look at them—they tend to attack certain paranormals in groups."

They turn around to check out what I'm talking about, and now that I've figured it out, it's easy to see. The ones near the vampires are carrying a bunch of red pouches, while the ones going up against the gargoyles are all carrying the purple pouches, like the one that killed poor Rodrigo. We just need to divide and conquer.

"Hudson, you need to mobilize the Vampire Guard and go after that group over there," I tell him, pointing to the huge contingent of hunters with purple pouches. "But stay away from the ones with the red bags.

"Artelya, you and the army take everyone else—just don't tackle any of the hunters with purple pouches unless you have the element of surprise."

By the time I'm done speaking, Hudson is already gone and Artelya is just about. As she disseminates my orders to her teams, I turn to Mekhi and the Shadow Queen.

"What can we do?" he asks.

But the Shadow Queen is already grinning. Because a giant wind has just whipped through the field, coalescing into what looks like a tornado. I know it has to be of supernatural origin—Alaska doesn't get tornadoes. And it sure as hell doesn't get them in the middle of a clear early-December evening.

Sure enough, the Bloodletter and the Crone come crashing back across the sky just as the wind whips into a frenzy. The Crone buries a fist in the Bloodletter's face. Blood spurts from her nose and sprays all over the Crone, who howls in outrage.

And in that one moment of distraction, the Bloodletter shoves her sister away from her.

The Crone goes flying through the air, straight into the small twister that just spun out of nowhere. It catches her, whips her into its eye, and then keeps her there, imprisoned as she screams and screams.

121

It's a Love/Fate Relationship

Once the Crone is captured, my grandmother's tornado deposits her inside a phalanx of gargoyles immune to her magic. My army simply gathers tighter around us, until they are just close enough for the tips of their wings to touch.

As they do, a powerful burst of energy rips through the air around us, creating a force field that imprisons us, imprisons her, within their circle. The remaining hunters—of which there are few—waste no time now abandoning the field. Artelya sends several members of the army after them to ensure that they don't decide to double back, but then she and the rest of the army gather around the Bloodletter, the Crone, and me.

My mind is whirling with several ideas of what to do with the Crone—and I'd be lying if I said one of them didn't involve repeatedly punching her in the face. Still, that's not exactly the way I want to start my tenure on the Circle, especially not when I've spent a lot of time thinking recently about tolerance and forgiveness and the way I want to rule.

So instead of kicking the Crone's ass—no matter how satisfying that may be—I turn to my grandmother instead. "She's your sister," I tell her. "What would you have me do with her?"

At first, the Bloodletter doesn't answer. Instead, she just looks between me and the Crone for several seconds. But as her sister continues to howl, she sighs heavily and says, "You're the gargoyle queen. Do with her what you will."

Now that I'm over the need to draw blood, I think about using the Crown to drain her power so that she can never cause trouble like this again. I'm not sure it would be possible, but it's worth a try. But even as I reach for her and the tornado falls away, I can't help thinking that it's a mistake.

Which makes no sense. Not when she has proven time and time again that she can't be trusted with the power that she has. Not when she's proven time and time again that her bitterness and hate will always win out over rationality and right.

And still, her strict adherence to order has a purpose. It's always had a purpose—to balance out the chaos that is so much a part of the Bloodletter's nature. The same chaos that is so much a part of my nature as well.

"The universe needs balance," I finally say. "Chaos and order."

"I was hoping you'd say that." My grandmother smiles. "Do you have something for me?"

My heart plummets, though I already know she's right. Because of the Crone's prejudice against paranormals and her determination to stomp us out of existence, there's only one way to ensure the balance of chaos and order that the universe requires to thrive.

And so, with my entire Gargoyle Army and all my friends looking on, I turn to my mate, who has just returned and is on the outside of the Circle. But who, as gargoyle king, can pass through the force field in a way that almost no one else can.

Before I can even ask him if he's got what I'm looking for, he reaches into his pocket and pulls out the beautiful stained glass vial the Curator gave me.

He hands it to the Bloodletter, who uncorks it before raising it to her lips. "Don't look so sad, Grace," she tells me. "This is how things were always meant to be. Chaos and order. Bitter and sweet."

And then she tips the vial back and slowly drinks every last drop of honey.

122

Two Crowns Are
Better than One

The Crone snarls as the Bloodletter recorks the empty vial. And as the Gargoyle Army stands down, I half expect her to attack either my grandmother or me. But she must know when she's beaten, because instead of coming for us, she just disappears.

"We need to go after her," I say.

Mekhi and Lorelei step into the circle. Now that I'm seeing them up close, I realize just how much better they both are looking now that the Shadow Realm has been destroyed. Their eyes are bright, their skin lustrous with health, and both look so much stronger than they did even a few days ago.

"Don't worry about her," Mekhi tells me, flashing the smile I've missed so much these last few months. "We're on it."

"There's nowhere to hide from the Prince of Shadows," Lorelei says with a wink. "Mekhi will find her."

Surprise rips through me at Mekhi's new title, but I can't say it doesn't suit him. He looks better than he has in a long, long time. "Thank you," I tell him, moving to give him a hug. "We appreciate your help."

"Always," he answers me before shifting his attention to Hudson. "Lorelei and I have a surprise for you," he says.

"Yeah?" Hudson raises a brow. "Besides the fact that you're a prince now?"

"Oh, I think this is a little better than that." Mekhi pulls his backpack off and unzips it.

I can feel Hudson tense as he suddenly realizes what's happening. "How—"

"Turns out you Vegas aren't the only ones with really cool Descent powers," he says with a grin. "Now that I'm healed, I realize I can do some pretty fancy shit. Most notably, turning shadows three-dimensional. Which means they can exist outside of the Shadow Realm. Or, at least, one particular umbra can."

And then he pulls a sleeping Baby Smokey out of his backpack and lays her in Hudson's waiting arms. Smokey looks the same as she always did—only *more*, now. She's round and adorable, and her little nose is absolutely precious. As is the look on Hudson's face.

Hudson looks back and forth from Smokey to Mekhi, and I'd swear that there are tears in his eyes as he does. It's like that, sometimes, when all your dreams come true. The joy is so sharp that it hurts. I should know. Right now, I feel the exact same way.

"Thank you," he says, his voice hoarse with the realization that we'll get to take Smokey home. And that we'll never have to leave her again.

"Anytime," Mekhi answers, going in for a one-armed hug and then clapping him on the back. "Any time."

"We need to get going," the Shadow Queen says from her spot outside the circle. "We don't want the Crone to get too far ahead."

"And if I'm not mistaken," the Bloodletter intones, "we still have an invocation to perform."

I can't believe I almost forgot in the rush of everything that's happened in the last hour. "Yeah, we do," I tell her as Hudson and I turn to make our way back to the dais.

It's a much faster trip now that we're no longer standing on ceremony. Even better, whatever lingering nerves I'd had are long gone. Nothing like beating down a god and her hunters with your mate, your best friends, and your grandparents to make you feel like maybe you've got this leader stuff on lock after all.

Still, I can't help but think of Rodrigo, as well as the others who gave their lives in the frantic battle against the hunters, and feel a heavy sadness settle on my chest, right alongside the massive griefs of the last year. I guess that this sadness, this responsibility, will be a part of my life as a ruler as well.

Macy comes running up to me as we approach the stage. "Good

job out there," she says, and there's an energy in her voice that I haven't heard in way too long.

"Same to you. Don't think I didn't see you take down that hunter with the long hair and monocle."

She shrugs. "A witch has got to do what a witch has got to do. Speaking of..." She sweeps a look over me from head to toe. "I need to change you back to your dress. Just give me—"

"No." I stop her with a shake of my head. "That dress is beautiful, but this is even better, because it's me, Grace. Gargoyle. Queen. Girl with a heart that can break and mend a million times. I want to be inducted the way I plan to rule."

"I think that's perfect," she tells me. "And so are you."

She starts to turn away, but Hudson stops her with a gentle hand on her arm. "Grace looks amazing like that, but is it too much to ask for a little tuxedo refresher?"

Macy cracks up, but when she finally settles down, she tells him, "For you, anything." Then she gives a little wave of her hand and Hudson is back to his normal sartorial elegance.

We're both grinning when we step out onto the dais a couple of minutes later, and instead of scary, this time it actually feels really good. Because Hudson and I are doing this our way, on our terms. And that makes all the difference.

The other members of the Circle are already seated around our thrones, and Alistair and the Bloodletter—the outgoing heads of the Circle—are standing right in front of them, waiting for us.

We slide into our seats without another word. Hudson still has Baby Smokey cradled in one arm while his other hand is holding tight to mine.

"Let's try this again," Alistair tells us with a grin I can only describe as a little impish.

"Yes, let's," I tell him.

And then our smiles fade as the importance of the moment comes back to us. Because Circle or no Circle, Crown or no Crown, this moment is about one thing only. Our people—*all* people—and Hudson's and my determination to do right by them.

"Grace and Hudson, the honor bestowed upon you today is a great and a grave one. You have faced every challenge to yourself, to your family, and to our people with bravery and selflessness, and in doing so you have proven yourself worthy of leading the ancient and powerful Circle."

The gravity of the situation comes back to me in a burst of icy nerves. But before it can take hold, a sudden burst of warmth comes down my mating bond, filling up all the oh-so-cold places inside me.

I grab onto the warmth—grab onto my mate—and promise myself that I will serve my people well. If not for my bravery, then because no one will work more tirelessly to keep peace among paranormals than I will, and no one will work harder to keep the world in balance than I will. After a thousand years spent trapped in time, my people deserve that much from a leader.

You are brave. Alistair's voice echoes inside me even as on the outside he continues with the pomp and circumstance of the ceremony.

You are powerful.

You are deserving.

My eyes meet his faded gray ones as his words echo in my head. And in his eyes, I see all my own doubts. All my own fears. All my own mistakes.

A good leader should be afraid, he continues, speaking inside me. *She should be worried that she will make a mistake so that she works hard to avoid doing just that. But she must also know when to let that fear go and believe in herself and the vision she has for her people. Can you do that, Granddaughter?*

Yes. The answer is a knee-jerk one, and it comes from deep inside my soul. But the moment I've given it, I know that it's true. *These are our people, and I will do my best by them, always. And so will my mate.*

Good. A smile tilts the corners of Alistair's lips at my assurances. *That is all I, or anyone, can ask of you. Except this.*

Except what? I start to ask, but before I can, Alistair's strong, rich voice fills the air around us.

"Are Your Majesties willing to take the oath?"

Your Majesty? Oath? I have only a moment to get used to the words before both Hudson and I answer, "We are."

Alistair nods approvingly. Behind him, the crowd appears to be holding its collective breath, hanging on his every word—our every word.

"Do you swear to use the power vested in you here, today, in this place of knowledge and learning, to ensure law, order, and justice for your people?"

I start to nod, then realize that he needs to hear my answer—that all of these people, gathered here today, need to hear our answer. So it's my turn to clear my throat before answering alongside Hudson. "We will."

"Do you swear to govern without personal interest and to put the needs of your people above yourself at all times?"

"We will."

"And finally, do you swear to govern with fairness and compassion toward all?"

It's the easiest question he's asked me, and my voice is strong as I answer, "We absolutely do."

Alistair nods his acceptance, then requests, "Please kneel here before the people you serve."

Hudson and I do as he wishes, kneeling at his feet with our hands clasped in front of us. When I look out over the fields and mountains of Katmere Academy, I can see the other gargoyles leaning forward, straining to see what I know is a sacred moment for our people. It certainly feels sacred to me, even before Alistair pulls a long, decorative sword from the scabbard at his hip.

"This is the Sword of Galandal," he tells us. "Forged in the deathly fires of Etna, carried only by those who wear the Crown, it has defended the Gargoyle Army and all under its protection for two thousand years."

He swings it over his head before gently bringing the flat of the sword down on first my right shoulder and then my left. "With this sword, I dub thee Protector of the Gargoyles. Do you accept this role?"

"I do."

He lifts the sword over his head again before bringing it down on Hudson's shoulders this time. "With this sword, I dub thee Protector of the Gargoyles as well. Do you accept this role?"

Hudson's voice rings loud and true when he answers. "I do."

Alistair nods, then hands me the heavy sword, jeweled hilt first.

I grab onto it and hold tight, determined not to drop it despite how heavy it is.

"Then with all the power vested in me, I crown thee Queen Grace and King Hudson."

A giant cheer sweeps through the field as soon as he says the words.

And just like that, Hudson and I are the new grown-ups in the room.

123

Hold on to
Your Horns

As shouts of "long live the queen and king" echo all around us, Hudson turns to me with the wicked grin I've come to love so much.

"You ready to do this thing?" he says.

"More than ready," I answer.

The other monarchs come to the front of the dais, prepared to congratulate us on our new positions. Hudson and I take a moment to shake each of their hands, and then we step back.

"Your service has been greatly appreciated," Hudson tells them. "You've held the Circle together under extraordinary odds, even when the last gargoyle king and queen went missing and the last vampire king and queen grew bloated with delusions of power. Your steadfastness in the face of all of that will always be appreciated."

"Why do I get the sense that the other shoe is about to drop?" Nuri asks, eyes narrowed as she looks between Hudson and me.

"Because it's time for a new way," I tell her. "One that honors the past but moves forward into the future we need to create for our people and for one another."

"I like the trajectory my future is on just fine," Linden tells us with a scowl. "So if you two think you're going to come in here with some new rules and shake things up, we're going to need to have a talk."

"No new rules," I tell him. "As for shaking things up...you can talk all you want. But our time of being told what to do is long over."

"What exactly are you planning?" Angela asks.

"Something that will make sure what's happened over and over again in our history never happens again," Hudson answers. "Our people can't afford another dictator with the power to destroy everything they've worked so hard to build."

I can see the moment the truth of what's about to happen dawns on the other members of the Circle. The witches look enraged. The wolves look scared. But the dragons, Aiden and Nuri, simply look intrigued. Then again, for a monarchy that is as embattled as theirs currently is, this may very well be the lifeline they need to see it through.

I turn to the front of the stage, where so many of our people are waiting for us to give our first official speech as heads of the Circle. Little do they know what's coming.

Hudson steps up to the microphone and holds a hand up to quiet the celebratory crowd. When everyone in the field finally grows quiet, Hudson says, "Grace and I would like to thank you for taking us into your hearts today and every day in the future. We'd like you to know that we have done the same for you. And with that in mind, we have some very big news we'd like to share."

He turns, holding the mic out for me to take.

Our fingers brush as I do, and even in the middle of all this, I can't help the way my heart skips a beat or twelve. But I don't have time to think about that right this second—not when we have such serious work to do.

I lift the mic to my lips and stare out over these grounds that started it all for me, that changed my life and taught me not just who I am but who I want to be.

I came to Katmere a year ago, lost and damaged and desperate to escape the pain of my parents' death. When I got here, I wanted nothing more than to be left alone to wither and cry. But Katmere Academy never gave me that option—and neither did the people I met here. I thought I had lost everything, but a lot has happened in the ensuing year, and as I stand here now, all I can think about is how grateful I am to this school. To these people. To this world that has taken me into its heart and helped me understand my place on the earth.

Both rock and seed. Protector and nurturer. It has given me friends to cherish and mourn, people to lead and learn from, and a mate to love forever.

I've found myself, and I've found a family.

I've made hard decisions, and I've faced the consequences.

And now I'm learning how to grow strong in all the broken places.

It is that strength—from my friends, from my family, from my mate—that gives me the courage and the conviction to stand on this stage right now and share the dream Hudson and I have for our people and our world.

"After thousands of years and countless setbacks and challenges to the Circle that brought hardship and fear into your lives, Hudson and I have decided that our first act as rulers of the Circle is to change the Circle from a body ruled by a select group of paranormals to one ruled by all of you."

My words echo over the snow-covered fields as people stop talking and cheering and start to *listen*.

"In the coming months, we will be establishing an elected body that represents the diverse and beautiful paranormal community in which we all live. One in which every paranormal group has a voice—not just the five factions that have *always* had one, but every single one of you—from the giants to the mermaids to the chupacabras to the manticores. And if our plan works, if we all find a way to live and love and support one another, it will no longer be a circle at all, but a chain in which all of our links connect. And one in which we pool our strengths and our resources to ensure that there are no weak links. This is how Hudson and I want to rule, and this is how we believe that we can all grow a healthy, powerful, thriving community."

"We ask you to join us on what will be a long and rewarding adventure that will culminate in a better future for all of us." Hudson continues where I leave off. And then he gives the entire audience—including the other members of the former Circle—the mischievous grin that gets me every time. Judging by the way the audience responds, it gets them, too. Even before he says, "But there is time for all of that. For now, I want to thank our hosts, Imogen and Linden Choi. Personally, I think you should hold on to your horns, because I've heard witches really know how to party!"

And just like that, loud music fills the air. Fireworks explode, outdoor grills fire to life, and the aurora borealis dances across the sky.

I grab Hudson's hand, and at this point there's only one thing left to do. Shut Up and Dance With Him.

124

Shake, Rattle, and Rule

Within seconds, my friends crowd around us. Congratulations fill the air as Macy flings her arms around me. "You did it!" she says as she hugs me so tightly she nearly cuts off my air supply.

"We did it!" I answer, hugging her back nearly as tightly.

I'm passed from friend to friend as the crowd continues to cheer around us. Eden gives me a fist bump and a "hell yeah." Flint tosses me in the air like a rag doll and says, "Not bad, New Girl. Not bad at all." And Jaxon—Jaxon just grins down at me and asks, "What shakes, rattles, and rules?"

"I have no idea."

"A gargoyle who's going to change the world." And then he sweeps me into the biggest hug imaginable—one that goes on and on. "Looks like we both found the mate of our dreams," he whispers to me.

I pull back, eyes wide. "You and Flint? You finally mated?"

"After the Chamber—" He breaks off, blows out a long breath before starting again. "After the Chamber, I begged him not to leave me. And because he's a better person than I'll ever be, he said yes."

Thank God. "About damn time you came to your senses," I tell him as the last tiny little cracks in my heart finally heal. "Although I hope he made you grovel."

Flint gives his mate a big, goofy grin as he slings an arm over his shoulders. "So much groveling," he says. "So, so much. It was a thing of beauty."

Jaxon rolls his eyes, but he's smiling just as wide. And I realize it's the first time I've ever seen Flint look at Jaxon like that—really, truly happy without having to pretend he's not dying inside. It's a really great look—a really great grin—and I can't wait to see it a lot more in the future.

Flint catches me looking and waggles his brows at me before sliding back into the laughing, dancing crowd.

"You did good," I tell Jaxon when we're alone again. "Though it took you and Hudson long enough to learn that you aren't the only ones who have to sacrifice."

"Maybe it's just that we both knew we had a lot to make up for."

"You've both done that very well." I hug him again. "It's time for you to just be happy now."

"I like the sound of that." He lets me go just as someone clears his throat behind me.

"May I cut in?"

"Go find your man," I whisper to Jaxon before I turn to see my uncle Finn standing there, staring down at me with my father's eyes. "I'm proud of you," he tells me as he, too, wraps me in a hug. "We're all so proud of you."

"Thank you," I whisper as another part of my broken heart mends. "For everything."

As he steps away, my grandmother takes his place. And, per usual, I have no idea what she's thinking. "Walk with me," she says, and the moment I step away with her, we're no longer on the side of Denali. We're alone on the boardwalk of my favorite beach in San Diego, and there's a cluster of chess tables right in front of us.

"Sit," the Bloodletter says, and I do, because even in the midst of a celebration, there are things we need to say to each other.

As she reaches for a chess piece, I still her hand. "I have something to propose to you."

She lifts a brow. "I already know what you're going to say, and I accept."

"Good. You'll make one hell of a vampire queen."

"Oh, Grace, darling." She laughs. "I already did. This is just the refrain." Again she goes to pick up the queen on the board, and again I stop her from doing so. "You don't want to play?" she asks, surprised.

"No," I tell her. "I don't. You taught me a lot, but I'm going to be a different kind of ruler than you."

For a second, I think she's going to take a bite out of me. But then she just smiles and says, "I think that's probably for the best," as she reaches out and sweeps all of the chess pieces off the board.

Epilogue

I check the bloody clock for the twentieth time in the last ten minutes. She isn't here yet. Why isn't she here yet?

I feel like a total tosser getting this worked up about Grace being a few minutes late, but I've been keeping this secret for months now, and I can't wait much longer to see her face.

Too bad it looks like I'm going to have to.

Figuring I might as well keep busy while I wait for her, I grab my phone off the corner of the desk and make a beeline for the office door. But as soon as I pull it open, I end up plowing straight into Grace.

"Sorry I'm late!" she tells me with a little laugh. "I've spent the last half hour mediating between Thomas and Dylan."

"Again?" I ask. "What are they fighting about now?"

She rolls her eyes. "Dylan's goat got into Thomas's room and ate the left half of his sneaker collection."

"Only the left half?" The thought hits me where it hurts. I've spent the last year getting my Versace underwear collection back in order. I don't know what I'd do if Dylan's goat ever got its teeth on my blue Baroccos.

"Thomas claims it was in a particularly vicious mood."

"I can't say that I disagree," I tell her. "Eating only the left shoe of every pair seems pretty diabolical to me."

"That's what I said. Dylan didn't seem impressed."

"He rarely is," I say as I pull her in for a hug.

She smells like cinnamon and apples, which means she's been hanging out in the kitchens again in between her mediation duties. She's determined to learn how to cook. I keep telling her she'd be better off taking a few cooking lessons from our local Sur La Table in San Diego, but she's determined to learn her way around our medieval keep's kitchen...much to the chagrin of Siobhan and the other gargoyles.

She cuddles closer, thankfully, and I bury my face against her hair and just breathe her in for a minute, taking comfort from her for what's coming next.

Eventually, though, she pulls away with a quizzical look. "So why'd you want to meet here? Do you have something going on?"

"You could say that." I take her hand and tug her gently toward the door. "I've been working on something for quite a while. Today seemed like the perfect day to share it with you."

There must be something in my voice, though, because the laughter goes out of her eyes, and she studies me for several seconds like she's trying to figure out what's going on inside my head.

"You okay?" she asks.

"Yeah, of course. Everything's tickety-boo."

"Every time you say that, it's a surefire sign that everything is not actually tickety-boo," she answers with an arch of her brow.

She has a point, but it's not like I'm about to admit that to her. She already sees too fucking much.

I settle for taking her hand and urging her gently down the hallway to the main room we portaled into all those months ago. It was the first one I had completely remodeled. Maybe that's why it's my favorite. Or maybe that's because of what I plan on using it for.

"Close your eyes," I whisper to her when we get to the soaring white arches.

"Is this another one of your paint sample things?" she asks skeptically. "Because I really don't feel like I'm up for a fight about the different shades of white we could paint the west wing of the Vampire Court, not after spending the last hour looking at a hundred and twenty-seven half-eaten shoes."

"A hundred and twenty-seven?" I shudder. "Jesus, that's brutal."

"You have no idea." She shudders right along with me, though I think we're traumatized about different things.

"Can I open my eyes?" she asks, the second I get her into position.

"Yes," I answer, then immediately regret it when a fucking wrecking ball full of nerves slams into me. Why the shite did I think today was a good day to do this?

I look at anything but Grace as I wait for her reaction, but when she doesn't have one, I finally force myself to meet her eyes.

"What is this?" she whispers as she traces the letters on the sign with her index finger.

"Vega Academy," I answer.

"I can see that." She turns to face me, wrapping her arms around my waist like she somehow already knows what this means to me. "What is Vega Academy?"

"It's nothing yet. But in a few weeks, it's going to be a school."

"A school?" Her eyes go wide. "Like Katmere Academy?"

"Yes," I answer. "And no."

She lifts her brows. "Well, that helps me out quite a bit."

"I don't want it to be for the kids of the elite, not the way Katmere Academy is. Here, anyone can come no matter how little or much their parents make. I love teaching and I love kids, and I realize there's no better healing for this Vampire Court—or for me—than to create a place where learning and knowledge flourish."

I hold my breath, waiting to hear what she thinks. Thankfully, she doesn't make me wait long.

"I think it's the most beautiful idea you've ever had," she tells me.

"Yeah?" I search her face, looking for some sign that she hates what I've done. But there's nothing there besides support and love and a quiet understanding that makes me feel bloody itchy.

Because Grace always sees too much.

"I actually have a present for you," I tell her in order to get that look off her face. "You want to see it?"

"A present?" She sounds half intrigued and half wary. Not that I blame her. This is the Vampire Court, after all. Bad shite happens all the time.

"A small present." I guide her down the hall and around a curve until we finally get to a room I spent months pretending didn't exist. And then spent several more months trying to figure out what to do with.

Grace stiffens as soon as she realizes what room we're standing in front of. "We don't have to go in there," she tells me as she starts to back away.

"I want to go in there," I tell her.

She looks skeptical. "You do?"

"It's kind of the point of this whole visit," I say, pulling the door open to my father's old study so I can hold it for her. "You can't get your present without it."

She gives me another searching look, but then she walks through the door I'm holding. I can tell the second she really starts to see what I've done with the place, because her gasp could probably be heard halfway around the world. It's come a long way from what it looked like after I took a sledgehammer to it.

"You— This—" She breaks off and swallows, then tries again. "This is what you've been keeping secret? This room and this school?"

"It is, yeah."

"Why?" She spins around in a circle. "Why wouldn't you tell me? You had to have known I would support you!"

"Maybe that's not what I wanted from you."

This time when she pulls back, she looks wary. "What does that mean?"

I don't have a fucking clue. It just kind of came out. But she's waiting for an answer, so say the only thing I can think of.

"It's a safe space," I tell her a few minutes later as she starts to explore the room. "Books, craft kits, drawing stuff. All things that can be done to quiet the mind and help kids feel better about themselves or whatever's going on in their lives."

"It's amazing," she tells me. "And I really can't think of a better use for your father's old war room."

"Me neither, considering the shit he plotted in here through the years." Shit that included torturing his own kids.

She keeps walking, looking at the different books and projects that are offered here. In typical Grace fashion, she's interested in everything and has a million questions she wants answered.

After the first few, I start to relax, because it feels like maybe she's not going to push me anywhere I don't want to go. She's not going to ask any of the hard questions I've been dodging answering.

But then, just when I think I got away scot-free, she stops in front of the quotes I have painted on the wall. I can tell she recognizes it because she gets quiet. Very quiet. But she doesn't say a word as we both stare up at it, until finally I just wrap my arms around her and read it aloud.

"Time does not change us. It just unfolds us."

At first, she doesn't say anything or do anything. She doesn't even look at me. She just stares up at the fucking wall and reads the quote again and again and again.

But then she takes my arms and wraps them around her waist and holds me. Grace just holds me as she says, "I'd love to hear more."

And just that easily, the knot that's been inside forever starts to loosen. And I realize that, no matter what happens, we're going to be okay.

And for now, that's enough.

Actually, it's more than enough. It's everything.

ACKNOWLEDGMENTS

Writing a long-running series, especially one with as many characters and storylines as this one, isn't easy, so I have to start by thanking the two women who even made it possible: Liz Pelletier and Emily Sylvan Kim.

Liz, we left it all on the pages of this series, so now all that's left is to thank you from the bottom of my heart. You are a marvel.

Emily, I have no idea what I would do without you. This last year has been challenging in so many ways and I don't think I would have made it through without you. Thank you, thank you, thank you.

Stacy Cantor Abrams, this has been one for the record books. Thank you for all your support for me and this series through the years. And thank you so much for that phone call that started it all.

Hannah Lindsey, my fabulous tour companion, intrepid problem solver, and copy editor extraordinaire. I've had a truly incredible time getting to know you and working on this book with you. Thank you for everything. You are a goddess.

To everyone else at Entangled who has played a part in the success of the Crave series, thank you, thank you, thank you, from the bottom of my heart. Jessica Turner, for your unfailing support. Bree Archer for making me ALL the beautiful covers and art all the time. Meredith Johnson for all your help with this series in all the different capacities. You make my job so much easier. To the fantastic proofreading team, thank you for making my words shine! Toni Kerr for the incredible care you took with my baby. It looks amazing! Curtis Svehlak for making miracles happen on the production side over and over again—you are awesome! Katie Clapsadl for fixing my mistakes and always having my back, Angela Melamud for getting the word out about this series, Riki Cleveland for being so lovely always, Heather Riccio for your attention to detail and your help with coordinating the million different things that happen on the business side of book publishing. A special thank-you to Veronica Gonzalez and the amazing Macmillan sales team for all the support they've shown this series over the years, to Julia Kniep at DTV for her eagle-eyed reading, and to Beth Metrick and Lexi Winter for working so extra hard to get these books into readers' hands.

Eden Kim, for being the coolest. No one in the world has a better beta reader than you and I am so grateful for everything. Next time I'm in New York, shopping is on me!

In Koo, Avery, and Phoebe Kim, thank you for lending me your wife and mom for all the late nights, early mornings, and breakfast/lunch/dinner/midnight conversations that went into making this book possible.

Stephanie Marquez, thank you for your joy in this series from the very beginning. Your love and support is one of the most amazing parts of my life.

For my three boys, who I love with my whole heart and soul. Thank you for understanding all the evenings I had to hide in my office and work instead of hanging out, for pitching in when I needed you most, for sticking with me through all the difficult years, and for being the best kids I could ever ask for.

For Jennifer Elkins, for sticking with me through everything that's come our way these last thirty years. I adore you, my friend.

And finally, for fans of Grace, Hudson, Jaxon, Macy, Flint, Mekhi, Eden, Heather, Gwen, Xavier, Luca, Liam, Rafael, Byron, Calder, Remy, Izzy, and Katmere Academy, thank you, thank you, thank you, from the bottom of my heart for your unflagging support and enthusiasm for these books. I can't tell you how much your emails and DMs and posts mean to me. I am so grateful that you've taken us into your hearts and chosen to go on this journey with me. I hope you enjoyed the Crave series as much as I enjoyed writing it. I love and am grateful for every single one of you. xoxoxoxo

Ready for your next YA vampire obsession?
Enter the dangerous world of...

SIGN
OF THE
SLAYER

SHARINA HARRIS

Read on for a sneak peek...
Available in stores and online summer 2023

CHAPTER TWO
That Ain't No Jackal

Raven

I'm jarred awake as my head slams against the back of the seat in front of me. The felt material that scrapes my forehead feels like steel, and I know I'll have a carpet burn.

Instrument cases fall like raindrops and crash like thunder from the racks above our heads. I duck and dodge the raining horns and flutes and clarinets.

Deidra screams beside me. My head snaps toward the sound of a *crack*. She grabs her bleeding forehead and looks down at her hands. Her fingers shake with blood.

Deidra whimpers. Her mouth moves soundlessly. Strings of saliva drip from between her lips.

"Shit." I grab her head, holding her together. "We had an accident. I'll get help."

She grabs my wrist, keeping me in place.

"Okay. I'll just…" I look around. The bus has stopped. People are standing and scrambling—struggling to get out of any open window.

A high-pitched scream fills the air. No, not *a* scream. Screams near the front of the bus.

"R-Raven?" Tears roll down Deidra's cheek.

Someone must've died.

A low growl from outside curls around my bones. Something rams against the side of the bus and knocks it clean off its axis. It teeters and totters and finally rights itself, but not before my mouth fills with blood. My tongue throbs.

The growling grows louder, nastier. *Closer.*

The screams bouncing around inside the battered steel grow scarier.

I peer out the window. Stare at the hulking shadow moving along the side of the bus.

A bear? No, that's impossible.

"Raven?" The pain in Deidra's voice grabs my attention. Even in the dim light, her eyes look unfocused, as if she is about to pass out. I press harder on the wound. "You'll be okay," I say, desperate to help her, to take her pain away, to focus only on her...when the *thing* from outside suddenly fills the front of the bus.

My hands fall from Dee's head. How did *it* get inside?

Air clogs my throat. I blink once, twice, not believing my eyes.

This is no animal, not a bear, not a jackal. It looks like a man. Skin as pale as the moon highlights ruby lips. The irises of his brown eyes are tainted crimson, while the surrounding whites transform to obsidian. Like a snake making room for a larger prey, his jaw unhinges as his fangs, dripping with thick, yellow saliva, lengthen.

Holy crap. That's not... It's not what I think it is. It can't be.

I lean closer to Deidra and press my palm against her forehead. I pull her close when I feel her shivering.

Dr. Jeffries pushes himself from the seat.

"Kids. Go outside the back exit. Now." His voice is calm in the storm, and he snaps his command as if we're running drills at practice.

Everyone scrambles, but I'm rooted to my seat, one arm around Deidra's shoulder, one hand against her forehead. Her sticky blood seeps between my fingers.

Dr. Jeffries shoots the thing a hard glare, and for a split second, I think maybe, just maybe he can reason with it. "You need to—"

His words are cut off.

The thing, the monster, grips his gnarled finger around Dr. Jeffries's throat. His extended fangs sink into his neck. He sucks down Dr. Jeffries's blood, grunting like a wild hog.

"Oh my God," I whisper while everyone screams. "A v-vampire?"

God, how can this be real?

Deidra grabs my fingers and whimpers. I squeeze back as cold realization hits me. We're sitting ducks packed in a tin can.

For a few heartbeats, silence fills the air. And then pandemonium breaks.

Cam, who sits behind me, bangs against the window, but it's jammed.

"Do something, gal." I hear Grandma Lou's voice urging me to fight.

I can't. The screams from my bandmates lock my muscles. The vampire is a mere forty feet away.

"You gonna let me take you down? You ain't ready for the world." In my mind, I see Grandma Lou standing over me, cane pointed at my neck.

I struggle to stand. I feel another tug from Deidra, but I shake off her hand. Shake off my fear.

"D-don't go." She shakes her head. "Don't leave me."

I hear a second howl from outside the bus.

"There's another monster out there. Get under the seat!" I yell.

The whites of her eyes stretch, but she slumps down.

I take a step. The monster tosses the dead bodies through the shattered front window.

A few people stand between Deidra and the monster and me. The others had managed to climb out through the windows, and from the skin-rippling screams, I guess they didn't make it far.

They're picking us off.

"Do like I taught you!" a voice inside me orders.

The creature's attention swings to me. I hold my breath, back away. "S-stop!"

He doesn't stop. He rushes me, swings his fist, and lands a punch on my face. The sheer force of his blow sends my body soaring into the air until my back slams against the exit door.

Somehow, I stand, groaning. Everything hurts.

Tiny explosions detonate inside my skull. The headache from hell doubles my vision, triples my pain so much that it seizes my muscles.

Lava incinerates my veins. I claw at my wrists. They burn and itch as if something foreign is invading my body.

The pain drops me to my knees. "Wh-what…what's happening to me?"

It feels like liters of sweat are soaking through my T-shirt. All I can do is breathe—breathe through *their* screams, *my* pain, and *our* fear.

The pain finally cedes.

The monster stares at me, licking his bloodied mouth. An eerie, Pennywise-the-killer-clown smile stretches his lips. He takes one step and then another. Slowly stalking me, eyes glued to me like I'm the snake and he's the mongoose. I swallow what feels like a cotton ball clogging my throat. He's deliberately taking his time to amp up my fear.

And sweet baby Jesus, it's working.

But Deidra needs my help. Gotta save me, save my friends.

My mind clears and my heart pumps with purpose.

"He's here!" someone with a deep, guttural voice yells. The vampire, now only ten feet away, snaps his overlarge teeth at me, a silent threat that freezes my heart. With a growl, he whirls, then, in a blur of motion, is off the bus.

My head droops like a wilted flower. I close my eyes, grateful for the reprieve but dreading what comes next. I inhale and instantly regret it when the smell of copper—the smell of blood—fills my nose.

I open my eyes slowly and find the glassy eyes of Cam staring back at me. I look away. An hour ago, those eyes were like a puppy dog seeking my attention, wanting...more from me. And the regret that pooled in my stomach for months now turns into lead.

Another explosion rocks my entire body. An overwhelmingly bright light fills my eyesight. I kneel over as my muscles twist around my bones—compressing and stretching, like they're trying to fit into another mold.

A thousand hot and sharp needles jab into the flesh of my palms. My screams are loud and as high as a whistling teapot. It feels like a hot poker emblazons my skin. Circles appear in real time, as if someone is etching them into my hands.

"Raven!" Deidra shouts, but it sounds like I'm underwater.

"I..." I pant. "S-something's happening to me."

She crawls to my side. "You're glowing." She grabs my hand and waves it in front of my face.

The light dims, but it's the shit on my hand that doubles the knots in my stomach. I stroke the intricate design—two inverted triangles, surrounded by a hexagon, two large circles, and three smaller nodes.

"What the hell is this?" I ask, though right after my question, the answer rushes me with clarity.

Deidra points to the nodes. "That's mercury, sulfur, and salt."

I nod and swallow. Science nerd to the rescue. "It looks like some witch shit."

She shakes her head. I wince when I notice the blood caked at her temples. "It's a circle, not a pentagram. But I think it has something to do with that demon. That's what it was, right?"

Something in my head, my heart, whispers, *Vampire*.

I flex my hand and stand. "I think I need to go. Stay here and don't move."

"I don't think I can." Her eyes are misty. "Don't leave. Don't get yourself—"

I point to the dent on the back door. "I did that. I can handle it. But I can't handle you getting hurt. So please stay here and let me go."

We have a stare-off. A long howl from outside jolts my resolve. I'm not as afraid as I was five minutes ago.

"Fine." Deidra slumps to the ground, like her worry for me was giving her strength to sit upright. I wait until she's wedged herself between the two seats in front and behind her.

I dash outside and find three men fighting in the middle of the road. A highway light blinks overhead, casting a chilling spotlight. Two vampires attack another guy who's built like a football player. But he's not dressed like one. He's wearing a navy-blue suit with a blazer, pocket square and everything. And the bizarre thing is, the guy doesn't seem to break a sweat. With a swipe of his fingers, he launches one monster across the pavement. The other one flies, like Superman or something, rushing him in mid-air. The guy in the suit narrows his eyes, and it looks as if an invisible force is lifting the vampire in the air. Then the vampire's body flies up and slams down like a mallet to a Whac-A-Mole against the pavement.

He's literally beating their asses with his mind.

While the suit repeatedly slams the vampire, the other one creeps behind him.

The one who attacked the bus and killed my friends.

A rash of red fills my vision. And suddenly all my tension shifts outward, and I sprint before he can make his sneak attack and slam my body into his.

The vampire topples over with a loud *thud* onto the ground and rolls hard over the asphalt. He lifts his arms in the air, taking inventory of the road rash along his limbs, with pebbles and bloody gash marks.

But just as quickly, his skin knits back together.

Like, it's legit healing.

He shakes out his arms, jumps to his feet, and crouches low. "Slayer."

A slayer? Where? I scrunch my forehead.

Oh. Him.

I look at the guy in the suit. His eyes widen when he sees me. "Why are you out here?"

"Because I can help." I tell him the truth.

"It's too dangerous. Return to the bus immediately."

Um, excuse him. I just tackled a whole-ass vampire. "I seem to be doing okay."

He shakes his head as if he's trying to add sense to the situation. I mean, he's the one who's kicking vampire ass with his mind. In a suit.

"Get behind me. Vampires from the Saqqara clans are tricky."

"Who?"

"The flying one."

"Oh. Superman with fangs."

"Yes. Him. Stay out of the way." His rough and rumbly voice reminds me of a monster truck, with monster tires, that just rolls and crushes over anything in its way. Not that his voice sucks, but there's something about it that plucks at my nerves. Something that offends me.

My attention snags on the scarred tissue around his neck, the only slight imperfection on his pretty-boy face. It looks like someone ripped his throat open, threw some hydrogen peroxide on it, and was like, *You good, bro.*

I clear my throat. "I think you meant to say thank you."

"You surprised him, that's all. But there won't be a next time." He jerks his thumb behind him.

I quickly do what he asks. Clearly, he knows what he's doing. But I don't cower. I move into a fight stance—feet spread, arms up, eyes alert. The two vampires close in on us, their eyes on the biggest threat—him.

"You'll never be king," the one with brown scraggly hair taunts.

"You'll never *see* me take the throne," Pretty Boy vows.

The vampire yells and flies toward him. Pretty Boy moves to the side, grabs his arm, and throws him across the other side of the road.

The vampire in front of me takes advantage of Pretty Boy's opening and swings out his claws, nearly clipping his ribs.

Nearly. I step in and do the same move and toss him away like yesterday's garbage. Except, instead of tossing him a few feet away, he's landed a few *hundred* feet away.

That's not what I expected or what I'd meant to do. I look down at my hands, then at the vampire, then my hands again.

Who am I? Did I eat or drink something that made me stronger? I had a PB&J, popcorn, Coke. Nothing outside of the usual.

I don't do drugs, not even weed. Okay, I had that edible brownie a few months ago, but that should be long out of my system. Edibles don't turn you into Wonder Woman.

A voice whispers in my head. The better question is, *What* am I?

I'm strong. Like, really, really strong. Simple as that for now.

A *thud* from the bus catches my attention. What is Deidra doing over there?

My focus drifts back to the vampire I'd thrown.

He looks at the bus, sniffs, and then looks at me. He's standing near the back of the bus—near Deidra.

"No." I stare at him, probably with a wild look in my eyes. He grabs my arm and tosses me like a Frisbee, just as I'd done to him. Then he runs toward the bus.

I scramble to stand, to get to him, to Deidra.

Her screams propel me to pump my legs, my arms. Wind slaps my face. I jump over the three steps on the bus. But by the time I arrive, the vampire disappears.

Grabbing the top of the bus seat, I hopscotch over bodies and scattered limbs to get to the exit door. There are so many bodies, I don't see her. "Where are—?" The question dies on my tongue when I find her wedged between Cam and Malia.

I ease the bodies away and grab my friend. Deidra's chest shudders hard like an overstuffed washing machine, while her legs, bent at an angle, remain motionless. One hand grips her flute. She wields it like a weapon.

Her wide eyes stare at mine. No impish grin, just crinkled grooves around her lips and between her eyes. Blood spurts from her red-stained mouth. I look down at her throat and it looks just like Pretty Boy's clawed-through neck.

With firm hands, I place my palms on either side of her throat. Red rivers gush through my fingers. It's hard to keep a grip. The blood makes it too slippery.

"It's not bad. It's not bad at all." Salty tears settle on my lips. My hands shimmer, a metallic silver on my right and gold on my left. But I don't let go of her to figure out what the hell is going on. I can't. I'm the only thing that's holding Deidra together.

Her eyes lock on mine, asking me all sorts of silent questions I don't know how to answer. The blood, the slashed throat, the wide-eyed fear all feel familiar—like I've seen this before.

I shake my head. I can't wallow in my strange déjà vu. Not when she's…

"Hurts." Tears gather in her eyes, slip down her cheeks.

"It's not bad. I'm gonna fix it. I—I promise."

I fix everything for her. If someone gave her shit, I always had her back. I won't stop now.

"Friends forever?" she asks, as she'd done time and again.

She releases her last breath. In the span of seconds, I see our past—the girl who kicked the boy in the nuts when he called me the Wreck-it Raven during art class. The girl who made me a "Boys Suck" playlist when Deon broke my heart.

The girl who tried but failed to sneak me out of the house to see an R-rated movie. But really, her goal was to sleep over. Something Grandma never allowed.

I see our future sailing away. Double dates in college. Marathon movie nights in our dorm rooms.

Darkness edges my vision. I can't see her. I can't see anything. Just like that time before. I'm losing it. I'm losing control, and for once, I don't want to stop it.

"Forever and ever," I vow.

The Da Vinci Code *meets* Riverdale *in the new YA fantasy from #1* New York Times *bestselling author Alyson Noël*

Stealing Infinity

My life goes completely sideways the moment I meet the mysterious Braxton. Sure, he's ridiculously hot, but he's also the reason I've been kicked out of school and recruited into Gray Wolf Academy—a remote island school completely off the grid. I never should have trusted a face so perfect.

But the reality of *why* Gray Wolf wanted me is what truly blows my mind. It's a school for time travelers. *Tripping*, they call it. This place is filled with elaborate costumes and rare artifacts, where every move is strategic and the halls are filled with shadows and secrets.

Here, what you see isn't always what it appears. Including Braxton. Because even though there's an energy connecting us together, the more secrets he keeps from me, the more it feels like something is pulling us apart. Something that has to do with this place—and its darker purpose. It's all part of a guarded, elaborate puzzle of history and time…and I might be one of the missing pieces.

Now I have all the time in the world. And yet I can't shake the feeling that time is the one thing I'm about to run out of…*fast*.

A thrilling and unique fantasy based on Korean legend
perfect for fans of Iron Widow *and*
These Violent Delights

LAST OF THE

TALONS

SOPHIE KIM

After the destruction of her entire Talon gang, eighteen-year-old Shin Lina—the Reaper of Sunpo—is forced to become a living, breathing weapon for the kingdom's most-feared crime lord. All that keeps her from turning on her ruthless master is the life of her beloved little sister hanging in the balance. But the order to steal a priceless tapestry from a Dokkaebi temple incites not only the wrath of a legendary immortal, but the beginning of an unwinnable game...

Suddenly Lina finds herself in the dreamlike realm of the Dokkaebi, her fate in the hands of its cruel and captivating emperor. But she can win her life—if she kills him first.

Now a terrible game of life and death has begun, and even Lina's swift, precise blade is no match for the magnetic Haneul Rui. Lina will have to use every weapon in her arsenal if she wants to outplay this cunning king and save her sister...all before the final grain of sand leaks out of the hourglass.

Because one way or another, she'll take Rui's heart.

Even if it means giving up her own.

Let's be friends!

🐦 @EntangledTeen

📷 @EntangledTeen

f @EntangledTeen

♪ @EntangledTeen

📰 bit.ly/TeenNewsletter

Visit to learn more about the school with bite:

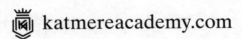 katmereacademy.com

entangled teen

an imprint of Entangled Publishing LLC